Roses Have Thorns

ROSES HAVE THORNS

Beverley Hughesdon

CENTURY
LONDON SYDNEY AUCKLAND JOHANNESBURG

First published in Great Britain in 1992 by
Random Century Group
20 Vauxhall Bridge Road, London, SW1V 2SA

Random Century Australia (Pty) Ltd
20 Alfred Street, Milsons Point, Sydney, NSW 2061
Australia

Random Century South Africa (Pty) Ltd
PO Box 337, Bergvlei 2012, South Africa

Random Century New Zealand Ltd
PO Box 40–086, Glenfield, Auckland 10
New Zealand

The catalogue data record for this book is available from the British Library

ISBN 0 7126 4768 6

Typeset by Deltatype Ltd, Ellesmere Port
Printed and bound in Great Britain by
Mackays of Chatham PLC, Chatham, Kent

Dedication

To Mum and Dad, with love

PART ONE

Chapter One

Borrell, Wiltshire — September 1898

'Amy Roberts be a bastard, a bastard – Amy Roberts be a bastard!'

I stopped, bewildered, as the boys came surging past me, their voices loud and jeering as they chanted again: 'Amy Roberts be a bastard, a bastard!' Amy Roberts – that was *my* name. 'Amy,' the teacher had said today, 'Amy Roberts – come and sit here, next to Lizzie,' and I'd sat down on the long wooden bench feeling so proud because it was my first day at school – but now the boys were calling after me in the street.

'Amy Roberts be a bastard, a bastard!' That last word was so harsh and ugly that although I didn't know what it meant I shrank from it, pressing closer to Emmy – Emmy who'd been told to take me home. But as the boys swung round to face us, Emmy suddenly tugged her hand away from mine – and left me!

They were jostling themselves into position around me; I was alone in the midst of my tormentors. I looked up at them, stiff with fear, and saw their faces split into wide gap-toothed grins. 'See Billy, she dussent know she be one o' *them*.' The biggest boy nudged the one next to him; his round blue eyes were glistening with excitement. My legs began to tremble.

'Amy Roberts be a bastard, a bastard!' Their circle was complete now, trapping me inside it as the heavy boots thudded down on the stony road with each chanted: 'Ba–stard, ba–stard!' I looked desperately round for Emmy – Emmy was a big girl, Emmy had been kind to me today – but now she was only a briefly-glimpsed pink face between the boys' circling shoulders, and even as I saw it, it slid away. Emmy had gone; only the swaggering, crowing boys remained.

I was shaking all over now, my eyes darting from side to side frantically seeking escape. The bodies parted for a minute, I moved one boot tentatively forward, then the boys surged inwards

3

and at once I backed away. But still they came on, looming dark and threatening above me. 'Into ditch, Billy – herd 'er into ditch!' They were forcing me backwards, and out of the corner of my eye I saw the ditch deep and dangerous behind me. I spun round, desperately trying to brace my legs for one panic-stricken leap – but they were too short, too frightened – and with a wail of despair I toppled sideways and splashed full length into the muddy water. Even as the triumphant laughter burst out above me, pain pierced my knee and I screamed – high and shrill as a rabbit in a snare. Then I slid hopelessly down into the mud.

There was a sharp tug at my plaits; one of the boys was hauling me out. A voice, doubtful now, said, 'Look at 'er knee, Albert. Old man Roberts'll be rare an' put out if he sees state of her.'

'Must've bin a stone – they baint got no right to leave sharp stones in ditches like that.'

'Me dad'll give I a thrashing if he do find out.'

'Don't be soft, Billy. We was only having a bit o' fun.' But even Albert sounded uncertain now.

I dared to open my eyes. The mud and slime was dripping down my face and I tried to wipe it away as the boys stood in a huddle, staring at me. Then one of them pointed. 'Look at 'er now – she'm bleeding like a stuck pig!' My eyes dropped to the bloody gash on my knee, and lower – to my boots: they were all scratched and scored by the stones in the ditch – my new boots! And my pinafore, it was soaking and streaked with mud – my best pinnie, clean on today. My bottom lip started to tremble. Grammer would be so angry, so terribly, terribly angry. I began to sob.

'Cowardy, cowardy custard! Cry baby!' The boys were edging forward, confident again, as the tears trickled down my dirty face.

'Whatever is going on here?' A voice spoke, sharp and angry. At once the boys backed away from me and I heard the girls' murmurs of, ''Tis Mrs Roper. 'Tis governess,' as they came closer, watching. 'You, Albert Yates! What mischief have you been up to now?'

'Nothing, ma'am – we baint doing no harm, ma'am. Amy Roberts 'ere, she did fall in ditch. She weren't looking where she was going – and Billy 'ere pulled her out, didn't 'ee, Billy?'

'Yes ma'am, that's right.'

Then a voice shrilled out from the group of girls, 'Thee bist

4

telling lies, Albert Yates – and you in choir an' all.' The schoolmistress turned her head to face the speaker. 'Them boys, they been real bad, ma'am. They did push Amy in thic ditch, and afore that they was calling her,' the voice paused, before rising in excited accusation, 'they was calling her bad names!'

Mrs Roper flushed, and there was a moment of hesitation before she rounded on the boys. 'I've no doubt *you* were the ringleader, Albert Yates. Mr Roper will see you tomorrow, first thing.'

Whispers of, 'The stick!' rippled through the group as Albert's voice was raised in protest. 'But ma'am, 'twas her fault! She wasn't looking –'

'Be off with you now, or you'll all be in trouble.' With a shuffling of boots the boys melted away.

I stood in the road, bedraggled and hiccupping from my sobs. Mrs Roper bent down and tied her handkerchief round my bleeding leg. 'Now wipe your hands on the grass.' As I crouched down to obey she addressed the girls. 'Why didn't you stop those boys tormenting little Amy? Jane Philips, a big girl of eleven like you should have known better.'

Jane spoke quickly. ''Tweren't nothing to do with us, ma'am,' then, drawing a deep breath she added deliberately, 'Besides, 'tis true what them boys said. I've heard me Dad say – Amy Roberts, she *do* be a bastard.'

I looked up into the shocked silence, to see Jane's mouth set in a tight, defiant line. When Mrs Roper finally replied her voice was quiet. 'I never want to hear you use that word again, Jane. Now run along, all of you.'

'Yes'm. 'Yes'm.' They scattered.

Mrs Roper took me home to Grammer. As we walked along the village street she tried to explain that my mother had done something very bad, wicked, so wicked that people would also blame me for what she had done. I listened but I didn't understand, because I knew I didn't have a mother – only Grammer and Granfer.

As soon as we came through the door Grammer began to scold me for my torn pinnie and muddied boots, and then she ordered me up into the loft, as she always did when she was angry. I scuttled up the ladder and crouched on the boards to wait until her

5

anger died down, but today I sensed something different. For a start, Mrs Roper came right into the kitchen. Grammer wouldn't like that, she couldn't stand other folks traipsing in over her clean floor and poking their noses into what didn't concern them. And then, when Mrs Roper spoke, Grammer wouldn't listen – I heard her voice, loud and angry as she interrupted the school-mistress: Grammer always spoke loud. It was because she was hard of hearing, Granfer said – but today she was almost shouting.

I could hear every word through the cracks. 'I been punished, punished for my pride in that one's mother – coming to us late when we'd been wed more'n twenty years and never been blessed. I thought she were the infant Samuel, I did. I were proud of her glossy curls and her pretty ways – though I were always strict, I brought her up God-fearing, I did. But Mister Roberts,' I heard the bitter carp, 'he spoiled her, he did, just as he does that one up in the loft – and so she ruined us, so now I can't hold up my head in this village for very shame.'

Mrs Roper spoke low but Grammer's harsh voice broke in. 'Charity! I know nought of charity, ma'am – only of sin and damnation, and the sooner that one knows the shame she brings on us the better.'

I heard the latch lift, then Mrs Roper's footsteps fading. Grammer called me down and washed my knee with hard, bony hands. As soon as she'd bound it up with a piece of old rag she fetched her strap and hit me sharply over the back of my legs, once for spoiling my boots and once for dirtying my pinafore.

I thought the strap hurt, but it only hurt my legs. What Grammer told me afterwards, that hurt me deep inside my chest, so I thought the pain would never go away. She told me I'd been conceived in sin and born in sin – I didn't know what conceived meant, but I knew from the tone of her voice that it was something dreadful. And then she used that word, the one the boys had used, that ugly, forbidden word – and she used it to me. 'You, you – you be a bastard – a child without a name.'

I was so frightened I dared to protest, 'I do have a name. I be Amy – Granfer he do call I Amy, and governess, she said today I be Amy Roberts –'

Grammer held up a hand that was curled like the claws of a bird and silenced me. 'Roberts be your Granfer's name, not yourn. *You* be nameless.'

The stone flags shifted beneath my feet and nothing was safe and secure any longer. I stared up aghast at Grammer until the red spots on either side of her nose quivered and spread and I couldn't see her face clearly any more for the tears which oozed out and trickled down my cheeks. Then she sent me up to the loft again where I wept with despair because I was nameless, a child without a name.

So I learnt the meaning of sin: sin that was not of my making but which I would have to carry for the rest of my life. I was branded. Everybody knew. Grown-ups had never been unkind, they'd spoken to me, called me 'Amy', or 'Mister Roberts' grand-daughter', but now I knew I had no right to my name – Grammer had spoken true. Grammer who never called me Amy, only 'her' or 'thic child', Grammer who never 'thee'd' me – only teachers and the Rector's wife said 'you', but Grammer always said 'you'. 'You – stop your chatter. You – fetch them sticks. You – get up thic ladder.'

However hard I'd tried to please her I'd known I was a terrible burden to Grammer, for I'd heard her say so, often. She'd take me out the back to catch the pegs in my pinnie while she fetched the washing in, and Mrs Rawlings from next door would come out and reach up for the sheets, 'To save your arms, Mrs Roberts.' Then I'd hold out the skirt of my pinnie so Mrs Rawlings could drop the pegs in and as she did so she'd smile at me and say, 'My, young Amy's a big help to you already, Mrs Roberts.' But Grammer's mouth would turn down at the corners and she'd say, 'She's a terrible burden to me, Mrs Rawlings, a terrible burden.' And now I knew why – and I hid in the loft for shame.

Granfer came home, but I didn't come down. I heard him asking Grammer where I was, and the bitter anger of her reply made me shrink back against the chimney-breast. Oh Granfer, do you hate me too? Nothing was certain now.

Then the rungs of the ladder creaked. Granfer was climbing up; he came right up into the loft, and still I did not move towards him. But he came to me. He came to me and crouched down so that his whiskery face was level with mine and then he told me, 'Don' 'ee

7

fret, my maid – for thy old Granfer, he do love thee.' And at his words I flung myself into his arms in a storm of weeping. He held me close, rocking me, until Grammer's harsh croak from below summoned us both downstairs.

After tea I sat on Granfer's knee while he smoked his pipe, just as I always did, but tonight I felt too heavy and sad to chatter, and when Grammer sent me up to bed I went without a backward glance.

Up in the loft memories became dreams and turned into nightmares, so that I woke shaking, too frightened to sleep again. Then I heard Granfer's voice. 'Amy, bist thee awake, my maid?'

'Aye, Granfer.'

'Come to thy Granfer then.' I wriggled out of the blankets and padded over to the trapdoor. 'I got something to show thee, my maid – but thee must be quiet as a liddle mouse.' Granfer began to drop down the ladder, placing his boots carefully on each rung; I followed, stretching out one searching toe after the other, safe between his arms.

Just as my feet touched the cold stone of the flags at the bottom I heard Grammer's rattling snore rise up and pause – and I shrank back against Granfer – but the snore settled down again into its usual rhythm and Granfer bent and swung me up into his arms. I twined my fingers together behind his neck and buried my face in his familiar smoke-smelling whiskers.

Putting each large boot down very gently, so the nails wouldn't strike, Granfer carried me silently across the kitchen; then, with only the faintest of creaks as the latch was lifted, we were outside in the cool air of the night. I began to lift my head, but Granfer's strong hand pressed it back. 'Dussent thee look, my maid, until I tells 'ee to.' Obediently I screwed my eyes up tight as Granfer's boots rang on the brick path.

'Down with thee, now.' His hands gently slid me down; I felt the rough cord of his trousers brush my bare legs and then I was standing upright as his fingers on my shoulder swung me round. I stood with my eyes still tightly closed, smelling the tang of the mint and the mustier scent of the sage, and hearing the faraway hoot of an owl; then I sensed Granfer crouch down behind me, and felt the warmth of his breath on my neck. His fingertip touched my cheek. 'Open wide, my flower – and look.' My eyes followed his pointing

8

finger up into the dark blue bowl of the sky – and there, silver-white and beautiful, hung the perfect crescent of the new moon – outshining all the stars. I gasped, and clutched Granfer's hand. 'She be born again thic very night, and now thee bist a big maid and a-going to school thee maun give her three curtseys – for 'tis the custom.'

With my eyes fixed on that shining silver crescent I curled my toes against the rough brick of the path and reached down for the hem of my nightie. Slowly, carefully, I lifted my skirt in the air and bent my knees until thy almost touched the ground: one curtsey, two curtseys, three curtseys. And the silver moon winked back at me every time I dipped and rose.

'She saw I, Granfer – she did smile at I!' I pressed myself against his solid legs, beaming up at him in delight.

He reached into his waistcoat pocket and took out a tiny silver threepenny bit. 'Gi' I thy hand, Amy.' He placed the coin in my palm. 'Thee maun turn it over three times where she can see it – then she'll bring thee luck.' The silver in my hand winked as I turned it: once, twice, thrice – and each time the silver moon winked back.

'Now 'tis thy turn, Granfer.' And the little coin almost disappeared between Granfer's broad fingers as he turned it three times, too. Then he slipped it back into his pocket, swung me up into his arms and carried me indoors. He kissed me from the midst of his bristles, set me on the ladder and gave me a gentle pat on the behind to send me scampering up to my loft. When I closed my eyes on my pillow the silver moon still shone behind my lids, until her tranquil beauty lulled me to sleep.

Chapter Two

Granfer – how I did love my Granfer.

Each afternoon I'd watch for that moment when Grammer hobbled over to the dresser to fetch the blue and white striped bowl; once it was set down on the table the preparations for tea had begun – and once tea was cooked, then Granfer would come home. I'd run to the flour crock, into the back kitchen for the suet, over to the dresser for salt and pepper – and then, as Grammer's knobbly fingers began to mix the dumplings I'd rush out to the shed for the vegetables. The smooth brown potatoes Granfer grew on his allotment, the bright orange carrots and plump juicy onions that came from the back garden: I'd pile them up in the skirt of my pinafore and carry them in to Grammer at the table. Her knife would flash and slice and then they'd all be tumbled into the big black pot together with a square of fat bacon and I'd be sent out up the garden for a bunch of sage leaves and a sprig of parsley, and maybe a cabbage, if it was in season. The cabbage would be chopped and bundled in its net ready for adding later while I ran out again to dip the jug in the water pail and bring it back to Grammer. While she poured it in I'd poke the fire up so it burned bright as bright and then Grammer would carry the iron pot over to the hearth and hang it from the hook above the leaping flames. As soon as it was bubbling Grammer would drop the dumplings in and then she'd ease herself down into her wooden armchair and reach for her big black Bible. Very few grammers could read, and even fewer could write, but my Grammer could do both. Her father had been a preacher, Granfer had told me. 'He did learn 'er her letters when she was only a young maid – she's a main clever 'oman, thy Grammer.'

I'd sit quiet as a mouse while Grammer's lips moved soundlessly above the page until the snap of the Bible closing told me it was time to fetch the knives and forks from the dresser drawer and climb up on my stool to set the table. By now the smells from the pot would be tickling my nose and my ears would be all of a-quiver with listening for Granfer coming home. I'd hear the cackle of hens and the squeal of next door's pig wanting his tea and through the wall the hungry yelling of Mrs Rawlings' latest baby – that'd be cut off quick as she put him to her breast – and then at last it came: the steady clump of boots on the brick path.

At once I was off my stool and running to the back door, straining up on tiptoe to reach the latch, tugging at the heavy wooden edge – until with one great heave the door flew open and there, on the step, was Granfer. The minute he saw me his wrinkled face would slit into a huge, beaming smile, and as I flung myself forward into his outstretched arms I felt as though my whole chest would burst with joy. He'd swing me right up until I could look down on the greeny-black dome of his bowler hat with his whiskers sprouting either side of the brim, and then as I came down I'd seize his beard in my hands and twine my fingers in it as if I'd never let go, crying, 'Granfer, Granfer!'

But then Grammer's voice would come from inside. 'Master, I do be dishing up,' and Granfer would quickly set me down. I'd run indoors with his jacket and hat and then jump for the piece of towel behind the back kitchen door and carry it out to where Granfer was clanking the handle of the pump. When the trough was full he'd reach his big brown hands down into the water and sluice his face with it until his whiskers shone with silver drops – and then he'd shake his head. I'd dance back from the sparkling shower exclaiming, 'Granfer, thee bist wetting I!' until Grammer silenced our laughter with her stern rebuke, 'Master, stop thic foolery – thy vittals be a-cooling.'

We'd hurry back to the step, and I'd kneel at Granfer's feet and wrestle with the mud-caked laces of his great heavy boots, tugging and pulling with my fingernails until the knots were free, and Granfer would wait patiently while I struggled even though he could have unfastened them quicker himself – but he knew I wanted to take his boots off for him, because I loved him so. And when they were both off he'd crack his knobbly toes inside his socks and say, 'My, that do feel good, that do,' and I'd glow with pride.

Grammer wouldn't let me speak while we had our tea, but I didn't mind, because while I stood at my stool eating my cabbage and dumplings Granfer would be telling Grammer where he'd been that day, and all the jobs he'd done – and I'd drink in every word he said. Granfer worked for Mr Thomas, whose farm was the largest in the whole of Borrell. Of course, it wasn't his really, he was a tenant of Sir Hugh – all the farmers were – but Mr Thomas was the most important person in Borrell after Sir Hugh and the other gentry, so it was right that it should be him Granfer worked for. Granfer was the oldest of his men, more than three score years and ten, Granfer was – so he knew more than all the others. He never said that himself, but I knew because Mr Thomas often asked his advice, and I'd heard Mr Rawlings next door say to Mrs Rawlings, 'Mr Roberts, he do know a thing or two – there baint much he hasn't seen afore, and he do remember. I disremembers last harvest, sometimes, but Mr Roberts, he'll remember what went amiss five and forty year ago – and how to put it right, too.' Granfer could do lots of jobs better than the young men could: he'd lay a whitethorn hedge so every twig was level and perfect, and everyone knew which ricks Granfer had thatched – they were neater than the others, and he always put a fine yellow cockerel on the topmost point, to stop the lightning from striking or the witches from landing.

Of an evening Granfer tended his own garden. He grew the best vegetables in the whole of Borrell: his peas were so plump and juicy they'd be bursting out of their pods, while his broad beans were as big as florins. So after tea he'd put on his old smock, ready for digging or hoeing, but then he'd sit down again in his wooden armchair by the fire. I'd run and fetch his pipe and his tobacco and stand ready with the spill, and then, when his pipe was drawing nicely he'd settle back in his chair and listen while I told him everything I'd done that day. He'd exclaim: 'Well, I never did hear the like afore!' and 'My, what a clever liddle maid thee bist!' so that my whole chest swelled with pride.

That half hour was my favourite time of the day. Before I turned four and went to school I'd sit on his knee and poke my fingers into the spaces between the stitching on his smock front, counting the gathers – snail creepers, Granfer did call them. But once I was at school, Grammer said I was too old for sitting on laps, and it was time I learnt to sew.

Grammer was powerful good at sewing; she'd made all Granfer's smocks for him long ago, but now her hands were too stiff with the rheumatics for her to do fine work and she needed me to learn so I could help with the mending. I wasn't always as neat as she wanted yet, but I was learning – because Grammer ripped all my stitches out if one of them was the least little bit uneven. When the nights began to draw in Granfer brought home a special candlestick for me to see by while I sewed: it had a round glass ball either side of the frame so it shone brighter over my needle. He got it from an old lady in Pennings who'd used to make lace by it when she was a child.

Pennings was the next village from Borrell, along the high road that went over the hill. I'd never been there, but I'd heard tell there were shops either side of the main street, instead of only on the one side – and there was a doctor living at Pennings, and a horse doctor, too. Folk said Pennings was almost a town. It didn't belong to Sir Hugh – everything the west side of Borrell did, right up to the main road to Bath – but Pennings and all the land to the north, near as far as Malmesbury, that belonged to Lord Warminster.

We often saw Sir Hugh riding through the village, while Her Ladyship, she'd drive out in her carriage. If they came past when we were out playing we'd have to stop what we were doing and bob to her, while the boys tugged at their caps – or their hair if their caps had come off from running about. But people said Lord Warminster never ever came to Pennings, although he owned a great white house there with fountains in the garden and a grotto – I didn't know what a grotto was, but I thought it sounded exciting. When the cottage roofs leaked at Pennings or the farms were being let, Lord Warminster sent his agent. Sir Hugh had an agent too, but sometimes if Sir Hugh was in a very good mood you could ask him about having your thatch mended or a new pump handle fitted – and then it'd be done quicker. People said the agent always made you wait a full year, just in case the roof mended itself.

Our cottage belonged to Sir Hugh, just like everyone else's, and Grammer kept the rent in a tin box on the mantelpiece for when the bailiff came round to collect it. I'd hear women talking about the rent – if money was short then you had to go without boots, or eat less, but the rent had to be paid, because if it wasn't then you had to go into the workhouse. I'd never seen the workhouse – it was over by Pennings – but Hannah Fuller, her uncle was in there.

13

He'd gone for a soldier and lost his leg in a big battle away in Africa; he'd managed at first with a wooden leg, Hannah said, but as he got older he couldn't get little jobs any more. The Guardians allowed him a couple of shillings every week and two loaves of bread, but he had to use the shillings to pay the rent, so he only had the bread to live on, and workhouse bread was horrible, everyone knew that. Old Mrs Tucker, she had workhouse bread, and so did Dummy Drew and his mother, and the loaves were dirty, just like the van that brought them. Once Mrs Tucker had found a dead mouse in her bread – right inside the loaf it was, and she'd eaten its tail before she realised what it was, she told Hannah's Mam. But she'd never dared complain in case the Guardians stopped her money – and even then she had to take washing in to get by – but the Relieving Officer mustn't ever be let know, and folk paid her in eggs and potatoes, not money.

Hannah's uncle, now, he'd fallen ill and used the shillings to pay the doctor, so Sir Hugh's agent had turned him out and he'd been taken off to the workhouse. Hannah and her mother got a lift in the carrier's cart one day and went to see him, and Hannah said her uncle had cried, even though he'd been a brave soldier, and Hannah's mother did too. The House was like a great grey prison, and once the iron gates clanged shut behind you, you never got out again, except to be carried to the churchyard – and a pauper's funeral, that was a terrible disgrace.

When she'd finished telling us Hannah looked at me sideways and said, 'My Mam said *you'd* have been put in the workhouse, Amy Roberts, if your Grammer and Granfer hadn't've taken you in.'

Just then the bell rang for the end of playtime, and we had to run to get in our lines, but all through spelling I felt sick and shivery, thinking of being trapped all my life behind those high grey walls. I was so upset I spelled tail, tale – although I knew it was one on a horse, and Mrs Roper said I wasn't attending and rapped me hard over the knuckles with her ruler.

That night I dreamt the Relieving Officer came to lock me up in the poor law van, to take me off to the workhouse; the grey loaves were piled up in the corner with a little mouse crawling out of every one – and none of them had tails because they'd all been eaten. The sides of the van closed in on me so I couldn't breathe and I cried out in panic and despair. The next thing I knew I was awake and sobbing on Granfer's lap. ''Tis only a nightmare, my flower – don' 'ee be afeard. Thy Granfer, he'll take care o' thee.'

I pressed myself against Granfer's warm chest, burying my face in his scratchy, tobacco-smelling neck, and slowly my heart stopped its frantic pounding, until I fell asleep in the safety of his arms.

Chapter Three

In June the roses came. Granfer did love his roses, and so did I. He grew others flowers too: lavender and sweet william, wallflowers and pansies. I liked to look at them all and smell their scents – but the roses, they were special. Roses had faces, so you could talk to them. Granfer, he talked to all his plants. 'Come on now, thee get thyself up thic pole, smartish,' he'd say to his runner beans, and the next day strong green stalks would be twining their way obediently up – but I only talked to the roses, and they'd bob their heads to show they were listening.

Some of the other cottages in Borrell had roses climbing up their walls, but none of them climbed as high as our Seven Sisters did; other folk might even have a bush or two in their front gardens, but they'd grow all straggly because they weren't tended like Granfer's roses were. Come March he'd be outside first thing on a Sunday morning cutting away the dead wood so the new growth would be strong and hearty. I'd run out to watch him whenever Grammer'd let me, dancing a little from the cold and putting my hands into the warmth of my armpits to stop the pain of my winter chilblains.

In May the buds began to peep, but they were only little glimpses of pink amidst the leaves – and they looked so shy and timid I'd think they'd never be bold enough to open. I'd stroke them, trying to coax them out, but Granfer would shake his head, chuckling, and tell me, 'Thee cassent hurry 'em, my flower – they'll bloom when they be ready, and not a minute afore.'

And he was right, because in June when the sun was warmer, then the tight little buds would loosen, and the petals would begin to unfold. 'She's nearly out, Granfer!'

' "Nearly" baint out, Amy.' His eyes would twinkle at my impatience. 'Gi' her another day.'

Next afternoon I'd be out of the front door and running down the path as soon as Granfer came into sight. I'd tug him home crying, 'She be out, Granfer – she be out!' He'd stand looking down at her, and then a slow smile would spread over his face and he'd reach out one horny hand and stroke the new-born petals with a touch that was as gentle as the flutter of a butterfly's wing.

Soon I'd be coming home from school to a front garden that was a mass of pink and white and red, with here and there the deeper tones of purple. The white petals of the Blushing Maiden would be flushing a delicate pink at the bold glances of General Jack, resplendent in his bright red coat, while the two moss roses were easing off their furry green buds to face the sun; Willy Lobb proud in his purple, the Countess dressed in bridal white. In front of them was the Rosamund rose, with every petal striped pink and white –named for a poor maid poisoned by a jealous Queen, Granfer told me. York and Lancaster, he was a pied rose – in every bloom some of his petals would be white for York and the others red for Lancaster – to remember how once a King of Lancaster had married a Princess of York, and so ended long years of war, Granfer said.

The Seven Sisters, she grew up the wall, but you never knew where you were with her. Her flowers came in clusters, but in each cluster some would be white, some the palest of pink, others so deep a pink as to be almost red, and one or two would be purple! She was a forward one, she was – she'd creep right up to the eaves and try and butt her way into the loft. She couldn't count, either. I'd pull a cluster down and there'd be eight blooms, or ten, or even more. I'd scold her, 'Thee hast too many sisters, my rose – thee do need to practise thy mental,' but as soon as I let her go she'd toss all her heads in the air as if to say, why should I care?

By the end of June all the roses would be out, and the old apple tree would be bearing a second crop of blossom – it was the Garland rose, falling like a great white shawl of lace over its branches and down to the gateposts, so that you had to lift her honey-scented fronds aside to go in.

I loved every one of Granfer's roses, but my favourite of them all was the Cabbage rose. I felt so sorry for her, being so beautiful and smelling so sweet, yet having a name like that. Her heads seemed to be always drooping in shame, so whenever I went in or out I'd stop and stroke her swirl of pink petals, telling her as I did so, 'Thee bissent never a cabbage – thee bist the most beautifullest rose in the whole o' Granfer's garden.' But I always whispered it, so the other roses wouldn't hear me and be upset.

17

Then one day Granfer had been to see Mr Marsh, who was head gardener up at the Hall, and when he came back he told me she had another name, too – the Hundred Petalled Rose. Immediately I rushed outside to tell her the good news – and to start counting, too. But as I pulled her down to begin my count of her petals one of her sharp thorns stabbed my hand. I jumped back, staring at the bright red bead of blood on my finger – and caught my arm on Willy Lobb's stem, so now a red smarting line ran along it. I pressed myself back against Granfer's legs as the tears filled my eyes. 'They be so beautiful, Granfer – but they do bite.'

Granfer's hand clasped my shoulder. 'There baint never no roses without thorns, my maid.' He added softly, ''Tis like life, my Amy. Joy and sorrow, pleasure and pain, they be all twined together, like brier roses in a blackthorn hedge – thee must suffer the pain o' the one to gain the joy o' the other.' Then he bent down and kissed me, though it wasn't bedtime.

Up in the loft that evening I thought about what Granfer had said, and realised it was true; there was no taste of fresh-baked bread without the ache in your arms from kneading the dough, no smooth, glossy feel of ironed linen without the weight of the flat-iron and the scorch of its heat, nor the joy of the new moon without the nights of darkness before. Pain and pleasure, they went together, just like Granfer said – and the greater the pleasure the higher the price that had to be paid for it. Sunday was like that: Sunday afternoon was the most special time of the whole week, but Sunday morning, how I did dread Sunday morning – and chapel.

On Sunday morning Grammer put on her big black bonnet and stood over me while I buttoned my boots and tied the strings of my little bonnet, then, with Granfer beside her and me behind she'd set off down the village street. We'd walk slowly past the big stone church, where the gentry in their fine clothes were alighting from their carriages, past the middling-sized brick chapel where Hannah and her family were all trooping in, and on to the little tin chapel set on the edge of the fields. All the way a worm of fear was wriggling in my chest, and as we walked through the chapel door, past the 'Thou Shalt Nots' on the wall and down to the narrow wooden bench just below the pulpit the worm grew bigger and bigger until it became a snake which slithered down to settle in my

18

belly. And when Mr Wilcox began to preach the snake began to bite. 'The fiery pit of Hell, it be there, waiting for you all – for all of you sinners.' My soul shrivelled, and I longed to put my hands over my ears, but I knew I had to listen to every word, because I was a sinner. 'All on you, you will all burn in the fires of Hell!'

There were little flecks of froth on Mr Wilcox's beard, and as he shouted 'burn' a round grey gob of spittle jumped from between his yellow teeth and spattered the brim of Mrs Rawlings' best Sunday hat. His eyes bulged, he leant even further over the edge of the wooden pulpit and his voice rose to a shrieking, strangled howl. 'You – you – you – ' the stubby finger pointed, 'you'll be in thic fire, dancing on them hot embers as'll never cool not in a thousand years – screaming in agony for time eternal. You, all o' you,' my gasp of terror was cut off in mid-flight as Grammer's black brim dipped and Grammer's glittering eye held mine. I crouched, silent, as the shriek rose ever higher, 'You be all sinners! Every last one o' you, from the oldest man to the youngest girl-child, you be sinners – every day you do sin – and Hellfire and damnation will be your punishment!' His eyes flared and his knuckles went white as milk where they clutched the edge of the pulpit; nobody dared even to take breath.

Then one by one his fingers opened with a succession of bony clicks, he reached into his top pocket, pulled out a large handkerchief and wiped his mouth and beard very thoroughly. When he'd finished he pushed it back into his pocket and said, 'Reckon us'll have a hymn now, brothers: *O Gentle Breeze That Breathes O'er Eden.*'

There was a rustle of starched Sunday petticoats and I half fell onto the wooden floor from the high pew; my numb legs would scarcely hold me up. Grammer's body began to creak upright beside me. I felt her bony hand squeeze my shoulder so that my knees nearly buckled under me. Her fingers pinched harder, until I looked up into her veined, wrinkled face. Her lips moved, though no sound came as the harmonium began to wheeze, but I knew what she was saying. 'You,' she mouthed, 'you be conceived in sin and born in sin – you be a sinner.' And the red fires of Hell flared up around me in that stuffy chapel. Desperately I pulled my eyes away and turned my face to look up at Granfer's whiskers, but he only stared straight ahead. I put out my hand, tried to touch

19

his – but it stayed still as a stone, it was no use. And Grammer's fingers pinched harder and harder until I could feel the bruises coming under my brown Sunday frock, so I dropped my hand and began to sing, while the flames of Hell licked at the toes of my boots.

But after chapel came Sunday School; Sunday School was Church, but all the children in Borrell had to attend because Her Ladyship said so. If you missed one week she'd ask you why next time she came into school to inspect our needlework – and woe betide anyone who hadn't been ill or got a good excuse.

I wouldn't ever have dared tell Grammer, but I liked going to Church Sunday School. The schoolroom seemed different from weekdays with everyone wearing their Sunday best, and Miss Mary, the Rector's youngest daughter who took the bottom class, she was different from a schoolteacher. She wore coloured dresses and a pearl brooch that winked in the sunlight, and she smiled a lot, even laughing sometimes.

Miss Mary would tell us about God, too. Church God, He was stern and strict, but He wasn't so angry as Chapel God, and Church Hell wasn't near as hot as Chapel Hell. Miss Mary said you needn't go to Church Hell at all if you were truly sorry for your sins, and promised to be good for ever after. Being good meant ordering yourself lowly and reverently towards your betters, and obeying them always. Your betters were the Rector and all the other gentry – with Sir Hugh and Her Ladyship best of all; not that anyone in Borrell would have dared to disobey them, else they'd have lost their jobs and been turned out of their cottages.

Being good also meant keeping the Ten Comandments. I thought I could manage eight of them with no trouble, but Number Seven was a problem because Miss Mary never told us what 'adultery' was, so I used to worry sometimes that I was committing it without realising. Then there was Number Ten: 'Thou shalt not covet'. Miss Mary explained that coveting meant to want something that someone else had, and I did – I coveted a mother: a mother who'd kiss my leg better when I fell over and tie the tapes on the end of my plaits into nice bows, and who'd look up and smile at me when I came home from school. But I didn't want anyone's else's mother, just one of my own – so perhaps that didn't really count as coveting. I did hope so, because I knew that even for Church God I had to be more good than everyone else, because of being conceived in sin and born in sin.

Being good wasn't just obeying, it was doing your duty, too, Miss Mary said. I knew all about doing your duty because Grammer referred to it a lot. If I stayed out in the dunnekin watching a spider spin its web after I'd finished my business, or ran into the lane to play 'catch leaves and wishes' under the ash tree when I was only supposed to be taking the potato peelings round to Mrs Rawlings' pig, then I wasn't doing my duty – and Grammer would scold me angrily. If Granfer was at home and he tried to excuse me, saying I was only young, then Grammer would round on him. 'I've done my duty by her, master – now she must learn to do hern.'

One Sunday, instead of our scripture passage Miss Mary made us learn a poem about it. It began: 'Stern Daughter of the Voice of God! O Duty!' and as I heard it I imagined God, sitting on a cloud and frowning, like the Rector when we hadn't learnt our Wednesday Psalm word-perfect – and God, He'd tell you exactly what you must do, even though you didn't want to, not one little bit. As I learnt the poem I vowed I'd try very hard to do my duty, and then Grammer would be pleased and tell me I was less of a burden to her.

Next Miss Mary would tell us a story. I did like to hear stories, and hers were always about the same kind man who'd lived a long time ago and gone fishing and helped people when they were ill. As soon as the story was over prayer books would be given out so Church children could learn their catechisms. Chapel children, they didn't learn catechism, because years ago, when Mr Wilcox first came to Borrell to be cobbler and preacher at the chapel, he'd gone up to the Hall to see Her Ladyship and ask if chapel children could be excused catechism and creed and prayer book at Sunday school, and on Wednesdays when the Rector came to school. Everyone had thought he was extremely brave and very fool-hardy, but eventually Her Ladyship had said yes, so as soon as the prayer books appeared you could have spotted the chapel children a mile away for the smiles on their faces – and at Miss Mary's signal we all jumped up and filed out, leaving behind some very glum Church looks. Although I liked Sunday School I liked leaving early even better.

Emmy Rawlings had to see me home, but she always dawdled of a Sunday, chattering to her friends, so I'd stand and sniff the tantalising smell of everybody's Sunday joints roasting in the bakehouse oven just across the green. Borrell looked different on a Sunday: the women had taken their aprons off and the men's faces were all clean and smooth after their weekly shave. Even the older men like Granfer trimmed their beards and whiskers and polished their boots on a Saturday night ready for Church. If you didn't go to chapel in Borrell then you had to be in Church, like the servants up at the Hall – or Her Ladyship would want to know the reason why. She didn't miss much, Her Ladyship – and what she missed the Rector'd spot and tell her about. But folk in Borrell didn't dare complain. Besides, as they said, she was a real lady – not one of those jumped-up tradesmen's daughters who'd bought herself a husband from an old family that had run short of money. Lady Blanche was an earl's daughter, and she knew what was right. If there was illness in a cottage she'd send her housekeeper down with special dainties to tempt the invalid's appetite, and as soon as a girl left school she'd find her a place in good service. Girls from Borrell were lucky, they never had to go to the agency in Bath.

When Emmy had said goodbye to her friends she'd take me by one hand and her little sister by the other and then we'd set off sedately down the street. We'd walk past the post office, the general store and Mr Wilcox's shop all in one group, then there was a gap before we got to the blacksmith's and the wheelwright's. We'd often stop and watch there on weekdays, but on Sundays there was no clanging of metal on anvil or hiss of steam as an iron tyre was being fitted so we went straight on to the pond. Dummy Drew lived opposite the pond with his mother; their cottage always looked lonely and sad – the thatch was ragged and untidy, like a woman's hair in need of a comb, and there were no flowers in the garden because Dummy had never learnt how to dig.

When we reached the beerhouse we'd turn left down Hill Lane, speeding up because our mouths'd be watering at the thought of Sunday dinner. And as we turned the corner more often than not I'd see Granfer at the gate, waiting for me. At once I'd tug my hand from Emmy's and start running down the slope until I arrived flushed and panting, to be swung up in Granfer's arms

22

until my face was level with the sweet-smelling white petals of the Garland rose. Then Granfer'd give me a Sunday kiss and we'd set off back up the lane together to fetch our joint of pork from the bakehouse.

I was allowed to use a knife and fork on a Sunday, and afterwards there'd be jam rolypoly; I'd feel so full I could hardly walk to the pump to fetch water for washing the pots. When everything was tidied away Grammer would lower herself into her chair and say to Granfer opposite, 'Master, thee bist weary – bide in thy chair this afternoon.' And my heart would stop as I waited for his reply.

Granfer would fiddle with his clay pipe and say, not looking at Grammer, 'A liddle walk in the Lord's fresh air'll be rest enough for I.' Grammer would drop down her chin and press her lips tight together, but I'd already be at the door reaching down my sunbonnet.

When I walked out with Granfer on a Sunday afternoon the birds would sing sweeter, and the flowers, they'd dance in the hedgerows. I'd run ahead of him, putting clover to my lips to suck the tiny drop of honey, then I'd chew the tangy leaves of the sorrel, poke my fingertips into the bells of foxgloves, and make poppy dolls with waists tied by a blade of grass. Next I'd leave my old favourites to search for new treasures, clambering down into the ditch bottom and across to pull the grass aside and exclaim, 'What be the name o' thic blue 'un, Granfer?'

Granfer would come closer to peer and then tell me, ''Tis birdseye, my maid.'

I'd catch at the trailing white trumpets. 'And thic, Granfer?'

''Tis withywind – see how it do wind itself around thic old hedge, Amy.'

'What be thic called, Granfer?'

'Grace o' God. 'Tis St John's own flower and a powerful healer.'

I'd gaze at the bright yellow stars respectfully before moving on. 'Thic 'un, Granfer – what be thic 'un called?'

He'd chuckle and say, 'What a maid thee bist for knowing names!' But he'd always tell me.

If we came upwind of a hare, and saw its long ears quiver before it sprang away I'd ask, 'What be his name, Granfer?'

'He be a puss, Amy – you know that.'

23

'But they all be called pusses – what be *his* name?'

He'd laugh and say, 'Joey, then – thic 'un be called Joey.'

Even the rabbit that ran across our path with its white scut bobbing had to have a name, so Granfer would call it Alfie, or Ted, and then I'd be satisfied; I couldn't bear to think of it with its lovely soft fur and big dark eyes – and yet being nameless.

Sometimes, when we took the path through Frog Wood, we'd see Dummy Drew – and I'd shrink back against Granfer's corduroy-covered leg. I was frightened of Dummy, with the great hump on his back and his odd, shuffling walk that made it look as if he were going sideways all the time. And when he came closer his face bothered me; his tongue wouldn't fit into his mouth so it always stuck out a little, and there was a damp patch on his jacket from the dribble. He couldn't speak properly, that's why folk called him Dummy, but Granfer said we must always be polite and say, 'Afternoon, Dummy,' and my voice would echo Granfer's, a little shrill with nervousness. Dummy's small eyes would peer at us, then he'd gobble and splutter, and when he'd finished Granfer'd reply, 'Aye, 'tis a fine day, Dummy – a fine day indeed.' Then Dummy would shuffle past us, his head lolling sideways as he watched us.

As soon as he was out of earshot I'd whisper, 'I be afeared o' he, Granfer.'

'Now don't thee bist a foolish maid – he be only a poor mazed creature, as wouldn't never do thee no harm.' But whenever I saw Dummy I'd always cross my fingers against the evil eye, like Granfer had shown me – on both my hands.

As we came back along the path beside Goosey Meadow my feet would begin to lag, because Sunday afternoon was nearly over and soon it would be Sunday evening, and chapel again. We'd all stand up while Mrs Wilcox pedalled the harmonium, and then the opening bars of the first hymn would wheeze out and we'd begin to sing:

> *'There is a dreadful Hell.*
> *And everlasting pains,*
> *Where sinners must with devils dwell*
> *In darkness, fire and chains . . .'*

Chapter Four

The haycocks had been loaded on to the high-piled waggons and the horses had hauled them off to the farms. School had finished, ready for harvest, but Granfer said it would be several days yet before the corn was ripe enough for cutting, so the horses could rest a while before having to begin their slow, sweating plod across the wheatfield, dragging the reaping machines behind them. Today the sun was shining, the bees were a-buzz – and it was Sunday afternoon.

As he lifted me off the stile at the end of Goosey Meadow Granfer asked, 'Canst thee keep a secret?'

'Aye, Granfer.'

He set me on my feet and crouched down beside me. ''Tis thy birthday today.'

My birthday! I hadn't thought I had one. Other girls had birthdays – Hannah had had one just before school ended. The bigger girls had held her arms and legs and bumped her eight times on the ground – but I'd always thought I didn't have a birthday, like I didn't have a mother and father. When we stopped school after haysel I was still six, and when we went back at the end of harvest I was seven – it just happened – but now Granfer told me in a whisper, 'Thee bist eight year old today, but thee maunt tell thy Grammer.' So I had a birthday, too.

Granfer stooped to tug at his bootlace. I stood waiting with my back against the firm wooden rail of the stile, gazing at the bars of green shadow and golden light painted by the sun shining between the trees onto the track ahead. Above me a bird called, and I looked up to see the flash of its wing and the bright pure blue of the summer sky high above. It was all so beautiful – and it was my birthday.

Granfer held out his hand. 'Come along, my maid.' With a hop and a skip to clear the ruts I was beside him, and we set off down the golden-green track. One two three – hop, 'Look at thic squirrel, Granfer.' One two three – hop, 'I seed a rabbit, Granfer.' One two three – hop, 'Where we'm going today, Granfer?'

'We'm going up to the Hall, to see Mr Marsh.'

The Hall! I stopped hopping at once and walked very sedately beside Granfer up to the gate and out and down Pie Lane to the East Lodge. Mr Marsh would sometimes invite Granfer to step up and take a look at a plant, but Granfer had never taken me with him before.

I was all eyes as we went through the small gate that was set to one side of the big, curly iron ones. Everything was different inside those gates: the road smoother, the trees growing so regular at either side, and the buildings around the stable-yard were bigger than a row of cottages. When we went through still more high, curly-patterned gates into the kitchen garden I could scarcely believe what I saw. It was so big, and yet so neat: rows of cabbages and onions and carrots and other vegetables I'd never seen before, were all bordered by little low hedges, and there wasn't a blade of grass out of place. The air was warm and still, and fruit trees grew like fans up the pink brick walls, with their crop basking in the sun. Mr Marsh's cottage was built right into one of those walls, and with its pointed windows and lacy white wooden trimmings to porch and roof it looked as pretty as a cottage in a fairy tale.

When Mr Marsh came out to meet us in his dark suit and black bowler and stiff white wing collar I bobbed at once – he looked just like one of the gentry, even though I knew Tommy Marsh was in the Infants class at our school. When he saw me Mr Marsh called Tommy out and told him to take me to pick some raspberries while he had a word with Granfer. The soft fruit were growing in great cages, to keep the birds off, and Tommy had to open a little door to let us in. Once inside he didn't say anything, he just seized handfuls of raspberries and crammed them into his mouth. Seeing as Grammer wasn't there to scold me I did the same; they were so sweet and juicy I kept pulling off more and more – until I saw the big red stain right on the front of my clean Sunday pinafore.

I turned and ran back to Granfer with tears in my eyes, and Granfer looked worried too, when he saw the state of me. But Mr Marsh said I mustn't cry, because Mrs Turnbull, Her Ladyship's housekeeper, would know how to get the stain out, so Grammer would never be any the wiser.

I could hardly breathe for excitement as I stepped over the

threshold of the Hall. Mr Marsh led me along a wide high passage, over flagstones scrubbed until they shone as white as snow. Then we climbed up a short flight of stairs and came to Mrs Turnbull's sitting room. Mr Marsh left me there, but I scarcely noticed him going – I was struck dumb with wonder. The whole room was full of furniture: deep red plush armchairs, cupboards that shone as though they were mirrors, and a huge oval table covered in a red furry cloth with bobbles all round the edge.

Mrs Turnbull, rustling in a dress of black silk, took me down to the stillroom – and that was even more wonderful. It smelt of roses and violets and lavender, and warm baking, while the walls were lined with row after row of jars of preserves which glowed ruby red and clear yellow and dark green and warm golden orange: it was like being inside a rainbow. Mrs Turnbull took a little bottle from a cupboard and dabbed at my pinafore until it was white, then she rinsed the damp patch over the gleaming white sink and hung it to dry by the range. Afterwards she gave me a gingerbread man on a fine china plate, then pressed a button by the door.

A beautiful lady came in and set an iron to heat at the range. She said it was one of the special pair she used to iron Her Ladyship's silk nightdresses, and when she'd finished my pinafore would be as good as new. She lifted me on to the big scrubbed table and gave me three jelly moulds to play with; I didn't know what jelly was and I was too shy to ask, but the shining pink metal was shaped like rabbits, crouching down with their ears flat, so I christened them Dan and Dick and Sally and sat stroking them.

I could hear the low murmur of voices by the fire as the lady waited for the iron to heat. 'Who is the little girl, Mrs Turnbull?'

'She's Mr Roberts' grand-daughter, Miss Evans.'

'Oh, what a shame – and she's such a pretty child, too.'

Mrs Turnbull sighed, and her voice dropped still lower. 'She's the image of Agnes at that age – the same fair hair with a nice little curl in it. Agnes had blue eyes, though – this child's are brown. You don't often see brown eyes with that colour of hair.'

The other lady glanced up, and smiled at me. I smiled back and she came closer and tipped up my chin. 'No, they're not brown – they're golden, like her hair. You have little yellow speckles in your eyes – did you know that, Amy?' I shook my head. 'Wait until I've finished your pinafore, and then I'll find you a present.'

27

She whisked away while Mrs Turnbull was helping me on with my pinafore, and when she came back she gave me a beautiful blue shiny ribbon – and she didn't even know it was my birthday.

When I showed it to Granfer later he told me that the lady was Her Ladyship's own personal maid, who mended her frocks when they were torn and helped her to dress in the mornings. I thought how lovely it would be to spend all day caring for the lovely dresses that Her Ladyship always wore, and mending the frills with the tiniest of tiny stitches.

In bed that night I put the ribbon under my cheek and remembered every wonderful sight I'd seen that day: the table-cloth with the bobble fringe, the rows of gleaming jars and, almost best of all, the shining white bowl I'd sat over when I'd told Mrs Turnbull I needed to go. When I'd finished she'd pulled a long chain and there'd been a great rushing of water – pailfuls and pailfuls of it swirling round and round the bowl until it was clean and shining again. If we had a dunnekin like that I'd be running up behind the cabbage patch every half hour – it was lovely.

When we went back to school after harvest Mrs Roper told me I was to go up into Standard III. I felt very proud of myself because I was only just eight and the rest of Standard III were nine, and several at the other end of the row were already ten. I couldn't wait to tell Granfer that evening.

But the very next week something even more exciting happened. We finished our spellings a bit before dinner, so Mrs Roper set the babies to chant their ABC and came to give us ten minutes mental. She'd ask the question, then, quick as a flash she'd call out a name – if it was yours, you had to answer.

'If three oranges cost tuppence how much do three dozen cost? Jack?'

'Add twenty-five, twenty-six and twenty-seven and divide by three. Dora?'

'If the inkwells in a desk are two feet apart, how many will be needed for three desks each eight feet long? Billy?'

'If a gentleman gave nine men three half-crowns to be shared equally between them, how much will each man receive? Amy?'

The little figures darted across the inside of my head until I saw the answer, clear as clear. 'Tenpence each, ma'am.'

28

The next question came rattling out. I did like mental, even though Standard III questions were a lot harder than Standard II.

The church clock began to strike for midday and the boys started to fidget, so Mrs Roper asked them a couple more questions, just to show who was in charge, and then closed her book. On the bench in front of me I saw Hannah sit up straight – she was bell monitor for that week – but Mrs Roper didn't call her name. Through the partition we could hear Mr Roper speaking to Standards IV and V before he dismissed them, so we waited.

'All the girls must make sure they're clean and tidy before they come back from dinner, and no scuffing your boots in the dust. Her Ladyship is coming to inspect your needlework.' I saw Hannah pull a face at Molly. Last lesson, Mrs Roper had made Hannah unpick the stitches of the side seam of the calico drawers she was making, because they'd been crooked. Her Ladyship was sure to spot the tell-tale needle pricks, so now she'd be told off again. 'Bell.' Hannah got up rather slowly, lifted down the brass bell and shook it, but I could see her heart wasn't in it today.

Outside she glared at me. 'It's all right for *you*, Amy – you're Her Ladyship's pet.'

'I dussent know for why,' Dora chipped in. 'She must know Amy be one o' *they*.' I sidled out behind them.

But when we got back at two o'clock and Mrs Roper gave out our needlework I was comforted by the sight of the neat, regular stitches of my seam; I did sew the tiniest stitches of all the girls – Grammer had seen to that.

The church clock had struck three before we heard the clip-clop of hooves slowing down and then stopping outside. Mrs Roper ordered, 'Sit up straight,' and her own back went stiff as she patted her hair smooth, and checked her bun. The footman threw open the door and we all jumped to our feet – as *two* ladies came in. We stared; we'd never seen the lady who was with Her Ladyship before. She was tall and slender and she seemed to glide into the room, her heels barely clicking on the wooden floor. Her nose was so straight and her face, it glowed like the pearls in Miss Mary's Sunday brooch; and I could see the pale gold of her hair sweeping up in one shining curve to nestle under the wide brim of her hat. She was beautiful. I gazed up at her, so lost in admiration that I'd have forgotten to bob if Dora hadn't dug her elbow into my ribs.

29

Mrs Roper brought her own chair forward, and sent the monitor rushing next door for Mr Roper's, then the two ladies sank down on the seats with a silken swish of petticoats, and Her Ladyship told us we could all sit down. Then she lifted one hand in its grey kid glove and said, 'Lady Warminster is staying at Pennings, and so she has come with me to inspect your needlework.' All our necks craned towards the tall lady, who was a countess, the wife of a lord, not just a 'Sir' like Sir Hugh. 'Lady Warminster is a particularly good judge of needlework, because she comes from France, and in France the nuns do the best sewing in the world.'

Mrs Roper gave the smallest of sniffs, quickly converted into a little cough, then she began to call us out, one by one. Her Ladyship made her usual comments: 'This buttonhole of Emily's is rather large, but we always feel her stitches are strong ones.' Lady Warminster swayed forwards to view Emily's combinations, but her finely shaped mouth with its little droop at the corners never moved. Piece after piece was inspected, and always Her Ladyship made some remark: 'This is better, Mary, but your stitching there is rather uneven.' 'A seam must always be *straight*, Bessy,' and still Lady Warminster said not a word. Then it was the turn of our bench.

Her Ladyship tut-tutted over the marks where Hannah had had to unpick – and Hannah came walking back red-faced and with her mouth set in a sulky line; then it was me walking out to the front. I held out my nightdress and Her Ladyship took it and displayed the yoke to Lady Warminster. 'Amy here is one of our *best* little seamstresses, Lady Warminster – just look at this feather stitching.'

The shining bird's wings on her hat dipped forward as I stood in front of her with my heart in my mouth. Then the wings slowly lifted, and eyes blue as forget-me-nots looked into mine – and gradually the drooping curve of her mouth straightened. 'This stitching is good, Lady Blanche, very good. Even little French girls taught by the nuns could do no better.' I heard Mrs Roper's sigh of relief, but my eyes were fixed on Lady Warminster's face as her mouth curved into an almost-smile. 'You must be a lady's maid when you grow up, ma petite – stitches as fine as these deserve to be set in ninon or guipure.' She had spoken to me! I gazed at her beautiful face in adoration. She reached out one gloved hand and gently patted my cheek; the scent of rose petals filled the air. 'Assieds-toi – sit down, little one, you have done well.' My feet seemed scarcely to touch the floor as I walked back to the bench.

I told Granfer all about her and what she'd said to me that evening while he was smoking his pipe – but Grammer broke in angrily saying nuns were wicked women who believed in false gods, and I should be ashamed of being compared with girls taught by such as them. The glow faded.

But later, when Granfer came up to the loft to say goodnight, he whispered that I was a clever little maid and had done well – and the glow came back a little. Then he dropped his voice even lower. 'Wouldst thee like to go for to be a lady's maid, Amy?'

'Oh Granfer! But Grammer –'

He bent his head so his beard brushed my ear. 'We'll see if thy Granfer can arrange it for thee. I could mebbe make a shilling or two by planting some extra veg – and if I put the old sty in order . . . But –,' he put his finger to his lips and nodded towards the floor.

I whispered, 'No, Granfer – I won't tell nobody.'

Chapter Five

Dimpsey, my beautiful Dimpsey: Granfer brought her home one afternoon in a sack. It was January, the wind was blowing outside and I'd spilled lamp oil on the table so Grammer had been angry; the tear streaks were drying on my cheeks as I scrubbed and scrubbed at the stain. Then Granfer opened the sack and lifted her out. She lay in his arms, her four tiny trotters hanging limply down, with only her little eyes alive – and frightened. Granfer sent me to the shed for a box, then he lined it with the sack and slid her down into it, beside the hearth. She gave a tiny, despairing squeal and at once I dropped on my knees beside the box and lifted the warm little body out, hugging and rocking it. 'There, there – don't 'ee fret. Amy'll look after thee.' Her little wet snout nuzzled my hand – and I loved her.

She was the dilling – the sow had had thirteen piglets, Granfer told us, 'And she'd only the twelve titties, so thic little 'un were starving.'

'Let I feed her, Granfer.' I dipped my finger in milk and put it to her mouth; I felt her little tongue lick me, and then she began to suck. Granfer had fetched home a bottle with a teat, and holding her in my arms I coaxed her to feed, and watched her throat quiver as she swallowed the good milk. When I could feel her small belly round and full under my hand I put her gently back in the box, and she snuffled like Mrs Rawlings' newest baby before settling herself down to sleep. Stroking her soft downy back I looked up at Granfer and asked, 'What be she called, Granfer?'

'She be a Tamworth pig, Amy.'

'But –'

His face crinkled into a smile. '*Thee* canst choose her name, my maid.' So I christened her Dimpsey, because Granfer had brought her home in the dimpsey, at twilight.

I heard Granfer get up in the night to feed her, so I climbed down to blow on the sticks and warm the milk, then I held the bottle – and after that I always fed her if I was at home. She'd be watching the door when I came in from school, and her little eyes would light up as she squealed with pleasure at seeing me.

When she got bigger Granfer mended the old sty, and then she went to live outside. I missed her watching me when I was doing my chores, but I knew she was only up at the end of the garden. I kept telling Grammer I had to go to the dunnekin – I always managed to squeeze a few drops out, so I wasn't telling a lie – then I'd rush out still buttoning my drawers and climb up on the stone Granfer had put there for me so I could lean over the wall of the sty. Even if Dimpsey was snug and warm in her little house she'd always come out to see me. Sometimes I'd climb right over and into her pen so I could put my arms around her neck and rub my cheek against her hairy one; then I'd whisper secrets to her, and her high, pointed ears would quiver – to show she was listening to every word.

The Rawlings had a pig, too. They had one every year, but theirs was a dirty white colour, with blotchy black spots – not a beautiful golden pig, like my Dimpsey. Its face was all fat and squashed, whereas my Dimpsey had a long elegant snout and a neat little pink nose; and its ears were all drooping instead of standing up straight. Even its tail wasn't a patch on Dimpsey's; it just hung there, completely straight, not flicking up into a nice curl like hers. And the Rawlings' pig, it waddled, while my Dimpsey, her little feet tip-tapped across the pen, stepping as daintily as Lady Warminster had in her high-heeled shoes.

As spring came on I'd go looking for tasty tid-bits for her in the ditches at the end of the lane: dandelion leaves, sow thistles and, best of all, fresh snails for her to crunch up. Granfer'd been fetching a can of skimmed milk for her to drink every afternoon, and for me, too – so we'd both grow big and strong; only Dimpsey drank more of it than I did. She liked her milk, did Dimpsey. But as the days got longer Granfer was home later from work and besides, he had to tend to the vegetables, so Grammer said I must go to fetch the milk instead. I had to walk along the path beside Goosey Meadow, right through Frog Wood and then down the track to the farm. My arms ached carrying the pail on the way back, but I didn't mind, because I was doing it for Dimpsey.

As summer came and Granfer's roses began to flower, so too did Goosey Meadow. Mrs Roper had told us in one of our object lessons that the sea looked like a meadow in June, and as I climbed over the stile I'd imagine that the rippling, swaying grasses were grey-green waves, and the moon daisies drifts of white foam. But as soon as I'd jumped down onto the path, then I saw the flower heads, one by one: ragged robin with its torn pink petals, spikes of speedwell, blue as the sky, purply scabious, crimson knapweed, yellow rattle, golden buttercups, white cuckoo flowers – all dancing amidst the green-grey grass.

Sometimes I'd put down my can and crouch on the path, just looking and listening: looking for green-gold beetles running shining across the bare earth, for hoppers, jumping like tiny green frogs from one stalk to another; watching bumble bees sauntering and honey bees searching while high above me I could hear the hoarse croak of the corncrake. All round me were the drifting specks of colour that were butterflies: blue, white, brown, pied – they would flutter past me to alight on a flower and spread their jewel-bright wings in the sun. I'd crouch, still as a statue until one, more careless than the others, would land on my hand – and for a fleeting moment I would feel the gentle brush of its wings, before it realised its mistake and fluttered leisurely away.

Then I'd remember Grammer, and the chores – and jumping up, I'd seize my can and set off running along the path and over the next stile under its arch of brier roses, only to slow down again as soon as I was in the woods. The trees, they cast a spell over me, and I'd dawdle along the track listening to the gentle rustling of the leaves, and watching them making green, ever-changing patterns against the blue-white of the sky.

I loved the woods. I was safe there under the green ceiling, treading soft on the fallen leaves of last autumn which were slowly mingling with the dark earth. The trees were kind, and sheltered me; if the wind blew sharp or the rain fell cold and wet then the wood offered me its protection. Sometimes I set down my can and left the track, threading through the undergrowth, in among the tree trunks to where an oak grew oddly, so that one of its boughs curved low and almost touched the ground. I'd spring up so I could sit down on it, and press my face against the rough friendly bark of the trunk, reaching my arms around it as far as they would go, clinging to the everlasting strength of the living wood. Above me the rustling leaves would endlessly whisper my name, 'Amy, Amy.'

34

But one day, when I came back to the track, a dark shape stood looming over my milk can. I stopped dead, and it turned and looked at me – it was Dummy Drew. My heart began to thud in my chest, so that I thought he must hear it, then forcing his tongue back into his mouth he tried to speak – but no sound came. His large red hand came up, and beckoned; I was frightened as I walked towards him. He put one finger up to his swollen lips, then turned and slid, clumsily but silently, between the trees on the other side of the track. I looked at my can, then back at him as he swung round to see if I was following; his little eyes were round and pleading, just like Dimpsey's when she was begging for her tea, so slowly I tiptoed after him. He stopped, his fat finger pointing downwards – and I saw it: a little ball of golden fur, hanging from a bindweed stem. Great dark eyes shone out above a quivering pink nose; the tiny fingers on its hands and feet held it firmly anchored, while its fluffy golden tail curled up over the whiteness of its belly. The dormouse's whiskers trembled as I gazed entranced at those shining dark eyes and whispered, 'What be thy name?' Suddenly, with a flick of its tail it uncoiled its body and there was a flash of pure gold as it jumped, lithe and sleek, across to a twig and away.

The large, awkward body beside me turned, and the misshapen lips worked until at last Dummy managed to get out a 'D – d,' and I realised what he was trying to tell me, and waited for the eventual, stammering, 'D – dor – dor – mouse.' Then he lumbered back to the track, picked up my can and held it out to me, his red-rimmed eyes imploring.

I reached out my hand and took the can from him, saying, 'Thank you, Mr Drew.' His distorted mouth rearranged itself into what I knew was a smile, so I smiled back before setting off over the ruts and down to the gate.

After that day he often waited for me by the stile, and lurched awkwardly through the wood at my side. His hand would point and there'd be a flash of blue-barred wings and black tail as a jay flew up, or he'd show me a fat furry caterpillar feeding on a leaf, or stab the ground close to the whorl of a snail's shell, its horned head poking blindly out as it oozed along a root. But he never hurt anything, Dummy didn't.

Sometimes he'd be there at the gate as I came back, and then he'd take the heavy can from me and lurch through the wood with it – holding it stiffly in one hand, so as not to spill a drop. But he never came out of Frog Wood – he liked to hide in there.

When I got home Dimpsey would be waiting for me, giving little grunts of excitement. I'd dip in a mug and drink my share, then I'd pour the rest of the can into the little taters Grammer had set to boil in the pot liquor from yesterday's vegetables. When I'd mashed it all up with some barley meal I'd take the pailful out and pour it into her trough as she squealed in ecstasy. She liked her tea, did Dimpsey.

When she'd finished eating I'd scratch her back with the special stick I kept propped up against the wall of the sty and she'd shudder and squeal with delight. The minute I put the stick away she'd flop down against the wall of the pen and turn her face up to mine – and I'd reach right over so I could stroke the soft skin behind her ear. She'd gaze at me from under the golden fringe of her eyelashes, her eyes loving and happy, and when I drew back to leave her she'd kiss my hand with her soft wet nose, to tell me she didn't want me to go. But I had to, because Grammer needed me to do the chores.

I did a lot of the work around the house now. On Monday as soon as I arrived home at dinner-time I'd climb up on my stool by the wash-tub and rub and rub on the ridged board until my hands were red and wrinkled from the soda; in the evening I'd feed the clean clouts through the mangle while Granfer turned the handle for me. If it didn't rain I'd be using the smaller pair of flat-irons on Tuesday to iron the linen. Thursday was baking day – Grammer wouldn't have boughten bread in the house – so I'd get up early to knead the dough and then set it to rise in front of the fire; Grammer still lit the faggots in the oven and raked the hot ashes out, but soon I'd be old enough to do that, too.

On Saturday every nook and cranny had to be cleaned ready for the Sabbath. I'd scrub the table and dust the chairs and polish the dresser and the chest of drawers where Grammer kept her grave clothes; then the bedroom had to be given a good going-over, and the loft swept and tidied. Back downstairs the floors had to be scrubbed and the flags in the back kitchen whitened with hearthstone. Last of all I had to take my brush and pail down to clean the dunnekin. I'd never felt quite the same about our dunnekin since I'd seen the one up at the Hall. I'd scrub the two seats until the wood dried snowy white, and raddle the bricks so they glowed a nice warm red – but it still smelt. I couldn't do anything about that. The smell got worse and worse all summer, until even the honeysuckle round the door seemed to give up trying, and then, the day Granfer emptied the pit in the autumn! The entire garden reeked, and even with all the doors and windows closed it seeped into the cottage down the chimney.

Saturday was hard work, but once I was sitting in the bath behind the sheets with the fire warm at my side, then I felt a glow of satisfaction that everything was clean and tidy for Sunday. Besides, all of us girls had to do chores now we were older – that's what being a girl meant. We'd be playing out in the lane at 'Thread the Tailor's Needle' or 'Nuts in May' and then a mother would come out in the road and call, and whoever was called would have to go rushing in. Grammer never called, she'd just open the door a twitch and then I'd know and run back as fast as I could. She'd say, 'Fetch the potatoes,' or, 'Thic water pail's empty,' then I'd run out the back feeling important, because I'd know her rheumatics were paining her, and she needed my help. I did like to be needed.

Some dinner-times I'd have to run all the way back to school, and arrive with a stitch in my side and no time to play in the yard. I was sorry to miss the games, but at least there were the afternoon lessons to look forward to, especially now I'd passed Standard III and moved up to Standard IV. Hannah was still in Standard II, and she said schooling was a waste of time, and she'd rather do chores – but then it was different for Hannah, because her chore was a baby. Mrs Fuller had a new one every year in the spring, and then Hannah would be put in charge of the old one – carrying it around and teaching it to walk and talk. Lots of girls had babies to look after, not just Hannah, and I'd have liked one myself. Once, when I wasn't very old, I'd asked Grammer if I could have a baby, too; her face went very red, and the veins on her forehead bulged with anger. I knew better than to ever ask again. But now I'd got Dimpsey I didn't envy Hannah her baby any more.

I loved Dimpsey more than ever; her golden-red coat was long and glossy and her face was plump and happy – she'd grown so much since she'd first come to us in January. But when Mr Rawlings leant over the sty of an evening and said to Granfer,

37

'Thic pig be fattening nicely now,' I didn't swell with pride any more. Instead, I felt a worm of uneasiness wriggle in my mind, and my chest would go tight, so I'd run back indoors saying, 'Be there aught else to do, Grammer?' And when Granfer was smoking his pipe after tea and I'd be telling him how clever Dimpsey had been that day, or how she'd tried to tip over her trough even with the ring in her nose, he didn't seem to want to know, and he'd start telling me about something he'd done that day, instead.

It was harvest-time again; the sheaves of corn stood golden in the fields, waiting to be tossed up onto the big waggons and carried away to the barns. The roses drooped, and soon their faded petals lay scattered on the ground. Cuckoo and corncrake fell silent, and then it was September and time for school to begin again.

First morning back I could see straight away that Hannah had something to tell us. All of us girls were supposed to be learning our weekly Psalm, but Hannah tried to whisper to Dora, then, when she saw Mrs Roper glaring at her, she edged over to me – but as soon as she opened her mouth Mrs Roper came marching up and rulered her hand, so she had to keep quiet until break.

The minute the bell rang the three of us went over behind the dunnekins, and Lizzie Hale came panting up behind us – she'd been watching Hannah, too. Hannah peered round to see that none of the boys were listening and then announced, 'Our Tom's getting married.'

Dora exclaimed, 'Thy Tom? But he baint old enough!'

'That's what Mam said, but Da, he said if Tom be old enough to go meeting Jenny Wells in the woods, then he do be old enough to put ring on her finger – so now they'm got to get wed.'

I felt panic rising. 'But – I do meet Dummy Drew up in Frog Wood most every afternoon when I go to fetch the milk. Dost that mean I do have to marry him?' Dora burst out laughing, and the others joined in. I looked from one to the other, bewildered. 'I dussent, do I?'

Dora gave Lizzie a knowing smile, then said, 'Depends what he did to thee, Amy.' Her voice dropped. 'Did he put his diddler in thy cunny?' I just stared at her. Dora's voice became jeering. 'She dussent know how it do happen!' She leant forward, putting her face very close to mine. 'A man, he do put his diddler in a woman's

38

cunny and gives her a squirt, and then she has a baby – but she orter be married first.'

Hannah butted in, 'My Mam, she said it baint fair on our Tom. She says no decent girl ever lets a boy take liberties, so it were Jenny's fault. But Da, he said Tom's still got to marry her, and soon – else baby'll be a bastard and branded for life – like Amy be.'

Three pairs of eyes swivelled in my direction, and there was a little silence. I felt my cheeks go hot, then Dora spoke. 'How do it feel Amy, being a bastard?'

'I – I dussent know.'

Dora's eyes narrowed. 'Fancy knowing your Mam let men put diddlers in her cunny, without her being married to 'em – eugh!' They all edged away from me. 'I did hear my Mam say once as your Mam were too pretty – it were bound to happen.'

'You be pretty, Amy – you be prettiest girl in school.'

'Like mother, like daughter – that's what they say.' Dora leant forward and jabbed her finger in my ribs. 'Are thee *sure* Dummy Drew didn't put his diddler in thy cunny, Amy?'

'No!'

The others looked at each other, and I heard their sniggers – then the bell rang and I turned and ran as fast as I could to the girls' door.

It was dictation next, but I couldn't seem to put my mind to it. I wrote 'until' with two l's in the very first line and Mr Roper noticed and shouted at me for being careless. I did try to concentrate, but I couldn't forget what Dora had said – it made me feel all hot and shivery inside.

After school I set off as usual with the can, but my legs lagged through Goosey Meadow, then I jumped off the stile and began to trot through Frog Wood, hoping Dummy wasn't there today. But he came lurching out from behind two oak trees, his face working, all excited because he'd got something to show me – and I remembered Dora saying. 'Did he put his diddler in thy cunny?' and as I looked at his slobbering mouth I went so hot I thought I'd burn to a cinder. As he came up to me I said, 'I dussent want to meet thee in the woods, Dummy Drew – not never again.' I gripped my can and hurried quickly past him, keeping as far away from him as I could. He tried to say my name, 'A – Am –' but he couldn't get it all out, and then I'd left him behind. I turned and looked back once, frightened in case he was following me, but he was just standing there with his humped back sagging; and as I looked at his face I saw the tears shining wet on his cheeks, then I turned and ran as fast as I could to the gate.

I brought the full can back the long way round, along the road, and I was late so Grammer was angry and Dimpsey was squealing with impatience. When she'd finished I put my arms around the place where her neck used to be and wept against her soft ears, but I didn't want Dummy to put his diddler in my cunny, I couldn't have borne it. I had to go back through Frog Wood eventually because Grammer got annoyed when I took longer, but Dummy never met me again. Once I saw the dark shape of him through the trees, and the white blur of his face as he looked at me – then he turned and ran, lurching and stumbling, away into the dark depths of the wood.

Chapter Six

October. There was mist in the early morning now, and the boys were squabbling over the conkers from the two horse chestnuts by the pond. The trees had donned their autumn coats and soon, so soon, they began to doff them. I played 'Catch Leaves' under the ash tree in the lane as I did every year, but now I leapt more frantically for each precious leaf – I was desperate for wishes this autumn. Every time I caught one golden trophy I made my impossible plea: 'I wish, I wish – that November will never come.' But all too soon the ash tree was a gaunt grey skeleton: November had come.

As I walked to the farm each afternoon the oaks in Frog Wood were shedding their leaves, but I didn't play 'Catch' any more. The dead and dying leaves rustled under my boots as I plodded along the track, and on my way back it was an effort to put one foot before the other. The can weighed heavier and heavier and I felt so tired. By the time I got home my arms were aching, my back was aching, and my neck – it never seemed to stop hurting. Often as I fed Dimpsey I'd feel the tears trickling down my cheeks, and would dash them quickly away so I could smile at her as I scratched her back.

One morning Grammer said I mustn't give Dimpsey any breakfast. When I went up to the dunnekin her small, bright eyes smiled at me; then she nudged her trough with her snout. I stood up on the stone and leant right over the wall, putting my arms as far around her as they'd go; she grunted, and nuzzled my chest. I rubbed my cheek against her rough, hairy one, and kissed the soft furry fringe of her ear; her wet nose kissed me back. Then it was time for school.

In the yard I heard Johnny Yates calling to the others boys, and as I came nearer I heard their excited shouts: 'Pig-sticker's coming tonight!' I stumbled, and almost fell – then I told myself, it's for the Rawlings' pig, I know it is. But half my spellings were wrong that morning, and in mental the numbers wouldn't add up.

After dinner I stayed up the garden, scratching Dimpsey's back and tickling the special spot behind her ears; she gave little squeals of delight, grunting her thanks. I couldn't bear to leave her, and I was late back to school. Mr Roper rulered my hand, but I didn't seem to care, today.

When I got home Grammer sent me for extra water; she'd got the fire blazing and barley cooking in the pot. She told me not to go for the milk today. Instead I must scour the can until it was spotless; then she set me to shredding bread and suet and preparing fresh herbs. My hands shook as I chopped, so I could scarcely handle the knife.

Granfer came home early, and I ran to him as I always did – but he didn't smile at me tonight, instead his eyes slid to the floor. 'Granfer?' My voice trembled, and then he looked at me, smiling – but it wasn't a proper smile. He went out again, still wearing his boots.

It was almost dark; there were voices outside. I heard Mr Rawlings' gruff tones, others I didn't recognise, the excited shouts of boys – then, high above every other sound – a shrill squeal of fright. I ran to the door, but Grammer called me back, pointing to the can. 'Bring that.' Then she set off up the path, and I followed on legs that trembled.

The sty door was open, my Dimpsey had gone; there were folk milling round among the apple trees to the side, moving under the lanterns, casting dark shadows on the grass. Grammer's fingers hard on my shoulders drove my stiff legs on – and then I saw her, my Dimpsey. She was lying on a bench with her little trotters tightly bound and her golden flank heaving with terror. I dropped the can to run to her, but Grammer's fingers closed like a vice. 'Pick up thic can.' And out of the darkness between the lanterns came a man, and the light glinted on the knives in his belt. 'No – not my Dimpsey!'

'Take thic can – you maun catch the blood.'

'No, Grammer – I cassent.'

Mrs Rawlings' voice: 'I'll hold can for her, Missus Roberts – she be only a young maid.'

'She's old enough to learn. Go!' Grammer's finger pointing, Grammer's voice commanding – like the Voice of God. Dimpsey's little eyes rolling in fear, then, as she caught sight of me, looking straight into mine, begging me to save her. Grammer's hand, iron on my shoulder as the knife flashed and there was a high-pitched scream of terror and little bound feet were frantically scrabbling as a voice shouted, 'She baint dead yet, Charlie.' My Dimpsey's eyes – a slash, another shriek, cut off as her eyes dulled – and her blood spurted out.

'Catch it.' At Grammer's harsh command I fell on my knees by my Dimpsey and held the can to her torn throat as her life-blood bubbled into it. A spoon was thrust into my hand. 'Stir it,' and I stirred.

'Keep stirring.'

'Make a nice black pudding that will, Mrs Roberts.'

'Lovely flavour – with a few herbs to season it.'

'Keep stirring.'

I stirred and stirred until the blood slowed to a dribble and the white of her windpipe showed through; then Granfer took the can from me. I looked up into his face, but his eyes wouldn't meet mine.

I stood there while they tossed straw onto my Dimpsey and set light to it; they burnt my Dimpsey, and her beautiful golden coat flared up and filled the air with the reek of singed hair. The men with the pitchforks were devils, and the flames, they were the searing flames of Hell; my heart in my chest seemed to burn with Dimpsey.

Grammer let go of my shoulder at last, but I still stood watching, until the flames died down and her poor bare skin showed, all brown and scorched. Then the pig-sticker pulled off her dainty little feet and threw them to the boys, who cheered and scuffled for them – and then began to gnaw at them, all blackened with soot as they were.

As the water was flung over her, and the pig-sticker began to scrape her steaming body Grammer jerked her head, and I followed her back to the kitchen.

I boiled her blood and stirred in the herbs and barley. Then, forcing my shaking hands to be steady, I poured the dark mixture into earthenware dishes, for baking next day. But when Grammer took out the pan and began to fry her liver I turned away without a word and climbed up the ladder into the loft. I crept under the sheets without taking my clothes off, and huddled there, shivering. I heard Granfer climb up and call me, but I wouldn't answer. He pulled himself right up into the loft and stroked my hair with his hand, but I stayed still as a stone. After a while he went away. I couldn't cry, there was no point. I just lay there, staring into the darkness. All I could see were Dimpsey's eyes, begging me to save her as I stood there, holding the can to catch her blood – like Judas.

Mrs Rawlings came in and helped Grammer cut up the flear, and it bubbled on the fire until its fatty smell filled the whole cottage. Dimpsey's body lay on a slab in the larder, soaking in salt; and every day I had to get down on my hands and knees and mop up the brine which oozed out of it and seeped across the back kitchen floor.

Grammer lit the oven and baked faggots and pies; she made brawn and stuffed sausages, then cooked them for tea. But I wouldn't touch any of them. She didn't say anything at first, until one day she took hold of my jaw and tried to force my mouth open – but it stayed locked against her. She was white with anger and I was afeard of her, but I wouldn't eat my Dimpsey.

Soon I could hardly eat anything else, either. The ache in my throat had got worse, it seemed to have almost closed up – and when I put my hand to my neck I could feel great lumps swelling out under my jaw. Granfer fetched me fresh milk from the farm, and soaked bread in it; I swallowed it, but it gave me no strength. I could scarcely drag myself to school and back, and at playtime I sat huddled on the cold ground in a corner of the yard with my head on my knees until the bell rang. As I did my chores at dinner-time and in the evening my whole body ached, and the weight of my needle as I sewed was almost more than I could bear.

Once Mrs Rawlings said to me, 'She was just a pig, Amy – and pigs do have to be killed. 'Tis only nature.'

I whispered, 'She wasn't just a pig – she was my Dimpsey.' And I wouldn't eat her.

Eventually Granfer fetched the doctor from Pennings. He held my wrist, peered down my throat and listened to my chest, before prodding the lumps in my neck with his hard hands. Then he told Granfer the milk had poisoned me, and I must have no more. He said I was to stay in bed all day and all night until the lumps went down. Grammer told him she needed me downstairs to do the chores and run errands, but he turned on her and shouted that if it wasn't done as he said then he wouldn't be answerable for the consequences. So Granfer said he'd pay Emmy Rawlings to come in each day to help, and Grammer didn't speak again.

I crept upstairs and got undressed and crawled into bed. It wasn't even dark, but I didn't want to go downstairs ever again – not with Dimpsey's body hanging from the beams down there.

I woke the next morning as I heard Granfer moving about below, and began to force my legs out of bed, then I remembered the doctor had said I mustn't get up. I put my tired head back on the pillow and stared up into the darkness of the thatch. The world had gone all wrong since Dimpsey had died, and now, lying in bed when I should be up lighting the fire and packing Granfer's nammet in his basket, that was all part of the wrongness. Granfer brought me a cup of tea and a slice of bread and lard, but I wouldn't look at him. Then I heard his boots on the flags and knew he'd gone to work.

I lay dozing, remembering Dimpsey, with the tears trickling slowly down my cheeks because my hands were too tired to wipe them away. Then I heard the door opening below, quick footsteps and Emmy Rawlings' voice calling, 'Missus Roberts, I be y'ere.' Soon after, Emmy's head appeared over the trapdoor. 'Bist thee awake, Amy? Give I thy chamber'n I'll empt en.' She came panting back with a bucket half-full of water, then carried up a steaming jug and my soap and flannel. 'There y'are! Thy Grammer said to tell thee: "Cleanliness be next to godliness", so thee must wash thyself all over every morn.' My arms and legs were heavy as lead, and the lumps in my neck ached worse than ever; I was so slow, the water in the bucket was cold by the time I'd finished. But Grammer was right: I must always keep myself clean.

Emmy came back at midday and brought up my dinner. I saw the pieces of bacon floating in the broth and my throat closed up. Emmy said, 'Mr Roberts, he did say as thee must eat it. 'Tis doctor's orders.' I looked at the bowl, but I wouldn't reach out for it. Granfer had held her down on the bench – and let Grammer make me hold the can. Emmy came closer, and put her finger to her lips, whispering, 'Thy Granfer said to tell thee it be all right' – she pointed into the bowl – 'thic bacon baint hern. Last night,

45

when thy Grammer was asleep, he and my Da, they did change all the flitches over. So thic be our pig, not yourn.' Grammer called from below and Emmy thrust the bowl and spoon down in my lap and scuttled to the ladder. The smell of the broth wafted up and tickled my nose; I picked up the spoon and began, very slowly, to eat.

Granfer came up that evening with my tea; I didn't look at him. He shuffled awkwardly from one foot to the other, then said, 'Amy, me love – I be main sorry I ever did bring thic little dilling home.' And I remembered Dimpsey, and what a lovely little piglet she'd been – and began to sob. Granfer came over to the bed and knelt down and put his arms around me. I climbed onto his lap and cried and cried as he rocked me, stroking my hair with his work-roughened hands. Mrs Rawlings was right, pigs had to die; and I knew Granfer couldn't have helped letting Grammer make me hold the can. He was afeard of her, just like I was.

Chapter Seven

The days were very long up in the loft, but at least there were voices to be heard out in the lane, and if I turned on my side I could see the bare branches of the ash tree waving in the wind. But after Emmy had drawn the curtain and gone back next door I just lay staring up at the dark rafters, and the even darker strips of thatch between, waiting for Granfer to come home.

I'd hear the sound of his boots on the scraper, then the click of the latch and the creak of the door as it opened, and the shadows would lighten a little. But I knew he'd only be able to put his head over the trap for a minute or two, because Grammer was waiting for him to fetch the water and bring in the coals – and besides, she'd want to complain about Emmy not doing this or that right.

Later, Granfer'd bring up my tea and stop for a word or two, but Grammer's voice'd call out, annoyed, 'Thy vittals be a-cooling, master,' and he'd pat my shoulder and climb down the ladder, quick.

So I'd have to wait until Grammer had gone to bed and I could hear her snores rattling out, and then, after a few minutes, there'd be the pad of Granfer's stockinged feet on the flags and he'd climb up the ladder and reach his arms out to me. I'd clamber on to his lap and he'd hold me, rocking me like I was a baby, just loving me until the loneliness of the day had worn off. Then he'd wrap me up tight in a blanket and settle down with me next to the warmth of the chimney-breast and I'd whisper, 'Tell I a story, Granfer. Tell I the story o' thic men as seed the moon shining in a pond, and did try to pull en out with a hayrake.' And he'd settle my head against his shoulder and say, 'Well, it were in this way . . .'

Another night I'd ask for the story of Tom and the three sillies, and Granfer'd tell me about the boy who fed the hens with boiling water, thinking they'd lay eggs ready cooked, and the man who kept jumping high up into the air of a morning to get both feet into his trousers at once. ' "Git out, you girt gawk," says Tom. "Why dussent 'ee put one foot in at a time? 'Tis as easy as shelling peasen, then." ' And Granfer's voice would get slower and deeper as he went on, ' "Well, to be sure," says the chap. "What a gurt silly I be. I never thought o' that!" ' Next day I'd lie in bed and remember the story, and Granfer's voice sounding so surprised as he said, 'I never thought o' that!' and the ache in my neck would ease a little.

Some nights I'd slip my hand into Granfer's waistcoat pocket and take out his lucky stone with the hole in it, and ask him to tell me about how he'd found it when he was a little boy and had been out in the field, bird-scaring. Granfer'd had to go out to work when he was only six year old – his mam had needed the money – so he'd never gone to school and learnt to read and write. Besides, there'd been no school in his village then, and schooling had to be paid for in those days. It was different now, you had to go until you were thirteen – unless you could pass Standard V and get your Labour Certificate – then you could leave as soon as you were twelve.

When he was young Granfer had lived in Somerset, over beyond Bath. Granfer'd been to Bath more'n once – a great city it was, of high stone buildings and such traffic as you'd never believe. Then he'd got the wanderlust and come to help a shepherd in Wiltshire, on the Downs over by Salisbury, in a village owned by a lord who was so important he had a whole town named after him. 'And what lord might that be, Amy?'

I'd whisper, 'Lord Warminster. Lady Warminster, she did praise my feather-stitching, Granfer.'

'So she did – but it were a long time ago as I'm talking of, so I reckon it weren't same lord as she be married to.'

Then Granfer had decided to go back to Somerset, so he'd set off over the Downs, walking and getting lifts from carriers, but one day he'd stopped at the back door of a fine big house to ask for a drink of water, and a maid with hair as yellow as daffodils in the sun had come to the door and given him a piece of rabbit pie with his water. So Granfer had gone to the next village and got a job – because that maid was Grammer. 'Terrible pretty she were, with eyes that were blue as the cornflowers after a shower in summer.' And I'd think of Grammer, with her grey hair all dragged back in a bun and her back bent over with the rheumatics, and decide that Granfer must be remembering wrong.

Eventually I'd fall asleep on Granfer's lap, and wake up the next morning back in bed, with another long, lonely day in front of me. If I lay very still the mice would come out to eat the crumbs from my breakfast: their bright eyes and quivering whiskers would make a bit of company, but the minute I moved or tried to talk to them, they'd go scampering back into their holes and I'd be left alone again.

But one day Granfer came up the ladder with something bulging in his pocket. 'See what I hast for thee, Amy.' He tugged and tugged – and suddenly out came a little hairy man! 'He did belong to Miss Mary at the Rectory, but she sent en along to thee, for being a good liddle maid in Sunday School.'

I gazed at him, then at once I pulled myself up in bed and held out my arms; Granfer put him into them, and I cradled the soft furry body. As he looked up at me with his brown button eyes I asked, 'What be thy name?'

Granfer said solemnly, 'Miss Mary, she never said nothing about no name, so thee must christen him thyself.'

And at once I knew what he was called. 'He be Esau, because he be an hairy man.'

Granfer chuckled. 'He baint never no man, Amy. He be a liddle monkey – look, he do have a long tail!'

But I knew he was a man, just like Esau in the Bible, who was tricked out of his birthright by his brother Jacob, all for a mess of pottage. I never had liked the sound of Jacob, who was a smooth man – now I felt really angry with him for cheating my Esau.

After Esau came, the days didn't seem so long. I'd whisper to him all the stories Granfer had told me the night before, and his eyes would blink and his head would nod as he listened to me. I held him clasped to my chest at night, and when I woke I wasn't so frightened by the dark now, because I knew Esau would look after me; and if my neck hurt he'd put his furry arms right around it, and gradually the ache would go away, and I'd be able to sleep again.

Every week or so the doctor would come to see me. I'd hear his voice saying to Grammer, 'I was just passing by,' and then he'd come climbing up the ladder, much quicker than Granfer ever did. He'd hold my wrist, then he'd unwind the bandages and feel my neck. When he'd done them up again he'd tell me I was a good girl and ask if I'd stayed up in the loft all the time, like he'd told me to.

I'd answer, 'Aye, sir. I baint never been downstairs since you did a-come thic first time.' He'd smile, and leave me two more bottles of medicine before he dropped down the trap and away.

I took a spoonful of each medicine night and morning, as he'd told me. One smelled of fish and was thick and oily, the other tasted sweet and bitter both together. Iron it was, the doctor told me once, and I imagined it making little horseshoes in my stomach, all pointing the right way up, so I'd be lucky. Granfer brought a third bottle, but that had to be a secret; he'd fetched it from Missus Miles, who was a wart-charmer over beyond Frog Wood. Folk said she was a witch, and always crossed their fingers when they passed her in the street, but Granfer reckoned she knew some powerful spells, so I took a spoonful of her potion every night too, and three when the moon was new. But he said I mustn't tell Grammer or the doctor, so we hid the bottle behind the chest of drawers.

Slowly the lumps in my neck grew smaller and smaller, and the doctor grunted in a pleased way when he came. I asked, 'Can I get up now?'

'Not just yet, child. Are you getting bored?'

I nodded. 'The days, they be main long up here. Granfer, he do come up after Grammer be a-sleeping, and then he tells I tales – but he be out at work all day long.'

'Can you read yet?'

'"O" course I can. I do be in Standard IV already.'

He smiled. 'What a clever girl you are – then I'll see what I can find for you.'

A couple of days later he stopped by again, and came up the ladder. 'Here, you can read your own tales now. My daughter enjoyed hearing these when she was in the nursery.' He dropped a whole book onto my lap.

'For I?'

'Yes, you can keep it.'

'Oh thank 'ee, sir, thank 'ee.'

Straightaway I opened it and began to read: 'There was once a very rich merchant, who had three daughters . . .' and I became lost in the story about the merchant's youngest daughter, whose name was Beauty. She loved roses, just like I did, and so she asked her father to bring her one back when he went on a journey. Her

50

father couldn't find one to buy, so he stole a rose from the gardens of a great castle – but both the castle and the rose belonged to a hideous monster, and when he saw what Beauty's father had done he roared at him in a fury, telling him he must die, unless one of his daughters consented to give herself up in her father's place. Beauty, she offered to, and came in fear and trembling to the castle, to be the captive of the terrible Beast. She was expecting him to eat her, but although he was so frightful to look upon he never did harm Beauty. No, instead he was kind to her, and gave her fine clothes and jewels and embroidery silks so she could sew; she had little apes to wait on her as servants, and her own special room in the castle, with beautiful furniture and all the books she could possibly want to read – and outside she could wander whenever she wished in the Beast's beautiful rose garden.

She never saw the Beast, except in the evening when he came to sup with her. Then he'd speak to her in his harsh, rasping voice – but what he said was so kindly and sensible that she became quite fond of him, despite his awful appearance. Only every evening before he left Beauty, he asked her if she would marry him, and of course she had to tell him 'no', and then the Beast was so sad that Beauty was sorry for him, and I was, too.

Along with her other presents the Beast had given Beauty a magic mirror, and in this mirror she could see her home, and that her father had fallen ill with pining after her, so one evening she asked the Beast if she might go home on a visit, to cheer her poor father up. The Beast didn't want her to go, because he'd miss her so much, all alone in his great castle – but he told Beauty he'd rather be unhappy himself than have her fretting, so she could go, even though he would die of grief if she never came back. At this Beauty wept, and promised faithfully that she would return to him at the end of a week.

But Beauty was so happy to be home she forgot her promise to the poor Beast, and it was ten whole days before she put on the magic ring he'd given her and was transported back to the castle – and when she got there, there was no Beast to be found! She became very upset, and so did I as she searched and searched for him; then at last, she found him lying unconscious in his rose garden. She was so stricken with grief to find him dying that at once she fell on her knees beside him and flung her arms around his furry neck crying that she would marry him, she would.

Immediately there was a flash of lightning and a clap of thunder – and she found she was embracing a handsome prince! He told her he'd been put under a spell by a wicked fairy, and had been condemned to live as a hideous Beast until a beautiful girl consented to marry him and so set him free. Beauty and the prince promptly got married, and lived happily ever after. I sighed with pleasure when I'd read the last word – it was such a lovely story.

I turned over the page and saw the title *Cinderella*. This story began: 'There was once upon a time, a gentleman who married for his second wife the proudest and most haughty woman that ever was known . . .'

I read all day, entering a magical world where nothing was as it seemed to be. The frog was really a prince and the miller's daughter spun straw into gold and so became a queen; even the homely beanstalk was a ladder to the sky. A cat wore boots and spoke to a king, mice became horses and a rat turned into a coachman; a princess pricked her finger and slept for a hundred years, awaiting the kiss of her prince. Glass slippers and poisoned apples, witches and fairies, giants and dwarfs – and a boy no bigger than a thumb –I read about them all.

As I lay alone in the loft, with only the book for company, the boundary between the real world and the story-tale world blurred and shifted; reality and illusion mingled and became one. After I'd read each story I'd lie imagining it all in my head: Jack climbing Granfer's beanpoles, right up to the sky; Snow White wandering in Frog Wood, looking for the dwarfs' cottage; the princess sleeping up in the housekeeper's room at the Hall, with everyone else asleep around her – Mrs Turnbull, Miss Evans, Mr Marsh – right down to Tommy Marsh, with his face all smeared with raspberry juice.

It was a wondrous world, a fairy-tale world – and gradually I became part of it too. I was Snow White, sheltering in the miniature house of the dwarfs, sinking my teeth into the tempting, rosy apple that would poison me. And it was I who lay in that glass coffin, waiting for my prince to lift it up and shake the piece of poisoned apple free. I was Bluebeard's wife, desperately trying to clean the magic key, shuddering with revulsion at the slippery feel of the blood on my fingers. I was Jack, climbing the beanstalk, Red Riding Hood dilly-dallying in the woods as I looked for flowers and innocently telling the wolf where I was going. I was the sleeping princess waiting for her kiss, and I was Beauty in the garden of the Beast, weeping over his great dying body as he sadly whispered, 'You forgot your promise, Beauty.'

That was my favourite story – the first one I'd read. Not just because it was the first, and started with a rose – but also because no one got hurt in that story: there were no knives, no blood, no cruelty – except for the Beast shouting at Beauty's father at the beginning. But he'd only done that because he was desperate for Beauty to come and stay with him, and break the spell. Besides, he must have been so lonely, the poor Beast, living in that great castle all on his own.

Every evening I told all the stories I'd read to Granfer, then I asked him if he knew any tales about princes and princesses, but he shook his head, then he said he knew a couple about lords and ladies, so I asked for those instead. One was about the cruel Lord of Dunster, who was going to take the common land from the poor people. His gentle lady begged him not to, so he said he wouldn't, as long as she walked all around the common in a single night – barefoot. He didn't think she'd do it, because she was ill of a fever and it was the depths of winter, but she rose from her bed and began to walk. The people of Dunster pleaded with her to stop, she was so poorly – but she walked on and on, right round the common; only as dawn came she fell down in a dead faint, and her Lord had to carry her home. 'Were he kind to her then, Granfer?'

'I dunno, my maid – I daresay he were.'

The other tale Granfer had from a shepherd who came from up north, and I liked it better. It was the story of the Lord of Duncombe; one day he saw a pretty servant girl in a sunbonnet swinging on a gate – and fell in love with her, there and then. He sent her off to school to learn her letters, and when she came home again he married her, because she was so pretty and he did love her so much. I wondered if maybe a lord would fall in love with me one day – and I wouldn't need to go away to school because I'd already passed Standard III.

It was the very next day that I began to make up my own story – it was about my mother. She'd been beautiful, with hair as golden as the lilies in the Rectory garden and eyes as blue as speedwell. One day she'd met a gentleman and he'd fallen in love with her,

53

just like the Lord of Duncombe. He'd taken her off to a little church and put a golden ring on her finger, and they'd been married before the Rector, all right and proper. But one evening he'd fallen off his horse into the river – the big river Granfer had told me of, that ran through Bath – and he'd been drowned. My mother, she'd put her hand in the water, trying to save him – and her ring slipped off and floated away – so folk who were unkind, folk like Hannah and Dora, wouldn't believe she'd ever been married. And when I was born they said cruel things, and she'd pined and died of a broken heart. But she had been married, I knew that, so I wasn't a bastard – and Esau nodded his head to show that he knew it, too. But I didn't tell my tale to anyone – not even Granfer.

Chapter Eight

I was content now up in the loft; I had Esau for company and my book of fairy tales to read – and then there was my own story. I told it to myself every evening without fail. The days drifted by and I was almost frightened when the doctor said I could get out of bed and sit on my stool by the window, as long as I wrapped myself in my shawl and wore my stockings. It was strange to see the outside world again; I'd lived so long with my tales that now they seemed more real than Hill Lane did.

Often I saw Dummy Drew lurching down the lane on his way to Frog Wood. From up in the loft he seemed small and sad, with his humped back and shambling walk; I noticed how he backed away and tried to hide when he saw folk coming, because he was frightened of them. One day he was later than usual and the boys were on their way home for dinner; as soon as they came round the bend they began to run towards him, shouting and jeering. He tried to run but his legs got all mixed up and he stumbled and nearly fell over and then they were all around him, and I saw Johnny Yates bend down and pick up a stone. Dummy saw it too and put his hands over his face, rocking from side to side; then the stone hit his shoulder and he squealed – and Mrs Rawlings came running out in her apron, her voice loud and angry. The boys skulked off and Mrs Rawlings went back inside, so Dummy was left alone in the street, still rocking and hiding his face behind his clumsy red hands. As I watched him I remembered how the boys had shouted at me on my first day at school, herding me into the ditch – and suddenly I was shaking just like he was, even though I was safe up in the loft.

At last he lowered his hands and peered back up the lane, and in that moment I saw the look on his face: it was the same as that day up in Frog Wood when I'd told him I never wanted to meet him there again. Although I hadn't been up long I slipped off my stool and crept back to bed; there I pressed my face into my pillow and cried just like Dummy.

55

I told myself the tale of my father and mother over and over again, and then I read the story of Sleeping Beauty, but I still felt sad and shivery when Granfer came home at tea-time. When he brought up my tea he said, 'Governess did speak to I in the street today, asking if thee bist perkier these days, and I did tell her as how thee wast getting up of a morn now.' He paused, and his voice dropped. 'An' I did tell her too as how thee'll be needing longer schooling, for being a lady's maid.' He was whispering now. 'An' governess did say as thee bist a bright liddle maid, and mebbe with an extry year thee could pass Standard VII – so long as thee didst work hard.'

'Oh, Granfer!' He patted my shoulder, then Grammer's warning voice called, 'Master . . .' and quickly Granfer went to the trap and began to lower himself down, but before his head disappeared I saw his finger raised to his lips – and then he smiled.

I could hardly eat my tea for excitement. Standard VII! Hardly anyone ever did Standard VII. Mr Thomas' daughter had passed it two years ago, but she was going for a teacher. Jane Wilcox, there was talk of her taking Standard VII next year, but then Mr Wilcox had a good business, making boots for the gentry as well as us – it was different for folks like that. But if Mrs Roper said I could then it must be true; I put my spoon down in my bowl and lay back against the pillows, basking in the glory of it.

The lumps in my neck had gone small and hard and I didn't ache any more, or feel hot and shivery by turns, so the doctor said I could come down from the loft on the first day of May – but there must be no school for a week, and no chores for a fortnight. As May Day fell on a Sunday Granfer was at home to steady me on the ladder, and by the time I reached the bottom my legs were shaking so much I could barely stand upright. I looked around the kitchen and felt very odd, as if I'd just hatched from an egg and was a new Amy – and I was, because I knew now that I wasn't really a bastard at all, I'd discovered that up in the loft – but I wouldn't tell Grammer, of course.

She was peeling the potatoes at the table and I walked towards her on my wobbly legs saying, 'Hello Grammer.'

She glanced up for a moment. 'So you've come down, then.' Her eyes dropped back to her knife as she began complaining to

Granfer about Emmy and how she'd not scrubbed the floor properly yesterday.

I said, 'I'll be doing chores for you soon, Grammer.' She didn't answer, but I knew she was glad I was up and about again.

Granfer said he'd best see me safe to the dunnekin the first time, so I wrapped myself up in Grammer's old shawl and set off down the path, clinging to his arm. As we came up to the end of the garden I thought I heard a pig squeal; I stopped, but Granfer hurried me on. As soon as I came out afterwards he beckoned me. 'Come round back, my maid.'

Behind the dunnekin Granfer looked all around, as if to be sure no one was watching, only with the apple trees in the way and just the field beyond no one could have been. When he was satisfied he crouched down and eased out a couple of bricks from the dunnekin wall, then he took out a tin box and opened it. Inside were two gold sovereigns! I gasped, and he put his finger to his lips and whispered, 'They be for thee, Amy. Thee must learn dressmaking afore thee canst go for a lady's maid, so I be saving up for thy premium.' He put the tin and the money carefully back then pulled himself up. ''Tis our secret, my maid – dussent thee tell nobody.' I shook my head. 'Only it baint near enough, yet, so I be selling half a pig to butcher afore Christmas. Come along in, now.'

As we came back and I saw the sty, Dimpsey's sty, I asked, 'Willst I have to feed en, Granfer – for my chores?'

'Aye, once Emmy baint coming no more.' And I heard the squeal again. I went right over to the sty and stared in. It was a male pig with ugly black blotches all over it and big flopping ears. It saw me and came to the wall wanting its back scratched, looking up with hopeful little eyes. I turned round and went straight back indoors.

Next day I sat at the window and watched as the May Day procession went past: Emmy walked in front of the Garland wearing the special white dress that was kept in the schoolroom cupboard and only brought out each year for the May Queen. Emmy had been eleven at Christmas and she was the best girl at needlework on her bench; Mrs Roper always chose from the girls who were still eleven because some of them would be getting their Labour Certificates and going into service at the end of the year so she said it was only fair they should all have the chance before they

57

left. In a couple of years' time I'd be eleven, and then it would be my turn, because I was the best at needlework of all the girls my age. Some years the procession walked as far as Pennings. I thought, suppose Lady Warminster saw me in the white dress leading the Garland – maybe she'd tell me I could come to her as lady's maid, just as soon as I'd learnt dressmaking.

Next Monday I went back to school. Mr Roper said he was glad I was better, because if I'd stayed off any longer I wouldn't have had enough attendances to be allowed to take the examination in July, when the Inspector came. 'Now you must promise to work very hard and catch up,' he added.

'Aye sir, I do promise.'

I worked hard all week, but it was difficult because I'd missed so much; all the others in Standard IV had learnt to do long division, so I had to stay in each break practising sums for Mr Roper. By Friday I could barely walk home, I was so tired. On Saturday Emmy came in as usual, but Grammer said there was mending to do, and mending didn't count as chores because you sat down to do it, so all day I darned and patched by the window. I could hardly lift my fork to my mouth at tea-time, and it was a relief when Grammer sent me straight to bed afterwards. Then it was Sunday, and chapel.

'So thic Ahab, he were a weak man as was led astray by his wife, Jezebel.' Mr Wilcox paused, and leant over the edge of the pulpit to glare at Johnny Yates. Johnny stopped wriggling and slumped down on the bench. Mr Wilcox drew a deep breath and suddenly roared, 'And Jezebel – she were a harlot!' Johnny's shoulders snapped up. 'Yes, brothers, she were a harlot – with her red raddled cheeks she did look out of her window at Jehu in his chariot below, and she smiled at him with her painted lips. But Jehu, he were a God-fearing man, so he called out loud – loud as a brass trumpet he did call, "Throw 'er down!" ' Mr Wilcox brushed the spittle from his beard before drawing another rasping breath. 'And my brothers, they did throw her down, wicked sinner as she was. She landed heavy, did Jezebel, right on the hard cobbles far below and her body was smashed so that her blood spurted up and splashed the bellies o' Jehu's horses –' my stomach seemed to turn right over as I heard his words '– and the dogs o' thic town they did come to lap up rest of her blood with their long pink tongues, so you could hear the slurp of it.' Desperately I swallowed, but the sickness kept rising. 'Then thic dogs, with their yellow, pointed fangs, they did tear the flesh from her bones, and crunch up them bones as had been her arms and her legs – crunch 'em up they did, until there was none of her left but the liddle white bones of her fine long fingers and small dainty feet.' I was panting for breath as he cried, 'And the Lord said: "The carcase of Jezebel it shall be as dung on the face of the field." For Jezebel, she were a terrible sinner – and a harlot!'

I gasped, 'Granfer!' Granfer caught hold of me and there was the blur of white faces – then I was outside, being sick on the grass.

There was no walk with Granfer that afternoon. I lay shaking in the loft while the pictures of Jezebel bleeding went round and round in my head, until in desperation I picked up my book and made myself read: 'There was once a very rich merchant . . .' and slowly Mr Wilcox's voice faded as I became Beauty, wandering in the gardens of the Beast.

At last I fell asleep, with Esau clasped in my arms. When I awoke it was evening, and outside in the ash tree a nightingale was singing. I lay listening to its soaring song and imagined that I was Sleeping Beauty in the woods, waiting for her prince to kiss her awake. Soon after, Granfer came padding up the ladder. 'Amy, bist thee awake, my maid? I brought thee a nice hot cup o' tea.'

'Thank 'ee, Granfer.'

He put the cup down and gently stroked my hair before saying, 'I were looking at the roses 'safternoon – old Willy Lobb, he be showing a bud already. Summer be on its way, my maid, and then the old sun, he'll make thee brave and well again.'

That summer the roses were more beautiful than ever. As their scented petals brushed my cheek I thought of Beauty, strolling in the enchanted garden of the Beast. So many summers had passed since then, and the roses had flowered in every one of them; they were old as time itself – yet their lives were so short. One day they were dancing in the breeze, confident in their beauty, on the next their petals curled, their heads drooped – and their moment of fragile perfection was gone for ever. Tears came to my eyes at the sadness of it. The tightly folded purple silk of Willy Lobb's buds, the faintest of pink flushes that warmed the heart of the Blushing Maiden, the swirling pink and white stripes of the Rosamund rose

– I rejoiced in each birth and mourned every death; they were so lovely, and so short-lived, the roses.

July arrived, and with it the Inspector. We sat in our best starched pinnies, waiting to be examined. I was nervous and uncertain, and when he called a question to me I hesitated as the numbers jumbled themselves up in my head. Then I saw Mr Roper's confident face and all of a sudden the numbers were little soldiers, marching to the answer. I told it to the Inspector and he nodded, before moving on to Bobby Yates. Spelling, dictation, composition – and then our trial was over as the Inspector turned his attention to the children in Standard V.

Lots of people passed Standard V, and Mr Roper beamed with pride, but Johnny Yates, he failed it again, so he wouldn't be able to leave until the spring, when he was thirteen. His Dad had told him he'd leather him if he didn't pass for his Labour Certificate this time, because they needed the money, so when Johnny got outside he stuck his bottom lip right out and kicked the wall – muttering that the Inspector was a gurt, maggotty old toad. Dora said, 'Baint no use blaming Inspector, Johnny Yates. Truth is, thee bist half-skim, just like your Albert – he had to stay till he were thirteen, too.' Johnny's face went bright red and his freckles stood out, then he lunged at Dora – but she jumped out of his way and shot into the girls' yard. As soon as she was safe behind the railings she called out, 'Boys, they be stupid – look at Amy Roberts, she baint even ten yet and she'm passed Standard IV already.'

Johnny's face went redder and redder, then he yelled at the top of his voice, 'But she be a bastard! Amy Roberts be a bastard, and her Ma, she were a harlot – a Jezzybell!' I put my hands over my ears and turned and ran out of the yard.

The tears were still prickling behind my eyelids as I was cutting the cabbage for tea and fetching the potatoes from the shed, and even when Granfer came home and praised me for passing Standard IV I still felt upset. But that night in bed I pulled Esau close to my mouth and whispered the story of my mother, all the way through; and as I told it to him I saw it happening, in little bright pictures in my head. I cried for my mother when the gentleman she'd married was drowned, and I cried even more when she died; but afterwards I felt better, and fell asleep.

It was August: the vivid scarlet of the poppies and the pinker red of the corncockles flowered amidst the ripening wheat – and were all cut down together by the whirring blades of the reaper. September brought the blackberries, nestling in juicy temptation against their thorny stems while the yellow crab apples dropped unheeded to the ground. By October the pink spindleberries were splitting to show their orange seeds as the berries of the bryony twined along the hedge, scarlet and dangerous.

The leaves of the ash tree in the lane began to turn, and one day a wind whipped up the branches, so that as I came home from school the leaves were whirling down. Almost without thought I leapt up and caught one – a wish. I remembered last year and was about to cast it from me – but a wish must not be wasted so I said aloud, 'I wish, I wish – I wish that a lord will marry me.' Then I went inside to do my chores.

November: the black and white pig was very fat by now. I fed him three times a day on barley meal and taters and skimmed milk from the farm in the village. Then one morning there was no breakfast for him. My legs moved very slowly as I walked home from school that afternoon, but as soon as tea was over Granfer sent me straight out again, up to the Hall with a message for Mr Marsh. When I'd delivered it to him he said Mrs Marsh had a lot of mending to do tonight, and she'd wondered if I'd be so kind as to give her a hand, seeing as I was a clever little maid with my needle. I nearly ran to the pretty little cottage in my relief.

I sat in the warm kitchen darning Mr Marsh's socks and trying not to think of the black and white pig screaming when he saw the knife flash down; even ugly pigs must be frightened. 'Are you cold, Amy? Move a little closer to the range.' As Mrs Marsh spoke I concentrated very hard on my needle, so I wouldn't remember Dimpsey.

It was quite dark before I set off down the drive, but the moon was out and her clear silver light comforted me. Then, as I reached the gate, I heard a loud gulping, sobbing noise, and I stopped. Mrs Atwell came out of the lodge and whispered, 'Don't 'ee be afeard, 'tis only Dummy Drew. He do get terrible upset on pig-killing nights – he cassent abide the squealing.' She raised her voice. 'Be off, Dummy – 'tis all over now, and thy Mam'll be waiting for thee.'

He shambled forward into the light from her open window; his face was all smeared and filthy with mud where he'd been fisting away his tears and his little eyes were frightened. 'Poor soul, he's mazed with the thought of it. He's allus been fond of animals, has Dummy. Thee'd best see him safe home, Amy – else he'll run off into woods and catch his death o' cold.'

For a moment I was frightened, remembering what Dora and Hannah had said, then I thought, I'm ten now, and in Standard V – so I walked forward and held out my hand. 'Come along wi' I, Dummy. I'll take thee home.'

And the fear gradually went from his eyes, and they looked at me clear as a baby's as he put his great, damp, muddy hand into mine and mumbled, 'Tek I 'ome.'

I knocked on Mrs Drew's door and she came out shivering in her shawl – there was a barely a glimmer of fire on the hearth. She seized Dummy's sleeve. 'Where've 'ee been? Git in, git in.' He let go my hand and shambled past her. She peered out. 'Thank 'ee for bringing him back.'

I said, 'He were up at the lodge, Mrs Drew, so I did fetch him home.'

She pulled her shawl tighter round her shoulders, 'Oh, 'tis thee, Amy Roberts. November's a bad month fer him – not that any month's good. But we do all have our crosses to bear, even young 'uns such as thee. Good night.'

After that evening if I ever saw Dummy out I always spoke to him, and waited for him to answer. He liked you to speak to him did Dummy, even though it was difficult to understand what he was saying, most of the time.

Chapter Nine

Annie Fuller was May Queen next spring. She wore the white dress and I walked in the procession behind the flower-decked Garland as we visited each house in Borrell in turn and then moved on to the outlying farms. We got as far as the lodge gates at Pennings, but the woman there told us the big house was closed up, as Lady Warminster wouldn't be coming for another fortnight or so. I was disappointed, but then I thought I'd rather wait until next year; I was sure she'd be at Pennings earlier then – and she'd see me in all my white-dressed glory.

We came back the shorter way, over the fields, because the Garland was getting heavier and the boys were complaining. They liked having a day off school for May Day, but they always said it was sissy and began to squabble over the carrying by the afternoon. As we climbed over the stile we could see a high grey wall in the distance, with a big bare building showing inside. Hannah nudged me. 'See thic, Amy? 'Tis the House.' I stared at the high walls and rows of blank windows – like a prison it was. I shivered, then jumped quickly off the stile with my face turned the other way.

When the Inspector came that summer I passed Standard V – with the top marks in the whole school! In the autumn I started working for Standard VI. I liked being in that class – there were only five of us and we were often set work to do on our own, and although the sums were difficult it was more exciting when you got them right. Florrie Black, the wheelwright's youngest daughter, was taking Standard VII this year and I peeked at her reading book when I was monitor and tidying the cupboard. It said on the cover it was a play called *A Midsummer Night's Dream*, by a man named William Shakespeare. The title sounded lovely and I could hardly wait for next year to come so I could read it myself – only I'd never dare tell Grammer; she said plays were the work of the Devil, and shouldn't ever be allowed.

Spring came round again; there was another gold sovereign in

Granfer's tin box and soon it would be May Day – my heart thumped with excitement at the thought. The last Wednesday in April Her Ladyship came in to inspect our needlework as usual, but this week would be a special inspection, because the Rector had come with her and she'd show him our stitches, too – then, when we'd all been up to her chair he'd clear his throat and announce who was to be this year's May Queen. Last year everyone had been on tenterhooks, because Annie and Joan and Sally were all as good as each other, but this year everyone knew it would be me that was chosen, because Her Ladyship praised my stitches most times she came.

We were called up one by one; Her Ladyship barely glanced at my seam today, though I'd tried extra hard, 'Yes, Amy – you may sit down now.' I sat down again, waiting.

But as Lizzie came back to our bench Mrs Roper moved over to Her Ladyship and the Rector, and spoke to them. We couldn't hear what she was saying because she had her back to us, and spoke very softly. The Rector's voice was much louder. 'Surely the child must realise – ' Her Ladyship put up her gloved hand and he was silenced, then she turned to Mrs Roper and nodded her ostrich plumes – and I saw Mrs Roper's tense shoulders relax. The next minute Her Ladyship was rising and we were so taken by surprise we didn't get to our feet until the Rector barked us to attention with an angry glare. Then, all of a sudden, they'd both gone. We sat in astonishment, staring at Mrs Roper when she came back in until she said quietly, 'The Rector will be in tomorrow morning to tell us who is to be May Queen next Tuesday,' and we all relaxed again. The other girls glanced at me and Hannah muttered to Lizzie, 'Reckon us don't need no telling this year, with Amy being Her Ladyship's pet.' I pretended not to hear.

At the end of the afternoon Mrs Roper said, 'Amy Roberts, stay behind.' I stood beside Mrs Roper's desk while everyone else filed out, wondering what I'd done wrong. When the room was empty she put down her pen, closed the register and said, 'Amy, Lizzie Hale is to be May Queen this year.'

I stared at her in disbelief. 'But, ma'am –'

She said quickly, 'The Rector kindly agreed to delay the announcement, so that I could speak to you privately.'

64

I still couldn't believe I'd heard aright. 'But Her Ladyship, she do allus praise my stitches –'

'It's nothing to do with your sewing, Amy.' And the serious way she spoke, then I knew. 'The girl who leads the May procession is representing Borrell school, and Borrell village, so she must be –' She broke off, then said very quietly, 'You are not as other girls are, you know that, Amy.'

I was fighting back the tears as I whispered, 'I did think, if I were extry good –'

'You are a good, obedient girl, Amy – but nothing will ever change the circumstances of your birth.' Grammer, her voice had been shrill with anger as she told me; Mrs Roper, she only sounded sad, but they were both saying the same thing – that I was branded, for life. 'And Amy, there is another matter – it's best you should understand it now. Your grandfather told me he hoped you might become a lady's maid, but you must realise this may not be possible, not for you. Such servants occupy a position of especial trust, and most ladies would not be prepared to employ as a personal maid a girl who was born out of wedlock.' She reached out and patted my hand. 'I'm sure you will pass Standard VII and become an excellent dressmaker, but don't build your hopes too high, my dear.'

'But Lady Warminster, she did say when she came –'

Mrs Roper stopped me. 'Lady Warminster was a stranger; she did not know about your – circumstances. I'm sorry, Amy.' She stood up. 'You may go now.'

I ran out to the lobby and sobbed and sobbed between the coat pegs; then I said to myself, 'But it baint true – I *baint* a bastard.' And I dried my eyes and went home.

Only next day, when the Rector announced that Lizzie was to be May Queen, my cheeks burnt with shame as the ripple of excitement ran round the room. Mr Roper rapped his cane down hard, but not before I'd heard Hannah murmur, ''Tis because Amy be one o' *they*.' My cheeks still burnt with humiliation as I walked in the procession behind the Garland – and I was glad when it began to rain at dinner-time and we had to come home early. Grammer sent me up to the loft so I wouldn't disturb her afternoon nap, and I lay on the bed and thought through the tale of my father and mother over and over again. At last the humiliation faded a little; one day they'd know the truth, and then they'd all be sorry. But I was still smarting with the pain and injustice of it when the letter came.

It came on the day they took Dummy Drew to the workhouse. Mrs Drew had died but no one knew until the Relieving Officer came round with the money and she didn't come to collect hers. Then Mrs Tucker went in and found her sitting dead in the chair. She must have been dead for days, Hannah said – she was all slumped down, but Dummy'd been going in and out as usual, so no one knew. They buried Mrs Drew in a pauper's grave, and then next day they came for Dummy.

There was a big crowd round the door and I wanted to slip past but Hannah gripped my arm. 'Look Amy – look!' The Relieving Officer in his bowler hat went into the cottage with the pauper who drove the bread van – only now it was a different van with a little barred window in the back. They came out with Dummy between them, but Dummy didn't want to go – when he saw the van he started bawling and struggling to get away, but they hung on tight. The Relieving Officer called out, 'Some of you, give me a hand,' but no one stepped forward out of the crowd and finally they got him into the van somehow and slammed the doors shut behind him. The Relieving Officer took off his bowler hat and wiped his forehead with a big white handkerchief, then he climbed up in front, the pauper driver said, 'Giddup,' and the crowd parted so the horse could clop away. There was a terrible howling from the back, like a dog – but it was Dummy. He'd found his voice at last.

As the van speeded up one of the boys shouted, 'Good riddance,' and the one next to him cheered, but Mr Sutton the blacksmith was standing right behind them and he seized them both by their collars and lifted them off their feet. There was a loud 'crack' as he banged their heads together – that shut them up.

Hannah let go of my arm and the crowd melted away. 'Poor ole Dummy.' ''Tis a terrible shame but still, 'e couldn't look arter 'isself, could 'e?' 'No, best place fer 'im, really.' 'I 'low 'e'll hate being shut up, though – he did like to roam, did Dummy.' 'Aye, he did that – but he couldn't look arter 'isself, could 'e?' I thought of the high grey walls closing around Dummy, and the great iron gate clanging shut behind him – and my eyes filled with tears. Poor old Dummy.

But when I got home the letter was waiting. Grammer said Aunt Agnes had written from London – she was ill, and she needed me to go and look after her and the boys. I stood staring at Grammer in surprise. I hadn't known I had an Aunt Agnes, in London, or anywhere else. I thought of leaving Granfer, and not being able to go on to Standard VII; but after May Day I hadn't wanted to stay on at school so much – and besides, Grammer said I had to go. 'But how will you manage wi'out I to do chores, Grammer?'

'I'll manage.' Her mouth shut in a tight line. Then she added, 'Be easier without you coming in and out all day, tramping mud over my clean floors.'

After that everything happened very quickly. Granfer went to see Mr Roper at the schoolhouse and Mr Roper said he was sorry I wouldn't be able to take Standard VI in July, when the Inspector came again, but he'd arrange for me to get my Labour Certificate, since I'd already passed Standard V and I'd be twelve over the summer holidays.

Then Granfer took me to see Mr Wilcox, and bought me a pair of new boots: they had kid on their tops and they buttoned halfway up to my knee. Granfer said they were so strong they'd last me for years. As we carried them home I said, 'I dussent want to leave thee, Granfer.'

His face went sad and tired and his whiskers drooped. 'And I dussent want thee to leave, my maid. But thy Aunt Agnes, she be poorly, so she do need thee to help her – and 'tis only right thee shouldst go. But when she's well again thee must come straight back to thy old Granfer, and tell him all 'bout thy doings in London Town.' I reached up and rubbed my cheek against his shoulder. I'd grown tall this last year, and Granfer, he seemed to have shrunk.

Grammer sent me to the shop to buy a length of calico, and I sat up late each evening sewing two new chemises and two new pairs of drawers. Because there wasn't much time Granfer asked Mrs Marsh up at the Hall to run up two red flannel petticoats on her sewing machine, and a couple of winter dresses of striped Oxford shirting. Grammer said my last year's print ones would do for summer since there were three more tucks in my skirt that could be let down later. I said, 'I baint a-going to grow that fast, Grammer,' but she didn't reply.

Grammer had told me the night before I left that I'd have to wear both sets of new underthings for the journey, because there wouldn't be room for them in my basket, so first thing next morning I pulled on two chemises, two petticoats and two pairs of drawers –I did hope I'd be able to find the buttons on both flaps if I needed to go in a hurry. I could only wear one pair of black stockings, though, else my old boots wouldn't fit – and Grammer said the new ones were too fine to scuff on the train. The train! My heart leapt with excitement – and fear.

I rolled up my nighties and made them into a bundle with the rest of my clothes, tying them tight with the string Grammer had given me. Then I picked up Esau, gave him a hug and laid him safe in the bottom of my basket, alongside my Labour Certificate. I wrapped up my new boots in brown paper, and packed them round with my stockings and vests and pinafores. I'd wanted to take my book of tales, too, but the basket was already half-full, and Granfer had said I must be sure to leave room for the fresh vegetables I was to take to Aunt Agnes, so reluctantly, I put my book away in the chest of drawers for when I came back.

Grammer was already up when I clambered down the ladder, and as soon as I'd plaited my hair she told me I must coil the braids in a bun on the back of my head, because I wasn't a child any longer. The hairpins she gave me stabbed my scalp, but I didn't dare complain.

After breakfast Granfer stepped outside to gather the vegetables, then he went out a second time, and came back with a bunch of roses in his hand. 'I picked 'em for Agnes. She were main fond o' my roses, when she were a liddle maid.' And just for a moment I was jealous of this Agnes, who'd been Granfer's 'liddle maid' before I was; then I remembered she was a grown-up woman, and my aunt, and the jealousy vanished – because I knew that even though I was grown-up now, with a bun, I was still Granfer's liddle maid, and always would be.

As I swept the floor I watched him wrap damp moss around their stems, then swaddle them close and tight in my old sunbonnet. 'Thic 'un'll keep they thorns from thy fingers, and mebbe it'll come in handy. I daresay as how even in London the sun shines of an afternoon.'

And suddenly it was time to go. Granfer put my bundle on his shoulder and lifted my basket; I picked up the bunch of roses while Grammer went to the front door and pulled it open. Gripping the roses firmly I walked over the stone step and out into the sunlight. I turned round. 'Goodbye, Grammer.' I smiled up into her wrinkled face, although I knew she wouldn't smile back, she never did. 'Goodbye, Grammer,' I said again, and at last she replied, ''Tis time you were gone.'

I swung back anxiously to Granfer. 'I mustn't miss train – Aunt Agnes, her do need I.'

'There's plenty o' time, my maid – church clock's only just struck the hour.'

He set off down the path, and I followed close behind. At the gate I stopped and looked back, to wave to Grammer – but she'd gone in and closed the door; only the roses bobbed their heads in farewell.

Hay-making had begun in Goosey Meadow – Granfer would be back to help directly he'd seen me off from the station. Soft beneath the jingle of harness and the whir of the blades I heard the steady swish, swish, as the new-mown grass fell in thick swathes, and the rich, heady scent of it filled the air. At the stile I stopped and looked back: rusty red sorrel, pale mauve vetch, bright shouting yellow buttercups, and drift after drift of white moon daisies – they all lay mingled with the pale green grass. Then Granfer touched my shoulder. 'Us'd best be getting along, Amy. Thee mussent miss thy train.'

We waited on the platform, Granfer's large hand holding mine. He heaved a great sigh, and his hand tightened on my fingers. 'I'll be back, Granfer – soon as Aunt Agnes is well again I'll come back home.'

'Aye my maid, and then us'll get thee apprenticed to a dressmaker. Thy old Granfer'll see thee a fine lady's maid yet.'

Then the rails began to tremble, and soon I saw the great size of the engine close to. I pressed back against Granfer – then the stab of the pins in my hair reminded me I was grown-up now, and I stood up straight, gripping my roses.

Granfer swung in my basket and bundle, and I climbed up onto the step – then suddenly I turned and threw myself back into his arms, covering his whiskery face with kisses. 'Ah, Amy my love, thee bist a good liddle maid. Now mind thee do come straight back to thy old Granfer as soon as thy Aunt Agnes be well again.'

'I will, Granfer, I will.'

'In wi' thee now – thic old guard be getting his green flag out.' Granfer bundled me back in and closed the door.

I thrust my head out through the window. 'Granfer –' but the shriek of the whistle and the blast of steam drowned my farewells, and Granfer's beloved face wavered and blurred as the train moved away and the tears streamed down my cheeks. By the time I'd wiped them away he was already out of sight.

PART TWO

Chapter Ten

Lambeth, London — June 1906

The fields rushed past me – little houses were there one moment and gone the next; tiny cows and even smaller sheep suddenly appeared and then vanished from sight again. The speed was frightening and exciting both at once. I was too hot, sweating in my double set of underwear, and my stomach began to churn so that I felt as if I was going to be sick. I closed my eyes in panic, and saw behind my lids Granfer and the cottage, the roses dancing, the ash tree swaying –and they were all getting smaller and smaller, as if they were going to disappear. My hands clenched tight, and I felt the sharp jab of a thorn – and the pain brought me to my senses. I hadn't left the roses behind, I carried them with me – Granfer's roses, that he'd picked himself this morning. My racing heart slowed.

But every time we came to a station I started up in panic – only folk were kind and reassured me, and at Andover Junction, where I had to change, I was carefully directed to the London platform and wished 'Godspeed'. In the next compartment, too, my anxious questions were patiently answered; we stopped at Basingstoke and at Woking, and then they told me we wouldn't be stopping again, so I sat back in my seat, my eyes fixed on the fast-moving scene outside. Gradually the houses appeared, until eventually there was nothing but houses: rows and rows of them, stretching away into the distance. I'd never have believed there could be so many houses in the whole wide world, let alone just in this one city. Then the wheels began to slow, there was the bustle of baggage being taken down from racks – and with a dying hiss of steam the train drew tiredly to a halt. Trembling, I picked up my bundle and my basket and followed the other passengers out of the safety of the carriage and into a new, strange world.

London was bigger and noisier, hotter and dirtier than I'd ever dreamed possible. In the great, echoing cavern of Waterloo I stood still as a fieldmouse at harvest – watching the bright silver blades of the reaper coming closer, but unable to move. Then a big, burly porter loomed above me. 'Nah then, ducks, where might you be bound for?' And his voice was quick and sharp, not like anyone's I'd ever heard before.

I whispered, 'Lambeth. Granfer, he did give I money for a cab.' He set off, and I scurried after him, my eyes fixed on his broad back as he shouldered his way through the crowds.

The cab window was smeared with grime and the straw on the floor was dirty; I sat crouched on the edge of the seat, bewildered by the constant rumble of wheels outside. The sweat was trickling down my chest and I was panting with the heat and the fear; my grip on Granfer's roses tightened until my knuckles were white with the strain.

When at last the cab stopped and the driver came round and opened the door, my cramped legs almost fell down the steps, and my fingers trembled as I found the right coins. Then he jerked his thumb towards a great high archway, and left me on the pavement. The smell of horse piss was sharp in my nostrils – but there were so many others I'd never smelt before my nose was bewildered; and my ears could scarcely take in the rattling, rumbling thundering of all the traffic. But it was the buildings that most astounded me. They were so high I had to crane my neck right back on my shoulders before I could see where they ended and the sky began. My eyes watered as the London sun glared brassily down at me, then I blinked and bent to pick up my bundle.

The archway led to a courtyard, enclosed by high brick walls and rows of windows; I whispered the number to a woman passing by and she stopped and pointed. 'That way, duck, then keep going up the stairs.'

Flight after flight of stone steps led up through the very heart of that great tall building; gripping my bundle and basket still more tightly I began to climb. I came to a narrow landing with a pair of little gates at either end, beyond which were balconies, open to the air. There was a number on the wall beside each gate. I peered at them anxiously in turn, but the one I wanted wasn't there, so I began to climb again. By the time I'd inspected the numbers on the next landing little rivulets of sweat were running down my face, but I had to climb on.

74

I'd reached the fifth landing before I found the number I was looking for and pushed open the little gate. My heart was pounding as I stepped inside the tiny enclosure; there it was like the front of a house, with a front door and a small window beside it – only it was all under cover, and instead of a garden there was just the bare space in front of the balcony. The front door was set wide open, so I walked through into a cramped lobby, with more doors all around it. The ones either side were tightly closed, but the one ahead stood ajar, so I tapped gently on the panel, but there was no reply. I tapped again. Still no answer – so in desperation I pushed it fully open, and saw a woman sitting in a chair by the window. Her hands were folded over her swollen belly, her head was drooping and her eyes were closed. I put down my basket and straightened my cramped hand, then dropped my bundle; at the sound her head jerked back and her eyes opened, and she stared at me. I walked towards her. 'Be you my Aunt Agnes?'

She still sat staring, until at last she whispered, 'Amy, Amy' and her voice caught, as if in a sob. She pushed herself up from the chair and clutched at the windowsill, swaying. 'Amy – at last.'

I explained, 'Mr Roper, he did have to arrange for my Labour Certificate and then there were my new boots – Granfer, he did say I maun have new boots for Lunnon, but I did come soon as they was ready.'

And now she smiled, a lovely welcoming smile, as if she were really pleased to see me. I smiled back, holding out the bunch of roses. 'Granfer, he did send thic roses for you.'

'Feyther's roses.' She took them from me, very gently, and held them against her cheek, breathing in their rich scents.

'There be a Cabbage rose and Blushing Maidens, General Jack and old Willy Lobb – he did gather from each bush, saying as how you'd likely remember all on 'em.'

'Oh I do, I do. Thank you, Amy, thank you.' But even as she fondled the roses her blue eyes kept gazing at me. Then suddenly her voice became brisker. 'But whatever am I thinking of? Come and sit down. I must make you a cup of tea – you look so hot.'

'That be on account o' Grammer. Her did say I maun wear two of everything – to save packing 'em.'

'Two of *everything*?'

I nodded, then leant forward. 'I even got two pairs o' drawers on!' And at that Aunt Agnes began to laugh, sounding so happy that the tight knot in my stomach dissolved and I started laughing, too. London wasn't frightening any more.

By the time I'd taken off my extra underwear Aunt Agnes had come back with the tea. She set the tray down on the table and began to fold up my underthings. 'I'll see to 'em, Auntie.'

'No Amy, you sit yourself down and cool off. Did you have a good journey?'

She sounded as if she really wanted to know, so I told her all about the train – how fast it went, and how kind folks had been, and how frightened I'd felt at Waterloo, only Granfer had given me the money for a cab, so I hadn't got lost – then I broke off and jumped up. 'He did send veg for you.' I ran to my basket and unloaded it on the table.

Aunt Agnes hurried over. 'Oh, Feyther's own growing!' She touched the glossy carrots, then picked up a pod of peas as if it were a gold sovereign, stroking it in her palm. She lifted the broad beans right up to her nose, sniffing them. 'Aren't they beautiful, Amy, and don't they smell lovely – so fresh and clean?'

I said, 'I reckon roses smell nicer.'

She smiled. 'They're *all* beautiful – thank you so much for bringing them to me.' Then she came closer, reaching out her hand to touch my hair. 'And you're beautiful, too, Amy – such pretty hair you've got.'

I flushed. 'Grammer do say as good looks be the work o' the Devil, and do lead young women into sin.'

Aunt Agnes drew her hand away quickly, as if she was embarrassed. 'But you're not a young woman, Amy – you're only eleven.'

'I do be grown-up now, Grammer did say so – 'sides, I got my Labour Certificate.' There was a loud, piercing wail and I jumped, stopping short in alarm.

Aunt Agnes smiled. ''Tis only Taffy, he's woken up. I'll go and fetch him.'

She went into an inner room and came back leading a curly-haired toddler by the hand. As soon as he saw me he stopped in the middle of the floor, staring. 'This is Amy, she's come to stay with us, Taffy.' His round blue eyes kept staring, and I didn't know what to say to him. Aunt Agnes went on, 'His real name's Alfred, but when he was a baby he had a shock of brown hair, and Albie said it was just the colour of toffee – so now we always call him "Taffy" – don't we, my pet?' He turned and buried his head in Aunt Agnes' skirt. 'Don't be shy, Taffy.' Aunt Agnes lifted him up and then sat down with him on her lap. He pressed his cheek against her breast and stuck his thumb in his mouth, looking at me out of the corner of his eyes. Aunt Agnes kissed the top of his head then asked me, 'Did you have to leave *very* early this morning, Amy?'

I was just telling her about them mowing the hay in Goosey Meadow when there was a sudden clatter of boots on the steps outside, and a child's voice calling, then another and another – until a great clamour of shouts and yells and running feet seemed to fill the air outside. Taffy wriggled round on her lap, straining towards the door. 'Nedanalbie, Nedanalbie coming!' His face was flushed with excitement.

Aunt Agnes smiled as she set him down, 'Yes, Ned and Albie'll be here soon.' Taffy's face broke into a huge, beaming grin, as he set off towards the door. Aunt Agnes turned to me. 'He thinks the world of his brothers – and they're so good with him.'

An army of boots was thundering up the stairs with shouts and shrieks, then the door burst open and two boys catapulted into the room, with a second, shorter pair jostling at their heels. 'Ma –' they all skidded to an abrupt halt, looking at me in surprise.

Aunt Agnes stood up. 'Boys, this is your Cousin Amy – she's come up from the country to help me. Say "Good afternoon" to her, now.'

'Arternoon.' 'Arternoon. Ma, can I have a slice of bread and jam?'

'Ma – Tim Morris cheeked Teacher and got the stick!'

'Ma – I got ten out of ten for my mental today.'

I sat beside the window feeling lonely and out of place as Aunt Agnes listened and answered them all. Then, as rapidly as they'd come they vanished again, taking Taffy with them. I was happier alone with Aunt Agnes, helping her peel the potatoes and prepare the evening meal, but then there were more boots on the landing, only heavier this time. Aunt Agnes glanced at me, her face anxious. 'Here's Alf, your Uncle Alf.'

I stood nervously by the table as a short, stocky man in working clothes came into the room. 'Aggie, I –' He saw me and stopped in mid-sentence. Then he said flatly, 'So she's come, then.'

'Yes, Alf. This is Amy.'

I said, 'Good afternoon, Uncle Alf.' His eyes narrowed and he stared at me, tugging his bristling moustache, but he didn't reply. He turned away, saying to Aunt Agnes over his shoulder, 'I've been sweating like a pig all day – I'll go and sluice meself down in the scullery.' He pulled the door firmly shut behind him.

Aunt Agnes' fair skin flushed. 'Alf, he can be a bit funny with people he doesn't know – it's just his way.'

Uncle Alf chewed steadily through his mutton chop while the rest of us spooned up our bowls of stew and dumplings. He questioned the boys about their lessons, but never once spoke to me. As soon as he'd finished eating Aunt Agnes pulled herself up and reached for his plate, 'Sit down, Aggie. Let her do that – seeing as the only reason for her coming is to give you an 'and.'

'Alf, she's had a long journey . . .' But I was already on my way to the scullery with his plate.

After he'd gone out again and I was helping Aunt Agnes with the washing up she said, 'I'm sorry if Alf seems a bit unfriendly.'

She paused, and I saw she was upset about it, so I said, ''Tis all right, Auntie, I be used to folk not talking to I. Grammer, she be just the same.' She looked at me, startled. I explained, 'Grammer, she never do speak to I if she don't have to.'

And now Aunt Agnes seemed even more upset. 'Oh, Amy – I am so sorry.'

'Baint *your* fault.' I saw the tears come into her eyes, so to cheer her up I told her, 'Granfer, he did say I maun be sure and give Aunt Agnes his love, along o' thic roses.'

She smiled then. 'How is Feyther – thy Granfer – keeping these days?'

'He be brave and well, save fer the odd twinge of rheumatics, but he do carry a potato in his pocket to cure thic.' I went on talking about Granfer and she listened and asked me more questions; I thought how much I liked Aunt Agnes and how I wished she lived nearer to Borrell. I was so glad I'd come up to help her for a while.

When we went back into the kitchen – the living room, Aunt Agnes called it – she told me that a friend of hers, called Beat,

Beat Harris, would be looking in for the evening. Aunt Agnes said Beat was a very old friend: they'd worked together once years ago, before Aunt Agnes had married Uncle Alf. She explained that Beat always came on a Monday evening because she served behind the bar of The Rose and Crown over beyond the New Cut until midnight or later all the other days. But Monday was her evening off, so she came to sit with Aunt Agnes while Uncle Alf was at his club.

I was a bit nervous in case Mrs Harris didn't like me either, but as soon as she pushed open the door her face broke into a broad smile. 'So she's come then! 'Ello, young Amy.' Her hand pumped mine vigorously. 'Let's 'ave a look at you. My, Aggie, ain't she a little smasher! Give 'er a year or two and you won't be able to get out on that balcony for the crowd o' boys queuing up to court her!' My face went so red I thought it'd burst into flames. Beat gave a great shout of laughter. 'Look at her blushing there!' Then her voice dropped. 'Seriously, duck, I am real glad to see you – your Auntie's been proper poorly these last months. I knows you'll be a big help to her.'

I sat quietly listening while Aunt Agnes and Beat chatted to each other. Beat's voice was sharper and higher-pitched than Aunt Agnes', and at first I couldn't follow everything she said – it'd been the same with the boys and Uncle Alf at tea-time – but gradually my ears began to adjust. Beat was older and bigger than Aunt Agnes, with a broad red face. She looked like a woman who'd stand no nonsense from anybody, but her eyes had a twinkle in them and her laugh was loud and jolly. Aunt Agnes laughed more softly, her voice was lower and gentler – and she was much prettier. Her hair was pulled back into a knot on her neck, very plainly, but it was a lovely colour – pale gold like wheat ripe for harvest, and her eyes were the clear blue of cornflowers. Every so often she'd half-turn from Beat and look at me, smiling – and I'd smile back. Once she reached out and took hold of my hand, squeezing it gently as she said to Beat, 'Oh, it is lovely to have Amy here – I'd quite given up hope of her coming.'

She looked so pleased I felt warm and welcome – and glad I'd come. Then we heard the music. Beat heaved herself to her feet. 'It's the barrel organ. Let's go out for a free look.' We followed her out onto the balcony, and I pressed forward to look over the iron railings. Down in the courtyard below was a piano on wheels – but the man wasn't playing the keys, he was winding a handle and as he turned, the rippling, tinkling tune danced up into the warm summer air. Children were running towards him; I saw a crust of bread fly up and a little brown figure on the top of the organ caught it in one paw. It was a monkey, a real live monkey. 'Aunt Agnes, look! He be wearing a liddle red jacket!'

The children were forming a ring, the little ones jigging up and down in time with the tune, and my feet began to jig too. Beat laughed. 'You'd best get down there, young Amy.'

'Can I go, Aunt Agnes?' At her smiling consent I began to run – through the gate, along the landing and down the stairs – flight after flight of them. And as I ran other girls rushed out of doors and off balconies and ran down beside me. As we burst out into the courtyard the tune changed its rhythm and speeded up; the girl in front of me turned round and seized my hand – 'Come on' – a second girl caught hold of me on the other side and now we were all in a circle around the barrel organ. Our boots tapped in time to the music, then all at once we began to move; faster and faster we whirled around until my hairpins fell out and my plaits flew free behind me – as we danced, and danced, and danced.

Chapter Eleven

It was so exciting, living in London. There was always bustle and noise and a sense of things happening. Even ordinary chores like beating the mats over the balcony in the morning were interesting in the Buildings, because you could watch people hurrying and scurrying across the courtyard and wonder where they were all going. The stairs, too, were always busy – from first thing in the morning when men and women stumped down on their way to work, until late at night when others came back from the late shift and fumbled their way up in the darkness because the gas was turned off on the landings at eleven o'clock sharp. Even when you were inside the flat you could hear folk all around. The walls weren't that thick and most people seemed to shout – besides, there were just so many people living in the Buildings it was like a city all of its own.

I thought the flat was wonderful, too. The dunnekin was so handy, and it was just like the one up at the Hall – one tug of the chain and the basin was white and shining again. There was a tap in the scullery – you just flicked it round and the water came gushing out – and it seemed like a miracle after having to clank the pump-handle at Borrell. The water ran away by itself, too, and disappeared under the floorboards; I thought there must be an enormous pond of dirty washing-up water under Jubilee Buildings, but Aunt Agnes said no, it was all taken off in pipes to a place miles and miles away. Aunt Agnes was rather worried about my sleeping in the scullery. She'd offered me a choice of putting the folding bed in there or behind a curtain in the bedroom, where the boys slept, but I preferred the scullery with its tap and smart yellow sink and gas-ring on the draining board. As soon as I heard Uncle Alf and Aunt Agnes getting out of bed in the living room next door I'd fill the kettle and set it to boil on the gas-ring – thinking all the time how fast and convenient it was, not having to fetch water from the pump or light a fire.

The range in the living room didn't have to be lit until much

81

later, when we were ready to cook the tea. It was much more convenient cooking with a range than over an open fire, and it had an oven at one side and a boiler at the other, for heating water for our Friday night baths. I even enjoyed scrubbing the floors in the Buildings. They were covered with linoleum which was much easier to keep clean; although everything did get terribly dirty in London, I had to admit that. All the chairs and stools had to be scrubbed every week, not just the table.

I liked dusting, too, especially the ornaments on the mantel-shelf. Aunt Agnes had a pretty blue vase, and two china dogs with brown spots and floppy ears; she said I could christen them as she'd never got round to giving them names, so I called one Toby and the other Ben, and patted them as I dusted their shiny black noses. In pride of place right in the centre was Uncle Alf's ship in a bottle. I wasn't allowed to dust that – no one must touch it except Aunt Agnes, and Uncle Alf, of course, when he took it down of an evening for a closer look. Sometimes he'd show it to the boys, explaining how the rigging went and telling them the names of the sails – lovely names they had, like Royals and Skysails. Uncle Alf had sailed in that very ship: although he was a time-served moulder, one day he'd decided he wanted a change and so he'd gone to sea and sailed round the world near a dozen times; then he'd felt like settling down again, so he'd come back to work at the foundry and married Aunt Agnes. The ship had a tiny brass nameplate on it; it was called *The Wanderer*. It was the last ship Uncle Alf had sailed on, and he said it was the most beautiful ship in the whole wide world. I thought so too, and I loved looking at it, even though I wasn't allowed to touch it – it was so brave and free with its little white sails all gaily blowing before the imaginary wind.

Although the living room was bigger than the kitchen at Borrell there wasn't a lot of space in it, not with Aunt Agnes' double bed in one corner and the big table in the middle. But at tea-time there were enough chairs and stools for everyone to sit down. I'd never eaten sitting down at a table before and I felt very grand. Uncle Alf was strict at meal-times, just like Grammer; he watched the boys' table manners and they weren't allowed to speak unless he spoke to them first. As he never spoke to me I couldn't say anything at all, but I didn't mind because I'd never been allowed to talk at meal-times at Borrell either.

82

If there were no boots to be mended or kindling to split Uncle Alf often went out of an evening, to his club or to visit his friends in one of the other Buildings. There were four blocks of Buildings close together, two on one side of the street and two on the other: Albert, Edward, Alexandra and our Jubilee. At first when I went out I couldn't tell them apart, but I soon realised they were all different – especially the window-boxes and what people put on their balconies. Albert was particularly different, because the Superintendent there wasn't as strict as ours in Jubilee, so folk sneaked pieces of washing out to dry on their balconies, although it was against the rules – all washing had to be hung to dry in the drying rooms on the seventh floor, and only on your appointed day.

Uncle Alf and his friends would sit on one of their balconies and smoke; sometimes they'd come and sit on ours, then Aunt Agnes would close the front door so it didn't look as if we were eavesdropping. I was rather sorry, because I liked eavesdropping – I knew you weren't supposed to do it, but you did find out all sorts of odd things that way. On Friday nights Uncle Alf was paid, so after he'd had his tea and counted out the housekeeping money he went out to The Goat and Compasses while we had our baths in front of the range. When Uncle Alf came back from the The Goat he was always more cheerful than usual; he'd give Aunt Agnes a big smacking kiss and then pat her on the behind, smiling – he even smiled at me, too. Sometimes the pat on Aunt Agnes' bottom would turn into quite a hard squeeze, and then I think it must have hurt her, because she'd go all red and flustered and shoo us very quickly to bed.

I'd lie on my bed in the scullery with Esau's head on the pillow next to mine and listen to the footsteps on the stairs and the creaking and squealing of the bedsprings next door as Uncle Alf gave Aunt Agnes her goodnight cuddle. I'd mentioned to her once about Uncle Alf being a restless sleeper and Aunt Agnes had poked up the fire until her face became quite pink with the heat, and then she'd told me that husbands liked to give their wives a cuddle of a night. I thought how nice and friendly that must be, and what a kind husband Uncle Alf was, because I could hear him giving Aunt Agnes her cuddle every night without fail – even on a Saturday when he went to The Goat for the whole evening and came in very late and hardly able to walk steady because he'd had a drop too much.

The shops were exciting in London, too. The first time I went shopping with Aunt Agnes I could hardly believe what I saw: there were so many people, hundreds, even thousands of people, just in one street – and every one a stranger. I kept very close to Aunt Agnes, for fear of being swept away into that swirling mass of bodies and lost forever – and yet mixed with the fear was excitement. There was so much to see.

Shop after shop had their wares hanging outside: brushes and brooms, pots and pans, huge bloody joints of meat that made my stomach churn and row after row of fishes, their scales glittering silver in the sunlight and the harsh reek of them making my nostrils twitch. Outside the shops, too, there were goods for sale, because men and women were selling on the kerb. A man with a box hanging from his neck was offering bootlaces and collar studs, 'Two a penny!' An old woman was holding out a tray of nose-tickling camphor balls; another had a handful of needles to sell – and then I saw a man with a huge basket full of greeny-yellow bunches. I stopped still, peering in astonishment, then turned and tugged at Aunt Agnes' sleeve. 'Auntie, thic fellow be selling groundsel! But 'tis a weed, it do grow everywhere.'

Smiling she whispered, 'Not in London, Amy – here people have to buy it for their pet birds.' As she drew me on I twisted my head round to take another look, so I could store the sight away in my memory for telling Granfer when I got back home – how surprised he'd be! But in London, everything was for sale.

Yet within a few weeks I'd learnt to find my way around, and the once-strange shops had become familiar landmarks. Here was the newsagent's on the corner, with pens and pencils displayed around a red and gold scroll; next came the grimy window of the shop that seemed to sell nothing but rags and bones and old empty bottles; then there was the toyshop with wax dolls in the window, their glass eyes staring blankly back at me, so I transferred my affections to the wooden bear with his friendly snarl.

When I reached the oil and paint store where the plump Spanish onions nestled cosily beside the boot varnish and washing soda, I'd go in for my regular purchase, a bottle of Uncle Alf's special sauce. Once it was in my basket its fierce red label would glare up at me, and I'd wonder what it tasted like, but none of us was allowed to sample it – it was reserved for Uncle Alf. He liked something tasty on his food; sometimes he'd have a sudden fancy for pickled onions, and Albie would be sent out to the farthing shop with an old jam jar to buy a ha'p'orth of them. We'd hear his boots clattering down the stone steps and all sit waiting quiet as mice while our teas cooled, until his boots came thudding back up again. The frown on Uncle Alf's face would clear as he tipped all the little onions onto his plate with a reproachful, 'You *know* I always fancy a nice pickled onion with cowheel pie, Aggie – you should keep 'em ready.'

'I'm sorry, Alf,' Aunt Agnes would murmur quietly, though we all knew there was no predicting Uncle Alf's fancies. Sometimes he felt like a helping of cooked eel when he came back from his club, or maybe a plate of winkles, and he'd sit there looking aggrieved if they weren't ready and waiting – but often when Aunt Agnes said, 'I wonder if Alf'd fancy a few whelks this evening,' and bought them in beforehand, then he'd like as not push them away. 'You *knows* I can't take whelks Aggie, not when I've had a drop of beer,' and she'd murmur, 'I'm sorry, Alf, I forgot.' We'd all remember how he'd got Albie out of his bed the very last Friday to send him out for a plate of those same whelks, saying reproachfully, 'You *knows* I always fancy 'em on a Friday night, Aggie,' but we knew better than to remind him.

Best of all I liked shopping on a Saturday night. At home I'd woken of a Saturday with a sinking heart – it'd stretched ahead as an endless round of chores, with Grammer's face getting frostier and frostier if everything wasn't done just so, but in London Saturday was different. As soon as Uncle Alf had gone off to work the boys would get up and chatter and laugh with Aunt Agnes while they ate their breakfasts. Then George and Jim would head for the door and either Albie or Ned would hoist Taffy up on his shoulders and carry him pick-a-back out to play with them in the courtyard. Aunt Agnes would glance at me and say, 'There's just time for another sup of tea, Amy. If you run out and put the kettle on I'll set a cup and saucer ready for Beat.'

Beat would come panting in, her broad face red and cheerful. 'Every time I come there's more o' them stairs – they're breeding, Amy, I'm sure of it.'

85

'They can't be, Mrs Harris – stairs, they don't have babies.'

'You get out there and count 'em, young Amy, and see if I'm not right. There's a couple o' little'uns come extra just at the turning, I swear it.'

I'd actually gone out and peered down at the bend, until I'd heard Beat's hearty gust of laughter from the open doorway behind me, and come running back flushed and foolish.

Aunt Agnes spoke gently. 'Don't tease her now, she's never been used to it.' She turned and pointed. 'Just look at the shine on that range – that's Amy's handiwork, Beat. It looks better than new, doesn't it?'

Beat bent down. 'So it does – and there's some elbow grease been used on them fire irons, you'd think they was silver. I do declare I can see my face in this poker.' Beat picked up the poker and held it in front of her like a mirror, patting and tweaking her hair into place. Aunt Agnes smiled, glancing my way and inviting me to share in her amusement. Then Beat suddenly pounced on the tongs and flicked them up to stand on the mantelpiece, with the poker propped facing them, the other side of Uncle Alf's ship in the bottle. 'There, you can get rid of those china dogs now, Aggie, these look smarter any day.' And now all three of us were laughing together.

When Beat had gone off to work we'd start preparing Uncle Alf's dinner for when he came home at two o'clock, but it was easier on Saturday with no Taffy to get under our feet, and we could take our time because we wouldn't be going shopping until the evening. Then, just at the time when Grammer would have been sending me up to the loft, Aunt Agnes and I began to get ready to go out shopping.

Albie or Ned would pick up one basket – depending on whose turn it was to stay in and look after George and Jim and Taffy – then I'd take the other and the three of us would set off down the stairs. Out in the courtyard other women would be moving purposefully towards the big archway, all on the same errand as us. Heads would be nodded in greeting. 'Evening, Mrs Reeves.' 'Warm today, ain't it, Mrs Thomson?' ''Ow are you keeping, Mrs Smith?' 'Mustn't complain, Mrs Wilson, mustn't complain.'

Albie would forge ahead through the crowd while we followed more slowly; Aunt Agnes' step was getting slower and heavier as the summer wore on. Lots of the women we greeted held babies close wrapped in their shawls, and I'd peep at the tiny pink faces so snug in their nests and think how nice it'd be when Aunt Agnes' baby arrived and I could help her look after it, and take it out for an airing all on my own, just as the other girls did in the Buildings. I'd envied Hannah with her baby sister to carry around, but now I'd soon have one of my own – but not a sister, exactly. I tore my eyes from one small, crumpled face and turned to Aunt Agnes. 'Auntie – is a cousin almost the same as a sister?' Her face was startled, and she caught her breath with a quick gasp. 'Have you got a stitch, Auntie?'

'Just a little one, Amy.' Then her voice became firm. 'Yes, a cousin is very like a sister.'

'Good!'

Albie quickened his pace, we turned the corner – and suddenly we'd arrived at the New Cut. The noise welled up and rushed towards us in a great foaming river of sound. 'Look at this luverly tea-set – every plate edged wiv real gold. The King 'isself ain't got a better one, not in the 'ole of 'is palace!'

'Stomach trouble – you got stomach trouble? These pills'll make you ferget you ever 'ad a stomach!'

'Kippers – three pairs a penny!' 'Trotters – luverly trotters!' 'Ices, ices!' 'Whelks! Lemonade! Cockles! Bloaters! Toffee, toffee!' All the shouts merged into a single clamorous cry: 'Come buy! Come buy!'

Aunt Agnes moved slowly from stall to stall, inspecting potatoes here, carrots there: judging, pricing, choosing. Gradually the baskets filled, but it was too early yet to buy the joint for Sunday dinner. Aunt Agnes turned into a side street. 'I'll just lean against the wall here and mind the baskets, while you two look around.'

Albie and I went dashing off to watch the young men puffing vigorously into the lung tester, or showing off to their friends as they braved the shocks from the galvanic battery. Then we went to listen to the one-man band with a drum on his back, a cymbal under his foot, a trumpet in his mouth and bells on his twitching head. As soon as the cap began to come round we melted back into the crowd and rushed off in search of new delights: the bird picking out fortunes with his beak, or the juggler dropping one of his oranges to the jeers of the spectators.

Albie seized my arm. 'Look Amy – it's the rat charmer!' Shuddering I pulled away and went running back to Aunt Agnes, leaving Albie to elbow his way into the excited throng of boys.

As soon as he came back we joined the jostling crowd all heading for the butcher's shop. Red-faced, his boater tipped back on his head, the butcher lifted a joint and swung it high above his head. 'Luverly piece o' beef, fit for the Queen 'erself – what am I bid?' For all the butcher's extravagant claims we knew that this one night we had the upper hand – he had to sell to us, for the meat wouldn't keep until Monday.

Our Sunday joint purchased and deposited safely in my basket we walked together back to the Buildings, up the stone steps and into the warm cosiness of the living room. Aunt Agnes sank onto a chair. 'Are your legs hurting, Auntie? I'll fetch the buffet.'

'Thank you Amy, that's lovely.' She reached out and patted my hand. 'You'd best go to bed now, Uncle Alf'll be back soon.'

Tired but happy, I stretched out in bed and lay listening to the steady footsteps and cheerful voices of returning shoppers on the stairs; London was so very different from Borrell.

Chapter Twelve

I enjoyed staying with Aunt Agnes – but I did miss Granfer. I wanted to tell him about all the exciting things I'd seen and done in London, only I couldn't, because he was far away in Borrell. I had sent him a letter: Aunt Agnes had given me the money for a stamp and a piece of paper and I'd written to say I'd arrived safely and was well, and that I hoped he and Grammer were too. I knew he couldn't read it himself so I'd drawn a little rose underneath my name. It was supposed to be the Cabbage rose only I couldn't manage to fit a hundred petals on the page, but I was sure Granfer would recognise it and know it meant that I missed him. I knew he'd be missing me too, and I thought perhaps Grammer might be as well, just a bit, so I put the address of the Buildings on the top of the letter, in nice clear capitals, in case she wanted to write back. But she didn't.

And yet despite missing Granfer part of me was glad I wasn't at home in Borrell, where everybody thought I was a bastard and nameless, and not fit to be May Queen. No one shouted out after me in London, or said unkind things behind the dunnekins; in London I was simply Amy, Mrs Thomson's niece who'd come up from the country to help her.

I did like helping Aunt Agnes. She never told me to do chores, but always asked: 'Amy, would you just sweep the floor now?' or 'Would you mind turning the handle of the mangle for me, Amy?' Afterwards she'd say 'Thank you,' and sound so pleased that however much mangling I'd done my arms hardly seemed to ache at all. One Friday evening, when I'd fetched the bath from the balcony and filled it with pails of hot water from the range, she said to me: 'Oh Amy, it *is* such a help having you here. All that pulling and lifting these past months used to make me feel as if my back were going to break in two. You *are* a good girl.' I glowed with pleasure.

The following Monday, when Beat had come round, I saw her watching anxiously as Aunt Agnes walked very slowly out to the

89

water closet – she seemed to be breathless just from the walk across the living room. Beat leant towards me. 'I'm so glad you've come, Amy – your Auntie's chest was real bad last winter, and ever since she's not been able to get her breath proper. O' course, being in the condition she is don't help.' She sighed. 'She's proper wore out is Aggie, with another youngster coming regular as clockwork every eighteen months the way they have.'

I said, surprised, 'Not *every* eighteen months, Mrs Harris, surely? Jim, he be a lot older'n Taffy.'

Beat glanced round to see the door was still closed and then she whispered, 'She don't like to talk about it, but she lost a couple in between. Tom, he was always ailing – so it weren't unexpected – but Danny, he seemed sturdy enough only your Auntie fell with Taffy when he was less'n four months old and so she lost her milk. And then there was a warm spell . . .' She shook her head, sighing. 'They never thrive, babies as is fed by hand – especially not in summer. Poor Aggie. She was heartbroken, losing two boys like that inside a year.'

I suggested, 'Mebbe the next baby'll be a little girl. I dare say Aunt Agnes'd like a girl for a change.'

Beat said, 'Yes, I think she would. Shush – she's coming back.'

I was certainly hoping the baby would be a girl. Boys always seemed so noisy, and they were so like boys, even when they were just babies. Taffy wasn't two yet and he was still in petticoats, but there was no mistaking what he was. I started looking at other people's babies, wondering what ours would be like when it came. It wasn't difficult to look at babies in the Buildings, there were so many of them around; when you went down the stairs of an evening there'd be women sitting on their balconies or out in the courtyard trying to catch a breath of cool air, and almost every one of them would have a baby at her breast. I wondered what it felt like, having a baby nibbling at your chest like that, but I was too shy to ask Aunt Agnes.

I thought a lot about babies and husbands and wives now I was living in the Buildings – it was partly because of the wash-house. The wash-house was up on the top floor, next to the drying rooms; there were rows of coppers and sinks and every woman had her special time when she had to go and do her washing. Aunt Agnes' time was Tuesday morning and I used to go up with her, but even with my help she'd be panting and wheezing long before we'd got to the mangling stage, and she'd have to lie down most of the afternoon to get her breath back. Then the Superintendent changed Aunt Agnes' time to Thursday afternoon. She was upset, but she didn't argue – nobody argued with the Superintendent in Jubilee – only the first time she had to wash in the afternoon she was so exhausted I suggested that perhaps I could manage on my own, the next week. Aunt Agnes said no, but when Uncle Alf found out about the change he told her I'd got to do it by myself – so that was that.

My arms would be aching by the time I'd finished; there was a lot more to do than there had been at home, and everything got much dirtier in London, but I didn't mind because it was so interesting listening to the other women talking. Aunt Agnes told me I shouldn't – she didn't really like the Thursday afternoon women, I'd realised that as soon as she'd had to change – but of course I did listen to them, and I found out all sorts of things, especially about 'It.'

Aunt Agnes hadn't quite told me the truth. Husbands didn't just cuddle their wives, they did It to them – and It was what Dora had told me about behind the dunnekins at Borrell. In fact, lots of husbands didn't cuddle at all, although their wives would have liked them to – instead, they just took their boots off, did It to their wives and then turned over and started snoring.

I'd always thought that a man only did It to his wife once a year or so, to give her a baby – like dogs – but I learnt different in the wash-house. Husbands had to have It regular – and although some only wanted It twice a week, or maybe three times, there were other men who wanted It every night and twice on Sundays, and if they didn't get It they sulked and wouldn't hand over all the housekeeping. But besides needing the housekeeping a woman had to give her husband It, however tired you were and however much your back ached, because it was a wife's duty – like washing his dirty clothes and putting his tea on the table the minute he walked through the door. Even if your back didn't ache no decent woman liked having It done to her, of course, but it was the price you had to pay for having a husband and being called 'Mrs ' – and you had to be a wife, it was a terrible failure not being married. There was a woman in the Buildings who was quite old – thirty or more, they said – she'd never been married and lived with her parents. Folk were pleasant enough to her, but they looked down on her, everyone did; and although she was so old she was always called by her Christian name, Gracie – even the children called her that, instead of Mrs Wilson or Mrs Smith.

Besides, women wanted to get married so they could have babies – babies were what made women special. Babies looked up at their mothers as if they were the only thing that mattered in the whole wide world – and mothers would look back down at them in exactly the same way. I thought how wonderful it would be when I had a baby of my own who looked up at me like that.

I learnt a lot about having babies in the wash-house. Dora had told us about 'monthlies': her sister had started having them before she went away into service, but now I discovered that that was how you could tell whether or not you were in the family way. If one of the women in the wash-house was late the others would ask her every week: 'Have you seen yet, Mrs Wilson?' and she'd shake her head and say, 'No – me luck's out, this time.' That was how I realised that although mothers loved their children they didn't want to go on having more and more new ones. At first I thought it was because it meant more mouths to feed; then I began to see it wasn't just that – it was because having babies did things to women: it made parts of your insides shift, and never go back to their proper place, so your back always ached like Mrs Wilson's. Or else your legs got all knotted with veins and sometimes they burst and bled and bled – I felt sick as I leant over the sink when I heard Mrs Smith describing that. And then there was the mysterious, 'Never been right since I had such a time with our Jenny,' and, 'It was my first as did the damage – they had to fetch the doctor to use his instruments and I was tore all the way up. Agony it was, I couldn't sit down for weeks, and now whenever me trouble comes again it splits open. I never been right since.'

At night, after I'd been up to the wash-house I'd hear the bedsprings creaking and groaning next door and know that Uncle Alf was doing It to Aunt Agnes. Uncle Alf was obviously one of those men who wanted It every night and twice on a Sunday, because he got very annoyed the afternoon when Jim kept being sick and couldn't go to Sunday School with the rest of us.

I turned over on my side on the narrow mattress and wondered what it felt like, having a man doing It to you. I knew it hurt the first time, because I'd heard the women talking about that one day – but surely it must always hurt, having a man's rod poked up your cunny like that? Cautiously I put my hand down between my legs and felt myself; there was no hole there – would I grow one later as I got older? Or did your husband make the hole when he did It for the first time? Was that why the first time hurt so much, and made you bleed? And then however did it get large enough for the baby to get out? I was still puzzling when I fell asleep.

By October Aunt Agnes was very large; as she came back up the stairs from shopping she would pant, clinging to the rail, and every third step she'd have to stop and rest before she could go on. Taffy seemed to sense that he'd soon be ousted and he was fractious and whining. Aunt Agnes was always patient with him but I wasn't; when he grabbed a handful of flour out of the basin and flung it all over the floor I shouted, 'You naughty, *naughty* boy!' and he set up a loud wailing and ran to Aunt Agnes.

She hugged him tight, stroking his hair and kissing his cheek. 'He doesn't understand, Amy – he's only a baby.' Tight-lipped, I went to fetch the broom.

Aunt Agnes' time came in the last week of October. When I got up she was already out of bed and walking slowly up and down in front of the range. Uncle Alf gobbled his bread and bacon and gulped down his tea – he seemed anxious to get away. As he left he put out an awkward hand and touched Aunt Agnes' shoulder – 'Be all over by teatime, Aggie' – then he was clattering down the stairs. Aunt Agnes turned to me and forced a smile, until her face suddenly changed and she gasped and caught at her back; her breath came in quick, strained pants.

I looked at her anxiously. 'Be it hurting, Aunt Agnes?'

She began to say, 'Not very – ' then she suddenly stopped and looked straight at me with her clear blue eyes. 'Yes, Amy – it does hurt.' And I heard Mr Wilcox's voice in the chapel bellowing: 'The Woman, she did sin, terrible her sin was, for she tempted the Man and led him astray – so the Lord, he did curse the Woman for all of eternity, saying: "In sorrow shalt thou bring forth thy children." ' And I watched Aunt Agnes' face contort in pain – and I was afraid.

I lit the range and filled the boiler, then as soon as Taffy woke up I took him to Mrs Morris, across the landing. Aunt Agnes asked me to peel the potatoes ready for tea and then slice the bread for the boys to eat at dinner-time; it was a relief to be out in the scullery for a while. I came back into the living room to sweep and dust, trying not to look at Aunt Agnes as she paced up and down, white-faced and panting. As I dusted the chest of drawers I thought of the baby clothes all washed and ready in the top drawer, and imagined how nice it would be once the baby was born and lying in the bed beside Aunt Agnes. Then she gave a sort of groan behind me, and there was a splashy, trickling sound before she said, very faint, 'Amy, my waters have broken. Could you be a good girl and mop up?' I fetched a cloth and knelt to swab the floor; the water was warm, and smelt strange and frightening. Then the shout of the milk boy came up from the courtyard so I picked up the jug and ran down. As I held it under the churn my hands were shaking so much I nearly spilt the milk.

When I came back Aunt Agnes was sitting crouched on the edge of the bed. She raised her face to me; there were dark circles under her eyes and her forehead was beaded with sweat. 'I know it's better to keep walking – but I'm so tired, Amy, so very, very tired.' Her voice faded so I could hardly hear her. 'People say the first time's the worst, and it was bad, so bad,' she closed her eyes a moment, 'but since then, every year, it seems to have hurt more and more. I lie in bed all those weeks before and try to tell myself it's not as bad as I remember, but then the pain starts and – oh . . .' She bent double with a long gasping cry as I stood rooted to the ground. When the pain was over she looked up at me and whispered, 'Amy, you'd better go across to Mrs Morris's. Tell her I sent you, and that I want you to stay there until it's over.'

I almost ran to the door, then I managed to stop myself and force out the offer, 'I'll bide wi' thee – if thee do want.'

She gave me a lopsided smile. 'No, Amy. I'm not very brave, and you shouldn't be seeing me like this. I'll call Mrs Morris when it's time for you to fetch Mrs Jackson.'

I sat huddled in Mrs Morris' living room while she bustled about doing her chores. Every ten minutes or so she'd ask me to give an eye to the children while she popped over to Number 25. I'd hear her asking, ' 'Ow are you getting along, Mrs Thomson?' and Aunt Agnes' faint reply. Mrs Morris would return with a, 'No change, Amy. Ah, you finished them onions – ta, duck.'

But then she came back and told me, 'Your Auntie says as you'd best nip over to C Block, to Number 84, and ask Mrs Jackson if she'll kindly step down.'

I ran as fast as I could; Mrs Jackson was elderly and lived in one of the one-roomed flats up on the sixth floor so I had a stitch in my side by the time I was knocking on her door. She opened it at once. 'Come in and wait, dearie, while I put myself to rights.' She banked up the fire in her range and set the kettle to one side before pulling her shawl around her shoulders. 'I'd best not leave anything to spoil – your Auntie always takes her time.' I trudged behind her down the stairs; my boots weighed heavy today.

The boys arrived home for dinner, and Mrs Morris gave them their bread and dripping on the stairs before shooing them off to play in the courtyard. She offered me a slice of bread and marge when her own children had dinner, but I couldn't face food today. Taffy grizzled and wouldn't eat his either, until Mrs Morris sprinkled it with sugar. Outside there was the usual deafening clamour in the yard, then the shouts and yells died down and were replaced by the sound of boots pounding through the archway. The last straggler clattered down the stairs and there was silence – and then I heard the scream.

My back went rigid as I looked at Mrs Morris. She shook her head, sighing, 'Your Auntie always has a bad time.'

The scream came again, high and thin, then the door was thrown open; it was Mrs Jackson. 'It's upside down – I thought I could get it out, but I can't. Amy, get down to Doctor McIntyre and ask him to come quick – Prince Street, you'll see the sign.'

My legs wobbled, then I began to run. As I turned the corner of the street my eyes were searching frantically for the lamp – then I saw it halfway down and panted on. I gabbled out my message to the maid and she went back inside to fetch the doctor. He came out still pulling on his coat, with his hat and bag in his hand. 'Mrs Jackson, you say?' His mouth tightened. 'I'd best get a move on – she doesn't panic easily.' He set off along the pavement with long, loping strides; I forced my shaking legs to trot after him.

We could hear the screaming as we reached the bottom of the stairwell and he took the steps two at a time. I followed, my breath coming in deep sobbing gasps. I rushed into Mrs Morris' and fell onto a chair, my hands pressed over my ears – but I could still hear it.

Then there was just one more scream, very high and piercing – followed by silence. Mrs Morris put her hand on my shoulder. 'It sounds as if she's been delivered, Amy. You keep an eye on the youngsters while I pop across and see if they need an extra pair of hands.'

It seemed a long time before Mrs Morris came back. I looked up at her, not daring to ask. 'She'll be all right now, but she's had a bad time. It's lucky you're here to look after her.'

'And the baby – is it a little girl?'

Mrs Morris' voice softened. 'The baby was born dead, lovey. With coming upside down and the doctor having to use his instruments – the poor little mite, she just gave up the ghost.' And as I stared at her, uncomprehending, she added, 'Mrs Jackson said could you take her down to the undertaker, and ask him if next time he's got someone ready for burying, he'd slip her into their coffin?'

The baby was completely wrapped in a piece of old sheeting, pinned at the front; cradling her in my arms I carried her down the steps and along the street to the address I'd been told. When I got there I handed the undertaker the half-a-crown and the letter Mrs Jackson had given me, and asked him very politely if he'd be so good as to put her into the next coffin that had a space in it. He said he would. 'Just put it down on the shelf over there.'

I laid her gently down and touching the top of the sheet whispered, 'Goodbye, baby.' Then I went back to the Buildings, my arms empty.

Chapter Thirteen

Aunt Agnes was ill for a long time after the baby was born dead. Mrs Jackson said she'd been torn inside and had had to be stitched by the doctor. When he came again to take the stitches out he told me to stay in the living room while he did it; I closed my eyes very tightly. Aunt Agnes only gave little whimpers of pain – I think she was too tired to cry out properly. Then the doctor got out his stethoscope and made her say, 'Ah,' several times. As he put it away I saw he was frowning, then he pointed to Taffy. 'Does the youngster still sleep with you, mother?' Aunt Agnes nodded. The doctor said brusquely, 'You'd better put him in with his brothers, from now on.' Then he swung round to me. 'How old is your daughter?'

Aunt Agnes spoke very quickly. 'Amy is my niece – she's twelve.'

His frown deepened. 'Then she should be in school.'

I explained, 'I do have my Labour Certificate. I did pass Standard V more'n a twelvemonth since.'

His eyes narrowed. '*You're* not a Cockney – not with that accent.'

'I did come up from Wiltshire, to help Aunt Agnes.'

He gave a great, angry sigh. 'Not a country child! Slip out of your pinafore and unbutton your dress.' Now it was my turn to say, 'Ah.' Aunt Agnes watched anxiously from the bed as he slowly folded up the rubber tubing. 'Her chest seems all right at the moment.' He spoke to me directly. 'Ever had any bad coughs, or a fever?'

I shook my head. 'No – I always been brave and healthy, 'cepting when I had the lumps in my neck and had to stay in bed until spring. The doctor from Pennings he said I been poisoned by the milk.'

His face changed, and the frown became less angry. 'Let's feel your neck.' He pressed and prodded, then said, 'You can do yourself up now.' Snapping shut his bag he turned back to Aunt

97

Agnes. 'When you're on your feet again, mother, you'd better pop along to the hospital and let them have a look at that chest of yours. In the meantime, don't get too close to your sons.'

Aunt Agnes said anxiously, 'But Doctor, what about Amy? Can she stay with me?'

He nodded. 'I think we can risk it – as long as you don't get too close to her, either.' Then he smiled at me. 'And you, little Miss Country Maid – you can say a prayer of thanks for that poisoned milk; it's done you more good than harm.'

Aunt Agnes whispered, 'Give the doctor his money, Amy.'

I ran to the mantelpiece and collected the three-and-sixpence set ready by Uncle Alf's ship. 'Thanks. Now, mother, don't you forget to go to the hospital.' Bag in hand he swung out through the door.

Aunt Agnes looked at me. 'Oh, Amy – whatever would I have done if he'd told me to send you away?'

And the catch in her voice as she spoke made the ache in my arms and legs suddenly disappear. 'Don't 'ee worry, Auntie. I'll look after thee.'

I did look after her, but I'd never worked so hard in my whole life before as I had to when Aunt Agnes was bedfast after the baby.

Mrs Morris offered to mind Taffy along with her youngsters for the first few weeks, and that was a relief because I couldn't seem to keep him amused like Aunt Agnes did – he'd get under my feet and then I'd snap at him and he'd run wailing to Aunt Agnes, trying to climb into bed with her. But as soon as she'd cuddled his tears away he'd start bouncing up and down and then her face would go white with pain, so I was very grateful to Mrs Morris. Beat helped too: I don't know how I'd have got through the washing that first week without her. Just bundling up the blood-stained sheets and towels from Aunt Agnes' bed had made my stomach heave, then Beat pushed open the door and told me she'd done a swap with one of the women who washed on Mondays so she could give me a lift. Up in the wash-house she rolled her sleeves up over her brawny arms and plunged the sheets into cold water; at the sight of the stains I gulped and put my hand over my mouth. Beat glanced at me. 'You all right, Amy?'

I muttered, 'I be afeard o' blood.'

She winked at me. 'You wait, my girl – the day'll come when you're glad to see it regular. Go and see if that copper's come to the boil yet.'

I'd always been so proud of myself when I did the chores for Grammer, but London was so dirty, and there'd only been the three of us to do for at home, whereas now I had to cook for eight; and Uncle Alf's dinner had to be on the table ready the minute he walked through the door – and it had to be something tasty, too, though there was less money to go round now. Calling the doctor to use his instruments had cost a whole guinea, and then Mrs Jackson had had to be paid, and Uncle Alf wasn't giving Aunt Agnes so much housekeeping these days – he stayed out later in the evenings while Aunt Agnes was poorly so he needed more of his wages for buying beer.

I got behind after the first couple of weeks so Aunt Agnes said she'd ask Uncle Alf for an extra shilling on the Tuesday, to tide us over until pay day. While she was dozing I slipped into the boys' bedroom to make the beds. I was glad she hadn't seen me because I should have done it earlier, only I'd been so rushed. Uncle Alf came in while I was still there, so I heard her asking him. He said, 'Look, Aggie – a man's got to 'ave some pleasure in his life. There's lots of husbands who wouldn't 'ave waited like I 'ave.'

'But the doctor said –'

'The doctor ain't going without – I am.' He sounded annoyed.

After a pause Aunt Agnes said, 'Perhaps, if you were careful –'

When I came out of the bedroom Uncle Alf was sitting in his armchair by the range, whistling as he read his paper. He glanced up, then fished in his pocket and took out sixpence. He tossed it on the table. 'You can have that, young Amy, seeing as you've got into trouble with the 'ousekeeping.'

I thought very carefully about that sixpence. Then after tea I went down to the butcher and asked for twopennorth of bones. I smiled at him with my very best smile and said, 'I'd take it kindly, mister, if you'd mebbe leave a liddle bit o' meat on thic bones.'

He left quite a lot of meat on them, and I set them to simmer all evening in Aunt Agnes' biggest iron saucepan. Later I lay awake while the bedsprings creaked next door, and planned exactly what I was going to do with that pan of bones. Even through the wall I'd heard Aunt Agnes' gasp of pain followed by Uncle Alf's, 'You all right, Aggie?' She'd muttered some kind of reassurance but every time the bedsprings squealed I seemed to feel a pain in my own cunny. I wasn't going to waste one single farthing of that sixpence.

In the morning I lifted the dripping off the top of the pan and set it aside for the boys' dinners. Next I dug the marrows out to tempt Aunt Agnes' appetite, then scraped and scraped at the bones until every scrap of meat was off them. When I'd been out for a pennorth of flour I made a pastry covering with some of the dripping and draped it over the meat. It made a lovely pie, and luckily I'd plenty of potatoes because Albie and I had bought them on Saturday night, as usual.

I still had three pennies left on Wednesday so I bought twopennorth of potherbs – the greengrocer gave me a good mix of onions, carrots and turnips – and then a pennorth of barley at the farthing shop. When I'd cooked them all up together with the bones and broth I had a nice big stew, and it was so tasty that Uncle Alf had second helpings. The boys wanted them too. 'Aw, go on, Amy – there's loads left.'

'That's for tomorrow,' I said, ramming the lid down tight. It just did for Friday's tea, and although Uncle Alf muttered about having the same meal twice he ate a good plateful – and then handed over all of the housekeeping. Aunt Agnes' eyes closed a moment in relief, before she passed it to me to put in the little teapot on the mantelpiece for safe keeping.

Aunt Agnes was still in bed when the first fog came in November. Albie and Ned had told me about London fogs – how you couldn't see a thing from the balcony, not the other side of the Buildings nor even the yard down below but I'd never believed them until it happened. Aunt Agnes had been coughing all night, and when Uncle Alf went out to work the air came in in grey, curling wisps, setting her off coughing again worse than ever. Later, when it should have been morning, I couldn't even see the balcony railings from the scullery window; the whole world was covered with a choking yellow cloud.

We had to keep the gas on all day, and when I went out to the shops I walked with my hand stretched out to the wall, hearing the faceless warning shouts of carters and draymen so muffled by the fog that they sounded like lost souls. I felt as if I'd been out for hours by the time I got back, and my hands and face were streaked with black; out in the water closet I discovered that my starched white petticoat was now a horrible limp grey – I felt as if I'd been up a chimney.

The fog cleared in a couple of days, but it seemed to have settled on Aunt Agnes' chest and she coughed and coughed. Uncle Alf got very annoyed at night – through the wall I could hear him shouting at her – but, of course, he needed his sleep so he could work at the foundry and earn the wages to keep us. Aunt Agnes started creeping out of bed as soon as he was snoring and going in to sleep with George and Jim.

She was up and about again by Albie's birthday at the beginning of December. He was eleven, George was eight just the next week and then it was Taffy's turn – 'My Christmas babies,' Aunt Agnes called them. Ned and Jim had been born in the summer, like me. By Taffy's birthday Aunt Agnes was doing all the cooking again, though I still scrubbed the floor and did most of the washing, because heavy work soon made her breathless.

The boys stayed in of an evening now winter had set in properly and it was too cold to play on the stairs or the courtyard for long. Some days Aunt Agnes would send Albie out for a bag of chestnuts; then we'd sit around the range roasting them in the fire and Aunt Agnes would tell tales until Uncle Alf came home and it was bed-time.

I loved listening to Aunt Agnes' tales; as she told them her voice would change and soften, until it sounded exactly like the way folk spoke in Borrell, and I'd feel cosy and warm and safe as I heard her. Sometimes she'd tell us about the children she'd looked after when she was a nursemaid, and the big house where she'd first gone into service after leaving school. She described the fine rooms and the lovely big gardens and the beautiful horses – and I'd think about how I'd live in a house like that one day, first just as a lady's maid, of course, but later, if maybe a lord fell in love with me . . . Other times she'd tell the stories that Granfer had told me: about the three sillies and the men who tried to rake the moon out of the pond. She used exactly the same words as Granfer did, so I'd be happy and yet sad, thinking of him and wondering how his rheumatics were getting on in the damp weather, and whether he'd tell me I'd grown when I went back home after Christmas. I hadn't actually mentioned it to Aunt Agnes yet, but she was

101

getting better now and I reckoned she'd be able to manage without me in a month or so. I'd be sorry to leave her, and the boys – I'd even miss Taffy – but I knew Granfer'd be wanting me back; and Grammer, I was sure she'd be glad when I came back, too – even if she didn't say anything.

Some of the tales Aunt Agnes told were the same as the ones in the book the doctor had given me: it was like meeting old friends to hear of poor Cinderella sitting in the ashes longing to go to the ball, or Snow White being tempted by the rosy apple, and Beauty dining every evening with the Beast. Once, in the New Cut, I'd seen a bear – a real live bear – huge he was, with big brown paws and a long furry snout. He'd raised himself up on his hind legs and danced in the street, while the man with him had collected pennies and ha'pennies; I hadn't been able to take my eyes off that bear, and now I imagined the Beast looking just like it – only uglier, of course. Aunt Agnes would quicken her voice when Beauty came back to the castle and couldn't find the Beast, and as she ran up and down the garden paths looking for him I felt my heartbeats quicken too. When she found him lying there, a great sad mound of fur, and fell on her knees beside him crying because she thought he was dead, then tears came to my eyes, too – even though I knew they were both going to live happily ever after. But Aunt Agnes didn't tell my favourite tales very often because the boys always clamoured for Jack the Giant Killer or Tom Thumb.

During the weeks before Christmas Aunt Agnes had managed to save a little from the housekeeping each week, and on Christmas Eve Uncle Alf came out shopping with us and bought a goose. I put it in the oven first thing next morning, creeping in to the living room while Aunt Agnes and Uncle Alf were still asleep and then going back to my own bed. By midday our mouths were watering at the delicious smell, and we all sat watching eagerly as the crisp, brown flesh was carved. Afterwards we ate the puddings I'd made, and when Uncle Alf said they were nearly as tasty as Aunt Agnes' I glowed with pleasure.

When we'd cleared all our plates and were quite full up Uncle Alf had forty winks in his armchair, while the rest of us sat quiet as mice so as not to disturb him. As soon as he woke up he sent Jim for his boots and said he'd take the boys out for a walk up by the river. The boys went rushing around, talking at the top of their

102

voices as they got ready, then Uncle Alf hefted Taffy up on to his back so he could ride; Taffy's little round face was one broad beam of delight as he fastened his arms tight around his father's neck. After they'd all trooped out Aunt Agnes turned to me, smiling. 'Alf's a good father, and he's a steady worker, as well – I've been lucky in my husband, Amy.' She sat back in her chair, folding her hands in her lap. 'And I'm so pleased to have you here, too – it's made it a perfect Christmas Day. Let's brew another pot of tea – just for the two of us – then we'll do the washing up.'

The washing up was soon done, with the water piping hot from the range boiler and two pairs of hands to do the work. Afterwards Aunt Agnes sat down with a little sigh of relief. 'You've been such a help to me, Amy. I don't know how I ever managed before you came.'

'I like helping you, Aunt Agnes – and to think, this time last year I didn't even know I *had* an Auntie!'

She raised her head and looked at me. There was an odd expression in her eyes, and she opened her mouth as if to speak, then closed it again without saying anything. There was a little pause, then she drew a deep breath and asked, 'Amy, do you ever want to know about your mother?'

I'd never told anyone about my mother before, but I liked Aunt Agnes so much and she'd been so kind to me that suddenly I wanted to tell her my secret. I said, 'I do know about my mother, already.'

She spoke very quickly. 'Did your Grammer tell you?'

I shook my head. 'Grammer, she dussent know. When the boys called bad names after me in the street she did say my mother'd been wicked, a terrible sinner, and that cause o' her I did have no name.' My voice caught in my throat, remembering my pain, before I added firmly, 'But it baint true. My mother, she were married, I know it.' And then I told her my tale, about my mother being so beautiful that a young gentleman had fallen in love with her, and she with him, and how they'd been married – but secretly, because his family were so high and mighty. Then one evening he'd fallen off his horse into the river and drowned, and in trying to save him my mother had lost her wedding ring, so that later, when I was born, folk were cruel and said unkind things – until she pined away and died. So now no one knew the truth. 'But I know. I

103

know my father, he did be a fine gentleman, and my mother, she weren't a sinner, not never.'

It was almost dark in the kitchen now, with only the glow from the range, and Aunt Agnes just sat quiet and didn't say anything; but I was glad I'd told her my secret, because I did like her so much. 'I'll light the gas, Auntie.' I jumped up, lit a spill and turned on the gas – it hissed and popped at first and then settled into a steady glow. I turned round to Aunt Agnes, but she didn't look at me, she just sat looking down at her hands, where her wedding ring glinted gold – and then I saw there were tears on her cheeks. My talking like that must have reminded her of the baby. And though I'd been too shy to ever refer to it before I felt at ease with her now, so I murmured, 'Bist thee sad, Aunt Agnes, wi' thinking of the baby? I be terrible sorry you lost your little girl.'

She looked up at me, her eyes so unhappy, and said, 'Yes, I'm sad because I've lost my little girl. Would you fill the kettle please, Amy? Alf'll be back soon, with the boys.'

Chapter Fourteen

After Christmas I asked Aunt Agnes about going home. 'When you're quite better, o' course, Auntie.'

She looked at me, startled. 'But – I thought you were happy here, Amy.'

'So I bist, but Granfer'll be missing I. And Grammer, when her rheumatics be bad she do need me to help wi' the chores.' I paused, and then added, ''Sides, I do miss Granfer.'

She didn't answer at first, then she said very quietly, 'We'll start putting a little bit by from the housekeeping each week, to save up for your fare. We should have enough by the spring.'

The spring! All of a sudden I thought of the lane, and the cottage, with the big ash tree standing beside it all fresh and green in its new coat of leaves, and Granfer's roses with the new shoots coming –and Granfer. 'Thank 'ee, Aunt Agnes – thank 'ee.'

But halfway through March Uncle Alf lost his job. He came in on the Friday, threw the housekeeping money down on the table and said, 'You'd better make the most of that – I've been turned off.'

Aunt Agnes' face went white – literally white as a sheet – and she gasped as though she'd been hit, before whispering, 'Oh, Alf!'

We never did find out exactly what had happened. There'd been some sort of argument with the foreman – he'd come in new and Uncle Alf couldn't abide him – there'd been a shouting match and at the end of the week Uncle Alf was told not to come back. He'd been at the foundry seven years without a break, earning good money – and now, suddenly, it was finished. He'd been out of work before, just after Ned was born, but there'd only been three mouths to feed then, and Albie being a toddler he'd not needed much. Besides, they'd been living in one room in Watson Street, Aunt Agnes told me, so the rent was much lower.

The rent – it was due every Monday without fail in the Buildings, that was one of the rules. There were a lot of folk who wanted to live in the flats there, so if you couldn't pay the rent, you had to go. We managed to pay it at first, and Uncle Alf said he'd soon get another job – he was a skilled man, there'd be openings – but no one seemed to be taking on hands and besides, he'd been black-listed; he found that out when he started looking. He did look: he tramped miles each day and came home exhausted and then had to get out his last and patch his worn-out boots with scraps of leather, but nobody would take him on.

He had five shillings a week due from his Friendly Society for the first month, and the men at his club had a whip-round and he brought home twenty-three shillings – but they had families of their own, they couldn't keep doing that. Then Beat slipped Aunt Agnes a few shillings. She left them on the mantelpiece and Aunt Agnes didn't want to take them. 'Beat's got little enough herself, and that's what her eldest boy sends her, the one in the Navy,' Aunt Agnes told me, her face drawn with concern. But we spent those shillings because we had to eat.

Aunt Agnes sent me down to the pawnshop. I felt ashamed the first time I walked under the three golden balls into the sour-smelling gloom behind. I handed over a bundle of tablecloths and spare bed-linen and when the man pushed half-a-crown back beneath the grille along with my ticket I seized them and almost ran for the door. But after I'd been a few times all I thought about was how many shillings and sixpences I was going to take away with me – although when I saw my best boots disappear under that high mesh grille the tears came to my eyes, remembering Granfer being so pleased when he brought them home and said they'd last me for years. But Granfer wouldn't have wanted us all to go hungry for want of my boots, so I picked up the grubby coins and left. The mantelpiece over the range was almost bare now. Toby and Ben were down in the pawnshop, along with Aunt Agnes' pretty blue vase; only *The Wanderer* remained. Aunt Agnes did suggest taking that, instead of my best boots, but Uncle Alf flew into a temper and said he'd rather starve than lose his ship.

I did mental arithmetic all day now: 8s 6d for the rent – the rent had to be paid first, the looming dark threat of the workhouse made sure of that – then there was 10d a week for the gas, and 1s for the coals. The burial insurance cost 10d a week, too, but Uncle Alf insisted the payments had to be kept up – he wasn't going to have any of his family disgraced by a pauper's funeral. And although it made the housekeeping more difficult I knew he was right. Our food had to come out of whatever was left once our regular payments were met, so every time I went shopping my mind was one continuing, frightening sum which never added up right.

Uncle Alf picked up a few shillings here and there some days, doing casual labouring, but other afternoons he'd come home soaked to the skin from waiting about outside for a chance which never came. Then we'd have to put more coal on the fire to dry his clothes; I'd watch the flames leaping up and think of coal at 1s 6d a hundredweight, trying to work out the price of each lump. On days when he did earn some money Uncle Alf'd often keep back threepence or fourpence even, and go out to the pub. In April he read in Mr Morris' newspaper that *The Wanderer* had been wrecked, run down by a steamer on her way to Germany. He came in very upset, and taking down his model he sat looking at it, sighing and saying what a beautiful ship she'd been, and how there'd never be another like her. Afterwards he went out and got drunk, so we had to live on bread and marge all the rest of the week.

Albie and Ned started going up to Waterloo station straight after school; anyone who looked as if they couldn't afford to tip a porter, they'd go up to and offer to carry their bags for a penny. Sometimes they had to carry them a long way, and they came home exhausted –but whatever they earned they handed straight over to Aunt Agnes: 'For the rent, Mam.' Albie was half-supporting Ned one day when they arrived back late. They'd carried two parcels for a lady right over beyond Kennington Park, and then she'd only given them a ha'penny for it. I poured hot water onto broken crusts, sprinkled the bread with salt and pepper and then added the tiniest knob of margarine. As they gulped the pobs down Aunt Agnes turned to me and said, 'We'll have to leave the Buildings.'

She went out herself and found a couple of rooms not too far from the Buildings; the woman who rented the whole house let off the upstairs. Endell Street was a respectable street, not like some, and as Aunt Agnes said, that was very important. The rent was two shillings a week less than the Buildings; besides, as Beat pointed out, one of your own kind might be prepared to wait a few days for the rent, or even a week if you asked them nicely, unlike the Buildings where they never would.

The rooms were small and poky: the bedroom just had room for the boys' two double beds pushed together, and when Aunt Agnes' bed and the table were both in the kitchen there was barely room to move. But what there was, was a little slip of a back room used as a scullery; it wasn't a lot bigger than a cupboard. Part of the main room had been partitioned off just leaving space for a small table with a bowl on it – but there was room at night for my folding bed, and I was glad of that. There was no tap in the rooms, so all the water had to be carried up from downstairs; the tap was out in the yard, along with the water closet. Mrs Carter did keep that reasonably clean, but the pan was cracked, so there was always a nasty ooze coming out of it and seeping over the floor.

The main problem was the fire. There was no range or gas-ring so all the cooking had to be done over the open grate; it wasn't a good grate like Grammer's, and when there was a wind blowing smoke'd come swirling back down the chimney so the food tasted of it. Not that the food tasted very nice even without the smoke. Aunt Agnes and the boys and I lived mostly on bread and margarine, and as we had to buy the cheapest margarine we could it was horrible and left a nasty taste on the tongue. Often I'd remember Grammer's fresh lard with its delicate flavour of rosemary – and then my mouth'd start watering just at the thought of it. Uncle Alf still had to have something more sustaining, of course – he was the breadwinner, when there was any to win. So we'd have to budget every day for his breakfast – an egg, a bloater, or most often, a rasher of bacon. But even that I couldn't cook for him properly because there was never enough fat, so it sat in the frying pan and just frizzled.

I didn't enjoy shopping any more, either: it was a constant worry, knowing that however careful I tried to be there simply wasn't enough money to buy the food we needed. And then there was the rent; we could always eat less – but suppose we couldn't pay the rent? I started walking the long way round to the shops, so I didn't have to go past Lambeth Workhouse – but I could still see its high brick walls looming up over Brook Street, imprisoning everyone inside. Whenever I caught a glimpse of them I remembered Dummy Drew being forced into the workhouse van at

Borrell, and couldn't stop myself shivering. Suppose Uncle Alf fell ill – we'd be thrown out on the street, and where would we go then, save through that high, forbidding gateway? And once inside we'd all be split up. The boys'd be taken away and I'd be separated from Aunt Agnes – I couldn't stop my mind dwelling on that terrifying possibility as I walked to and fro from Endell Street.

London was a different place now – or maybe I saw it as it really was. When I'd first arrived there must have been litter and rubbish in the gutter, but in my excitement at the novelty I'd not noticed it. Now I saw how every street was fouled by fish-bones and slimy cabbage leaves scattered amongst the crumpled newspapers and discarded cigarette packets. And those folk offering their pitiful wares on the edge of the pavement – matches, bootlaces, packets of pins – now I saw the desperation in their faces and shrank from it. Once as I turned into the Cut I heard a man playing a hurdy-gurdy, accompanied by a tap, tap on the cobbles. I went towards the sound and saw a crippled man dancing. He'd only got one leg, with just a crutch in place of the other. There was an old cap lying on the pavement in front of him for collecting pennies and ha' pennies and he was dancing to the hurdy-gurdy, his single boot and his crutch trying to bob up and down in time to the music. He couldn't get it quite right – he was always half a beat behind – so some boys in the small crowd were jeering at him: 'Get a move on, Hoppity, get a move on – or they'll never 'ave you in the front row o' the chorus!' 'Call that dancing? You wanner get the other one cut orf 'n'all –you'd do a better job on a pair o' stumps!' The man's face was grey and gaunt, and his sunken cheeks glistened with sweat as he tried desperately to catch up – but he couldn't. My hands tightened on the handle of my basket as I turned my head and almost ran down the street to get away.

Still the incessant sums drummed in my head: shillings, pennies, ha'pennies, farthings – and they wouldn't add up. Aunt Agnes sold her sewing machine to the wife of the Superintendent at the Buildings, who couldn't sew but said she had a fancy to try; that kept us going for several weeks. Then Uncle Alf got some casual work shifting scenery at the theatre, and Aunt Agnes managed to scrape together the 6s 6d for the rent by Friday. She had it ready on the mantelpiece when Uncle Alf came in. He was in a bad mood and when he saw the stew I'd made of a cod's head with potatoes and carrots he swore and said it was pig food, not fit for a man, so he was going out for a plate of stewed eels and mash, with a pint to wash it down. We watched, frozen in horror, as he picked up half the rent and put it into his pocket. Aunt Agnes said, 'But Alf, that's for the *rent*! We must pay it, or we'll have to go into the House.'

He swung round. 'There's some 'ere as might as well go in.' He pointed straight at me. 'Look at 'er – she's left school, she should be earning her keep.'

'Alf – I couldn't manage without Amy's help!'

'If she weren't 'ere you'd 'ave to manage, wouldn't you? And there'd be one less mouth ter feed. I'm off.'

My face was burning, but I didn't say anything because of Aunt Agnes – there were tears in her eyes and they wouldn't meet mine. At last she whispered, 'I'll go down and see if Mrs Carter will wait for the rest of the rent this week.'

Next day Aunt Agnes sent me along to the pawnshop with her boots; she said she didn't need to go out, so she could do without them. She never referred to what Uncle Alf said, but first thing on Sunday I went down to Beat's room and asked her if she'd help me find work.

Chapter Fifteen

Beat found me a place as a buttonhole hand. I had to provide my own thread, but she lent me the money for the first week and I started eight o'clock on Monday morning. It was a sweatshop, and although the factory regulations were stuck up on the wall they weren't always kept to, but from what the other girls said there were plenty worse places. There was a machine, and once the forewoman had shown me how to use it I got started on the shirts that were being made there. It was piecework; I was paid 5d for each dozen shirts, and every shirt had seven buttonholes. I was slow at first, and by the time seven o'clock came and the missus shouted, 'Stop work!' my fingers were sore and my back and neck ached with the strain. All the way home I did sums in my head –and knew I must speed up. By Saturday afternoon my fingertips felt like pin cushions, but I forgot the pain when I saw the expression on Aunt Agnes' face as I handed over 6s 3d; I'd almost paid the rent.

By the end of the evening we had all the rent safe on the mantelpiece and a little over, even when Beat had been repaid for the thread. Albie had been earning, too – he'd got himself a Saturday job as a lather boy at the barber's. By the time he came home he could hardly stand up from tiredness after twelve hours on his feet, but he smiled with pride as he held out the shilling he'd earnt. 'For the rent, Mam.'

Aunt Agnes was exhausted, too. I'd helped her with the cleaning of an evening and Ned and Albie had run all the errands but otherwise she'd had to manage. Beat had popped in whenever she could, and she'd asked the headmistress of the Infants' School if she'd take Taffy since there was sickness at home. The headmistress said she would as long as he was clean in his habits, so Aunt Agnes cut off his hair and altered a pair of Jim's old breeches to fit him and the boys took him off with them.

Beat came round on a Monday evening and helped with the washing. Aunt Agnes said, 'Beat, I'll never be able to thank you enough for all you're doing.'

Beat tossed her head. 'You don't need to, Aggie. I remembers what you did for me when my Bert was bedridden all that time afore he died. I'm only paying me debts.'

It was hot and stuffy in the workshop, and by evening my head would be aching as I tried not to think of spring coming far away in the country. The other girls were all older than I was. I'd only been taken on because I had my Labour Certificate, and apparently you didn't get those in London: girls had to stay on until they were fourteen. But although they were older they weren't unkind, and the two who sat between me and the end of the table, Flo and her friend Bessie, offered to share a milk can and teapot with me at teatime, and they'd often include me in their conversation. I thought that at least no one here called me 'one o' *they*,' and that was something to be said for Lambeth: I'd left the past behind me.

But one evening, as I was walking back to Endell Street, I looked up above the gas lamps and saw the silver crescent of the new moon, shining in the sky. I remembered Granfer carrying me outside to curtsey to her three times – and the clear shape of the crescent blurred and almost disappeared. But when I'd blinked the tears away she was still hanging there, still shining. I bent down and gripped the hem of my dress, lifting it ever so slightly, before bobbing three times to her beauty. Then I felt in my pocket and found a farthing I'd got in change from buying the thread. It wasn't silver but I knew she'd understand as I turned it over three times in her light. I felt better as I trudged on towards Endell Street, and she did bring me luck because the next three weeks I earnt seven and sixpence, then seven and eleven pence – and then eight whole shillings and fourpence. Aunt Agnes was so pleased and grateful.

But just when I'd got quick and confident with my machine we were put on short time. It meant I could get home earlier and help Aunt Agnes prepare tea – but there just wasn't the money, so we were back on bread and marge again.

On the Friday I heard Flo say to Bessie, 'I've not got the rent this week.' She sounded very depressed and I felt sorry for her, because I knew that while most of the other girls lived with their families Flo was an orphan, and had to fend for herself. But then she added, in an undertone, 'I'll have to go out this evening and earn it.'

I pricked up my ears. I was only taking 3s 6d home that week, which wouldn't even cover half the rent – and Uncle Alf hadn't been too lucky with casual jobs. The rest of us would be on potatoes and bread, unless I could earn some extra. So I followed Flo outside, and as soon as she'd said goodbye to Bessie I caught her up and asked, 'Are you going to earn some money this evening?' She turned and looked at me, her face unfriendly, but I persevered. 'I'm willing to work hard – is there any chance of a job at the same place? Mebbe I could come with you and ask?'

She just stood there, looking at me. Then she snapped, 'You silly little cow! Go back home to your Auntie – and be thankful you got a home to go back to.'

Her voice sounded so angry I flinched away from her, but by the time I'd got to Beat's to give her a message before she left for The Rose and Crown I was annoyed myself. She could have explained to me nicely if there wasn't enough work for both of us. I told Beat what Flo had said, expecting her to sympathise with me, but Beat just looked at me for a moment in silence, then said firmly, 'Amy – she did you a favour.'

I was bewildered. 'But we need the money, and I don't mind hard work. It couldn't be worse'n making hundreds of button-holes.'

'There's work and work, Amy. That girl was going on the streets.'

'You mean selling something – like bootlaces?'

Beat sighed heavily. 'She ain't got no bootlaces, you heard her. And when a girl ain't got nothing left to sell, then she has to sell herself. It's either that or the workhouse. Now you do as she said – go home to your Auntie, and be thankful you got her.'

I walked home in a daze, thinking of Flo and what she was doing; I couldn't get her out of my mind all weekend. On Monday morning I heard Bessie whisper to her under the cover of the noise of the machines, 'Did you make your rent all right?'

Flo nodded. 'And a bit over. I walked all the way up West. I was fagged, but they pays better so it was worth it.'

Bessie warned, 'You want to be careful, Flo. Suppose you gets yourself in the family way? It'd be all up with you, then.'

Flo shook her head. 'One of the girls I met told me once as it's when you 'as one bloke regular that you're likely to get caught. She said if you takes a dozen quick, one after the other, then you don't usually fall. So I always takes thirteen, just to be on the safe side – even if I've earnt enough before then.' Flo tied off her thread and then stopped for a moment, her hand over her face. 'Oh, Bessie, if only I didn't have to do it. I feel dirty, so *dirty*.' Then the forewoman looked our way so Flo picked up the next shirt and slid it quickly under the needle.

I felt dirty, too – all summer. The whole of London seemed to be covered with a layer of filthy dust that stuck to us as we sweated in the stuffy heat of the workshop. Although I tried to have a wash down every day at Endell Street I still didn't feel really clean – and anyway, I had to put my grubby clothes back on again the next morning. Besides, summer had brought out the bugs.

The first time a bed bug dropped onto my pillow I thought I'd be sick. Uncle Alf had been scene shifting that week so there was some money coming in; Aunt Agnes sent Ned out to buy some wallpaper and then she begged Uncle Alf to put it on. He complained, but he did hang it on Sunday evening and for a couple of weeks the bugs were kept at bay; then the weather got warmer still and they must have nibbled their way through and out again. I hated waking up in the morning with my arms and chest all red with bites. I felt unclean, but the boys didn't seem to mind too much – I used to hear their triumphant shouts of 'splat!' whenever they squashed one. I'd try and kill as many as possible in the scullery at night before I went to bed, but even that little splash of red upset me; ever since Dimpsey's death just the sight of blood had made me feel queasy.

I used to dream about Dimpsey that summer. I got so tired sewing buttonholes all day in the hot, stuffy workshop, and yet when I got to bed I couldn't sleep properly. I kept having nightmares in which memories of Borrell were all mixed up with what I'd seen in London that day. Once I had to go past the workhouse when people were queueing for the spike. Everyone in that dingy line seemed so hopeless; sagging against the wall looking as if they couldn't bear the thought of going into the casual ward. Yet the eyes of the late arrivals were never still as they darted up and down the queue, counting the heads in front, desperate in case they failed to get their meal and bed for the night – even though they'd only be fed on bread and skilly and would be imprisoned all of the next day paying for it by picking oakum or

114

cleaning the yard. Beat told me no one was allowed to stay in the same casual ward more than the two nights – with the day's labour in between to pay for it – so I imagined them forever dragging their ill-shod feet over dirty streets in an endless round of misery. I couldn't get the thought of them out of my mind. As I watched Uncle Alf eating his dinner and saw the dejected droop of his shoulders panic would tighten my chest. Suppose he fell ill and couldn't work at all? My wages wouldn't even keep me, let alone all eight of us. One night I dreamt of Dummy Drew, struggling to get away from the van – only then he stopped struggling, and stood waiting for the spike. He was right at the back of the queue and his little eyes were hopeless and frightened above his slobbering mouth; just as he got to the gates they were slammed shut in his face, and he stood outside, alone and crying. When I woke up there were tears on my cheeks.

I was having so many nightmares I started taking Esau to bed with me again. I felt ashamed as I knew he was a toy and I was grown-up now, but I wanted the comfort of him. As soon as the scullery door was closed for the night I reached into the orange box where I kept my spare clothes and fetched him out for a cuddle. When I woke up later sweating and frightened I'd press my face against his furry one, and it did help.

But nothing helped the night after I saw the bear. It was a very old bear, and he couldn't stay up on his hind legs to dance. His owner put the whip to him, and the old bear did try – but he kept losing his balance and falling down on his front paws. The crowd got restless and started shouting: 'What sort o' dancing bear is that, mister? You won't get nuffink from us – 'e aint worf a farving.' The owner whipped harder, and the bear tried again, but he just couldn't do it. A man at the back of the crowd called out, 'That bear's a gonner, mister – let's 'ave some fun. I'll set me dog on him and we can all lay bets on 'ow long 'e lasts.' There was a roar of assent from the crowd, but the man with the bear looked doubtful; then the bear made one last despairing attempt to stand up on his hind legs – and failed.

His owner picked up his cap and held it out. 'All right – but I want ter see the colour o' yer money first.' The coppers flashed in, and even some silver – the crowd was seething with excitement. Then the dog was unleashed. He was a smooth, tan animal, obviously still young and with sharp, pointed teeth. He went straight for the bear and began to snap at him – and now at last the bear did get up on his back legs and stay there. The crowd jeered, shouting, 'That's made him dance! Come on, you old bugger – dance!'

The bear was a lot bigger than the dog, with huge paws, but he was such an old animal. His snout was quite grey, and when he opened his mouth there were hardly any teeth – not that they'd've done him any good, because being a dancing bear he was wearing a muzzle. He did try: he batted at the dog with his big paws and growled and snarled, but the dog was young and agile and simply jumped out of his way before coming in to attack again with his sharp white teeth. He circled the bear and attacked him from behind; the bear was too big and clumsy to get his paws round in time and the dog's teeth sank deep into the dusty brown fur – when he leapt back there was blood on them. The bear turned and turned, trying to fend off the dog – but he was always too late, and the dog bit again and again. The crowd roared every time the dog's teeth closed, and their shouts of excitement drowned the bear's piteous yelps of pain, but I could still hear them, and at last I managed to uproot my feet and push my way out of the crowd to run, panting and desperate down the street. Just as I got to the end I heard a great roar from behind me. 'E's down! At 'im boy, finish 'im orf!'

I tried to tell Aunt Agnes why I was crying, but I couldn't get the words out – then the boys came in full of excitement, saying they'd seen a dead bear in Parker Street. I flung myself down the back stairs and was sick in the drain. Aunt Agnes came panting down after me, asking what was wrong – but it was no use, the bear was dead now.

That night even Esau couldn't stop my nightmares, and when I woke up I kept seeing the bear in my head – his grizzled muzzle and his little baffled eyes as he tried to dance and kept falling down. Then I seemed to hear the men jeering again, and saw the dog's lithe tan body dashing in and out as it attacked. Eventually I got up, crept downstairs and went out into the backyard. It was a little cooler there and Mrs Carter had a couple of geraniums in pots on her scullery windowsill, so I sniffed the sharp, tangy scent of them and thought of Granfer's roses. They'd still be in bloom

116

now: the Seven Sisters, the big, full Cabbage rose, mossy Willy Lobb and the Countess – and the Garland, climbing over the front gate like a bridal wreath and smelling of honey and sweet oranges. Then I thought of how one day I'd be a lady's maid, just as Granfer had promised, and go to serve Lady Warminster in the big white house over at Pennings – and with thinking of that, and the roses, I eventually became calm enough to take Esau upstairs again and go back to bed.

Chapter Sixteen

One day in November, just after Guy Fawkes' Night it was, Uncle Alf came in and said, 'I've got a job – at the foundry over by the Tower.' Aunt Agnes flopped down on the edge of the bed and began to cry. Uncle Alf sounded aggrieved. 'You might look more cheerful about it, Aggie.'

'Oh Alf, I'm so thankful, so thankful.'

He asked her if she'd like to apply to go back into the Buildings, but she said she didn't feel up to the move yet, and besides, Endell Street was cheaper. So much had gone into pawn it would take a while to get everything we needed back together again. Then Uncle Alf decided that part of my wages should be put aside to buy back Aunt Agnes' sewing machine. The Superintendent's wife wasn't really using it – she'd only bought it out of kindness, we thought –and Uncle Alf was keen to get it back because he'd given it to Aunt Agnes as a present when they were first married. It was January before he carried it in and set it triumphantly down on the table, his moustaches bristling with pleasure as Aunt Agnes exclaimed, 'Thank you, Alf! Thank you so much – you are so good to me.' But Aunt Agnes didn't seem to have the energy to use it these days, so I had to do most of the mending in the evenings and on Sunday afternoon. I'd given up going to Sunday School when I'd started working, as there wasn't the time.

With the sewing machine back I asked Aunt Agnes if I could be allowed to keep back sixpence a week from my wages, to save up for my train fare, now she was getting better. She said quietly, 'Yes, Amy – I'll speak to Alf about it.' She sounded very tired, but she was managing all the housework and cooking again now, so I was sure she'd be quite well again by the summer, and then I'd be able to go home.

February came and smeared the streets with grey slush – even snow was dirty in Lambeth. We'd just finished our dinner at the workshop when Mrs Carter's eldest son arrived red-faced and panting. When he saw me he shouted, 'Ma says yer got ter come 'ome quick – yer Auntie's collapsed!'

I ran all the way back with him. As I reached the top of the stairs I glimpsed Aunt Agnes lying in bed, her face very white and her eyes closed. Mrs Carter came out and pulled the door to behind her. 'She's come round now, but she's not so good, Amy. She's not been well for weeks – I've heard 'er coughing her heart out some mornings, then today I heard this thump – made the ceiling shake, it did – and afterwards I couldn't hear a dicky bird, so I got worried and come up. Soon as I opened the door I saw 'er lying there, in a dead faint. Took me ages to bring 'er round and then she was so shaky I could hardly get 'er onto the bed. You tell your Uncle as 'e'd best get the doctor to 'er.'

The doctor came and left her some medicine, then said she must have her own spittoon – like Uncle Alf did – and always cough into that, and be sure to put some turps in the bottom of it. She was so weak she couldn't even get out of bed, and Uncle Alf said I'd got to stop work at once, so I could stay home and look after her. It had given him a shock, seeing her so ill; I didn't even hear the bedsprings creaking that night.

I'd got used to going out, and talking to the other girls; my fingers had developed little pads on the tips so they didn't get sore any more and I could make buttonholes without even having to think – now I didn't really like being at home all day. Aunt Agnes couldn't get up at first, so I had to keep running up and down stairs and out to the back yard with her chamber. Often one of the Carters'd be inside, and I'd have to stand there holding it out in the open where everyone in the whole terrace could see me, my face getting redder and redder as I waited. And of course, now I wasn't working I had to do all the washing again, downstairs in Mrs Carter's cramped, steamy scullery.

Since I wasn't earning there was less money for the housekeeping, but Ned got himself a job helping with an early morning milk round, so he brought in 1s 6d a week, and with careful shopping I was able to squeeze out 2d to put into my railway fare jar at the end of the first week. I was sure Aunt Agnes would be on her feet again in a few weeks, and then I'd be able to go back to work and save up properly. It was the winter that was making her poorly; she'd feel better in the spring, and by summer she'd be quite well again –

then I could get back to Borrell just in time to see Granfer's roses coming into bloom. I thought I'd like to come and stay with Aunt Agnes and the boys again one day, but for now I'd had enough of London. I wanted to go home.

It was Beat who told me. Aunt Agnes sent me down to her with a piece of pie I'd made, and when Beat had thanked me she asked how Aunt Agnes was today. 'Oh, she got up this morning and sat in Uncle Alf's chair for half an hour or more. She'll soon be well, once spring's here.'

Beat looked at me. 'Amy, your Auntie's asked me to tell you – she was too embarrassed to do it herself – she's in the family way again.' I just sat, staring at her as she added, 'If you'd been doing her washing you'd 'a realised she's not seen anything for months.'

I licked my dry lips before asking, 'When?'

'She reckons she fell at the end of October, just before Alf got his job, so the baby's due in July.' I couldn't say anything. Beat went on, 'She won't have a chance of getting back to anything like normal until her trouble's over – and it'll take her a while then. The doctor told her that. He said as how her chest's bad and her heart's been strained with having too many little 'uns. He was narked with her, because he'd told her after she lost the last one that she mustn't ever get that way again.' Beat shrugged. 'But what can a woman do? A man's got his needs – and he'll take what he wants, regardless. She's been lucky to go so long. But her luck's run out now.'

I walked back from Beat's very slowly. The wind blew grit into my eyes as I looked at the dirty scraps of paper and old vegetable peelings littering the street and tried not to breathe in the stench from the tannery. I was trapped in Lambeth now; there'd be no roses for me this summer – and no Granfer.

I knew it wasn't Aunt Agnes' fault, but part of me couldn't help blaming her. The minute I came in she looked up at me and asked, 'Did Beat tell you?'

'Yes, she did.' I went out to the poky little scullery and began to peel the potatoes. When the boys came in for dinner I gave them their bread and dripping and then took her a cup of tea. As I gave it to her she whispered, 'I'm sorry, Amy.'

I shrugged like Beat. 'Baint your fault,' and turned away.

I knew really she hadn't had any choice; it was a wife's duty. A man needed his clothes washed, his rooms cleaned, his meals cooked, and he needed It, too, regular – his wife had to provide them all. Aunt Agnes hadn't been able to do the washing and cleaning and cooking because she was ill – so I'd done them for her – but obviously I couldn't do the other. Uncle Alf needed It, whether she was ill or not. I'd heard him tell her so through the scullery wall when she'd told him she wasn't feeling too well that night. He'd said, 'It ain't no good fer a man, Aggie, doing without it when he feels the urge.' Besides, he'd added, as she was lying in bed all day it didn't make any difference to her, anyway. Of course, I knew it did; it wasn't a nice thing to have done to you at the best of times, but when you were feeling poorly it felt much worse. I'd learnt that from listening to the women in the wash-house of the Buildings. But you couldn't expect Uncle Alf to realise it – he was a man. It was the way things were: a woman couldn't manage on her own, she couldn't earn enough even without having to care for her babies – so she needed a husband to support her and her children. But in return she had to give him what he wanted. I knew that, but I still blamed Aunt Agnes for being in the family way again. She'd got enough children already – she didn't need any more. Especially when she wasn't well enough to look after them and I'd have to do it instead, staying in filthy London for ever and ever and never being able to go back home to Borrell.

Whenever I was cooking over the fire I'd look up from stirring or basting and gaze at the model of *The Wanderer*, with its sails all set as if it wanted to fly far away, over the sea. But it couldn't, because it was cooped up in a bottle – trapped, just like I was.

So although I did all the chores and fetched and carried for Aunt Agnes I didn't speak to her very much these days. She'd ask me who I'd seen while I was doing the shopping, and what the weather was like outside, and I'd answer – but only briefly, so as not to be rude. Anyway, talking made her cough. I didn't like that, either. I'd hated emptying the spittoon for Uncle Alf, and now I had hers to see to as well. And sometimes, after she'd been coughing, her handkerchief would be all spotted with blood. I liked that even less – handling anything stained with blood always turned my stomach.

Then something happened that upset me even more. I'd been

out shopping one afternoon and when I took the basket into the scullery I saw that Taffy had been at my box as soon as he came in from school. All my things were tumbled about with half of them tipped on the floor – and Esau was missing. I ran through the kitchen straight into the boys' bedroom; Taffy was in there with Esau – and he'd torn him in half, so he had a gaping wound in his chest and all his stuffing was coming out. I grabbed hold of Taffy and boxed his ears as hard as I could. 'You've killed him – you've killed my Esau!' He ran howling out of the room and I stood screaming and crying by Esau's ravaged body.

Aunt Agnes must have dragged herself out of bed because she stood swaying in the doorway, with Taffy clinging to the skirt of her nightdress. 'Amy, what is it?'

'He's killed my Esau.' She came over and put her hand on my shoulder, but I thrust it away. 'Leave me alone! Go away, go away.'

I threw myself down on the boys' bed and lay there, sobbing. When at last I got up and went back into the kitchen Aunt Agnes was up and dressed, sitting by the fire. She looked dreadful, but she had her sewing box out and a needle in her hand; on her lap lay the remains of Esau. She glanced up at me, quickly. 'I think I can mend him for you, Amy.'

I turned my back on her and reached under the bed. 'Thic chamber needs emptying again.' I walked past her and out of the door. That night I wept because Esau was dead. Esau, my old friend, my only friend.

She was so tired she could only put in a few tiny stitches at a time, then she'd have to put him down on the bed and rest. But somehow she kept on sewing, and after a week he was mended. She held him out to me. 'I know the tear still shows, Amy – but I've done the best I could.'

I muttered an ungracious, 'Thank you,' as I took him from her. I put him in the bottom of my box; I was too old for toys now.

It was the very same night that the toothache started. I'd had twinges before, but I'd always pretended it was just the way I'd bitten – now it was a definite ache. Sometimes it'd go away for a while and I'd tell myself I'd just imagined it, but it always came back again. One night I woke up as I heard the church clock strike two, and the pain was so bad I never got back to sleep again. As soon as I got up next morning Aunt Agnes exclaimed, 'Amy! You look so ill – whatever's the matter?'

'My tooth, it be hurting. I daresay it'll stop by and by.' But it didn't.

When Beat came Aunt Agnes asked her to fetch me some oil of cloves. I rubbed a few drops on my gum but it only eased it temporarily. Then Aunt Agnes staggered out of bed, sewed a little bag and filled it with hot salt. She gave it to me to hold against my cheek as I lay in bed; it helped a little – but not for long.

Next morning my face was all swollen up, and Aunt Agnes must have spoken to Uncle Alf about it because he dropped a sixpence on the table, saying, 'Get down to the doctor. He'll pull it out for you.'

I stammered, 'I – I don't want –' I was terrified.

Uncle Alf shrugged and reached out his hand to the table. 'Well, if you're not bothered . . .'

Albie's hand shot out and closed around the coin. 'Ned'n me 'ull take you, Amy, before we go to school.' My face hurt so much by now I thought nothing could be worse, so after I'd done the washing up I took off my pinny and went with them. The boys were excited. 'Can I 'ave it, Amy, arter he's pulled it out?'

'Yes – yes.'

I sat in the dark little waiting room shaking with terror. Then we were in the surgery.

'What's the trouble?'

'It's her tooth, mister.'

'Sit down here – I'll soon have that out.' A pair of enormous pincers came towards me and crunched shut on my tooth. I tried to scream and couldn't – then an agonising pain seared through my head and it seemed to split in two. Blood splattered onto my face. 'No need to make such a noise, my girl – it's out now.'

'Can I 'ave it?'

'No, she said *I* could, Albie. I wanner swap it fer a fag card –'

I staggered back clutching my bloody mouth, but when I reached the house in Endell Street I felt so ill I had to crawl up the stairs on my hands and knees. I reached the landing and collapsed into a weeping heap on the floor, remembering my pain and terror.

'Amy – oh, Amy!' Aunt Agnes stood swaying in front of me.

123

'Here, let me help you.' Somehow she got me up and into the kitchen, where I fell onto her bed. She sat beside me, stroking my hair and trying to comfort me. 'Amy, my poor little Amy.'

I raised my head and looked up at her, the tears streaming down my cheeks as I sobbed, 'Granfer. I want my Granfer – I want my Granfer!'

She sat beside me until my sobs died down, then she said quietly, 'I'm sorry, Amy. I'm sorry for everything.' Then she bent down, and for a moment I felt her cheek rest on my hair before she told me, 'You will go back to your Granfer, I promise.'

Chapter Seventeen

The following week Beat popped in early on Thursday morning. As soon as she arrived Aunt Agnes asked me to go out and buy a couple of bloaters. I resented being sent out like that – Beat's jolly laugh always made me feel a bit better so I didn't want to miss her visit, but Aunt Agnes was surprisingly firm. Beat was still there when I came back, but she wasn't laughing; she kept darting anxious glances at Aunt Agnes, and didn't seem to be listening properly when I told her I'd seen a rat running out of George's Pudding Shop: 'Bigger'n Mrs Carter's ginger tom, he were.'

Beat just nodded. ''Is kitchen's alive with 'em – but they don't spoil the flavour o' George's puddings, never 'ave done. Are you sure, Aggie – certain sure?'

Aunt Agnes said quietly, 'Yes Beat, I'm sure. It's the only way.'

Aunt Agnes lay with her eyes closed most of the rest of the day, although she didn't sound as if she was asleep, so in the afternoon I got her sewing machine out to turn George and Jim's top sheet sides to middle. When I'd finished she said, 'Amy, I want to give you my sewing machine. I never use it now, and you're very handy with it.'

I looked up in surprise. 'Thank you, Auntie.'

She went on, 'And if you ever needed some money, then you could pawn it. Take it to Harvey and Thompson's, they'll give you a fair price.'

'But now Uncle Alf's working –'

She interrupted me. 'Just remember, Amy – for my sake.'

'All right Auntie, I will.'

I noticed later that Aunt Agnes' hairbrushes had gone from the shelf. They were a nice pair, backed with ebony, that Granfer'd given her when she first went out into service. They'd been in pawn, but we'd managed to get them back – now they'd gone again. 'Auntie, where are –' She glanced quickly in Uncle Alf's direction putting a finger to her lips, so I stopped my question, and forgot about asking her later.

The next Monday, Aunt Agnes asked if she could borrow my boots. 'But Auntie –'

'I'm going out for a little while, with Beat.'

'You baint fit.'

'I have to go, Amy.' There was something about her voice which stopped me arguing, so I took off my boots and gave them to her. They were a bit small, but she said she could manage. Beat arrived and they set off, with Aunt Agnes leaning very heavily on Beat's arm.

They came back in a cab; people were staring at it because cabs were a rare sight in Endell Street, but I saw why they'd had to use one when Beat and the driver between them half-carried Aunt Agnes up the stairs and lowered her down on to the bed. Beat took my boots off and gave them to me, then told me to help her undress Aunt Agnes and get her under the bedclothes. Beat hardly spoke a word; when we'd finished she sat down in a chair by the fire, picked up one of Albie's socks from the mending basket and began to darn it. Aunt Agnes just lay in bed with her eyes closed.

The boys came in for their dinners and I cut and spread their slices of bread and dripping and sent them out again so as not to disturb Aunt Agnes. When they'd left I went into the kitchen. 'Auntie, would you like a slice of –' I broke off in dismay; her face was a greeny-white, and there were big beads of sweat on her forehead.

She gasped, and then suddenly doubled up, clutching her belly. 'Beat – oh, Beat – help me!'

As Beat ran over to her she ordered, 'You go and sit in the scullery, Amy.'

I sat out in the poky scullery feeling left out. I'd done my best while Aunt Agnes had been ill, so why had I been sent out now, as though I were a child? I wasn't a child – I'd be fourteen in the summer, and I was doing all the housekeeping – it wasn't fair. But underneath I knew that if Beat had called me in I wouldn't have wanted to go. And as I heard Aunt Agnes moaning with pain I became more and more afraid.

There was one last, despairing cry and then Beat thrust the scullery door open and came in. She was holding a bowl, which she dumped down on the table. Lying in the bowl was a baby. It was

126

tiny, unbelievably tiny, but it was a real baby, with arms and legs, fingers and toes and a miniature head with every feature perfect. You could see the shape of its nose and the curve of its mouth – and its little eyelids looked as if they'd just closed in sleep. I stood gazing at it, and as I watched one of its tiny arms moved and seemed to reach out – its fingers curled. 'Beat – she's –' My voice was silenced by the expression on Beat's face.

'If you ever tell your Auntie it were still alive I'll flay you, young Amy.' She spoke softly but very distinctly. 'I must get back to her – she's in a bad way.'

I grabbed frantically at her arm, pointing to the bowl. 'But Beat, what shall I do?'

Beat whispered, 'She won't last long, Amy – she can't, poor little mite, she weren't ready. Just cover 'er up with a clean cloth. I gotter get back.'

I stood in the dark little scullery looking at the baby; despite the blood and the mess I couldn't take my eyes off her. Besides, she was alive – I couldn't just cover her up and leave her. Her arm moved again, and her little hand seemed to be reaching up to me. I put out my own hand and gently touched hers with my fingertip, whispering, 'I'm here, baby – I'm here.' Her skin felt warm and waxy on mine, then her arm dropped back again. I don't know how long I stood there watching her, but eventually I realised that the tiny movements had stopped. She was dead.

Beat came back with a bundle of bloody towels and sheets, and some old newpapers. She wrapped the baby up in the papers and put it in her basket. 'I'll see to that later. Look Amy, I was going to take these home to wash myself, but your Auntie wants me to stay with her until Alf gets home. Can you take 'em downstairs and wash 'em now? You tell Mrs Carter as your Auntie's had a fall and lost her baby, then she'll let you use her scullery if she's finished. Give 'em a good soak in cold water while the copper's heating.'

I couldn't speak, but I managed to nod and pick up the bundle. When I told her what had happened Mrs Carter let me have a couple of pailfuls of hot water from out of her range, to give the copper a start. I dumped the towels and sheets in the sink and went out to the tap. I had to stop a couple of times to go out and retch over the drain in the yard, but I did get them done at last. Mrs Carter turned the handle of the mangle as I fed them through, and then cleared some space on her line so I could peg them out. Luckily it was a fine, sunny day – spring had come, even to Lambeth.

Losing the baby like that seemed to have weakened Aunt Agnes as much as if she'd gone the full time and had all the birth to go through. I could see it would be quite a while before she was properly on her feet again and I could think about going home, so I didn't say anything to her about it. In any case, I'd only managed to save elevenpence towards my fare, so there was no point bothering her about it while she was poorly. Most of the time she just lay there looking at the ceiling. Once or twice I tried to cheer her up by telling her about something funny I'd seen in the street or up the New Cut; she'd turn her eyes and look at me as I talked, but I could tell she was only pretending to listen, so I stopped bothering.

Once she suddenly said, 'Amy, would you take down your hair and then undo your plaits?' I stared at her. 'Please, Amy.'

I did as she asked, and shook my hair out – it would have come down to the top of my legs, except that the wave in it lifted it up a bit. She just lay there looking at it, while I felt rather foolish, having my hair loose in the middle of the day. Then she said, 'Your hair is beautiful, Amy, like brown satin sewn with gold. And your eyes look golden, too.' As she spoke something echoed in my memory: Her Ladyship's maid saying, 'You have little yellow speckles in your eyes,' – and Mrs Turnbull, she'd talked about my hair, comparing it with somebody else's – but it'd been a name I'd never heard before, and I couldn't remember – it was so long ago, now. Aunt Agnes lifted herself a little way from the pillow. 'You're going to be beautiful when you're grown-up, Amy.'

I said, 'Grammer did allus say as good looks be the work o' the Devil.'

Her face twisted, as if in pain. 'No, Amy. She's wrong – I'm sure she's wrong. Only God can create beauty.' She got so agitated saying that, that she made herself cough. When she lay back again, panting, her hankie was streaked with blood and I turned away, feeling queasy as I began to re-plait my hair. Then she spoke again. 'But Amy, you must – take –' she was panting between the words ' – care. Always, take care.'

'Yes, o' course I will.' I always was careful. Even after nearly

128

two years in London I was wary of the traffic; I never dashed across the road in front of a tram, or got in the way of the horses pulling the empty drays back to the brewery, like Ned and Albie did sometimes.

'And Amy, please remember – please remember that I never meant it to be like this.'

I was bewildered – like what? But she was getting agitated again so I said, 'No, o' course not. Thee bist fair wore out wi' all that coughing – I'll mek thee a nice cup o' tea.'

She managed to smile at me. 'Thank you, Amy. You're a good girl.'

I felt guilty when she said that; I hadn't been a good girl for months. I'd been too squeamish when I'd helped her onto the chamber or changed her linen, and I hadn't talked to her when she'd obviously wanted to chat; I'd been too impatient and resentful at being trapped in Lambeth. And then that tiny baby had upset me – I couldn't get the sight of those little fluttering limbs out of my mind. But that was more than a month since now, and there was no point dwelling on it. And, well, I hadn't wanted it to die, but now I wouldn't be needed to look after it, so I could go back to Borrell as soon as Aunt Agnes was better. With the summer coming she was sure to pick up. It was May already, and the speedwell would be little blue flecks in Goosey Meadow, dancing amidst the growing grass. How green the grass was at home; there was no grass in Lambeth except in the churchyard – and that seemed to go dusty and grey almost as soon as the new shoots came through. But still, it was better than nothing, so the next time I went out I made a special detour to look at it, and the two trees by the wall at the end that had just come into full leaf.

When I got back I told Aunt Agnes what I'd seen, then I said, 'It's almost summer – you'll feel brave and well once summer's properly here.'

She smiled, but she didn't say anything, only her usual, 'Thank you, Amy,' when I brought her a cup of tea. I went back out into the scullery to peel the potatoes, but no sooner had I got started than I heard her coughing. It seemed worse than usual, as if she was almost choking with it, so I slowed the knife, listening and then I heard her gasp, 'Amy!' I dropped the knife on the table and ran back next door. She was reared up in the bed and there was a

129

terrible gurgling sound as she tried to speak – but no words came. Instead, the blood gushed out of her mouth like a dark red river – and I stood there, staring at her terrified blue eyes and the scarlet tide spreading out over the bedclothes, frozen with terror. Then she slumped sideways onto the bed and the gurgling stopped. All I could hear was my own voice – screaming, screaming, screaming.

Mrs Carter came up; I could feel her shaking and shaking me until the screams stopped. Then she said, 'Your Auntie's dead – you'll have to fetch the doctor.' But she had to send someone else, as my legs wouldn't hold me up. I collapsed on the hearthrug shaking – all I could see was that spreading scarlet tide.

They got Uncle Alf home, and he fell on his knees by her body, sobbing, bawling like Taffy. Mrs Carter sent the boys to Mrs Morris at the Buildings, and then she and another neighbour stripped the bed and washed her and laid her back in clean linen. All the time I sat huddled on the floor by the hearth, cold and clammy with horror. They brought me a cup of tea, but I couldn't drink it, so they left me alone.

Later that evening, Alf was sitting in his chair with his face in his hands when the door opened – it was Beat. She went to the bed where Aunt Agnes lay, pale as wax, and stood looking down at her, her lips moving. Then she crossed herself, and turned away. She saw me, crouched by the hearth, and came straight towards me. As she reached me she bent down and put her arms around my shivering body, hugging me to her warm, sweaty bosom. Then at last I began to cry.

Chapter Eighteen

Uncle Alf arranged a good funeral for her. He said she must have the best; there were nodding black plumes on the horses' heads and the hearse shone like a glass coach. The whole street lined up on the pavement to see her go, and there was a big crowd of women outside the Buildings as we drove past, all waiting to pay their last respects. Afterwards I discovered that he'd sold her sewing machine to pay for it; the insurance money hadn't been enough for a really first-class funeral. I remembered Aunt Agnes saying she'd given the sewing machine to me – but it hardly seemed to matter now. I was so stunned by her dying, and the terrible way she'd gone, I could scarcely think straight enough to add up the cost of the shopping.

The boys were very shaken, but they had each other; Albie and Ned took Taffy everywhere with them now. I remembered once hearing Aunt Agnes say to Beat, 'The boys, they'll look after each other – Taffy'll be all right.' I hadn't understood what she'd meant by that, but now I did; she must have known she was dying, but she hadn't told me. I thought she should have done. She should have given me a chance to be nicer to her – she shouldn't have pretended like that.

But that wasn't the only thing she'd pretended about. Uncle Alf came in late one evening, when the boys were already in bed. He'd been out for a couple of drinks after tea and now his eyes were red-rimmed and miserable. Sitting there, slumped in his chair, he looked so unhappy that I tried to cheer him up. 'You were a good husband to her Uncle Alf – she often said so.'

He looked up at me, his face haggard. 'And she was a good wife to me – even if she had slipped up before I met 'er. But I never threw it back in her face, like some would've done. I said you 'ad to go, o' course – a man's got 'is pride – but no word o' reproach ever passed me lips again, not once we was wed.' I stared back at him, my thoughts frozen. 'I told 'er she'd got to put you right out of 'er mind, and she did. Then, when she was took poorly, she

131

'appened to say: "If only Albie or Ned 'ud been a girl they could've given me a hand with the housework." And I thought, why not? She's been a good wife. So I said, "You can send fer your daughter, if you want." So she wrote to your Grandma and asked her to send you. But I told her you'd got to call her Auntie – a man's got his pride.'

He sat there, staring into the fire. I couldn't speak, and after a while he continued, 'I went to meet her at the station, the day before we were wed. She'd just taken you down to the old folks and she was grizzling, with 'aving to leave you behind. But I said, "You got to forget about 'er now – it's all over an' done with. I'll soon give you another one to take 'er place." And I did: young Albie was born nine months to the day from the wedding.' He heaved a great sigh. 'I remember she had a nice blouse on when I met 'er that evening – little pink squares it was – and the front was all damp. She was still in milk, you see, from feeding you. Funny, the things yer remember.' He fell silent for a moment, then he said again, 'She was a good wife to me, Aggie was.'

I stood up and went into the scullery and got my bed down and lay on it. My mind couldn't take in what Uncle Alf had said. It couldn't be true, it couldn't.

Next day Beat came in to see how I was getting on. I rounded on her. 'Uncle Alf – he did say as Aunt Agnes, she were my –' I broke off, I couldn't get the word out. 'It baint true, be it?'

'Yes, Amy. Aggie was your mother.' I looked at her, my mind in shock. 'I nagged at her to tell you, Amy – on the quiet, without letting Alf know – and she promised she would, that first Christmas you were here. She was going to lead up to it gentle-like, and then tell you the truth. But after that she told me she couldn't bring herself to do it – said she didn't want to spoil things for you.' Beat shook her head. 'I reckon myself she was too ashamed – she didn't want you to look down on her. And o' course, Alf'd always been very funny about it. She'd begged him to let her keep you, when he first asked her to marry him, but he wouldn't hear of it.'

I cried out, 'So she sent I away. She sent I away so she could marry Uncle Alf! She didn't care!'

'She loved you, Amy.'

'No she didn't, not never. If she'd a' loved I she'd never've

132

married Uncle Alf – she'd a' kept I with her instead. She was cruel – cruel and wicked!' The tears streamed down my cheeks as I spoke.

Beat stood up. 'She was my best friend, Amy. I'll not stay here and listen to you abusing her. P'raps one day, when you're grown-up, I'll tell you what drove her to it, and then you'll see why she did what she did.'

I burst out into a torrent of weeping. 'She'd never've sent the boys away, never – but she sent I, she sent I.' But Beat had already left.

I kept on with the cooking and cleaning, there wasn't anything else to do. I tried not to think about what Uncle Alf had told me; I couldn't bear to think about it. Instead I'd spend hours worrying about whether to have giblet stew instead of cowheel pie when the money was running short on a Wednesday and Thursday, and if the little sliver of soap I'd got left would do another day or not. I did rouse myself once. I'd been past the old women selling ha'penny bunches of mint and sage, so that evening I asked Uncle Alf if I could go back to Granfer.

He said, 'Who's going ter look after me and the boys then? Besides, you reminds me of her.' And he reached out his hand and laid it on my arm, then squeezed it, hard, his eyes looking a bit strange – I was glad when he let go again. I knew he was only trying to be friendly these days – he'd come into the scullery to say goodbye before he went out to the pub, for instance, but there wasn't much room in there and when he was standing behind me he seemed to be pressing against my behind, and it made me feel uncomfortable. He'd say, 'Ta ta for now, Amy. Why don't you have a kip on the big bed this evening, get some beauty sleep? Not that you look as if you're in need of it,' and he'd laugh.

Once I saw him eyeing my chest, and when he saw I'd noticed he leant forward and asked, ''Ow old are you now, Amy?'

'I do be fourteen, come July.'

He nodded, half-smiling to himself. 'Grown-up, near as makes no odds.' I heard him whistling as he went down the stairs. I never slept on the big bed; I always stayed in the scullery. I didn't know whether to mention it to Beat, the way Uncle Alf was behaving, but although she popped in regularly we didn't seem to have a lot to say to each other these days, and the boys seemed to want to

133

talk to her all the time, telling her the things they used to tell Aunt Agnes. Besides, I was sure it was only that Uncle Alf was feeling lonely and missing Aunt Agnes.

But one night when he was back late from the pub he came right into the scullery, pushing the door to behind him. I smelt his beery breath on my face as he leant over me. 'Amy – you awake, Amy?'

I lay absolutely still, with my eyes closed. Then I heard the pad of bare feet and the door creaking open as Ned's voice called, 'Amy –Taffy's bin sick!'

Luckily, Albie had realised what was happening and pushed Taffy's head over the edge of the bed, so I only had to clear up the mess on the floor. Taffy was grizzling for Aunt Agnes, so I found his old dummy, dipped it in a tin of condensed milk and popped it in his mouth; he gulped, and then began to suck at the sweet stickiness. Albie got back into bed with him and put his arms around his brother. 'There y'are Taff – you go to sleep now.'

I had to go back through the kitchen with the bucket and Uncle Alf was sitting in his chair, watching me. I felt all hot and embarrassed at him seeing me in my nightie like that, so I decided that in future I wouldn't get properly undressed until he was home and safely snoring.

The next evening, as soon as the boys had gone to bed I went into the scullery and lay down fully clothed. I heard him coming up the stairs and held my breath – but he went straight into the kitchen. He must have just wanted a drink of water the night before, like he'd told Ned. I listened to him hawking and spitting, and then as soon as I heard the rattle of his snores I got up and put my nightie on.

He mustn't have been thirsty the next night, either – but I was so tired I fell asleep, still wearing my boots, and never even heard him come in. The night after, I was fast asleep and dreaming when I felt a hand grip my shoulder. I woke to the reek of beer, and began to sit up, but the hand pressed me back again, while another hand started pushing my skirt up. I tried to pull away, but a heavy knee pinned down my thighs and strong fingers seized hold of both my hands and thrust them back behind my head so I couldn't move. As he shifted on to me I heard the crack of his head against the table edge – he cursed, but his grip never slackened. Then he began to speak, his voice hoarse and panting. 'Amy – I need you, I need you. I got to 'ave a woman – and you're 'er daughter, it's only right I should 'ave first crack at you, seeing as I didn't get it with 'er. Besides, you bin leading me on, sticking your chest out, jiggling your little bum, trying to get me excited –'

'No, I never! Please, no –'

A hand covered my mouth, cutting off my pleas. 'I know you women – you don't mean that, you want it just as much as I do.' He groaned. 'I bin wi'out for weeks. I got to 'ave it – stop wriggling – I got to 'ave it.' He drew back, and in the gloom I could see his trousers were already open and his huge swollen rod was jerking and jerking as he reached for my drawers, tugging and tugging at the flap until the buttons gave.

The hand over my mouth shifted and I whimpered, 'Please, Uncle Alf, let me go. Let me go!'

'I got to 'ave it, I got to 'ave it.' His fingers thrust between my thighs and then suddenly his whole body was rocked with an enormous belch. The stench of his breath smothered me, but even as it did his grip relaxed and he exclaimed, 'Sod it – I'm gonner throw up.' He twisted sideways and a stream of foul-smelling liquid gushed out of his mouth and onto the floor. I threw myself forward, and leapt at the door. 'Amy –' He was on his feet behind me but I was running down the stairs, out of the house and full tilt along the street. I heard the pounding of boots behind me and ran faster and faster, twisting down alleyways, flinging myself round corners, and all the time the boots came nearer and nearer – until a boy overtook me and went charging off down the street on some last errand of the day. I collapsed against the wall gasping for air, doubled up with the pain of the stitch in my side.

When I'd finally got my breath back I realised I was completely lost. But in any case, I couldn't go back to Endell Street, not with Uncle Alf there. Panic rose in my throat, threatening to choke me – then I remembered Beat. She'd be at work now: I'd go and find her there, and then she'd look after me. I began to walk slowly along the street. A woman came towards me weaving from side to side in the gutter, but I stepped in front of her and asked, 'Please could you tell me the way to The Rose and Crown?'

She hiccupped, 'Which one, ducks? There's three as I know of – and none of 'em serves a decent glass o' port.' She gave a second, louder hiccup and pushed past me.

I looked round for someone else to help me and saw a group of men coming round the corner at the other end. I began to move towards them, but then I noticed there were women standing outside doorways down the length of the street. I walked up to a pair who were chatting together and waited for a chance to interrupt, but one of them noticed me and swung round. 'Clear off, this pitch's taken.' Her voice was hard and angry. I shrank away, and moved on to the next woman, but just as I came level with her a man went up to her, and they linked arms and went into the house.

I looked round, uncertain – and the group of men quickened their pace and then stopped beside me. One of them touched his cap and said, 'Evening, miss – out for a little walk are you? How'ud you like to walk along of us?'

He smiled at me, and gratefully I smiled back. 'I be walking to The Rose and Crown but I dussent know which on en I do want. Only 'tis thic one that Mrs Harris do work at, behind the bar. Mebbe thee dost know?'

'I reckon we can take you there – eh, boys?'

All the others were grinning now, and one of them said, ' 'S'all right by us, Jim. You go first and we'll follow.'

My knees trembled in relief. 'Oh, thank 'ee, thank 'ee.'

'But perhaps you'll do us a little favour in return?'

I nodded in gratitude, and the one who'd spoken took my arm. I didn't like to pull away when he was being so helpful. We turned up a narrow entry; as we came round the bend I saw there was a wall blocking the end. I stopped. 'Are you sure 'tis up here?'

'This'll do fer a knee-trembler. Hup you gets on the step. You're a bit of a short arse fer this job, but you looks a clean 'un.' His hands gripped me tight under the armpits, lifting me up on the step and pushing me back against the wall. I watched in horror as he unbuttoned his trousers and his swollen rod poked out, jerking. It was like a nightmare where the same terrible thing happened over and over again.

'No – no! I –'

'Come on, get your petticoats up. There's others waiting.' He reached out and put his hand under my skirt, pulling the dangling flap of my drawers to one side. He sniggered. 'My, you're the fussy one – drawers an' all – but I see you got 'em undone and ready for business! Stop wriggling.' His voice was getting harsher, his grip harder.

'Please – no!'

He shouted, 'It's too late to change your mind now – you offered!' He slammed me hard back against the wall and I cried out in pain and terror.

'You wanter keep off 'er – she'll give you a dose o' the clap.' It was a woman's voice, loud and clear.

The hands gripping me loosened their hold. 'Wotcher mean? She's only a youngster.'

'Young she may be, but she discharged 'erself from the Lock this afternoon – she told me only ten minutes since.'

His hands dropped back as if they'd been stung. 'Christ – at 'er age!' I felt a stinging slap on my cheek. 'You dirty little bitch!'

The woman walked further into the entry. 'I'll see you right, mister – you and yer mates – but I'll check the colour o' yer cash first.' There was a clink of coins. 'Another tanner, *hif* you please. Right, that'll do.'

As I watched she lifted her skirt and leant back against the wall opposite, with her legs splayed apart. I saw the dark V of her cunny and the pale stretch of flesh above her garter and realised she wasn't wearing any drawers. Then the man dropped his trousers to his knees and stuck himself into her. He pushed and pushed, then gave a short grunt and after a moment backed away, already pulling up his trousers. The other men came round the corner one by one; she didn't even bother to let her skirts down in between. The last two came in together, and one stood watching, fingering his rod while he waited; then he took his turn, there was the final chink of coin and I heard the sound of their boots receding down the street.

'You can come out now.' And as she spoke her voice seemed softer, more familiar. I crept forward. 'You daft little brush. Have you run away from home?'

I whispered, 'Uncle Alf, he'd drink taken – and he did try to –' My voice shaking I added, 'So I ran out, and got lost.'

'Talk about out of the frying pan into the fire!' Then she said abruptly, 'You come from down Wiltshire, don't you?'

And then I knew why her voice had sounded familiar. 'Aye, but I bin in Lunnon near two year since.'

137

'Time enough for you to learn some sense. Stop snivelling and tell me where you were trying to get to when you fell in with that crowd.'

'I be looking for Beat. She do work at The Rose and Crown – but a woman told me as there be three of 'em, and I don't know which it be.'

She laughed. 'Three! There must be a couple o' dozen this side o' the river alone. You can't go wandering round looking at this time o' night – not a daft liddle donkey like you. You'll have to stay here, this entry's my pitch so you'll be safe enough – then when I've finished work for the night I'll take you back to our place.' Boots sounded on the pavement outside. ''Ere, get back in the shadow –some of 'em don't like anybody watching.'

The next man didn't even bother to drop his trousers; it was like a dog mounting a bitch – but dogs had a lightness about them, capering and playing – there was no playing here. I closed my eyes, but I could still hear. Some grunted all the time, some only once. One or two said, 'Ta, Peg – see you next week' – they were all different and yet all the same. And each time there was the chink of coins. I huddled in a doorway, praying they couldn't see me, until eventually she counted her money and decided she'd earnt enough, then she took me back to her room in the next street.

She lit the gas, set a match to the fire and then sat down, kicking off her boots. 'Thyrza's not back yet, you can sit in her chair.' For the first time I saw her clearly: her hair was young and springy, but her face looked much older. I sat down gingerly. 'Soon as the fire's drawing I'll make us a cup of tea.'

I said quickly, 'No, I don't want anything, thank you.'

She suddenly jumped up and came to stand in front of me, legs apart and arms akimbo. 'Don't you look at me like that, as if I were something the cat'd dragged in! If it hadn't a' bin for me you'd a' bin bleeding all over that entry – and then you would've had something to snivel about, by the time that lot'd finished with you.'

'I – I – thank you.' Then I got control of my tongue and said, 'I be main grateful for what you did.'

Her voice dropped. 'I suppose I was soft, but when I heard you speak I remembered my little sister – not that she'll be so little now.'

But as I looked at her I still saw the men's backsides ramming into her, followed by the chink of coins. And she read it in my face, so that as she sat down again she said quietly, 'I wasn't always doing this. I used to be a housemaid in one o' them big houses in the West End. I only ever went with one man. He was a footman there, and I loved him – so I let him have whatever he wanted. He told me he loved me – he swore it on his heart – and I believed him. But when I told him I was in the family way he laughed in my face. He left the next day, found another place – but the other footmen wouldn't tell me where he'd gone. Hung together, they did.' She leant forward and put a couple of coals on the blazing sticks. 'I kept going as long as I could, but in the end the housekeeper guessed and turned me off, so I went home. Me Mam would have taken me in, but Feyther wouldn't hear of it. He said if I didn't go quick he'd have me put away as a "moral criminal" – them's the very words he used. He was local sexton, Feyther, so he liked to show off his education.' Her voice was bitter. 'I dunno what he'd call me now – he'd need a few longer words an' that, I reckon. I was soon through me savings; I'd been sending part of me wages home every month, the way you do, so I had to start this game – but I only meant it to be temporary, till I was over my trouble. I had to go in the workhouse infirmary when my time came, so he was born in there, but what else could I do?'

Her voice softened. 'He was a beautiful baby, and as I looked into his innocent blue eyes I vowed I'd make a fresh start. The matron found me a place as a general servant, and I put him out to nurse. Nearly broke my heart to part with him, but of course, I had to do it. An hour a week I used to have with him, on my afternoon off, and it took me half an hour on the tram each way to get there. But I'd've managed, somehow – for his sake; only after I'd been in the place a month it started. The master, he had me in the bathroom when I was running the bath. There was nothing I could do, I'd lost my character, see. He said if I breathed a word to the missus he'd swear I'd made advances to him, and I'd be turned off. He always had girls like me, from the workhouse, then when he got them in the family way he turned them out, saying they was bad blood. He took me whenever he fancied after that, and there was nothing I could do. Nothing I could do,' she repeated, staring into the leaping flames. 'Then the woman looking after my boy, she asked for more money, and I wasn't earning enough to give her any extra. So I thought, that's it – if I'm going to have to put up with it anyway I might as well be paid for it, so I left.'

She glanced up, her eyes harder now. 'I give 'im something to think about before I went, though. The last morning, I waited till he was well stuck in and then I screamed for the missus. O' course, she turned me out there and then – but I was leaving anyway. I reckon he had some explaining to do. I could've taken my baby back into the House – but I'd have been lucky to see him once a month, in there. They separate you, see, soon as your little'un's weaned. Besides, there was the disgrace. It was bad enough him being born what he was, and in that place – without being labelled a workhouse brat for the rest of his life. I've been on the streets ever since, for his sake. So don't you look at me as if I'm dirt.' She paused, then said, 'I *am* dirt – but my boy don't know it. He thinks his mother and father are dead, he calls me "Auntie", and I give him everything he wants. I don't earn what I used to, of course – in this job you get worn out fast – but as long as I can keep going until he's set up in life then I'll be satisfied.'

All I could do was whisper, 'I be sorry, I be terrible sorry.' Then there were footsteps in the hallway and Thyrza came in.

I dozed in the chair for the rest of the night, and next morning Peg told me the way back to the Cut; it wasn't far, it was just that Aunt Agnes had said I wasn't ever to go in that direction, because the streets weren't respectable, so I'd not known where I was.

I went straight round to Beat's room; she was still in bed, but she got up at once and I told her everything that had happened. She sighed, then said, 'I'm sorry, duck, I should have expected it. Alf don't mean no harm, it's just the way he is – especially when he's had a drop too much. Only I've been that upset about Aggie going I didn't think to warn you. We'll have to do what she always wanted, and get you back to your Granfer.'

'Granfer – I can go back to Granfer?' Then my heart dropped. 'But I baint got no money for the fare. There's only fivepence in my jar.'

Beat went to her cupboard and rummaged in an old saucepan. 'I've got three bob put by – you can have that.'

'But it baint enough.'

'I knows that, Amy – I got me thinking cap on.' Then her face

cleared. 'O' course! That'll be just the ticket. You come along wi'
me.'

I hung back when we got to Endell Street, but Beat chivvied me
on. 'It's all right, Amy – he'll be at work by now.' Beat marched in,
went straight to the mantelpiece and lifted down Uncle Alf's ship
in the bottle – his precious *Wanderer*. 'We oughter get enough on
this.'

'But that mustn't ever be pawned – not never!'

'Today's never, duck. Be putting your things together while I'm
gone.'

There was a pool of foul-smelling vomit still on the kitchen
floor; I'd just finished cleaning it up when Beat came back. She
slapped a pawn ticket down on the mantelpiece. 'Right! He'll find
it when he comes home fer 'is tea.'

'He'll be main angry.'

'I'll deal with your Uncle Alf, duck – I got me methods.' She
winked at me. 'Do 'im good to keep off the beer fer a few weeks
while 'e's saving up to get that thing back. Now you'd best come
home with me for a bite – you got a long journey in front o' you.'

As I walked back with Beat I kept remembering what Peg had
told me, and by the time the herrings were cooked for our meal I
couldn't stop myself asking the question, although I was
frightened of what the answer might be. 'Aunt Agnes – how did
she manage, afore I was born?'

Beat carefully spat out a bone, then said, 'It weren't easy for
her.'

I felt cold. 'Why didn't she go home? Granfer, he wouldn't
never a' turned her out.'

'He weren't there when she arrived, see, only your Grandma –
and when she saw the condition poor Aggie was in she wouldn't let
her over the doorstep. Said she didn't have no daughter any more,
and called her a string o' names, from the Bible.' Beat shook her
head. 'Terrible for Aggie, it must've bin, her own ma turning on
her at a time like that. When your Gran shut the door in her face
she set off walking back to the station, and she was just going up the
slope when she heard her name being called. It was your Grandad,
he come after her. She was that relieved, thinking he was going to
take her back – that he'd made the old gel give in – but he hadn't.
Aggie said your Gran had allus worn the trousers in that house,

and she weren't fer taking them off now. But your Grandad did what he could – he brought all his savings, and he gave her his watch. So Aggie caught the train to London – she'd been here when she was in service, with the family, and she thought there'd be more chance of earning a bob or two. She found a room and sewed shirts, but she wasn't at all well – she had to call the doctor and the money was running out, so she knew once that was finished she'd have to find regular work.'

Beat mopped her plate with a piece of bread, popped it in her mouth and went on, 'By the time you was born she'd got nothing left, but then she managed to get a job behind the bar at The Goat and Compasses. Old Nolan said she could live in and keep you with her; she used to nip up and feed you whenever she got the chance –lucky you was a good baby. That's when I met her. My old man was still alive then but he'd bin knocked down by a tram and lost the use of his legs. Aggie'd do extra fer me so I could pop home to give 'im his tea. She was a good friend to me, Aggie was.' Beat dabbed at her eyes. 'Then Alf came along, offering to marry her – but he said you 'ad to go. She thought your Gran'd feel different about you – an innocent babe, and ever such a pretty one as you was. Besides, your Gran had been a good mother to Aggie – strict, but fair. Only Aggie was a bit more careful-like this time, so she wrote to the next door neighbour and asked her to read her letter to your Grandad, asking him to take you. And when she went down with you he was there at the station, waiting. He took you in his arms, she said goodbye to him – and she never saw him again.' Beat heaved a deep sigh.

Granfer! Granfer taking me, holding me, loving me – and suddenly I realised that I'd be back with Granfer today. This very evening he'd come home from work and find me waiting. And I'd kneel down on the mat and untie his bootlaces, just like I used to do, while he patted me on the head and called me his 'good liddle maid'. 'Is it time for the train yet, Mrs Harris?'

'Yes, duck – we'd best be on our way.'

When we reached the ticket barrier at Waterloo she put her arms around me, hugging me tight. 'You be a good girl now, Amy.'

'Aye, I will. Say goodbye to the boys for me. And thank 'ee, thank 'ee.'

When I got on the train memories came flooding back: Uncle Alf's probing fingers; the men in the entry; the look on Peg's face as she told me about her son – I began to tremble. Then I thought, it doesn't matter any more. Nothing matters, not now I'm going home to Granfer. I hugged that thought around me like a cloak, and it kept me warm all the way back to Wiltshire.

As I walked along the path by Goosey Meadow I saw the hay stacked in cocks, ready for carting, and breathed in the fresh scent of it until my nose tingled with joy. I climbed over the stile and began to run. I was still running when I turned the corner of Hill Lane and saw the cottage in front of me – then I stopped dead, in the dust. The roses, Granfer's roses: they'd all gone.

Chapter Nineteen

I walked very slowly up to the gate. There were potatoes growing where Granfer's roses had bloomed. As I stood looking at them a woman came round the corner of the cottage with a child clinging to her skirts; I'd never seen her before. She glanced at me, half-smiled, and then bent to pull some spring onions from the place where the Rosamund rose had once danced in joy.

I walked on, and up the path of the other cottage, to where Mrs Rawlings' door stood open. I knocked, and she came through out of the scullery, wiping her floury hands on her apron. She gasped in surprise. 'Amy – Amy Roberts!'

I asked, 'Where be my Granfer?'

Her expression changed, her cheeks sagged. 'Didn't thy Grammer write thee? Thy Granfer's dead, Amy – he died more'n a year since.'

Granfer was dead, dead for so long – and I hadn't even known. He'd had a seizure last spring, Mrs Rawlings told me, and lain on his bed not able to move or speak. She'd gone in to help Grammer nurse him, so had the other neighbours, but after a couple of weeks he'd died. 'It were a blessing, Amy – he were as helpless as a newborn babe – and him such an active man.'

'Where be Grammer? I maun go find Grammer.'

Mrs Rawlings looked down at the flags, her face reddening, then she said, 'We did what we could, but with the cost o' fetching the doctor to thy Granfer, and his funeral – she buried him proper, you'd a bin proud to see it, Amy – even if she could a' got relief from the Parish, with her rheumatics so bad –' She stopped, took a deep breath and then told me, 'She's had to go in the House, Amy.' Grammer – in the workhouse – Grammer! 'She hung on till autumn, but by then I reckon she'd had enough. I remember it were just after Dummy Drew hanged himself – they shouldn't a' let him keep his braces, but he were always cunning, were Dummy. She went in then. We thought she'd written to 'ee, but that thee'd chosen to stay in London with thy Mam, as 'twas only natural.'

144

I said, 'I'll get a place, then I'll find somewhere – just a room. I'll work, I'll look after her – I won't let my Grammer stay in there.'

Mrs Rawlings patted my shoulder. 'Thee bist a good maid. Thee canst bed down with my girls till thee've sorted things out. Lucky 'tis visiting day this Sunday – thee canst go and see her then.'

I was so stunned by everything that had happened I hardly noticed the rest of the day. It only started coming to me that night, as I lay crammed against the wall with Alice Rawlings' knees sticking into my back. It was so quiet outside after London it didn't seem natural, and in the silence I kept thinking of me in the loft next door – and how Granfer had slept down below, keeping me safe. Oh, Granfer – but I stopped myself crying. I must be strong, for Grammer's sake. I planned how I'd find a daily place, and a little room, and care for Grammer first thing before I left, and then of an evening after I came home. I'd work hard for Grammer because she needed me and she'd be so grateful that I'd come back to save her from the House that she'd smile at me and call me her 'good liddle maid'. So at last I fell asleep.

But when I woke up the next morning there were shillings and pennies darting about in my head, just like there'd been at Lambeth. Living was cheaper in the country with rents being so much lower, but there wasn't the work. I could machine button-holes, but there were no sweatshops in Borrell – maybe if we went to Bath, but I'd never heard of them there, either – and likely rents were dearer in Bath, it being a city. I'd have to go into service, but only a daily place, because of looking after Grammer – and daily places didn't pay much, and I'd have to buy my own food . . . The sums kept going round and round in my mind so that I scarcely heard Mrs Rawlings telling me what had been happening in Borrell as I helped her with the chores.

Up in the stuffy bedroom I lay awake next to Alice, still worrying. Then suddenly the bedpost shone silver – it was the moon, and she showed me the way. Very quietly I eased myself out of bed and crept downstairs. I lifted the latch of the back door and slipped out into the moonlight. At the top of the garden I slid through the gap in the hedge, trod silently under the apple trees, past the sty with its snoring occupant – and came to our old dunnekin. Round the back I crouched down, found the loose bricks and pulled them out. The tin box was still safe in its hiding place, and when I opened it a cluster of gold sovereigns shone silver in the light of the moon. Next morning I showed them to Mrs Rawlings, and asked her to keep them safe for me until I'd been to Pennings and fetched Grammer out of the House.

On Sunday I set off over the fields to Pennings. I shivered when I came to the high iron gates, but I stepped up to them and tugged at the heavy bell-pull. The harsh clamour brought the porter out from his lodge, the keys jangling at his waist. I said, 'I be come to see my Grammer.' He told me to wait, and went back inside, dipped his pen in the inkwell and entered my name and the time of my arrival in the huge ledger on his desk.

Then he asked, 'Where's your card?'

I whispered, 'I dussent have no card – I be just come back from Lunnon.'

He frowned, then jerked his head to the right. 'Apply at the Master's Office – that way.'

On legs that trembled I passed through the high iron gates and into the shadow of the great grey walls. I was frightened, so frightened – but I would get Grammer out, I would.

The Master questioned me, then gave me permission to visit Grammer. 'Through that door and up the stairs on the left.' As I came into the gloom I saw the wizened face of an old man peering hopelessly through the iron grille that cut the corridor in two. Quickly I turned my face from his despairing eyes and walked away, the heels of my boots echoing on the bare stone flags.

Up in the large whitewashed room the wardmistress inspected my card carefully before handing it back and saying, 'Roberts is down at the far end.'

I saw a group of old women sitting round the empty hearth, and for a moment I hesitated – they all looked alike in their uniforms – then I spotted Grammer and ran forward crying, 'Grammer, Grammer – I be come back!' She turned, very slowly, because of her rheumatics, but her face was just the same under the white mobcap. She didn't smile, but then Grammer never had. I repeated, 'I be back, Grammer.'

'I can see that for myself, there's nought wrong with my eyes.'

I said, 'Mrs Rawlings did tell I about Granfer.' My eyes filled with tears.

' "The Lord gave, and the Lord hath taken away." It was his time.'

I said, 'Grammer, now I be come back, I'll fetch you out o' thic place. Granfer, he did leave money for I, so I can rent a room for both on us – then I'll find work. Don't 'ee worry, Grammer – I'll look arter thee.' I waited, smiling down at her.

At last she spoke, her voice high and cracked as she said, 'I'd sooner stay here.' I flinched back, as though she'd struck me, but she hadn't finished yet. 'I'll not share a roof with *you* again. I never would a' had you in my house in the first place, but Agnes, her sin made her cunning.' Her face creased with bitterness. 'When he came back from thic station with you in his arms I stood at the door, barring his way. But he said he couldn't take you back because he didn't know where she was going to be living – with her husband.' She almost spat the word. 'But I wouldn't let him in, only he fetched Mr Wilcox, and Minister told me it was my duty as a Christian woman to take you in – bathed in iniquity as you were. He said I must rear you with a proper notion of good and evil, cleansing you from your sin, so I did my duty. But it's over now. I brought you up – and then *she* sent for you, and tainted you. You should a' stayed with her.'

I whispered, 'Aunt Agnes is dead, Grammer.' Something flickered in her eyes for a moment, and then went out.

'She been dead to me these fourteen years, I'll not mourn her passing now.' And the terrible rasping croak continued, 'I baint never being dependent on *you* for my daily bread – better be a pauper and dwell in the halls of righteousness forever. Be gone – and don't never come near me again.' Slowly, painfully, she deliberately turned her back on me.

I stood there, sinking deeper and deeper into the black pit, then the old lady sitting next to Grammer got very shakily to her feet and put her hand on my arm. 'Maid, willst thee help I back to my bed?' In a daze I walked her down the long bare room until she stopped, with her hand on an iron bedrail. She turned, and her rheumy blue eyes smiled into mine. 'Thee maunt mind thy Grammer, she do have strange notions. Thee bist a good liddle maid. Now do thee go thy way in peace.' And the touch of her frail fingers on mine drew me up out of the mire, so I was able to walk out of that high grey prison, back into the world beyond.

I told Mrs Rawlings that Grammer had said she'd rather stay in the workhouse than be beholden to me. She stood shocked, then put her hand on my arm saying, 'I daresay thy Grammer's thinking what's best for thee – she dussent want to be a burden on thy youth.' I looked at her bleakly, without a reply, and she gave a big sigh and said, 'She's been cranky for a long time now. It curdled her, your Mam getting into trouble like that. She'd been the apple of your Grammer's eye, had Agnes – and after, your Grammer couldn't live wi' the shame of it.'

I slept with the girls that night, and helped Mrs Rawlings with the washing the next day, but I knew I couldn't stay much longer – there were six still at home and another baby coming. When the mangling was finished and the clean clouts hung out to dry I asked Mrs Rawlings whereabouts Granfer was buried. As soon as Alice came home from school she sent her down the churchyard with me to show me where he lay. He was under the green mound two graves in from the yew tree in the corner, but Alice was more interested in Dummy Drew's grave. 'Rector wouldn't have en in churchyard proper, seeing as he done take his own life, so he do lie out there, on the other side o' the wall.' She went running off to play with her friends.

I walked out into the lane, and picked wild roses from the hedgerow, for Granfer. Carefully I arranged them in a neat bunch, and placed it where I thought his hands would be, folded over his chest. I said, 'I did come back to thee, Granfer, but it were too late,' and I knelt on the grass and cried. When I'd no more tears left to cry I whispered, 'I dussent know what to do, Granfer. Nobody do want I, and I've nowhere to go.'

And as I knelt there I seemed to hear his voice, just like it used to be, asking, 'Would thee like to go for a lady's maid, Amy?' and my own young voice exclaiming, 'Oh, Granfer!' He'd worked and saved to get together those gold coins, and now I knew he wanted me to use them. I whispered, 'Thank 'ee, Granfer – thank 'ee.' Then I uncurled my cramped legs and went back to Mrs Rawlings.

Next day, after school was out I went to see Mrs Roper. I could tell by her face that she'd heard about Grammer; the whole village knew. She listened while I told her about Granfer saving up to pay my premium, and then I said I wanted to be apprenticed to a dressmaker, and learn to sew.

She arranged everything. She went to see Her Ladyship at the Hall, and she told Mrs Roper who to write to, and then Mrs Roper took me to Bath herself, on the train. We went to see a lady called Mrs Bryant, and Mrs Roper told her I needed to live in, as I was an orphan, and my grandmother was now too infirm to make a home for me. Mrs Bryant said it suited her to have an apprentice on call, and then she made me sew all the different stitches I knew. Mrs Roper told her Lady Warminster herself had praised my sewing, and gave her the character Lady Blanche had written for me, and then it was all settled.

As I was walking back from the station with Mrs Roper she began to speak. 'Amy, I don't know whether I've –' then she broke off, and it was a while before she continued, her voice firmer. 'The question must be for my conscience, I have no right to burden yours. Amy, when I went to ask Her Ladyship for your character she was in a hurry to go out, so she wrote it very quickly, then gave it to me to check. I noticed at once that she had omitted any reference to the unfortunate manner of your birth. I thought this was probably an unintentional omission – but I chose not to draw her attention to it. Today, I did not tell Mrs Bryant any falsehoods, but some might say I'd been sparing with the truth.'

I said, 'So Mrs Bryant – she dussent know?'

'I didn't feel there was any good reason for her to know. Amy, I may be wrong, but I'd like to make a suggestion – that unless you are directly asked, you do not reveal the fact that you were born out of wedlock. Your incomplete birth certificate will betray it at once, but there are very few circumstances under which you will need to produce that document.' She stopped and turned to face me. 'No one in Bath will know, so you can put the past behind you and make a fresh start – and later, you'll be free to follow whatever path you choose.'

I understood; I could go to be a lady's maid, because no one would ever know. 'Oh, thank 'ee, Mrs Roper – thank 'ee.'

'But Amy, there is one time when you must be totally honest. You must tell the truth to any young man who wishes to marry you. If he is planning to honour you with his name, then you must tell him that you do not have one of your own. If he truly loves you, he will overlook the taint, but since you will be his wife, and the mother of his children, then he has a right to know. So please promise me that you will tell him, Amy.'

'I do promise, Mrs Roper.'

Next day I went back to the churchyard. I'd picked more wild roses from the hedgerow, and once again I laid them on Granfer's grave. 'Goodbye, Granfer.' But as I got to my feet I picked one of the roses up again, and took it out to the green mound beyond the wall. I set it carefully down there, saying, 'And goodbye to you, too, Dummy Drew.' Then I went back to Mrs Rawlings' to pack my basket.

Chapter Twenty

Mrs Roper had told me to put the past behind me and make a fresh start, but I couldn't. I'd be sitting with a needle full of thread and suddenly realise that the hands of the clock had moved on five minutes and I hadn't even put it into the cloth, then I'd panic and stab frantically at whatever I was doing and the stitches would be pulled too tight and pucker the stuff I was working on. Mrs Bryant only put me on easy tasks at first: tacking linings and over-sewing seams – the kind of sewing I'd been doing for years – but my fingers seemed to have got clumsy and slow, and my brain had too. Mrs Bryant or Miss Worthing, the first hand, would give me instructions and I'd nod and say, 'Yes, ma'am' – but ten minutes later they'd completely gone from my head. All I seemed to be able to think about was Aunt Agnes being my mother, and never having been married to the gentleman who was my father; and how she'd got rid of me because she wanted to marry Uncle Alf; and how Grammer had never wanted to look after me, not even when I was a tiny baby, and now she preferred staying in the House to living with me – and Granfer, Granfer dying and leaving me. Nothing else seemed to matter besides that awful truth: that nobody in the whole wide world had ever wanted me – and nobody ever would.

I'd get through the day somehow, then pull myself up the three flights of stairs to huddle on my bed in the little boxroom. But there was no relief to be found there, either, because when I did finally drop off to sleep, then the nightmares came. I'd be back in the kitchen at Endell Street with Aunt Agnes, and suddenly the blood'd come pouring out of her mouth like a great scarlet wave – and I couldn't move. Frozen I'd be, just watching while her eyes looked at me pleading for help – and I couldn't move, I couldn't speak. Then her face would change and it would be Dimpsey's golden snout, with her dainty feet drumming on the wooden bench, but still there were those pleading eyes, and the blood, that terrible tide of blood. I'd wake with my cheeks wet and my pillow sodden, and scrabble frantically for matches and candle, terrified that blood was flowing out of me, and that I was dying too. Other nights it was men's hands, reaching for me, seizing hold of my legs, tearing at my drawers. I'd pull away and run, only to hear the pounding footsteps behind me and feel the huge fingers pinion my shoulder, and slam me against the wall – and that awful, jerking rod would swell larger and larger, until it was all I could see. Then, just as it was about to ram itself into me I'd wake up, drenched in sweat. One night I got Esau out, but when I saw the neat little stitches mending his fur I thrust him away again at the bottom of my chest of drawers. I had nobody, now.

I'd been in Bath a couple of months when Mrs Bryant gave me a silk dress lining that needed the seams over-sewing; the order was for a good customer who wanted the dress in a hurry, so she told me to concentrate, and not start day-dreaming the way I had all morning. I began to sew so quickly I didn't notice I'd torn my nail while I was attending to the irons – now the snag caught in the fabric and puckered the whole panel of silk. Mrs Bryant was very angry, telling me I couldn't be trusted – and Janet, the improver, was annoyed too, because she had to stay late into the evening cutting and fitting another skirt panel.

Next day Mrs Bryant took me on one side and told me she thought I was wasting my time, and hers, trying to learn dressmaking. She said she was willing to give me my premium back, less a guinea for the nine weeks' board and lodging, but because I was so young I must go and talk to my grandmother first, to ask her advice. I must go that coming Sunday, she said.

I only had one of Granfer's gold sovereigns left in my pocket, and I knew I mustn't break into that, so I would have to walk. I didn't know the way by road, but I remembered Granfer saying once that the canal which ran through Pennings went all the way to Bath. So on the Sunday I asked for directions to the canal and set off walking. My boots were too small for me now; they pinched my toes, and I was so tired and unhappy I felt like lying down beside the towpath and never getting up again. But Mrs Bryant had told me I must see Grammer, so I hobbled on.

When finally I arrived at the iron gates and pulled at the bell the porter came out of his lodge and barred the way. Timidly I whispered, 'Please, mister, canst I see my Grammer?' Without speaking he jerked his thumb towards the printed notice and I read: '*The time appointed for the visitation of inmates other than those in the Sick Wards is the first Sunday in the month between the hours of 2.30 and 4.00 in the afternoon.*'

When I'd finished reading he said, 'Today's the *second* Sunday,' and turned to go back into his lodge.

Desperately I ran after him. 'Please, mister, I did walk all the way from Bath and Mrs Bryant did say I maun see my Grammer – she'll be terrible angered if I dussent.' Reluctantly he turned round. 'Please, mister, please.'

He pursed his lips, then grudgingly moved towards the gates. 'You can try your luck with the Master.'

I was lucky, because the Matron was there as well, and after I'd pleaded with her husband she spoke up for me. 'The poor child looks exhausted. I'll send up to Mrs Roberts to say her grand-daughter's here, and would she come down and step outside to the female airing ground.' She smiled at my relieved face. 'You can have a word with her there, child.'

I whispered my thanks before the Matron rang for the pauper maid and gave her the message, then she sent me out into the bare, walled yard to wait. I stood there in a daze of relief. Grammer would be angry with me, but at least she'd tell me what I should do. But when the pauper maid came back she was alone. I asked anxiously, 'Be Grammer's rheumatics worse?'

The pauper shook her head. 'She says she don't want to see you. She says she told you that afore.' I couldn't believe what the dull voice was saying, but then she thrust a folded piece of paper into my hand. 'She said you was to take that away wi' you – 'tis your birth certificate, and she don't want it soiling her marriage lines.'

I took the piece of paper, pushed it into my pocket and went back into the gloomy corridor. The Matron was coming out of the office. 'My, that was quick.'

I told her flatly, 'She wouldn't come.'

The Matron's face creased in concern. 'What a shame for you, my dear, when you've walked such a long way – but I'm afraid old people can be very crotchety.' Then she touched my arm. 'Come into the office and I'll take down your name and address, seeing as you're her only kin.' I gave her Mrs Bryant's address, although I didn't suppose I'd be there much longer, but I hadn't got any other. She blotted the ledger carefully before saying, 'I expect

153

she'll come round in a little while, and then she'll be asking after you. When she does, I'll send for you – but remember, visiting is on the *first* Sunday.'

'Yes, ma'am. Thank 'ee, ma'am.'

I walked down the long drive and out through the high gates. I didn't know what to do or where to go – I didn't seem able to think for myself any more. I'd been so sure Grammer would see me and tell me what I must do – now I was completely adrift. There was a woman walking ahead of me down the lane, so I turned that way and followed her; it was all I could think of.

When I'd walked for a while I came to an ornate iron gate, and a small pretty lodge and I recognised them – I'd been here before, walking behind the May Garland when I was a child. I stopped and stood by the gate, looking up the drive – and remembered Lady Warminster with her shining golden hair and fine drooping mouth, which had smiled only at me. Maybe if I stood and waited she'd come driving out in her carriage, and as the gate was being opened her blue eyes would light up and she'd call me over, saying, 'Aren't you the little girl whose needlework I praised at Borrell School? Would you like to come and be my sewing maid, my dear?' And it was as if I actually saw her, and heard her speak, and it was so real that I began to cry tears of relief as I forced my tired feet into a little run – then a woman in an apron came out of the lodge door. 'Bist thee looking for someone?'

The words tumbled out of my mouth. 'Lady Warminster – I be looking for Lady Warminster. Be she at home today?'

She shook her head. 'Bless you, no. She's not been to Pennings these two year past – or mebbe 'tis longer 'n that.' I lowered my head as I fought the tears of disappointment. The woman came closer. 'Thee dost look fair wore out, my maid. Hast thee come far?'

'I did walk from Bath.' My voice had almost gone.

'From Bath! Then 'tis no wonder thee bist tired. Come inside and rest thy feet awhile. I'll fetch thee a drink – the roads be main dusty this time o' year.' I sat dully sipping the cold water as she chattered on. 'No, last time Her Ladyship were here were just arter our Tom was wed, and he's a got a fine youngster now – a liddle boy and another on the way – so it must be more'n two year since. His Lordship, he's got another house over by Salisbury –

154

with a fine garden full o' roses, they do say – so mebbe she's staying there, seeing as His Lordship do never come to Pennings. Only Her Ladyship do come here, and the young lord, her son – as handsome a young gentleman as you ever did see, and a lovely way with him. I never opened thic gate for him but he had a friendly word and a "thank you" – not like some o' the gentry. Yellow-haired he be – takes after his mother, luckily – and you could tell she fair doted on him.' I held out my empty mug and she took it, saying, 'Bist thee going back to Bath today?' I nodded. ''Tis a long way – mind thee dussent get lost.'

'I did follow the canal.'

'Ah, 'tis further that road, but 'tis safer.' As I stood up to go, she suggested, 'Why don't you cut across the Park? It'll save you a tidy step. There's a Mr Benson and his family renting the house now, but they're away in Lunnon for the week, so there's nobody there to mind. Look for the stable block and keep to the left of it. You'll come out by the West Lodge, then 'tis only a cock's stride to the canal.'

I walked very slowly up the drive; my feet were made of lead and I scarcely had the strength to lift them. As I rounded a bend the house came in sight – and my dragging feet stumbled hopelessly to a halt. I couldn't go on. Even after what the woman at the lodge had told me I'd still hoped she might be there – but every blind was drawn. I stood looking at it with the tears streaming down my face, but nothing stirred behind those blank windows.

I must have managed to lift my feet because the next thing I knew I was crouching on the grass much closer to the house, and the memories were coming crowding back to suffocate me. Looking up at the golden pillared walls I sobbed, 'Help I, please help I.' And like a miracle, they did: they told me what to do. I would build a house, just like this one – I would build it in my head. Then I would open the door and push inside all my memories, and once they were all in I would close the door and shutter the windows and never let them out again. And as I knelt there I did just that.

The door clicked shut behind the final memory – the pauper handing me the piece of paper from Grammer – and I felt an enormous weight slip from my shoulders. I was light and empty. Empty. There was nothing behind me and nothing ahead: nothing to remember and nothing to look forward to. My life was empty. And with the nothingness came despair.

Again I whispered, 'Help I, help I,' but it was a hopeless whisper. I didn't expect another answer – yet one came. It came from the one memory I hadn't shut away, that of Lady Warminster herself. And now as I gazed at her house, she told me again, 'You must be a lady's maid when you grow up, ma petite.'

Deliberately I refilled my head and peopled it. When I had finished my apprenticeship I would be a lady's maid, and come here and serve her. She would speak kindly to me, praising my looks and saying, 'I can hardly believe you were born in humble circumstances in a little village – you look so like a lady, ma petite.' Then, because she was kind, I'd tell her my story. As soon as she heard it she'd clap her hands and exclaim 'I'm sure your father is not dead. Some accident befell him and so he lost touch with your mother – now we must find him for you.'

She'd call Lord Warminster, and although I'd never seen him I knew exactly what he looked like – tall and distinguished with silver-grey hair and just the slightest of stoops. He would ask with a smile, 'What is it, my dear?'

And when she'd told him my story she'd say, 'You must find Amy's father for her.'

He would raise her hand to his lips. 'How kind you are, my dear. Of course I will do as you wish.'

Not long after, Lord Warminster would send for me to go downstairs, and he would be in a room lined with books – like the one Sir Harry had at the Hall. There would be a gentleman with him who was younger, and had curly brown hair, and as I came in Lord Warminster would say. 'Amy my dear, I have a surprise for you.' But of course my father had already recognised me and was holding out his arms. I'd run into them, crying with relief and joy. It was a lovely story, and when I'd finished it I felt so much better. I stood up, said, 'Thank 'ee,' to the house, then set off on the long walk back to Bath.

All the way back as I trudged along the towpath the story grew and grew in my head. I knew the exact colour of the dress Lady Warminster was wearing when she called His Lordship to her, and I saw how his hair curled at his temples. Now the story didn't finish when I met my father for the first time; he was so pleased to have

156

found me he took me straight home with him, to a house very like the one at Pennings – he was an earl, too. He'd never married because he'd never forgotten my mother, so I became mistress of his great house. Lady Warminster asked if she could take me out in society, and I went to a ball, wearing a dress of shiny green satin with roses sewn all round the neck and the hem. The first man I danced with was Lady Warminster's son, the young lord, and I never danced with another because he fell in love with me and asked me to marry him that same night. I saw the candlelight shining on his fair head as he knelt at my feet to propose. Blushing, I accepted him, and at once he took me off to his parents. Lord Warminster smiled kindly, but Lady Warminster opened her arms to me, and I hid my face against her scented bosom as she said, 'My dear, I'm so happy – at last I have a daughter.' Soon after I was on my way back from church in a dress of white satin, with a wreath of orange blossom in my hair; as I stepped out of the carriage Lady Warminster put her arm around me and kissed my cheek. 'Welcome home, my dear.' And so I had a family at last.

Chapter Twenty-One

That certainty buoyed me up all the journey back, and as soon as I got in I asked if I could see Mrs Bryant. I begged her to let me stay and try again. Her face looked doubtful, so I pleaded, 'Please, ma'am, I will try main hard – I do promise faithfully.' I waited anxiously until at last she said she'd give me one more chance.

It wasn't easy because Mrs Bryant and Miss Worthing watched me like hawks every time I picked up a piece of material, but I tried very hard to concentrate on whatever job I was doing, and to shut everything else up in the miniature house in my head. Only Granfer wouldn't stay locked up there: I'd catch a glimpse of a late-flowering rose in one of the square gardens when I was out on an errand, or see an old man with grey whiskers that bristled like his, and then tears would prickle my eyelids and I'd have to fight to keep them back – because Granfer had loved me, I knew that. So one day I decided I wouldn't lock Granfer away any more. I'd let myself remember him – but only the times we'd been happy together. Life became a little easier after that.

Then one day I found the rose. Because I was the only apprentice living in, I used to eat my breakfast and supper in the kitchen with the servants. I liked sitting there in the warm listening to their soft country voices that sounded so different from the way folk spoke in London, and although they were all old they were always kind to me. Mary and Saranne were the two maids and Mrs Dawes was the cook. Mrs Dawes had 'legs' and they pained her terribly when she first got up of a morning, so I used to run down early to fetch and carry for her. I preferred being busy all the time: that way it was easier to keep the door of the little house closed. One day she sent me out after breakfast to tell the gardener she'd need an extra cabbage for dinner; I couldn't find him near the house so I walked up the narrow path between the vegetable beds, and there on the wall behind the runner beans, was a rose. I thought it couldn't be at first, because there were blooms, and it was well into September – but she was there all right. She was a white rose, but when I came nearer I saw that her buds were pink-tipped. She wasn't a big, full rose, like the Cabbage, nor a brisk, sturdy one like the York and Lancaster – no, she was soft and delicate, with a light, sweet scent. But she'd managed to climb a long way up the wall, and now her dainty heads were drooping a little as if tired with the effort, and they trembled in the lightest of breezes. I fell in love with her at once.

I cupped my hand around one white cluster and told her, 'Thee bist beautiful, my rose.' Her silken petals gently stroked my fingers in reply. 'Tell me, my rose, what bist thy name?' But she shook her head and was shy.

When I found Mr Eliot, the gardener, I asked him what she was called – but he didn't know. He said she'd always been there: he gave her a bit of a prune in the spring and she'd start flowering in June and stay in flower all summer until well into the autumn. He said she was a very good-tempered rose, but I knew that already.

I had to go in then, but every day after, I'd slip out to see her first thing in the morning when the dew was still on her petals, and then ask Mrs Dawes if I could pop out before supper to wish her goodnight. Mary and Saranne used to tease me, saying I was going to meet a sweetheart who'd climbed over the wall – but they knew I wasn't really. One day they said they'd both come with me to see this marvellous rose for themselves. They didn't know her name, either, although they said she was very pretty – but she was more than that, she was beautiful. When her last petals turned brown and dropped off I wanted to cry, but Mr Eliot said I mustn't fret, she'd bloom again next year – and her leaves were still glossy and green, so she hadn't quite gone away.

Seeing the rose made me remember the fairy tales, and I started telling them to myself in bed at night – but best of all I liked my own story, and now I added another scene to it. I decided that although the young lord fell in love with me at that very first dance he was too shy to propose to me there and then, so he invited me to walk with him in his father's rose garden. He would show me a beautiful pink Cabbage rose, and I'd exclaim, 'Baint she a lovely rose!' Then he'd gaze into my eyes and reply, 'But she's not half as lovely as you are, my dearest Amy.' And next minute he'd be on his knees on the gravel path asking, 'Will you be my wife?' Blushing, I'd say, 'Oh, this is such a surprise,' and 'I never expected such an honour,' but when I'd finished saying that then of course I'd accept.

I'd learnt what I should say from the books Saranne and Mary used to read aloud after supper in the kitchen; in these stories handsome lords were always falling in love with poor governesses and humble housemaids and asking them to marry them – so they helped me to get my dreams exactly right. Mrs Dawes said Mary and Saranne were filling my head with romantic nonsense, and lords in real life didn't marry outside their station; but I knew she was wrong because the magazine Mrs Dawes herself took had a Society Page, and it was always telling you about lords who'd married Gaiety Girls who came from humble backgrounds. Denise Orme, now – she'd married the son and heir of Lord Churston, while her Cousin Dorothy had married Lord Bridport's son the following year. Then there was Rosie Boote, who'd been Marchioness of Headfort for years, and had three little children now.

Saranne said one day, 'Thee bist such a pretty maid, Amy, I do believe thee couldst go on the stage one day – and then marry a lord.'

Mrs Dawes was annoyed. 'Amy's going to be a lady's maid, and that's the finest career any girl could have.'

Mrs Dawes had been in service in a big household before her legs flared up, and every Sunday morning while I was helping her prepare the vegetables she'd tell me tales about her life there. I loved hearing about the Upper Ten and the Lower Five; the Upper Ten were fewer than ten, and there were many more than five in the Lower Five, because they were all the other servants, but it was the Upper Ten who really mattered. They were so important that while they were eating their main course in the Servants' Hall no one else was allowed to speak, then they would all get up and walk in procession to the housekeeper's room – always called just the Room – to have their dessert there, in the comfort that befitted their station. Personal servants like valets and lady's maids were members of the Upper Ten, of course, together with the Heads of Department – the butler, the housekeeper and the cook, who'd been Mrs Dawes herself. She'd sigh as she told me of those past glories. 'To think I had three under me, Amy, one in the kitchen and two in the scullery. I never thought then –' She shook her head sadly, then said, 'Still, I'm lucky to have got such a good place here, my legs being the way they are.' She'd smile at me and add, 'And I don't miss a kitchenmaid when I've got you helping me the way you do. You're a neat, handy girl, Amy, and always willing – not like some of those flighty modern pieces.'

I felt rather guilty when Mrs Dawes said that. Although I liked helping, I did it partly because unless I kept busy all the time I couldn't keep the door of the little house in my head quite closed, and the minute it opened a crack I'd see Grammer's pale bitter eyes peering out at me, or Aunt Agnes' despairing blue ones.

Besides, Mrs Dawes was always kind to me. The other apprentices brought their dinners from home to eat in the little back room where the dressmakers' dummies were stored, so Mrs Dawes could have just given me bread and cheese – but often there'd be a nice piece of pie, or a little hot-pot ready warmed, followed by one of her special apple tarts. At our tea break she'd send up a scone or a piece of cake, and when I thanked her she'd say, 'Growing girls need their food.' Every so often she'd leave a pair of stockings by my plate at supper-time: 'For all your help, Amy.' Saranne and Mary were kind, too. When they'd finished with an old dress or a nightie they'd give it to me to alter for myself. I'd have been hard-pressed to look decent without their help, because Granfer's last sovereign had been spent long ago on having my boots mended. Then, just when my soles were worn paper-thin and couldn't stand any more patching, Janet the improver brought in a pair of boots her sister had grown out of – she said perhaps I could oblige her by making use of them. Then Miss Worthing arrived with one of her old hats, and showed me how to trim it so it looked as good as new. I was very proud, the first time I went out wearing a proper grown-up hat.

I needed a new hat for going to Church. Not for chapel, where Saranne and Mary took me every Sunday evening. I could wear my old straw there; I didn't want to go at first because the preacher was very fond of Hell, like Mr Wilcox, but I learnt to close my ears and think about my story instead. But going to Church was different, because I only went to weddings. Most of Mrs Bryant's customers were older ladies, but sometimes a bride came to be dressed. Bridal gowns were always special to sew – yards of silk or satin and lace, all of the purest white. On the wedding day itself either Miss Worthing or Janet would go to check that everything was in order, first to the house then on to the church – and they'd take one of us apprentices with them to hold the pincushion or needle case. I always offered, and as the other girls preferred to be at home on Saturday afternoons I was generally the one to go. I'd feel the excitement mounting as Janet fanned out the train in the church porch and tweaked the veil into position, then, as the organ soared out, we'd slip into one of the back pews and watch our handiwork being married.

Although I'd know the bride a little from when we'd been to fit her, once she was standing at the altar I forgot about her and imagined it was me standing there in my white gown and veil – being married to Lady Warminster's son, who loved me. His voice would be loud and firm as he vowed: 'I take thee, Amy, to my wedded wife, to have and to hold from this day forward . . .' Then I would plight my troth in turn and we'd come to the part of the service I liked best of all. He'd turn to me, hold out the shining gold ring and then slip it gently on my finger before saying those magical words: 'With this ring I thee wed, with my body I thee worship, and with all my worldly goods I thee endow; in the Name of the Father, and of the Son, and of the Holy Ghost. Amen.' I'd feel faint with joy at the very thought of it. I did so like wedding Saturdays.

By the time spring came round I'd learnt to braid a skirt and set in a waistband, I'd sewn hundreds of tiny gold sequins on a chiffon evening dress, and best of all, I'd made a whole blouse myself; I glowed with pleasure when Mrs Bryant praised the set of my sleeves. I even enjoyed the back-breaking job of picking pins up off the floor. Each one I found was like a little sliver of silver, and knowing I was getting the irons just the right pitch of hotness – that was satisfying, too. It was my task to tidy up the workroom when everyone else had gone home, and I loved picking up the scraps of fabric to put them in their proper boxes: the fragile lightness of ninon, the smooth shinyness of satin, the soft deep pile of the velvet – they all spoke to me through my fingers. I could have stayed there for hours, caressing them, except that I'd be getting hungry and looking forward to Mrs Dawes' good supper.

The one job I didn't much care for, though, was sewing

162

buttonholes. Despite them all being made by hand at Mrs Bryant's they still sometimes made memories ooze out from under the door of the little house. Then, towards the end of spring, something else happened which upset me. I knew what it was, of course, and that it happened to every woman, but seeing the blood on my drawers frightened me, and the idea of it coming out of my body made me feel sick and ill. Mrs Dawes was very kind and found me some old rags to wear, then she asked Saranne to fill a hot water bottle. 'Poor little Amy's got a pain under her pinnie.' But it wasn't painful, more a feeling of being unclean. I used to wash extra carefully at those times.

The blood brought my nightmares back, too – Dimpsey and Aunt Agnes became all jumbled up together in my dreams. I could keep my memories shut up in the daytime, but I lost control over them while I was asleep. Every evening as I prepared for bed I'd feel myself going shaky, and as soon as I put my head on the pillow I'd have to start telling myself my story, very quickly, to stop the trembling. I didn't like doing that. I preferred to keep it as a treat; I didn't want it to get used every day and become worn and shabby.

One night after my monthlies started I dreamt of Aunt Agnes screaming before the baby was born dead, and the other tiny baby coming before its time and dying on the scullery table. When I woke up I was shaking – and then I suddenly realised that I could have a baby now. Part of me wanted one, a baby of my very own that would feed at my breast and smile up at me – but the other part of me was frightened, very frightened. I climbed out of bed and went rummaging in the chest of drawers to find Esau; I took him back to bed with me, and lay cuddling him until I fell asleep.

The rose helped me, too. The last week in May Mr Eliot left a message with Mrs Dawes: 'Tell the liddle maid thic rose do be in bud.' I gobbled my pie at dinner-time and then asked Miss Worthing if I could go out in the garden. I ran down the path to the back wall and there, standing bravely out in front of the dark green leaves were the first clusters of scarlet-tipped buds. I said, 'Good afternoon, my rose – I bist so pleased to see thee,' and her buds smiled shyly back at me in greeting. I was so excited I plucked up the courage to ask Mrs Bryant what the rose's name was – but she didn't know, either. She said it'd been there when she and Mr

163

Bryant first came to live in the house, and Mr Bryant had wanted to have it chopped down because he said roses were prone to pests and a lot of trouble in the garden. I gasped in dismay and Mrs Bryant smiled as she said she'd persuaded him to leave it a while and see how well it bloomed, and now he'd got used to it – but neither of them knew its name.

At the end of my first two years at Bath Mrs Bryant began paying me half-a-crown a week, on top of my board. The first weeks' wages just melted away: I'd mended until my underwear seemed to consist of nothing but patches and darns, and I had to save up for a new winter coat – my old one was so tight over my chest I could hardly breathe when it was buttoned up. But eventually I managed to start saving, although sometimes when I saw a pretty ribbon or a decorated comb for my hair I couldn't stop myself giving into temptation and buying it. I'd feel guilty afterwards, but then Mrs Dawes gave me a little account book, and that helped. I wrote down in it every single farthing I spent, and then added up the columns each week to see what I'd saved. I knew I must save, because ladies' maids had to supply their own outfits, and pay to have hair-dressing lessons as well.

I did manage to learn some different hairstyles from Mrs Dawes' magazine: she'd let me borrow it, and I'd take it upstairs and prop it against the mirror on my chest of drawers while I practised on my own hair. There were useful tips in the magazines, too, and I bought a cheap exercise book so I could copy out instructions on 'How to clean kid gloves' or 'How to cure muddiness of the complexion in youth'; not that I had any kid gloves, or a muddy complexion, either, but the young lady I was serving might well have both. Mrs Dawes had explained to me that before I became a proper lady's maid I'd have to get a place as a young lady's maid, so as to learn my duties. At first I'd been disappointed, but then I thought that of course I would need to get some experience before I went to Lady Warminster, so I went back upstairs and wrote down the instructions for cleaning white ostrich feathers and removing tar from the hem of a skirt.

When I was seventeen Mrs Bryant made me head apprentice and gave me a rise. She said in another year I could look for a place as an improver – perhaps somewhere where I could work with fur and get some tailoring experience – she'd give me a good character. But I explained that before then I should have enough money saved to apply for a place as a young lady's maid – if she'd still give me a character. She smiled and said she would. Then just after Christmas a message came to me from Pennings: Grammer had died.

Chapter Twenty-Two

I couldn't take it in at first. I listened while Mrs Bryant said I could have the day off tomorrow so I could go over to Pennings to make 'the necessary arrangements' and all the time I kept nodding my head like a puppet in a Punch and Judy show. 'Yes, ma'am. No, ma'am. Thank you, ma'am,' – but I still didn't believe it.

When I came down for supper Mrs Dawes patted my hand and Mary and Saranne spoke in subdued voices – then Saranne said, 'We never knew thee hadst a grammer living, Amy – we thought thee wast an orphan, wi' nobody o' thy own.' Her voice had a slight edge of reproach.

'Grammer, she been ill since afore I did come to Bath.'

Mrs Dawes said quietly, 'Mebbe with her being poorly it would have heartened her if her grand-daughter'd paid her a visit from time to time.' I sat looking down at my plate, my throat too choked to reply – besides, what could I have replied? I couldn't tell them Grammer hadn't wanted me; I couldn't, I couldn't. There was a silence, then Mrs Dawes sighed. 'Still, youngsters don't think, it's not in their nature.'

The minute I'd forced down my supper I pushed back my chair and got up, managing a strangled, 'Good night.' As I closed the door behind me I heard Saranne say, ''Tis strange they didn't send for her, when they knew the old lady was ready to meet her Maker.'

Upstairs I crouched on my bed, shaking. I'd never really thought Grammer would die like that, without my ever seeing her again. Underneath – for all the way I'd shut my dreams in the little house – I'd always thought she'd send for me again. Not to say she wanted me to make a home for her – Grammer wasn't like that – but just to let me know she hadn't forgotten me. Then I'd have offered again, and when she said, 'Yes,' I'd have had her out of the House so quick, now the old age pensions had come in. They'd started the first winter I was in Bath. Mary and Saranne had talked about them a lot. 'He's a lovely man, that Mr Lloyd George, even

166

if he is Welsh. He's known what it is to do without.' And Mary had added, 'Every night I'll be down on my knees giving thanks, now I've got something to look forward to instead of the House.'

Five shillings a week wasn't much, but I could have found a daily place. Grammer never had eaten a lot and I could manage with less, like I'd done in Lambeth. Grammer must have known about the new pensions, so I'd expected to get a message then. When the months had gone by and it hadn't arrived I'd decided Mrs Rawlings was right: Grammer didn't want to be a burden to me while I was still young, but when I was full grown then she'd feel differently. Maybe she was waiting until this summer, when I'd be eighteen – she knew the date of my birthday, even if she never referred to it. That was it, I'd decided; she was going to send for me this summer. But now she was dead. Only, as Saranne had said, they'd have sent for me from the House, when they knew she was dying – they always did. Perhaps it happened so quickly . . . But I knew I was deceiving myself even as I thought it. They hadn't sent for me because Grammer had refused to see me, even on her deathbed.

It all came back to me then: the bitter anger in Grammer's voice on my first day at school, after the boys had herded me into the ditch: 'You – you be a bastard – a child without a name.' Grammer's glittering eyes boring into mine when Mr Wilcox preached of sinners burning in Hell – Grammer, who never even looked my way if she could help it. Grammer closing the door on me the day I'd left for London – before I'd even reached the gate. And later, when I'd gone to her in the House and offered all I had, she'd rejected me.

Grammer hated me; she'd always hated me – and she'd gone to her death still hating me. I was shaking so much I could hardly breathe. It was as though Grammer were choking the life out of me, trying to take me with her – no – because she was going to Heaven, she knew that – she was sending me to Hell, and I could feel the heat of the flames as they licked at the soles of my feet. I twisted and turned in panic, gasping for breath, then jumped up and threw myself against the small window, and as I did so the curtains swung aside – and there, serene and shining, was the moon. And as she bathed me in her silver light I remembered Granfer carrying me outside and setting me down on the path so I

167

could curtsey to her. She wasn't a new moon today, she was already three-quarters full – but she was there. I knew I had to get out of that stifling little room where Grammer was choking the life from me; I had to get outside, into the open air, where Grammer never went – even on Sundays going to chapel Grammer had walked like a snail, carrying her house with her, her eyes fixed on the ground. The open air belonged to Granfer and the moon – and the roses.

I tugged my coat up over my arms and put my hat on with hands that wouldn't stop trembling, then I picked up my boots and tiptoed downstairs. Mrs Dawes slept in a small room off the kitchen and I held my breath as I pulled back the heavy bolts on the door – but they didn't make a sound, and then the cold night air came rushing in. I pulled on my boots by the light of the moon, and she guided me across the backyard and up the garden path – straight to my rose. She wasn't in flower, of course, but I could see the outline of her branches where she climbed up the wall, and she still had a few leaves – she never lost them all, even in winter, and now they were edged with silver. I reached out and touched her stem; it was firm and living under my fingertips, and as I stood there the moon bathed me in her clear, cool light. Slowly, the terrible thudding in my chest began to ease. When my legs were steady enough I took my hand from the rose and lifted the hem of my nightie; bending my knee I dipped in a curtsey – once, twice, thrice. And my beautiful moon smiled back at me.

The sharp air had cleared my head, and my feet were cold now inside my boots – I felt their coldness gladly. I was not going to go to Hell: Grammer would have sent me if she could, but I wouldn't let her. Stepping back so I could see the moon and the rose together I remembered Granfer: Granfer who'd loved me. I spoke to the moon, hoping he'd hear me, too: 'I be going to serve a beautiful lady, and then one day my father will come and take me back to stay in his fine house – until a young lord do fall in love with me and make me his bride. Then we'll all live happy ever after.' I gazed at the moon harder and harder, until I could see her nose, and her eyes and her smiling mouth – then I curtseyed once more. A wisp of cloud floated across her face like a veil – she was saying good night.

I gave Grammer a good funeral; she was my Grammer so I owed

her that. I couldn't let her be wrapped in a shroud and tumbled into a common grave with paupers. She had a proper elm coffin with brass handles and a brass nameplate; the eight bearers all wore gloves of black kid, and the mourning bell tolled as she was carried through the village. I followed her in my new black dress which I'd cut and sewed myself, wearing a black coat, black hat and a pair of black gloves, all bought new for Grammer's funeral.

After the service she was carried out and buried where she'd have wanted to be, in the churchyard at Borrell, beside Granfer. A lot of people came to pay their respects. Mr Wilcox spoke first; he shook my hand and said what an upright, God-fearing woman Grammer had been. I smiled politely and then turned to the next person. Everyone was very kind, and Mrs Rawlings invited me in for a cup of tea afterwards. She told me all the news of the village, and I listened politely, but I didn't belong there any more. I didn't want to, I had a new life to make. Mrs Rawlings said the path beside Goosey Meadow was firm with the frost and wouldn't muddy my boots, but I told her I'd walk back to the station the long way round, by the road; I wasn't 'liddle Amy Roberts' any more.

As I came past the last cottage I saw that there was a man ploughing in Ten Acre. He and the boy were turning the plough on the headland close to the road and when the ploughman saw me he told the boy to hold the horse and came trudging over to the gate. He took off his cap. 'I did hear as thee wast burying thy old lady today.' After carefully wiping his hand on his corduroy trousers he thrust it out and we shook hands solemnly. 'Thee bist working over by Bath, my Mam did say?'

'Yes, with a dressmaker. But next year I be going for to be a lady's maid.'

He shook his head in admiration. 'My, thee's done well for thyself. But then, thee always wast a fine-looking maid, Amy – and smart too. I can see thee've not changed. Good luck to 'ee.'

'Thank 'ee, Albert.'

He put his cap back on and raised his hand in farewell. I smiled in acknowledgement and continued on my way; Albert Yates hadn't herded me into the ditch today.

Chapter Twenty-Three

I'd had no choice, I'd had to bury Grammer properly, but afterwards came the full realisation of what it had cost me: except for a few shillings, all my savings had gone. I would have to find a place as an improver, and start to save up again, but it would take me years – if I ever managed it at all. Dressmaking was really only for girls who had families. I'd be hard put to live on my wages, once I had to pay for a room and my food – let alone save.

I decided I'd have to go into service now, as a housemaid, and then try and work my way up, but when I told Mrs Dawes of my plan she shook her head very firmly. 'It's no use, Amy. If you do that you'll be classed – you'll never be able to move up and become a personal servant.' Seeing my downcast face she patted my hand. 'I'll see what I can do.'

Next day Mrs Bryant sent for me and said I could stay on with her at the same wages, with perhaps a rise in the summer; I was overwhelmed with relief. But after relief came depression. It would take me a long time to save up again, and I couldn't get the thought of Grammer out of my mind. I began to think she'd died deliberately so her funeral would stop me being a lady's maid. I was so out of sorts my monthlies didn't come at the usual time, and when Saranne asked me where my rags were for washing her voice sounded so sharp and suspicious I burst into tears, stammering, 'I wouldn't – I never –'

Saranne's face cleared, and she put her hand on my arm. 'It's all right, Amy. I know you're a good girl, for all you're so pretty. It's just we had a housemaid once who . . .' She broke off, and added, ''Tis likely the shock of your bereavement, making you late – it do take some folk like that, so I've heard.'

My monthlies did come eventually, but I didn't feel a lot better for it. As always the sight of the blood made me queasy, and I couldn't shake off the feeling of Grammer hating me, even though she was dead. The next two years seemed to stretch endlessly ahead, dull and dreary, with nothing to hope for – then the very next week Miss Annabel came.

Her great-aunt, Miss Hurst, was one of our regular customers and she sent her footman round with the carriage and a note for Mrs Bryant saying that she had a special commission which needed to be completed quickly. Mrs Bryant went to put her hat on at once; Miss Hurst was a great lady in Bath and she always paid her account regularly – as Miss Worthing said, the two didn't often go together. Miss Hurst was so important that normally Mrs Bryant would have taken Janet with her, but poor Janet was streaming with a cold and had to keep blowing her nose – that wouldn't do at all for Miss Hurst, so Mrs Bryant took me instead.

I'd only ever travelled in a proper gentleman's carriage a couple of times before; now I sat looking out of the windows as we bowled along the familiar streets imagining it was *my* carriage, and that I was a fine lady on my way to pay an afternoon call. Miss Hurst's maid, Miss Lovell, met us in the hallway and took us straight upstairs, explaining as we went, 'Miss Hurst's niece is here on a visit with her mother, and she's been invited to a fancy dress dance. Her mother said she couldn't go at first, because she isn't Out yet, but now Miss Annabel's managed to get round her – only it's this coming Saturday, so everything's got to be done in a rush.'

Mrs Bryant repeated, '*Fancy* dress?' She didn't sound at all happy about the idea. Apart from the brides most of her customers were too old to dance, let alone dance in a fancy dress.

We were shown into a bedroom while Miss Lovell went to fetch Miss Annabel. All of a sudden the door burst open and a young lady came in like a whirlwind, exclaiming, 'How spiffing – you've come to make my dress!' Her dark eyes were shining and a glossy black plait bounced on her shoulders. I stood gazing at her, lost in admiration – Miss Annabel was beautiful, the most beautiful girl I'd ever seen. As she walked towards us, so tall and slender, she looked born to be a princess; I couldn't take my eyes off her.

Miss Lovell murmured, 'This is Mrs Bryant, who dresses Miss Hurst.'

The girl's smile flashed out. 'I've been thinking about it all morning, and now I've finally decided – I want an Egyptian costume.'

Mrs Bryant blinked, then said in a worried voice, 'I'm afraid I've never dressed an Egyptian lady before.'

Miss Annabel laughed aloud. 'Not a *modern* Egyptian – they're

171

covered from head to foot with veils, which wouldn't do at all. No, I want to be an *ancient* Egyptian – a queen. I want to be Cleopatra herself.' She smiled engagingly. 'Auntie says you're the best dressmaker in Bath, so I know you'll construct me a simply gorgeous costume.' She gave a rapturous sigh. 'I'm so looking forward to Saturday. It's my very first dance and I want to be the belle of the ball.' She swung round. 'Unhook me, Lovell, so they can take my measurements.'

There were beads of perspiration on Mrs Bryant's forehead as she turned to me in a mute appeal for help. I found my voice. 'Please, miss, do you mebbe have a picture o' the dress you got in mind – then we'd be sure it were what you did want.'

Miss Annabel twisted her head to look at me. 'What a good idea. Hook me up again, Lovell, and I'll run down to the library.'

She came back with a big fat book. 'Here you are, Egyptian paintings – they painted the inside of their tombs, you know – terribly jolly.'

We peered at the drawings; they looked very odd. I said, 'They be all flat, like folk as've been squashed flat by a steamroller!'

Miss Annabel turned so her laughing dark eyes met mine. 'Yes, they do, don't they? It's the way people drew in those days – they didn't know about perspective.' Nor did I – but I knew she was clever as well as beautiful. I did so want to dress her like an Egyptian queen.

But Mrs Bryant was speaking. 'Miss Annabel, I've never made a fancy dress before. I'm afraid I really can't –' She was interrupted by Miss Annabel's wail of dismay, but she ploughed on, 'I understand there are businesses, theatrical costumiers, who hire out fancy dress costumes –'

'No! No!' Miss Annabel shook her head so vigorously her plait bounced against her cheek. 'I had *such* a time persuading Mama, and when she did finally say yes she said I mustn't even *consider* hiring – because of germs, you know. She only agreed to let me send for you because you make all Aunt Maud's clothes. You *must* help me, you simply *must*.'

I looked at the pictures again before saying, 'Mrs Bryant, thic dress be quite a simple pattern, I reckon – 'tis the decorations as do make it look special. Mebbe if we could borrow the book –'

'Take it, take it.' Miss Annabel thrust the book into my hands, smiling straight at me. 'I knew you'd think of something the minute I saw you – you look so pretty and clever.' I blushed with pleasure. 'Unhook me, Lovell, so this girl – what *is* your name?'

'Amy, miss.'

'So Amy can measure me.'

She had a lovely figure and I knew she'd be a joy to fit; I could hardly wait to start transforming her into an Egyptian queen.

Mrs Bryant took me off all my other work and said I could have any help I needed, as Miss Hurst was such an old and valued customer. I sat in the corner of the workroom poring over the little pictures and reading the description that went with them, learning that the dress was made of white linen and was pleated like a kilt – but the pleats went all the way round. Next I made little sketches of what it would look like without the decoration, and then drafted the pattern. I went back into the workroom after supper – Mrs Bryant had said I could if I wanted – and it was eleven o'clock before Saranne came in and insisted on turning out the gas.

I dreamt of that Egyptian dress, and first thing next morning I went out to buy the material and trimmings I'd need. I cut and tacked, and by the afternoon it was ready for fitting, so Mrs Bryant said I could go straightaway, in a cab. I pinned and tucked while Miss Annabel fidgeted with excitement; the instant I stood back she began twirling in front of the mirror and I could hardly persuade her to stand still so I could position the big collar. When it was in place she exclaimed: 'It's going to look just how I wanted! You *are* a clever girl, Amy.'

She sent a maid for her mother and then waited impatiently, chattering all the time about how she would arrange her hair. As soon as her mother came in she began twirling again, until I felt quite dizzy just from watching her. Mrs Hurst was plumper and shorter than Miss Annabel, but she had the same dark eyes; they studied the dress carefully before Mrs Hurst pronounced that it was quite charming – but perhaps it fitted a trifle too well over Miss Annabel's posterior; it would have to be let out. Miss Annabel gave me a little grimace so her mother couldn't see while I was altering it, then I was sent away to put in the permanent stitches.

By the following afternoon it was virtually finished, and I took it round for the final fitting. It looked wonderful on Miss Annabel; as she stood in front of the mirror her eyes flashed fire, outshining

173

the brilliant blues and reds of the costume jewels in her deep collar. I set the headdress carefully on her glossy black hair and stood back, drawing a deep breath of admiration: she looked wonderful. Then her eyebrows creased in a slight frown. 'I tried to persuade Mama to let me paint my eyelids to match the blue stones – I was only going to use *water* colour, but she said it wasn't ladylike.' She sighed. 'It would have just been the finishing touch.'

I said, 'Miss Annabel, you don't need to paint – you couldn't look beautifuller than you do already.'

She smiled with pleasure. 'How sweet of you to say that, Amy.' Then she leant closer to the mirror. 'It's lucky my hair is so straight. I've always wanted curls, but just for now I'm glad I haven't got them.'

I shook my head. 'Curls are a nuisance, miss – they be a terrible trouble to get neat sometimes, while if you got straight hair you can always use curling tongs if you want.'

'What a sensible point of view, Amy – I must remember that next time I'm complaining.' She pirouetted round in front of the mirror. 'I do like this outfit! You're a very clever dressmaker, Amy – you must come to London and set up a costumier house there, and when I'm married to my duke I shall come and patronise you.'

'No, miss – I only be learning dressmaking so I can go for a lady's maid.'

'A lady's maid?' Her eyebrows arched in query.

'Yes, miss, 'tis what I've always wanted to be – ever since I were a liddle maid in school.' And because I liked her so much I confided, 'Lady Warminster, she did tell I to be a lady's maid.'

'Lady *Warminster*? How curious, because –' Then she checked herself and smiled. 'It seems almost as if it were meant, and you're so neat and handy. Put my wrap around me and I'll go and show my costume to Mama, she's just along in her bedroom.'

When Miss Annabel came back Mrs Hurst was with her. She pointed at me. 'There, Mama, look how clean and tidy she is – and so pretty, too.'

As I blushed Mrs Hurst shook her head in reproof. 'Annabel, you're embarrassing the poor girl.' Then she turned to me. 'My daughter tells me you intend to become a lady's maid?'

'Yes, ma'am. Leastways, a young lady's maid, to start with.'

'There you are, Mama –'

'Shush, Annabel. Now, my daughter will be needing her own maid soon, and she's asked me if she can have you, subject to a satisfactory character from Mrs Bryant, of course.'

'Oh, ma'am!' I just stood there, gazing at Mrs Hurst. 'Oh, ma'am – there baint nothing I'd like more in the whole wide world than to take care o' Miss Annabel!' Then the mourning bell tolled in my memory and I felt my face crumple. 'But I cassent – I don't have no money fer my dresses and things.'

'But –'

'Quiet, Annabel.' Mrs Hurst frowned. 'Surely Mrs Bryant pays you a wage – you're not a spendthrift, are you?'

I shook my head in vigorous denial. 'No, ma'am. I been saving up for more'n two year now, an' I did have nearly enough. But my Grammer, she died last month, so I did have to use all my savings for burying her.'

Miss Annabel exclaimed, 'But surely you can get people buried for nothing, on the poor rates!'

I just looked at her. Mrs Hurst said quickly, 'Shush, Annabel – you don't understand how these people feel. A pauper's funeral is a terrible disgrace.'

I nodded gratefully. 'Yes, ma'am – I couldn't've let Grammer be buried on the Parish.'

'But Mama –'

'I think it's time Amy went back with the dress – she's still got the finishing touches to add.' She smiled at me. 'We'll see you tomorrow.'

I had a hard time trying not to weep over that dress as I finished it off. It was like seeing the gates of Paradise open in front of you – and then having them slammed shut in your face just as you set foot on the threshold. If only Grammer'd waited a bit longer to die, then the money would have already been spent . . . I pulled myself together – it was wicked to think like that.

I'd completed the dress by next morning, and the dance wasn't until the evening, so there was plenty of time for any last-minute alterations that needed to be done at Miss Hurst's. It would only be a matter of a tuck here or a stitch there, Miss Annabel being such an easy young lady to fit; I began to fold it carefully into its box.

Miss Annabel looked magnificent; the perfect Egyptian queen. She swung round to me from the mirror, her eyes alight with pleasure. 'It's wonderful, Amy – exactly as I'd hoped. You have worked hard – thank you so much.'

I gazed up at her in adoration. ''Twere my pleasure. I baint never enjoyed making a dress so much as thic 'un.'

She laughed. 'What a quaint accent you have! It's even stronger than that of our servants over in Hampshire – but I like it, it's so soft and soothing.' I vowed there and then that I'd never try to change my way of speaking, before springing forward to help Miss Annabel take off her costume.

When it was hanging safely in the wardrobe she went to her dressing table and shook out her long hair. 'Would you just brush my hair for me and plait it, Amy? It'll be the last time – after tonight Mama says I can put it up.'

It felt strange at first, handling someone else's hair, but I'd brushed and plaited Aunt Agnes' for her when she'd been so ill, and now my fingers remembered. Aunt Agnes' hair had been a pretty colour, but later on it had become dry and brittle; Miss Annabel's hair was quite different; like her it was young and full of energy, flowing through my fingers like strong silk. I was sorry when I'd tied the second ribbon; I could have handled it for ever, it was so lovely and smooth to touch.

'Thank you, Amy. Oh look, there's a pin on the floor there.' As I dropped on one knee to retrieve it she said, her voice sounding deliberately casual, 'By the way, I asked Mama if I could lend you the money for your dresses and hairdressing lessons, and she said yes, if you're willing to work the first year without pay. She says that would be a fair bargain.'

I knelt there with the pin in my hand, thinking I'd not heard a-right; then she turned and smiled down at me. 'So you can be my maid after all, Amy – if that arrangement is agreeable to you.'

I gazed up at her. 'Oh, Miss Annabel – I'd work for you forever without pay, if so be you needed I to!' She threw back her head and laughed. Still on my knees at her feet I exclaimed, 'Thank 'ee, Miss Annabel. Thank 'ee – and I do promise to serve thee true.'

PART THREE

Chapter Twenty-Four

Nether Court, Hampshire — February, 1912

I worshipped Miss Annabel. From the very first minute I arrived at Nether Court I became her willing slave, with all my time and energies devoted to her service. As soon as the housemaid came in with my early-morning tea tray I'd jump out of bed and plan my day as I was dressing. First I'd iron her shoelaces – freshly washed the night before – then thread them carefully into her shoes and set them ready. At eight o'clock I'd go down to the stillroom, collect her tray and bring it upstairs. Pushing open the green baize door, the hard linoleum under my feet changed to soft carpet, the plain walls came alive with colour and pattern and I breathed in the lovely scent of fresh beeswax mingled with the hint of woodsmoke from newly-lit bedroom fires. I loved to go into the front of the house.

I opened her bedroom door very quietly, holding down the handle so it wouldn't click – Miss Abbott, Mrs Hurst's maid, had shown me the right way to do it – then I almost tiptoed across the carpet to set the tray gently down on her bedside table. I spoke very softly but clearly, 'Good morning, Miss Annabel.'

The dark plaits twitched as her face pressed itself even deeper into the white linen pillow, and there was the usual muffled, 'Go away.'

'It's a lovely morning, Miss Annabel.' I heard a groan behind me as I glided over to the high windows and drew the curtains back in one smooth movement, taking care there was no rattling of the rings. Then I was back beside the tray, pouring the amber tea into her cup and lifting the sugar tongs.

Suddenly the bed erupted, bedclothes flying in every direction. 'Give me my tea – quickly! I'm going riding today. My blue habit, Amy – no! My brown one.'

'What be you wearing for breakfast, Miss Annabel?'

'Oh, any old skirt will do – my navy serge. Choose a blouse for me. Hurry up Amy, do!'

I rushed along to the bathroom and turned on the gleaming taps; as the hot water gushed out I arranged the fresh white towels just where she could easily reach them, then squeezed exactly half an inch of toothpaste onto her brush and laid it ready on the shelf. After testing the water I went back to her bedroom and she dashed past in a swirl of silk dressing gown. While she was in the bath I bustled around opening drawers and laying out her clean under-wear: chemise, corset, drawers – only they had narrow legs and Miss Annabel called them knickers – camisole and petticoats. By the time I'd rolled her stockings so that all she had to do was slip her feet into them, she was back. Along in the bathroom I pulled out the plug, picked her nightdress off the floor and rinsed her toothbrush clean, then scampered back along the corridor to wait outside her room until she called me in to lace her corsets. I held out each garment in turn until I came to the blouse. 'That blue won't go with my olive serge.'

'But Miss Annabel, you did say –'

'I've changed my mind.' As I rushed back to the drawers her voice followed me. 'Do *hurry*, Amy.'

The minute I'd slipped the skirt over her head and before I'd had time to finish fastening it she was darting over to the dressing table. 'Quick, my hair! It's such a lovely day I don't want to waste a second of it.'

I unplaited her hair and brushed it until it shone like black satin, then I carefully looped and pinned it into a Grecian knot; Miss Abbott had shown me how to do that, but I'd have to go for hairdressing lessons as soon as we went up to Town. 'Quick, Amy, quick – ouch, that pin's digging into me!' Hastily I fumbled to adjust the offending pin, then she sprang up and almost ran to the door, flinging a 'Remember, the *blue* habit,' over her shoulder as she left.

I toured the room picking up everything she'd dropped. Her dressing gown lay all rumpled on the floor where she'd flung it off, her damp slippers were kicked into the corners of the room – she was so fast-moving that by the time she'd been up five minutes her bedroom always looked as if it had been hit by a whirlwind. Miss Abbott had warned me about this, saying, 'Old Nannie spoilt her, Miss Roberts – you'll have to train her to be tidier otherwise you'll be making a rod for your own back.' But I couldn't imagine 'training' Miss Annabel; besides, I liked waiting on her and knowing she needed me to care for her.

At first the bootboy cleaned her shoes with mine and left them outside the door of my room early in the morning, but I wasn't completely satisfied, so when one day I saw Mr Morton at work in the boot hall – he was valet to Miss Annabel's great-uncle – I went in and asked him if he'd show me the best way to polish shoes. I didn't realise then that every valet had his own secrets which he guarded jealously, so I shouldn't really have asked Mr Morton, but he was very kind and agreed to teach me his method as long as I promised not to pass his tips on to the footmen. I promised, and sat down for my lesson. 'Now, let the polish sit on the shoe a little while, so it can soak in.' We sat and watched it soaking, then Mr Morton picked up the polishing brush. 'Never, *never* scrub at a shoe, Miss Roberts. You'll ruin your brush and still not get a good shine. You try, my dear.' He sat with pursed lips, while I wielded the brush. 'Too hard, too hard – you're not a kitchenmaid blackleading the range. Quick and light, that's the ticket. Good, good.' Later, 'Now, don't forget to polish the instep, for when your lady kneels in church,' and, 'Chamois next, make a pad of it and buff all over – it gives a much deeper shine, you'll see.'

When I'd finished he made sure the door was properly closed and then put a pair of old Mr Thomas' boots on the table and showed me how he boned them with blacking. 'Front leg of deer, this one comes from – a female for choice. There's nothing like the shine a good bone can give, you see if I'm not right, Miss Roberts.' He smiled at me. 'No use for you, though. Ladies' boots are made of daintier leather – they won't stand boning.' I exclaimed in admiration at the brilliance of the black shine and Mr Morton beamed with pleasure, the sweat still standing on his forehead from his exertions. When I left, he gave me a pair of his old brushes, and I begged a chamois leather from Mrs Harper, the housekeeper, to go with them; from then on I always cleaned Miss Annabel's boots and shoes myself.

The household at Nether Court ran as smoothly as a well-oiled sewing machine. Mrs Harper and Mr Davenport, the butler, were experienced heads of department; nothing escaped the eagle eye of Mrs Harper – a smear of polish or a rug left crooked resulted in the offending housemaid being summoned and reduced to tears.

One day Mrs Harper showed me her linen room. It was beautiful: in every cupboard there were piles of neatly folded linen, every item marked with its monogram and each dozen tied with a ribbon of different colour, according to where it was to be used. Even though Miss Annabel's nieces and nephews were only occasional visitors there were two whole sets of nursery linen, tied up in blue bows – then there were red ribbons for the kitchen, green for the staff, and satin ones of pale pink for the finest quality linen used only by the family. Down in the stillroom every surface shone white and spotless, and I loved to linger in the doorway drinking in the scent of new-made cakes and scones, while the fresh pots of marmalade stood cooling in their orange glory.

Mr Davenport was kind and helpful, too. Soon after I'd arrived he took me on a tour of the front of the house – one afternoon when the family had all gone out, of course – so I'd know where the different rooms were when Miss Annabel sent for me. Nether Court was like a palace: the dining room with its long, gleaming table, the great curving staircase, the high, light drawing room looking over the terrace to the green lawns below – I admired them all. Even though it was winter there were bowls and vases of flowers in every room, as if spring had already come. We came to the pretty morning room which Mr Davenport described as smaller and cosier than the drawing room, but it still looked enormous to me. Next door was the library, with more books in it than I'd ever seen in my entire life, and then, right at the end of the passage beside the garden entrance there was the billiard room with its huge, green-baize covered table.

Everywhere was cleanliness, luxury – and warmth. Nether Court had radiators as well as fires; Mr Davenport pointed them out to me with pride. 'Madam had these installed when she married the late master – being American she has modern ideas. And the electric light, that was put in the year Miss Caroline was married – we were the first house in this part of Hampshire to have our own generator. Of course, she brought money with her, did Mrs Hurst, although old Mr Hurst, her father-in-law, had plenty of his own – factories in the North. But we don't speak of that, Miss Roberts, seeing as it was trade.'

'No, sir.'

'There's nothing like that now,' he added quickly. 'It's all tied up in land and solid gilt-edged investments. And Miss Caroline married a very nice gentleman with a property in Surrey, an old family – but not titled.' He moved a little closer and his voice dropped. 'We're all hoping for a title for Miss Annabel, with her being a beauty as well as an heiress. There were no sons, you see.' He shook his head sadly before escorting me back below stairs.

If Miss Annabel needed me while she was downstairs she'd ring for a footman, and he'd send a housemaid to fetch me. I'd arrive panting to be met with, 'I've lost my embroidery, Amy – find it, would you?' or, 'That book I left by my bedside table – I need it now.' And I'd go scurrying off on my errand. But if she was upstairs she'd ring directly. There was a bell in her room which connected to one in mine, so she could summon me any time of the day or night. 'Amy, I'm going for a walk with Earl – my tweeds,' or, 'Amy, I've torn the hem of my dress,' and 'Amy, there's ink on my blouse – I must change.'

I never knew what she'd need next so all her clothes had to be clean and ready. I knew how to handle delicate fabrics, and how to make repairs with stitches so small as to be almost invisible, but at Mrs Bryant's I'd only dealt with new material – now Miss Abbott instructed me on brushing, cleaning and the removal of stains. She told me that if Miss Annabel spilt her breakfast coffee onto her woollen skirt then I was to brush the spot with glycerine, but if the drop fell on the sleeve of her linen blouse then I must use egg-yolk dissolved in a little tepid water. Wine stains, grease stains, ink stains, jam stains – Miss Abbott told me how to deal with each in turn, and I wrote busily in my small notebook.

I learnt to only ever brush velvet with velvet, and always down the nap, and how I should use the special brush with straw bristles on Miss Annabel's tweed skirts every time she'd worn one. Her skirts were always a problem because of Earl; Earl was her Great Dane and he used to press against her legs and leave his hairs all down the side of her skirt. I asked Mr Morton's advice because his gentleman had a dog, too. He told me he'd tried everything, but the only real answer was to pick the hairs off one by one – so I did.

Although Nether Court had its own laundry in a special range of buildings off the service courtyard, Miss Abbott told me she always washed Mrs Hurst's lace herself, in her own room, and she'd advise me to do the same. So I fetched rainwater from the butt outside the scullery door and boiled it with a little rice, for stiffening – 'Starch must *never* be used on lace, Miss Roberts.' Then I spread a clean cloth on my ironing board and pinned out the lace – one pin to each tiny point. It took a long time, but I knew that once the lace had dried its shape would be perfect, so after I'd finished I sat by the fire mending in a warm glow of satisfaction.

My room was my workroom: I had a nice large table, a set of small irons and a sewing machine, all for my own exclusive use. It was next door to Miss Abbott's room, just up the back stairs from the Room, where we of the Upper Ten ate. I was so proud of being one of the Upper Ten, but the other upper servants were much older than I was, and sometimes when I heard gusts of laughter coming from the Servants' Hall I wished I were in there with the housemaids and stillroom maids and the footmen. But then I'd remind myself that the housemaids were all called by their Christian names – Ida or May or Gladys – while I was Miss Roberts, even to Mr Davenport and Mrs Harper. I did have to wear a print frock and apron like the housemaids in the morning, because I was still only a young lady's maid – but in the afternoon, when they changed into their black dresses and white aprons and caps, I took off my uniform and wore instead a navy skirt and white blouse, or a dark dress. My clothes had to be discreet and without any trimming, of course, because when we went up to London I would have to escort Miss Annabel whenever she went out without her mother, and there must be no possibility of anyone being unable to tell which was the mistress and which the maid.

Those first weeks there was so much to do and so many new skills to learn I never set foot outside the house, until one afternoon Miss Abbott told me I must get into the habit of taking a little exercise and fresh air every day. 'But I dussent have time, Miss Abbott –there be so much to do.'

She shook her head firmly. 'If you want to be a good personal servant, Miss Roberts –'

'Oh I do, I do.'

'Then you must learn to take care of your own health; you can't expect the mistress to think of it – she's got more important things on her mind. Now, Mrs Hurst and Miss Annabel won't be back until dinner-time, so go and put on your hat and coat – then we'll take a little stroll around the gardens.'

The gardens at Nether Court were as beautiful as the house; although it was only February there was lots to see. In the beds on the terraces were neat little evergreen shrubs all sparkling with brightly coloured berries, ivies shading from green to cream – and bushes warm with golden leaves. A flight of steps curved down between ornate stone balustrades, and there at the bottom of the lower terrace was a great bronze dolphin whose mouth spouted a shining arc of water into the pool beneath his leaping body.

Miss Abbott led me round and down to the kitchen garden, so she could introduce me to Mr Peake, the head gardener. 'I'll ask him if we may visit the plant-houses.'

As soon as he saw us Mr Peake removed his bowler hat and ushered us into his office. Miss Abbott introduced me and I gave a little bob. 'Good afternoon, sir.'

His fierce blue eyes smiled briefly from under bushy grey brows. 'I'll take you both around the houses myself, Miss Abbott.'

With murmurs of gratitude we followed him through the far gate and out into a city of glass-houses, their myriad panes glinting in the pale winter sun. We passed the vinery and the other fruit-houses, then Mr Peake opened a white painted door and suddenly we were transported into summer: warmth, scent and colour. I gazed enraptured at the blue and pink, orange and white, deep purple and clear pure scarlet. 'Oh, baint they beautiful – the most beautifullest flowers I ever did see!' Mr Peake's stern face relaxed into a smile, then he began leading us down the aisle, pointing at the flowers and telling me the name of each.

'Hyacinths, cyclamen, strelizias, cinerarias, aurum lilies, azalea . . .' I repeated the names after him in my head, determined to learn them all.

We moved on into the damper, hotter air of the stove-house, where several gardeners were busy with soil and pots. As we drew level with one of them Mr Peake tapped the man's arm with his stick. 'No, Fred, that's far too firm – do it again.' The man flushed, then carefully tipped the soil away from the thick, fleshy root and began to scoop it gently back. 'An ixora won't thrive in firm soil, you should know that by now. What's the point of using sandy peat if you go and ram it down the way you were?'

185

'Sorry, sir.'

Fred's face was brick-red by now and Mr Peake was still frowning, so I asked him quickly, 'What be the name o' thic plant, Mr Peake?'

He turned back to me. 'That's an acalypha sanderi, Miss Roberts. When it's full grown it'll have crimson tassels instead of flowers – just like lambs' tails. And this here's a bougainvillaea; its flowers are mauve and shaped like trumpets – grows lovely up a pillar, it does.' We moved slowly away from poor Fred.

Next came the orchid-houses, where Mr Peake's stick pointed angrily at a flower spike as he shouted, 'You've missed a snail here – you young good-for-nothing!' A boy came panting back down the row and picked off a minute snail. Mr Peake turned to Miss Abbott with a snort. 'These modern youngsters! If you don't watch 'em every minute of the day they'll skimp any job they're put to.' He swung back. 'One more slip like that, my lad, and you'll be paid off.'

The boy ducked his head, mumbling, 'Sorry, sir,' before backing away.

Odontoglossums, dendrobiums, cattleyas, laelias – even my appetite for names was sated by Mr Peake. As we came to the door of the cool orchid-house he smiled at me. 'Now, Miss Roberts, tell me your favourite flower and I'll see if I can show it to you.'

'You won't be able to do that, sir, 'cos 'tis only February – and my favourite flower, she be the rose.'

He threw back his head and laughed so loudly that the boy washing plants against thrips jumped like a startled rabbit. 'The rose is *my* favourite, too, Miss Roberts – the Queen of Flowers. But as to my not being able . . . Come along with me now.'

He took me by the arm and shepherded me past another glass-house, then threw open the door of the next – and there they were, roses, blooming in February.

I just stood gaping. 'Oh, Mr Peake! Baint they lovely!'

His chest swelled. 'It's just a question of knowing the right technique, Miss Roberts. Mrs Hurst is very partial to roses, so I always keep a supply for her.'

I bent my head to a beautiful bloom of deep pink, drinking in the delicate tea scent. 'What be her name, Mr Peake?'

'The Bridesmaid, and this here's the Bride herself – then we've

186

got Lady Alice, and Lady May Fitzwilliam.' He drew forward a head of pale, salmon-pink petals, 'And here's a little favourite of mine – Caroline Testout.'

May, Alice, Caroline . . . I exclaimed, 'Why, they be all names o' girls! I do wish as there were a rose named for I.'

I heard the laughter of Miss Abbott and Mr Peake, then the latter said kindly, 'Roses are named after ladies, Miss Roberts, not lady's maids. Why, there's Lady Penzance, Lady Curzon, the Marchioness of Londonderry, the Duchess of Bedford and a score of others I could name.' He smiled. 'Now, if Miss Annabel were to marry a title . . .' Miss Abbott smiled too.

I kept remembering those roses all evening, flowering so bravely in the depths of winter. How astonished Granfer would have been to see them. Then I seemed to hear Mr Peake's voice again: 'Roses are named after *ladies*, not lady's maids.' But I would be a lady one day. My father, he was a gentleman, a lord – and I was going to marry a lord too, I knew it.

Chapter Twenty-Five

When March came Miss Abbott didn't need to shoo me outside: the Lenten roses were blooming in the beds on the terraces, alongside clumps of large white flowers, each of which had its own yellow eye. Mr Peake told me they were called Gilbert's Harbinger. 'Harbinger means messenger, Miss Roberts, and that's what they are, messengers of spring.' Then he went on to grumble about the mice nibbling his crocuses, but they couldn't have done much harm because the yellow heads stood straight as soldiers in all the beds while gardeners knelt over them, tying each purple hyacinth spike to its own special stick.

Of course, while Miss Annabel and her mother were at home in the drawing room I had to keep well clear of the terrace – her great-uncle didn't matter because he stayed in his rooms which looked out over the lake – but I was allowed down in the pleasure grounds where the violets smiled at me from their tiny, laughing faces. Mr Peake said I was welcome to visit the plant-houses at any time, as long as I didn't distract the men from their work, and one day he took me along to the rose garden. The bushes and standards were still bare and gaunt but he told me what each one was as we walked along the straight gravel paths. His stick would point, 'Noisettes there, all pale pink. Bourbons opposite, for a deeper shade. Albas in the crescent beds, to give a patch of white.' Each bed was cut into a precise shape, crescent, oblong, oval, and each shape was used for four matching beds. When you stood at the top of the steps the dark earth made a pattern as exact as that on a piece of printed fabric.

The gardeners were busy with their pruning knives, and as we came to one Mr Peake would stop to peer over his shoulders: 'Cut right back there – no more than one or two eyes.' Then, turning to me, 'There's some I could mention who leave pruning their hybrid perpetuals until March is halfway over.' There was a disapproving shake of the head. 'But the sap's in full flow by then, Miss Roberts, so you risk malformed flowers, and that's no good at all. Perfect blooms are what I want in my rose garden, perfect.' We walked on to the next bed. 'Now noisettes, they're different – Noisettes are tender and should be left until April, the same with teas, but your hybrid tea's ready for pruning by the middle of March,' he swung round to face me, his brows beetling, 'and don't let anyone tell you different, Miss Roberts!'

'No sir, certainly not.'

Some days I'd stand at the top of the steps looking at the bare earth and the leafless bushes and try to imagine how the garden would look when the roses were all in flower in June. But I knew I wouldn't see them, because by then I'd be in London, and would have been there for weeks. Miss Annabel was to be presented at the very first Court in May, and there was a lot of preparation to do before that. Once she'd been presented she would be officially 'out', and Miss Abbott warned me about how busy I'd be then. While I was brushing Miss Annabel's hair she'd talk about all the exciting things she was going to do in the Season: there'd be balls and dinner parties, concerts and plays, afternoon garden parties and evening receptions – then there'd be the races at Ascot, the river at Henley, cricket at Lords . . . I felt breathless just listening to her.

One evening, while I was pinning up her hair and she was telling me about all the places she wanted to go to, Mrs Hurst came in. I ran to pull up a chair for her, then she waved me back to the dressing table before saying, 'Annabel, what is this ridiculous story Davenport has just told me, about Earl?'

Miss Annabel stared straight back at her in the mirror. 'Earl, Mama?'

'That you're planning to take him to Town.' Miss Annabel didn't reply. 'It's out of the question. He's far too big a dog for London – however will he get enough exercise?'

'I'll take him with me when I walk in the Park.'

'Annabel, he'll need at least *three* good walks a day – you simply won't have the time for that.'

'One of the footmen can give him a run first thing.'

'The footmen will be far too busy.'

I inserted the final hairpin and held up the hand mirror so Miss Annabel could see the back. She nodded absently, then suddenly her eyes sharpened and she exclaimed, 'Amy! Amy can take him

189

for his early morning walk. That's what lady's maids are for – Betty Stonor's maid always exercises her dog.'

In the mirror I watched Mrs Hurst's bosom swell. 'Betty's dog is a Pekingese!'

There was silence, then Miss Annabel rallied. 'I don't see that it makes any difference, Mama – a dog's a dog. It only has to be taken out the same number of times, whatever its size – and Amy loves walking. She'll be quite happy to take Earl out for a run.' She swung round to face me directly. 'Won't you, Amy?'

I glanced nervously at Mrs Hurst, then back at Miss Annabel's determined brown eyes. 'Yes, yes of course.' I turned to face Mrs Hurst. 'I'll be happy to take Earl out, madam.'

Miss Annabel smiled. 'That's settled then.' And it was. Miss Abbott told me Miss Annabel was spoilt, and that Mrs Hurst would have been much happier if I'd said no – but how could I say no to Miss Annabel? I did wish Earl wasn't quite such a large Great Dane, though – his head was as high as my elbow.

The next day we began to pack. The oddman brought the large domed trunks down from the boxroom and Miss Abbott summoned me into Mrs Hurst's bedroom. 'The art of packing, Miss Roberts, is to ensure that the clothes come out of the box at the end of their journey in exactly the same condition as when they went in, without one single crease.' Ida arrived with piles of snowy white tissue paper. 'Plenty of tissue and careful attention to folding, Miss Roberts – that's the secret.'

I thought I knew all about folding with being at Mrs Bryant's, but Miss Abbott soon punctured my pride. 'Fold the collar *back*, Miss Roberts. That dress is made of *silk*, not cheap flannelette. Put the tissue *right* inside the sleeve. You've left a *wrinkle* there, Miss Roberts.' My legs were trembling with exhaustion by the time those big trunks were finally filled – and there were still the dressing-cases, hat-boxes and shoe-boxes to do.

When at last we'd finished packing for our mistresses, Miss Abbott gave me some tissue paper to use on my own clothes: two skirts, two dresses, four day-time blouses, two dress blouses for wearing in the Room of an evening, spare underwear, nighties, my boots, my straw hat for summer – and a silk petticoat. Miss Annabel had given it to me because she'd caught the hem in her heel when she was romping with Earl on the lawn, and I'd sat up late into the night under the clear brightness of the electric light bulb, carefully mending the long rent. When I'd shortened the hem and the straps I slipped it over my head and swayed from side to side so the cool silkiness caressed my bare legs. I was very proud of that petticoat, and I swathed it in sheet after sheet of tissue paper before packing it.

The day of our journey, I was even more excited than Miss Annabel as I said goodbye to those maids who were staying at Nether Court and climbed into the big waggonette that was taking us all to the station. The footmen looked after the luggage on the train, so Miss Abbott and I were free to sit back and admire the scenery, while she gave me some extra tips on how to behave in Town.

We arrived in London – and the station was Waterloo. As I stumbled to my feet the memories came flooding back, of Beat waving me goodbye after Uncle Alf – Aunt Agnes and the boys . . . the pictures were jostling each other in their haste to invade my mind – the girls at the sweatshop, Uncle Alf's hands tugging my legs apart, the frantic pounding of my boots on the pavement, the men in the street, Peg . . .

'Come along, Miss Roberts.' Unseeing I turned towards the voice, which softened in concern. 'My dear, there's no need to be alarmed –' a hand took my arm, guiding me '– though I know London can be a little frightening when you've never been here before.'

But I was frightened of London because I *had* been here before – but I mustn't think of that, I mustn't remember. The past was over, behind me – I must forget it, hide it, conceal it utterly – because no one must ever know.

By the time we reached Belgrave Square my memories were all shut away again, completely hidden behind the door of the little house in my head. I looked around me eagerly at the wide streets and tall white terraces, at the sparkling windows and pillared porches. It was a world away from grimy Lambeth.

We trooped down the flight of steps to the basement door and the footmen headed for their pantry while the kitchenmaids scuttled along to the kitchen. Gladys, who'd come up the day before, met us with a smile. 'I'll show you to your rooms, Miss Abbott, Miss Roberts.' Nether Court had come to Town.

My room was up in the attic, and tiny. I'd have to work in Miss Abbott's room next door, but then London houses were always cramped for space, Miss Abbott said. 'And so many stairs,' she added with a sigh. But I didn't mind – I liked running up and down them when Miss Annabel rang, or first thing in the morning when I went to fetch Earl for his walk. He slept in the mews at the back, and as soon as he saw me opening his door his great tail would begin to wag, his soft brown ears would cock and his eyes would brighten as he gave a gruff 'woof' to say hello. Despite his size he was a gentle dog, and one of the Nether Court gamekeepers had trained him, so he was very obedient. 'Except,' Miss Annabel had warned me, 'when there's – er – a lady dog in the vicinity who's – um,' she paused, her cheeks rather pink.

I said helpfully, 'You mean when he do get a whiff of a bitch as is on heat?'

Her cheeks turned crimson. 'Yes. He may try to pull away then, so do hold him tightly.'

Luckily there weren't many bitches around in the Park first thing, so he padded placidly along beside me on his huge paws until I broke into a run – then he'd speed up too, loping easily along beside me and not even being out of breath by the time I came to a halt, panting and flushed. 'Good boy Earl, good boy.' I'd stroke his head and his large pink tongue would lick my hand in reply. I was glad Miss Annabel had got her own way and brought him with us.

However I usually only ever took him out in the morning, as Miss Annabel had persuaded the gnarled old man who came with the house as caretaker to give him his midday and evening walk, because I was far too busy. Although the Season hadn't officially started yet I had to escort Miss Annabel to dressmakers and milliners; young ladies must never go out alone in London, so I walked beside her, proud to be her guardian.

It was an odd sensation, standing idly by while other fingers were busy with pins as holland foundations were fitted. My hands felt empty without the familiar shape of tape and pincushion tucked into my palm. But at the milliners' I could only stare in wonderment at the glories on display. There were hats with wide brims, drooping brims, curving brims, brims turned up at the back or swept starkly high at the front, their severity softened by a covering of lace. Every style of hat was to be seen, too: shepherdess shapes, marquise shapes, toques, berets and simple shady river hats of broderie anglaise. But it was the decorations which really fascinated me. It was as if every beauty of nature had fallen prey to the London milliners; there were feathers – plumes of ostrich and aigrettes of heron, flowers – every one that ever grew, from the full-blown rose to the tiny blue forget-me-not; and fruit – from plump shiny cherries to small, luscious strawberries that looked good enough to eat. Velvet, lace, taffeta and tulle, in all the colours of the rainbow, were set on Miss Annabel's sleek dark head. With each new model she would purse her lips, narrow her eyes, lift her chin, tilt her head first to one side and then the other, and then she would smile. And I would see a hundred Miss Annabels stretching into infinity in those silvery mirrors – and every one was smiling, too.

She smiled down at me as I twitched out the hem of her Presentation dress, then she straightened her shoulders and stood sheathed in gleaming white satin with the three ostrich plumes curving proudly over her head. She was so tall and slender and beautiful; I knelt on the floor at her feet, worshipping her.

When she'd left in the carriage with Mrs Hurst I began to tidy up her bedroom, feeling suddenly forlorn. We'd worked so hard to make her look beautiful for the Court and now it was done, and she was gone. But a few minutes later Miss Abbott came bustling back with a parcel. 'Miss Annabel's parasol has just been sent round, Miss Roberts. It's been re-covered.' I watched as she unwrapped the narrow box, took off the lid and lifted out the tissue-wrapped contents. The tissue paper fell to one side and with a deft flick the parasol opened.

I gasped; the whole of the lining inside the shade was decorated with roses – clusters of beautiful pink roses. 'Oh, baint it lovely!'

Smiling, Miss Abbott held it out to me. 'Look at the handle, my dear. It's carved from ivory, and very valuable.'

Bending closer I saw that the handle was a girl wearing a loose, flowing dress – and she was picking roses. I looked up at Miss Abbott in amazement. 'I never seen anything like it afore, not in the whole wide world.'

'It belonged to Miss Annabel's grandmother. It had a cover of needle lace – Brussels *point de gaze* – quite charming, but Miss

Annabel thought it looked rather old-fashioned so she sent it to be re-covered.'

Miss Annabel was tired when she came back from the Palace. She said she'd had to wait hours to make her curtsey and the chairs were all spindly and most uncomfortable. As soon as I'd lifted her dress over her head she flung herself down on the bed. The minute I'd finished at the wardrobe I rushed over to take off her shoes; she wiggled her toes then yawned. 'It was all rather a bore, really, not as exciting as I'd expected.' Hoping to cheer her up I fetched the parasol and showed it to her. 'Yes, it looks quite nice now. I'm glad I had it re-covered.'

'Miss Annabel, what be she called?'

'Called? Who called?'

'No – thic girl picking the roses – what be her name?'

She threw back her head and laughed. 'Oh Amy, you are a little goose sometimes! Parasol handles don't have names – they're just handles. Go and ask Mrs Hobbs for some slices of cucumber – I want to lie down and freshen up my eyes before this evening's festivities.'

Chapter Twenty-Six

It was just as Miss Annabel had told me: once the Season had started she was never in the house for more than a couple of hours at a time, except when she was asleep. And even then she seemed to need less sleep than anyone else, so I was always busy.

Miss Annabel had asked Mrs Hurst if she could rearrange the furniture so that her bedroom became a bed-sitting room. 'Mama has her boudoir – I need somewhere private, too.' So several afternoons a week her girlfriends would come up to sit gossiping over cups of tea, and as I was going in and out seeing to her clothes and her underthings I'd be able to listen in to what they were saying. Once sandy-haired Miss Fenwick jumped up and went to peer into the dressing-table mirror. 'Oh, I look *dreadful* this week. I'm *so* journalière – sometimes I might as well be a ghost for all the colour I've got. Last night my lips were positively *sore* from rubbing them so hard.' She swung round. 'You are *lucky*, Annabel. You can dance till all hours and still look fresh as a daisy.'

I glanced from her pale face to Miss Annabel's vivid one. It was true, Miss Annabel always did look beautiful – and so alive, from the minute she got up to the time she came bounding home well after dawn: 'Swept out of the ballroom *again*, Amy! Oh, it *was* fun – dances only really warm up in the wee small hours.' She began to leap around the room. 'Look, this is the cakewalk,' then slowing, her arms rippling sinuously, 'Now I'm doing a valse.' As she reversed around the end of the bed without missing a beat she exclaimed: 'It was a simply *ripping* dance tonight, Amy. Late on Tom Verney arrived with this *gorgeous* man – he stood in the doorway surveying the assembled company like this.' She stopped dead and struck a haughty pose, her expression very superior. '*Just* as if he were a Sultan inspecting his harem – *don't* tell Miss Abbott I said that – then he saw me and came straight over to ask me to dance. It was *so* exciting, we danced the Kitchen Lancers and at the end the men all lifted up their partners and swung them round and round in the air. It was just like flying, and I flew higher than anybody – he was so *strong*!' Her eyes were sparkling with delight.

'And were he a lord, Miss Annabel?'

'I haven't a clue, Amy. When Tom introduced him he just said: "Miss Hurst, meet Quin – he's an idiot but good fun!" And he was, he was! Unhook me quickly Amy, I must get my beauty sleep.'

Carefully I unhooked the green chiffon, and then unfastened the deeper green taffeta bodice beneath, catching the shimmering folds of the rustling skirt as she stepped impatiently out of it – then I saw the damage. 'Miss Annabel, you've torn your underskirt again – and I only mended the hem a couple of days since.'

My voice was reproachful, and she coloured before saying guiltily, 'I am sorry Amy, but this Quin, he whirled me round so fast I got my skirt tangled up with Joan Fenwick's. Her dress was ripped *much* worse than mine, and poor Joan's terrified of her maid because she's so old and strict, but I knew *you'd* understand, Amy.' She smiled up at me from the dressing-table stool and, tired though I was, I felt a warm glow of pleasure as I realised how much she relied on me, and needed me. Suppose she did marry a lord – say an earl, or a duke? Then I'd go into the Room for dinner in front of all the other lady's maids. Except, of course, that I was going to marry a lord myself. Only sometimes with all the mending and cleaning and pressing I had to do I forgot that, but every night without fail, as soon as I put my head on the pillow, I dreamt my day-dream; though often, when Miss Annabel had been out late I was so tired I only reached the point where Lady Warminster said: 'You must come to be my lady's maid, ma petite,' before falling asleep.

But I was never late for two nights running because Mrs Hurst said Miss Abbott and I were to take turns waiting up for her and Miss Annabel. Miss Abbott said I should be very grateful to Madam for her consideration, and I was – but I would have been quite happy to sit up for Miss Annabel every night. After all, she was often so late I'd had the best part of a night's sleep in the chair by the time she came in, and I'd always been an early riser. Besides, I knew Miss Annabel preferred it when I was on duty, because as soon as I'd unlaced Mrs Hurst and brushed her hair I hurried along to Miss Annabel and then she could tell all about her evening, whereas she said Miss Abbott was always yawning and trying to make her hurry up and get into bed. 'But I feel so alive after I've been out enjoying myself, Amy – I'm just longing to tell someone about it!' So I listened as she told me her tales of dinner parties and dances, plays and concerts – brushing her hair with long, even strokes so it would be fresh and shining when she woke up later in the morning. Even if I felt dull and headachey from having to sit up most of the night I soon perked up at hearing Miss Annabel's stories; I began to feel as if I knew the people she described, and she talked so vividly it was almost as if I'd been there myself. Almost, but not quite. Just once I'd have liked to go to a ball; I was sure I'd be able to dance lightly and gracefully if I did, not like some of the clumsy girls Miss Annabel told me about, but I'd never danced since the days in the Buildings when the organ grinder came with his monkey and we danced to his tinkling tune in our boots.

When her friends came to tea I'd remember what Miss Annabel had told me about them: how Miss Fenwick had a hopeless crush on Bobbie Bynge, and how Miss Stonor's father was very mean and only gave her a hundred pounds a year for her dress allowance. 'Of course, it's totally inadequate – poor dear Betty's always in debt.' When Miss Annabel said that, I started to do sums in my head: 6s 6d for the rent – that must be paid – 10d for the gas, 6d for potatoes, 3½d for a loaf, Uncle Alf had to have his haddock, that was a whole 2d gone . . . It would have seemed like a miracle to Aunt Agnes and I if we'd had a whole £2 a week to keep the eight of us, but I forced the sums from my mind; it was different for the gentry. I made my face look sympathetic as Miss Annabel told me about poor Betty's problems in managing. 'Her kid gloves positively *reek* of petrol, Amy – her maid has to keep cleaning them over and over again. By the way, that pair of mine I've been wearing,' she gestured over to where she'd flung them down on the bed, 'they're almost grubby now, and they won't stand cleaning a second time – you can have them.'

The gloves were soft white kid, just like ladies wore – I was thrilled with them. Miss Annabel's hands were bigger than mine, of course, but with ladies always wearing their gloves so close-fitting they were quite snug enough round my fingers. Whenever Miss Annabel put on her gloves to go out I had to use her ebony stretchers and dust inside each finger with fullers' earth, and even

197

then she couldn't get them on without my help – she'd prop her elbow on the dressing table while I smoothed the glove over her hand. It really wouldn't have done if they'd been so tight on me, since I had to put my own gloves on. I didn't have a pair of stretchers, either.

She told me about the young gentlemen she met, too, and occasionally when I was escorting her to the milliners, or to visit a friend, we'd see one of these gentlemen out walking. He'd raise his grey top hat with an immaculately gloved hand saying, 'Good morning, Miss Hurst,' or sometimes it was, 'Good morning, Miss Annabel,' and then I'd know that Miss Annabel must like him, because she'd given him permission to address her in that way. One, Mr Verney, actually called her 'Annabel'. She looked a little embarrassed and said to me afterwards, 'I feel he's a very old friend, since I know his sister,' but she blushed as she said it. They never did more than speak about the weather; that was because I was there. Although I walked on ahead a little and pretended not to listen, everyone knew I was Miss Annabel's chaperon – 'duenna' she called me, laughing. Young ladies out on their own didn't chat to young gentlemen in the street or the Park: it wasn't done.

I even had to stay with her when she was sitting for her portrait, although the painter, Mr Venn, was so old that what was left of his hair had gone completely grey. One day he told Miss Annabel it was his birthday, his half-century he said, and he certainly looked fifty – he stooped and had a pigeon chest, and he was so thin I thought a good puff of wind would have blown him away. But Miss Annabel said he was a very famous artist, and I could see she was flattered when he confided in her one day that he was a martyr to neuritis and could hardly lift his left arm some days. I got rather bored, just sitting in his great bare studio with nothing to look at except the statue of a young man that stood in the corner; although he was very handsome I didn't like to stare at him too much as he was only wearing one large leaf. Miss Annabel told me later it was a fig leaf, because he was a Greek god. I did wish I could be sent to chaperon her at dances sometimes instead, but of course, it wouldn't have done. On that sort of occasion her chaperon had to be a lady, and a married lady at that. It didn't matter how young she was, like Miss Annabel's cousin, Mrs Bellingham, who was only twenty and danced as much as Miss Annabel did – she just had to have that magic gold circlet on her finger.

One morning Mrs Bellingham called just as we were setting out to go to the dressmaker's for a fitting, so I wasn't needed. I was glad of the time because Miss Annabel had torn a lace flounce on one of her ball-dresses and it was a fiddly job to repair it, but when Miss Annabel came back and rang for me I was sorry I'd not been with her, because she'd met the gentleman called Quin. 'He raised his hat to me so we stopped and had a little chat. Lucky it was Sadie with me, she's such a good sport – Mama would have insisted on my introducing him to her, and I don't even know whether "Quin" is his surname or his Christian name!' She burst out laughing; she was looking happier than ever today.

I went to unpin her hat, and then I noticed. 'Miss Annabel – where's your parasol?'

Her hand flew to her mouth. 'Oh Amy – I've lost it! I still had it with me when we saw Quin, then the sun went in and I took it down. Whatever did I do with it then? We met Quin just as we were crossing Broad Walk and he strolled a little way with us – oh, whatever did I *do* with it? Mama'll be so angry. Let me think . . .' Suddenly her face cleared. 'I remember now! We ran into Joan just by the bandstand and she'd just bought a new hat, so I asked her for a peek and her maid was making such a hamfist of untying the string – I'm sure she was doing it on purpose, she doesn't approve of people unpacking parcels in the Park, miserable old killjoy – so I seized it off her and undid the knots myself.'

I prompted, 'And your parasol, Miss Annabel?'

'I hung it on the railings, of course – and it's still there. At least, I *hope* it's still there. Amy, put your hat on this minute and run as fast as ever you can. It wasn't that long ago, so I'm sure if you get a move on you'll be in time to retrieve it. Run, Amy, run!'

I ran so fast I had a stitch in my side by the time I came in sight of the bandstand, and I had to slow down. My anxious eyes searched the railings, but they were empty. I quickened my pace again – it must be there, perhaps it had fallen off – then I saw it, tucked under the arm of a gentleman! I couldn't believe my eyes. I stopped and stared. He was standing beside the railings as if he were waiting for somone, but why ever should he be carrying a parasol? It did look so odd. Perhaps it wasn't Miss Annabel's parasol at all – perhaps it belonged to his sister who'd rushed away to speak to a friend . . . But there were no ladies nearby, and besides, it did look very like Miss Annabel's parasol. I circled round him, trying to peer at it and there, poking out from under his immaculate grey elbow, was the girl picking roses – so it *was* hers.

I didn't know what to do. I edged a little nearer, and suddenly his head swung round and there was a flash of sparkling blue eyes – then he was looking straight ahead again. But as I watched, in one smooth movement he drew the parasol out from under his arm and flicked it open. I gave a gasp of surprise as he lifted it up and held it over his grey top hat. Then he began to speak to the empty air in front of him. 'Parasols are handy things – they keep the sun from spoiling a fellow's complexion.' I thought, he must be mad – gentlemen don't *have* complexions. Next thing I knew he'd stretched out his right arm and balanced the girl's ivory toes on the tip of his finger, then he spoke again. 'What's a pretty maid like you doing, hanging about the Park on her own? Let's dance!'

I said, 'I don't never –' Then my voice trailed off, because I realised he'd been talking to the ivory girl, not me; and now he was twirling her round and round on the end of his finger so the cream silk fringe of the parasol spun out shining in the sun and she danced underneath it.

He turned his head to look directly at me, his blue eyes smiling. 'There – she *did* want to dance!'

I exclaimed, 'You be making her dizzy, twirling her so fast!'

'Oh, we can't have that!' He tossed the parasol up in the air and caught it with his left hand. 'There, she's stopped.' He lowered the shade then lifted the handle to speak to it directly. 'No more dancing for you, my girl – besides, where's your sense of decorum? A lady should never dance with a gentleman until she's been introduced. What's your name, fair maiden?'

'Miss Annabel says she don't have no name – she's just a handle.'

'How very unkind of Miss Annabel!' He turned to face me and stepped forward. I didn't move away – I didn't want to, and even though he was a stranger he looked very friendly. Besides, he was still holding Miss Annabel's parasol. When he was close by me he smiled down saying, 'Shall we christen her, you and I? What name do you suggest for this fair maid, fair maid?'

'She do have a look o' the head housemaid at Nether Court.'

'And in what appellation does the head housemaid at Nether Court rejoice?'

It took me a moment to work out what he meant, then I told him: 'Gladys.'

'Gladys! Oh no, that won't do, it won't do at all. She's obviously a Grecian maiden – and whoever heard of a Greek girl called Gladys? You'll have to do better than that.'

I shook my head. 'I dussent know no Greeks.'

'Mm, then I'll have to put my thinking cap on.' He reached up and tipped his top hat right down over his eyebrows, so I could see the sleek yellow hair behind his ears. He narrowed his eyes and pursed his lips in an exaggerated frown of concentration while I waited with bated breath. Then all at once his face cleared and his white teeth flashed in a smile of satisfaction as he tipped his hat back up again. 'I've got it! She's called Penelope – because she's waited so patiently on the railings.' Then he added very quickly, 'And what are *you* called?'

'Amy – Amy Roberts.' I blushed.

He peeled off his glove and held out his bare hand. 'How do you do, Miss Roberts? But I shall call you Amy.'

His strong hand was so warm and friendly as it shook mine that I spoke without thinking. 'And what be your name?' He blinked in surprise and I blushed hotter as I said quickly, 'I be sorry for presuming,' and added, 'sir.'

His hand squeezed mine tighter as he commanded, 'Don't call me "sir", any friend of Penelope's is a friend of mine – you can call me Frank.'

I shook my head. 'But – you be a gentleman. I cassent – mebbe Mr –?'

He hesitated a moment, then laughed. 'If you insist – then it's Mr Dunn. Ah, I'm forgetting my manners. Amy, may I introduce Penelope?' He dropped my hand then drew the parasol out from under his arm and held the handle towards me. 'Greet her properly, Amy and say "How do ye do?" '

I put my fingers round Penelope's slim body and said, 'How do you do, Penelope?'

A rather growling squeak replied, 'Pleased ter meetcha, Amy me old cock sparrer.' And suddenly we were laughing and laughing.

An old lady walking past lifted her lorgnettes to glare at us before saying loudly to her companion, 'The way people behave in the Park these days!'

Mr Dunn bent down and whispered in my ear, 'It's Penelope's accent – she's not quite –' He lifted his hands in mock dismay before adding, 'And her dress is a little outré for Town, don't you think?'

I didn't think, I just looked at him. Then as he stepped smiling back I asked, 'What were she waiting for?'

He looked puzzled for a moment before exclaiming, 'Oh, you mean Penelope. It was for her husband – he went away to fight in a war and didn't come back for twenty years.'

I exclaimed, 'She waited *twenty years*?'

'Yes – women are so much more faithful than men in these circumstances. She had other suitors who told her her husband was dead, but she fended them off and carried on waiting, because she loved him.'

I gave a sigh. ''Tis a lovely story.'

'Mm – *not* a very likely one, though. Now let's forget about Penelope, she's served her purpose. When can I see you again, Amy?'

I gasped, 'But, I cassent. I –'

'My dear Amy, if you wish to restore this most attractive and no doubt valuable parasol to your mistress you will have to stop gaping like a rather lovely goldfish and give me a time and place.'

'But I dussent get no regular time off. I be Miss Annabel's *personal* maid, and I have to be there in case she needs me.'

He lifted the parasol high above his head, announcing, 'If you don't give me a time and a place I shall hurl this pretty object at tremendous speed through the air all the way to Park Lane, where poor Penelope will undoubtedly be crushed to death by a passing motor cab.'

He looked so determined I had to give in. Anyway, I did so want to see him again. 'I do bring Earl for a walk in the Park, every morning, regular.'

He dropped his arm, looking puzzled. 'Earl? Is this Earl a child – an American child, perhaps?'

I shook my head. 'He be a Great Dane.'

'Then he should be called Hamlet. I'll have to accompany you – you're far too small to handle a Great Dane.'

I was indignant. 'I baint small – I be five foot three!'

'Thank you, Amy, that saves me the trouble of measuring you. Time?'

'Half-past six, or mebbe a twitch later.'

He exclaimed, 'Half-past six – in the *morning*?' I nodded. 'Good Lord, what sacrifices you women expect of a fellow. Still, you've given me a time and place, and that's what I asked for, so here's Penelope.' He held out the parasol and as I took it he swept off his hat and bowed, just as though I were a lady.

'Thank 'ee, Mr Dunn.'

'Farewell, five foot three Amy.' He dropped his hat back and with a parting smile turned and strode away. I watched his straight, slim back until he was out of sight, then I set off back to Belgrave Square, my heart pounding.

Miss Annabel had a friend with her when I got back so I didn't have the chance to tell her about meeting Mr Dunn, and later I was glad I hadn't. I wanted to hug the secret to myself: it was private, like my day-dreams. But that night in bed instead of my usual dream I imagined I was in the Park next morning, and Mr Dunn was striding towards me with a smile on his face as he lifted his hat and said, 'Good morning.'

Only it didn't happen like that. It was raining the next two mornings, and though Earl and I stayed out so long we got thoroughly wet, he never came. I felt low and sad both days, but it was probably the weather, because the third morning was fine and sunny and I felt as though I were bubbling with excitement as we walked sedately to the Park. It was such a lovely day I decided to run with Earl, but he ran faster and faster until I could hardly keep up – then suddenly footsteps were racing along behind me and as they drew level a hand reached out and a voice said: 'Give that to me!' The leash was torn from my fingers as Mr Dunn overtook me and went running ahead, his long slim legs bounding over the grass with Earl galloping along beside him. While I was watching, his hat toppled backwards and off so I began to run again, panting after him to pick it up. And as I took hold of it and felt the silky firmness of the brim in my palm – then all at once I knew I loved him.

I took out my handkerchief and began to dust it down; far ahead of me he reined in Earl and then turned, waiting for me to catch up. His hair shone yellow as a daffodil in the sun and as I came up to him I saw his blue eyes were smiling at me. He didn't stay long – he said he'd been up all night, 'Dancing and such-like frivolities,' but I didn't mind, because as he left me he said, 'I'll be seeing you again, five foot three Amy.'

That night I decided to change my day-dream; now, instead of Lady Warminster's son kneeling at my feet asking: 'Will you be my wife?' it was Mr Dunn. I gazed down at his smiling blue eyes and breathed, 'Yes – oh yes, please.' When at last I fell asleep it was in a warm glow of happiness.

Chapter Twenty-Seven

'Quin is Lord Quinham!' Miss Annabel burst out the minute she opened the door. 'Stop fussing with those boring old drawers, Amy, and take off my hat.' I ran to the dressing table as she sank down on the stool so I could slide out her hatpins. Leaning forward she peered into the mirror. 'I look in good face today, don't I, Amy?' She laughed. 'I sound just like Joan and Betty, always fussing over the state of their complexions, but it does matter – because I've seen him and he's going to be at the Thornleys' tonight and –' she jerked her head back suddenly so her toque nearly fell on the floor before I caught it '– and he's asked me to dance with him! "As many as your chaperon will allow," that's what he said, and as my chaperon tonight will be Sadie . . .' She sprang up and began to whirl around the room. 'How can I bear to wait five whole hours! Oh Amy, he is so frightfully handsome! I know Mama says one shouldn't judge a man on his looks, but they always judge *us* on our looks, so why shouldn't we girls do the same in return? You must make me especially beautiful tonight, Amy – and for now I'm to lie down with cucumber on my eyes so that they sparkle.'

I helped her out of her dress and into her wrap and was heading for the door when she called me back. 'While you're fetching the cucumber, get the *Debrett* from the drawing room.'

'I dussent know what that do look like.'

She said impatiently, 'You can't miss it – it's red and very fat.'

I wondered if it was some kind of toy – for Earl, perhaps – but in the end I had to ask Mr Davenport. He went straight over to the fireplace alcove and took if off the shelf – it was a book. I was glad I hadn't given myself away to Miss Annabel – she would have made fun of me over it.

Her head lifted from the pillow. 'You've remembered it – good. Luckily Mama's out – she says it's very vulgar for a girl to read *Debrett*, so you'll have to read it aloud to me while I've got the cucumber on my eyes.'

While I was slicing the cucumber she told me that she'd met Quin while she was in the Park with Mrs Bellingham. 'And Sadie's such a sport. She knows I like him, so she said Earl was pulling rather, and would he take the leash for me. Of course, the darling wasn't doing any such thing, he's far too well-behaved – darling Earl, I mean.' She giggled, and then laughed outright. 'I may have to change Earl's name! Anyway, he walked with us for simply ages, and then not long after he'd gone we ran into Tom Verney so I said to him, "You've got to tell me Quin's proper name – it was so embarrassing not being able to introduce him properly to Sadie." And Tom said, "We've always called him Quin because his name's Quinham, Lord Quinham." '

'Oh, Miss Annabel – so he's a *titled* gentleman.'

'It's better than that, Amy. He's a lord because he's the eldest son of his father, who's an Earl – the Earl of Warminster!' She glanced at me, smiling.

My thoughts went round in a whirl as I exclaimed, 'But that do mean he be *Lady* Warminster's son!'

She laughed. 'It would seem likely, Amy.'

'But Lady Warminster, she did come to school and praise my stitching. She did say I –'

Miss Annabel interrupted me. 'Yes, I remember you telling me – that was when I decided I simply *must* have you as my maid. You see, this house actually belongs to Lord Warminster.'

I stared at her. 'But I thought it were madam's –'

'For the year, yes, but she only rents it. Lots of peers rent out their Town houses. Mama told me that Lord Warminster doesn't ever use it – he stays in the country all the year round. I never bothered to ask about him because he didn't sound at all interesting – an elderly reclusive peer who was only concerned with his garden, but now . . . Quick, Amy, put my cucumber on and then get that *Debrett* open. It's alphabetical by title, so flick through until you find "Warminster", then read the entry to me.' There were hundreds and hundreds of pages before I reached the W's and Miss Annabel called impatiently, 'Whatever are you *doing*, Amy?'

'I be sorry, Miss Annabel, only I never did realise there were so many lords.' Then I saw it, in big black letters: WARMINSTER, EARL OF. 'I found it – and there be a picture!'

'That's the coat of arms. Just read the bit beside it.'

I read slowly, 'Leonidas –'

'Don't sound so mystified, Amy – it's a Greek name, the brave King of Sparta who died with all his men at Thermopylae.'

With relief I added more rapidly, 'Arthur Hector.'

'Goodness, what a collection of heroes!'

The next word was double-barrelled. I took a deep breath then gabbled: 'Fitzwarren-Donne.'

'Fitzwarindon – that'll be the family name.'

'Seventh Earl; b. May 2nd, 1868; s. 1886?' My voice was puzzled.

' "Born" then "Succeeded". Lord Warminster's father must have died in 1886, so he's been an earl for ages. Keep reading, Amy.'

'Ed.?'

'Educated.'

'At Eton, and at Trin. Coll. Camb.'

'Trinity College, Cambridge. You're reading this as though it were a foreign language – do speed up.'

'Is patron of five livings: m., be that "married", Miss Annabel?'

'Mm.'

'Married 1889, Jeanette Joséphine Marie-Louise.' I stared at the names – *my* Lady Warminster, printed in a book.

'Carry on, Amy.'

'Who d. 1910 – what does "d." mean, Miss Annabel?'

'Died.'

'Died! She can't have done! Lady Warminster, she cassent be dead!' My voice caught in a sob. 'She was so beautiful!'

'That wouldn't stop her dying, Amy. Keep going.'

I forced myself to stumble on: 'Only dau. – daughter – of the late Marquis de Montjean, of St Valéry, France, and has issue.'

'Ah, now we get to the really interesting section.'

'Arms, sable within –'

'Skip that bit, Amy – move on to his son.'

'Son living.' I hesitated, then admitted, 'I can't say his name. It's spelt F,R,A,N,C,O,I,S.'

'That's pronounced "Franswa". It's French.'

'Peter, *Jean*?'

'Shun. It's a man's name in France, meaning John – after his mother, of course.'

207

'Then it says in brackets: "Viscount Quinham", and he was born on February 2nd, 1890 and educated at Eton and at Magdalen College –'

An impatient exclamation from Miss Annabel interrupted me. '*Maudlin*, Amy. You don't know how to pronounce anything, do you? Lady's maids are supposed to know some French, at the very least.'

I was glad Miss Annabel had her cucumber on – my cheeks were scarlet under the tears now. I mumbled: 'Oxford.'

'Speak up, Amy. Has he any brothers and sisters?'

'No.'

'We'll forget the rest of his relatives, then. In any case, Mama'll be back any minute – you'd better return it at the double.' As I left the room I heard her murmuring under her breath, 'So he's twenty-two – and he was at Oxford, like Tom.'

All the time I was dressing Miss Annabel that evening I couldn't get the thought of Lady Warminster out of my mind. She'd died two whole years ago, and I'd never known – now part of my dream had gone, just like that. Besides, she'd been so beautiful, and so kind to me. The tears kept welling up. That night I clothed Lord Warminster all in black in my dream, what was left of it. Then I realised I could salvage it, for how could Lord Quinham fail to want to marry Miss Annabel, with her being so beautiful and so clever? And then old Lord Warminster would die soon, of a broken heart, and it would be his son's turn to be earl – and so Miss *Annabel* would be Lady Warminster, and she and Lord Quinham that was would find my father for me – only who would I marry, if I couldn't marry Lady Warminster's son? But I knew the answer to that already – Mr Dunn, of course. I remembered the mornings when he'd walked with me and Earl in the Park, and fell asleep, comforted. Next morning the bell woke me just after five and I went down to undress Miss Annabel. Her cheeks were flushed and her eyes sparkling; she'd danced nearly every dance with Lord Quinham, she said – so I knew my altered dream was going to come true.

In the middle of June Mrs Hurst decided that Miss Annabel had had too many late nights and needed some country air, so we went down to Nether Court for the weekend. I was so pleased to be there again, sleeping and working in my own big room and saying

208

'hello' to Mr Morton and the other servants who'd stayed behind. The minute Miss Annabel and her mother had gone out for a drive I went rushing outside to the rose garden. The roses were in full flower; I stood at the top of the steps and looked down at the patches of red and white and pink. Every rose seemed to match the one opposite it, in a precise pattern. The ones in the centre beds were all standards; they had lots of blooms – but their heads seemed too heavy for their bare, spindly stems. There were proper bushes around the edge, but they were all trimmed into different shapes: a white one like a little pyramid, a pink one that was completely circular – and the differing shapes all repeated themselves in a regular pattern. In each corner the red roses were trained down over a stand like an umbrella, while the pink ones in front of them were pegged firmly down on the ground.

After a while it all began to seem rather sad. Those roses were so very much under control – and they looked as if they knew it. Granfer had always let his roses go where they wanted, and they'd been free and happy, whereas these were cowed and obedient, like prisoners. I walked down the steps and among them, and saw that each bloom was large and perfect, just as Mr Peake had said. I told them so, but they just looked back at me, listlessly – Mr Peake's roses didn't seem to know how to smile.

Presently Mr Peake himself came along to the garden, and told me about the splendid wood the roses were making. 'It's because of that fine hot summer we enjoyed last year, Miss Roberts, I'll be bound. Terrible for rhododendrons, but it's done my roses a power of good. Look at that pillar there. The Dorothy Perkins is getting quite out of hand – it needs a good trim.'

I followed his pointing finger: a bright pink rose was tumbling down from the top of a pillar in a mass of frilly blooms. She was the only rose in that garden who looked as if she was enjoying herself, and I exclaimed, 'Oh no, Mr Peake – she be beautiful just as she is!'

He escorted me round every rose in turn, telling me the names. He didn't need to read the little china labels at the foot of each stem; he knew them all by heart. In some cases there were two or even three labels for the same plant, because several different types of bloom were growing on the one standard – trick budding, Mr Peake called it, and he was very proud of the way they'd all

209

taken. I admired them politely, but I didn't really like them – the roses didn't look as if they enjoyed being treated in such an undignified way.

The next day I went round the rest of the garden; there were roses against the walls in several places, and I looked carefully at every white climber, but I never found my white rose from Bath. I was sorry not to have discovered her name – she'd been my faithful friend all those years – but in a way I was glad I hadn't found her. I didn't think she'd have been happy at Nether Court.

Soon after we'd returned to London Mrs Hurst held Miss Annabel's ball. Miss Annabel had been rather casual about it at first, because Lord Quinham had told her he'd be out of Town that week and couldn't come, but as her new dress took shape her spirits began to rise. She'd had a big argument with her mother about that dress – Mrs Hurst had said it wasn't girlish enough – but when I'd finished dressing her that evening I knew she'd been right – she looked stunning. Over a close-fitting bodice and underskirt of heavy ivory satin was a shimmering gown of black silk net, with all the borders picked out in a pattern of gunmetal-grey sequins, while trailing sequin leaves curved across the bodice and up from the hem. Her hair was piled up in the most elaborate coiffure Monsieur Paul had taught me, and was glossy black over her broad white brow and sparkling dark eyes. Her pink cheeks glowed with excitement and good health.

The gaily striped awnings were in place, the carpet had been laid down the stone steps at the front and the footmen were arrayed in their dress livery, with their hair powdered so stiffly white that they seemed strangers – as indeed some of them were, because Mr Davenport had had to hire extra help for the occasion. Miss Abbott and I had been invited downstairs along with the housemaids to see the preparations: the folding doors between the reception rooms had been thrown back, the carpets removed, the floors french-chalked – and everywhere there were flowers and ferns, so that the ballroom was like a great indoor garden. The supper was already prepared, and Miss Abbott reeled off the names of the dishes until my head was in a whirl: quails in aspic, galantine of veal, salmon mayonnaise, lobster salad – and then there were the sweets: vanilla meringues, coffee éclairs, pistachio cream, strawberries in jelly, pineapple ices . . . I'd never seen the like before. There were so many different colours and scents that I exclaimed: 'They do look good enough to eat!' And then blushed at my foolishness as all the housemaids laughed.

As soon as the guests were due to arrive I was on duty in one of the bedrooms set aside as a cloakroom, receiving wraps and keeping my needle and thread at the ready in case any running repairs were needed. Every time the door opened I could hear the music clearly from below, and the lilting tunes twitched my toes until I longed and longed to dance, even if it were only around the bedroom. But I was far too busy, and it was only much later, when it was already dark, that I could stop and put my hot face out of the window to look down at the linkmen below, with their torches flaring in their hands.

Late, very late – long after the new day had dawned – Miss Annabel came up to bed, flushed and triumphant. 'It was wonderful, Amy – wonderful. If only Quin could have been here then it would have been quite perfect.' I knew exactly how she felt. If Mr Dunn didn't come to the Park for a while it was as though the savour had gone out of my life.

But she met Lord Quinham at Ascot; he told her which horses to back and they all won. 'Isn't he *clever*, Amy!' And I fervently agreed as she gave me ten shillings from her winnings. He went with the party Miss Annabel arranged for Wimbledon. 'He enjoys tennis, Amy, and when I told him I did too he said we must play together some time.' And, 'Lord Quinham gave me his arm at Henley. He's so divinely handsome the other girls were positively green with envy.'

Meanwhile there were the Saturdays to Mondays: Mrs Hurst had a lot of friends within easy rail distance of London, and Miss Annabel was invited to visit them whenever they had a group of young guests staying. I went too, of course. At first I was rather nervous, being responsible for the luggage, and having to find bathrooms for Miss Annabel to use and then distributing the tips before we left. I'd be shy of eating with strangers, and it was especially odd being called 'Hurst' in the Rooms of these different houses. But the households were all run like Nether Court, and I soon learnt the importance of being extremely polite to the housekeeper and resident lady's maid, politely friendly to the butler and valet – and very distant with the footmen. When Mrs

211

Hurst and Miss Abbott came with us once Miss Abbott said after the visit, 'I'm so glad, Miss Roberts, that you never flirt with the menservants. Most girls with your looks would be tempted, but as I said to Madam, "Miss Roberts is *not* a flighty girl." ' I was pleased when she said that, but it wasn't really any credit to me. Obviously I wouldn't want to flirt with other men when I loved Mr Dunn.

Then, at the very end of July, Miss Annabel went away and I couldn't go with her – there wasn't room for me, so a housemaid would have to look after her. I was sorry about it, even though it meant I'd be free all Saturday – until I told Mr Dunn in the Park and he invited me to spend my day off with him. I couldn't believe it was true – it was so wonderful looking forward to it – and the day itself was even more wonderful.

Sometimes I'd feel I wasn't really in my body – it was as though I were up in the air watching myself, or like being in a fairy tale. I was the princess and he was the handsome prince who would waken me from my dream with a kiss. Not that he did kiss me – though once I thought he was going to.

We went to Surrey, travelling in a first-class compartment, and he told me I must call him Frank, for today at least. At Weybridge he took me on the river in a punt. He looked so handsome, dressed in his white flannels, that I was sure I was the envy of every other girl on the river. He handled the heavy punt pole as if it weighed no more than a feather; when the sun grew hotter he took off his jacket, tossing it to me to hold, and then rolled up his shirtsleeves. I watched the muscles rippling in his forearms, but mostly I watched his face, waiting for the times when his blue eyes would flash in their familiar smile – so I could smile back.

We tied up in a quiet part of the river, and he opened the hamper he'd brought with him, saying, 'I feel lazy today, Amy. I'll lie back against the cushions and you shall feed me.' So I pulled the delicate flesh of the chicken from the bone, and slipped choice morsels between his parted lips. Then I fed him bite-sized pieces of sandwiches, followed by strawberries, each one dipped in cream and sugar. When it was time to open the wine he sat up slightly. 'I'll hold the glass myself as you might spill it, but you must entertain me. Talk, Amy.'

So I chattered on about Miss Annabel: how she could play the piano so well and speak both French and German, and even read Latin, and how she'd studied Shakespeare's plays and knew all about art and paintings. I told him about how I dressed her hair in all the different styles I'd been taught at Monsieur Paul's in Bond Street, and how I'd learnt to fix on a double plait, or pin a puff cluster so that nobody could tell it wasn't her own hair.

He sat up with a jerk. 'You mean – her hair's *false*?'

'Only little bits of it,' I said quickly. 'She do have lovely hair, but it dussent curl, so it do look a mite flat at times, even after I've back-combed it. So then I do give it a liddle help.'

'By Jove.' He lay back again before asking, 'And what about yours? Is your hair all your own?'

I laughed. 'I baint got no money for spending on hair pieces. 'Sides, mine do curl.'

He replied slowly, 'Yes, it does. You keep it that way, Amy. Sitting here in the sunlight today you're a golden girl, do you know that? Golden hair, golden eyes, skin with the bloom of a sun-warmed peach. You are a little peach, Amy – I'm sure that if I bit into your cheek you'd taste as sweet and luscious as a ripe fruit.' He sat up, and began to slide towards me. When he put his arm around my waist I didn't move away – I just wanted to sit looking up into his face for ever. He bent his head closer until I could feel the warmth of his breath on my cheek – and suddenly there were shouts and laughter as a boat came shooting round the corner, and a man called, 'This'll do, Harry – we'll tie up here.'

Mr Dunn muttered, 'Damn,' and began to withdraw his arm – but very slowly as if he didn't really want to move it. I was sure he would have kissed me, if that other boat hadn't arrived when it did.

He went back to his rooms in London to change, then that evening he took me out to a music hall. People on the stage sang and danced and told jokes; and we both laughed and laughed until our ribs ached. He took me back to Belgrave Square in a cab, and he cut short my thanks saying, 'I have enjoyed myself today – girls of your class are such jolly company. You are a little love, Amy.' He squeezed my hand tight. 'We must do it again, some time.' In bed that night I kept repeating his words over and over again to myself; I was too excited to go to sleep, so I dreamt my daydreams instead.

213

Miss Annabel came back full of complaints. 'It was dreadful without you. The housemaid was quite efficient at unpacking and laying out my clothes, but it was disgusting getting up in the morning to find yesterday's hairs still in the brush – ugh.' I was sorry she'd been upset, but I couldn't regret my day with Mr Dunn.

A couple of weeks later Miss Annabel went out of Town for the day, and he took me to the Zoo in Regent's Park. I watched enthralled as the bears climbed their pole for buns, and cried out loud as the lions roared – clutching at Mr Dunn's arm in fear. I'd have liked to stay longer, but he said he had an engagement so he sent me home in a cab. I thought about those wild animals all evening, and then dreamt about him.

Then it was August and Cowes Week, so we went down to stay on the Isle of Wight, and I saw the sea for the very first time. I would have been sorry to leave London, except that Mr Dunn told me he was going away too. I felt my face fall and he laughed. 'Cheer up, little five foot three Amy. We'll meet again.' So I knew we would, because he'd promised.

Miss Annabel's married sister had taken a house for Cowes Week, so we stayed with her. Miss Annabel had told me that she was looking forward to seeing her nieces and her nephew, and I was pleased at the idea of having children around, but I hadn't understood – in practice I hardly ever saw them. They spent all their time up in the nursery, except for when the elder girl and the boy came down to the drawing room after tea; 'children's hour' Miss Annabel called it, and she said how much she enjoyed playing with them. 'They're such fun, Amy! This afternoon I put the hearthrug over my shoulders and crawled around on my knees growling. Little Lucy squealed and squealed, so Timmy said, "Don't be frightened, Lucy – it's only Aunty Annybelly"!' She laughed. 'Young children are so restful after a busy day.'

I'd seen them being walked around the grounds by their nanny, with the nursemaid wheeling the baby in a pram – she was just over three months, Miss Annabel said. Then Mrs Bonham, Miss Annabel's sister, went over to the mainland for a couple of nights – and the baby was still here. I said to Miss Abbott, 'Baint she a mite young to be weaned?'

'Mrs Bonham isn't feeding her – it would ruin her figure. You

214

can always tell a lady who's nursed her babies herself, Miss Roberts, however good her corsetière.' Her voice lowered, 'Dropped bosoms. I happen to know that Mr Bonham did suggest that Mrs Bonham should nurse herself when Master Timothy was born, but she wouldn't hear of it. Quite right too; once the damage is done it's done for life.'

'But they used to say in the Build –' I amended hastily '– in the place where I did live, as babies brought up by hand didn't never thrive.'

Miss Abbott leant forward, her voice low and confidential. 'There was a little trouble with Miss Lucy. She was such a sickly baby – madam did suggest hiring a wetnurse but she told me that Mr Bonham put his foot down over that.' Her voice dropped even lower. 'They're often women who've had their babies out of wedlock, Miss Roberts – and besides the moral aspect, there is the risk of certain types of disease. Now I don't want to discuss the matter any further, my dear, with your being still so young.' She stood up to return to her own room. 'But you can rest assured that Nanny Wilkins is totally competent.' After she'd gone I thought about all the women I'd seen at Borrell and in Lambeth, suckling their babies and looking down at them as if they were the most precious thing in the whole wide world, and I decided that if – when – I was married to Mr Dunn then I'd beg him to let me nurse our babies myself.

The weather was very bad, the worst Cowes Week for years, people said. The wind and the high waves kept lots of yachts from going out of harbour, but I didn't mind, because he sent me a telegram: *Meet me on the pier at Ryde, 3.30 Tuesday. F.D.* It was lucky that Miss Annabel was out visiting all afternoon, and even luckier that she'd given me that ten shillings from her winnings at Ascot, otherwise I'd have had no money for my fare.

As soon as I arrived Mr Dunn handed me a parcel, saying that he'd been lucky at *chemin de fer* and won £230, so he'd bought me a box of gloves. He laughed away my thanks and went to buy us an ice apiece; we stood close together under a shelter as we ate them, watching the white-capped waves toss their spray high into the air. He asked me what Miss Annabel had been doing, and whether she had many admirers. I told him she had lots of them. 'And how does she feel about the poor chaps – doesn't she like any of them?'

215

'I think she do like Lord Quinham the best.'

'So he's to be the lucky fellow?'

I shook my head. 'I dussent know. He hasn't asked her yet.'

He was staring out at the grey sea, and I sneaked a glance at the clean-cut lines of his profile – then suddenly he turned, and his eyes were alive with laughter as he said, 'I daresay he will.' But in a moment his head had jerked back to the waves and he was exclaiming, 'I knew that silly ass would come a-cropper.' I watched in horror as a small yacht keeled right over into the water. Mr Dunn put his arm around me and hugged me close. 'Don't worry, he'll bob up again. There, I told you so.'

He had to leave soon after, so I was back in good time. I dressed Miss Annabel for a dinner at the Yacht Club, and then waited up for her – it was my turn. When she came in she looked radiant, and I guessed what had happened even before she exclaimed, 'Amy – I'm engaged! He asked me to marry him – and I said yes!'

Chapter Twenty-Eight

The next day we were due back at Nether Court; our news caused a great flurry downstairs. Miss Annabel marrying a title – she'd be a countess one day! We couldn't stop talking about it in the Room. Lord Quinham ran down from Town one day to see Mrs Hurst, and Gladys caught a glimpse of him as he was alighting from the carriage. She said he was tall and slim. We pestered Mr Davenport who'd been there to open the door in person, and he said he seemed 'a very pleasant young gentlemen', but he wouldn't tell us any more, because Mr Davenport didn't believe in gossip. We wished it had been one of the footmen on hall duty as usual – we'd have got more out of him.

Miss Annabel told me that Mrs Hurst had given her consent to the engagement. 'Now it's just the boring old settlements to sort out, and I won't see him for simply ages because he's got to go on to Scotland, as soon as he's been down to Wiltshire to tell his father.'

'At Pennings?' My voice wavered a little as I asked. I was frightened. Pennings was so near Borrell, suppose Miss Annabel found out about me?

She shook her head. 'No, he lives at Eston – it's to the west of Salisbury. Of course, you come from Wiltshire, don't you, Amy? You'll like to go back there. Quin says we'll have to go to Eston, because his father never travels in the summer – he won't leave his precious rose garden. Isn't it lucky he likes roses? With Mama being so fond of them they'll have something to talk about.' She suddenly jumped to her feet and began to twirl around the room crying, 'Amy, I'm so happy I can hardly bear it!' I knew exactly how she felt, because before he'd left me at Ryde Mr Dunn had said, 'I'll be seeing you, little Amy – sooner than you expect!' Now I dreamt about him every spare moment.

Two days later a letter arrived from Wiltshire. Lord Warminster had written inviting Mrs Hurst and Miss Annabel to Eston at the beginning of September. Miss Abbott told me he'd asked Mrs

217

Hurst to act as hostess for the week, and suggested that she might like to invite some of her and Miss Annabel's friends to come with them. 'A very handsome gesture, Miss Roberts, don't you think?'

Miss Annabel thought so too. 'How very kind of Lord Warminster – I shall write to Joan and Betty tonight.' In the mirror I saw Mrs Hurst's smile of approval. Miss Annabel added, 'Quin told me several of his friends are coming too, so it should be good fun.' My heart gave a little leap. Suppose Mr Dunn was one of Lord Quinham's friends, and that's why he'd said he'd be seeing me again so soon? But I had to put the thought from me; Miss Annabel wanted her hair Marcel-waved that evening, and I needed all my concentration for manipulating the comb with one hand and the heated tongs with the other.

I scarcely had time to think during the next couple of weeks, either. It had already been arranged that Miss Annabel and Mrs Hurst were to stay with old friends in Gloucestershire, and on the way Miss Annabel insisted on stopping off in London to order a new evening dress for Eston. I took her for a fitting on our way back to Nether Court, and then the dressmaker's telegraphed to say it wouldn't be ready until the Thursday evening – and that was the very day we were going to Eston. Lord Quinham was coming first thing to meet Miss Annabel's great-uncle and stay for luncheon, then he was going to escort Miss Annabel and her mother to his home, himself. He was bringing the engagement ring too, so there was no question of changing those arrangements. Miss Annabel was so angry about the dress she was crying tears of rage, and I didn't know how to calm her down – then Mrs Hurst arrived and took charge. She told me that I must go up to London on the Wednesday, go straight round to the dressmaker's and insist that Miss Annabel's dress be finished at once. I was to spend the night in Belgrave Square and then take the dress down to Eston the next day. 'Telegraph the housekeeper as soon as you know which train you'll be catching.'

'Yes, madam.'

'We won't be arriving until four-fifteen. I've written to Lord Warminster, but just remind the butler.'

'Yes, madam.'

When I arrived at the dressmaker's they were all at sixes and sevens because two girls had gone down with a fever the previous week. Miss Annabel's dress was trimmed with beaded embroidery and they simply hadn't been able to finish it. I told them I'd sew the rest of the beads on myself, and by nine o'clock that evening it was all ready. I took it back to Belgrave Square in a cab and knocked up the old caretaker and his wife who lived in the basement. Next morning I put on a pair of the fine new gloves Mr Dunn had given me and set off for Waterloo, to catch the train to Wiltshire.

I had to wait for my connection at Salisbury, and I realised I'd have missed staff dinner at Eston by the time I arrived, so I had a cup of tea and a pie in the third-class refreshment room, carefully noting down the details in my account book, for when I presented it to Miss Annabel at the end of the month. There was a dogcart waiting on the forecourt outside Eston station as I came out, and the driver waved his whip and jumped down. He came to meet me, smiling, and took the box and my basket from my hands. 'You'll be Miss Roberts – Mr Tims, he sent I down to meet 'ee.' He wasn't much older than I was, and his teeth flashed white in his sunburnt face as he added, 'I be Jim Arnold, at thy service. Now do 'ee come up in front and sit alongside o' I.'

It was lovely to hear people speaking Wiltshire again, and I felt a lift of my heart as I settled my skirts down on the narrow seat beside him. We set off up the slope and turned out onto the bottom of a long village street. I exclaimed, 'My, baint it pretty – thic cottages, they do all match one another!'

Jim turned his head with a grin. ''Tis an estate village, Eston, that's why. They was all on 'em built at the same time.'

I looked at the nearest pair of pink brick cottages, a mirror image of the ones opposite and of those either side: they had steep-pitched red tiled roofs decorated with curly white barge boards under the eaves, and the same lacey white pattern edged the small pointed porches and ornamented the diamond-paned windows either side. The cottages were all set well back from the street, with neat little brick paths running through gardens ablaze with brightly coloured flowers. Then I noticed the roses; almost every cottage had one climbing up its pink walls, and several still had a few blooms bobbing their heads, even though it was already September. I said to Jim, 'I never did see the like afore. Did Lord Warminster build 'em all?'

'Nar – 'twas Her old Ladyship, His Lordship's mam. She grew

up at Eston – belonged to her dad it did – then she married the old lord and goes to live way over t'other side o' the county. Only when me Grammer were a liddle maid a terrible fever struck, and half a dozen or so on the young 'uns, they dies. Her Ladyship, she were in foreign parts then, with her man being a powerful soldier – a general he was, all the Warminster Lords were generals, so I heard tell. And the old lord was fighting in thic there Crimea, 'gainst the Russkies – won a battle there, by all accounts, so Her Ladyship dussent know nothing about the fever till she comes back. When she does, she be so upset she gets a big doctor down from Lunnon, and he says as 'tis drains as have done the damage, and they maun be mended. But Her Ladyship, she dussent stop wi' them – she orders the whole o' the village to be rebuilt. Tidiest cottages for miles around, thic 'uns at Eston.' He raised his whip to point. 'There's ourn, opposite the post office.'

Even the shops matched – all pretty pink and white. The paintwork sparkled, and I'd not seen a single tile out of place. 'Is His Lordship a good landlord?'

'Oh aye, he be that all right. He keeps his eye on things, and sees repairs are done smartish, like his mam afore him.'

We passed a wide side street, and Jim gestured to it. 'Church be up that away, with Rectory, and Mr Selby's house, His Lordship's agent he be. And doctor, he lives up there too, you can see his lamp at the corner, though I hopes as you won't be needing to send for him for your mistress – leastways, not till she's been married a few months, eh?' He dug his elbow into my ribs, grinning.

Blushing, I hastily changed the subject. 'Be it far to the house? I'd like a morsel o' time for getting prepared for when Miss Annabel arrives.'

He laughed. 'So would everyone else, I reckon. Mrs Johnstone's been flapping round like a headless chicken this morning, sending the housemaids back and forth as though 'twere the Day o' Judgement! They dussent know whether they be going or coming by now, Clara says.'

I thought of Mrs Harper, so stately and so methodical. 'At Nether Court the rooms are all dusted and the beds aired whether guests are expected or not.'

He threw back his head and laughed. 'Don' 'ee try telling that to Mrs Johnstone!' He leant closer, so his breath tickled my ear.

'Truth is, she's taken it easy these last years – and she's got a sight too fond of her cowslip wine!'

'A housekeeper wouldn't never be drunk!'

'Well, sure as eggs be eggs she baint often sober. There's the East Lodge – it baint more'n cock's stride from the village.' The lodge was the same as the cottages, and just as spick and span. As we pulled up at the gate a woman came bustling out to open it, and Jim leant down. 'This be Miss Hurst's maid, Aunt Mags, come on ahead.'

A pair of friendly brown eyes smiled at me. 'Welcome to Eston, me dear.'

Jim interrupted my reply with a wink at his aunt. 'I reckon if the mistress be only half as pretty as the maid His young Lordship'll be dancing round like a dog wi' two tails!'

She laughed as the blush warmed my cheeks. 'Don' 'ee take no notice o' Jim, my maid – proper honey tongue, he has.' She drew the gate fully back, then said to me, 'We be all pleased as punch at the news – 'tis time there were a lady up at the house. Good day to 'ee, and I hopes as 'ee enjoys thy visit.'

I waved, and then turned eagerly back to look ahead. The drive curved, and it was a while before the big house came in sight; when it did I was disappointed. It was built of brick, not white stone, like Lord Warminster's other house at Pennings, and although it was big there was nothing special about it – no tall towers or pointed turrets like at Nether Court. We veered left well before we reached the front entrance, and followed a driveway up beside a high brick wall and round into the stable-yard. A lad ran out to hold the horse's head and Jim helped me down, before hefting out my box and basket; I followed him through a service courtyard, and up to the back door. He threw it open and yelled, 'Clara!' at the top of his voice; Mrs Harper would have had a fit.

A housemaid with ginger hair and freckles came to meet me. 'I be Clara, Clara Chandler.' I told her my name and she said, 'I'll take you up to your room, Miss Roberts.' As she swung round I couldn't help noticing the large port-wine birthmark staining the side of her left cheek, but I pretended not to have seen it, since she was obviously trying to keep that side of her face turned away from me. She called over her right shoulder, ''Tis only just ready. Mrs Johnstone couldn't make up her mind where to put all on you, wi' us not being used to parties.' She stopped so suddenly I almost cannoned into her. 'What manner o' lady be she – thic Miss Hurst?'

'She be beautiful – tall and dark, and slender as a willow wand.'

'No, I mean to work for. Be she pernickety?'

We were on the back stairs by now, and the woodwork was smeared, as if it had been polished too late, and in a hurry. I replied firmly, 'She do expect everything to be just so.'

'Oh dear.' Clara sounded flustered. 'Mrs Johnstone, she be all of a caddle – she'm had us running up and down like yo-yos, so nothing baint properly finished.' We stopped on a landing. 'Your room's here. 'Tis only small, but at least you don't have to run all the way up to the attic.' My room was quite well lit, with a full-sized window, but I could see the dust lying on the sill and the top of the chest; the creased counterpane was crooked, too. 'I'll take you down to your mistress' now.' Clara paused by the door. 'I hope thic bell still works – I think it do. Lord Quinham had a couple of friends to stay in the spring, and one on 'em had a valet that slept in this room – no one did complain.' She didn't sound too sure, though.

Miss Annabel's room was big and light, although the furniture was very old-fashioned. I ran my finger over the dressing-table top, but it was spotless. Clara reddened. 'I turned thic one out myself – 'tis clean as a whistle.'

I said quickly, 'I be sorry – 'tis just a habit o' mine.'

Clara's voice was flat. 'I seed you eyeing up the state o' your room.' Then she shrugged, 'Bertha's supposed to take care o' yourn, and she –' Clara stopped, then added, 'Anyway, after that I baint surprised at you checking thic 'un – I'd a' done the same myself. But Mrs Johnstone, she don't care, not as long as His Lordship's rooms are clean, and she puts me on them, 'cos she knows I don't skimp.' She gave a half-grin. 'Me mam'd kill I if I did, she learnt I right.'

I said, 'My Grammer were just the same.' And we smiled at each other; I liked Clara already. 'Mebbe if you did have a minute to spare, you'd be so kind as to show I round, afore the guests arrive. 'Tis a big help in a strange place.'

'I be glad to, Miss Roberts.'

As we came out onto the corridor I asked, 'Mebbe the bathrooms, first.'

''Tis down the end o' the corridor, by the housemaid's pantry that's on the way to the bachelors' wing.'

'Only the one?' Clara nodded. I told her, 'Why, at Nether Court we got two just for the staff – and madam, Mrs Hurst, she do have her own private bathroom, wi' a door leading to it from her bedroom.'

Clara said quickly. 'So do His Lordship – but no one else maun use it, the door to the corridor be always kept locked. Ah, but there's the one opening off the Countess' bedroom – I hadn't thought o' that one. None of the guests've been put in the bedroom, His Lordship wouldn't like it – but the bathroom's the other side.' She said more slowly, 'I suppose if I found the key and unlocked the door to the corridor, then your lady and her mother could use that bathroom.'

She still sounded doubtful, so I said firmly, 'I'd take it kindly, Clara, if you'd arrange that.'

'I will then. By the way, there is one for the staff, but 'tis in the basement, and creepy-crawlies do find their way in from the ivy over the window. I prefers a nice clean all-over wash, meself.'

I nodded. 'So do I. But the gentry –' We both shrugged simultaneously, grinning at each other. I thought what a pity it was about the mark on Clara's face – she'd have been quite a pretty girl, otherwise.

Clara said briskly, 'I'll take 'ee down the main staircase now.'

'Won't His Lordship mind?'

Clara shook her head. 'He's never indoors in the day-time, not this time o' year.'

The woodwork wasn't much better on the main staircase. There was no deep shine like at Nether Court, which was a pity because it was a handsome stair, and well set off by a whole sequence of portraits of gentlemen in shining breastplates or red coats. I lingered beneath one with his hand on his sword and read the words underneath: *Arthur, 5th Earl of Warminster*, then, in smaller letters: *Spain and Waterloo*. Then I realised Clara had reached the bottom, and I hurried after her, asking, 'Were His Lordship a soldier, too?'

She glanced round. 'Didn't your lady tell you –' She broke off in mid-sentence as there was a scurrying of footsteps below and another housemaid appeared. 'What's the matter, Bertha?'

I eyed Bertha's dirty apron and crumpled cap as she panted, 'Clara, thee maun come quick – Mrs Johnstone's screeching fer 'ee like a banshee. I reckon she's two sheets in the wind already – I dussent know what she puts in thic cowslip wine o' hern.'

Clara snorted. 'His Lordship's brandy, most like. I be busy now, Bertha –' The other girl caught at Clara's sleeve, and I noticed the black rims round her fingernails as Clara said impatiently, 'All right, Bertha – I won't be a minute.' She turned back to me and began to point at doors, spinning round and reeling off the names of the rooms behind them, until she finished with a breathless: 'And the billiard room be down the far end o' thic corridor. Come and find me if you need anything more, Miss Roberts.' She disappeared at a run through the door opposite which led to the dining room and the back stairs.

The slatternly girl called Bertha stayed behind, staring rudely at me. As she began to open her mouth I cut in sharply, 'Be you the maid as is supposed to have cleaned my room?' She nodded; her sullen face was as grubby as her hands. 'Then I'll see to it myself, while I'm here. Your standards baint what *I've* been used to.'

She glared at me, before snapping, 'Then you can fetch your own tea tray of a morning.'

I retorted, 'I intend to – I dussent like dirty fingermarks on *my* cup and saucer.' Her face went brick-red, and she flounced off back stairs.

Flushed with the triumph of sending that slammock packing I stood and surveyed the scene, memorising the information Clara had gabbled at me. I decided that it wouldn't be too difficult to find my way about Eston. It was obviously quite a simple design, just a long oblong with three of the main rooms projecting out at the front. The big entrance hall was the middle one of these three, with the morning room opening off it on the left, and the library to the right. The main staircase came down into the back right-hand corner of the hall, and the door that led to the dining room and the back stairs was directly opposite it on the left. Judging by the furniture the entrance hall was used as a drawing room too, but the main drawing room was actually at the back, overlooking the terrace, Clara had told me; it was obviously a very long room, because one door to it was next to the dining-room entrance, whereas the other was at the foot of the main staircase. I stood peering along the corridor that ran behind the stairs. Clara had told me the billiard room was at the end, but there were a couple of doors before that – I'd have to find out where they led to later. I'd need to find my way about Eston properly, because we'd clearly be spending a lot of time here in the future.

Once I was sure of the layout of the rooms I studied the entrance hall more closely: it was a fine big room, with four pink marble pillars along either side supporting some kind of balcony. I craned my neck to look up at the ornate plaster ceiling far above my head; the whole room was more impressive than any at Nether Court but it looked uncared for, neglected. I walked over to one of the matching fireplaces that stood under each balcony; the fire surround was of pink marble, too, with a pair of smaller pillars supporting a carved marble panel under the mantelpiece. The carving was pretty, a flowing design of leaves and flowers, but when I leant closer I saw that the back of the leaves were all coated with dust – thick as a rabbit's fur it was, that dust. I shook my head; Mrs Harper would have had something to say about *that*. It was a bit gloomy under the balcony, too, I thought: three or four nice big mirrors wouldn't have come amiss. Mrs Hurst had lots of mirrors in all the main rooms at Nether Court and it made them extra light and airy. Still, with girls like that Bertha being responsible for the cleaning, perhaps mirrors wouldn't be a good idea at Eston.

I still kept staring round; I knew I shouldn't be loitering in the front of the house like this, but I couldn't resist the opportunity of having a good look while His Lordship was safely outside. I wanted to think about Lady Warminster: to imagine her sweeping down this very staircase with a loving smile lighting up her face as she caught sight of His Lordship waiting for her below. Tears came into my eyes – how sad he must be now. I blinked them away, relieved that there was no sign of the footman on hall duty – I didn't want him laughing at me. On the other hand, where was he? Perhaps the butler was drunk, too, or more likely the bell was answered from back stairs, since this hall was used as a room.

Reluctantly I began to drag myself away, but I slipped back for one last look at the first of the red-coated generals. He was labelled *Hector, 6th Earl of Warminster*, then *Afghanistan and The Crimea*, so he must be Lord Warminster's father, and the husband of the old countess who'd rebuilt the village. I stared at his face –

he looked exactly as a general should look, with a hawk-like nose and fierce dark eyes under bushy black brows. Suddenly I thought, Lord Quinham – he must look like this, only younger. What a handsome couple he and Miss Annabel would make when they stood at the altar . . . but just then I heard a door slam, so I scuttled quickly across the big hall and up the back stairs.

I found the housemaid's closet and collected the cleanest box of dusters – Clara's, I'd be bound – then took it up to my room, along with a dustpan and broom. When it was clean and tidy I went down and unpacked Miss Annabel's dress. As I shook out its gleaming folds I heard the stable clock strike three, and realised there was some time to spare before the guests started arriving. Glancing at the window, I saw it was still fine outside – why shouldn't I go and see if I could have a look at Lord Warminster's rose garden? I decided there and then that I would, not that I had very high hopes of it – it'd likely be the same as Mrs Hurst's garden, only bigger, and with even more captive roses. Still, I might at least find out the name of my rose from Bath. Spurred on by this hope I set briskly off to the back stairs.

Chapter Twenty-Nine

Down in the service corridor I spotted what was obviously the door of the butler's pantry; it stood open to reveal two footmen, languidly cleaning the silver. Cleaning the silver in the afternoon! Mr Davenport would have had something to say about that. One of the men caught my eye and called, 'Can I help 'ee, miss?'

I said, 'I were wondering if I could mebbe have a look around the gardens afore the guests did arrive. Perhaps you could tell I where to find the head gardener?'

The man nearest the door jumped up, pulling off his green baize apron. 'I'll take 'ee, me dear.'

'Here, Thomas – I seed her first!' But Thomas ignored the protesting shout, and seizing me by the arm rushed me along the corridor.

I heard the clang of saucepans followed by a yelp of pain. A woman's voice screeched: 'Yer silly cow – o' course it were 'ot!'

Thomas winked at me. 'Best keep away from there – Mrs Procter baint in the sweetest o' tempers today, what wi' all the extry work. We'll use the other door.' He steered me across the service court and through into the stable-yard. 'Kitchen garden's over the back here – nice and handy for the horses' muck. Nothing but the best for His Lordship's vegetables, eh, me dear?' He leered at me, tightening his grip on my arm, and I was relieved when I caught sight of the dark-suited, bowler-hatted figure of the head gardener talking to one of his assistants. Thomas' voice became more respectful. 'Here's a young lady as'd like to ask you a favour, Mr Hicks.'

The stern face turned to look at me, and I quickly dropped a half-bob before explaining, 'I be Miss Hurst's maid, Amy Roberts, come early wi' one o' her dresses, and I did wonder if I could mebbe have a peep at the rose garden. I do be powerful fond o' roses.'

Mr Hicks stroked his moustache, considering my request, then the young gardener with him spoke. 'His Lordship did say as how

227

he were going over to Horley 'safternoon, and the guests, they baint due till the four-fifteen train – Jim Arnold told me.'

Mr Hicks nodded a grave assent. 'In that case, I don't see why not, Miss Roberts. But you wouldn't have any fanciful ideas about picking a nosegay for your mistress? We couldn't allow that.'

'No, Mr Hicks, o' course not.'

'Then you may have a look around. Joe here's just going back to the glass-houses, he'll show you the way in.'

Joe was stocky, with well-muscled arms below his rolled-up sleeves and a bristling brown moustache. He touched his cap and grinned, showing two rows of strong white teeth. 'This way, me girl.' As soon as we were out of earshot he said, 'You don't look old enough to be a lady's maid.'

'I were eighteen thic summer.'

'That be only a *young* lady's maid, I reckon – so I'll call you Amy. My name's Joe – Joe Dempster.' I knew I shouldn't allow him to be so familiar, but he didn't seem the kind of man you could easily argue with. He pointed to the right. 'Them's the glass-houses for the new roses – the trial grounds are beyond. I be journeyman for the roses; 'tis a big job here at Eston, what wi' breeding new 'uns too. Now, I've got work to get on with, so I'll leave 'ee here. Follow the path round by the wall till you come to a white gate, then go in by that, and you'll be able to find your way to the main rose garden.'

'Thank 'ee, Mr Dempster.'

He said firmly, 'The name's Joe – dont 'ee forget that, 'cos I'll be seeing more o' you, young Amy.'

I stepped through the gate and under an arch of green leaves. A path led me on between high green hedges and under more leafy arches, until I came to a small clearing where the path split into two. I hesitated, uncertain which way to take, and then I saw the dog – at least, I knew it was a dog really, but for one heart-stopping moment I'd thought it was a lion, like the ones I'd seen in Regent's Park with Mr Dunn. It was golden, with a curling mane and wavy coat; I'd never seen the like of it before. I walked towards it, and as it saw me coming it rose to its feet. I could see now that it wasn't actually big enough to be a lion – it wasn't even as big as Earl – and besides, it was carrying a hat in its mouth. I glanced up the path and saw that there was a bare-headed gardener at work further along, so it was obviously his hat. The dog walked purposefully forward, offering me the battered old panama. I took it, saying, 'Thank 'ee kindly,' and she smiled, actually smiled – I'd never seen a dog smile before, so I smiled back as I told her, 'But this baint my hat – we maun give it back. Come along wi' I.' I patted her soft golden head, and her plume of a tail waved in acknowledgement as she padded along beside me.

The gardener had a humped back and he didn't turn round as I came level with him, so I put the hat down at his feet – and saw one of his boots had a built-up sole, three or four inches or more. He must have been lame, poor fellow, as well as being a humpie. I was going to slip past but the dog dropped down on the ground and rolled over on its back – *her* back, I could see now, so I'd been right about that. Crouching down I stroked the silver-gold velvet of her belly, asking, 'And what be thy name?' She smiled at me again, her soft brown eyes crinkling at the corners, and I exclaimed, 'Ah, thee bist beautiful – the most beautifullest liddle dog I ever did see! But I maun leave 'ee, if I be going to get a peep at thic rose garden 'safternoon.' I gave her a parting pat and stood up, then I glanced at the gardener, wondering whether to ask him which was the best way to go. But the back of his dark head was still to me. He obviously didn't want to speak to a stranger – maybe he was frightened of them, like Dummy Drew used to be – so I started to walk past him; then I saw the flash of a knife.

As I watched he sliced quickly down, pulled a cane out, and then reached into the basket at his side. He was pruning, pruning in September! He must have made a mistake. Perhaps he was deaf, and that was why he hadn't looked round – and so he hadn't heard Mr Hicks' instructions, either. He dabbed paint on the cut and then began to raise the knife again. I stepped forward and said, quite loudly, 'I dussent think thee shouldst be pruning roses at thic time o' the year.' The knife stopped, just like that – but he didn't turn his head or speak, and thinking of Dummy Drew again I wondered whether this gardener was half-skim too, so I explained, 'Pruning, 'tis best done in the spring.'

At last he began to turn, but not just his head – he swung round his whole body, all of a piece, as if he couldn't move his head separately. And once he'd started turning I saw it wasn't just that his back was humped: his neck was all twisted, too, fixing his head sideways as if he were always trying to look over his shoulder. He had to swing even further round before his face was towards me – and when it was I nearly jumped backwards in surprise. It was as if a giant had taken hold of the right side of the man's face with his huge hand – and squeezed it, hard; so now it was much smaller than the left. The eyebrow was lower, the eye smaller, his nose was lopsided – and the two corners of his mouth didn't match. One bigger eye and one smaller one stared at me, looking as surprised as I felt. He didn't say anything.

I smiled into his mismatched eyes and began again. 'I daresay thee didst mishear when Mr Hicks did tell 'ee what to do. Mebbe he meant thee to deadhead – there be a powerful lot o' deadheading needed, to keep a rose garden looking nice. That's what Mr Peake always did say.' He still stared at me, silent. So I explained, 'Mr Peake, he be head gardener to Mrs Hurst, her as be mother to Miss Annabel, that be betrothed to Lord Quinham.' His lips tightened a second, so I knew he'd heard of her. 'I be Miss Annabel's maid,' I added, 'her *personal* maid. Anyway, Mr Peake, he did always set his men to pruning in the spring; and Mr Hicks do look strict, so I wouldn't want 'ee to be getting into trouble for doing it wrong time o' year.'

At last I saw his lips beginning to move, but he couldn't get the words out at first. I waited, as I used to with Dummy, until he managed to speak. 'These – are ramblers. Ramblers – are pruned – in the autumn.'

There were long gaps between his words, but I could understand him easily enough. I still wondered, though, so I asked, 'Bist thee *sure*?'

'Quite – sure.' Then he drew another breath and added, 'Wichuraianas are best – pruned soon after – they finish – flowering.'

And somehow he didn't sound like Dummy at all now; there were still those long gaps, but he spoke as if he knew what he was saying was right. Besides, Dummy would never have used a long word like Wichuraiana – I hadn't come across it before myself. 'I never heard that name afore. What colour be thic Wich –' I tried again, 'Wicharanas?'

'Wichuraiana. It's the name – of the species. This rose is called – Dorothy Perkins.'

Then of course I remembered the pillar at Nether Court. 'Oh, I know what *she* do look like – she be a very lively rose, tumbling over herself with all her petals pressed close together like they were pink frills on a petticoat hem. And she do smell lovely, too.'

'Yes, she does.'

I was puzzled. 'But why does she have two names?'

'Wichuraiana is her – surname. The species is – rather like a family. It denotes a rose's origins.' He pulled off his glove and reached up to one of the leaves; his hand was large with a mat of dark hairs all over the back and running up to the knuckles of his fingers – yet he touched the leaf very gently, stroking its glossy green surface. 'A German called Wichura – brought the first plant back – from Japan.'

I gazed at the dark green leaves. 'So she did come all the way from Japan?'

'Not this one – but her – grand-father.'

I exclaimed, 'Well, I never! Fancy a rose having a granfer – just like folk do.'

And his oddly-shaped mouth twitched a little, as if he was almost smiling, then the dog gave a short bark. 'Quiet, Nella.' He reached down and patted her head – black fur on golden – then I saw Mr Hicks come round the curve of the path, with his hat in his hand. I'd been talking to this poor fellow and kept him from his work, and from the look on Mr Hicks' face he wasn't at all pleased.

So as the head gardener came closer I smiled at him, my nicest smile, and said quickly, 'I just been hearing as thic here rose do have a granfer.' Mr Hicks' face went rigid, so I added, gesturing towards the gardener, ''Tis my fault thic fellow baint working – I did start talking to 'ee, but 'tweren't more'n a minute or two –'

Mr Hicks simply turned his back on me and said, 'My lord, Dempster has reported signs of black spot on the White Maman Cochet. Do you still prefer the potassium permanganate spray?' And the man with the humped back bent to pick up his glove – which was not an ordinary pruning glove at all, but a fine, dogskin driving glove which only gentlemen wear.

I stood transfixed as he reached for his panama and placed it over his dark hair – which was grizzled at the temples because he was older than I'd realised. I still couldn't move or speak as he raised himself to his feet and stood looming over me, with his lopsided face clean-shaven – far too well shaven for any gardener. With a slight dip and sway of his twisted shoulder he moved to one side to step around me, and then at last my tongue unlocked itself and I whispered, 'I be sorry, my lord, terrible sorry – I didst think thee wast,' I stumbled, desperately trying to retrieve my words, 'I thought you were – a gardener!'

His odd, misshapen face looked down at me, and his mouth began to work – but before he could speak my feet uprooted themselves from the grass and I turned and ran up the path between the curving hedges, my eyes prickling with the tears of humiliation. How could I have been so stupid as to mistake Lord Warminster for a gardener? And I'd 'thee'd' him, too! What must he be thinking of me? And Miss Annabel – whatever would she say when she heard?

'Amy, how *could* you have been so silly? Whatever must Lord Warminster be thinking of me – having a maid who commits such a stupid blunder? And I did *so* want to make a good impression. How on earth could you have mistaken a peer of the realm for a gardener?'

Miserably I tried to explain. ''Twas with him having a hump, and his face being all lopsided – and then, when he couldn't speak properly, I just thought –'

Miss Annabel looked so surprised my voice trailed off. She asked, 'Are you *sure* this man was Lord Warminster, and not one of the gardeners playing a trick on you?'

'I be sure. Mr Hicks be head gardener, he wouldn't play no tricks.'

She shook her head in puzzlement. 'I just don't understand. Lord Quinham didn't tell me anything about this.' She paused, then added, half-speaking to herself, 'I suppose he's so used to him, he didn't think. Only what'll happen when the girls meet him? Joan wouldn't stand gaping, but Betty can be so childish sometimes.' Her head lifted again and she addressed me directly. 'Amy, you say he looks odd – *how* odd? Is his appearance so unusual that people who didn't know him might stare?'

'Oh yes, Miss Annabel. You'd stare if you did just pass him in the street.'

She said decisively, 'Then I'll go and warn them now – and

Mama.' After she'd gone I felt sick with worry. Suppose His Lordship was really, really angry, and made Miss Annabel dismiss me at once – whatever would I do then?

While Miss Annabel was down at tea I waited in her room, fidgeting with clothes I'd already unpacked; it seemed a long time before she came back. She swept in, kicking off her shoes and waving her hand in a great curving arc, so that her engagement ring flashed fire. 'Isn't it beautiful? I do so love diamonds!'

I whispered, 'Did His Lordship say anything about –?'

'You can take that hangdog expression off your face, Amy. He did demand your instant dismissal, but I managed to gain a reprieve of twenty-four hours.' The blood drained from my face. 'Amy – whatever's got into you today? I was only joking. I apologised on your behalf, but he didn't seem at all annoyed – in fact, he said he appreciated your concern for the well-being of his roses. I didn't really understand what he meant by that – what *were* you doing, Amy? Anyway, it doesn't matter now, what matters is that I'm sure he likes me. He talked to me for simply ages, even though it was obviously difficult for him, with his impediment, and Lady Burton – she's a neighbour whom he invited to tea to act as hostess until Mama had settled in – she told me afterwards that he never talks to women, not unless he's known them for ever.'

I scarcely heard as Miss Annabel chattered on; my legs were trembling with relief, but I tried to look interested as she said, 'Lady Burton's quite old – her son was at Eton with Lord Warminster, he's something fearfully grand in the Army now. Her son I mean, not poor Lord Warminster – apparently all the Earls of Warminster have been generals or such-like ever since the time of Marlborough, but of course, the tradition's broken now. Except that Lord Quinham may go in the Army, he told me on the way down. He'd look so dashing in a Guard's uniform, or perhaps he might apply for a commission in the Household Cavalry, and wear a plume on his helmet – he's a marvellous rider, Tom told me . . .' Normally I loved to hear Miss Annabel talk, and I always knew when to say: 'Oh, Miss Annabel!' or 'Just fancy,' or a quiet 'Mm?' – but I found it difficult to say them in the right places tonight.

I'd barely recovered by nine o'clock, and staff supper. Miss Abbott and I and the visiting lady's maids went down together.

There were only two men in the Room: Mr Tims, the butler, and Lord Warminster's valet, Mr Wallis. Lord Quinham didn't have a valet – he and the other young gentlemen were being looked after by the footmen, Clara had told me when she came to turn down Miss Annabel's bed. She said Henry and Thomas were looking forward to the tips.

Miss Abbott had the first place, but I was given the second – as maid to the future Lady Quinham – so I sat next to Mr Wallis. He had a wrinkled face and sandy hair that was going thin on top. Mr Tims was even older, being almost bald except for a sparse white fringe. His expression seemed to be permanently anxious, and I'd heard him say to Mrs Johnstone as we went in, 'Henry's gloves were grubby at dinner – I'm sure Mrs Hurst noticed. I suppose I should speak to him, but . . .' His voice trailed off uncertainly. I thought of how stern Mr Davenport would have been with a footman who wore grubby gloves at Nether Court – not that any of the Nether Court footmen would have dared to do such a thing. Mrs Johnstone wasn't a patch on Mrs Harper, either. She was smiling, but her eyes had an odd, glassy look, and she held out her glass to be refilled long before any one else had finished theirs – obviously Jim Arnold had told the truth. After her third refill she knocked her glass and spilt some wine on the tablecloth; as she mopped it up with her napkin she giggled, 'Oops, clumsy me!' Miss Stonor's maid began to snigger, and Mr Tims hastily made a comment about the weather. Mr Wallis replied with an anecdote about a storm at sea – his brother was in the Merchant Navy, apparently – and the awkward moment passed.

By the end of the meal Mrs Johnstone was noticeably slurring her speech; when she invited us visitors to stay behind for a glass of her special cowslip wine Miss Abbott declined, politely but firmly. The other lady's maids stayed seated, but I felt I had to leave with Miss Abbott. Clara was hovering outside, and she beckoned to me behind Miss Abbott's back. 'Mary and me, we'm going up to the balcony. Thomas said as the guests be all in the hall, and we can look down on 'em from there. We've not seen your mistress yet, or her Mam – will you come with us, and point 'em both out?'

I hesitated. Suppose Lord Warminster spotted me, after what had happened earlier? 'Won't they see us?'

Clara shook her head. 'No, there be a wooden screen we can get behind, but it's got holes in it, as part of the pattern, so we can look through 'em.'

I did want to go. I told her, 'I baint never seen Lord Quinham yet, or his friends, except for Mr Verney.'

'Then come up now – you can spy Miss Hurst for us and we'll spy Lord Quinham for you.'

As there was no electric light at Eston we were in shadow on the balcony, even without the screen. Clara whispered, 'You can only see half the room at a time, but Mr Tims is taking in more coffee, he told us, so they'll be moving round.'

I spotted Mrs Hurst in her green dress, and murmured her name; then Miss Annabel came into view and I told them who she was. Clara exclaimed softly, 'My, baint she beautiful!' and I glowed with pride.

Mary whispered, 'That's Lady Burton, talking to the Rector – but I can't see our Lordship.'

Clara replied, 'He'll be keeping under the balcony – 'tis darker there. I cassent see His young Lordship, either – ah, he's walking over to talk to your lady's mother – do you see the gentleman standing beside her now? That's him.'

My eyes searched for the green dress again, and Mrs Hurst's familiar face. Then I saw a fair head bending towards her. 'No! It can't be, it can't be!'

Mary's voice spoke in my ear. 'O' course it is – that's Lord Quinham all right.'

As I clutched at the screen and stared down at the handsome face below, my heart beat loud as a drum – because Lord Quinham was Mr Dunn.

Chapter Thirty

I hardly knew how I got away from that balcony and back to my room. Once there I sat shivering in the dark. Clara must have made a mistake – she'd not understood which lady was Mrs Hurst, that must be it. Mr Dunn simply happened to be staying here too, as I'd half-expected – he was a friend of Lord Quinham's. But Lord Quinham was Lord Quinham, and Mr Dunn was Mr Dunn. Their names were quite different, and so were they – different people. Gradually I became warmer, and soon I'd lit the lamp and begun sewing while I waited for Miss Annabel to send for me.

It was much later when she did ring. 'Just help me out of my dress and unpin my hair – I'll brush it myself tonight, as Miss Fenwick and Miss Stonor are coming along shortly.' I began to unhook her. 'By the way, Amy – you'll have to learn to read *Debrett* correctly, or you'll be drummed out of the Steward's Room.' The last hook was unfastened, and I lifted the frills of lace and satin. As her head emerged again she added, 'You told me the Warminster family name was Fitzwarindon.'

''Twas what it did say.'

'No – it's Fitzwarren hyphen Dunn.'

I exclaimed, 'But – I do remember plain, the end were spelt Donne.'

'Donne is always pronounced Dunn – like the poet.'

Dunn! As I held out her wrap I said carefully, 'Miss Annabel, you did say as "Jean" were same as John; that name, Franswa – be it like an English name, too?'

She shrugged her wrap on, and lifted her arms so I could tie the belt. 'Yes of course – Francis. That's what I'm going to call him – Quin's only a nickname, and I prefer Francis to Frank.'

The room seemed to be swaying around me, then the door flew open and Miss Fenwick and Miss Stonor swooped down upon Miss Annabel. With hands that shook I began to put away Miss Annabel's dress, while they clustered around the hearth, their hair hanging loose over their shoulders. 'Rather sticky at dinner,

236

wasn't it, Annabel? I felt sorry for your poor Mama, stuck with Lord Warminster. He does talk – so – terribly – slowly – when he talks at all, that is.'

'It certainly wasn't because he was busy eating, Betty – like that fat little Rector. I never saw Lord Warminster take a single bite – I suppose with his neck being at that peculiar angle he can't find his mouth to put his fork in it!'

Miss Annabel glanced at me, saying, 'You can go now, Amy.' I left them all brushing their hair in unison.

So now I understood. He'd said, 'You can call me Frank Dunn,' and it was his name – only everyone else called him Lord Quinham. But why should he tell me his other name? I was bewildered for a moment, until I realised why. It'd been for *my* sake, because he knew I was only a servant, and he didn't want to make me feel awkward. But with the relief came another question – why had he got engaged to Miss Annabel when he was courting me? And him being Lord Quinham, Lady Warminster's son, it was right that he should be courting me – it was my dream coming true, just as I'd always known it would. And then I knew the answer to my second question; his engagement to Miss Annabel was a mistake. She'd misunderstood him, and he'd been too polite, too chivalrous, to put her right – gentlemen were like that, I knew from Saranne's novelettes. Besides, the mistake was partly my fault, because I'd told him at Ryde that Miss Annabel liked him best of all, so naturally he'd not been able to disappoint her. But as soon as she discovered the mistake she would release him, and then it would all come right in the end, just like my story – I knew it would. So I was safe again, safe in the arms of my dream.

Miss Annabel said to me next morning, 'You're rather subdued today, Amy. You're not still worrying about your gaffe with Lord Warminster, are you?' Before I could answer she went on, 'I'm sure you don't need to. He didn't seem at all annoyed, and when I asked him not to tell Mama he promised at once. Shall I wear my blue linen costume this morning? Mm, yes, I think I will.' She slipped on her ring and held it up to the light. 'I do so love diamonds.' I turned away, and went to the wardrobe.

I kept glancing around whenever I was on the main corridor, hoping I'd see Mr Dunn, Lord Quinham, for I knew he'd reassure me, but the bachelor's rooms were all together beyond the back stairs, and only the housemaids were allowed to go along there. It seemed a very long day, knowing he was in the same house, yet not seeing him.

That evening the bell in my room rang early – a long, jangling peal. I rushed down to Miss Annabel's room and found her standing by the dressing table with flushed cheeks and flashing eyes. She tugged at her finger. 'That odious, odious man! How could I ever have –' The diamonds sparkled, then spun in a curving arc to land with a tinkle on the silver back of a hairbrush, before rolling slowly off. I stood staring at it. 'Of all the thoughtless, arrogant men! Amy, go and fetch Miss Fenwick.'

I ran towards the door, but it opened before I got there and Miss Fenwick came rushing in. 'Annabel, what happened? You looked so angry!'

'He's hateful, hateful! Do you know what he –'

Miss Fenwick took her arm, interrupting. 'Annabel – *pas devant les domestiques.*'

She glanced in my direction, and Miss Annabel stopped abruptly. After drawing a deep angry breath she said quickly, 'Unhook me Amy, then you can go.' By the time she was in her wrap Miss Stonor had arrived as well. Miss Annabel spoke sharply to me. 'Stop fussing with those clothes – you can clear up tomorrow. Just go, now.'

Normally I'd have been hurt at Miss Annabel speaking to me like that, but tonight I only wanted to be on my own. Upstairs I collapsed on a chair, remembering the shining arc of Miss Annabel's engagement ring as she'd flung it away. He'd told her, he'd told her that he loved another, and she wasn't sad, only angry – and she'd set him free. I'd known my story must come true. I felt faint with relief and thankfulness.

As soon as I entered Miss Annabel's room next morning with her tea tray I looked at the dressing table; the ring still lay where she'd thrown it. She pulled herself up in bed. 'Wrap that, that *thing* up in a parcel, Amy. I don't want to even *see* it again. Diamonds are hateful, so hard and uncaring – like him.'

At breakfast Miss Abbott whispered quietly to me that Miss Annabel had wanted to leave at once, 'But naturally madam wouldn't hear of it, especially with her acting as hostess. She told Miss Annabel she must put a brave face on it and entertain the guests; Miss Annabel wasn't best pleased. Of course we won't discuss the matter below stairs, Miss Roberts.'

'No, Miss Abbott.'

'If anybody should fish – mum's the word.'

'Yes, Miss Abbott.'

I wanted to dance along the corridor as I went back to Miss Annabel. She was sitting at the writing desk in her room, her pen scratching angrily. 'When I've finished this letter I want you to – bother, who's that?'

I went to open the door and Clara's face appeared. 'Mr Tims gave me this for Miss Hurst, from His Lordship.'

Miss Annabel almost snatched the envelope out of my hand and tore it open. Then her movements slowed. 'Oh, it's from Lord Warminster.' She scanned the short message. 'He says he'll be driving round the estate this afternoon, and he wonders if I'd care to accompany him. How thoughtful. He must have realised at breakfast how unpleasant it is for me now that – yes, I'll go. Mama can hardly object to my leaving the guests to spend time with my host. Amy, go and find him and tell him I'll be delighted to go with him.'

There was another tap at the door, and this time it was Miss Fenwick's face that appeared. Miss Annabel called, 'Do come in, Joan – I'm longing to talk to you.' She swung back to me. 'Take your time with that message, Amy, there's no hurry – as long as you tell him before lunch.'

Mr Tims was in his pantry, and he told me Lord Warminster was always out in the gardens at this time of day. 'Guests or no guests, he won't neglect his roses.'

I found Joe Dempster in the kitchen garden, just coming out of the toolshed. 'I got a message for His Lordship, from my lady.' Joe stood looking at me, without saying a word. I added, 'Mr Tims, he did tell I as he'd be wi' his roses.'

Joe shook himself. 'Reckon you look like a rose yourself this morning, young Amy.' Then his sunburnt face reddened. 'He's mebbe in the autumn rose garden – but he often takes that yellow bitch of his down to the pond for a swim of a morning. She likes her swim, that dog does. Tell you what, you go along to the autumn rose garden, and if he baint there carry on through the gate in the far wall and down the track to the pond. That garden's over the other side of the house, so I'll show you the path that runs along behind the hedge – that way you won't be seen from the windows. Mr Hicks says we maun be careful, with guests being here.' When I thanked him for his trouble, he said firmly, 'Baint no trouble about it, young Amy – 'tis my pleasure.'

I reached the gate in the wall, opened it – and stepped into a fairy tale. The air was warm and heavy with the scent of a thousand roses. I could see them joyously growing in bushes, gaily climbing up into trees, and exuberantly scaling every available piece of wall. Blush pink, pure white, dark red, palest of golden yellows – I laughed aloud with delight at the sight of them, and every one laughed with me. I walked onto the soft turf holding out my hands to them on either side, and their velvet petals brushed my fingers in greeting. When I reached the small green lawn at the heart of that garden I stopped and looked around me. Truly, it was an enchanted garden. I had been quite wrong in thinking that Lord Warminster's rose garden would be like the one at Nether Court – this wasn't a rose garden, but a garden for roses. A garden for roses, where they could bloom safe and happy behind their sheltering walls.

There were no clipped pyramids or spindly standards here; these roses weren't forced to go where they didn't want to. Instead they were helped, with discreet wooden supports slipped under their stems, when they wished to ramble further than they could safely reach. They were not trained but guided – guided into a warmer corner, or up onto a wall where they could fan out and bask in the autumn sun. They were enclosed in this walled garden, but not as captives – no, they had chosen to grow here, here where they knew they would be protected, cared for – and loved.

Wandering amidst those roses I spotted an old friend, and ran joyfully to greet her. The Seven Sisters was sunning herself on a wall; she bore great clusters of blooms, in all the shades from white to pink to mauve – and every one of them was smiling at me. Nearby, in the corner, climbed another rose I recognised from Nether Court; there the pretty Blush Noisette had been chained to a pillar, her heads drooping like captive maidens, but here she tossed her petals so vigorously that every one had blushed with delight. Even her buds were jaunty and carefree, seeming to say to me: 'Look at us – baint we pretty!' 'Aye, thee do bist so,' I replied

240

– and in gratitude she showed me her secret. There was a recess let into the corner where the two walls met, with the arched entrance almost hidden by her hanging sprays. Gently I lifted one and slipped inside a small, circular room which had a wooden seat running all round it and a white domed ceiling. I sat down, breathing in the spicy scent of the rose, and looking out though the lacy veil of her blooms – looking out to yet more roses, to roses everywhere.

As as I sat there I fell under the spell of that enchanted garden: I became Beauty in the rose garden of the Beast, living in a fairy tale. But gradually the fairy story merged with reality, and became the truth. I knew now why this beautiful garden had been created – because the Beast had fallen in love with Lady Warminster. She was beautiful, and he was crippled and twisted – so he had grown a garden for her, just as the Beast had done for Beauty. And living in his house, walking in his garden, she, like Beauty, had come to love him.

I rose to my feet and stepped out into the warm, scented air, treading gently over the soft carpet of fallen petals. I closed my eyes and stood breathing the scent of her flowers and caressing the blooms on her rose bushes – until I seemed to hear the rustle of her silken skirts, and could see, behind my lids, the smile on her beautiful face and the silver-gold of her shining hair curling up under her beribboned hat. She stepped delicately across the lawn in front of me – and when I raised my lids my eyes seemed to catch the last flicker of her skirts as she glided past. I held my breath a moment in wonder, and then the tears came to my eyes as I remembered that she was dead, and the Beast was alone now in his great house, mourning her. But then my heart lifted, because her son – he was alive and loved me. I was sure of that now as I stood in her garden. I knew he would marry me and take care of me, just as his father had loved and cherished his mother; and my sadness turned to joy at the thought of him.

It was then that I saw the white rose; she was climbing the wall in the other corner, happily, light-heartedly, but a little shyly – because she was a shy rose. There was no mistaking the deep green of her leaves or the way her flowers clung together, nestling up to each other for company, and as I ran towards her I saw the pink tips of her plump buds – those distinctive plump buds of my rose from Bath.

I reached out my hands to cradle a cluster of her delicate white blooms, exclaiming, 'I found thee – I did find thee at last.' Her velvet petals brushed my fingertips as I told her: 'I bin looking for 'ee everywhere, and thee bist hiding in thic corner all o' the time. I did look for thee at Nether Court, but thee wasn't there.' She shook her head, as if in apology. 'Oh, thee maunt be sorry for that – thee wouldn't've been happy in thic there rose garden. Roses there be all clipped and trained, proper kept in their places, they be. Thee bist much happier blooming here, I can see that. Only – if thee'd been at Nether Court I'd a' found out thy name, from them liddle china labels, but now I still dussent know it.' She looked at me as if she were longing to tell, so I asked her directly: 'My rose – what bist thy name?'

And a voice said, 'Her name – is Amy Veebare.' There was a rustling, and a huge dark shadow spread over the grass. I looked up, and there, looming in the archway, stood the Beast.

And because I was in his enchanted garden there was no fear in my heart, so smiling up into his crooked face I exclaimed with delight, 'Then she be named for I – my name, 'tis Amy.' The Beast twisted his ungainly body and raising his huge furry paw, very gently snapped a stem and held out one perfect white spray. Dropping a curtsey I said, 'Thank 'ee, my lord.' And took it from him.

Then the air shimmered and wavered, the spell lifted – and Lord Warminster stood before me with his twisted neck, humped back and sad, mismatched eyes. Nella padded out of the recess and thrust her wet nose into my palm. Bending to pat her soft head I delivered my message: 'Miss Annabel, she did say she would be pleased to drive wi' you thic afternoon.'

His sadness lifted a little as he replied, 'Tell – her I – will be waiting.' Then he turned and lurched back into the small room with his newspaper in one hand and Nella at his heels.

Miss Annabel was alone again when I got back. She jumped up from her desk with an impatient, 'Well, did you give him my message?'

'Yes, and he did say he'd be waiting.'

'Good. What's that you've got in your hand?'

''Tis a rose that be called for me. Amy, Amy Veebare, he said her name be.'

'How kind of him. There's a vase on the mantelpiece, you can put it in water. Apparently he never allows his roses to be picked and brought into the house, so I am honoured.' I opened my mouth to say that he'd given it to me – but of course, he hadn't. It was the Beast who'd given it to me; Lord Warminster would have meant it for Miss Annabel. I picked up the vase and took it along to the housemaid's pantry to fill it.

Miss Annabel sent for me straight after lunch. 'Quickly, get out my hat-boxes. I must choose the prettiest.' She ran to the mirror and peered in. 'I'm in good looks today, aren't I, Amy?'

'Yes Miss Annabel, you always are.'

She spun round, her dark eyes sparkling and her cheeks pink. 'I'll show that oaf what he's lost. Bring me those hats.'

She looked lovely when she was ready to go. 'Am I smart enough to drive with an earl, Amy?'

'Oh yes, Miss Annabel. That colour do suit you.'

'I prefer earls to their sons! By the way, take that parcel back to him today – now – it's polluting my room. Deliver the letter as well.'

My heart was thudding – I was going to see him. Mr Tims almost managed a smile. 'You are busy today, Miss Roberts. His young Lordship went down the corridor that leads to the billiard room – he's either in there or in the gunroom.'

I found him in the billiard room. He was slumped in an armchair with his long legs sprawled out in front of him and his hands jammed into his jacket pockets. He looked up without smiling. 'Oh, it's you, Amy. What do you want?'

With hammering heart I held out the little parcel and the envelope. 'Miss Annabel sent I wi' these.' Then I added, for the first time, 'My lord.'

His eyes were fixed on the parcel. 'I can guess what *that* is.' He took the envelope, ripped it open and scanned the sheet inside. His mouth set in a grim line, then he crumpled it up and scudded it into the empty hearth. 'See if I care. Where is she, your mistress?'

'She be gone for a drive – with His Lordship.'

'Oh, has she indeed?'

I held out the little parcel. 'Thic be for you, too.'

'I don't want it.'

'But she did say I maun –'

He interrupted angrily, 'You have it, Amy. You like jewellery, don't you? All girls do.'

'But – I – I couldn't!'

He shrugged. 'All right, toss it over.' He thrust it into his pocket, unopened.

I stood gazing down at him, until I'd plucked up the courage to say, 'My lord, I didn't know as you were Lord Quinham, not till I did come to Eston.'

He looked up, raising his eyebrows. 'Didn't you? I thought you'd have guessed by then.' I watched his face changing, becoming more cheerful. 'Good fun, wasn't it? Do you remember that day on the river?'

'Oh yes,' I said fervently. ''Twere the most wonderfullest day o' my whole life.'

He laughed. 'I enjoyed it, too – lying back at my ease while you popped morsels of chicken into my mouth.' He suddenly sprang to his feet, towering over me. '*You* don't think I'm a selfish, overbearing oaf – do you, Amy?'

'No, oh no!'

'Loyal little five foot three Amy.' He moved closer. 'And you're even more beautiful than she is.' His face as he looked down at me seemed darker, more intent; his voice deepened. 'God, you're a lovely girl. You're like a ripe peach. I told you that when we were on the river – do you remember?'

'Aye. I do remember every word you ever did say to I.'

'Amy, that day, I wanted to – but it wasn't possible then. But now, you're here, looking so beautiful, so tempting – I'm a man, Amy, with a man's needs. Do you understand?' I couldn't answer, but I felt my whole face burning. 'Of course you do – you're a warm, loving little girl.' He was very close to me now. 'Amy, do you love me?'

I whispered, 'Yes.'

'Then let me come to your room tonight.'

I was drowning in his gaze, but I shook my head. 'No – it baint right.'

'But you say you *love* me, Amy.'

'But –'

'It's very simple. Either you love me or you don't – and if you love me then you'll let me come to you tonight.' I couldn't answer.

His voice became more insistent as he said, 'Amy, I *need* you – and I want you so much.' I could sense his longing. 'Please, Amy.'

I looked up into his blue eyes. 'Do you love me?'

He laughed. 'So that's what's worrying you.' He reached out his arm and pulled me close against his chest. His face nuzzled my hair and I felt the touch of his lips on my ear as he murmured, 'Of course I do. I'm deuced fond of you, Amy, you must know that.'

So I whispered, 'Yes.' It was a sin, I knew it was a sin – but how could I say no?

He released me, asking, 'Which is your room?' He had to repeat the question; then, with my head bent so I didn't meet his eyes, I told him – before turning and running out of the door.

Chapter Thirty-One

I knew it was a sin, a terrible sin – but he needed me. I shut my mind to everything but that one thought. He needed me, and so tonight he would come to me and I would give him all that I had, because I loved him; and afterwards we would belong together, for ever.

Miss Stonor came in for a gossip while I was dressing Miss Annabel for dinner. My hands moved mechanically with comb and hairpins and I scarcely heard what Miss Annabel was saying about Lord Warminster, and what a good landlord he was, but then I heard her refer to 'Francis' – and at once my body was taut and aware. She said, 'He was playing tennis with Tom as we drove past, and they must have just finished their match, because I saw him leap right over the net – what a horrid show-off he is! I don't know why I ever thought I cared for him.' Relief made my head swim; she didn't love him any more, so she wouldn't mind when he married me. She caught my eye in the mirror. 'You're very quiet this evening, Amy. You're not *still* fretting about having offended Lord Warminster, are you?'

Before I could collect my wits and reply Miss Stonor broke in with a giggle, 'I'm sure she doesn't need to – judging by the state this house is in he's far too easygoing with his maidservants. Shall I go and fetch Joan, Annabel? Then we can all go down together.'

Down in the Room at supper Mrs Johnstone pounced on me. 'Is it true, Miss Roberts – Henry says your lady wasn't wearing her ring at lunch?'

'I – she'm sent it back to Lord Quinham.'

'Well, I never! That *was* a short engagement!'

Miss Abbott's firm voice interrupted us. 'Miss Roberts and I do *not* discuss our employers' private affairs, do we, Miss Roberts?'

'No, Miss Abbott.'

My mind kept repeating, 'tis a sin – but my heart replied, he loves me and he needs me. Besides, it was only fornication, not adultery which was a Commandment – and I was willing to sin for

246

him, suffer for him – because I loved him so. My head stopped whirling, and I became calm. He loved me and he needed me – that was all that mattered.

Miss Annabel came up early; she said she was tired and wanted to go straight to bed. She hardly spoke, except to scold me for tugging her hair as I plaited it. The minute she dismissed me I rushed upstairs to my room. With shaking hands I undressed, washed and put on my clean nightie. Then I climbed into bed and lay there trembling, waiting for him.

I didn't have long to wait. The door-handle turned softly, and before I had time to move he was inside my room. 'Good evening, Amy.' He stood there, his fair hair gleaming in the lamplight, and the hint of a smile on his lips. Then he held out his hands to me. I stood up and went to him, but I was too shy to lift my head; the fierce gold dragons on his brocade dressing gown shimmered and danced before my eyes. Gently his hands cupped my chin. 'Let's have a look at you, Amy.'

I raised my face to his, gazing up at him, and a silken lock of hair fell forward onto his forehead as he stared down at me. His breathing quickened. 'You're beautiful, Amy – absolutely beautiful. And you're more beautiful than ever tonight, looking at me so adoringly with those golden pansy eyes of yours – and blushing. You blush like a rose, Amy, petal by petal.'

I couldn't look away, I was drowning in his gaze. He bent his head and his lips covered mine, firm and warm – then I felt his tongue probing and sprang back, trembling. He laughed. 'So it *is* the first time for you, Amy – my shy little golden rose.' I saw the pleasure on his face as he said, 'To think – all this beauty, and *I'm* to be the first man to enjoy it. Come here.'

As I moved towards him my eyes never left his. He pulled me into his arms, then, still holding me tight, he took my right hand and guided it inside his dressing gown. Underneath it he was naked. I tried to draw away, but his grip was too strong. I felt his heart beating under the silken smooth skin of his chest, then he pulled my hand sharply down and there was the crispness of hair, and then –

'No!'

'Yes, Amy – yes.' And he was stronger than I was; he forced my fingers open and pushed his rod into my palm. It was warm and full and throbbing. 'That's for you, Amy – all for you. Just a little pain, and then he'll give you all the pleasure in the world.' Then his voice changed, becoming deep and urgent. 'Now you see why I couldn't wait any longer – and I can't now. Quickly, over to the bed.' And suddenly everything happened at once. Even before I'd scrambled onto the bed he was tossing up the skirt of my nightie and the minute I was on my back, confident hands gripped my thighs, separating them. I closed my eyes as my body began to shake with fear. 'You'll only feel a little prick, Amy.'

I heard his laughter, then it stopped abruptly and the pain came. It was like the blade of a knife tearing me apart and I cried out against his muffling chest, 'No – please – no!' But there was no reply, only the knife slicing into me again and again. I clenched my fists until at last he stopped moving and the knife was finally stilled.

I was sobbing as he lifted himself off me. 'Poor little Amy, did I hurt you, my pet? Never mind, it's all over now.' He pulled me close against his chest and I clung to him while the pain slowly eased to an aching soreness. He whispered in my ear, 'No doubt about your maidenhead, was there? At first I thought I wasn't going to get in!' He drew away and lay back, stretching. 'God, it's so long since I've had a virgin I'd forgotten how exciting it is – and how messy.' He reached over me to where his dressing gown lay crumpled on the floor. 'Lucky I came prepared.' He shook out a white silk handkerchief, and through tear-blurred eyes I watched as he carefully wiped his blood-smeared rod. When he'd finished he smiled at me. 'You'd better go and wash that pretty little fanny of yours.'

Shaking, I scrambled off the bed and went over to the washstand. Once there I looked back to where he lay sprawled out on the bed. He grinned. 'No point being shy now, Amy.'

I whispered, 'Willst thee close thy eyes? Do 'ee promise?'

He laughed. 'All right – I promise.' I watched until his long fair lashes had dropped, then I seized hold of the soap and flannel.

I'd nearly finished washing myself when I heard a match striking behind me. I turned my head quickly – and saw that his eyes were wide open, and focused on my behind. 'Lovely little arse you've got there, Amy.'

'You did promise you wouldn't look!'

He threw back his head, laughing. 'Promises like that are made to be broken. Come back and keep me warm while I smoke my cigarette.'

I ran back to nestle close against him; flinging his free arm around my shoulder he gave me a quick hug. I lay cuddled close to his chest, with my head tucked into his shoulder, gazing down at the smooth curve of his hip and the long, shapely length of his leg, with its dusting of fine golden hairs leading to the narrow, arched foot. His body was as perfect as the statues of the Greek god which had stood in Mr Venn's studio.

I breathed in the exciting, unfamiliar scent of gentlemen's cigarettes as he silently smoked, and knew I had to tell him. Without looking up I whispered, 'There be something as thee ought to know about I – I should a' told 'ee afore.'

He asked lazily, 'What's that, Amy my pet?'

I drew a deep, painful breath and said, 'I were born out of wedlock.'

'Good Lord!' He sounded surprised, but not angry. Then he added, 'I bet your mistress doesn't know about that.'

'No – nobody do know.' My voice quavered.

He pulled me closer for a moment. 'Well, don't worry, Amy. Your secret's safe with me.' Relief washed over me. He knew, and he didn't mind – his voice had been so calm, so matter-of-fact. I turned and put my arms tight round his chest. 'Ready for more already? I thought it wouldn't be long.' He reached over and stubbed out his cigarette in my candlestick-holder. 'But let's get rid of this nuisance of a nightdress first, shall we?'

'No, I couldn't . . .'

Laughing he said, 'Amy, you are a little goose.' Then his voice became firm as he ordered, 'Stop all this false modesty and take that nightdress off.' Trembling I turned my back on him and did as he'd commanded. 'Turn round – I want to see you properly.' I backed into the shadows, but he sprang to his feet, picked up the lamp and came walking towards me. 'Stand still, Amy.' He lifted the lamp up high, so I stood full in its light, naked before him. He began to speak, slowly and softly. 'God, you're lovely. The whole of your body is perfect, from those small rosy virgin's nipples to that faint smear of virgin's blood on your thigh. You're a pocket-sized Venus, Amy. If only I could pick you up and put you in my jacket pocket and carry you around with me all the time, so that you'd be there, waiting for me whenever I needed you. Would you like that, Amy?'

I whispered, 'Yes – oh yes.'

'I need you now, Amy.' He nodded his head towards the bed and I ran to it and lay down. At once he was on top of me, and I heard him saying, 'You'll enjoy it this time, Amy,' as he parted my thighs. Now the knife was a red-hot poker burning deep inside me but he'd told me I'd enjoy it so in my head I kept saying over and over again, 'I'm enjoying it, I'm enjoying it,' and the poker still seared my body but it was as if I wasn't in it any more – there was just my heart and my mind, loving him.

Afterwards he said, 'There, you enjoyed that, didn't you?'

And I whispered, 'Yes – oh yes.'

'Me too!' He pulled me close, and the soreness didn't matter any more. I had pleased him, that was all that mattered in the whole wide world. I fell asleep against his chest.

He woke me again much later. 'Amy, Amy.' The faint grey light of early dawn showed at the window. 'Amy.' His voice became more urgent, as his hand squeezed my breast. 'Wake up, Amy – I need you again.'

I screwed my eyes tight shut and put the palms of my hands flat against his back, and the feel of his smooth strong muscles working helped me to endure the pain of the poker burning into my belly, until at last he'd spent himself again. Then he pulled away quickly, reaching down for his dressing gown.

I whispered in dismay, 'Bist thee leaving I?'

'Must do, Amy – the old man gets up cursed early. I don't want to be caught roaming around the corridors – and the traditional: "I was just looking for the WC" excuse will hardly wash here, since this is supposed to be my home.' I felt his lips brush my forehead – and then he was gone.

I got up straight away. When I'd lit the lamp I saw that there was a lot of blood on the bottom sheet – and felt weak with relief that I'd sent Bertha packing that first day, and now no one came into my room. I went to wash myself first, and saw fresh blood on my flannel. I clutched at the marble edge of the wash-stand, feeling sick and giddy, then I took a hold of myself. It was a sign of how much he loved me – he'd wanted me again, even though it was so early in the morning – he hadn't been able to wait. And I, I had given myself to him gladly, because I loved him so much.

Chapter Thirty-Two

By the time the damp sheet was spread out over the chair by the open window it was fully light. Automatically I began my preparations for the day ahead, checking over in my mind the outfits Miss Annabel might want to wear – then all of a sudden I realised what I'd done. I was a maid no longer. I ran to the mirror and peered at my face – did it show, would people be able to tell? As my shame burnt my cheeks I shrank back, trying to hide my guilt, but I knew that eventually I'd have to leave the shelter of that room.

As I took in Miss Annabel's tea tray I felt as though my face were branded; but her expression didn't change as she sat up and looked across at me. 'I think I'll wear my olive walking costume first, Amy – it's a little chilly today.'

That morning seemed to drag and drag. Once, when I was tidying Miss Annabel's room, I heard voices on the terrace below. I went to the window and stood at the side, peering down around the curtain at the gaily patterned parasols and creamy boaters below – they all sounded so happy. Then a boater tilted and I caught a glimpse of his face, flushed by the sun. My heart leapt, before he moved out of sight and I heard the sound of girls' laughter. I backed away into the room. I didn't belong out there – I was only a servant. Tears prickled behind my eyelids, then the soreness of my cunny as I moved reminded me – he loved me, he needed me. A thrill of pure happiness rippled through my body at the thought, and I went back to my work with a light heart.

After lunch Miss Annabel rang for me. 'Get out my tennis costume, Amy.' Her eyes were shining and she looked so very happy that I thought she could never really have loved him, else she wouldn't be so cheerful now. The guilt I'd been feeling towards her eased as I went to fetch her white linen skirt and blouse.

I was up in my room later, darning a pair of her silk stockings, when there was a tap at the door – it was Clara. 'Your lady's broken a shoelace – you'll have to take a spare out to her.'

Mr Tims told me that the tennis court was over beyond the kitchen garden. I heard shouts and the thwack of balls, and hurried towards them. As I came round the corner of the wall I saw that he was playing; his long, slim legs flashed as he ran forward, his racquet sliced through the air – and the ball sailed triumphantly over the net. Then I heard Miss Annabel's voice. 'Quickly, Amy – I'm playing in the next match.' I dropped to my knees in front of her and began to unlace her shoe. The minute I'd tied the bow she jumped to her feet. 'They've nearly finished. Betty, where's Tom got to? Ah, there he is! Tom – you're wanted!' I dared only one last, fleeting glance, before turning and walking back to the house on feet that dragged.

But as I was climbing the back stairs I heard swift footsteps behind me; I swung round – and it was him. His face glistened with sweat as he gave me a smile of welcome, and I ran back down to him, my heart thumping with joy. He caught my hand, tugging me along. 'Quick, I haven't much time.' I panted along beside him until suddenly he shifted his grip to my arm, propelling me sideways. 'In here. The maids'll be all downstairs by now.' And he bundled me into the housemaid's closet.

'But –'

'I know it smells a bit – but we won't be long.' He jammed the door shut with a broom-handle before turning back to me. 'God, Amy, you certainly know how to get a man excited, don't you? The way you were kneeling there with your little backside stuck up in the air – I could hardly keep my hands off you!' He shivered, and I smiled at him, but he was bending down, rooting on the floor. 'Only snag is, you're too short – still, this should do the trick.' He reached under the wash-up sink and dragged out a box. 'Stand on that, and lean back against the wall.'

I stepped up onto the box in bewilderment. 'Did you want to speak to me, in private?'

He glanced up, surprised; then his teeth flashed in a quick grin. 'You are slow sometimes, Amy. No, I want to fuck you – in private.' He began to unbutton his trousers. 'Now get your drawers down. I haven't got much time – I'm playing in the next match.'

My protests died unvoiced. With shaking hands I did as he bid me. As he came towards me I tried to back away – but there was nowhere to go. I was trapped against the wall. 'Stop fidgeting, Amy! How on earth can I get it in if you keep wriggling sideways? Here –' he seized hold of my behind and held it like a vice as he thrust himself into me. I gasped aloud in pain. He panted into my ear, 'Feels good, does it? I'll bet you've been waiting for this all day. Once girls of your class get a taste of it they can't have enough.' My back bounced against the wall as he rammed his rod into me again and again. Because I was up on the box I could see over his shoulder. Fighting to keep back the tears I focused my eyes on the chain opposite – the chain that hung down from the cistern over the slop sink. The brass links were dulled, and the wooden handle was greasy from much use – even the tiles behind it were splattered and smeared from carelessly thrown slops. How appalled Mrs Harper would be if she could see the state of this closet.

At last he stopped thrusting, and I felt him spurt inside me. As he spent himself I remembered a voice from the past: 'A man, he do put his diddler in a woman's cunny and give her a squirt.' He finished, and started to draw back; as he came out I felt the slimy ooze begin to trickle down the inside of my thighs. I dropped my skirts, not looking at him.

'Amy – you're still bleeding! For goodness' sake, if I've got blood on my white flannels . . .' He bent down to look. 'Seems to be OK, but you really should have warned me. I say,' his voice was suspicious now, 'it's not your monthlies, is it?'

'No, they baint due for a fortnight.'

'That's all right then.' He pulled his trousers up and took out his cigarette case. I bent to pull up my drawers, but his voice stopped me. 'No, leave them down – I'll be wanting you again in a minute.' He flicked his spent match into the wash-up sink behind him and inhaled. As he breathed the smoke out again he laughed. 'You've got a renewable maidenhead there, Amy my pet – you could make a fortune in a French brothel. Now you're going to have to learn another little French trick, because although I have every intention of presenting my compliments to you again this after-noon I am deuced short of time – so while I'm smoking you'll have to give me a rub.' I just stood there, staring at him as he sat on the wooden rim of the wash-up sink, his trousers gaping open. 'Come on Amy, jump down from that box and get a grip of it.'

I looked at where it flopped limply against the sweat-darkened hair of his crotch. 'I cassent –'

His voice sharpened with impatience. 'You were ready enough last night. Don't start playing the shrinking violet with me – I know better. Get hold of it.' Forcing back a shudder I reached in and took the slimy loose skin in my hand. 'For goodness' sake, Amy – I'm not interested in a circumcision. Get hold of it properly, *all* of it. Right now, up and down – no, not so quickly –' Eventually he was satisfied. 'That's it, just the ticket, it's doing me a power of good already. Tell you what, while you're at it, open the top buttons of your blouse.' My other hand moved mechanically as I fumbled with the buttons. 'Camisole as well. Now, pull yourself out a bit – not too much, I like a bit of a tease. Mm, that's nice, now you look like a girl who can't wait for another ration! And that's right, isn't it Amy? Can't wait, can you? And nor can I – you can feel it now, can't you?' I nodded dumbly as his rod began to fill and swell under my moving fingers.

He stubbed out his cigarette on the dirty china rim of the sink. 'That'll have to do. Nip back up on your box.' I shuffled awkwardly back up, my drawers tangling round my ankles. 'Skirts up – let's have a look at you – I never had time before. Mm – nice, very nice.' I felt my belly blush scarlet as he stared fixedly at my cunny, then he shook himself and looked up, smiling. 'More time for that tonight, eh, Amy my pet? But I'd better get a move on now. I'm not really ready yet, but I can't wait any longer. I'm due back on court – so you'll have to put it in for me.'

'Put it in?' My voice rose in panic. 'But I cassent –'

'Don't be silly – you must know where it goes. Open your legs – wider.' He braced his arms either side of me, his rod pressing against me. 'Put it *in*!' I took hold of it again and somehow managed to force it inside the aching soreness of my cunny. At once he began to push, hard – and soreness turned to the sharp bite of pain as he gripped my behind and pushed over and over again. It was like a nightmare, going on and on for ever, and then he said accusingly, 'You aren't bringing me off – you should be *helping* me, Amy.' His voice was sharp with irritation.

I whispered apologetically, 'I dussent know how.'

He gave an impatient sigh. 'No, I suppose not – you'll have to learn. I know, give me a kiss.' I turned my mouth to his. 'Open!' I opened my lips and his came down and covered mine. His tongue forced its way into my mouth and began pushing and thrusting in time with his rod below – deeper and deeper both of them – my mouth was full of him, my belly was full of him. I couldn't breathe, I couldn't move – my whole body had been invaded. Panic welled up and I began to choke, then suddenly his tongue withdrew and as I gasped for breath I realised his rod had stopped moving. I began to sag down against the wall but his hands caught me and held me pressed tight against his belly so he could spend himself inside me again. I stared at the chain of the cistern, waiting for him to finish.

He pulled away, panting, and sat down on the edge of the sink again. 'I'll have to get my breath back after that.'

I whispered, 'Can I – can I pull my drawers up now, please?'

'Lord, yes. You've sucked me dry for this afternoon.' He glanced up at my face. 'Sorry I was ratty, Amy. It's just that it's damned unpleasant for a man when he thinks he's not quite going to make it.' He grinned. 'And now I've got to go and play another game of tennis!' Then his face flushed red, and he looked away from me as he stood up.

I asked quickly, 'Bist thee coming to my room tonight?'

'Well – I don't know.' I reached out a tentative hand and touched his sleeve. He smiled at me. 'You want me to come, don't you, Amy?' I nodded. He shrugged, 'Well, it's happened now – another night or two won't make any difference. Besides, it's all your fault, Amy.' He reached down and pulled up his trousers. 'There I was, playing a peaceful game of tennis when suddenly this little serving wench appears and starts flashing her ankles and jiggling her arse at me, and –' He broke off with a rueful grin. 'We men are helpless in the face of feminine wiles – we don't have a chance when a woman sets out to seduce us. You're such a little tease, Amy, how could I help –' He shrugged again. 'Oh well, *tant pis* – and talking about pee, housemaid's closets are handy places, as I've discovered in the past.' He turned and put his cock over the low rim of the slop sink; I looked away quickly, but I could hear the splash and smell the sharp tang of piss. When he'd finished he swung round and fastened his buttons with one hand while unbarring the door with the other. 'Must fly, or they'll come looking for me.' He left.

Even through the tears welling up in my eyes I could see the squalor of that closet – and the yellow puddle of urine that lay at the bottom of the slop sink. With shaking hands I reached for the chain, pulled it hard and flung myself through the door and out into the corridor – then stopped dead. Lord Warminster was walking towards me. I heard swift footsteps receding behind me and turned for a moment to catch a last glimpse of my own lord's fair head disappearing down the servants' stairs. Lord Warminster was looking straight over my head to where his son had gone from view; I flattened myself against the wall of the corridor, praying he wouldn't notice me. But as he came level with me he swung his whole head and shoulders round, staring down at my crumpled skirt. Slowly his eyes moved up to where my sweat-stained blouse gaped open, and then on to my dishevelled hair. I stood frozen like a rabbit before a stoat as his gaze finally came to rest on my face. Disgust twisted his mouth and darkened his eyes – then, moving his huge body very deliberately, he drew as far away from me as he could, and continued his lurching progress down the corridor.

Back in my room I frantically pulled off my stained blouse and creased skirt, then ran to the wash-stand and poured water into the bowl with hands that wouldn't stop shaking; my cunny stung from the soap but still I scrubbed and scrubbed at it, desperate to be clean again. Then I stumbled over to the bed and flung myself down, pressing my face into the pillow – but still in my mind I was back in that wretched little closet, still seeing the chain hanging from the cistern, still hearing my lord panting and grunting as he drove his rod into me, still smelling the stink of the drains, and the reek of his sweat and his piss. I felt soiled, unclean – and finally the image I'd been desperately keeping at bay forced its way into my mind's eye; I saw Peg, standing with skirts lifted and legs splayed, serving the men in the dark alleyway, one after the other. This afternoon, my lord had used me in the same way. I began to sob and sob.

After I'd finished crying I felt limp and empty, but then I reminded myself that it wasn't the same, because he loved me. And I loved him. Yesterday I'd told myself that I'd willingly sin for him, suffer for him because I loved him so – I had no right to weep today. He had seen me on the tennis court and at once he'd left his friends to come to me – that showed how much he cared for me –

257

and he'd expressed his love in the simplest, most obvious way that a man could. Tonight, it would be different. He would take me in his arms and tell me how beautiful I was, and how he wanted to put me in his pocket and keep me with him always. Caressing me, he would smile as he called me, 'Amy my pet,' and when it was all over he would hold me close until I fell asleep against his warm chest. I got up and splashed my eyes, then I picked up my darning again, waiting until Miss Annabel sent for me.

She didn't ring until just before the dressing bell. As I went in she greeted me with a smile. 'Lovely, tea on the lawn. I do like Eston – it isn't as well run as Nether Court, but it has such an old-fashioned, gracious feel about it. Run my bath for me, Amy.'

She was humming to herself as I hooked her into her evening frock and went over to the dressing table. I backcombed her hair and arranged it in elaborate swathes and coils, so it framed the perfect oval of her face; then I picked up the hand mirror and held it to back and sides so she could inspect my handiwork. 'Mm – it was certainly worth sending you to those hairdressing lessons, Amy.' She smiled at me in the mirror. 'Now hand me my jewel case.' She took it from me, flicked up the lid, reached inside – and in one smooth movement slid a ring onto her finger. As she spread out her hand and lifted it to the light the stone sparkled and shone; it was a diamond – the diamond of her engagement ring.

I would have stood there for ever, just staring at it, but at that moment the door opened and Miss Stonor came rushing in. 'Annabel! Joan's just told me – I *am* so pleased. Now I can be a bridesmaid after all.' I heard Miss Annabel's laugh, and the rustle of silk as they embraced. Then Miss Stonor's triumphant voice rang out again. 'I guessed this morning, the way the pair of you were whispering together on the terrace. I said to Joan: "I bet the lovebirds have made it up," and I was right, wasn't I?' Miss Annabel nodded, laughing as the door opened a second time. 'Joan! Isn't it wonderful?'

My hands folded and tidied mechanically – hearing but not registering the high, excited voices punctuated by squeals of laughter, until the merciful release came with Miss Annabel's casual, 'You may go now, Amy.'

I didn't think, I was beyond thinking. My feet took me straight to the bachelors' corridor – there were no footmen in sight and even if there had been I was far beyond all caution. I ran from door to door until I found the label I wanted, and then I burst straight in. He was standing in front of the mirror in his shirtsleeves, knotting his white bow-tie. He turned quickly to face me. 'Amy – for God's sake! What are you doing? You can't come in here.'

His voice, with its clipped, gentleman's accent, halted my rushing feet. He moved swiftly past me to slam the door, then came back to where I stood – and my frantic courage oozed away in the face of his gleaming white shirt-front and the faultless line of his black dress trousers. I had to force myself to whisper, 'Miss Annabel – she be wearing your ring.'

He turned, reaching for his waistcoat, and I saw the faintest of flushes tinge his fair skin. When he'd fastened the buttons and settled the flaps he said, 'It appears she does care for me, after all, so it seemed a good idea to make it up.'

'But I thought – I thought you did love me?'

He reached out and seized both my hands. 'I do, Amy, I do. You're a delicious little thing and I'm deuced fond of you.' He grinned boyishly. 'Didn't I prove it to you this very afternoon?' He squeezed my fingers gently. 'And you enjoyed it too, didn't you? But Amy, my pet, whyever did you rush out after me like that? There I was, still buttoning up my trousers when I nearly cannoned into the old man and then seconds later *you* appeared – with your hair all over the place and skirt creased to blazes, looking for all the world like a girl who'd just enjoyed a thoroughly good fuck.' He laughed, before adding, 'As indeed you had. But Amy –' his smile changed to a frown '– because of your carelessness I've just been subjected to a most uncomfortable quarter of an hour in the library, being informed – between stammers – that my future income depends on my present good conduct while under this roof.' His frown deepened. 'The old hypocrite – he can nip up to his cosy little apartment at Kew whenever *he* feels like a bit of hanky-panky. Damn, there's the bell for dinner, and I'm not ready. Quick Amy, fetch my jacket.' He turned his back to me and automatically I slipped his jacket over his arms and lifted it to sit square on his shoulders. 'Is my tie straight?' I twitched it into position before he took a last glance in the mirror, then he strode over to the door saying, 'Now stay here for at least ten minutes, until you're sure everyone's gone down.'

259

He paused with his hand on the knob, and smiled at me. 'Don't look so sad, my pet. We'll have to keep apart for the time being, but it'll all come right in the wash. Now, stand well back from the door as I go out, and remember, don't move for ten minutes.' Raising his hand to his lips he kissed his fingers to me – and was gone.

I sat through supper in the Room forcing myself to chew the unwanted food and to make some kind of reply whenever I was spoken to. They were full of the news of the resumed engagement. 'I expect you'd guessed that they were going to make it up, eh, Miss Roberts?'

'No, no, I hadn't.'

'Quite right too,' Miss Abbott broke in. 'It's not our place to speculate about the emotions of our employers. Thank you, Mr Tims – I would care for a little more.'

It was very late when Miss Annabel rang. 'Poor Amy, had you dropped off? You do look washed out. Never mind, I won't keep you long – we're all brushing our hair together tonight.' As soon as Miss Fenwick and Miss Stonor arrived Miss Annabel dismissed me – then she called me back. 'By the way, Amy, we all went for a stroll in the autumn rose garden after dinner, so I asked Lord Warminster to show me the rose called Amy.' She paused for a smile before saying, 'You are a goose. It isn't Amy at all – it's a French rose called Aimée Vibert.' She threw back her head, laughing, and the other young ladies laughed with her. 'Anyway, it's started dropping now, so take it with you and throw it away.'

Outside in the corridor I laid my cheek against her white velvet petals; her scent had almost gone, and as I lifted my head more of her petals broke off and fluttered to the floor. Crouching down, I carefully picked up each one, then I carried her along to the rubbish box in the housemaid's closet. I told her, 'I be sorry my rose, but nobody do want us any more.' Then I dropped her in and closed the lid.

Chapter Thirty-Three

Upstairs I still couldn't believe it; this time yesterday he'd been holding me in his arms – and now it was all over. I looked at the pillow, and saw there was a dent in it from where his head had rested; I put my face down to that dent and the faint smell of his hair still clung to it. I lifted the pillow very gently off the bed, and set it down on a chair so I could put back the dry bottom sheet and make the bed for the night. When I'd finished I rested the pillow on top of the bolster in the exact place where it had been before. As soon as I was washed and wearing my nightie I climbed between the sheets and fitted my cheek carefully into the space where his head had lain. It was all I had left.

But in the middle of the night I woke up and realised that it wasn't. He'd spent himself inside me over and over again – and now I carried part of him in my belly. Frantic, I jumped up and squatted down on the floor by the bed, pushing and kneading at my belly, trying to force it out – but of course it was too late, I knew that really. I was carrying his seed, and if it chose to take root and grow inside me there was nothing I could do to stop it. And the full enormity of what I'd done finally hit me, so that I crouched shivering and terrified on the floor whispering, 'No – please, no!' But all I could see in my mind were the women in the Buildings, walking tired and slow, dragged down by the weight of their huge bellies. They had all worn wedding rings on their swollen fingers – but my hands were bare.

From then on it was as though I was two people living in the same body: one was the maid who took in Miss Annabel's early morning tea, who drew the curtains, ran her bath, dressed her hair; the other was a frantic mouse in a trap that kept whimpering, 'No – please, no!' I was constantly peering at my face in the mirror, convinced that it must show what I'd done, but nobody seemed to notice. We went back to Nether Court a couple of days later, and I thought it might be easier there, but it wasn't. When Mrs Harper spoke to me kindly or Mr Peake invited me to view his latest specimen in the glass-house I felt as though I were lying to them; they thought I was the same, but I wasn't. I'd done this terrible thing. And all the time my mind kept saying: 'No – please, no!'

I had to wait two weeks before my monthlies were due, and it seemed like two years. Then, early in the morning, I felt a dampness between my legs. I climbed out of bed trembling like an old woman, and stared down at my nightdress – it was dark with blood. I wasn't even a day late. I began to cry with relief.

But then I couldn't stop crying, and I realised it wasn't just relief. I was crying because I'd lost him. Worrying about the other had held my grief back, but now it all flooded out: he didn't want me. It was like that day in the workhouse when Grammer had cast me off; only worse, much worse, because underneath I'd always known that Grammer hated me, but my lord – he'd told me that he loved me, and I'd believed him.

Soon after we went up to London. The wedding was to be at St George's, Hanover Square, in the middle of November, so of course there was a lot to arrange. Going back to Belgrave Square where I'd dreamed about him as 'Mr Dunn' intensified my misery; my whole body seemed to be stretched and aching. I thought I couldn't bear it, but I had to. It helped that the worry and unhappiness had made me deathly tired, so at least I didn't lie awake any more at night. Sometimes I felt as if I was scarcely awake in the daytime, either – the tiredness helped, because it numbed my brain.

Then one day the old caretaker who'd come with the house was waiting for me as I came down the back stairs to supper. After looking furtively around to see no one was watching, he thrust a small package into my hand. ''E give it me – fer you. 'E said to tell you: "Don't let anyone see 'em." ' A brown mottled eyelid dropped over one rheumy eye in a grotesque wink and he sniggered, as he added, ''E always was a lad.' I turned round and ran back upstairs, carrying the small parcel as though it were made of the most delicate porcelain. As soon as I began to unwrap it I realised that it was a jeweller's box; with quickening heartbeats I eased up the lid, and there, nestling against the deep blue velvet lining was a pearl necklace. I stood looking at the glowing white beauty of it until the tears trickling down my cheeks blurred the three rows of separate pearls into one shining ribbon of promise. He still loved me.

That night I wove a new story: he had been too chivalrous to tell Miss Annabel that it was really me he loved, so he had allowed her to wear his ring again. But when he could, he would explain to her that his heart was given to another. She would release him and then he would come to me, his eyes smiling, his mouth laughing as he exclaimed, 'Amy, my pet – you didn't *doubt* me, did you?' I would not doubt him, ever again. Gently I placed the token of his love back in its box. Even in the seclusion of my room I wouldn't wear it around my neck; I would wait until he came and put it on with his own beloved hands – and then I would be truly his.

I never doubted him again, but I did begin to worry about Miss Annabel. What would she feel when he told her the truth? She would be so unhappy, and I didn't want her to be unhappy. Then Lord Warminster came to London, and gave me the solution. He invited Miss Annabel to Kew, to show her round the Botanic Gardens, and then he took her back to his apartment there, for tea. She didn't arrive home until very late, and her eyes were sparkling. I had to start dressing her at once – she was going out to dinner – and Mrs Hurst came in while I was doing her hair to ask her how she'd enjoyed her afternoon.

Miss Annabel smiled. 'It was most pleasant, Mama – he's such a well-read man, so cultured. It *is* a shame that he's so self-conscious about his appearance – after all, it isn't in any way repulsive, just extremely odd. And you know, if it hadn't been for that wretched torticollis he would have been *so* distinguished-looking. In profile he could easily be mistaken for Mr Forbes Robertson, when he played Julius Caesar that time, do you remember? Leonidas has the same splendid Roman nose and strong chin and noble forehead – and then he turns round . . . Oh, it is so sad.'

Mrs Hurst said, 'Leonidas? Did he ask you to call him that?'

'No, Mama – I told him he was far too young to be a father-in-law, so I would address him by his Christian name.'

'Annabel! That was extremely forward of you! Whatever must Lord Warminster have thought?'

'Oh, don't be stuffy, Mama – he likes me, I know he does. In fact, he's suggested that we make our home at Eston after we're married. I haven't spoken to Francis yet, but I'm sure he'll agree – it's such a lovely part of the country, and so healthy. We'll be in Town for the Season each year, of course, but London is no place for children. They'll be much better off in the country with their grand-father to keep an eye on them – I don't think it's right to abandon one's offspring entirely to the tender mercies of servants, as youngsters do pick up undesirable habits so easily. Oh, and Mama – I didn't tell you – Leonidas is going to teach me to read Greek! Isn't that marvellous? You know how I always wanted to learn, but Miss Lister only knew the alphabet – he *is* so kind.'

And suddenly I knew the answer. Lord Warminster was in love with Miss Annabel, and she liked him so much already that when my own lord told her he couldn't marry her after all, and she was sad, then Lord Warminster would comfort her. He would take her to walk in his rose garden every day, and slowly she would come to love him in return: it would be like Beauty and the Beast, all over again.

After Mrs Hurst had gone, and I was buttoning up Miss Annabel's gloves for her she said, 'By the way, Amy – how *did* you get hold of that white rose? Because I was telling Lord Warminster about Earl, and how the poor darling got restless in London, even though you took him out every morning first thing, and suddenly he said: "Are you sure your maid can be trusted?" And I immediately remembered that rose, and how Lady Burton told me he *never* allows his roses to be picked, and I thought, naughty little Amy, I'll wager she *stole* that rose – and he must have seen her doing it!' She glanced up at me, smiling. 'You look so guilty I know I'm right!' Picking up her fan she tapped my knuckles. 'You mustn't do it again, Amy – don't you remember your fairy tales, and what happened to poor Beauty when she stole a rose? Goodness, look at the time – I must dash.'

After I'd closed the door behind her I stood stock still, thoughts whirling in my head. But it was Miss Annabel who was to be Beauty and besides, it was Beauty's *father* who'd stolen the rose. In any case, I *hadn't* stolen it – Lord Warminster had given it to me himself. But that was before – and I knew why he'd asked her that question, and the knowledge made me shiver with shame and guilt.

But in bed that night I took out my box and opened it, and placed his pearls under my cheek, just as I did every night. And as they grew warm and comforting there I imagined my new story: it ran very smoothly right until the end, when Miss Annabel became a countess with a diamond tiara on her head, while I lived in a smaller house, and looked after my own lord's clothes myself. If his father was angry with him for marrying me, and didn't give him any money it wouldn't matter, because I could cook for him, and clean for him – and serve him every day. I kissed his pearls in the darkness, then put them back in their box. All I had to do was wait.

As I waited the trousseau began to arrive. Chemises and petticoats, camisoles and slip bodices, corsets, nightdresses and dozens of pairs of the finest silk hose were all delivered to the house, along with new frocks and costumes and hats. Then the presents started to come; so many presents, it did seem a shame they'd all have to be returned – except for one, the tiara and necklace of diamonds sent by Lord Warminster. They said in the Room how wonderfully generous it was of him, but then, they didn't know what I knew: that he was destined to be the bridegroom.

It was the day before the wedding, and still I waited for the message to come from my lord – and then, at last, it did. The caretaker slipped the note into my hand: *'Amy, meet me under the third lamp-post in Halkin Street. F. D.'* I stared at the scrawled words, my breath coming quick and shallow, then I seized my hat and jacket and ran down the back stairs.

He was already there, waiting for me. I paused a moment in my headlong rush, and stood clutching the stitch in my side – just gazing at him. So tall and straight and slim – then I saw him reach for his watch, and at once I panted on.

He saw me and came striding forward. 'Wherever have you been, my pet? I've been waiting for ages.'

'I –'

'Never mind, you're here now. I've only got a minute, so listen carefully. As soon as you're off-duty tonight come straight round to my rooms in Jermyn Street – Portland Chambers, Number Five. The porter'll send you up – I've told him to expect you.'

My head was in a whirl – it was to happen at last! He was turning to go before I found my voice. 'What shall I bring with me? What'll I need?'

'What?' Then he laughed. 'Oh, just the bare essentials.' Then his laughter deepened. 'Don't worry, my pet – I can give you

265

everything you need.' Suddenly he caught my hand and lifted it to his lips. 'God, Amy – you're even lovelier than I remembered! I can hardly bear to wait till tonight.' I felt the fleeting warmth of his kiss on my fingers, then with a murmured: 'Be as quick as you can,' he left me standing in the street, my heart ablaze with love and joy.

I could hardly stop myself dancing along the pavement on my way back to Belgrave Square. Gladys saw me coming in and smiled. 'My, you do look cheerful this afternoon, Miss Roberts. Anybody'd think it was you who was the one getting married in the morning.'

But I was the one! Tonight I would go to him, and tomorrow we would be wed. My heart sang as I ran upstairs and straight over to where I'd hidden my jewel box. I opened it and took his pearls in my hand, caressing them with the tips of my fingers – how could I ever have doubted him? Tonight he would clasp them around my neck, and tomorrow he would put his ring on my finger, and I would be his for ever.

My joy was checked when Miss Annabel rang for me, but I pushed the sense of betrayal aside. He didn't love her, he loved me. It was Lord Warminster who loved her, and soon she would learn to love him in return – and become a countess.

Miss Annabel hardly spoke to me as I dressed her; she said she was tired and would be going straight to bed after dinner. Later, when she was in her wrap and I'd nearly finished brushing her hair, Mrs Hurst came along to the bedroom. Miss Annabel turned to her mother with a smile. 'You may go now, Amy.' I rushed upstairs.

I found my basket. I would have to take my nightdress at least – men didn't understand – and a change of underwear; but he was right, there was no point in taking any of my clothes. As Lady Quinham I would have to dress quite differently. Lady Quinham! I'd hardly dared to even think those magical words, but now I said them aloud, savouring them. Oh, how I loved him!

I put on my best pink satin dress blouse, and black serge skirt, and coiled my hair up on my head in one of the elaborate styles I'd been taught at Monsieur Paul's. I wanted to be beautiful for him tonight. Then I remembered he'd told me to be quick – so I rushed to the chest of drawers, pulled out my things and hastily packed them in the basket, along with my precious box. Just as I was leaving I ran back and found Esau; I thrust him down the side, out of sight – but I couldn't leave him behind. Then I scampered down the stairs and out of the back door, into the stable-yard.

Once I was safely out of the house my feet grew wings, and I seemed to fly along Piccadilly. I was panting by the time I turned into St James' so I slowed down. I mustn't arrive red-faced and out of breath. Portland Chambers loomed over me, ornate and imposing, and I was frightened for a moment. Then I thought that there was no need for fear tonight, because I was going to my lord. I pushed open the great wooden door and walked over to the porter's desk. He grinned. 'Up the stairs to the first floor, miss, then turn to your right – it's just along the corridor.'

The corridor was carpeted; it was very hushed and still – except for the pounding of my heart as I pressed the bell. Then my lord himself opened the door, and at the sight of his eager face my whole being was flooded with happiness. 'Good girl – in you come.' As I stepped over the threshold I saw he was in full evening dress – for me. 'Off with your jacket, my pet.' I dropped my basket and felt his hands slide up my arms to clasp my shoulders for a moment before gently easing off my jacket. As I took off my hat his warm lips pressed a kiss into the nape of my neck – then he was striding ahead of me. 'In here first. You're going to dine with me tonight, Amy.'

Quickly I reached down for my necklace box, then followed him along the passage and into a spacious sitting room. There was a soft carpet under my feet, flames leaping in the grate, and light sparkling everywhere. A table was set for two in front of the red velvet curtains of the bay window. I was dazzled by the warmth and the luxury. ''Tis lovely!'

'Quite cosy, isn't it?' I watched him as he strode over to the sideboard. The faultless line of his evening jacket displayed the perfection of his square shoulders and slim hips; he was so elegant, so handsome – and I loved him so much. There was the pop of a champagne cork, and then he was holding out a glass. As his glass tinkled against mine he said: 'To us – tonight!' Bubbles fizzed in my nose as I drank, then he reached out for my other hand, the hand which held the jewel case. 'What have you got there, Amy?'

''Tis my necklace, that you did give I.'

'Oh, did you like it?'

''Tis beautiful!'

'Good.' He smiled, and tried to take it from me. 'But let's put it down somewhere now, shall we?'

I shook my head. 'I did bring it for you to put on.'

'*Me* put it on? Oh, you mean me to put it on you!' I nodded, and his smile became indulgent. 'What a romantic little thing you are, Amy.'

I told him, 'I baint never worn it afore.'

'Good girl – I knew I could rely on you. But naturally you want to see yourself in it now – vain little puss! Over to the mirror with you.' He took my hand in his. 'Just a minute, put down your glass and close your eyes – then it'll be a lovely surprise!' Obediently I did as he told me, following him trustingly over the carpet until he ordered me to stop. 'Now, no peeping until I tell you.' The pearls were warm from his hand as they slid round my neck, then I felt his fingers playing with the clasp before he exclaimed: 'There, Amy – you can look now.'

The mirror was full-length, and my straight dark skirt and plain blouse looked very dull against the black velvet lapels of his jacket and the gleaming whiteness of his shirt-front; but around my neck I wore his pearls – the pledge of his love. As I gazed into that mirror I saw two hands in shining white cuffs come stealing round my waist to hold me fast. 'Got you!' And then I saw his fair head bend over to kiss my neck – and at the touch of his lips my whole body seemed to light up. My face in the mirror was aglow with happiness.

He raised his head from my neck. 'By the way, while I remember – this is for you, too.' I watched him reach into his pocket and take out a key – an old iron door key. He swung it on his finger. 'Don't forget to take that with you when you go, or you'll never be able to get back in.'

'Back in?'

'Back into Belgrave Square tonight.' He laughed. 'Or tomorrow morning, I should say.'

I repeated, 'Back? I've got to go back?'

'Well, of course. Miss Annabel will be needing you – it's her wedding day tomorrow.'

I said very carefully, 'But Miss Annabel won't be getting married tomorrow, now.'

'Of course she will.' His face in the mirror looked surprised.

'But – I thought – I thought as you be going to marry me.'

'Marry you?' I watched as his jaw dropped in amazement. 'Marry *you*! But Amy, you're a servant – how could I possibly marry you?'

And as I saw the astonishment on his face the light went out inside me. But still I pleaded, 'But lords, they do marry actresses – I read it in Saranne's paper. That Mr Brett, he be the son of a lord, and he did marry an actress.'

'Yes – and got drummed out of his regiment for it! You wouldn't catch me marrying an actress, I've got more sense. But in any case, it's not the same thing at all. That Dare girl came from a respectable middle-class background – her father was a solicitor johnnie or something – whereas you . . . Good God, Amy, you told me yourself that night at Eston!' In the mirror I watched the light catch my tears as they began to trickle down my cheeks; he saw them too. 'Amy, don't cry. Here, my pet – look at yourself in the mirror. You're a very pretty girl, and I'm sure that one day you'll meet a young man of your own class who'll be prepared to overlook your taint.' As I gazed at his reflected face I saw his eyes darken, and felt his grip on my waist tighten as he pulled me back closer against his body. His voice was husky in my ear as he whispered, 'Though you'll have to play your cards cleverly, won't you my sweet? Because you're soiled goods now, *I* know that.'

And as I watched in the mirror I saw one hand move down, take hold of the hem of my skirt and pull it up until the frills of my drawers showed. The other hand moved now, over and under my skirt, lifting it still higher, so that I could see the hand slide down inside my drawers. I watched that hand as it tugged, hard, so that my drawers loosened and dropped down onto my hips and below – and in the mirror I saw strong fingers push themselves between my thighs and begin to fondle my cunny. I watched as the arm that was attached to the hand inside my cunny clamped itself tight against my skirt, holding it up so that the first hand was freed. That hand began to move now, travelling up over my breast to unfasten the top buttons of my blouse before forcing its way inside. I watched it all in the mirror. That girl with my face wearing my clothes – and a man's fingers handling her most intimate places. I closed my eyes because I couldn't bear to look any more and then I felt it instead:

269

the pain in my cunny as the fingers probed deeper and deeper, the ache in my breasts as they squeezed harder and harder, and the mounting pressure against my back as with steady, rhythmical movements he rubbed his rod up and down in the cleft of my behind.

Then, slowly, the hands began to withdraw. 'God, Amy, you're delicious. That soft golden down, those rosy pink nipples. Why ever did I tell that fellow to bring dinner up at ten? I should have guessed –' When he'd let go of me I pulled up my drawers and turned away from the mirror, my eyes still tightly closed. I only opened them again when I felt the warmth of the flames on my cold hands. I was shivering. 'You're excited too, aren't you my pet? I could feel you all swollen and ready for me. But it's no use, we'll have to wait, there's only ten minutes before dinner, and although I could – no.' He shook his head firmly. 'I'm not going to spoil the first time – it's always the best. Look, you pop along to the bathroom and get yourself tidied up before the man arrives. He knows what you're here for, of course, but,' he grinned, *'pas devant le domestique!'*

Desperately I swung round to face him. 'Why did you send me the pearl necklace, if you don't love me?'

'But I *do* love you, my pet – and tonight I'm going to show you just how much!' I still stood looking up at him. He leant forward and took my hand, squeezing it gently. 'Look Amy, this is the night before my wedding, my last night as a bachelor – and it's *you* I've chosen to share it with. The chaps offered to buy me any girl in Town and I told them "No." I said: "Look, you fellows, if you searched the whole city you'd never find a peach to compare with the one I've already got!" Now go and dry those silly tears and tidy yourself up – we're going to have a wonderful time tonight, you and I.' He turned me round, and gave me a gentle push on the behind. 'It's the last door on the left.'

Alone in the bathroom I buttoned up my blouse, tucked my chemise back inside my drawers and pulled my skirt straight. Then I went over to the mirror to tidy my hair – and saw the pearls. I heard his voice as he'd said: 'The chaps offered to buy me any girl in Town . . . I said: "Look, you fellows, if you searched the whole city you'd never find a peach to compare with the one I've already" – *bought*. Bought, with these pearls: not the pledge of his love, but the price of my maidenhead.

I raised my hands and unfastened the clasp, then I laid the pearls down on the glass shelf beside his shaving brush, turned round and crept out of the bathroom. I lifted my hat and coat off the peg in the passage, picked up my basket with Esau in it and went to the front door. It closed very quietly behind me – and then I was running full-tilt down the stairs. I was lucky: when I got back to Belgrave Square the area door was still unlocked. I went straight up the back stairs to my room without anyone seeing me.

When the door was closed behind me I made myself go over to the mirror, to stare at my reflection there – and for the first time I saw what I really was. Not a lady, but a servant – a bastard servant – and, worst of all, soiled goods. Even as I looked, a brown stain seemed to spread over my face; it was so pale it could scarcely be seen – but it was there. It would always be there, now. Somewhere my father lived, a gentleman, but no one would ever find him for me; and if they did, how could I face him, in my shame and guilt? My absurd dreams had deluded me, leading me on to the ultimate folly – and beyond. I had given myself to a man who wanted only my body, a man to whom I was no better than a whore. The reflection shimmered and changed, and became the one I had seen earlier this evening – reflecting those hands so casually making free with my body before preparing to use it again. The last rags of my self-respect were slipping from me – and then I remembered the pearls, the pearls which I had left on the bathroom shelf at Jermyn Street. He had set out to buy me, but I had not allowed myself to be bought. At the last, I had not played the whore. That was all I had left to cling to.

Chapter Thirty-Four

Next morning I dressed Miss Annabel in her bridal white; covering her shining dark hair with a veil of lace I set the wreath of orange blossoms above it. Then I lifted up her long satin train and carried it behind her down the stairs. She left the house on her brother-in-law's arm – and when she came back she was Lady Quinham.

I went on their honeymoon with them. I was Miss Annabel's personal maid; obviously she needed me. Before we left for the country house which one of Mrs Hurst's friends had lent them Miss Abbott took me on one side and explained that from now on I must wait outside the door until I was certain I'd heard Miss Annabel's reply to my knock – only then could I enter her bedroom. So I knocked and waited, listening to the muffled sound of voices, until eventually Miss Annabel would call: 'Come in' – and there on the pillow next to hers would be the dent his head had made. The thought of him lying beside her all night, holding her close, cuddling her, was more than I could bear – but I had to bear it.

Again and again I remembered that evening in Jermyn Street. If only I'd spent that one last night with him, however much he'd hurt me, however much shame and guilt I'd felt – still he would have held me close, caressed me, called me, 'Amy, my pet.' I wept for the time I'd not had. My pride had gone now, I only wanted to be back there again. I would still have returned that hateful necklace, but once I'd done that then I would have been free to give him my own gift – the gift of myself. But it was too late now.

Then the day of my monthlies fell due and I did not bleed. I realised then the terrifying price I could have paid for that one night. Now I knew it was only the effects of shock – it had happened that time before, for the two months after Grammer had died. I remembered Saranne touching my arm and saying: 'It's all right, Amy, I know you're a good girl . . . 'tis likely the shock o' your bereavement – it do take some folks like that.' And

272

now, again, losing him was like being bereaved, and my body knew it. But if I'd stayed that last night with him it wouldn't have been shock, for I was a good girl no longer. At least the necklace had spared me that.

But it was so hard to have to see the two of them together. Sometimes he came into her room before dinner when I was dressing her hair or putting on her gloves, and he'd wander round picking the glove stretchers up, opening and closing them, twirling her hairbrush in his hand, playing with her jewellery – touching the things which had touched her – touching them because he loved her.

I saw his love in his eyes, lingering on her bare shoulders; in his mouth, curving in greeting as she moved across to take his arm before going downstairs; and I saw it in his whole body bending protectively over hers as they left the room – together. I'd never seen them together before. If I had, I'd never have dreamt my pathetic little dreams.

He didn't ever speak to me, of course – I was only her servant.

She loved him, too. I saw that in the way her eyes sought his, every time he came into the room, but she didn't always look happy. She'd lost her glossy girl's buoyancy and she was often pale and tired. One morning she told me she wasn't feeling well and would stay in bed, but my lord kept sending messages up that he wanted her to go out for a walk, or to play a game of golf, so by lunch-time she'd dragged herself up and gone downstairs. That evening as I was brushing her hair last thing, I noticed how pale and drawn she looked in the mirror. Then next door, in his dressing room, my lord began to whistle, a cheerful, lively tune – and at the sound of it her whole reflected face seemed to sag, and for a moment her eyes closed. When she opened them again she said softly, 'I never realised – I just thought marriage would be like a dream come true.'

She looked so bewildered and sad I forgot my place and said to her, 'But men, they do have their needs – and they maun be met. 'Tis a wife's duty, however hard it may be.'

She glanced up at me in the mirror, and for a moment we were not servant and mistress, but only two women. As I put the brush down her hand reached out and briefly covered mine. Then she replied quietly, 'Yes.'

273

There was a tap on the connecting door. 'May I come in and say good night?'

She drew her back up straight. 'You may go now, Amy.'

Even as I was leaving I heard his voice behind me, 'Annabel, my pet, you look absolutely delicious tonight –'

Upstairs in my room I forced my memories into the little house in my head, just as I'd always done, but I didn't have any dreams any more, so now I was left with nothing.

We went back to Nether Court for Christmas. When I'd first gone there Gladys had told me all about Christmas: the great tree in the drawing room ablaze with candles, and how all the maids went in while the family were there to be given their presents. The special dinner for staff, the Servant's Ball on Boxing Day – I'd thought then how wonderful it sounded. But now I just wanted it to be over. I stood dully behind Miss Abbott, watching the tiny flames flickering against the dark green foliage, then bobbed to Mrs Hurst as my turn came and she gave me my parcel. 'Thank you, madam.' When we'd all received our presents Mr Davenport called for three cheers for the Family, and we dutifully responded before going back to the servants' hall.

The housemaids opened their parcels, complaining about the ugliness of the dress-lengths inside. Gladys sniffed. 'It's the same every place I've been in, always cotton print in some horrible colour! They don't want us to look like anything but servants – not even when we're off-duty.' My dress-length was cotton too, only a harsh blue instead of a crude pink. I was just a servant – I knew that now.

I dressed Miss Annabel in her wedding finery for dinner on Christmas Day, but she didn't look well. I knew from the gossip in the servant's hall that she'd been trying to persuade my lord to move to Eston, but he wouldn't agree. I was glad he'd refused. I didn't want to go back to Eston, not ever again.

Then on Boxing Day morning Miss Annabel told me that we were going over to Wiltshire that very day. 'I've sent a telegram; Lord Warminster is expecting me.' At the station she sent me to buy two first-class tickets; she said she felt rather faint, so she would prefer me to be in the same compartment as she was. Once I'd have been excited at the idea of travelling first-class – but nothing was exciting nowadays.

274

Twice she had to go to the lavatory to be sick, and as I helped her back the second time I said, 'You shouldn't have come, my lady, you're not well.'

She sank down onto the seat. 'I had to, Amy. Lord Warminster so much wanted us to make our home with him – how could I say 'no' in a letter? And at Christmas-time, too. I feel the least I can do is tell him in person.' She sighed, and picked up her book, then said, 'I do love Homer, but I can only read him in translation – Lord Warminster was going to teach me Greek, so I could study the original text.'

She sounded so sad I made myself suggest, 'Mebbe Lord Quinham could teach you?'

She gave a half-smile as she shook her head. 'You are droll sometimes, Amy.'

The carriage was already waiting at the station, and as we drove up to the house the front door opened and Lord Warminster himself came out and began his crabwise descent of the steps. Glancing at me Miss Annabel whispered, 'However shall I tell him?' Then she was stepping out, her clear voice calling, 'Leonidas, how kind of you to entertain me. Every last soul at Nether Court has gone hunting today, I'd have been left quite alone if you hadn't agreed to give me lunch.'

He stood to one side, letting the footman help her down from the carriage, nor did he offer her his arm as she came towards him – but his eyes never left her face, and there was no mistaking the warmth in his voice as he made his halting reply to her greeting: 'The pleasure – is – entirely – mine.'

The coachman dropped me at the entrance to the service courtyard, and Clara came out to meet me with Mary. 'Come into the warm, Miss Roberts.' As soon as we were inside the door she turned a switch on the wall – and at once the gloomy passageway was flooded with light. Clara laughed at my surprise. 'I still can't believe it – no more smoky old lamps! His Lordship had it all done for when your lady comes to live here.'

'She baint coming.'

'What! But she must, the whole house's been turned upside down these last months, getting ready for her. She can't say no to him now!'

''Tain't her, 'tis Lord Quinham.'

Mary glanced at Clara. 'Aye – it would be.'

Clara said, 'His poor old Lordship. You know, Miss Roberts, he's even been up prowling around the old nurseries, getting all the rubbish cleared out and the window bars renewed, he's that set on her coming.'

Mary broke in. 'Is she in the family way yet?'

The question was like a punch in the stomach. I stammered, 'I – I dussent know.'

'You must know. You sends her rags to the laundry, don't you?'

'She don't use rags – she has special pads as are thrown away.'

'What a waste of money! But surely, even then, you must – oh, there's herself ringing for me. I suppose I'd better go.' With a grimace Mary disappeared in the direction of the housekeeper's room, and to my relief Clara didn't demand an answer. I did know, of course, but I hadn't admitted it even to myself. Perhaps she was just late. I didn't want to think – I *wouldn't* think.

The day dragged on. I was grateful to Clara for keeping me occupied; she asked me if I'd help her cut out the material for a new dress she was making. Eston was the one place the maids weren't given ugly cotton print for Christmas; instead Lord Warminster let them go to the draper's at Tilton and choose their dress-length of any material they wanted, so Clara had chosen a fine brown wool. 'Bertha picked panne velvet – daft, I calls it. When'll she ever be able to swan around in a dress made of crimson velvet?'

I said, 'Mrs Hurst'd never have allowed *that*.'

Clara grinned through the fringe of pins in her mouth. 'That's the advantage of having no mistress, and Mrs Johnstone's too idle to check up on what we wear off-duty – or anything else much, for that matter. She weren't best pleased at the prospect of your lady coming to live here, seeing as she's done just as she likes since I don't know when.'

I exclaimed in surprise, 'But surely, Lady Warminster did tell her what's what, when she were still alive?'

Clara shook her head. 'She never lived here, not since I was a liddle maid. Even when they was first married she only stayed here for two, three month, then he took her back to France, so my mam told me. Lord Quin was born over there, and it was a goodish while afore they did come back – they say she was ill at the birthing. Then, just about the time he was learning to walk she upped and took him back to France – and His Lordship, he stayed here.'

'But – they were man and wife!'

Clara shrugged. 'The gentry, they do things different. She'd bring His young Lordship back for a month or so every summer, but they'd stay over by Bath – His Lordship's got a house over there, too. She'd come to Eston odd days with Lord Quin, but he never went to see them; you can't wonder sometimes at Lord Quin not being on good terms with his father. And whenever she did visit, Mr Tims says, there was generally words – terrible temper he's got, our Lordship. Sometimes he'll go for weeks with the black dog on his shoulder, either in the sulks or shouting at anyone as gets in his way, except for his yellow bitch – he don't never shout at her.' Clara put down the pincushion. 'I'll pop along to the stillroom and make us both a cup o' tea, Miss Roberts.'

My hands pinned mechanically as yet another of my cherished dreams lay in dingy tatters at my feet. He hadn't loved her at all, my beautiful French countess. I remembered my own lord talking about the apartment Lord Warminster kept at Kew, and how he met other women there. He must have been unfaithful to his wife, and she'd been so unhappy she'd gone back to France, in tears. No wonder her lovely blue eyes had been so sad; she too had been spurned, rejected by the man she loved.

Clara came back with the tea tray – and Joe Dempster. He was dressed in his best Sunday suit, but I noticed that his boots were coated with mud. He stood twisting his cap in his hand, his face still red from the cold outside. 'I heard as how Lady Quin were coming today, so I walked over to Eston, on the off-chance she might've brought you wi' her – and she had.' He thrust out his large horny hand. 'How are you keeping, Amy?'

I put mine into his strong warm clasp. 'Quite well, thank 'ee Joe.'

He stood there, just staring at me, until Clara said briskly, 'Sit down Joe, do. Mrs Johnstone won't mind you being in here the once, seeing as 'tis Boxing Day. I'll fetch another cup.'

As soon as she'd gone Joe leant towards me. 'I been telling meself as thee cassent be as pretty as I did remember, but I were wrong – thee bist even prettier.'

277

I felt my whole face suffuse with blood. Looking down at the floor I asked him, 'Have you come far, Joe?'

''Tis more'n five mile by road from our cottage, but I'd walk twice that and back, for the sight o' one o' thy smiles.'

I didn't know how to answer, and it was a relief to hear Clara's returning footsteps. The three of us sat talking, and gradually the other maids drifted in, followed by the footmen. The fire blazed halfway up the chimney and there was the sound of joking and laughter all around; I began to feel warm again – for the first time that winter, so it seemed.

After Joe had set off back to his parents' cottage Clara murmured to me, 'He's never stopped talking about you, Joe hasn't. You could go further and fare worse, Miss Roberts. His Lordship thinks very highly of Joe – he'll have his own garden one day, I shouldn't wonder.' I didn't know how to reply.

We left soon after; I knew Miss Annabel didn't want to upset my own lord by being late back. She looked very pale as she sat opposite me in the train, and she was silent for a few minutes, just staring down at her gloves. Then she lifted her face and exclaimed, 'Did you see the electric lights, Amy?'

'Yes, my lady. Clara, she did tell me the whole house was topsy-turvy for weeks, while it were being put in.'

Miss Annabel closed her eyes and whispered, 'He did that for me.'

Her voice was so sad I tried to reassure her. 'Well, it did need smartening up – 'twere terrible old-fashioned, Eston.'

She opened her eyes very wide and dark. 'But he preferred it like that.' She sighed. 'You see, Amy, he doesn't like bright lights. He only did it for my sake.' She added. 'He's even installed a telephone – a *telephone*, when he can hardly speak.' Then she exclaimed, 'So I couldn't disappoint him, could I? Not when he'd tried so hard to please me.' She took a deep breath and said firmly, 'We *are* going to make Eston our home – I've decided.'

'But – Lord Quinham . . .'

She leant forward, her eyes bright and confident. 'My mistake, Amy, was to assume that men are rational creatures, but they're not. Using logical argument is a waste of breath where they're concerned.' She smiled. 'Goodness, I've only been married seven weeks – I'm still a bride. I know I can persuade my husband to do

278

as I want, if I really try.' She picked up her book, flicked it open and settled back in her corner.

She did persuade him. The very next day it was all decided: as soon as the New Year had come in we went to live at Eston, with Lord Warminster.

PART FOUR

Chapter Thirty-Five

Eston, Wiltshire — January 1913

Mrs Johnstone made it very clear that I wasn't welcome in the Room. She never addressed a single word directly to me, and when Mr Tims tried to include me in the conversation she'd immediately interrupt so he had to turn his attention to her instead. Then Lord Warminster's valet, Mr Wallis, would drop one eyelid in a wink and say, 'Enjoying your dinner, Miss Roberts? Nothing but the best is served at Eston – or so Mrs J. always tells me!'

Mrs Johnstone would glare at him, but he wasn't frightened of her like the butler was; if he wanted to complain, he would. And there was plenty to complain about – the food certainly wasn't up to Nether Court standards. The cook, Mrs Procter, was as lazy as Mrs Johnstone. Clara told me she set the kitchenmaid to do most of the cooking for the dining room, so the poor girl hardly had time to attend to her proper job of the servants' meals. After a while the food got so bad I began to suffer from indigestion. I'd never been troubled by it before, but now I got this funny feeling in my stomach every so often, and heartburn, too. If I'd still been at Nether Court I'd have asked Mrs Harper for a glass of her special peppermint cordial, but I didn't reckon Mrs Johnstone'd even know how to make peppermint cordial – and if she had, I wouldn't have fancied it. The stillroom at Eston was positively grubby.

Miss Annabel kept saying to me, 'I must do something about that housekeeper, Amy. It's time she pulled her socks up.' But she didn't seem to have the energy. She sent me down a couple of times with messages for Mrs Johnstone – some flowers that were past their best, and an ormulu clock left undusted. I didn't like delivering the messages and Mrs Johnstone liked receiving them even less; in the Room afterwards it was as though she had icicles growing from her gums instead of teeth.

Miss Annabel didn't even have the energy to take Earl out, and she said she didn't want to bother Lord Warminster, nor did she feel she could trust the footmen to give him a proper run – with them being Eston footmen – so she asked me to take him out morning and evening without fail. I didn't mind, I wasn't so tired myself now, and I hadn't much to do, with so many of her clothes having been bought new for her trousseau. It was a relief to get out of the house, and Earl always looked so pleased to see me I was grateful to him. Then, after the first couple of evenings I heard footsteps behind me and a voice said, 'You didn't ought to be out after dark on your own, not a young maid like you.' It was Joe Dempster. He took Earl's lead from me until we were beyond the stable block and out in the park, and then set him free for his run. 'I'll come with you in future.'

'But, Miss Annabel –'

'She be in dinner now, that's why thee bist free, I know that. My sister's lady's maid over Bristol way.'

'But mebbe His Lordship –'

'His Lordship knows I do me work. He don't never interfere in how we do spend our free time.'

After that Joe came with me every evening. He lived in the bothy with the other young gardeners, and one of the housemaids cooked for them, so I knew he must be gulping down his supper and rushing out, but he was always there at the entrance to the stables, waiting for me. His Wiltshire voice was so familiar and comforting, and with him I could drop into dialect, and not have to worry about how I spoke. Not that I did speak much now – I didn't seem to feel like chattering any more – but Joe had enough to say for both of us. A lot of the time he'd be telling me about Lord Warminster's roses; he was a true gardener, was Joe.

I'd always thought roses just grew – red or pink or white, just as the fancy took them – but apparently some of the gentry bred roses, like sheep. Lord Warminster did, and one of his own roses had won a Gold Medal in London only last year. It was a dainty little pink one, Joe said – so tiny it was called a fairy rose. I did like the sound of that. Once he'd bred his roses Lord Warminster gave them names – the pink fairy rose he'd called Persephone, after some Ancient Greek maid. I made Joe spell it out for me, then I said it aloud; it tripped so delicately off my tongue I knew it must be an especially pretty rose.

Joe said Lord Warminster was set on breeding a golden rose now, but golden roses were the most difficult – and His Lordship's roses, they had to be perfect and grow true on their own roots; he wouldn't give them a name until they did. He'd spent years on Persephone, Joe said, long after most breeders would have been satisfied. And it wasn't just looks he cared about; he wanted a rose that was hardy, and wouldn't be attacked by pests, or fail in poor weather. ''Tis them rugosas he be working wi' now. They don't look much at first, being as they're only single, but His Lordship reckons as he can double 'em, and he do say they be o' sturdy stock.'

One afternoon when Miss Annabel was lying down and I'd just popped out for a breath of air Joe invited me into the glass-house where the new roses were bred. The house wasn't as big as the ones at Nether Court, but it was a prettier shape, like a big 'T' – and I could see green foliage in the two wings at the far end. 'Be they a-growing already?'

Joe laughed. 'Nar – them's His Lordship's pot roses. He do like to have a rose in bloom most o' the year. But we puts the seed pans in wi' 'em because they all need the same temperature.'

There was nothing to see in the seed pans but brown earth and labels, but as Joe talked I could imagine the roses blooming last summer, and the scissors delicately cutting into a flower so it wouldn't breed with itself. 'His Lordship showed me how to do it – he's a dab hand wi' the scissors, is His Lordship.' Then the camel-hair brush transferred the pollen; so tiny were the grains that a lens had to be used to inspect the flower afterwards, to see the job had been done. ''Tis difficult to be sure o' that, but His Lordship, he can always tell.' Next, Joe said, each pollinated flower was wrapped up in waxed tissue for a while, like a little parcel, 'To keep them bees from interfering.' Joe gave me a sidelong glance and whispered, 'Same as a man do make sure his wife be wearing a stout pair o' flannel drawers – he don't want no other fellow pollinating *his* blossom.' My cheeks went fiery red and Joe gave a great shout of laughter. 'You be even prettier when you blushes, Amy – I swear it.'

I spoke quickly, 'But surely, them hips won't ripen, not tied up in liddle parcels like that.'

'We unwraps 'em, soon as danger's over. Though last summer,

wi' the weather being so bad, I thought we'd lost 'em. Only His Lordship, he puts glass jars over each spray o' hips, to warm 'em up – and they ripened lovely.' Joe shook his head in admiration. 'He do know a trick or two, does our lordship. I reckon what he don't know about roses baint worth knowing. Now, I daresay you'd like a quick peep at the pot roses while you're here, Amy.'

It was a very quick peep, because as soon as we turned into the right-hand wing we saw Lord Warminster; he'd been there all the time, busy with one of the bushes. I shrank back, waiting for him to explode in fury, but when Joe touched his cap saying, 'I been showing the seed pans to Amy here,' Lord Warminster merely grunted before turning his attention back to his rose. He hadn't even looked at me.

Joe was very quiet as he walked me back to the house, then he said, 'I reckon I shouldn't't've passed that remark about flannel drawers – especially not with His Lordship listening. But in any case, it weren't respectful to you.' His voice deepened, and he stopped, turning to face me. 'The truth is, I think very highly of you, Amy – very highly indeed. In fact, there's something I want to ask you –'

I broke in very quickly, 'Joe, I must go back in now – Her Ladyship'll have woken up.' I began to run towards the back door.

But that evening he was waiting for me as usual, and this time I couldn't run away – when he asked me to marry him.

I whispered, 'Joe – I be main sorry, but I can't.'

'Dussent thee like I – just a bit?'

'O' course I do like thee, Joe, but you don't understand. I – I baint fit to marry you. I done a terrible thing once.'

He paced beside me in the darkness, silent. Then he said, 'I know that being a lady's maid, there's temptation put in your way but whatever you done, I still wants to marry thee.' He was so true and generous that I began to cry. He spoke gruffly. 'I'll not pester thee any more now, but be sure I'll ask thee again.'

That night I thought, if I were to marry Joe there'd be someone who cared about me, someone who needed me to cook and clean for him, and – my mind shrank away from that next thought. But I went back to it again. I'd do my duty, and then maybe there'd be a baby. I started to cry again, because I knew I wasn't fit for any man to marry now – and besides, I still loved my lord.

But I hardly ever saw him, and when he did come to Miss Annabel's room while I was there he barely glanced in my direction. Miss Annabel saw less of him, too, now we were at Eston. The pillow was still dented every night but he was out most of the day hunting or shooting. He even went up to London for a couple of days; I think he'd asked Miss Annabel to go with him, but she really wasn't well enough, so he went on his own and left her behind.

She spent a lot of time with Lord Warminster; I knew that from things Clara told me. I used to think that Clara was my only friend at Eston, apart from Joe Dempster, of course. I asked her to call me 'Amy' and she was pleased, and started coming and sitting with me in my room some evenings, while I was sewing after supper. Then she'd tell me what the footman had said in the servant's hall, about how Lord Warminster took tea in the drawing room every afternoon now. 'He never used to go near it afore, from one month's end to the next.' One day he'd taken Miss Annabel with him when he walked round the village; he did that regularly, Clara told me, because he was a good landlord. And anybody who was in trouble, he'd see they got help. 'No one's been put in the House from Eston village for as long as I can remember.' She leant forward, her freckled face serious. 'When our dad died Mam was at her wit's end – there were five of us, and not one old enough to work. Other landlords would have had us put out of our cottage, but His Lordship told Mr Selby – that's his agent – as he was to forget about the rent until my mam was on her feet again. She did what she could in the way of washing and such-like, but she said many's the time His Lordship would come in to ask how she was keeping, and after he'd left there'd be a couple of gold sovereigns on the mantelpiece. O' course, he do think a lot o' my mam, does His Lordship. She came into the nursery here to help Nanny Fenton when he were just a little lad – six year old he were that year, my mam said – and she stayed until he went away to school.' Clara sat back in her chair. 'Times are better now, the Lord be praised – me and my brothers are working and Mam does nicely doing the laundry for the Rector and the doctor – and that's without what she gets from confinements. She's a capital nurse, our mam, and she'll keep an eye on the other youngsters and turn her hand to any job as needs doing while a body's lying in, not like

287

some o' them fine nurses I've heard about. So there's no problem with finding the rent these days, but she hasn't forgotten. If she so much as sees His Lordship coming down the street she'll leave whatever she's doing and rush out to give him a curtsey and a "Good day". There's some villages where the gentry complain they don't get no respect these days, but nobody won't ever say that about Eston. I'll just put a couple more coals on thic fire, Amy.'

As soon as she'd put the tongs down again Clara settled back in her chair to resume her gossip. 'Mam invited your lady inside, and she said as she was very civil spoken – and His Lordship was like a dog wi' two tails, having such a pretty daughter-in-law.' She sighed. ''Tis a terrible shame Lord Quin don't get on wi' his father. They were at it again last night, Thomas said – arguing about preserving game. Our master's never gone in for that, o' course, but Lord Quin, he do want to shoot. Thomas said as your lady tried to calm things down by talking about how pretty them liddle pheasants be, and how 'twere a shame to kill them, and His young Lordship starts making fun of what she said – just teasing her, Thomas reckoned he was – but our Lordship, he took her side, and next minute he was shouting at Lord Quin, as best he can wi' his way o' speaking.' She shook her head. ''Tis a terrible shame – and he was so looking forward to her coming to live at Eston.'

Next morning as I was bringing Earl back I saw Lord Warminster and Miss Annabel coming out of the side door together. She called me over. 'Earl can come with us, Amy – he'll be company for Nella.' As the two dogs began frisking around each other Miss Annabel turned to smile up at Lord Warminster. 'Shall we be going, Leonidas – while the sun's out?' And I saw the expression on his lopsided face as he looked down at her as if, for him, the sun had indeed just come out – after a long winter. My heart twisted in my chest and I thought, it's not fair; Miss Annabel, she's got two men loving her, but nobody loves me. That night Joe Dempster asked me again to marry him.

I said to Joe. 'I got to tell you something.' I stopped, and had to force myself to go on and say, 'I was born out of wedlock.'

He didn't say anything for a full five minutes, but just kept on walking beside me with Earl. Then at last he spoke. 'I can't say it doesn't matter to me, because it does. Our family – there's never been anything like that. But I love thee, Amy, so I'd be prepared to overlook it.'

I felt a surge of gratitude but it was no use, I couldn't marry Joe, not after the way I'd sinned. 'I'm sorry, Joe. I'm grateful to you, but – there's something I done.'

He said firmly, 'I won't change my mind, Amy. I'll ask you again.' Then he began to talk about His Lordship's special Japanese roses.

Mr Tims came late to supper in the Room that night, his face creased with worry and his hands shaking. 'It was dreadful, Mr Wallis – dreadful. I didn't know where to put myself – and in front of Thomas and Henry, too.'

Apparently Lord Quinham had met this gentleman who'd told him he'd made a lot of money investing in Russia, and my lord had suggested that his father should buy some of these Russian bonds. 'It had been all quite amicable up to that point, Mr Wallis. Her Ladyship was sitting there between the two of them looking pleased because they were speaking civilly to each other, and then Our Lordship said he'd never invest in Russia because the Czar was a tyrant, and he was surprised at Lord Quin for even thinking of such a thing, with him having been born in France where they'd had a revolution to overthrow tyranny. At that Lord Quin starts getting heated and saying that that was a long time ago, and nothing to do with today. I could see Our Lordship was losing his temper the way he threw his knife down then he says, "I suppose it would seem irrelevant to someone who only managed to scrape a Pass degree in History!" Now that really did get Lord Quin angry and he said, speaking very loud and clear so we could hear every word: "With your beliefs in democracy I'm surprised you weren't in the House of Lords last summer, lending your support to the Parliament Bill," and Our Lordship starts spluttering a bit, because naturally he's never taken his seat – and then,' Mr Tims took out his handkerchief and mopped his brow, 'and then Lord Quinham leant right over the table and added, "But you'd be a laughing stock if *you* ever tried to speak in the House." There was just this terrible silence, before Her Ladyship cried out, "Francis – how *could* you!" Our Lordship, he just threw down his napkin and left the dining room, right in the middle of dinner. In the middle of dinner,' Mr Tims repeated. He put out one trembling hand to his wine-glass.

Mr Wallis shook his head. 'Poor old so-and-so – it's not as if he's getting much food at the moment, anyway.' He turned to me. 'He nearly starved when you were all here in the autumn, Miss Roberts. He can't bear to eat in front of other people, not even his own guests.'

Mrs Johnstone suddenly broke in, sounding resentful. 'I never could understand how he came to invite them in the first place – that was when all the trouble started.'

Mr Tims put down his empty glass. 'He only did it because his son goaded him into it, Mrs Johnstone. Lord Quin flicked him on the raw, implying his father wouldn't have the courage to invite them. And His Lordship, he just fell into the trap – he had to show Lord Quin he could do it, so he dashed off a letter to Mrs Hurst there and then.'

Mr Wallis reached out to refill Mr Tims' glass, and then took up the tale. 'Soon as he'd done it he realised he'd been gulled, but it was too late. So then it was nothing but sulks and tantrums! My life wasn't worth living for the next couple of weeks, I can tell you.' He grinned at me. 'You know what it's like in our job, Miss Roberts, when something's upset them.'

I replied primly, 'Miss Annabel – Her Ladyship – she be always pleasant spoken, however much she's been put out.'

Mr Wallis laughed. 'Well, I certainly can't say the same for His Lordship. If he's put out, we're all put out – eh, Mr Tims?' Mr Tims nodded as he lifted his glass again. Mr Wallis shook his head. 'Real pain in the backside he was, if you'll excuse my French, Mrs J., until your young lady turned up, Miss Roberts, and he fell for her pretty face hook, line and sinker. Now he's paying the price.'

There was a tap at the door, and Clara's worried face appeared. 'I'm sorry to intrude, Mrs Johnstone, but Her Ladyship's ringing her bell.'

I jumped up. 'I'll go.'

It was obvious Miss Annabel had been crying, but she didn't tell me what had happened. I put her to bed early with a hot water bottle and came away. She must have made it up with my lord, because there was a dent in the pillow beside hers when I took her tea tray in first thing. As she sat up she said, 'By the way, Amy, when you take Earl out this morning be sure to keep him on his lead, and well away from the stables. Nella's – ah – unwell.'

I replied automatically, 'Yes, my lady,' but I forgot. I seemed to forget things more than ever, now I was back at Eston. So I fetched Earl, put him on his lead and took him out the way I always did – through the stable-yard. I saw Nella sitting outside the tackroom, her lead looped over the latch, and I knew she was never normally put on a lead, but I still didn't think – until all at once there was this terrific wrench and Earl was away from me. His great brown body bounded across the yard – I ran after him – but by the time I caught him up Nella had broken free and he was already mounting her. I threw myself on top of him, flung my arms right round his chest and pulled and pulled. Suddenly a pair of arms came round my waist, gripping me so tightly I couldn't breathe – then with a great jerk I was torn free of Earl and seemed to be flying through the air until I landed with a bump on the cobbles. Seconds later Earl landed beside me, barking furiously. A lead was thrust into my hand – 'Hold her!' and Earl was dragged away, his legs stiff with protest.

A stableman came running up. 'I'll take him for you, my lord.' Earl, still wildly barking, was hauled off as I clung grimly to Nella's lead.

'You fool – you little fool! You shouldn't have him out if you can't control him!' Lord Warminster towered over me, and as I blinked up into the bright sunlight I saw that his face was distorted with rage. He stood there for a moment, glaring at me – then his eyes sharpened, and he kept on staring a few seconds longer before seizing hold of Nella's lead and lurching off with her.

By now I was in the centre of a small crowd of grinning men, and the elderly coachman began to laugh. 'Dang me, I ent never seen nothing so funny since me brother-in-law's bull got out and treed him.' He dug his elbow into the ribs of the man beside him. 'Thic there liddle bitch, all excited she were – thought her dream'd come true when that great dawg jumps atop o' her, and then,' he pointed his finger at me, 'thic here maid, she do jump on the dawg, trying to pull him off afore he's got properly stuck in, like.' The men's laughter changed its note, becoming deeper, suggestive. 'Me lord, he comes out o' the tackroom, sees what's going on and starts cussing and swearing 'cos he can't get hold o' the dawg fer her being in the way – then all at once he leaps on top of her!' He stopped, spluttering. 'I did think dawg had given him ideas – and he was a-going to have a go hisself!' I couldn't move; my face was burning with shame as the men laughed at me. 'Then he did seem to change his mind – lucky fer her, reckon it'd've been more of a mismatch than if them pair o' dawgs had mated!' They all roared with laughter, slapping their thighs in merriment; they were still laughing as they drifted back to work.

I turned to the man holding Earl. 'Please, can I take him now?'

'Best let I walk him this morning, you don't want another mishap. After all, you being such a pretty liddle maid, who's to say but His Lordship might be tempted to carry on and finish the job next time – and then where'd you be?' He leered at me before sauntering off, a despondent Earl trotting at his heels. I crept back indoors in disgrace.

But it was worse than that. The coachman must have told the story to my lord when he came back from hunting, so he came in while I was doing Miss Annabel's hair before dinner, sat down beside her and then described the whole scene to her – just as if I wasn't there. He repeated the very same words the coachman had used, mimicking his accent. I didn't know where to put myself.

He obviously found it all very funny, and even Miss Annabel laughed before she said, 'Amy – you really should have been more careful.' I was fighting down tears all the time I tidied up. Then I put on my hat and jacket and went down to collect Earl for his evening walk.

That night Joe Dempster asked me again to marry him – and I said yes.

Chapter Thirty-Six

I tried to tell him then, but I couldn't seem to get the words out and he didn't want to listen. He kept saying, 'Whatever you'm done, 'tis no matter now, we'll put it right somehow.' He took me in his arms and hugged me close; he was warm and alive, and I rested my head on his shoulder with a dull sense of relief. I didn't like it when he started kissing me. I could feel how much he wanted me, and I shrank from the thought of a man's hands pawing my body, doing 'It' to me every night – but I knew a woman hadn't any choice. It was the price she had to pay.

I told Miss Annabel next morning. She clapped her hands and exclaimed, 'Amy – I *am* so pleased for you! And he's such a steady young man, I know Lord Warminster thinks most highly of him.' Then she went to the dressing-room door and tapped on it. My lord opened it in his shirtsleeves; he'd just finished shaving and his fair hair was damp at the temples. Miss Annabel said, 'Francis, Amy's just told me she's going to be married – isn't that nice?'

His blue eyes looked at me very hard and cold before he said, 'Congratulations, Amy. What a clever girl you are.' He swung round and almost slammed the door shut behind him.

That night Joe told me he'd asked Lord Warminster for a cottage. 'There's one coming free down in Eston I know – old Mrs Holt's going to live with her son over by Tilton. 'Tis only small, but it'd do us for a start. So I asked His Lordship and he said yes, I could have it – but not yet. So I told him I'd got a bit put by and I'd rather not wait too long – and then he said a funny thing, Amy. He said: "That girl, she's got a mark on her face. Wait until it fades, then you can have the cottage – if you still want it." I thought it were an odd sort o' remark, coming from him of all people. 'Tis true, you have got a mark on your face, Amy, I noticed it that afternoon when I took you into the glass-house – like the shadow of a big, pale-brown moth it is – but it don't make you any the less pretty. In fact, it were true what I said on Boxing Day, as you were even prettier than I'd remembered. You've got a sort o' glow

293

about you now, and your hair, it shines like a new-minted coin. Oh Amy,' he pulled me closer, 'even if we do have to wait for the cottage, there's no reason why we should wait for – I mean, we be betrothed – and a man, he do have needs, Amy.' His hand gripped my behind, pressing it tightly against his body, and I felt his rod swollen and hard against my belly. His breath came warm in my ear as he whispered, 'Wi' thee coming out every night wi' thic dog, we could find a quiet corner – the dog, he won't tell no tales!' He laughed very low in his throat, and his voice became deeper, more urgent. 'Amy – I'm bursting for you.' His hand moved quickly, reaching down to get under my skirt – tugging, pulling, grasping. 'Amy – just let I – just the once –' His fingers pushed hard between my thighs, and at the feel of him touching me there I couldn't bear it – with a great wrench I managed to pull myself away from him.

'No, I couldn't!' He made as if to come after me and I put up my hands to fend him off. 'Please, Joe – you mustn't!' He stopped, still breathing heavily, then he began to move forward again and I cried, 'Please – no!' And at that moment Earl came bounding up to me and I flung my arms around his neck, clinging to him for protection. 'Please don't be angry with me, Joe, but I couldn't, I couldn't.'

Joe turned and began to walk back towards the stables; in silence I followed him, with Earl under my hand. As we came up to the stable-yard archway he turned, waiting for me to catch up. When he spoke his voice was low and serious. 'Amy, now I've cooled down I'm main glad you did stop me back there. I got carried away, but it would've been wrong. The truth is, a man he do try it on, 'tis only natural for him – but once he's had his way with a girl, then he don't respect her any more. But I respect thee, Amy – I respect thee more'n ever after tonight.'

Upstairs I thought, but what'll he say when I tell him that once I didn't say no, and that now I wasn't a maid any more? And I would have to tell him. I couldn't deceive him – it wouldn't be right. I went over to the mirror and peered at the mark on my face. Like the wings of a giant butterfly it was, though it only showed in a direct light; but it was there, and it wouldn't fade – Lord Warminster was wrong about that. But he'd recognised it for what it was – only of course, he would, because he'd seen me come out of the housemaid's closet that afternoon, with my blouse gaping open and my skirt creased and stained.

I put my hands over the mark and wept for what I'd done, and for what I'd have to do once I was married to Joe. Even with my lord I'd hated having It done to me – the pain and the shame of it, and the feeling of my body being invaded. I remembered the Buildings, and what the women had said in the wash-house, and me lying in the scullery listening to the bedsprings creaking night after night – and panic began to well up in my throat. Then I caught hold of myself, telling myself firmly that it was only what all women had to put up with and besides, in return I would have a husband: someone who cared for me, someone who needed me, someone I could look after – and there'd be the babies.

And at the thought of them I began to dream again. I dreamt of the little cottage, and me outside in the garden, pegging up the washing. There were two little girls with me: barely able to walk the younger one was – she was tumbling in the grass with her sister, the pair of them like a couple of puppies. The smaller one'd raise her chubby little arms to me, 'Mam!' and I'd reach down and pick her up, and kiss her rose-petal cheek. Then the other little girl'd press close against my legs looking up at me: 'Kiss I too, kiss I too,' and I'd bend down, kissing and hugging them both – until from inside the cottage I'd hear a wail, not angry, just calling me, letting me know I was wanted. At that cry I'd feel my breasts tingling – just like I remembered the women telling me – and I'd say to the little girls, 'We maun go in now – I got to feed thy brother.'

And as I stood there my breasts began to tingle, and it was as though the milk was already coming. I knew at that moment that even if Joe wanted me every night I'd never complain; not for the sake of that cottage – and those babies. But I'd have to tell him what I'd done; I'd have to tell him before we were married.

Next morning when I was dressing Miss Annabel after her breakfast – at Eston she always breakfasted in bed – she told me my lord had already left. He'd gone to stay with friends in Leicestershire for a couple of nights. 'The hunting's better there, apparently.' She tried to speak casually, but her eyes were red and swollen. I knew she hadn't wanted him to go. Clara had told me last night that when Thomas had taken the coffee into the drawing room to the two of them – Lord Warminster always took Nella for a run last thing – Miss Annabel had been pleading with Lord Quinham not to go away and leave her, but he wouldn't listen. 'He said Eston was too slow, and,' Clara leant forward confidentially, 'Thomas reckons as he muttered something about her not being any fun any more, then they both realised Thomas was still there, and shut up.'

Miss Annabel rested in her room most of the next day, but the morning after she got up straight after breakfast, and as soon as I'd put her bedroom to rights I went down for Earl. I'd just brought him back when Thomas came rushing along the back passageway. 'Miss Roberts, Mr Tims said to come quick – your lady's fainted!'

I dashed after him through the green baize door and along to the drawing room. Mr Tims threw open the door and there was Miss Annabel lying on the sofa, white as a sheet. I ran straight to her. 'My lady, wake up.' I put my arm around her shoulders and raised her head, like I'd seen people do in the Buildings, but she just flopped back. I looked up to where Lord Warminster stood, almost as white as she was. 'My lord, help I lift her up – we maun get her head down, that'll bring her round.' He half-bent over – but he couldn't bring himself to touch her and it was Mr Tims who helped me to get her propped up. I put my hand on the nape of her neck, pressing her head down to her knees – and she began to stir. Crouching beside her I said, ''Tis all right, Miss Annabel. I got thee safe – do 'ee rest thy head on my shoulder. There, don' 'ee move.' I looked up. 'Mr Tims, do 'ee pile all thic cushions up behind her, so she can sit up straight.'

As we made her comfortable the colour gradually came back into her face, but she still leant heavily against my arm. Lord Warminster stood in front of us, like a great ungainly bear; his face was appalled. She glanced up at him, managing to smile. 'Don't worry, Leonidas – I was only being silly.'

He suddenly burst out stammering, 'You're – ill. You're – ill!'

She shook her head, still smiling. 'No, Leonidas, I'm not ill. It's just that I –' She hesitated, then said firmly, 'It's just that I'm expecting a child.'

As I knelt with my arm still around her shoulders I saw the expression on his face – it was like sunrise after a moonless night. His mouth worked, but he couldn't get the words out; he just

296

stood there, looking at her, until Miss Annabel said gently, 'Sit down, Leonidas – you've had a shock, too. Amy, I'm fine now, you may go. And thank you.' She squeezed my hand, then I got up and left with Mr Tims. I felt cold and numb as I walked upstairs, but I'd known already – I just hadn't admitted it to myself.

It was half an hour before she sent for me again. She must have been talking to Lord Warminster, calming him down, because he was still in the drawing room when I returned. 'Amy, His Lordship insists that you help me upstairs, though I'm really quite recovered now.' She gave him a parting smile as we left. Upstairs she said, 'I feel much better now, but he's told me I must lie down for a while, so I will – just to please him.' Then a shadow crossed her face. 'I do hope Lord Quinham won't mind my telling his father first, but Lord Warminster was *so* worried – and now he's absolutely thrilled.' She smiled. 'I told him I wouldn't have time to learn Greek now, and he said, "Never mind – I'll teach your child instead." '

When she was lying down she gave an involuntary glance at the pillow beside her. 'I'm glad Lord Quinham's coming back today. I've been so longing to tell him, but I wasn't absolutely sure – and I didn't want him to think I was just making excuses.' She sighed. 'It will be such a relief not to have to *pretend* I feel well. I think maybe I will have a little nap now.'

She had lunch on a tray in bed, then decided she would sit up on the sofa in her room. She said we'd have to look at her clothes together – they'd need altering soon – several of her dresses were already rather tight over her chest. I took them out of the wardrobe one by one and talked of seams and darts. I tried to pretend that I was a dressmaker again, and she was merely a client – not the woman who was carrying the child of the man I loved.

I was just putting away her cream silk when the door burst open. It was my lord, with a face as black as a thundercloud. 'So when am *I* going to be let into this secret that the entire household already knows?' He strode over to Miss Annabel and stood glaring down at her. 'But I suppose I don't count, since I'm only the ruddy father!'

Miss Annabel's cheeks paled. 'Oh, Francis! I –' then she remembered me. 'Amy, go now,' but I was already halfway through the door.

Mr Tims told us what had happened. He was sitting in his pantry with his face chalk-white and his hands shaking so much he could hardly hold the cup of tea which Clara had made for him. I poked up the fire so that it burned more brightly as Clara said soothingly, 'There, there, Mr Tims. 'Tweren't *your* fault.'

'It was dreadful, dreadful.' His voice quavered. Clara said firmly, 'You've had a nasty shock. Best thing is to tell us about it – you'll feel better after.' She nodded to me and I closed the door, then we both sat down on the footmen's chairs.

'It was the telegram, that's what started it. If only he hadn't sent that telegram – he could have telephoned from the station, and then I'd have answered it though I don't like them newfangled things, but I –' He stopped, shaking his head.

'Who sent the telegram, Mr Tims?' Clara prompted.

'His young Lordship. I suppose he forgot about the telephone, seeing as it's new. I don't hold with it, if folk want to –'

Clara tried again. 'But what did the telegram *say*, Mr Tims?'

He fixed his red-veined eyes on her. 'I don't know, Clara, but I suppose it was the time of his train. I took it straight to Our Lordship in the library and he snatched it off the tray. When he'd read it he said, "Don't send the carriage – let him walk." Then he crumpled it up and just threw it into the corner of the room.'

Clara said soothingly, 'But there's no need to take on so about that, Mr Tims. His Lordship often throws bits o' paper on the floor when he's in a bad mood – I've picked 'em up myself, many a time. Baint nothing to get upset about.'

'I wasn't upset then, Clara – it was what happened later.' Clara was about to give him another prompt when he went on himself. 'Henry was on hall duty, but he came for me, because Lord Warminster was in the hall – walking up and down with a face like thunder. And Henry, he did think from the look on his face as there'd be mischief done, so he fetched me. We both waited, and then there was a great long peal on the bell but His Lordship got to the door before Henry – fairly threw himself at it he did, he'd got himself so worked up by then. Lord Quinham stood on the step, not looking best pleased as he'd had to walk up from the station, and at the sight of him His Lordship starts shouting. He don't falter so much when he shouts, Miss Roberts, and it was dreadful to hear him. All about how Lord Quinham had left his wife when she was ill – ill because she was carrying his child. And what a selfish –' Mr Tims shook his head. 'I couldn't repeat the word he used in front of you girls, but it was a terrible word for a father to use about his own son. Lord Quinham, he just stood there on the doorstep, looking at his father, his face going colder and colder. He didn't say anything until His Lordship finally ended with, "And you're not fit to black her boots, let alone be the father of her child." Then Lord Quin said, quietly but very clear, "Annabel's child is mine, you have no claim on it whatsoever. Nor on my wife." Then he pushed past into the hall, and I thought for a moment Our Lordship was going to hit him, but he didn't – instead he just went to the door and walked out.'

I asked the housemaid who cooked for the bothy to tell Joe that I wouldn't be taking Earl out that night because Miss Annabel had ordered dinner in her room, so I'd be waiting on her. She barely touched her food, and at supper in the Room afterwards Mr Tims told us that Lord Quinham and Lord Warminster had sat through the whole of dinner in total silence. Mr Wallis shook his head. 'They're like a couple of dogs fighting over the same bi– . . . bone,' he corrected hastily. 'But our Lordship, he's behaved like a fool. If he wants to keep her and her young 'un here then he needed to box cleverer than that. She's Lord Quinham's wife, and a wife has to do as her husband wants, heiress or no heiress. And the child ain't his.'

Mr Tims said, 'But it'll be his grand-child, Mr Wallis.'

The valet put down his knife and fork and said firmly, 'Lord Quinham's the father – that's what counts. Even Her Ladyship can't gainsay his rights there; in law a child's only got one parent – and that's its father.'

Mr Wallis was right. As I settled her down that night Miss Annabel told me that we'd be leaving Eston at the end of the week – for good.

Chapter Thirty-Seven

Next day it was as if there were a pall over the entire household. Miss Annabel stayed in bed, so I was up and down the stairs all day, seeing to her. Clara told me Lord Warminster had wanted to send for the doctor, but Lord Quinham wouldn't hear of it. I asked Clara if she'd take a message to Joe for me, explaining that I couldn't get out; then I told her what Miss Annabel had said about leaving and she shook her head. 'I baint surprised, not after what happened yesterday. I'll tell Joe – he'll be main put out at your going away.'

Over supper Mr Tims told us there'd been more words at dinner. 'His Lordship must have been asking Lord Quinham to change his mind while they were in the hall, because just as the soup was being served Lord Quin says: "Get this straight, sir. She is *my* wife and she is carrying *my* child. Because you were so besotted with her you settled an income on me at our marriage, now you've got no hold over me whatsoever. I'm going to take a house at the other end of the country and I'll make damned sure you never even *see* the child, once it's born." Then he takes a mouthful of soup and adds, "I'll make damn sure I employ a decent cook, too." Our Lordship, he couldn't answer, and Lord Quin looks straight at him and says, "If you want a child, you go and get one of your own – that's if you *can*, of course." At that Our Lordship throws down his napkin and walks out. Lord Quin he just kept on drinking his soup, cool as a cucumber.'

Mr Wallis shook his head. 'He shouldn't've spoken like that – not in front of servants.'

Mr Tims sighed. 'It's my guess he did it deliberately, because of the way Our Lordship swore at him in the hall yesterday in front of me and Henry. Lord Quin was getting his own back.'

Mrs Johnstone picked up her glass. 'Fancy saying that about Mrs Procter's cooking – the very idea!'

Mr Wallis snorted, 'Who are you kidding, Mrs J.?' And as he winked at me I felt the familiar fluttering of indigestion in my belly.

As soon as I could decently get away I left the Room and slipped along to the servants' hall. Clara and Mary were there, with Doris and Ivy from the laundry. Thomas had told them over supper about the scene in the dining room, and they were full of it. 'He didn't have no right to speak to Our Lordship like that – not his own father.' Clara was indignant. ''Tis only natural he be looking forward to becoming a granfer, at his age. He were that set on Lady Quin's childer growing up here at Eston. My Mam dropped a hint about it after the wedding and she said he looked as pleased as Punch at the very thought of it.'

Mary interrupted, 'I reckon 'tweren't so much his grand-children he were thinking about but his pretty new daughter-in-law. He's sweet on Lady Quin – always has been.'

Clara shrugged. 'Mebbe, but he were looking forward to the childer, too, I be main sure o' that.'

'I 'low you're right, Clara.' Doris leant forward, sharp elbows planted firmly on the table. 'I mind when my sister Maud came up to see me the other week wi' her two little 'uns. She left 'em to run in yard, and when I peeked out o' window – just to make sure as they weren't up to no mischief – I sees as they were playing wi' His Lordship's yellow bitch – letting 'em roll all over her she was, tugging her ears an' all. Well, I was just a-going to call 'em off when I sees His Lordship was there, standing in the shadow by the drainpipe – just watching 'em he was. And then little Jenny tumbled over and banged her knee on the cobbles. She set up such a howling, but afore we could do anything His Lordship comes barging into our sitting room shouting: "The child's hurt, the child's hurt – go to her, go to her!" I never seed Maud move so fast in her life! Though as she said after, you can't run to babbies every time they takes a tumble.'

Ivy reached for the teapot. 'Anyone fancy another cup?' As she poured she said, ''Tis a shame he only ever had the one o' his own – never saw much o' him, neither, not wi' Her Ladyship taking him off to France, and her never did have no more.'

Mary laughed. ''Tis always the way. Them as can afford a family don't get 'em, and them as can't gets more'n they bargained for!'

Doris nodded. 'You never spoke a truer word, Mary. I remember my poor Mam worrying herself sick every month in case she'd fallen again – and me and Maud, with us being the eldest and having to look after the babies, we'd be watching for her bloody clouts near as anxious as she was. The relief when we saw 'em soaking in the bucket!'

Ivy broke in, 'You were lucky, then. Our Mam, she couldn't tell whether she'd fallen or not.'

'Couldn't tell! A woman can always tell.' Mary's voice was disbelieving.

Ivy shook her head. 'Not my Mam, she couldn't. Wi' every one o' us she bled regular as clockwork for three, four months after she'd fallen. 'Tweren't till she quickened that she realised she was on the way. And the first time, wi' me, she didn't realise even then – thought I was indigestion, she did!'

The other girls all laughed, then Mary exclaimed, 'Fancy thinking you got indigestion, and then discovering it were a baby – what a surprise!'

'Oh, she knew the next time all right. She said it weren't a bit like indigestion, really – more like a moth fluttering in your belly.' And as she spoke the fluttering came in my belly. 'My Mam, she said once that happens there's no mistaking it. You can tell there's a baby in there, alive and moving.' And deep in my belly I felt a baby – alive and moving.

I stood up, very carefully, just managing to say, 'I – I best be going, in case my lady wants me.'

Clara glanced up. 'Oh, Amy – I nearly forgot. Joe says as you must pop out sometime tomorrow afternoon to see him. He wants a word wi' you – urgent.'

Somehow I thanked her, and got myself outside the door. I stood clutching the handle, listening to the carefree voices behind me, then I began to shuffle along the passageway, like an old woman.

My legs were shaking so much I could hardly climb the stairs, and I was shivering by the time I reached my room. But as soon as I'd bolted the door I began to undress. When I was completely naked I went over to the full-length mirror Miss Annabel had had fitted for me, and looked at myself in the bright electric light Lord Warminster had had installed for her.

The fullness of my belly barely showed – but when I turned sideways the swelling was there. I tried to pull it in, but it wouldn't go. I looked down, and under the bright light I noticed the brown line which ran like a band straight up the centre of my stomach. I licked my fingers and rubbed and rubbed at it – but I couldn't rub it away. I raised my trembling fingers to cup my breasts – and felt them lie hot and heavy in my palms. Fearfully my fingers tightened, squeezing, and as I watched small drops of liquid oozed from each full brown nipple – it was milk.

I put my clothes on again with fingers that shook so much I could hardly fasten the buttons. Once I was dressed you couldn't tell, and I thought, no – it's not true, it can't be true! Then the light caught my face and I saw the mark of the giant brown moth – and I knew now why Lord Warminster had told Joe: 'That girl, she's got a mark on her face – wait until it fades.' But it wouldn't fade, not until I was delivered.

Then I thought of Joe. I guessed what his message would be. He wouldn't want me to go to the other end of the country – he'd want to marry me, now – and if he did, my baby would have a name. I thought, in a cottage, by candlelight, he wouldn't see the mark on my belly, or the darkness of my swollen nipples; he wouldn't know until the baby was born that it wasn't his, and then it'd be too late and my baby would have a name. I seemed to see her, in the garden of that cottage, looking up at me so trustingly with her cornflower-blue eyes – blue eyes, my lord's eyes – because she wasn't Joe's baby and I couldn't pretend she was. I couldn't marry Joe Dempster now.

I hardly slept all night. I kept thinking that I was carrying my lord's baby and had been for months. It was the end of January now; he'd come to my room the first week in September and put his seed inside me – and it had been growing ever since. I slid my hand up under my nightdress and felt the smooth living roundness of my belly. Fear and panic clutched at my throat.

In the morning I asked Thomas where Lord Quinham was. He wasn't surprised; he thought I'd got a message for him, from Miss Annabel. 'He's in the billiard room, Miss Roberts.' The billiard room, where I'd gone to him to return Miss Annabel's ring – and told him he could come to my bedroom.

He was leaning over the green baize table, a long cue in his hand, casually potting balls. I closed the door behind me as he glanced up. 'Oh, it's you, Amy. What does Her Ladyship want now?'

303

I replied, 'I baint come from Her Ladyship.' My voice was a frightened squeak, and I had to swallow before I could continue. 'I be come for myself.'

'Oh?' He sounded very distant. 'And what do *you* want from me – a wedding present?'

I blurted out, 'I be carrying your child.'

'What!' The cue clattered down as he jerked upright. 'You can't be!'

'I be five months gone. I didn't realise, because I did bleed after, but I baint seen nothing for three months now – and I've quickened.'

'Oh my God!' His eyes closed for a moment. Then their blue flashed out as he snapped, 'How do I know it's mine? You must've met that gardener chappie by then.'

I gasped as though he'd hit me. 'No! Joe baint never– I baint never let him touch me. Thee bist the only man –' The tears were coming as I whispered, 'I do love thee – I allus have, and I allus will.'

He came closer, and I felt the warmth of his breath on my cheek as he asked, 'Then why did you walk out on me, that evening in Town?'

'Because thee didst give I the necklace.' He frowned in puzzlement, and I explained. 'I did think at first as it were a gift because – because you loved me. But then, when you said as how you could've had any girl in London, I knew you meant any – any –' I couldn't say that word. At last I whispered, 'I didn't want to be – bought.' He just stood there, looking down at me. I gazed back up into his blue eyes and told him, 'What I didst give thee, I gave thee because I do love thee. I didn't want nothing for it.'

His hand reached out, then checked itself. When he spoke it was very softly. 'I'm sorry, Amy – I didn't realise. If only – but you weren't to know. My cursed tongue. If it's any consolation, I'd give anything to have that time back again, and persuade you to stay.'

I whispered, 'So would I.'

For a moment we stood quite still, gazing into each other's eyes, then he seemed to shake himself before saying briskly, 'But it's too late now, the damage has been done. Though it's not as though it would have made any difference to you – you'd still have been in this pickle, since I'd already knocked you up. Anyway, at least you've got a husband lined up.'

'But I can't marry Joe now!'

He shrugged. 'You'll have to – unless you want your baby to be born a bastard.'

'No!'

'Then you don't have any choice, do you?'

'But it baint fair on Joe.'

'All's fair in love and war, Amy. Besides, it's been done often enough before, though I admit you've left it a bit late, you careless little thing.' His eyes narrowed until I flushed under his intent scrutiny. 'Luckily you're barely showing yet; I can tell the difference now I've had a proper look at you – but then,' he gave a small laugh, 'I've seen a lot more of you than the others have – and nobody else will ever see those tiny pink nipples now, will they, Amy? They've gone for good – they were my prize and I'm glad of it. That gardener chappie is going to have to make do with second-best – only you don't want him to guess that too soon, for all our sakes. Look, this is what you'll have to do. Next time he gets his hand up your skirt,' he paused, 'he *has* been trying to get his hand up your skirt, I presume?' My face crimsoned as I nodded. 'Yes, I thought so, any man who still had a complete pair would. You're a tempting little piece, Amy. Look how you tempted me – it's no wonder I succumbed. Women like you should be locked up in a convent and only allowed out on Sundays –' He stopped, with a wry grin, 'But I suppose I'd still have been scaling those nunnery walls! We'd best get back to business, my pet, before you start giving me ideas again. It really wouldn't do at present for me to be caught rogering my wife's maid on the billiard table. Besides, it plays havoc with the green baize, or so they tell me! Look, next time he tries it on, give in – let him do whatever he wants. But try and struggle a bit just at the last, then he mightn't realise that you're not intact. Inexperienced men often don't, I gather. Then as soon as he's finished start weeping and wailing – tell him he's ruined you and he's got to marry you at once. If he shows any signs of hesitating make it very clear that he can't have another taste until he's put a ring on your finger – that should bring him to heel.' He paused, and I saw his eyes were fixed on my breasts. 'God, Amy – you're more enticing than ever, with those extra curves.' He drew a deep uneven breath. 'I can't bear the thought of another man mauling you –' Then he dragged his eyes away and his voice became firm and businesslike again. 'But it's got to be done – I mustn't be selfish. Let me give you some advice, Amy. Once you are married keep your legs open all night – and all day too, if need be. Don't ever say no to him – however often he wants it. Being refused irritates a man, and you can't afford to do that, because as soon as this infant arrives he'll know he's been duped. At that point you'll just have to weep and wail again and say how sorry you are and that you'll give him one of his own straight away. By that time, with luck, he won't be able to do without you. Oh, and give him the necklace, to sweeten the pill.'

I stared at him. 'But I did give that back to you!'

'What?'

'I left it on the shelf, in your bathroom.'

'Good Lord! Then I know where that went – and I certainly didn't take *her* maidenhead. You silly girl, Amy – that's what it was *for* – in case this happened.' He sounded so exasperated I shrank away from him. He gave an impatient sigh. 'Stop looking like a stricken deer – I suppose you just didn't think. Look, I'll try to get some cash together and send it to you before the confinement – that gardener's owed something for taking you on in this condition. But the cards let me down last time I was in Town, and what with having to find a house . . . so you'll just have to wait, all right?'

I whispered, 'Yes. Thank 'ee, my lord.'

'And Amy, let me give you one last piece of advice. Don't ever let that fellow get worked up the way I was that night in Jermyn Street, and then walk out on him, will you? It makes a chap bloody angry, and then he does stupid things. You'd better go now, or the other servants'll be wondering what's going on.'

I was turning away, fighting my tears, when suddenly his hand shot out and pulled me back. My arm seemed to come alive where his fingers touched me and I gazed up into his blue eyes, which were smiling now. 'Take care, Amy my pet – and perhaps I'll come and see you and your baby one day.' He bent over me, and brushed my lips with his. 'Goodbye.'

At lunch-time Miss Annabel told me that my lord was going up to Town the next day to look for a house; so I knew I wouldn't see

306

him again until after I was married to Joe Dempster. But when at last I was free to go out and see Joe I knew I couldn't do what my lord had told me to; I had to tell Joe the truth. He'd said over and over again that he wanted to marry me whatever I'd done – he must mean it, he must.

Daylight was beginning to wane by the time I got outside, and I was shivering with the cold as well as with nerves when I found him over in the trial grounds. 'You'm looking starved wi' the cold, Amy. Come along into the glass-house, it'll be warmer out o' the wind.' He stumped ahead of me in his heavy boots, and for a moment I remembered my lord's easy, swinging stride – then I thrust the memory away from me. Joe was a good man, and I'd be safe with him.

I breathed in the reassuring earthy smell of the glass-house, then Joe shut the door, enclosing us safe inside its sheltering warmth. The rose bushes at the other end seemed to rustle their leaves in welcome, before falling silent once more. 'I'll light the lantern.' There was a spark, then a flame burnt steadily, and Joe and I were alone in the golden pool of light as the daylight outside was transformed into darkness by the glowing lantern. I saw the white gleam of Joe's teeth as he smiled at me, then his hand reached out and automatically straightened one of the seed pans. There were rose hips in those pans, buried deep in the dark moist earth, waiting to grow; just like the child I carried deep inside me – a child which would have no name, unless – and for a moment I hesitated, remembering my lord's advice, and the voice of temptation whispered in my ear: 'Go to him, offer yourself, deceive him,' – but I couldn't.

Then, as I was gathering all my courage together, he spoke first. 'Now, Amy, Clara told me what's happened and as how you're to be leaving at the end o' the week.' I nodded. 'Look, I can't a-bear to let thee go, so I'm going to speak to His Lordship again, and if he still don't agree about thic cottage then I'll find a room in the village somehow, then we can still be together. I'll see Rector about the banns this evening.' So I didn't even need to offer myself to him; I only had to keep silent, and my baby would be born with a name. 'Now, come 'ee here and give us a kiss to seal the bargain.'

I said, 'Joe, there be something as I maun tell 'ee first.'

I heard the good humour in his voice as he replied, 'Amy, you

307

been going on about this dark secret for weeks now, so if it's going to settle your mind, then tell me.' His teeth flashed in a grin. 'I can guess what it is already. I'll wager Lady Quin gave thee some money for fares and such-like – and thee didst spend it on thyself.'

'No, Joe, 'tis nothing to do with money.' I took a deep breath and said, 'I baint a maid. That's what I been trying to tell 'ee.'

'What!'

I dared not look at his face, but I heard the shock in his voice. I ploughed on, 'And now, yesterday evening, I found out there be something worse'n that.'

'What could be worse'n that?' He was almost shouting.

I braced myself for the final confession. 'I be carrying a child.' There was no answer. 'Joe, I didn't know that – not when I did say I'd marry you, I didn't know, I swear it.'

When he finally spoke he sounded dazed. 'But I never touched you. You wouldn't let me –' Then his voice became louder as he demanded, 'Whose is it? Who's done this to me?'

'It –' my voice stumbled. 'It was my lord.'

'His Lordship!' He exclaimed in disbelief. 'His Lordship'd never –' Then his voice changed, becoming flat as he said, 'You mean His young Lordship.'

He'd stepped back from the lantern, and the outside light had almost gone now. I couldn't see his face, only the stillness of his body. I moved towards him, my hands outstretched, pleading, 'But Joe, if you did marry me, and give my baby a name, then I'd be a good wife to you – I do swear it. I can cook and clean, I do be a hard worker – and Joe,' I hesitated, stumbling over the words, but I knew I had to say them, 'Joe, any time you wanted – even if it were dinner-time – I wouldn't never deny you. I wouldn't never say no – I do promise.'

There was silence as I waited, trembling, for his verdict. When he finally spoke his voice was quite level. 'No, I daresay you wouldn't. You baint had much practice in saying "no", have you? I daresay as you wouldn't say no to the baker, or the butcher's boy, neither.' He groaned. 'And I thought you were something special! The other night I was ashamed of myself for trying to –' His anger exploded. 'Hell and damnation! I should've put you up against a tree, taken my fill o' you and then walked away – that's all you're worth, you little slut! All the dreams I've had about you – you've trampled them into the muckheap – and that's where you belong!'

He came towards me, and one hand seized my arm. I saw the other go back – and then it swung forward hard across my face. Pain exploded in my cheekbone and I tried to pull back, crying, 'No, Joe! Please – no!'

'No wonder you got a mark on your face! Only it baint clear enough – it don't serve to warn decent blokes off – but it will. When I've finished wi' you your face'll be marked all right,' and as I cowered back he raised his hand again.

'Stop!' The command roared out from the depths of the glass-house.

Joe dropped my arm as if it stung, and swung round to face the shadows. 'My lord, I –'

'Get out, Dempster.'

'I –' Joe's voice tailed into silence as he turned and blundered out of the glass-house.

I saw the dark shape lurching towards me; as it reached the circle of light a huge, misshapen shadow crawled across the stone flags of the floor and began to climb up the wooden shelf supports, creeping towards me. I shrank away from it in fear – and at once the shadow stopped moving. Then the voice, pitched lower now, said, 'Go back – to – the house.' I turned and ran out of the open door.

Upstairs in my room I felt as though I were in the grip of a nightmare. I'd pinned all my hopes on Joe. He'd said he was willing to overlook my bastardy, that whatever sin I'd committed he would still want to marry me – and then I realised what I'd done; I'd believed my dreams again. That cottage, the little girls, the baby calling me indoors – they'd been nothing but my imagination. They'd never existed, and now they never would exist. I'd created another fool's paradise, just like my dreams of Lady Warminster, and my father, and of my lord marrying me. I'd never learnt by my folly: as each new dream was destroyed I'd simply made up another one, and believed that instead. I must have been mad to think Joe would still want to marry me once he knew I was soiled goods. And now it was worse than that – much, much worse.

The bell in my room rang; Miss Annabel wanted me. I went at

once, as I always did, but as I opened her door I cringed – suppose Lord Warminster had already told her? But as soon as I saw her face turned towards me I knew that he hadn't. She stared at the red weal on my cheekbone. 'Amy, what have you done to yourself? Did you trip and fall?'

'I –' My voice faltered, I couldn't answer.

She spoke for me. 'You silly girl, you could have put your eye out. You must be more careful in future.' She stood up and moved over to the mirror, peering into it at her too-pale face. 'I feel a little better this evening, so I shall be going down to dinner tonight.' Then she added in a voice that tried to be casual, 'Lord Quinham's dining with friends.'

As I entered the Room Mr Wallis asked, 'Walked into a tree, Miss Roberts? That dog try and get away from you again, did he?'

'No, it wasn't Earl's fault.' Mrs Johnstone sniffed.

Sighing Mr Tims said, 'Everyone's at sixes and sevens these days. His Lordship was like a cat on hot bricks at dinner.'

Mr Wallis snorted. 'Like a bull in a china shop, more like, smashing everything he plants his great hooves on. Got my head chewed off good and proper tonight. It'll be a relief when Lady Quin goes, his temper's worse than ever these days.' I pushed the potatoes around my plate, then tried to hide them under my fork. I couldn't eat a thing tonight.

I was shaking when I went into Miss Annabel's room to undress her, but it was obvious Lord Warminster hadn't told her yet. Then I thought, why should he tell now, when he's known all the time – known because he'd seen the brown butterfly on my face and understood what it meant, even before I had? Besides, he wouldn't want to upset Miss Annabel. I was safe for a few more days, and then, when we left Eston, I'd have to ask my own lord for help. I couldn't think beyond that.

But I'd reckoned without Joe Dempster. Next day as I came into the service corridor Mary passed me stony-faced, without even acknowledging my 'Good morning.' Behind her Bertha averted her eyes, as she very deliberately drew her skirts away from mine. When I came level with the pantry the two footmen were ogling me through the open doorway, and as I passed them Thomas nudged Henry. 'Not a bad looker for a whore, is she?' Their sniggers followed me down the corridor.

The men barely spoke in the Room. Mr Tims sat staring down at his plate; Mr Wallis only looked my way once, then shook his head murmuring, 'You daft little ha'porth.'

Worst of all was Mrs Johnstone's smile. 'Another cup of tea, Miss Roberts? After all, you've got to keep your strength up.' The smile came again. 'Let me help you to a second slice of toast – you're eating for two, remember!' She laughed out loud.

I got up and stumbled to the door. Behind me Mr Wallis exclaimed angrily, 'Leave the girl alone, Mrs J.!'

Outside I began to run along the passage – until Thomas and Henry barred my way. 'Well, well, look who's here, Miss High and Mighty Roberts – only she baint so high after all!' They closed in either side of me, penning me into the service corner. 'Did he give you a good time, His young Lordship?' Thomas' flushed face came closer. 'He baint the only fellow as can give a girl like you a good time – me and Henry, we knows a thing or two.' His hand closed on my breast and began to squeeze. 'Mm, that feels like a bit of all right. You have the other one, Henry.'

The two hands squeezed harder and harder; I gasped in pain. 'Enjoying it, are you? Hot-blooded little thing, I'll wager. Here, let's have a proper feel.' He jammed his knee into my belly as I struggled to get free, panting and frantic – but there were two of them, and they were much stronger than I was. As Thomas' hand pulled open my top buttons and thrust itself inside the neck of my blouse I felt Henry's swollen rod pushing against my thigh. Desperately I tried to twist away from it, but his hands caught at my buttocks and began to press and knead.

'No! Please, no!'

'You leave her alone, or I'll tell Mr Tims!' The two heads jerked back, and I caught a glimpse of Clara's angry face. Then Thomas' fingers resumed their painful probing.

'I baint afeard of old Tims.'

'Then I'm going to fetch His Lordship.' At once the two bodies backed off; I sagged against the wall, sobbing. Clara grabbed my arm. 'Get upstairs, Amy, and into your room. They won't dare come after you there.'

I sat huddled on my bed, the tears still running down my cheeks – then the bell pealed, an angry, jangling peal. As I came along the bedroom corridor Mrs Johnstone was walking towards me. 'Your

311

mistress wants you, at once.' I saw the sly smile on her face, and hardly dared to open the door.

Miss Annabel was standing by the hearth. I'd never seen her look like that before, and I cowered back in the doorway, not daring to meet her eye. 'So it's true, then – it's true.' Her voice rose to a shriek. 'Get out! Get out of my room, get out of this house. Go, go!' I turned and stumbled back upstairs.

Clara came in as I was trying to pack. She put her hand on my shoulder. 'You silly girl, Amy – you silly, silly girl. Why ever did you do it?'

I whispered, 'I do love him.'

Her hand gave my shoulder a brief squeeze, then she went over to the chest and pulled out a drawer. 'I'll help you pack.'

'Clara, whatever shall I do?'

She straightened up, and looked across at me. 'There's only one thing you can do. You'll have to go home and get down on your bended knees before your mam – and pray she can talk your dad round. That's all you can do now.' But it was more than I could ever do. Clara took out my spare skirt and brought it over to the bed, before asking, 'Have you got enough money for your fare home?'

'I've only got ninepence three-farthings.'

'What! Haven't you saved anything from your wages?'

'I did use all my savings to pay for Grammer's funeral, so Miss Annabel, she did lend me the money for my clothes and hairdressing lessons, so to pay her back I had to work without pay.'

She sat down with a thump on the bed. 'Oh, my goodness! Ninepence three-farthings won't get you anywhere.'

Timidly I asked, 'Has His Lordship left yet?'

She shook her head. 'I don't reckon so – I've just seen him downstairs.'

I felt a glimmer of hope. 'Then – please, Clara – would you ask him if he'd see me?'

She stood up. 'Yes, that's the best thing – I should have thought of it myself. I'll tell him as how Lady Quin's turned you off, and you baint got no money.'

I huddled in the chair, waiting, clinging to the thought of my lord. He'd help me, I knew he would.

Clara came back, her face flushed from running up the stairs. 'Quick – he was just on his way out.' I jumped up and followed her down. As she led me across the wide entrance hall the grim ranks of red-coated generals glared down at me. I shivered under those scornful stares from my lord's ancestors, but he would help me, he would. When we reached the library door Clara knocked and turned the handle. 'Go straight in – he's expecting you.' Hurriedly I slipped inside the door – and froze. The man sitting crouched behind the desk had a humped back and twisted neck; not my lord, but his father.

He raised his head in an impatient gesture, and I crept very slowly towards the massive desk. I didn't dare lift my eyes to his face. His right hand reached into his pocket, there was a jingling of coins and then he pushed a small pile of gold sovereigns over the red leather top of the desk, towards me. 'Take – those.' I stood staring at the gold, and it winked back at me, knowingly. '*Take* them.' He was getting impatient.

Slowly I picked them up. They were cold and hard to the touch. I managed to whisper, 'Thank you, my lord.'

Then he tossed a piece of notepaper across the desk. 'I will – inform Lord Quinham that he must make – some provision for you. Write down your home address.' A pencil bounced over and landed close to my hand.

I made no move to pick it up; I just stood staring at the thick, creamy paper. It was headed in confident black letters: *Eston, Wiltshire*. That was all. I pushed it away from me, saying dully, 'I baint got no home.'

He barked, 'Your family – where do they live?' And now at last I did look up at him. There was nothing to be frightened of any more, the worst had happened. There was no point keeping secrets, either: I'd kept too many of them in the past. So I said, 'I baint got no family either, because,' and my voice barely faltered before I spoke that ugly word, 'I be a bastard.'

He looked straight back at me; grey eyes he'd got, both the same colour, but they didn't match because one was bigger than the other. I saw his forehead crease into a crooked frown. 'Lady's maids do not – come out of – the workhouse. Who brought you up?'

'Granfer and Grammer – but they be both dead. And Aunt

313

Agnes –' I swallowed before adding flatly, 'She be dead too. So there baint nobody.' And I felt the tears coming so that his tilted head and raised shoulder blurred into one dark mass. I balled my hands and forced them into my eyes, knuckling the tears away; it was no use crying now. As my sight cleared I saw he was watching me, his mismatched grey eyes intent upon my face. I looked back, hopelessly, then I turned to go.

'Wait.' He flicked back the lid of the inkwell, picked up a pen, and began to write. When he'd finished I watched his huge hands splay out on the blotter as he rammed the piece of notepaper down on it. The thick hairs on the back grew almost the full length of his fingers; they looked very black against the white of the blotting paper. Then he reached for an envelope, slid the folded sheet of paper inside and wrote a name on it. When he'd sealed the flap he threw the letter across the desk. 'Take it – to this address.' He tossed a stiff white oblong of pasteboard over to land on the envelope. 'Give the letter – to the porter. You can stay there. I will be in Town – myself, at the end of – the week.' He dropped the lid of the inkwell. 'Go.'

Outside Clara asked me, 'Did he give you some money?' I nodded. 'I knew he would – His Lordship wouldn't let you be dismissed with nothing. You'll be able to go home now.'

'I thought – I thought it were Lord Quinham you'd asked.'

She looked at me in surprise. 'He left on the early train – didn't you know?'

'No, I didn't.'

'He baint coming back no more, he told Thomas this morning. He's sending for Her Ladyship when he finds a house.'

Clara helped me pack, and then went down to the back door with me. I picked up my basket and bag and set off walking to the station.

When I was on the train to London I took out the card he'd given me. Engraved in the centre in black copperplate lettering were just the three words: *Earl of Warminster*. In the right-hand corner below I read: *Eston, Wiltshire*, then opposite, on the left: *4, Richmond Mansions, Kew, Surrey*. It was the left-hand address he'd circled.

But even if my own lord hadn't told me the purpose of his father's apartment in Kew I would still have known why he was

314

sending me there. Thomas and Henry were young, and servants; Lord Warminster was elderly, and an earl – but they were all men. There was only one thing men would want from me now, and Lord Warminster wanted it too.

Chapter Thirty-Eight

I thrust the piece of white pasteboard into my pocket and out of my mind. Instead I began to dream. When I reached London my own lord would be there, waiting for me. He'd realised what was likely to happen, guessed I would be coming, and so was meeting every train. He would take me to a little room somewhere – quite a small room, in a lodging-house, but that was all I would need. No, not a lodging-house – it was the home of a former servant, his old nurse – someone he could trust, and she would look after me because I was carrying his child. I wouldn't take any money from him – she would already have a pension from my lord, so she would care for me because she loved him, just as I did.

Every week he would come to see how I was, and every week after he'd gone the old nurse would tell me that Lady Quinham wasn't well. She was coughing, she had no strength; the nurse looked grave. Then one day my lord came wearing a black armband and looking very sad – she had died of galloping consumption and been buried already. As I sat there in the train I felt the tears fill my eyes, but I didn't let them fall. My lord said simply, 'I know it's too soon, but we can't wait, Amy. We have the child to consider.' Early next morning he came for me, and we walked slowly to the church round the corner; there we became man and wife. And I walked back on his arm safe in the knowledge that now my child would have a name.

I dreamt my dream over and over again, filling in each tiny, precious detail: the furniture in the room, even to the bobble fringe on the red chenille tablecloth; his gentle expression and the loving words he spoke when he visited me every week; the old nurse's face, wrinkled like an apple in spring; even the clothes I sewed for my baby – every stitch was dreamt. It lasted me all the way to London.

I got out of the train at Waterloo and there was no one waiting for me at the barrier. I'd never thought there would be – it was only a dream.

I took out Lord Warminster's card with its circled address and read it again carefully, but I couldn't go to Kew and become a whore, so I took it over to the rubbish basket and dropped it in. I watched it fluttering down inside – and my dreams fluttered down after it. Then I picked up my basket and bag and set off for Lambeth, to look for work.

And as I walked I was back again in the world I'd known – and just as I had before, I began to calculate shillings, pennies and farthings: the cost of a room and my food, set against how much I could earn. I couldn't get a respectable position; I had no character, no reference. Even if I had, my condition would soon be obvious, and then I'd be turned off. The dressmakers' shops of the West End were closed to me, and even there I couldn't have earned enough to support myself – and a baby. So I turned my steps towards the sweatshops. If I forced my fingers to fly faster than ever before I could earn, maybe, ten or eleven shillings a week. A room would be perhaps five shillings, and with five shillings left for food I could just about manage. But when my time came, what then? Panic rose in my throat, but I fought it down. After all, Aunt Agnes had managed, hadn't she? But I remembered Beat telling me: Granfer, he'd given her his savings – she'd not been truly alone, as I was. So I knew where I would have to go, when my pains started, and I turned and walked there instead.

I made myself look at it; it was no use hurrying by on the other side of the street now. And as I stood there I tasted to the full the bitter brew of guilt. My baby – not only would her birth-lines bear the stigma of bastardy, they would also proclaim the shame of the workhouse. She would carry that disgrace with her for the rest of her life.

For the rest of her life: but what would that life be? I would not be allowed to leave her in the workhouse while I searched for work. No, to gain even that grim security for her I would have to stay there myself; we would be prisoners together – but not together. At the end of the first month she would be taken from my side and banished to the workhouse nursery, so that I hardly ever saw her. We would serve our sentences apart. And later, what was there for her then? Lord Warminster had said: 'Lady's maids don't come out of the workhouse,' and they didn't; only drabs and skivvies came from the workhouse. It had been

317

different for Aunt Agnes. She'd always known that in the last resort she could send me to Granfer, where I'd be safe in the country with only the jeering boys to fear, but now, in the same plight, I had no one to turn to.

As soon as she was born I would have to take her out of the House and find a woman to care for her while I went back into service. Not in a gentleman's establishment, not in a place like Nether Court, but I could at least be a general servant, because there were people who were prepared to employ fallen women from the workhouse – people like the man who'd employed Peg. I remembered Peg very clearly now I was back in Lambeth. I even remembered the very words she'd used as she'd told me: 'The master, he had me in the bathroom while I was running his bath. There was nothing I could do, I'd lost my character, see.' So Peg, she'd gone on the streets to pay for her baby's keep – as I would have to do.

My body was racked with shudders as I turned away from that high prison wall. No! It must be the sweatshop – I would manage somehow. I would feed the baby but not myself, so I could afford to pay a girl to look after her while I was at work. At work I would sew buttonholes until my fingers were bruised and bleeding, until the very bone showed through; only suppose there was no work, and the sweatshop was on short time – what would I do then? And I knew what I would have to do – the same as Flo, the girl who'd gone up West in the evening to earn the money for her rent.

But she'd only had herself to support; I would have the baby, too, so I'd have to go more often. The workhouse – and then the streets: or the sweatshop – and the streets. I closed my eyes and saw again the scene in that dark alleyway, with the men coming to be served one after the other. Then in my ears I heard Beat's voice: 'When a girl ain't got nothing left to sell, then she has to sell herself.' I too would have to sell myself.

I went straight back to the station, found the rubbish basket and dug my hand in among the slimy banana skins and empty cigarette packets. The white card was still there, just where I'd dropped it, together with my dreams. I left my dreams in the basket with the other rubbish, took out the white card and set off for Kew.

I still had the envelope with me, I hadn't thrown that away; perhaps all along I'd known that I was going to need it. After all, he'd given me more than my fare to London had cost, so I was already in debt to him – and there was only one way I could pay that debt.

After I got out at Kew Bridge Station I had to walk across the river. Stopping on the bridge I looked over the parapet – and there was another answer, flowing swiftly beneath my feet. I lingered, gazing down into the grey depths – and I was tempted, but then the fluttering came in my belly. My baby, she was alive – I had no right to kill her too. As I was about to turn away a policeman approached me, his face watchful. 'You wouldn't be thinking o' doing anything silly, miss, now would you? Remember, there's laws against it.' I shook my head and turned to walk over and off the bridge.

By the time I'd found Richmond Mansions it was beginning to drizzle. The imposing pillared entrance marked it as the residence of gentlemen; I had no place here, except as a servant – or a gentleman's mistress. I hesitated outside a long time, getting steadily damper, before I could pluck up the courage to walk between those pillars and knock at the door of the porter's lodge.

The head porter was summoned and handed Lord Warminster's letter. When he'd read it he showed it to the younger man, and they both grinned knowingly at each other before the head porter called his wife. She took me up to the apartment, pointed out the doors of the different rooms and showed me how to use the speaking tube in the kitchen for ordering meals. Then she took me along to the linen cupboard. 'I'll make up your bed – next door to His Lordship's dressing room, I suppose?' Her voice was quite matter-of-fact.

I tried to answer in the same tone. 'Yes, that'd be most convenient, thank 'ee.'

She gestured to the door at right angles to the cupboard. 'His Lordship's valet always has this one.' As she spoke I quailed at the thought of having to face Mr Wallis – he'd go back to Eston and tell Mrs Johnstone and Mr Tims – then I pulled myself up short; it didn't make any difference, not now.

When the woman had gone I went back to the kitchen, sat down at the table and made myself think quite coolly about what I was going to do. I told myself that it was much the most sensible move. At Eston I'd often heard tell of what a good landlord Lord

Warminster was; he always ensured that his farm labourers were paid a fair wage, and saw to it that his agent had repairs done promptly on cottage roofs and such-like. I remembered Clara saying that no one had been put in the House from Eston village for as long as she could remember – and the walls of Lambeth Union loomed a little less forbiddingly. If he paid me well for my services I could save – maybe even enough money to buy a sewing machine, and then I could set up as a dressmaker. It wouldn't be easy at first, because there were a lot of expenses and bad debts to face, but I'd manage somehow, if only I had some money. And I was sure he'd pay me a fair fee, as long as I satisfied him, pleased him, even – only then I remembered that I was already five months gone, and my spirits plummeted. I'd be bound to start showing soon, and he might not want me any more, then.

Uncle Alf, he'd wanted to do It to Aunt Agnes right up until the baby was due, but Lord Warminster, he was a gentleman, and the gentry were more fastidious; he might prefer to buy some other girl's services once I began to show. I might only have a couple of months to save up in. Then again, I knew whores like Peg were paid each time the man did It, and with Lord Warminster being quite elderly he might not want to do It all that often, so I wouldn't earn very much. I began to fret, then I thought, but maybe the gentry are different – perhaps they pay a kind of rent. After all, Lord Warminster paid for this flat in Kew even when he wasn't living in it, it just had to be available – maybe he'd pay for me to be available when he needed me, in the same way. Besides, he'd already given me money – I still had over a pound of that left which I wouldn't need because this was a service flat with all meals provided – so in a sense he was already renting me, even though he wasn't coming up to make use of my services until the end of the week.

At that point my calmness vanished; I began to shiver. I'd only done It with my own lord those few times, and although I loved him so much I'd hated the feel of him doing It to me – and it had been so painful, as well. My own lord – he was tall – but his father, despite being twisted sideways, was taller still; and he was broader and more heavily-built than his son, too. I'd heard the women in the wash-house at the Buildings say that the bigger the man the bigger the rod, and my own lord, his had looked enormous, so whatever –? I was really shaking by then, great heaving shudders. I got up and went out onto the small service balcony next to the dustbin, gulping in the cool air, trying not to retch. But it was no use; I was violently sick in the servants' WC beyond the dustbin.

Cleaning up afterwards calmed me down a little, and once I was back inside the warmth of the kitchen I told myself firmly, 'Thee bist a gurt fool, Amy. There be a babby got to come out o' thy cunny afore midsummer – and however big His Lordship's rod do be, it baint never going to be size o' that!' Then a bell rang over by the dresser, and when I picked up the speaking tube a voice said, 'If you put the kettle on now I'll send a tray up in five minutes. Do you want buttered crumpets?'

And suddenly I realised I was ravenously hungry, so I replied, 'Yes, please,' and went to fill the kettle.

When the bell rang again I pulled on the rope and the tray came up the shaft with a tea caddy, milk, sugar – and the crumpets, keeping nicely hot under a shining metal cover. I felt better as soon as I'd eaten them and drunk a cup of tea. I told myself it was silly to keep fretting about what was going to happen, because it wasn't going to happen until the end of the week – and I didn't have any choice, anyway. So I poured myself another cup of tea.

After I'd done the washing up and sent the tray down there was the whole empty evening ahead of me in that echoing flat. The kitchen was warmed by heated pipes and had a gas stove – there was no glowing range to sit in front of, and all the crockery and utensils were shut away in cupboards behind blank closed doors, like those doors along the passageway. Little tendrils of unease began to creep up my spine; suppose there was someone hiding behind those blank doors, suppose that later, when I was fast asleep. . . ? I caught hold of myself; I would go and check, now.

As soon as I'd made that resolution, fear was joined by guilt. I had no right to go prying into Lord Warminster's private rooms but I knew I had to look, else I'd never sleep a wink that night. I stood up at once. I would tour the flat, now, before I lost my nerve.

I went right back to the entrance lobby and started there; a door opened directly off it and I threw that open and snapped on the electric light. It was only a cloakroom, with a black and white tiled floor, a wash-basin and a WC in a cubicle at the end – there was no burglar hiding in there. I went back into the main corridor and walked along to the door opposite the kitchen; it opened to reveal a dark, gloomy dining room. The room next to it was obviously intended to be the drawing room, but there was no sofa and only a couple of armchairs; instead a huge desk dominated the room, while both chimney alcoves were filled with bookshelves. But what drew my eye were the paintings – they hung on every wall, and there was even a painting between the two windows. There must have been half a dozen larger ones, and some smaller – all brightly coloured and glowing under the bright electric light. I would have liked to stay and look at them, but I felt as though I were intruding, so I shut the door quietly and went through the swing doors to the bedroom corridor.

It was obvious which was the door to the master bedroom, but I couldn't bring myself to go in yet, so I turned right and went down to the linen cupboard. I checked it again, although only an extremely small burglar could have hidden in there; then I peeped into Mr Wallis' room – there was just a bed, a chest, a chair and table, and a wardrobe. Apart from the table the next bedroom was the same, just like the one with the bed made up for me. On the other side of the passage were the bathroom and WC, with a black and white tiled floor the same as the cloakroom. I wouldn't use his bathroom, of course – I'd wash in the scullery off the kitchen.

There were only two doors left by now. I opened the one to his dressing room; it was as large as the spare bedrooms, but with just a chest of drawers and the wardrobes. The mirror on the wash-stand was so tiny I wondered how Mr Wallis managed. There'd been no mirrors in the main rooms at all – any more than there were at Eston. I knew I was thinking about mirrors just to put off going into Lord Warminster's bedroom; but I'd have to go in there once he arrived, so I flung the door open – and nearly jumped out of my skin. There was a woman in there, standing between the windows – and she was completely naked.

I started to stammer my apologies – then I saw the pictures either side of her, and realised that she was painted, too. When my heartbeats had slowed, I moved forwards into the room – it was as if she drew me to her. She was tall, taller than any woman I'd ever seen, and she was beautiful. Her golden hair curled softly around the faultless oval of her face, and her eyebrows were two perfectly-matched crescents that curved down to the finely drawn bridge of her delicate nose. As I gazed at her in admiration her eyes looked straight back at me from below their golden-brown lashes – there was just a hint of a smile in them, and that hint was mirrored in her curving lips. She wasn't embarrassed at having nothing on; she was beautiful, and she knew she was beautiful – no one would ever make her feel ashamed.

The odd thing was that I recognised her. I knew I'd seen her before, yet I couldn't put a name to her, although I searched my memory for her likeness. But seeing her there was like meeting a friend when I'd least expected to, so I smiled at her, and in the dim light her lips seemed to move as if smiling back at me – and I was comforted. Gently I closed the door and went back to the kitchen.

It was a strange week, that week while I waited for Lord Warminster to come and make me his mistress. First thing the morning after I'd arrived I went out and bought a packet of starch. I washed my best nightdress, even though it was clean, and then I starched it as stiff as I could, before ironing it until every tuck and frill stood out straight and white. When it was aired I folded it up neatly and put it away – then I stopped worrying. I stopped thinking, too; I simply existed.

A maid was supposed to come up each morning to clean the flat, but I asked her if I might do it myself. I wanted to have something to occupy my hands – besides, while I dusted I could look at the paintings. I spent a lot of time looking at them: at the deep blue seas and the bright skies above, at the glowing white marble of the sun-warmed benches and pillars, at the clear water of the splashing fountains – those pictures were windows into another world. There were people living in that world: women dressed in loose flowing robes, mothers playing with their plump smiling babies, young girls who were slender and graceful to watch. Some of them had names – I read them in the titles below: Clytie, Nausicaa, Psyche, Balneatrix – strange names that I'd never heard before. The nameless ones I christened, and I gave them all surnames and families – mothers and fathers, brothers and sisters – they all had names in the tales I wove about them. Except for the naked lady in the bedroom – I couldn't think of a name good enough for her. Besides, I was sure she had one already, if only I knew it. I didn't make up stories about her, either. She was so real I wanted to know her true story.

I would stand in front of the huge painting trying to puzzle it out. The title below was *The Judgement of Paris*, but that didn't make sense because Paris was the capital of France, and a big city like London; but she obviously wasn't in a city because there were trees and hills in the background. And who were the two other women in the picture? They both had their eyes fixed on her, but she stood there taking absolutely no notice of their stares, even though she hadn't got a stitch on. And why had she taken her dress off? It was hanging from the fingertips of her left hand as if she were just about to drop it altogether – but it couldn't be because of the heat, since by the look of the blossom on the tree behind her it was only spring. Yet there was an apple lying on the grass at her bare feet and, even more curious, that apple was a pure, shining gold.

All the women in the other pictures were busy with their own concerns and with each other, but she was different – she was looking straight at me, as if she could see me, hear me. And so, because I was lonely and afraid, I made believe she was a real living woman and talked to her – and she seemed to listen to me, smiling her calm, confident smile.

My other comfort was the Botanic Gardens; I visited them every afternoon, staying until the gates closed at dusk. I would walk along the paths and between the trees until I grew chilly or it began to rain, then I would take refuge in the warmth of the great glass-houses and wander among the odd, outlandish plants, gazing at them in wonder. There were plants there the like of which I'd never seen before: strange swollen green pillars, with spikes in the place of leaves, round plants which crouched on the ground pretending to be pebbles, plants with little shopping bags hanging from the ends of their tendrils and ferns so tall their fronds were like fringed green parasols opening above my head. There were wide pools, too, with the enormous flat leaves of gigantic water lilies floating on their surface – as big as boats, they were, while in the great Palm House the trees rose to the roof high above me, so that I felt as though I were walking in the depths of a tropical forest. In the other houses the gardeners showed me plants which grew cocoa, cinnamon, nutmeg, bananas, coconuts; I was wide-eyed at the wonders revealed by Kew. Wandering through the warm moist greenery it was as though I'd been taken out of the real, frightening world and set down in this strange exotic place where no one could harm me.

On Friday I woke suddenly and thought, it's the end of the week – and panic clutched at my throat. Then I said out loud, 'The end o' the week be *Saturday*,' and I got up and had my breakfast as usual. After I'd eaten my dinner I went straight out to the Gardens. There was no wind and the sun came out. It was almost warm, so when my legs began to ache I found a bench in a sheltered spot and sat down to rest. There was nobody else about; I was completely alone. And as I sat there the loneliness seemed to seep into my very bones. I could look at the pictures, even talk to them – but they were only pictures. When Lord Warminster came he would enter my body, but he wouldn't talk to me either. I was only a servant. I'd had a fancy once that he was the Beast in the fairy tale who was kind and sat down with Beauty every evening while she dined – but he wouldn't dine with me; I would eat in the kitchen in my proper place. Later I'd go and lie down on his bed so he could put his rod inside me and spend himself, but as soon as he'd finished he would turn away and dismiss me, just as the men had done with Peg. I doubted if he would actually touch me, except where he had to. I'd never seen him even offer his arm to Miss Annabel, whom he loved, so he wouldn't touch me, whom he despised.

Because there was no one near me I let the tears overflow and trickle down my cheeks – and then it happened, she began to move. It wasn't the fluttering any more, which I still thought of as indigestion even though I knew it wasn't – no, this was actual movement. She was turning round, I felt her do it. And suddenly I could see her, like the baby on the draining board at Endell Street: complete and perfect, with her tiny feet and starfish hands, her small mouth, her button nose, the delicate curve of her eyelids. She hadn't opened her eyes yet, she was still blind like a new-born puppy – but she was alive. She was inside me, my baby, moving – waiting to be born. And I wasn't alone any longer.

I don't know how long I sat on that bench. While she was moving I stayed absolutely still – I just wanted to sit and feel her there, inside me. When she finally settled herself down, curled up and went to sleep then I very carefully rose to my feet. My back felt as though it were breaking in two but I didn't mind the pain, not now. I walked slowly along the path with my hand inside my pocket so I could hold it over my belly to protect her, and keep her safe.

The sun had gone in and it began to spatter with rain, so I took her into the nearest glass-house. It was the fern-house, and the high, feathery fronds curled protectively above me. There was the sound of voices, but they were far away; I was floating in the depths of a warm, green ocean – just myself and my baby. The ferns seemed to sway towards me, hiding me, keeping us both safe.

In a trance of happiness I moved unthinkingly through the whispering greenery, then the path turned, widened – and there, blocking my way, stood the great black shape of Lord Warminster. His mismatched grey eyes stared down at where I stood, rooted to the ground. Then the gentleman with him touched his arm. 'There's an interesting specimen of *Angiopteris hypoleuca* over here, Lord Warminster – Morrison brought it back from Java. We thought at first it wouldn't take, but as you can see it's doing well now.' The humped and twisted shoulder swung round away from me as they both bent over the large tub. At last my legs unlocked themselves and I brushed past and almost ran towards the door and out into the chill air of winter.

Chapter Thirty-Nine

My breathing was fast and frightened and there was a stitch in my side by the time I got back to the safety of the flat – only it wasn't safe any more. I was sobbing as I climbed the stairs, and then my stomach began to heave. Out in the servants' WC I retched and retched; by the time I crept back into the kitchen and collapsed on a chair I was cold and shivering.

I remembered the humped shoulder and twisted neck, those unequal eyes set in that contorted face – and the bile rose in my throat again. How could I offer myself to this deformed stranger, allowing him to invade my body and pay money for that intimacy which I'd given my own lord for love? The frightened thoughts chased themselves through my head and down into my shaking legs so that I stood up, preparing for flight, but as I moved, so did my baby. I put my hand over the place where she lay, clasping her – and sank back onto the chair. Because I had chosen to let my own lord come to me that night in September, so now I had lost my right to choose.

I bathed my eyes and tidied my hair; by the time I'd finished, boots were clattering along the corridor. I turned to face the door as Mr Wallis flung it open. 'Amy Roberts! Whatever are *you* doing here?'

My face burnt as I whispered, 'I didn't have nowhere to go, so Lord Warminster did send I here.'

'Well, I never did!' His eyebrows shot up in a pantomime of amazement – which suddenly ceased as his eyes slid away from mine. 'Still, ours not to reason why. Put the kettle on lovey, my throat's dry as a bone. I'll order dinner.' He picked up the tube and whistled down it. 'How's my beautiful Mrs B. this afternoon? And what's she got on the menu for us tonight, then?' He held his ear to the tube as I filled the kettle, then swung it round again to speak. 'He'll have the soup, as usual, then sole, a mutton chop and apple pie. Oh, and send up a bowl of nuts and one of oranges – he likes his fruit, does His Lordship. Miss Roberts and I will partake of the same. Seven-thirty on the dot – he's going out to one of his Rose Society meetings this evenings. Ta, Mrs B.' He replaced the tube on the hook, grinning at me. 'And yours truly's got a meeting this evening as well, in The Crown and Anchor with my brother. His ship's just docked, so His Lordship's given me the night off. Ah, he must've let himself in.' At the sound of the uneven tread of Lord Warminster's boots in the passageway I cowered back against the dresser, while Mr Wallis filled the teapot and set the tray.

When Mr Wallis came back I stammered, 'Did he – did he ask for me?'

'Nah – I told him you were in the kitchen and he just grunted. I'll take his bags along and get them unpacked. See you at dinner, young Amy.'

I crept down the corridor to hide in my bedroom. I could hear Mr Wallis whistling as he moved around in Lord Warminster's dressing room – and for a moment I wished it were him I had to go to tonight. He was getting on, but not as much as Lord Warminster, and besides, he'd always spoken kindly to me at Eston – but it was no use thinking like that.

Later there were the muffled sounds of Mr Wallis running His Lordship's bath, followed by the uneven footsteps going past my door, and then returning. Finally the dressing room door opened again and I knew it was time for dinner.

Mr Wallis was unloading the soup tureens from the lift as I came in. Setting the second one down on the tray he backed through the door with a wink in my direction. He returned so quickly I looked up in surprise and he explained, 'When he's on his own His Lordship won't have even me or Tims in the room while he's eating. I reckon it's with him having to feed hisself sideways – he thinks folk'll laugh at him. Ladle ours out, Amy, while I unload the rest and put it in the oven.'

I didn't know what to say to Mr Wallis as we drank our soup, but fortunately he began telling me about his brother, and how he'd been at sea since he was a boy. Then there was a buzz as the indicator jumped. 'Upsadaisy – put the sauceboat aboard, there's a good girl.'

He came back, slipped into his seat and began to dissect his fish. 'That should keep him quiet for a while, seeing as he's not eaten properly for weeks, not with young Lord Quin and his lady being there.'

Staring down at my sole I managed to pluck up the courage to ask, 'Is she – is my lady still at Eston?'

He replied briskly, 'She ain't *your* lady any longer. No, she was in such a state after you left, His Lordship telegraphed for her ma – and she came and took Her Ladyship back home. Pass the pepper, duck – Mrs B.'s a bit mean with the seasoning.'

So Miss Annabel was back at Nether Court – now everyone would know the terrible thing I'd done. Mrs Harper, Mr Davenport, Mr Peake, what must they be thinking of me now? My eyes filled with tears, and one plopped down into the cheese sauce. Mr Wallis sighed, 'You were a silly girl, Amy. You had a good place there, and you threw it away – now look at the pickle you're in. Lord Quin, he won't do anything for you. He wants to keep on the right side of his missus – he'll never risk upsetting her even more, especially not in her condition. You'd be left high and dry if it weren't for His Lordship in there.' He jerked his thumb towards the dining room and just at that moment the bell buzzed again. 'That's quick – he'll give hisself indigestion. He must've been hungry.'

I stood up as he did. 'I dussent want no more, thank 'ee Mr Wallis. I be going to my room now.'

As soon as I'd closed the door behind me the worries began again, but they were different worries now. He hadn't bothered to ask if I was there, waiting for him, and when Mr Wallis had told him that I was in the kitchen he'd only grunted. Perhaps he'd changed his mind, perhaps he didn't want me any more. I remembered that dreadful afternoon in the housemaid's closet, and my own lord becoming impatient with me because I didn't know how to help him satisfy himself. He'd said I'd have to learn, but perhaps Lord Warminster didn't want the trouble of teaching me. After all, the women he went to regularly must be experienced, and know how to give him pleasure – why should he want to bother with me? And the memory of the painted lady in his bedroom wasn't a comfort any more; *she'd* know how to please a man – I could see it in her face – but I didn't. Then I'd behaved so badly in the fern-house. I hadn't said: 'Good afternoon, my lord,' I hadn't even managed to smile at him. Instead I'd just stared, and then run away in horror – suppose now he thought I wasn't willing? I must show him I was, I must. I would go to him and tell him I'd come to please him, to pleasure him, and then, when he'd done It once – my mind darted back to my own lord, and what he'd told me about Joe. He'd said that once Joe had had a taste of me then he'd want me again and again. I must *make* Lord Warminster want me, I must.

Folding my hands neatly on my lap I sat up straight and began to plan. I'd been in his bedroom every day, in the morning to clean and in the evening to look at the picture, so I knew that when I went in tonight the lamp in the street outside would give me just enough light to see my way. I would go straight to where he was lying waiting in the big bed and tell him exactly why I'd come. He wouldn't answer, I was sure of that, but he'd be expecting me, so he'd grunt in acquiescence and then I'd lift the top sheet and climb in beside him and . . . Panic gripped me once more – I didn't know what to do next! Then I caught hold of myself again. I wouldn't need to know: he was a man, and a man of his age would have done It hundreds of times – thousands of times – he'd know what to do next. Then when he'd finished I'd ask him if he wanted me to stay so he could do It again straight away, or to come back later in the night if he wasn't ready again yet. He'd give me his orders, and I'd do whatever he required.

But suppose he didn't want me again, not ever? No, he would, he must.

When I heard the clock strike nine I began to make my preparations. I went along to the scullery and shut the door behind me, wedging it with a kitchen chair. Then I took off my clothes and scrubbed myself all over until my skin was taut and stinging. There were two types of soap beside the sink; I used the stronger one that was actually meant for the floor, but I wanted to be really clean. Then I brushed my teeth very carefully before going back to my bedroom and putting on my best nightie; the starch crackled as I pulled it over my head, and the firm stiffness of it gave me courage. I buttoned every button and tied every tape with exactly matching bows. I knew I must be neat as well as clean because Mr Wallis had often mentioned in the Room how particular Lord Warminster was about his dress; everything must be 'just so' for him, and now I must be 'just so' too.

I went over to the mirror and began to plait my hair; when they were finished I tied each plait with identical tape bows. One or two tendrils had escaped and come curling round my temples as they always did. I peered at them anxiously, before deciding that he probably wouldn't notice them in the poor light. Then I began to worry about my feet. My only slippers were very worn by now – they'd been an old pair of Saranne's that she'd given me back in Bath and they looked far too shabby for a gentleman's bedroom. Eventually I decided I'd leave them behind and go barefoot – besides, it'd be quicker for me to climb into his bed that way. When I was fully ready I pulled out the starched skirt of my nightie so as not to crease it and sat down on the edge of the chair to wait, and as I waited I rehearsed all my moves over and over again.

At last he came back, and his footsteps passed my door as he visited the WC opposite. I heard the cistern flushing and water running in the bathroom basin, then the sound of his footsteps returning. By straining my ears I could hear him moving about in his dressing room – then the muffled slam of the inner door, followed by silence.

I counted up to sixty five times, and then I unlocked my cramped legs and stood up. My whole body was shaking as I crept up to his bedroom door, and I stood outside trying to still my trembling legs, before forcing my hand to reach for the handle. I had to do it, I had to.

My fingers closed on the knob, I turned it quickly, pushed open the door and stepped inside – then stopped abruptly. He still had the electric light on, and he was sitting up in bed, reading. I'd thought he'd be lying down, waiting for me in the dark – the bright light confused me. As I stood there the whole top part of his body swung round to face me directly and his eyes flashed. Then he pulled off a pair of spectacles and asked, 'Are you – ill?'

I walked forward, stiff as a clockwork doll, my eyes fixed on him. He clicked the spectacles shut and closed his book, then he reached out to place them on the table beside the bed before speaking again. 'What do you – want?'

I was at the side of his bed by now, but I hadn't been expecting him to speak. My carefully rehearsed words were flying away from me as desperately I groped to retrieve them. 'I – I be come to –' My tongue stumbled, and I faltered before blurting out, 'I be come to please you.' He was staring at me as if he hadn't properly heard, so I amended, emphasising 'To *pleasure* you.' Then I reached out for the edge of the sheet and began to raise it. At once his arm dropped and pinned it down, so the sheet was twitched from my fingers. But I had to, I had to. Taking a deep breath I grasped the hem again, and tugged as hard as I could until it broke free of his arm and lifted. But even as I was climbing under it the sheet shot rapidly away from me, and in seconds it was tightly wrapped around his body.

He glared at me. 'No!'

I stopped, poised with one knee on the edge of the mattress. 'But – you did give I money, and send me here –' I couldn't control the quaver in my voice as I explained desperately, 'And I be *clean* – I did scrub myself all over.'

'I can – smell – that.' Through the blur of my threatening tears I saw that his face was less angry now, but he still kept the sheet tucked firmly around his body like a shield. In a last effort to make him understand I whispered, 'I be willing.'

His voice replied very decisively. 'But *I* am not.'

Slowly I slid back off his bed, the tears of humiliation spilling over as I asked hopelessly, 'Dussent thee want I?'

The tears were running down my cheeks now; I put my hands up to try to brush them away, but they kept on coming. When he finally answered his voice was quiet. 'Child, it's so long since I – associated – with a woman, that I have forgotten what to do. Go back to your own bed now. I will see you in the morning.'

Somehow I stumbled out, and back to my room. I crawled into bed and lay sobbing with exhaustion and fear. I'd been wrong, completely wrong. Lord Warminster didn't want me, he never had. Oh, whatever would happen to me now? And the baby began to twist and turn in small, frantic movements, as if sensing my distress. I whispered to her, 'I did try – but he dussent want I.' Then I cried myself to sleep.

When I woke the next morning I felt sick and heavy – and every time I thought of the scene of the previous night hot waves of shame engulfed my entire body. When I heard Mr Wallis go in next door I dragged myself out of bed and began to dress – and discovered that I couldn't fasten my button on my waistband. I'd known, but I hadn't admitted to myself, that my belly was swelling

– even the few days at Kew had made a difference. It wasn't just the brown butterfly wings on my face; my whole body now showed what I was – a woman with child. And my ringless finger proclaimed my shame.

I ate my breakfast in the kitchen with Mr Wallis. I hadn't heard him come back last night and he wasn't very talkative this morning, except for muttering, 'Oh my head. No, I *don't* want a fried egg, Amy – ta all the same.' After he'd cleared Lord Warminster's breakfast he told me, 'His Lordship wants to see you, in the drawing room.'

I went in and closed the door. Lord Warminster was sitting behind his desk with his spectacles on, writing. He was dressed in his London clothes: the black frockcoat that only older men wore nowadays; the double-breasted grey waistcoat; the navy-blue silk cravat tied at the neck of his high wing collar – all spoke of his age and his rank in society. He looked so stern, so remote, that I wondered how I could ever have dared to enter his bedroom, let alone try to climb into his bed.

He finished the sentence he was writing and blotted it carefully before removing his gold-rimmed spectacles and looking up at me. As I stood in front of him I saw his glance take in my straining blouse, and notice the way my skirt had ridden up at the front over my swollen belly. My cheeks flushed with embarrassment as I waited for him to speak. 'When – exactly – will the child – be born?'

My eyes dropped to my twisting fingers. 'At the end o' May – or mebbe June.'

He flicked back the skirt of his coat and reached into his trouser pocket. 'In the absence of Lord Quinham I must – take some responsibility – since your – seduction – took place under my roof.' He pushed a pile of sovereigns and half-sovereigns across the desk to me. 'You will have to find – somewhere to live; obviously you cannot – stay here – for any length of time. Take this, and secure respectable lodgings – until the birth. Tell the landlady – that you will be receiving a weekly allowance.'

I took the coins and put them in my pocket. 'Thank you, my lord.' Despite his odd face and twisted neck he still looked very much the gentleman – elderly, distinguished – however could I have been so presumptuous, so foolish! I blurted out, 'My Lord, I be terrible sorry about last night. Only I did think, with you giving me money, as I had to please you in return.'

As soon as I'd spoken I wished the words back again – he'd be angry, shout at me – but instead he replied quite calmly, 'You misunderstood my motives.' Then, to my astonishment, I saw one corner of his mouth lift slightly as he added, 'But if, in future, you should wish to – ah – please a man – do endeavour to look more than twelve years of age. And, perhaps, you should indulge rather less enthusiastically in your otherwise commendable quest for cleanliness.'

I exclaimed in surprise, 'But gentry, they do like their servants to wash regular!'

And now his mouth curved fully up before he replied firmly, 'Not with *carbolic* soap. You may go.' I crept out of his presence.

I went back to Lambeth; I didn't know where else to go. He'd said 'respectable lodgings', but what respectable landlady would take me in, in my condition? So I went to Albert Buildings, the ones furthest away from Jubilee, and asked if there were any vacancies. The superintendent said yes, he might have a single-room flat free, but – he looked at my waist and then at my ringless left hand. 'How are you going to pay the rent? I don't want men traipsing in at all hours. These are respectable Buildings – I won't have no goings-on.'

I said, 'His Lordship, he be going to make I an allowance until,' my tongue stumbled, 'until my baby be born.'

The superintendent frowned. 'When the money stops, you're out. The Five Percent isn't a charity. I've got some furniture in store – you'd require that if you took the room – you'll have to pay for it.' I understood and agreed. He asked more than the goods were worth, but I paid. Lord Warminster had been generous, and I had to live somewhere.

By the time I came back down the stairs it was the dinner hour, and the children were streaming into the courtyard from school. I stood watching them, seeing their pinched winter faces, their reddened running noses, their hands swollen and chapped from chilblains. One day my child would be among them, pinched and hungry-looking too. Except that as soon as my baby was born I'd have to leave the Buildings, and where would I take her then? How would I get the money to feed and clothe and house her?

Heavily I walked the mean, grimy streets that my own mother had walked, carrying the same burden. But she had had Granfer to send me to – I had no one. My baby moved, jerkily, as if in protest and then I realised: my Granfer was dead, but hers wasn't. Her Granfer was back in Kew, in his tailored frockcoat of best vicuna, his fine grey waistcoat and spotless white shirt. And so I had the answer.

He was out when I got back, and it was after tea before he sent for me again. I'd spent all afternoon in my bedroom, preparing what I would say – and praying for my baby's sake that he would agree. When I went into the drawing room he was behind his desk again. He reached for his pen. 'You have found somewhere?'

'Yes, my lord.'

'Give me the address.'

'Seventy-two Albert Buildings, Eden Street, Lambeth.'

His pen remained still as he repeated with a frown, 'Lambeth?'

'All thic Buildings be clean – and I did live there, afore.'

He was still frowning, but he wrote the address down. Then he said haltingly, 'I will arrange – for a postal order – to be sent to you – each week.'

He was about to dismiss me, so I moved forward and gathered all my courage together. 'My Lord, there be something I did want to ask you.' He stared at me, his bristling eyebrows raised – but in surprise, not anger. 'Miss Annabel, Her Ladyship,' his face began to close but I plunged recklessly on, 'she said as you did want her baby to live at Eston, with you, but Lord Quinham, he wouldn't.' His face shut completely. Desperately I changed tack. 'Aunt Agnes, who was my mother, only I didn't know it – when she did have me, out o' wedlock, she sent me to Granfer – to live with him.' I drew a deep, ragged breath and said loudly, 'My baby, *you* be her Granfer.' And then I couldn't go on, I could only wait for his explosion of anger.

But instead there was silence. It went on so long that I'd begun to edge towards the door before he broke it. 'Are you – offering me – your child?'

I whispered, 'Yes.'

There was another silence. I moved back again, towards the desk, and proffered a further inducement. '*My* father, he were a gentleman – I be sure o' that.' I risked a glance at his face. He didn't look as if he were angry with me, in fact he wasn't looking at me at all. His eyes were fixed on the wall above my head, where a painting hung – a painting of a girl playing with a plump, smiling baby. Putting my hand protectively over my belly I told him, 'She be a strong healthy baby – she do move, often.' And as if in response to my voice she stirred and began to turn. I exclaimed, 'She be moving now – she be turning over!'

His head jerked down and he stared at my stomach as if he couldn't believe his eyes. 'She's – turning over?'

'Aye, so she can settle herself down for a nap – she always do at this time o' day.'

'Good lord!' Then he seemed to give himself a little shake, and his eyes lifted from my midriff to my face as he asked, 'Why are you so sure – your child – will be a girl?'

'She will be – like I was.'

His lips twitched briefly before he said, 'All women with child were girls once.'

There was a tap at the door and Mr Wallis appeared. 'I'm sorry to disturb you, my lord, but Mr Pemberton has arrived.'

Lord Warminser spoke to me. 'I can't make a decision now – in the morning – ' Turning I fled back to my room.

Next morning I could hear him moving about very early. I got up too, and crept along to the kitchen while he was in his bath. Mr Wallis came in soon after. 'Good, you're up, Amy. His Lordship wants to see you now, before breakfast. I don't know what on earth's got into him today – he rang for me at the crack of dawn, and by the look of him he'd been up half the night.'

As soon as I'd closed the drawing room door behind me Lord Warminster said, 'I accept your offer.' My whole body sagged with relief – and sorrow. She wasn't even born yet, and I'd already lost her. Then I realised he was speaking again. 'You must eat properly – plenty of good, nourishing food – and fruit. I insist that you consume some fruit every day.'

'Yes, my lord.'

'And – there is another – matter. Infants brought up by hand – do not thrive – especially in summer. So I wish to employ you – as her wetnurse, until she is old enough to be weaned.'

The sorrow receded a little as I whispered, 'Thank 'ee, my lord.' He was about to dismiss me, but there was something else I had to ask. It was an effort to say it, but I had to, for her sake. 'My lord, she'll be born out o' wedlock so, she won't have a name, like – ' My voice faltered, dropping. 'Like I baint never had no name.'

He said quietly, 'I realise that.'

'I thought with you being a lord, an earl – when you did take her, mebbe you could make her less of a – ' I hesitated again, then added in a rush, 'less of a bastard?'

I saw the answer in his eyes, and my small flame of hope flickered and died. 'No. Only a prior marriage can legitimize a child.'

'Then, when she be old enough to go to school, mebbe you could go to meet her – so the boys wouldn't be able to call after her in the street.'

He said loudly, 'Nobody will call after her, I shall see to that.' Then he added, 'Besides, if she is a girl she won't go to school. Once she has left the nursery her governess will teach her.' He waited, but I had nothing more to say, so he dismissed me.

Back in my room I told myself that my baby would be grateful. *She* wouldn't be brought up in a slum, no – she would have nursemaids, a governess, fine clothes, everything she could possibly wish for – except her mother. The sobs wracked my body as I began to pack.

When I went to say goodbye to Mr Wallis he told me he was coming with me to Lambeth, to see me settled in. One of the chairs the superintendent had sold me had a broken seat. Mr Wallis pointed at it. 'That'll have to be replaced.' The superintendent went to fetch another one without a word. When he came back Mr Wallis made it clear that he was inspecting the room, and then he spoke loudly to me, with one eye on the superintendent. 'I'll report back to His Lordship, Miss Roberts – and if there are any problems you must let me know at once.' With a smile he held out his hand to me. 'Best of luck, Amy.' I shook it gratefully, then he and the superintendent both left.

I sank down on the new chair, shivering. I was back in Lambeth again, but this time there was no Aunt Agnes to welcome me, no boys to tease me, no Beat to gossip with – not even Uncle Alf to cook and clean for. This time I was completely alone.

Chapter Forty

The doors of my memory burst open at Lambeth. I'd managed to keep them closed over the week at Kew but now, as I sat huddled in that bleak little room, guilt and shame overwhelmed me. Miss Annabel, the memory of her face, her voice – all tormented me. From the very beginning I had deceived her. 'Lady's maids do not come out of the workhouse' – Lord Warminster had spoken the truth; if she'd known that I'd been born out of wedlock she would never have engaged me as her own maid. Personal servants, spending so much time with their masters and mistresses, could not come from the gutter.

The lesser sin had led to the greater: in my pride and stupidity I'd read my lord's casual attentions as love. Unmindful of my origins, my head stuffed full of silly stories of fairy-tale princesses and beautiful actresses, I had forgotten what I was – a servant and a bastard. And now, because of my sin, I was to bear another bastard. I was doing to my child what Aunt Agnes had done to me.

I remembered the slights, the taunts, the humiliations that I'd suffered in childhood, and now my child would suffer them too. Lord Warminster's rank would protect her at first, at Eston where he was in command – but what would happen when she grew up? Then his rank would be a curse to her, because she would not be able to hide her origins as I had done – the big red book would see to that. She would never be able to wear the three ostrich feathers and make her curtsey at court, as an earl's grand-daughter should do. He would buy her fine dresses, dainty shoes, jewellery – but everyone would know what she was: the bastard daughter of a servant. So she would be an outcast, and learn to hate the mother she had never known.

When she moved inside me now I sensed her anger and resentment, and she became a burden to me, a burden that had to be carried, although my back hurt and my legs ached. And when the time came for me to deliver her I would scream aloud in pain, as Aunt Agnes had screamed. Fear clutched my throat and crushed my chest, because I knew I was a coward.

Shame kept me imprisoned in my room. I would have stayed there always, except for the necessity of buying food. He had ordered me to eat, so that the baby would grow strong and healthy – for him. There was the postal order, too: it came on the second day, and I had to go out to cash it. I was too ashamed to go to a post office nearby, in the streets I'd known before, so instead I walked for a long way in the other direction, praying that no one would recognise me. As I walked I saw London as it really was: ugly, noisy and filthy. Over the last year I'd grown used to a different London, the London of the West End. The streets there had been bustling with people and traffic, but they'd been cleaned and swept – hosed down each night by an army of workers. There had been trees, parks, gardens in every square – all fresh with greenery that rested the eyes and gave promise of summer. Everywhere the well-kept houses with their gleaming brass knockers and gay striped awnings spoke of elegance and gracious living. There was none of that here. The only polished brass was on the doors of public houses, the only colour the garish hues of torn advertisements – otherwise the rows of grimy houses, the high, dark walls of warehouses and factories stretched drab and smoke-soiled into the distance, without the relief of even a single blade of grass. Once I'd lived in Paradise but, like Eve, I had sinned – and been cast out.

I hurried back to my room where already there was a veil of soot on the windowsill and the moulding of the door. Going into the tiny scullery I filled a bucket of water and took it back to the range boiler. When it had heated I scrubbed and cleaned until I was trembling with exhaustion. My back ached and my head throbbed, so that the scrape of boots on stone steps and the high-pitched shrieks of the children playing in the court seemed to stab into my very brain. I dragged myself across to the range and reached for a saucepan. The thought of food repelled me – but I had to eat, Lord Warminster had ordered me to.

At the beginning of the next week a second postal order came; it was for two pounds, like the first. I hadn't expected it. A pound a week would have been generous, but two pounds was too much – I had no right to it. But because he'd sent it I felt I had to cash it, so I went out at once. I clutched my shawl around me as I did each day when I went to the shops, and each day my belly had become more swollen, my condition more obvious. Now I walked with my eyes fixed on the ground, so I couldn't see the look of contempt on people's faces. At the post office counter I saw the clerk notice my ringless hand and watched her eyes sharpen; seizing the coins I blundered out.

I was panting and there was a sharp stitch in my side as I climbed the stone stairs, yet I quickened my steps still further, desperate to return to the safety of my burrow. But when I reached it it was empty, unwelcoming – a refuge, but not a home. I was so terribly lonely.

I poked up the range and cooked my solitary dinner, then dished it up and put it down on the table – and there was only my plate. Until I'd left Eston I'd never eaten a meal alone in my life, and suddenly I couldn't stand it any longer. I pulled up the other chair, set a box on the seat and propped Esau up on it. Carefully I arranged his body so that his short furry arms were resting on the table opposite me – only then could I bear to sit down to my own meal.

When I'd finished eating I began to talk to him – there was no one else. I told him the story of Snow White, just as once I'd told it to him in the loft at Borrell, so many years ago. And now, as then, his small button eyes seemed to wink back at me, listening. Then came the rap on the door.

Startled, I jumped to my feet. It couldn't be for me – visitors often came to the other three doors on the landing, but never to mine. The rap sounded again, louder. I went to the door and pulled it open a crack, peering out; it was Mr Wallis. 'Hello, Amy – aren't you going to let me in?' I opened the door wider. As he came inside he glanced around the single room. 'What've you done with your visitor? I could hear you talking.'

My face went red and hot as he waited for my reply. At last I whispered, 'I were talking to Esau.'

'Esau?'

I put my hand to where his furry body sat up at the table, opposite my plate. 'I been so lonely – I did have to talk to somebody.'

He didn't speak for a moment, then coming closer, he patted my shoulder. 'Well lovey, you can talk to me now.' As the tears began to trickle down my face he said gently, 'I'll make us both a cuppa while you mop yourself up.'

When the tea was made Mr Wallis picked Esau up and laid him down on the bed with a friendly wink in my direction. 'He'll be more comfy there, eh Amy?' He sat down in the vacated chair. 'Now, how've you been keeping? You look very peaky to me. You've not been staying in all day, have you?'

'No – I been out to the shops, and to cash His Lordship's postal orders, only he be sending I too much. The rent be only five shillings a week, so I don't need – '

He cut me short. 'Let His Lordship be the judge o' that. But Amy, I'm not talking just about doing your shopping – haven't you been to see your friends?'

'Friends?' I stared at him.

'His Lordship's under the impression that you took a room in these parts because you used to live here, so he thought there'd be folks to keep an eye on you.'

'I did live here, once, but – I couldn't – ' I began to cry again. 'I be so terrible ashamed, I couldn't let people see me like this.'

'Here, you'd best have my handkerchief – yours is sopping already. I'll pour the tea.' He pushed a cup and saucer over. 'Dry your eyes and wrap yourself round that, lovey. Now, tell me exactly who you *do* know in this part o' town.'

I spoke reluctantly. 'There's Uncle Alf, and the boys – but I couldn't go and see them, not Uncle Alf. After Aunt Agnes died he, he – '

As my voice faltered I saw by Mr Wallis' face that he understood. 'I daresay even as a youngster you were a pretty girl. All right, we'll cross Uncle Alf off the list. Now, your Auntie, she must have had – '

I broke in, confessing, 'She wasn't my aunt, really. She was – my mother . . .'

He said gently, 'I'd guessed that, Amy, but we'll call her your Auntie, shall we – if that's the way she wanted it. Now, if she was bringing up a family here she must have had neighbours, friends.'

I said, 'There was Mrs Harris, Beat – she was her best friend. Beat did help me go back to Borrell. She gave me some money, and pawned Uncle Alf's ship in the bottle, for my train fare.'

341

'Right, then. First thing tomorrow you go and find this Mrs Harris.'

'But I couldn't, not like this, with no ring on my finger.'

'Amy, she's obviously a good-hearted woman – I can't see her turning her back on you. Besides, London folk, they're more tolerant. I know, I'm a Londoner myself.' I shook my head again. He spoke very firmly. 'Amy, when I report back to His Lordship tonight he'll say exactly the same thing – and you don't want to get me into trouble with him, do you? He's bad-tempered enough at the moment as it is, with losing – well, losing his company.'

I knew who he meant and I couldn't stop myself asking, 'Miss Annabel – hasn't she come back?'

He shook his head. 'They won't come back, either of 'em. She's living in Town now – with Lord Quinham, of course.' My heart twisted at that 'of course', as Mr Wallis continued, 'She's written to Our Lordship and I know he's worried about her – she's not too good in her health. Still, no doubt she'll feel better once she's got her baby in her arms.' He smiled. 'Same as you will.'

I shook my head. 'No. I be giving her away – to her granfer, to Lord Warminster.'

Mr Wallis gave a low whistle of surprise. 'So *that's* why he's been prowling round the old nurseries! Well I never. That's a turn-up for the book and no mistake. Gawd knows what Lord Quin'll say when he finds out. Still, it's none of his business now, is it?' He stood up. 'Don't look so downcast, young Amy – it'll be for the best in the long run. You can put it all behind you and make a fresh start. A pretty girl like you – I daresay you'll find a man who's willing to overlook a little slip, just like your ma did. Now, don't forget what I told you. Go and see this Mrs Harris first thing tomorrow – and I daresay I'll be back next week to see how you've got on. I'd best be off, before that cabbie loses patience and decides to scarper. Cheerio, Amy – and keep your pecker up.'

Mr Wallis' words drummed in my head. 'It's none of his business now, is it?' They were so final. I'd known he'd never be mine once he married Miss Annabel, but at least I'd still seen him, however much it had hurt to watch him with her. And if I'd married Joe I'd have stayed at Eston; I'd have been living where he lived – he'd have been bound to come back sometimes, there would have been precious, fleeting glimpses – but now there was nothing. I'd never see him again. I'd lost him, lost him forever – and soon I'd lose his baby, too. But I mustn't think of him. For just one last time I let myself remember him; his flashing smile, his teasing voice, his laughing blue eyes, and the sun shining on the pale gold of his hair – then I opened the door of the little house in my head and pushed him inside. I must not think of him, not now. I picked up Esau, and with a voice that wavered began to tell him the story of Jack and the Beanstalk. I told him all the stories, one by one – even the terrifying tale of Bluebeard and the blood-stained key. By the time I'd finished my voice was hoarse and I was so tired I fell asleep.

The next day I set out to find Beat. I went to the place where she'd had her room; the landlady told me she'd moved, but gave me her new address – it was a road leading off Endell Street. It felt very strange walking past that house where Aunt Agnes had lain a-bed until she died. Then I turned the corner and began searching for the right number. When I found it I drew a deep, apprehensive breath before tapping on the door.

'Amy!' It was Beat. Then her eyes dropped to my belly, and flicked back to my bare finger. 'Oh my Gawd!' I began to back away, but her large hand reached out and took hold of my arm. 'Come in duck, come in. Sit down here, where it's warm.' She stood in front of me, her face set. 'Look Amy, don't worry – we'll manage somehow. I still does three evenings at The Rose and Crown. I could do more – and besides, things are much easier now, with Albie and Ned both working.'

I looked up at her. 'Albie and Ned?' Then I saw it, standing on the mantelpiece in all its shining glory – *The Wanderer*.

Beat watched my eyes fasten on it. 'I promised your ma I'd look after the boys – and this was the simplest way o' doing it.'

'You married Uncle Alf?'

'No duck – I ain't *married* him. Once is enough for me. Bert was a good husband in his way – I don't feel the need for a second. I'm prepared to share Alf's board – and his bed, seeing as how I'm past worrying about the kind of complications as you've found yourself in – but – I reckoned I'd hang on to me freedom. Keeps Alf on his toes too, knowing I could walk out any time. Don't you worry about Alf, Amy – he'll give you a home if I tells him to. Besides, he owes it to you, the way you looked arter Aggie afore she died. And to tell you the truth, he was ashamed of what happened that last night. He wouldn't've done it if he hadn't been grieving, and took a drop too many. We'll look arter you, you and the little 'un, when it arrives.'

So I hadn't been on my own, after all. I'd had somebody to turn to all the time – only I hadn't realised. But it was too late now. I shook my head. 'I've got to give my baby away.'

'Give it away! You can't, Amy. Nobody wants babies – there's orphanages and workhouses bursting at the seams with 'em.' She shook her head. 'Even them 'as been born in wedlock – nobody wants 'em, not any of 'em.'

'Her granfer, he do want her, and he be a gentleman, a lord.'

'What!' Beat stared at me in astonishment. Then she seized the black iron kettle. ' 'Ere, I'll make us a cuppa, then you'd better tell me what you've been up to, young Amy.'

So I told her about Granfer being dead, and my going to Bath, and then becoming Miss Annabel's maid. I told her about meeting my lord – Mr Dunn, as I'd thought he was – and loving him, how I hadn't known I was carrying until I was five months gone, and how when Miss Annabel had dismissed me I'd only had ninepence three-farthings to my name, so Lord Warminster had given me money and sent me to Kew. But I didn't tell her about offering myself to him there, only that I'd offered him my baby, because my own lord had quarrelled with his father and taken Miss Annabel away, to stop him seeing his grandchild. So I'd offered him his other grand-child – and he'd accepted.

When I'd finished explaining, Beat said, 'So you're gonna keep it till it's weaned, and then hand it over.' She sighed. 'Just like your ma did with you.'

I exclaimed, 'She didn't have to, she didn't. Granfer, he did give her money – '

'She'd run through that long afore.'

'But she had a job, and a place where she could keep me – she didn't have to marry Uncle Alf. Or she could have told him she wouldn't, unless he agreed – ' My voice rose to cry out, 'She could've waited!'

'No, Amy, she couldn't.' Beat's eyes were steady on mine. 'I said to you once, when you were old enough to understand I'd tell you. I reckon by the state of you you're old enough to be told now.

344

Old Everett at The Goat and Compasses didn't give her a job out of the kindness of his heart – not with her having a baby in tow. She had to pay for that job, Amy – the way a woman always has to pay. His wife were bedfast, but although he were getting on in years he was a lusty man – that's why he took Aggie in. And she was desperate. It were that or the House – so she paid.' Beat gave a deep sigh. 'And your ma, you know how easily she fell. She'd had a couple of scares already, when Alf asked her to marry him – so what could she say? Besides, living like that, it was eating her up, raised respectable the way she had been. She needed a ring on her finger, did Aggie. *I* told her to take Alf, Amy – I persuaded her. Blame me if you must, not her. I said to her: "It's only a matter of time, Aggie, before you're in trouble again. Old Everett'll throw the pair of you out then, before you can say knife – I've seen it afore. And the workhouse – they treats you bad enough if it's your first slip up, but if it's your second – " ' She broke off with a shudder. 'So I told her to do what Alf said, and send you down to her parents. And your granfer, he thought the world of you, I knows that from the way you talks of him. You was cared for, brought up respectable.' She paused, then said, 'But Amy, with you knowing what'd happened to your own ma, however could you have been so silly?'

'I loved him. I did love my lord from the first moment I saw him.'

Beat sighed yet again. 'That's just what your ma said about your father. She told me she saw him galloping towards her on horseback and as he came close he raised his cap to her, so his hair shone golden as the sun itself. From that minute it was all up with her.'

'Galloping on horseback' – so I'd been right, he was a gentleman, my father. 'Beat, did she ever talk to you about him?'

Beat nodded. 'She was talking about him not long afore she died. She never forgot him, she still loved him, even though – ' She broke off, cocking her hand to her ear. 'That's the boys home for their dinners.' George and Jim and Taffy burst in, then stopped, staring at me; they looked much older. Beat said, 'Do you remember Amy, then?' Taffy shook his head, but George and Jim grinned at me, before turning to Beat. 'Ma, Tom Jones burst our bladder – will yer ask butcher fer anovver?'

I left as soon as I could; I didn't belong there any more. But the very next day Beat came panting up the flights of stone stairs to my room – and when I saw her broad red face and beaming smile I could have wept with relief.

She came to see me two or three times a week after that, and I would sit listening as she gossiped about the boys and her neighbours, and the customers at The Rose and Crown. She didn't mention my father again, and I didn't ask. I couldn't try and find him now, now that I'd sinned, but it was enough that my dream had been true. He was a gentleman, and Aunt Agnes had loved him until the day she died – just as I would always love my lord.

I never went to see her again, and Beat didn't press me to. Once Albie came round with a message and we stood talking awkwardly for a minute or two before he left. We were brother and sister, but Albie didn't know that, and I would never tell him.

Mr Wallis came back the following week and asked if I'd been to see Beat. I told him I had and he said, 'I thought you looked a bit perkier, soon as you opened the door.' He'd brought a hamper with him. 'His Lordship's orders, you've got to get outside of this little lot.' In the hamper were apples and oranges, pears and bananas. I ate them all, one by one – feeding his grand-child for him. She was his baby, not mine – I'd given her away. She kicked hard, hating me for my treachery.

Chapter Forty-One

Outside, the barrel organ began its tinkling tune. Beat put down her cup. 'Let's go and have a listen, Amy.' Slowly and heavily I dragged myself up from the chair and followed her out onto the balcony. She sniffed the air. 'The sun's come out – ain't that nice? I always feels that once April's arrived then winter's really over.' She pointed down. 'There 'e is – it's a proper pianner organ an' all, not one o' them hurdy-gurdy boxes.'

Down below the children were flocking towards the music: boys in too-short trousers and too-big boots; girls in pinafores, the older ones trailing toddlers by the hand; women carrying babies bundled up in their shawls – all were drawn out into the bright spring afternoon. Then the girls moved forward, separating out from the boys and dropping the toddlers' hands; boots began to tap on the cobbles and in seconds it had happened: a space had cleared around the barrel organ, a circle had formed – and the girls began to dance.

Clutching my shawl around me I stood beside Beat with tired legs aching, with ankles that were puffy and weak – and I watched the girls dance. Beat left me, but I hardly heard her parting words; still I watched the girls, their pigtails flying, their skirts whirling as they danced in the spring sunshine – dancing as once I had danced. But spring was over for me now, and would never come back. The music ended and turning I stumbled heavily away into my room.

Because my hand was shaking I spilt the milk. The jug toppled and all its contents splashed out and down the front of my shawl. My precious, all-concealing shawl – it would have to be taken off and washed at once, otherwise the milk would sour and make it smell. By the time it was clean and hanging dripping over one of the chairs on the balcony I was bent over with the pain in my back, but the range boiler still had to be refilled. When I'd finished doing that I had to haul myself up by clinging to the mantelpiece; it was then that I caught sight of my face in the mirror. The mirror was damp-speckled – it'd been in the superintendent's basement store a long time – but I could still see what I looked like. My hair hung lank and lifeless, and the unsightly brown shadow of the giant moth was spattered with red spiders' webs where small veins had broken. I lifted the mirror and tilted it: now I could see how my bulging, shapeless breasts sagged on to my distended belly and how my puffy ankles were swelling over my too-small shoes. All my life when men had looked at me their eyes had lit up with pleasure – just as my lord's eyes had done. He wouldn't have looked at me so now. My pudgy fingers replaced the mirror and I went over to the bed, to Esau. As I picked him up his black button eyes blinked at me, and at once I laid him back on the blanket with his face turned towards the wall. I didn't want even Esau to look at me now.

And then I heard the footsteps. They were heavy – and halting: the steps of a man with one leg shorter than the other. I froze in fear as the built-up boot scaled the last flight of stairs and came towards my door. It must be Mr Wallis – he'd been several times by now – but I knew it wasn't. A rap came on the door. It was sharp, peremptory – because it was made not by knuckles but with the silver knob of a gentleman's cane. I shuffled over to the door and opened it – the huge dark bulk of Lord Warminster filled the doorway. I tried to bob, but stumbled, and had to clutch at the door-frame to steady myself. Then I stood aside to let him enter.

He lurched after me to the chair. 'Please to be seated, my lord.'

He stood hesitating, then shifted his ungainly body so he could survey the whole room. It seemed to shrink as he stood there, filling it. 'Where – is – *your* seat?'

I began to explain. 'The other chair, 'tis – ' And then I remembered, I'd lost the protection of my shawl. My hands flew to cover my straining blouse and the unbuttoned placket of my skirt – and I saw he'd noticed them before he turned his head a fraction, averting his gaze. I whispered, ' 'Tis outside. My shawl – I did spill milk on my shawl – I had to wash it, so 'tis drying over the chair, on the balcony.'

'You must sit.' He stood waiting, his hat and gloves in one hand and his silver-mounted cane still under his arm. I went to the bed to pick up Esau and move him out of the way, and as I did so Lord Warminster's eyes flickered in momentary awareness, so that I knew Mr Wallis had told him about my talking to a toy. Flustered, I quickly dropped Esau onto the pillow before perching

348

myself awkwardly on the edge of the mattress. Then at last he sat down, but before he did so he shifted the chair; not much, but just enough so that when he sat opposite, his face was towards me even though his body was twisted sideways. And for a moment it was as though I saw the room and its two occupants from the outside: he with his ungainly, misshapen body – and I with mine. We were both deformed now.

Then he began to speak. 'Are you – well?'

I replied quickly, 'Yes, thank 'ee my lord.'

'You are – eating – properly?'

'Yes, I do cook every day.'

'Fruit?'

'Yes – see, there in the bowl.'

He craned his head to inspect the apples and oranges, before continuing his catechism. 'The woman – your mother's friend – does she visit regularly?'

'Oh yes, my lord. Beat, she were here just this afternoon. She been main good to I.'

His whole head and shoulders twisted as he looked all around, then he said, 'This room – is – very bare.'

'But 'tis clean, my lord – there baint never been no bugs in thic Buildings.'

Suddenly he seized his hat and gloves and jerked to his feet. As he stood there he asked abruptly, 'Do you – still wish to surrender your child?'

I looked at the deep true black of his frockcoat, so expensively tailored that it fitted his humped back and twisted shoulder without one single wrinkle; looked at the snowy whiteness of his linen; I looked at the glossy sheen of his silk top hat. And as I looked at those unmistakable signs of wealth and position I knew that down the road the emaciated, ragged queue would already be forming, outside the gates of the Lambeth Union – and I answered, 'Yes.'

He swung his built-up boot round and in two strides was almost at the door. I rushed forward to open it for him. As my hand closed on the knob a voice behind me asked, 'The baby. Does she – still – turn herself over?'

I told the door panel, 'No, she be too big now – instead she do kick, every day.'

Turning the knob I opened the door and stood to one side. With a final 'Good afternoon,' he put on his hat and left.

I closed the door quickly, but I could still hear those boots dot-and-carrying down the stairs. And my baby began to kick, angrily, resentfully – because I'd given her away, and still she would have no name. I whispered, 'I be sorry, terrible sorry, but thy granfer, he do be a lord, he'll take care o' thee.' But her sturdy foot kicked harder than ever, because even he couldn't make her less of a bastard. He'd told me plain: 'Only a prior marriage can legitimize a child,' and her father, my own lord, was already married to Miss Annabel. He'd been married even before I'd known she'd been conceived. Stumbling over to the bed I huddled on it, weeping: weeping for my shame, my guilt – and for my lost love.

Mr Wallis came the next day, just as it was going dark. He was carrying a box, and the cabbie was behind him with a second. He told the man, 'Put it on the table, then wait for me downstairs.' Mr Wallis smiled at me. 'Light the gas, lovey, so I can see what's what.' When I turned back to face him, blinking at the brightness he asked, 'How are you keeping?'

'I be quite well, thank 'ee Mr Wallis.'

'Well, I know it's not polite to contradict a lady – but frankly, Amy, you look terrible. Sit down, do. Now,' he fumbled in his pocket and brought out a clutch of sovereigns, 'His Lordship sent this, to buy yourself a new frock with. He said your clothes were far too tight for you. I was surprised he'd noticed, but I can see now he'd have to have been blind as a bat not to.' He shook his head. 'I reckon young Lord Quin should be kept on a collar and chain, the state you two girls are in.'

'You've seen her – Miss Annabel?'

'Only for a minute. I had to deliver one of these, and she was in the drawing room, lying on a sofa. She looked like a ghost and her maid told me on the way out it was the first time she'd been out of her room for a fortnight. Doctor's coming every day, and there's a hospital nurse been engaged.'

I couldn't stop myself asking, 'Her maid – she's got a new maid?'

'Of course she has, Amy. She couldn't manage without, could she? And before you ask, she's fifty if she's a day, and with a face like the back end of a horse tram. Her Ladyship's learnt that lesson all right.'

350

'Did you see – ?' My voice faltered.

'No, I didn't see Casanova hisself – he was away for a couple of days – that's how his nibs managed to sneak a visit to Lady Quin yesterday. And seeing the state she was in put him in mind of coming on here to see how you were getting along. By the time he'd finished his sick-visiting I reckon if Lord Quin had walked through the door he'd have got a size twelve boot up his backside, son or no son.' He flicked the small pile of gold coins. 'Best put these somewhere safe, Amy – you can't be too careful.'

I shook my head. 'No, I don't need any more money. The postal orders, they be more'n enough.'

'Keep 'em. If I take 'em back I'll get me ear chewed off – we're on a very short fuse these days. Still, I suppose it's not surprising, the way he's fretting about Lady Quin. Now, this is your fruit – I'll just unfasten the lid for you, then I'll get the other unpacked.' There was the sound of splintering wood. 'Gently does it.' He reached in and took out a tiny bush – a rose bush. I gasped in surprise. 'It's just in bud now, but it'll be out in a few days if you put it by the window. Let's see, if I move that chest – ' Mr Wallis busied himself rearranging the furniture to his satisfaction. 'Right, that should do the trick. Here's the saucer to hold the drips. There, how's she looking now?'

'She's beautiful!' Reverently I touched the tiny leaves – I couldn't believe it.

Mr Wallis wiped his hands on his handkerchief. 'His Lordship telegraphed down to Mr Hicks yesterday evening, and it came up on the train this morning – along with one for Lady Quin. Hers was full-sized, of course; anyway, she's got more room than you.' He picked up the empty box. 'I'll be on my way now, Amy – remember to buy yourself that new frock. Oh, I nearly forgot – His Lordship said to tell you its name is Persephone.'

Persephone, the fairy rose: I kept looking at her all evening. She smelt of damp earth and growing things; she was green, and her buds were plump with promise.

Next morning I went out first thing and bought a sewing machine. It was only small, with a handle, but when I tested it in the shop it ran well. The man said he'd send it round after dinner, so then I went to the draper's and bought a length of cotton print ready. As soon as the machine arrived I sat down to work, and by the evening I'd made a couple of blue and white check pinafores, like the ones the women in the Buildings wore when they were expecting. Next day I bought navy striped shirting and made a dress: it had a yoke, and the skirt fell straight down from it in long full gathers without a waist, but you could still see my condition – there was no use trying to hide it any longer.

I'd positioned my machine so that every time I raised my eyes from my work I could see Persephone. Whenever I got up to ease my aching back I went to her, peering at her buds – and on the third day the first one opened. It was pink: a true, deep rose-pink, with a perfect double frill of petals. I bent over to breathe in the faint, delicate scent, then put my face still closer, so that her petals gently stroked my cheek. A rose in bloom in April; truly she was a fairy rose.

I showed her to Beat and she exclaimed, 'Fancy His Lordship taking the trouble to send that! You ain't 'alf been lucky, Amy, when you think what reg'ly happens to girls as slips up like you. And him willing to take the child off yer 'ands an' all – it's for the best, I s'pose. A gentleman like that, he can give her everything.'

I cried out, 'Except a name! She won't have no name, like I don't.'

'You should've thought of that before you got yourself into trouble, Amy – it's too late now. More'n that, it's time you was thinking about a doctor. Now, there's young gentlemen at the hospital as is still learning – they'll come out for free – '

I broke in, 'I dussent want no doctor.'

In the end she took me to see Mrs Jackson, who'd delivered Aunt Agnes. 'Dearie me – what a terrible shame, Mrs Harris. But don't you worry, when her time comes I'll look after her.'

After I'd panted back up the stairs to my room I went straight across to Persephone. As I gazed at her delicate pink blooms I remembered Joe telling me of how Lord Warminster had given her a name – but even he couldn't give one to my baby, because her father was already married to Miss Annabel, Miss Annabel who was so poorly the doctor was having to visit every day. The thought came unbidden into my head: suppose Miss Annabel became so ill that she died – then he could marry me and give my baby a name. At once I was horrified – how could I even have thought such a wicked thing! I swung round to Esau exclaiming, 'I didn't mean it, I didn't mean it!' His black boot-button eyes seemed to wink back at me, slyly. Oh, my lord – how I loved him, how I longed for him.

It was the first day of May: down in Borrell the children would be walking proudly behind their May Garland. In London it was raining, and dark sooty drops ran down the windowpane behind Persephone's small pink blooms. I had to stop now after every few steps, to catch my breath. Looking at me Beat said, 'Not much longer now, I reckon Amy. Only a few more weeks to go.'

My voice was low as I told her, 'I be afeard.'

She shook her head. 'You should 'ave thought o' that afore. I'll put the kettle on.'

We were drinking our tea when I heard the uneven footsteps on the stairs. I turned and looked at Beat, who exclaimed, 'Whatever's the matter, Amy? You've gone as white as a sheet.'

The sharp rap came at the door. I whispered, ' 'Tis His Lordship.'

'Well I never!' Beat jumped up. 'I'll let him in.' She swung the door wide open and I saw her momentary hesitation at the sight of him, but it was only for a moment, then she was saying loudly, 'Come in, my lord – come along in.' As soon as he was inside she held her right hand out to him. He looked surprised, then extended his own hand in turn. Beat pumped it up and down vigorously saying, 'Missus Harris – at your service.'

He replied with only the single word: 'Warminster.'

But Beat wasn't a bit abashed. 'I *am* pleased to meet you, Lord Warminster – me lordship – very pleased, seeing as how you've done so much for little Amy here, in her time of trouble. She's like one o' me own, she is, with her ma being such a good friend o' mine. And now, o' course, I'm – er, "friendly" with Amy's step-father.' I watched in horror as her eyelid dropped in a wink. 'So that makes me her step-mother – in a manner o' speaking.' Beat waddled over to a chair and carefully dusted the seat with her skirt. 'You sit down and make yourself at home, me lord, while I'll pour you a cup of tea.' Beat bustled around with teapot and milk jug. 'Sugar, me lord?' I winced as Beat dumped a spoonful of sugar into the cup and stirred briskly before handing it to him.

353

Then she plumped herself down on the bed to a squeal of protest from the springs.

There was silence. When Lord Warminster lifted his cup he had to hold it at an odd angle to get it to his mouth; the tea must have been too hot, but he drank it all the same. As he returned his cup to its saucer Beat said chattily, 'She keeps the room nice and clean, don't she? But then Amy always was a good little worker – she can get a real shine on a range, can Amy.'

At last Lord Warminster spoke. 'How – has – she been?'

'She's getting about, me lord. She goes out for a breath of fresh air every day, when she fetches her shopping, but,' Beat sighed, leaning towards him, 'the fact is, she's fretting – and it's not doing her any good at all. She spends half her time crying, 'cos her youngster won't have no name, like what she didn't. I tell her it's no use worrying now, what's done's done – and she's been luckier than most girls in her position. There's not many young gentlemen's fathers as would've behaved as handsome as you have, me lord.'

His face reddened as he moved his hand dismissively. 'I bear – a – responsibility.' Then he added abruptly, 'Have arrangements – been made, for the confinement?'

Beat replied briskly, 'Yes, my lord – it's all booked.'

'Is the doctor – competent?'

Beat shook her head. 'She won't consider a doctor – not with him being a man – even though you can get 'em from the hospital for nothing, them as is still learning. And there's the lady nurses – they're learning too, only for them you has to show your marriage-lines. I could've fixed for Amy to borrow a set, for a small consideration, but she didn't think as it were honest, so instead we've booked Mrs Jackson, from Jubilee Buildings.'

'Is this woman – qualified?'

Beat's brow wrinkled. 'She ain't got nothing on paper, if that's what you mean, but she knows what she's about does Mrs Jackson. She's delivered nearly every youngster in the four Buildings – and that's saying something. I've heard Dr McIntyre say she's the best midwife for miles around, and when she does send for him then he picks up his bag and runs, 'cos he knows she don't send for nuffink.' Beat jerked her thumb towards the door. 'And I've arranged with Mrs Smith opposite to send her eldest boy to fetch me as soon as Amy starts her pains. We'll look after her, me lord, don't you worry. Here, I'll take your cup off of you if you've finished.'

As soon as he'd been relieved of his burden he stood up to go, but before he did so he fished in his waistcoat pocket and took out an oblong of white card; the jingle of coins followed as he spoke to Beat. 'When she has been – delivered, would you be so good as to – telegraph to me, at Eston?'

'Certainly, me lord.' Beat took the card and the coins and slipped them into her large bosom.

Next he produced a wallet, and extracted a bank-note. 'For your trouble, Mrs Harris.'

Beat shook her head decisively. 'No, her mother were my best friend – I don't need paying to keep an eye on Amy here.'

He hesitated, then put the note away. 'Thank you, Mrs Harris.' He picked up his cane and gloves and swung round – but not towards the door; instead he went over to the window, to Persephone. He gently pressed the soil in her pot before murmuring, 'Good – not too damp.'

Beat beamed at him. 'She thinks the world o' that plant, me lord – she's always fussing over it, turning it round every day so all the flowers gets a share o' the light, and such-like. Say "thank you" to His Lordship for sending it, Amy.'

I whispered, 'Thank 'ee, my lord.'

He began to pull on his gloves. Beat bent down for his top hat and handed it to him, then rushed to fling the door open for him. 'Good afternoon, me lord.'

'Good afternoon, Mrs Harris.'

After he'd gone Beat came and sat down again. 'You never told me he were a humpie, Amy – and his face . . .' then she stopped, frowning in thought. 'No, it ain't a proper hump, it's because of his neck being twisted and tipping his face up, so the only way he can look a body straight in the eye is by half-crouching. He's put his own shoulder out, that's what that hump is. And with him being so big, you notice it more.' She paused, pursing her mouth. 'I'm glad I've had a dekko at him, only he weren't what I expected at all. The way you talked, I thought he were an elderly gentleman.'

'So he be.' I remembered back to the big red book. 'He be forty-six year old.'

Beat laughed. 'That's younger'n me, duck – and I ain't past it yet, not by a long chalk. Lumme, is that St James' striking? I'd best get back – the boys'll be pawing at the ground for their nosh. Ta-ta, Amy – look after yourself.'

I had to go out later to fetch some more milk. When I came back the children were playing in the courtyard. I stopped to catch my breath as they formed a circle, holding hands and singing:

> *'Up the streets and down the streets*
> *Round and round we twirl.*
> *Oh, isn't Annie Taylor*
> *A nice young girl.'*

I watched the girl called Annie let go of the children either side of her and run into the centre of the circle. They began to chorus the second verse:

> *'Annie made a pudding, she made it oh so sweet,*
> *She took it to her true love, and he began to eat.*
> *Hurray! Hurray! Don't let him run away,*
> *For next Sunday morning is her wedding day!'*

Turning away from those bright young voices I began the heavy, panting climb up to my solitary room. As I reached the balcony I could still hear the girls singing far below, *'For next Sunday morning is her wedding day.'* Fighting back the tears I opened the door and went in. It would never be my wedding day, now.

Chapter Forty-Two

'Not much longer now, duck, judging by the size of you. I'll pop in again first thing Monday and fetch yer washing – it'll save you being on yer feet all day.' I whispered my thanks, but Beat shrugged them off with a smile. 'No trouble, Amy – I won't even notice it along of ours. Ta-ta for now.'

I closed the door and had to lean against it before I could will my swollen legs to move. When I did pull myself upright the pain in my head hammered at the inside of my skull, as if trying to split it apart; and as I left the safety of the wall my head swam. I reached for the chair and clutched at its back for support, before stepping very slowly over to the bed and collapsing upon it. I wasn't comfortable there – I hadn't been comfortable anywhere for weeks now – but as long as I lay clinging to the iron frame then I was safe.

The giddiness receded a little at last and I managed to get to the table and sit slowly peeling potatoes and carrots. But fetching the meat from the scullery made my head swim again, and as I began to chop it my hand slipped. Petrified as a rabbit before a stoat I watched the bright red blood ooze out of my thumb – then nausea cracked the ice of my terror and I stumbled to the WC outside, my hand wrapped in my apron. Afterwards I managed to tie a piece of rag around my thumb, then I tipped everything on the chopping board into a saucepan, poured water on top and set it on the range. I crept back to the bed. Glittering knives, scarlet blood, Dimpsey's despairing eyes – Aunt Agnes – blood – screams . . . I lay in a waking nightmare of fear and panic.

Later I ate, because Lord Warminster had ordered me to, but the food tasted of ashes in my mouth. Then, suddenly, I knew what I wanted; reaching under the draining board I found the packet of starch and began to spoon it greedily into my mouth. How could I eat starch? But it was all my stomach craved.

Much later, when I got ready for bed, I had to wash my top half sitting down. Then I clung to the edge of the sink with one hand while I cleansed my private parts, and whimpered as the flannel touched my cunny – it was swollen and painful, like my fingers. In bed I fell into a fitful doze, but the nightmares came: the beautiful princess, sleeping the sleep of the dead, trapped in her castle. Snow White, imprisoned in her coffin of glass. Bluebeard's wife – she was alive, but the blood-stained key clung to her hand as that terrible scarlet tide lapped at her feet – she couldn't move, couldn't run even as her hideous husband raised his sword to kill her. I woke sweating with terror, and barely able to move my own cramped and aching limbs. As I lay in the darkness, weak from fear and exhaustion, I could control my thoughts no longer – and they turned to my lord. I pictured his fair head and smiling blue eyes, longing for him, craving for him – a sight, a word, a touch. 'My lord, my lord!' Desperately I used the thought of him to keep the nightmares at bay.

When dawn came I sank into an uneasy slumber, still dreaming of him. But in my dreams I was pleading with him: 'Please, please, my lord – my baby, she won't have no name.' And his face became cold and contemptuous as he replied, 'How could I possibly marry you – you're a servant!' 'Please!' His voice was hard and cruel as he told me, 'You're soiled goods.' When I woke my baby was moving sluggishly, resentfully, in my belly; I cried hot tears of guilt and shame.

I ate more starch that morning, but as soon as I'd swallowed it nausea rose in my throat and I retched and retched over the sink. My head throbbed and a fox seemed to be gnawing at my belly – I was being squeezed in a nutcracker of pain.

I made myself follow my daily routine: riddling the grate, picking out the cinders, carrying the ashes to the dust-chute; but every few minutes I had to stop, to clutch at a chairback or the mantelpiece – and when I looked in the mirror, red slits peered back from under puffy eyelids set above swollen white cheeks. My face was the face of a fairground freak.

I lit the range and set the kettle over the fire but then, suddenly, there were two kettles, two fires, two ranges. I swung round and saw two tables, two beds – and two rose bushes. I fumbled my way to the chair that was two where only one should be and groped for the seat before collapsing onto it, shaking and crying. I was so frightened. I wept for my lord, but he didn't come.

358

It was Sunday. I heard voices, footsteps, people all around me in the Buildings, but I huddled in my room – imprisoned by my treacherous eyes and unmanageable body. There were still apples in the bowl, so I chewed and swallowed one – but all I wanted was starch, and the twopenny packet was empty by now.

In the afternoon I pushed the chair over to the window and sat hopelessly gazing at the doubled rose bush on the doubled chest. Uncertainly I put out my hand. Would it close on a stalk – or on nothing? It closed on a firm, living stem and I snapped it off and lifted a cluster of tiny pink roses to my cheek. I held it there, with my deceiving eyes tight shut – and remembered Granfer, Granfer, who'd come to comfort me in the loft when I was ill. I whispered, 'Granfer, Granfer – help I, please help I.' But no-one came.

I spent all night with the roses on my pillow, and Esau held tightly in my arms. I had to keep a pail by my bed, the sickness came so often, but each time it passed I pressed the scented petals against my cheek and clasped Esau to my chest – and cried for Granfer, who was dead. My baby kicked slowly, less vigorously now, but she was still angry, angry with me because she would have no name. And then I began to cry for him, who was her father – but no one came.

It was light again, but I'd lost all sense of time. I lay with my head on the edge of the bed, crying for my lord, for Granfer. I leant over to vomit into the foul-smelling pail, and even that was double.

'Amy – oh my gawd! Look at the state of you!' Beat's two red faces swum above me. 'Here,' – a clean bowl, a cool cloth wiping my face – 'I'll send for Mrs Jackson.'

I lay crushed in my nutcracker of pain, moaning, 'My lord, my lord – I baint got no name – my baby, she won't have no name – my baby – my lord,' then, in a despairing whisper, 'Granfer, Granfer!'

'She's bad, Mrs Harris – it'll have to be the hospital.'

'No – no!'

Mrs Jackson's anxious face doubling above me. 'You got to go, Amy.'

Stepping, falling, Beat's strong arm supporting me – the stuffy, jolting cab – worried whispering voices. I thought, I be dying – what'll become of my baby? 'Granfer, my lord – '

Two starched white caps but only one woman's voice. 'She's got no subscriber's ticket – she should be in the Union Infirmary.'

A man's reply, 'She's too ill to be moved, Sister. We'll have to admit her.'

Beat, Mrs Jackson – four figures fading, leaving me. The chair I was sitting in began to move, silently – I clutched in panic at the sides – into a tiny room of metal. The room moved. I moaned, 'My lord – Granfer.'

A long room stretching into the distance, rows of beds – doubling, doubling. A woman spoke. 'Have you had to remove your wedding ring, Mrs Roberts?' Her voice was brisk, demanding answers.

'I baint married.'

'Then you've been a very foolish girl.'

Tears oozed from under my swollen eyelids. 'I thought my lord, as he did love I.'

'So you were in service?'

'I were lady's maid – '

'Then you ought to have known better.'

'I did love my lord. My baby, my baby – she won't have no name.'

'You should have thought of that before you sinned. Next of kin?' I stared up at her two stern faces. 'Your father, where does your father live?'

I whispered, 'I baint never had no father.'

Two pairs of thin lips tightened, the voice exclaiming sharply, 'Bad blood will out. Nurse!'

'Yes, Sister?'

'Undress her, wash her and put her to bed.'

Hands tugging at my clothes, telling me to lift my arms, the splash of water, roughness of a towel. 'In you get now, just lie still until Doctor comes.' She patted my shoulder and looking up into the pair of kindly eyes I confessed, 'I baint got no name and now my baby, she won't have no name.'

'It's far too late to worry about *that*, my dear.'

The rustle of starched skirts – starch, let me eat starch! 'Granfer – my lord – '

A strange man's faces hovered above me. 'My lord, my lord – my baby – she won't have no name.' Kind brown eyes gazed down

360

at me as the terrible truth welled up. 'My baby, she'll be a bastard – a bastard like I be. "Amy Roberts be a bastard, a bastard." ' My voice chanting, then in despair again. 'My baby, my baby – ' rocking, rocking.

'She's thrashing about and moaning like that all the time, Dr Haynes.' The white frilled caps came closer. 'Lie still – it's no use making a fuss now, you've been a bad girl.'

'Sister, have charity. She's only young – blame rather the employer who seduced her.'

He was angry, angry with my lord. I lifted my swollen hand and he bent over me, listening. 'No, no – it baint my lord's fault – I did let him come to my room.' Painful tears squeezed from under my eyelids as I told him, 'I do love my lord – I do love him so.'

A hand briefly touched my hair. 'He should be here, to see the state of you now.' Then the voice lost its anger, and spoke gently. 'Try to keep still, I want to listen to your baby.' The sister twitched my nightie up over the great mound of my belly, and the dark head bent over a tall wooden mushroom. 'Still – keep quite still.' The head withdrew. 'That's fine, I can hear a strong heartbeat. Your baby's in good shape – no problems there, yet.'

As his mouth smiled I tried to shake my head. 'But she won't have no name! She'll be nameless, like I.' He was drawing back, leaving me. I cried, 'Granfer, I want my granfer!'

The man's voice spoke decisively. 'We'll treat her expectantly, Sister – Sir Henry's usual régime. No solid food, plenty of fluids, a good strong purgative and an enema now, followed by colonic irrigation.'

'Very well. Dr Haynes.'

Other voices, starched skirts rustling, hands touching me, taking hold of me, invading me . . . Pain – 'No!'

'It's for your own good, my dear.' More pain, indignity, the foul smell of myself. In the distance a voice murmuring, 'She looks very poorly.'

'Dr Haynes says there's a good chance of saving her baby, though.' Footsteps receding, voices dying away. Poorly, very poorly: I lay drained and ill and knew that I was dying. But my baby, she would live – I must send her to Granfer. Grammer would care for her if Mr Wilcox told her it was her duty – 'Duty, stern daughter of the voice of God'. Grammer would obey the voice of God – but no, Grammer was dead, dead in the workhouse, but Granfer would come up to the loft to care for me and my baby. And then I heard them, Granfer's boots, slow and halting, coming to me. I moaned aloud, 'Granfer, Granfer – tell I a story.'

A voice spoke sharply, summoning me from my dreams. 'You have visitors.' There were shapes around the bed, doubling – then I saw the largest one move, lurch. He was twisted sideways and so I knew him – not *my* Granfer, but my baby's. I grasped at that knowledge before it slipped away from me. 'My lord, my lord.' With a great effort I reached out my leaden hand to him. 'My lord – my baby, willst thou care for my baby?'

For a brief moment his two faces merged into one lopsided one. I saw the uneven mouth move, and as the face disintegrated again I heard his voice promise, 'I will.'

My hand fell back. The kind man spoke, but coldly now. 'You were her employer?'

'She was employed – in my household.'

'Then look at her now, look at the state she's in.'

Beat's voice spoke. My eyes turned towards it; her two round faces wavered as she exclaimed, 'She was such a pretty girl!'

The kind man was angry. 'She isn't pretty any longer – that's what you and your kind have brought her to.' His voice spoke accusingly. 'We need to keep her calm, but she won't *be* calm. She can't stop talking about her child, and how it will be nameless, like herself. She knows, you see – she knows what it means for a child to be branded for life, as she has been. It's a terrible stigma, bastardy.'

As he spoke that word I cried out, 'Grammer, Grammer did tell I,' and I chanted her accusation: ' "You – you were conceived in sin and born in sin. You be a bastard – a child without a name." ' As Grammer's words died away my eyes sought out the only figure I could recognise. Gathering all my strength together I inched my pounding head up from the pillow, focusing on his wavering shape as desperately, hopelessly I begged, 'My lord, canst thee not give her a name?'

There was silence, then the other man spoke. 'Only marriage can legitimize a child.' And at his words despair engulfed me; my stomach heaved and I tried to turn my head. 'Nurse – a bowl!'

362

Curtain-rings rattled as the foul fluid burnt my throat, my mouth, my nostrils. 'There, there – better out than in.'

Time passing. 'Drink, my dear. You must drink.'

'No.'

'For your baby's sake.'

'My baby – she won't have no name.'

Time passing. 'There, we're feeling a little better now, aren't we?' The nurse was smiling – still two smiles, but they weren't wavering any more, and the pain in my head wasn't stabbing so deeply. She turned. 'Yes, Doctor, her pulse is slower. We've got rid of some of the poisons and that's eased her body – if only we could ease her mind, too.'

'I think we can, Nurse – I really think we can.'

Voices were arguing. 'She isn't fit to be moved – it's ridiculous!'

'Sister, if we don't agree, the child will be branded for life. He's got a licence ready, and the chaplain's willing, as long as we use the hospital chapel. It must be done, it must.'

'Then it's entirely *your* responsibility, Dr Haynes – *You're* answerable to Sir Henry when he returns.'

I heard my own voice hopelessly moaning, 'My baby – she won't have no name.'

Kind brown eyes fixed themselves on mine. 'My dear, your baby *will* have a name. Your precious "my lord" has agreed to marry you.' His words didn't make sense. I forced my mind to concentrate as he repeated, 'He's agreed to marry you – at once.'

I whispered, 'But he be married already.'

'He told me that his wife is dead, and so he's willing to marry you now, to legitimize the child.'

Miss Annabel. I had dreamed of her dying – it was my fault. Guilt hovered over me, trying to pierce me – but it was swept aside by a surge of relief. Only, before, he'd said he couldn't possibly marry me, because I was a servant – so why was he willing to now? Then I guessed what had happened. It was his father, his father had made him agree, so that his grand-child would have a name. I whispered, 'Did Lord Warminster. . . ?' My voice faded, but the doctor understood.

'Yes, Lord Warminster has arranged everything.' The brown eyes smiled. 'It's lucky that the Archbishop only lives down the road! You can be married this evening, and then your baby will be born in wedlock, and bear its father's name.' Relief, waves of relief, washed over my aching, throbbing body at those words. 'But he insisted that I must ask you whether you were willing to marry him?'

Through swollen lips I muttered, 'Yes, oh yes.'

Sister's voice spoke sharply. 'She was hardly likely to refuse, was she? I still don't – '

'Just look at her, Sister, she's calmer already.'

Time passing, but now all I had to do was wait. I must lie still, for the sake of my baby, for the sake of her father. Miss Annabel's baby had died with her – mine must live for him.

'Staff Nurse will take you down.'

'Into the wheelchair now, dear.' As they moved me my back felt as though it were breaking in two, and I moaned in pain. A voice spoke close to my ear. 'Be a good, brave girl – it won't take long, and when you come back you'll have a ring on your finger.' Today was my wedding day, my wedding day.

I was moving between the doubling beds – the corridor walls began slipping and sliding until I closed my eyes against them. My stomach lurched in the clanking descent. 'Nearly there, dear.' Fresh air was cool on my face. 'Up the step now.'

The smell of beeswax polish – I lifted my swollen lids – yellow flames wavered in front of me, candles burning; a white-robed figure stood waiting – but where was he, where was my lord? My eyes began to strain for a glimpse of him. Perhaps it was all an illusion, a dream because I was dying – and then I saw the black, hump-backed shape of Lord Warminster, his father – and knew it was true. My lord was going to marry me.

Beat's broad face swayed before mine. 'You've been a good girl, Amy.' I tried to smile back. But where was he, where was my lord? Had he changed his mind at the last minute and not come, refusing to obey his father?

Voices were talking, pitched low in tone. Straining to hear I caught the one, glad sentence. 'He'll be here with the ring any minute.' He was coming. I tried to turn my head, to look for him, but the pain came and I moaned. 'Stay quite still, my dear.' The nurse's hand steadied me.

The white-robed figure spoke. 'Wheel the bride closer, Nurse, right up to the steps – I must be able to hear her responses.' All I could see now was the starched whiteness of his surplice as his voice intoned above my head, 'Dearly beloved, we are gathered here in the sight of God, and in the face of this congregation,' but where was *his* face? And footsteps came quick and sure down the aisle behind me – he'd arrived. Now I could hear his rapid breathing, and although he was standing behind me I could see him in my heart. Comforted, I forced my tired mind to listen to the words which would bind us together for ever: 'To join together this Man and this Woman in holy Matrimony; which is an honourable estate . . . to satisfy man's carnal lusts and appetites . . .' The chain on the cistern swung before my eyes – but then came the promise for the future: 'It was ordained for the procreation of children . . .' My baby, my baby would have a name now. 'For the mutual society, help and comfort . . .' Pain came ripping through my belly. I cried out; Dr Haynes was beside me, bending over, pressing his hand to my stomach.

He looked up. 'Make it snappy, Parson – I think she's gone into labour.'

The voice was gabbling now, 'or-else-hereafter-for-ever-hold-his-peace. I-require-and-charge-you-both . . . any-impediment . . . neither-is-their-Matrimony-lawful.'

As he paused to draw breath a voice beside me muttered, 'No one's objecting, Parson – carry on.'

'Wilt thou have this Woman . . . love her, comfort her, honour, and keep her in sickness and in health and, forsaking all other, keep thee only unto her, so long as ye both shall live?'

There was silence. And then, behind me, a deep voice answered, 'I – will.'

'No, no!' My voice rose in horror – then the pain caught hold of me, crushing me. I gave a thin, wailing scream, and hands gripped my shuddering shoulders, steadying them. 'It's all right, my dear, it's all right. Hang on a moment, Parson, until the contraction's over.'

Slowly the pain receded. I sagged limply in the chair as the voice, faster again, asked: 'Wilt thou have this Man to thy wedded husband . . . Wilt thou obey him and serve him . . . keep thee only unto him, so long as ye both shall live?'

I stared at the white surplice, my breath coming fast and uneven. The doctor spoke into my ear, prompting: 'Say "I will".'

Bewildered, frightened, I half turned to him. His voice, more urgent now, ordered: 'Just say, "I will".'

I took a deep, ragged breath and whispered, as I was bid, 'I will.'

At once the other voice resumed his chant. 'Who giveth this Woman to be married to this Man?'

'I do, Parson. Come on, come on!'

The chaplain's voice was a low hiss. 'Your right hand, my lord – hold it out to your bride.' One large hand wavered before my face and became two. I closed my eyes. The hiss again. 'Here, my lord – take the book, read your vows – it'll be quicker. Nurse, lift her hand.'

My hand was gently raised and placed upon the soft, warm fur, Esau's fur – I was marrying Esau – but the voice behind me said: 'I – Leonidas – Arthur – Hector – take thee Amy – to my wedded wife – to have – and to hold – from this day forward . . . God's holy ordinance.' The pain came again and my fingers clutched at the mat of fur, caught at the skin and crushed the bones beneath. The hand did not flinch, and I clung to it desperately until at last the pain began to fade and the voice behind me resumed its halting progress. 'And thereto I plight thee – my troth.'

The chaplain's two pairs of eyes peered into mine. 'Say after me, "I, Amy . . ." ' All sense, all reason had gone, and like a puppet I repeated, 'I, Amy.'

' "Take thee Leonidas Arthur Hector".'

'Take thee Leonidas Arthur Hector.'

' "To my wedded husband".'

'To my wedded husband . . .' until my voice faded into the final, 'And thereto I give thee my troth.' Loud in my ear I heard the doctor's sigh of relief.

The nurse gently loosed my fingers as two gold rings shimmered before my eyes on two open books – then the rings became one and encircled my fingertip. 'With – this – ring – I – thee wed, with my, my – ' a long, struggling pause then, 'body, I thee – worship.' Pain gripped me again, my body arched up and the gold circlet flew from my finger to tinkle on the tiles. Pain stabbing, crushing – then, at last, it receded.

'Carry on now, my lord.'

The nurse held the ring in place. 'With all – my worldly – goods I thee endow. In the Name – of the Father, and of – the Son, and of – the Holy Ghost. Amen.'

366

'Let us pray. O Eternal God, Creator and Preserver of all mankind . . . Amen.'

'Lift her hand again, Nurse.' And he took my hand in his as the chaplain proclaimed, loud as thunder, 'Those whom God hath joined together let no man put asunder.'

'Forasmuch as Amy and Leonidas have consented together . . .' The world was spinning, turning, slipping from me. 'Pledged their troth . . . a Ring . . . Man and Wife . . .' My mouth was watering, filling, flooding – saliva began to dribble down my chin. 'Life everlasting. Amen.'

'The register's here ready.' A cloth wiping my mouth, the nurse's hand steadying mine on the pen – Mrs Roper's voice: 'Best copy book, children.' Laboriously I traced 'Amy Roberts' – then the pen jumped from my fingers, my legs were jerking, eyes slewing – and the Hand of God was closing round my body as a voice shouted: 'She's convulsing! Quick, Nurse – her tongue!' The giant hand gripped me tight and squeezed harder and harder – and then there was only darkness.

Chapter Forty-Three

Pain. A voice screaming – pain – screaming – voices, figures, hands – the Giant's hand seizing me, crushing me – Jack escaped down Granfer's beanstalk – but the Giant's knife flashed and cut the bean rows down, blood spurted from their stems – A voice calling 'Granfer! Granfer!' But there was only the Giant's hand gripping, twisting, crushing – and then darkness. Fee, fi, fo, fum – the Giant gnawing at my belly – snapping, biting – 'No! No!' The Giant's teeth tearing, the Giant's hand crushing . . . and a voice screaming, screaming . . .

At last the Giant's teeth bit deep and hard, 'Push, push.' A red hot poker driving, twisting, stabbing. 'Nearly there, now.' A high piercing scream, a gasping cry – voices speaking far away – and a last despairing whimper: 'Granfer, tell I a story, Granfer,' but nobody answered. I was alone in the darkness, alone.

Heavy eyelids slowly rising: light, a high window, green-tiled walls. I lay staring at those walls, and could remember nothing. I had been living in the Buildings, but the walls were brown in the Buildings, and the window there wasn't so high. I tried to turn over to see more, but my cunny still hurt. I remembered that, and lay still again. After a long time staring at the window I shifted my head a little and saw the door. The door had a handle, so it would be opened eventually and someone would come in and tell me where I was. I only had to wait.

At last the door did open, and a woman came in. She was wearing a frilled muslin cap and a starched white apron – a housemaid. 'Good, you're awake. Doctor will be pleased.' Not a housemaid, but a nurse. 'You'll be longing to see her. I'll go and fetch her for you.'

When the nurse returned she had a white bundle in her arms. She bent over the bed and pulled back the wrapping. 'Here she is, the little Lady Flora Elizabeth.' The bundle was a baby. I stared at the round face with its dainty fringes of golden eyelashes lying on plump pink cheeks. I'd never seen her before. 'She's still asleep, the little pet – barely stirred when I picked her up. Isn't she a pretty girl?'

The nurse smiled at me, as if expecting a reply, so I said, 'Aye, she do be pretty,' and wondered whose baby she was.

'Sister thought it best for her to be baptised at once, since there'd been problems before her arrival, but she's a fine, healthy child – over seven pounds. *Haven't* you been a lucky girl?'

She seemed to want me to be pleased, so I murmured, 'Yes, yes, I have.'

'Your husband chose the names.' Husband? I'd never had a husband, that was why . . . but the nurse was speaking again. 'I'll send him along to have a word with you now you've woken up – that's if he can bear to tear himself away from the nursery, and this little lady.' She laughed, and whisked out, still carrying the white bundle. Obviously she'd made a mistake; it was someone else's husband, just as the bundle was someone else's baby – mine wasn't born yet. No one would come.

Then I heard a man's footsteps outside – uneven footsteps. 'Here she is, my lord. Only a minute now, Sister said – she's still very weak.' Lord Warminster lurched through the door. I tried to raise myself. I should get up, curtsey – but the nurse shook her head. 'Stay quite still my dear, you must rest.' The door closed behind her, and I lay looking up at His Lordship, very embarrassed because I was in my nightdress, in bed.

He shifted his top hat from one hand to the other before asking, 'How – are you?'

'I be quite well, my lord.'

'You've seen – the child?'

'Aye.'

'She is – healthy, a strong baby, and she has – a name, now.'

He stood there as if waiting for me to reply so I said, 'Yes, thank 'ee my lord.'

'I hope – Flora satisfies you as a Christian name. I had to decide – quickly.'

'Flora be a very pretty name.'

'Good.' Then his knuckles tightened on the brim of his hat as he said loudly, 'And you – you have a name now, too. No one will ever call after you – in the street, now you are – Lady Warminster.'

I stared at him. Lady Warminster had silver-gilt curls and blue

369

eyes, and she was dead. 'No!' But maybe I was dead too, and dreaming. I exclaimed again, 'No! No!' His face stiffened as though he'd been struck and he lurched back as I cried out: 'No, I baint Lady Warminster, I baint!'

The door opened. 'That's quite long enough, my lord. She's getting over-excited – she must be kept calm.'

His ungainly body seemed to catapult itself back through the doorway as still I cried, 'No!'

'Shush now, or your milk won't come in.' She plumped my pillows up. 'Lie back and rest.'

I whispered, 'Nurse – be I dead?'

She threw back her head and laughed. 'Whatever gave you that idea? Of course you're not. I expect you had a bad dream while you were asleep.' She reached for my hand and nipped the skin on the back between her fingers. I flinched at the pain. 'There, you felt that, didn't you? You're awake now, you aren't dreaming. Poor thing, your fits have made you confused. It does happen with eclampsia, I know, Sister's told us.' She gave me a reassuring smile. 'Some patients even lose their memories. They forget everything that happened while they were ill, including the delivery!' She laughed. 'How convenient, to forget your labour pains! And here's something else to remind you: you can put it on now your oedema's gone down.' She reached into the locker beside my bed and took out a plain gold ring. 'Give me your hand – no dear, your *left* hand.' I watched in bewilderment as she slipped the ring over the knuckles of my third finger. 'Now, you suck this thermometer for me like a good girl, while I go and fetch you a nice cup of tea. Then when you've drunk it I'll wash you and change your pad.'

I lay with the glass tube poking out of my mouth and the gold band tight on my finger – and knew there'd been some mistake.

Later they brought the baby to me again. 'It's time you suckled her – it'll help bring the milk in.' They unbuttoned my nightdress and put her to my breast. Eagerly she seized hold of my tittie and pain pierced me as I felt the strong pull of her mouth.

On the third day my breasts were swollen and tender, and as she sucked I felt the tingling rush of warmth as the milk flowed from me. I held her while she drank her fill, and she lay warm and living against my breast – *my* baby?

370

Afterwards the doctor came. He smiled with his kind brown eyes, holding my wrist and telling me that I was much better. Then, as he stood up to leave he said, 'Good evening – Lady Warminster.'

That night I scarcely slept as one by one my memories came back. By morning I knew it was true: I was married to Lord Warminster.

At first there was only puzzlement. Why, oh why, had he done it? Was it because he wanted my baby? But I'd already given her to him; he didn't need to *marry* me to gain possession of my child.

But he'd believed that he did. It was Beat who told me why he'd done it. She'd sent him the telegram as soon as she'd left me in the hospital. She'd sent it early because I was so ill: '*Amy took very bad.*' And then she'd signed it and added her address. He'd arrived at her house in a cab. Beat had been mangling, because it was Monday, but she'd immediately taken off her apron, rolled down her sleeves, and come to the hospital with him. They'd let him in at once to see me: 'With him being a gentleman, a lord.' And as they'd walked down the ward they'd heard me crying for Granfer. 'You was lying there all swollen up like a bunch of sausages in the pan,' Beat said. 'I'd never've recognised you if it hadn't've been for the colour of your plaits – terrible you looked, Amy, terrible.'

As soon as he came near me I'd cried out to him: 'My lord' – so the doctor had misunderstood and thought Lord Warminster was the father of my child. Beat said, 'It didn't seem such a peculy idea – the state you was in that day you looked more of a freak than he did.' So when, in my despair, I'd asked Lord Warminster, 'Canst thee not give her a name?' the doctor had answered angrily, 'Only *marriage* can legitimize a child.' And Beat, she'd heard him – and that was when the idea had come to her: 'In a blinding flash, Amy. I'd been so upset for you, thinking you'd have to go through what Aggie did when your little 'un was weaned, and there was the answer, staring me in the face! The doctor, he made it easier for me, 'cos when he'd hustled us outside he told us your baby was healthy but you was likely going to die, then he looks at His Lordship and says, very meaningful, "And if that happens, I shall ensure that this child becomes its *father's* responsibility." And I sees Lord Warminster flinch, 'cos he knew, like I knew, that he

371

wasn't the father, that the father was really his son, what he didn't get on with. But the doctor, he was that angry he didn't stop there. He goes on: "And goodness knows what your wife will say to you then." His Lordship frowns, and says, "My wife is dead." At that the doctor turns on him, almost shouting, "Then you should have had the decency to marry the girl, once you knew she was carrying your child!"

'Lord Warminster, he looks as if somebody had dumped a ton of bricks on his head. His jaw just dropped, only it went sideways instead of down – I'd 'a burst out laughing at the sight of him if I hadn't've been so worried about you. Then, it was like Providence; afore he had the chance to collect his wits together and say as your trouble hadn't been none of *his* doing, a nurse comes up all agitated and calls the doctor away. So afore I could lose me nerve I turns on His Lordship and says, "Why don't you?" He still looks stunned, and he says, "Why don't I do what?" Obviously the idea hadn't even crossed his mind. So I pulls all me thoughts together and says, "Look, me lord – if you want your grand-child, there's only one way to be sure o' getting it, and that's to marry its mother now, afore it's born."

'He just stands there gawping at me, then he sort o' shouts, "How can *I* marry *her*?" Desperation made me bold, Amy. I says, quick as a flash, "Easy, me lord – you only need one o' them special licences from the Archbishop." He's trying to interrupt, but I don't let him. "The doctor, he'd fix it for you, 'cos he thinks it was you as got her in the family way in the first place." He shouts, "I wouldn't –" and I thought he was going to hit me, so I says fast, "*I* knows you wouldn't stoop so low, me lord, but *he* don't – and with Amy asking you to look after the baby for her, and you saying you would, anybody'd've thought the same." Then I decides to knock the nail on the head. "And you *did* promise her, didn't you? You told her 'yes' – but your son, the one as got her into trouble, what sort of upbringing will he give a by-blow, with his own wife expecting, too? Only Amy told me how you and him don't get on, so I reckons if poor little Amy dies he'll likely claim his own, just to spite you – and then farm the poor little mite out somewhere." '

Beat paused for breath. 'By this time, Amy, there was tears in me eyes, thinking o' you and thinking o' that innocent child and what might happen to it. But I couldn't stop until I'd said my piece.

372

I 'ad to say it, with you looking that bad and crying for your Granfer what was dead, so I says to him, "She ain't much more'n a child herself, and she's got nobody to call 'er own – and this is her dying wish, that her baby should have a name, like she's never 'ad. And she asked you, she asked you – you heard her. You could give her her wish and let her die happy – and then the baby'd be yours. Nobody could take it away from you then."

'I could see from his face I was getting through to him, tempting him, but he says, "I must – think." I replies, "Beg pardon, me lord, but there ain't time to think, not with the state she's in." All of a sudden he swings his leg up and goes marching off down the stairs, with me having to nearly run to catch up with him, and wondering whether he was so angry at what I'd said that he'd jumped into a cab and never come back no more. And once he's outside he does make straight for the cab rank, and me heart was pounding so much I could 'ardly breathe – then I hears him shout at the driver: "Lambeth Palace!" so I knew he was going to do it.'

Beat sat back and patted her chest. 'I can still feel that stitch in me side now, like a wet dishrag I was by then, what with worrying about you and arguing with him, and then having to chase after 'im like that – and I still had me mangling to finish an' all. Anyway, he comes back just as I'd done hanging out the sheets, saying as how he'd got the licence and arranged with the hospital, but with you being under age he needed your ma's death-lines and your birth certificate. I knew Alf had the one, and I prayed you'd got the other in the Buildings – and you had. I gave 'em to His Lordship and he takes a quick look at both and says, yes, Parson'd be satisfied as you were an orphan.

'Even then I thought we wouldn't make it, because His Lordship'd telegraphed to his valet to fetch a ring, and he was supposed to meet us at the hospital gates with it – but the feller wasn't there. So I says quick, "We can use mine if need be," praying we wouldn't because I haven't been able to get it off in years, not even with soap, but lucky for us the valet came rushing in just as Parson got going.'

Beat shook her head. 'Even then it was a near thing, Amy. I thought you'd fall to pieces afore the words'd been said. The Parson read as fast as he could, but with His Lordship being that slow-spoken . . . But you just managed to last out – and then you

373

went into that fit. He stood there looking horror-struck, as if he'd only just realised what he'd done and I thought, it's too late now, me lord – the knot's been tied. But then I couldn't think of anything but the state of you, Amy. Terrible you were, black in the face, foaming at the mouth, eyeballs rolling – I could hardly bear to look at you. I didn't sleep a wink all night for worrying, and Alf, he were upset too, when I told 'im. But when I came round to enquire first thing next morning they said as you'd had a little girl just after midnight, and that as soon as she was born you'd stopped fitting, and were ever so much better already.'

Beat sat back with a sigh. 'And to think that Aggie's little Amy's a countess – a proper lady! If only your ma were alive to see the day.' She dabbed at her eyes with her handkerchief before heaving herself up out of the chair. 'I must go now, duck – Alf'll be wanting his supper.' She bent to kiss me. 'You looks nearly like yer old self today, Amy – a treat for sore eyes, you are. Cheerio, duck. Give the little 'un a kiss from me.'

After she'd gone I lay shaking. Oh Beat, why did you do it? The thought of marrying me would never have entered his head in a thousand years, if you hadn't put it there. But it wasn't Beat's fault, it was mine. I'd forged the first link in the chain of disaster with my frantic plea of, 'Canst thee not give her a name?' And he had done so in the only possible way, by making her his legal daughter – so now she was the Lady Flora Elizabeth Fitzwarren-Donne. But to make her his daughter he'd had to take me as his wife. Only he didn't want a wife – I knew that from the night in Kew. Above all, he didn't want a wife like me, a servant, who couldn't even speak proper English, who'd been born out of wedlock – and who was soiled goods. Remembering the expression of disgust in his eyes as he'd seen me that time in the corridor at Eston I turned my face into the pillow and wept.

Guilt harrowed me. He'd only married me because Dr Haynes had told him I was dying – but I hadn't died. Instead I'd lived, to be a burden to him, just as I'd been a burden to Grammer: 'A terrible burden.'

They brought the baby to me and I fed her. I had plenty of milk, far more than she needed – my breasts overflowed long before she was due – but there was no pleasure in holding her small warm body, no pleasure in her mouth, eagerly suckling. There was only guilt, guilt towards her, guilt towards her grand-father – guilt overwhelming me, crushing me. And the burden of guilt grew even heavier after Sir Henry came.

He wore a pince-nez and a formal frockcoat, and he swept into my room at the head of a bevy of white-coated young men, Dr Haynes bringing up the rear with Sister. Sir Henry stood at the foot of my bed and addressed the young men – talking as though I were not there, listening. I didn't understand everything he said, but I understood enough. I'd been ill, very ill – but I had not been dying. Dr Haynes had misread the signs. Sir Henry was extremely polite to Dr Haynes, but he made that point quite clear. And now I would soon be well again. 'A girl from healthy peasant stock' – that was how he spoke of me. He said His Lordship had made a better bargain than he realised. He would have to wait for a year or so, but after that I would be able to bear him an entire cricket team of healthy sons – if His Lordship so wished! There was a ripple of laughter from the young men standing round him.

As they filed out after Sir Henry I heard the last one whisper to his fellow, 'With her looks I reckon he's got himself a damn good bargain – but I doubt whether he'll wait that year!' They both sniggered. I turned my face to the wall.

He didn't want me, not even as a man wanted a woman – he only wanted my child. He came to see her. Dr Haynes told me when he looked in that evening, 'Lord Warminster is enchanted by his daughter. I saw him in the nursery just now, and he was standing looking down at her in her cot as if she were the first baby that had ever been born!'

But he didn't come to see me. He didn't want me; nobody wanted me. Even the baby didn't want me, she only wanted my breasts – just as her father had only wanted my cunny. But Lord Warminster didn't even want that.

Nobody wanted me. Nobody ever had, not even Granfer. Granfer had loved me, but he'd have been happier if I'd never been born. Aunt Agnes, she hadn't wanted me, either – she'd sent me away, so Granfer had been forced to take me in, just as my baby's granfer had been forced to take me, too – so he could claim her as his own. But he didn't want me. Nobody did.

Chapter Forty-Four

As the days passed I slid deeper and deeper into the black pit of despair. I answered when I was spoken to, I did everything I was told; I even made myself smile back when people smiled at me. Beat, Dr Haynes, the nurses who tended me, I smiled at them all – but underneath that smiling mask guilt ate into my heart like acid.

They kept me in bed until the discharge on my pads was clear and white, then they told me I could get up and walk. My legs were weak and shaking, but I made myself use them. I didn't want to be a burden any more, so several times a day I walked slowly along the passage and up the stairs to feed the baby in the nursery. It was on my way back from one of these journeys that I met Lord Warminster. As I watched him limping towards me guilt rose in my throat like a bitter bile; turning my face away from his I shrank back against the wall. I heard the footsteps draw level with me, slow, stop – but I did not move. I stayed frozen there until they resumed their halting progress away from me and on up the stairs to visit the baby, his baby. Back in the small room I wept helplessly: hot, burning tears of guilt and shame.

Staff Nurse popped her head around the door several times a day. 'How are you, my dear? Baby still sucking well? Good – tell me if there are any problems.' But I couldn't tell her.

One day I tried to explain to Beat how I felt. She'd been talking about the baby, and how pretty she was, then she said, 'Them nurses tell me as how His Lordship came yesterday and couldn't take his eyes off of her – wanted to know her weight now, and if she was feeding all right. Proper taken with her, he is. Lucky she was a girl – I reckons he must have been wanting a grand-daughter all the time.'

I whispered, 'But he doesn't want me – he never comes to see me. It's only her he wants, not me.'

Beat pursed her lips. 'Now, Amy love, yer just gotter be sensible. Mebbe he ain't too pleased at the moment, with him being a lord and you being . . . But you're a pretty girl, a very pretty girl, and you've got your looks back, no doubt about that. He'll come round to the idea, once you're warming his bed for him, regular.'

'But he doesn't *want* me!'

'Look duck, every man wants a woman from time to time, and you being under his own roof, it'll save him having to go out looking for it when he gets the urge.' She stood up. 'I'd better be on my way, Amy – the boys'll be in from school any minute.' Bending to kiss me she said, 'Now stop worrying and do as I say. Don't take no notice o' what them doctors tell you – first night back home you go sidling into his room and show him you're willing, that'll do the trick. Ta-ta, duck.'

But Beat didn't understand. I had shown him, that night in Kew – I'd even *told* him I was willing – but he'd answered very definitely, 'But *I* am not,' and the pain of that rejection flayed me again. He'd only married me because they'd told him I was going to die – but I hadn't. And by living I'd done him a terrible wrong.

They brought a cot to my room. 'There, now you can get about again we'll leave your baby in here during the day, so you can give her a cuddle whenever you feel like it.' But I never cuddled her. When she cried and the milk came tingling into my breasts I would heave myself out of bed and give her my tittie, but as soon as she'd finished I put her straight back again.

When the nurses came in to change her they would tickle her tummy and pat her cheeks, telling her what a good baby she was – and she was good. She slept most of the time, and when she was awake she lay murmuring to herself, waving her tiny, star-shaped hands. I knew that, because sometimes I crept over to her cot and peeped in when she wasn't looking – but I never picked her up because she wasn't my baby, she didn't belong to me. I'd given her away before she'd even been born.

Then one evening Dr Haynes told me, 'You're well enough to leave now, Lady Warminster. Your husband is coming tomorrow to collect you.'

'I – I dussent want to leave.'

Dr Haynes smiled encouragingly. 'It's all right – Sir Henry's told him you're not strong enough to make a long journey yet, so he's arranged for you to stay at his rooms in Kew,' Dr Haynes laughed, 'while he's searching for a nursemaid whom he thinks is good enough to care for his precious daughter!'

'But –'

'Don't worry, you'll be well looked after. His Lordship is engaging one of the nurses on our private staff to care for you both in the meantime, until you're able to go back to Wiltshire.' To Wiltshire, to Eston – where everybody knew of my sin, my shame.

I scarcely slept all night. Guilt and despair kept me tossing and wakeful – I had done him a terrible wrong. And when morning came with its cold grey light I knew there was only one way to right that wrong. He'd given my baby his name in return for my death; but I had cheated him by living – so now I must live no longer. I knew I had to fulfil my part of the bargain. It was my duty. 'Stern daughter of the voice of God.' I had sinned, so this was my punishment. But I was a coward – I didn't want to die.

I knew how I must do it – the morning light piercing the glass panes had told me. The window of the room was set high above the hard grey road: all I had to do was climb up on the sill and take one step forward. One small step, that was all. But I was a coward, so I kept putting it off.

First I must give my baby her early-morning feed – then it was breakfast-time. I told myself it was not good manners to interrupt breakfast – and once that was over then she would soon need feeding again, so I waited. Lord Warminster wasn't coming to fetch me until after lunch, Dr Haynes had said, so I told myself there was still plenty of time. I fed her again, and then the lunch trolleys were rattling along the corridor. As soon as the trays were cleared I knew I shouldn't wait any longer – but she was hungry again, so I picked her up and put her to my breast. I wept as her warm mouth drew milk from me for the last time, and when she'd finished I held her very close for a little while, cuddling her, because it didn't matter now – and then I put her safely back in her cot and watched until her eyelids closed. I whispered, 'Goodbye, little Lady Flora Elizabeth – goodbye.' Then I went over to the window.

I placed the chair in front of it and climbed up on the seat, pulling myself upright by the ledge. I stood swaying for a moment until I got my balance, then I stepped up onto the radiator, feeling the ridged iron hot under my bare soles. Only another step, a very small step – and then I was on the windowsill, my hands tugging at the wooden frame. It was open, but not enough – it must be wide open. Then the sash gave, the window shot up in a rush and there was nothing between me and the grey street outside.

I looked down: there were people a long way below me, hurrying along the pavement. As I watched one of them saw me and waved; I didn't wave back in case I lost my balance, but I smiled politely as I stepped over the frame and on to the gritty ledge outside. Other people were waving now and I could see their mouths opening and shutting – they were calling to me, but I couldn't hear what they were saying above the roar of the traffic. Wagons, carts, vans, they were all rattling along below me until a cart stopped with a jerk. I saw the driver flick his whip, and all the traffic disappeared – and so too did all my doubts and fears. I knew that what I was doing would finally lift my burden. I would leave that terrible weight of guilt back in the room, and float down light as a feather to the empty road below. The cobbles were soft and welcoming, soft as a grey velvet cushion – and slowly I unclasped my hands and swayed forwards . . .

Screams, hands tugging – pulling, dragging me back – back into the black pit of despair.

'You wicked girl!' Sister's voice rang out high and sharp above the others. 'And you, Nurse – how could you have been so careless?'

Voices explaining, excusing, and then the rapid thudding of boots on the stairs. 'A woman, trying to throw herself out! Ah, you've got her!' A sweating red face above gleaming brass buttons on a blue uniform tunic. 'This'll have to be reported. Attempted suicide's a criminal offence.'

Dr Haynes' voice, loud and authoritative: 'Constable, her husband is a titled gentleman, a man of property. Surely –?'

The other head shaking firmly. 'Sir, the whole street was watching – it's more'n my job's worth.'

'Then I'll accompany you to the station, to see your superior officer.'

Beat came – I heard her at the door. 'I brought 'er clothes, like you asked. 'Ere, what's going on?' Then her anguished cry of, 'Oh my Gawd – they put folks away fer that!' Afterwards there was silence. Beat had left me, too.

Staff Nurse came in. She spoke to the nurse standing guard at the foot of my bed then raised her voice to address me. 'Your husband's come, my dear – he's with Sister now. I'm sure he'll do everything he can . . .' But the expression in her eyes belied her words. He wouldn't. He would take the baby away, just as he'd taken her from me already, and leave me to my fate. I was nothing to him, merely an unwanted burden.

Dr Haynes came back, and I saw by his face that he'd failed. He didn't look at me. Instead he spoke to the nurse. 'Has Lord Warminster arrived yet?'

'Yes, Doctor, he's in Sister's room.' Dr Haynes went out again at once. Everyone had gone, and left me.

But then they all came back. Dr Haynes, Beat – and Lord Warminster. The doctor commanded, 'Nurse, wait outside.'

'But, Doctor, Sister told me –'

'I'll be answerable to Sister.'

Slowly, she went. Dr Haynes shut the door very firmly behind her before swinging round to say, 'Lord Warminster, I've done my best. The local Sergeant's sympathetic, but it doesn't rest with him whether or not charges are pressed. And he says the Inspector's a stickler for the rule book – he's sure it'll mean a prosecution.'

'No!'

Dr Haynes ignored Beat's anguished cry. '*If* she's still here.' He raised himself up on the balls of his feet so that his face was level with Lord Warminster's. 'You must act quickly to get your wife away, out of reach of the law.'

Lord Warminster replied haltingly, 'The law – reaches – Wiltshire.'

'But not to France.'

'F – France!' His head jerked so that the whole of his body slewed sideways.

'My lord.' Dr Haynes' voice was forceful yet persuasive. 'It came to me while I was talking to the Sergeant – I think he was trying to drop me a hint. English law stops at Dover, they can't touch her once she's the other side of the Channel. God knows, it's been done before, and if she's not here they can't charge her. In six months, a year, the books'll be closed and you can bring them both back.' He reached into his waistcoat pocket and brought out a letter. 'I've written a note to a friend of mine who's working at the British Hospital in Paris – if you take this to him he'll find you a

competent nurse and a safe place for your wife and child to stay.'
Then he added urgently, 'That's all she needs, time and rest. The
law's an ass. She didn't know what she was doing – eclampsia can
cause a state of confusion, I should have been prepared for it. But
it's only temporary, I swear – in two or three months she'll be
completely recovered. It was my mistake, Lord Warminster, so
give her a chance, please – for my sake.'

He paused, waiting. Lord Warminster's mouth began to move,
but before he could get any words out Beat broke in, 'My lord,
what the doctor says, it'll be best for the baby – for your grand-
daughter. If they puts Amy away you'll have to bring little Flora
up by hand, and hand-reared babies, they don't never thrive.'

Dr Haynes added quickly, 'The woman's right – especially in
the summer. However careful your nurse is there's always a risk of
contamination. And wetnurses,' he shook his head, 'Nowadays
you can't persuade a respectable woman to leave her own child,
and the others – they're riddled with disease.'

Beat suddenly jumped up and rushed over to where I lay. She
pulled back the top sheet. 'Look at the front of her nightie – it's
wringing wet, she's running with milk! And the little 'un's as
bonny and healthy as could be on it – you know that.'

At last there was silence as both pairs of eyes fixed themselves
on Lord Warminster while he fought for words. Finally he
stammered, 'B-bring me – a – *B-Bradshaw*!'

Dr Haynes' eyes closed in a moment of relief before he said
briskly, 'I've already checked, my lord. The afternoon boat-train
leaves Charing Cross at twenty past two.'

'The nurse – must accompany – her.'

Dr Haynes shook his head. 'I can't allow it, Lord Warminster –
there'll be trouble enough for the hospital as it is. We'll have to say
you insisted on taking your wife away, but any nurse who went
with you would be dismissed.'

'*I'll* go with you.' Beat spoke up. 'I can manage her – I've got her
clothes over here.' Beat went to the door, there was a murmur of
voices then Lord Warminster and the doctor left and Beat came
quickly back with her basket. 'Come on duck, let's get you up and
dressed.' Beat tugged and pulled, dressing me as though I were a
rag doll. 'His Lordship's gone to his bank – he'll meet us at
Charing Cross.' She began to button my blouse. 'He wanted to

fetch his valet from Kew but Doctor told him as there weren't time, we'd miss the train. Upsadaisy Amy, there's a good girl.'

Dr Haynes came in with a white roll of cloths. 'Spare nappies, Mrs Harris – I'll slip them in the basket with her night-things. I've sent the nurse off on an errand – while she's gone get Lady Warminster down to the main entrance, and I'll bring the baby to you there.'

There was a motor cab waiting at the bottom of the front steps. Beat took the shawled white bundle from Dr Haynes. 'Thank you, Doctor, for all you've done.'

'Thank *you* Mrs Harris, for so valiantly backing me up.' He bent over the nest of shawls and gently tickled a dimpled chin. 'It's lucky she's such a good baby but,' he frowned in puzzlement, 'why ever did you refer to her back there as Lord Warminster's *grand-daughter?*'

Beat hustled me up the step and into the cab. When we were all safely inside she called through the window, 'Because that's what she is. His son was the milord who got Amy into trouble. Goodbye, Doctor!'

Dr Haynes stared after us open-mouthed as the cab drew smartly away.

Chapter Forty-Five

I obeyed Beat unquestioningly; I seemed to have no mind of my own. Lord Warminster was already at the station and Beat hustled me after him onto the platform as she told him that we must travel in a 'Ladies Only' compartment: 'So she can feed the little 'un. You'd best give me the tickets in case an inspector comes round.' She shoved me up the step. As soon as we were sitting down she removed her hat and used it to fan her hot cheeks. 'Well, looks as if we've made it, duck – terrible rush, though.' Jamming her hat back on her head she looked around her. 'I ain't never been in a first-class afore – nice piece o' plush on these cushions.' Then she peered at the two small pieces of cardboard and exclaimed: 'The cost of 'em! That's more'n Alf gives me in three weeks together.'

The baby began to stir and Beat handed her to me. 'Quick duck, get your tit in 'er mouth afore she starts squawking.' The two ladies sitting opposite turned to stare out of their respective windows. As the milk flowed the baby coughed and spluttered. 'Give 'er a chance, Amy. My, you could 'a fed half a dozen, the milk you've got.' There was a rustling as two pairs of grey-gloved hands opened magazines and stared resolutely down at them.

Beat took the baby back as soon as she'd finished and began murmuring to her: 'Ain't you a little love, ain't you the prettiest little poppet?' I sat with my eyes fixed on nothing, feeling as though I were in a waking nightmare. On that window-ledge I'd tried to make reparation – and failed. Now I was even more of a burden than before – 'a terrible burden'.

At last the clattering rhythm of the wheels changed as the train began to slow down. Beat leant forward. 'Amy, I'm not coming to Paris with you. Alf'll be raising Cain by the time I get back as it is.'

Slowly I lifted my eyes, whispering, 'He'll send me back, too.'

'No he won't. Fer one thing, His Lordship won't even know as I'm not there. I'm coming on the boat to get you settled, then I'm going to slip off at the last minute. With him being twisted you can walk right past him without him seeing you – if you picks your side

– so he won't know I've scarpered till you gets to France. And for another thing, he might look a bit of a freak but he's a proper gent. He won't let you down – he'll get you safe and sound to Paree.' The train slid smoothly into the station. 'Here we are – and here's your ticket. Keep it safe, it must've cost more'n the crown jewels!'

She took me along to the cabin area, and I watched Lord Warminster's money change hands as Beat spoke earnestly to the stewardess. Then she came and bent over me. 'Now Amy, I'm giving you your daughter. Don't leave go of her until you get to the hospital – right?' I nodded. 'Here she is, then.' I held out my arms and Beat gently put the warm, wriggling body into them; she was heavy, but I would hold her and keep her safe – my daughter.

Later the stewardess insisted on taking her from me to change her soiled nappy. I handed her over reluctantly, and only necessity compelled me to leave her with the woman while I went to the WC. As soon as I got back I took her into my arms again and lay down on the bunk. When the stewardess brought a tray I ate and drank with one hand, before unfastening my blouse and feeding my daughter again. Then with her held tight in my arms we slept together.

We'd docked by the time the stewardess woke me. 'I'd have left you longer, but the gentleman's getting impatient.'

My legs trembled as I walked slowly along the narrow passage-way, and the stewardess held my arm firmly as I climbed down the stairs. Lord Warminster stood at the bottom. His bushy eyebrows came together as he frowned. 'Where is – Mrs Harris?'

I whispered, 'She went back at Folkestone. She had to get Uncle Alf's tea.' The anger in his face made me flinch away from him.

The stewardess handed the basket to the waiting porter then spoke directly to Lord Warminster. 'She's a bit weak, sir – you'd best give her your arm.' A chink of coins – and it was the stewardess who helped me down the sloping gangway and onto the cobbled quay. The cries of seagulls, the smell of fish, voices speaking in strange tongues. I clutched my daughter even closer to my chest. 'I'll have to go back now, sir – it isn't far to the train.'

The woman left. A black-coated arm was extended very slowly towards me; his face was looking away, out to the sea. I muttered, 'I can manage, my lord,' and began to stumble after the porter. We reached a platform, but it was far too low, and all the signs were in a different language. Lord Warminster was stammering badly as he tried to speak; voices replied – so many voices – and hands were gesticulating, arms waving. He took out his watch, pointing at it, trying to form words and failing while the sweat started on his forehead. Standing in the midst of the blue-bloused porters he was like a great awkward bear trapped by a pack of quick-moving dogs. Then all of a sudden he shook them off and called harshly, 'Come!' and we were in another railway compartment. But this time the smells were subtly different and I was frightened – frightened of the place, frightened of the differences and, above all, frightened of the man who was sitting opposite me.

The clicketty-click of wheels on rails, the strange-looking houses rushing past – everything was so different. I clutched my baby to me, and sensing my fear she began to whimper. I shifted her until she was pressed against my heart, then she settled and fell asleep.

A man with a peaked hat came in from the corridor. When Lord Warminster gave him our tickets he shook his head, shouting, 'Non Paree, non Paree.' Lord Warminster tried to shout back, then took out his watch and jabbed a large finger at its face. A gentleman with a small pointed beard leant forward. He spoke oddly, but I could understand him. 'Monsieur, in France railway time is different – it is five minutes behind. You are on the wrong train.' The man in the peaked cap nodded vigorously in agreement. Lord Warminster's face twisted between the two men, baffled and angry. The bearded man spoke again. 'Permit me to advise you, Monsieur. You must descend at Amiens and await a connecting train there.'

But by the time we arrived at Amiens the baby was crying – she was hungry. As soon as I'd stumbled down onto the low platform I said, 'My lord, I maun feed her. I –' I looked round, desperately.

He set lurchingly off along the platform, then stopped abruptly to point his cane at a sign. 'Go – in – there. Here,' he reached into his pocket and held out coins. 'Give this – to the attendant.'

I gave the money to the woman inside and she ushered me to a seat. When I'd finished feeding my baby I felt her bottom – it was damp again. The woman produced a clean towel. 'Ah, quelle jolie petite!' As I began fumbling with the baby's pilch she took her

385

from me, deftly unwound the soiled napkin and replaced it with the towel.

When I came out again Lord Warminster was at the door, a porter beside him holding my basket. I saw by their expressions that the train to Paris had already gone. The porter led us to another platform. 'C'est lent, très lent – mais il arrivera.'

Lord Warminster paced up and down while I sat on a bench clasping my baby. My arms were aching and numb by the time the train eventually came in and I was frightened I might drop her; I tightened my grip still more as I clambered up.

It was dark by now, and we'd scarcely left the lights of the town behind when she began to cry. I tried to shush her – she couldn't be hungry, I'd not long fed her and she wasn't damp – but she wouldn't stop crying. One of the gentlemen in the compartment frowned and started to tap the floor with his stick. Her cries grew louder and louder; she was screaming now and there were tears glistening on her creased red cheeks. The tears of despair began to fill my eyes. I fought to keep them back but at last they overflowed and trickled down my face. Lord Warminster turned his body to look at me, then hastily swung back. The other Frenchmen were fidgeting with their gloves and shuffling their highly-polished boots by now, then the one who'd tapped with his stick leant forward, adjusted his monocle and addressed Lord Warminster directly. 'Monsieur, l'enfant n'aime pas voyager.' Lord Warminster didn't reply, but his gloved hands tightened on his cane and beads of sweat stood out on his forehead.

The baby's screams reached a new and more frantic pitch, 'Hush, please hush – oh please!' But the screams only intensified until I was sobbing and distraught, then the train began to slow. As the lamps of a station appeared in the darkness Lord Warminster suddenly flung himself upright and started to wrestle with the door. The minute it was open he shouted, 'Get – out!' I half-fell down the steps, my arms an aching band of pain.

A porter helped me into a musty-smelling station fly while Lord Warminster bellowed at the driver, 'L'hôtel, l'hôtel!' The carriage jerked into motion as I sat huddled in the corner, crouched over my screaming bundle. Then, mercifully, as the steady clip-clop of hoofs fell into a rhythm, the screaming started to slow down; by the time the driver reined in and brought the vehicle to a halt it had quietened to a despairing series of gulps.

The hotel was small and there was only one old woman there. She kept repeating, 'La fête, aujourd'hui c'est la fête,' and shaking her head.

Lord Warminster shouted, 'La femme – elle est fatiguée!' Then he held out a gold coin to her.

The old woman put it between her teeth and bit it then, satisfied, she held up one finger. 'Une chambre – seulement.' Slipping the coin into her apron pocket she picked up the lamp and beckoned. She led the way into a small room with an enormous white-pillowed bed in the centre. As soon as she'd lit the lamp Lord Warminster held up another gold coin. 'L'enfant – la mère,' he pointed at me.

She nodded her head vigorously then, seizing me by the arm, took me back into the narrow passage and out of a side door into a yard. She waved towards a small hut. 'Le cabinet, madame.' She reached out and took the baby from me, and I followed her pointing finger to the earth closet.

Lord Warminster had vanished by the time we got back to the bedroom. With a push towards the wash-stand the old woman ordered, 'Attendez.' I stood there, uncertain, until she came back with an enamel jug of hot water, and towels. Seizing the hiccuping baby from me she took her over to the bed. There was a carafe full of water and a glass on the marble top, and I was so thirsty I gulped down the entire contents of the carafe before starting to undress with hands that would barely obey me. While I washed myself I could hear her chattering in French to the baby, who'd fallen quiet at last.

With numbed arms I pulled on my nightdress then went over to the bed and climbed between the clean linen sheets. My baby was handed back to me and at once I put her to my breast. While she was suckling the old woman went out, to return with a cradle. Next she came back with a tray, and as soon as she'd settled the baby in the cradle the old woman laid the tray across my knees. I was so exhausted I shook my head at the bowl of soup, but she lifted the spoon to my lips crying, 'Buvez, buvez – pour le bébé.' She pointed to the cradle, 'Pour le lait.' My arm was shaking as I took the spoon from her and began to drink.

387

When I'd finished she picked up the tray and going to the door called, 'Monsieur! Entrez, Monsieur. Madame a fait sa toilette.' The dark-jowled face of Lord Warminster appeared in the doorway. As soon as he'd stepped inside she said, 'Faites une bonne nuit, monsieur, madame,' and closed the door firmly behind her, leaving us alone – together.

He came towards the bed where I lay rigid with apprehension, but he did not once look at me. Instead he told the wall above my head, 'I will – sleep – in the chair.' He lowered the wick of the lamp until there was only a tiny glimmer of light, then he unfastened his tie and took off his collar before lowering himself into the wooden armchair. He bent awkwardly down to untie his bootlaces, then, as he eased off his boots, he told me, 'You – must – sleep.' He'd never looked at me, not once.

I slept, and in my sleep the nightmares came. I was on the window-ledge again, looking down at the people waving far below. I swayed outwards, and fear caught me – too late. I was falling, falling – then I saw Granfer's beanstalk rising up to save me and I reached out frantically to grasp its sturdy stem, but a knife flashed, blood spurted from the green stalk – it toppled and fell –and I fell after it, down into the darkness.

Down in the dark I was Bluebeard's wife, trapped in the forbidden chamber, watching the red tide of blood creep over the flags to lap at my feet. Dropping my key I turned to run frantically out and down the steps, with Bluebeard's sword slicing the air behind me.

Out, out into the woods I ran, between the trees and into the safe depths of the forest, searching, searching – and saw a tiny cottage. I ran to the door and as I opened it I knew I was Snow White, fleeing from the wicked queen. Seven plates and seven loaves and seven tiny stools – the dwarfs would keep me safe. But there was a tap, tap, tapping at the window. It was an aged crone holding out an apple. So rosy-red and tempting was it that I seized it, biting into it eagerly – and the old woman cackled aloud in triumph. I looked up at her, and saw the eyes that were Grammer's eyes, and the face that was Grammer's face – and so I knew what I had done. I'd eaten Eve's apple, the apple of sin – and now I was poisoned for ever. I fell to the floor as if in death, and when the seven dwarfs came home to find me there they lifted me

388

up and laid me on a bier. They carried me out on to the mountainside and there they sealed me in a coffin – a coffin of glass.

The room was dim and shadowed, my head rested on a pillow, but I could not turn it, I could not move. Yet I could see. Then I knew why – my dream had become reality and I too lay in a glass coffin, like Snow White. But my prince would never come to rescue me. He'd cast me off long ago, so now I was trapped for ever.

And then a baby began to cry, crying for me. Even as I lay in my cold glass coffin I felt the warm milk rush into my breasts, ready for her – but I could not go to her, I could not move. Something was stirring in the room: a great distorted shadow moved black up the wall and onto the ceiling, then light came, and I saw the huge shape coming towards me, face twisted and darkly shadowed, with the tufts of black fur showing at its throat. It was the Beast: Beauty's Beast who never harmed her.

The Beast opened his mouth and roared, 'The child is crying,' but I wasn't Beauty, I was Snow White who'd eaten of the poisoned apple and been punished for my sin. I lay paralysed, staring up at him through impenetrable walls of glass. He came closer, asking, 'Are you awake?'

I saw him plainly now; he was the Beast who'd given me the rose, long ago in his garden – so, with a great effort, I tried to answer him. 'I be dead and in my coffin.'

'Nonsense!'

He did not understand. In a whisper of despair I told him, ''Tis a glass coffin. The dwarfs, they do watch – but the prince, he baint never coming . . .' My voice faded away.

Hopelessly I watched his brow furrow and his eyes darken – then all of a sudden he sprang forward. His great arms wrenched the lid off my coffin, seized hold of me and shook me, hard. As my head jerked forward I heard his voice loud in my ear, 'The apple, the poisoned apple – it's fallen out!' And I began to tremble with relief, because I was alive again.

As he laid me back against the pillows the baby's cries became louder. I knew I must feed her, but when I tried to move my arms I could not even lift them from the coverlet. I looked up at him with panic in my voice. 'I still cassent move my arms, they be numb.'

He spoke very firmly. 'That is because you have been ill – and you carried the child for too long, yesterday. The strength will come back in time.'

'But – she do need feeding now.' Her cries were high-pitched and demanding, they tugged at my breasts. I tried to roll over towards her – my body wouldn't obey – but she was hungry, she needed me. He just stood there, watching. 'Please,' I was begging him. 'You maun help I – you be her Granfer.'

At last he came closer and leant over the bed. As her cries became more insistent he reached out and slid his hands under my armpits, to lift me up against the pillows before asking, 'Can you – unfasten – your nightgown?' My hands were as limp as a rag doll's. I shook my head; he hesitated, but the baby's cries were becoming frantic now, so his dark-furred fingers reached down and undid the tiny buttons, then pulled the cotton flaps back to uncover my breasts. The milk was already coming, dripping steadily from my nipples. He froze for a moment, staring at it, then he swung round to the cradle and lifted her out. She stopped crying in surprise.

He put her down on my lap and now she could smell my milk her mouth opened wide like a fledgeling's – but she couldn't reach. She let out another yell of rage and frustration. 'Help I, help I.' I was almost crying as well by now. 'Do 'ee hold her up.'

'I will – have – to hold you, too.'

'Yes, yes!'

He lowered his heavy body down on to the edge of the bed and bent away. I heard the thud of his boots falling and then he slid his legs in beside mine, put one arm right around my shoulders and the other under her wriggling back. She rocked sideways for a moment before he pulled me close against him so both his hands could reach her, then he lifted her up, supporting her floppy head – and at last her gaping mouth snapped shut on my breast. There was a sudden, blessed silence.

As she sucked, the milk from my other breast dripped down onto his black-coated arm and I whispered my apologies, but he only murmured softly, 'It doesn't matter, it doesn't matter.' All the time she suckled he held me close; I didn't speak again and nor did he, but whenever I moved to ease my cramped body he would shift his to fit in with mine. Gradually I relaxed against him, letting my head fall to one side, until it rested against his neck, fitting into the space made by his tip-tilted chin. The steady beating of his heart, the warmth of his body, the smell of his sweat – they all reassured me; I was not dead and lying in a glass coffin, but alive, with my baby at my breast.

When she'd finished she drew her head back a little and looked up at me with her wide blue eyes. Gazing back at her I lost all sense of time and place; she was my daughter, and I loved her.

At last he spoke behind me. 'She is damp.' Then he added, 'More than damp, I suspect.' Bracing himself he held her in place against me with one arm while carefully withdrawing his other from behind my back. The fur on his hand brushed soft against my bare breasts as he pulled the covers over them and lifted her from me, then he was cradling her in his arms. He shifted his humped shoulder, bending awkwardly sideways so that he could look directly into her eyes. Gazing up at him she raised one small, curled fist towards him; tentatively he reached out a large finger to touch her palm and at once her hand closed on it, holding him prisoner. He kept quite still, as if scarcely daring to breathe, until she at last released him and gave a small whimper of discomfort, wriggling in his arms. He spoke to her alone. 'Your Papa will soon have you clean and dry, little Flora.' He lifted her up until she was safely clasped against his chest and then eased himself off the bed.

Without the support of his built-up boot he dipped and swayed as he crossed the room to the wash-stand. Once there he spread a towel over the marble top with one hand, then gently laid her on it and lifted her long skirts. He studied the arrangement of her nappy while she kicked her small legs, gurgling to him; then he reached down to unfasten the pin. His movements were slow and deliberate, yet never clumsy; his fingers had the deftness of a man who'd spent long years tending his roses.

The minute he'd pinned her clean nappy on and pulled down her skirts she was up in his arms again. I saw the whiteness of her bonnet above the darkness of his frockcoat – then she gave a little burp and possetted onto his fine, vicuna-clad shoulder. As he patted her back I heard a low, rumbling sound – and realised it was his laughter.

Dipping and swaying he carried her back to the cradle and lowered her into it. His hands moved, tucking her in – but as soon as he withdrew them she began to whimper. At once he put his hand back to stroke her, and the whimpering stopped. Twice more he took his hand away, and each time she whimpered until he put it back again. He crouched uncertainly over the cradle – then all at once he reached in and lifted her out. She gave a crow of pleasure, and I watched his mouth curve into a smile of response. Clasping her securely against him he pulled a blanket out of the cradle, wrapped it around her, and then carried her back to the chair. He eased himself gently down into it and folded her to his chest. Then there was silence.

Once I drifted into wakefulness and heard his voice, talking to her. It was pitched so low I couldn't hear what he was saying, but my ears caught one fragment: 'And when you are older, my Flora, I will teach you to read Greek,' then the voice dropped back again into its low murmur. There was no trace of hesitation in his speech, now.

Later my eyes flickered open; the lamp still burned but the grey light of morning showed through the curtains. From where I lay on my side I could see him in the chair, unmoving, the bundled shape of my baby still clasped to his breast. Waking, I drew a deep breath – and at the sound he moved, very quickly. When I opened my eyes properly his arms were empty, and from the cradle I heard her wail of protest. Then the cries became more determined – she was hungry again.

Automatically I pulled myself to the edge of the bed and reached down for her. My arms were trembling but they did my bidding. Lord Warminster stood up quickly, bent for his boots, and then shrugged himself out of his frockcoat. 'I will – go – to wash.' He left the room without looking at me. Outside I heard the clank of a pump-handle and the quick gush of water.

When he came back his greying hair was rumpled and damp, and silver drops of water glistened amidst the heavy growth of black stubble that darkened the lower part of his face. Without looking at me he threw down his towel and picked up his cuff-links. After he'd fastened his collar studs and shrugged on his waistcoat he told the window, 'When you – have finished – I will order breakfast.' He stood with his humped back to me waiting until I'd buttoned up my nightdress and I could tell him, 'I be finished, my lord.' He stumped out.

The old woman came in with a tray and set it on the bed in front of me: fresh rolls, butter and milky coffee – only the coffee was not in a cup, but a bowl. I was so thirsty, but there was no soup spoon to drink it with. I stared at it, baffled, while she brought in a second tray and set it on the table by the window. 'Monsieur.' He came in and sat down facing away from me; watching anxiously I saw him raise the entire bowl to his lips and drink from it. Eagerly I seized my own bowl and did the same.

When he'd finished he wiped his lips with his napkin then told the wall opposite, 'I have – sent for a doctor. He will be here – soon.' He didn't once look at me as we waited. Although we were in the same room together he was utterly separate from me. I snatched a glance at the sleeve of his frockcoat and saw the whitish stains on it, where my milk had dripped onto his arm. At the sight of them a hot wave of embarrassment swept over me: he wasn't the kindly Beast any longer, he was Lord Warminster, my husband – and my jailer. I shrank back against the pillows.

He spoke to the doctor in the passage outside before letting him come in to see me, then he stood staring out of the window while the doctor took my pulse and listened to my chest. When the examination was over the doctor turned to Lord Warminster and began to speak; I couldn't understand a word of what he said, nor of Lord Warminster's halting replies. I felt like an inconvenient package whose disposal had to be arranged for. When the conversation was over Lord Warminster turned to address the wall above my head. 'The doctor recommends – that you lodge with the Widow La Roche, who speaks – English. She will – nurse you, and her younger daughter will act as *bonne* – nursemaid to the child.' Then he rang the bell.

When the old lady came in the doctor spoke quickly to her. At first she protested, then money changed hands and she reached into her capacious pocket to draw out knitting needles and a ball of wool before sitting down in the wooden armchair.

I lay with my eyes closed listening to the clicketty-click of her needles; I felt so tired it was an effort to feed my daughter when she cried. The old lady sat guarding me until it was time to fetch my lunch, then a clean-shaven Lord Warminster came in and took her place. Apart from a quick glance into the cradle he sat with his eyes fixed on the door until she returned.

I dozed, and woke to the sound of a familiar English voice in the corridor. 'Of course I'll see her safely there, my lord.' It was Mr Wallis.

393

The old lady helped me to dress and then I picked up my baby; she lay in my arms like a lead weight as I walked to the door. Mr Wallis was waiting just outside. 'Give us the nipper and then catch hold o' me.' I clung gratefully to his strong right arm as I shuffled along the passage beside him.

A smiling, apple-cheeked girl was standing in the entrance hall. She swooped down on my baby, taking her from Mr Wallis' arms with a: 'Ah – quelle jolie petite!' She began to rock her, singing softly. The station fly was waiting outside; Mr Wallis had to half-lift me up the steps. As I sank down on to the dusty cushions I glimpsed the hump-backed figure of Lord Warminster, standing watching us leave. I closed my eyes.

Mr Wallis chuckled as we jolted forward. 'I don't know whether I'm on my head or my heels. First His Lordship disappears, and you with him – then I gets a telegram from Folkestone telling me to report to the British Hospital in Paris – pronto. I pack like a dervish, set off for gay Paree – and when I get there no one's even heard of His Lordship! Lost without trace, and you and the nipper with him. So I books in at a hotel nearby and goes back next morning to make a nuisance of myself there until a second telegram turns up, telling me to report to this neck o' the woods instead! So here I am. How are you, Amy? Oops, beg pardon – my lady, I should say.' Tears filled my eyes. 'All right, all right – don't answer that. But promise me not to go near any more windows, will you? I can't keep rushing all over the continent with His Lordship's baggage.' The fly began to slow down. 'Ah, looks like we're arriving. We'll soon have you safely tucked up in bed. Oh, by the way, His Lordship said I was to tell you he thought it wiser if you didn't use your full title, under the circumstances, so he's told the widow you're to be known as "Mrs Donne".'

I stared at him, then I began to laugh. My laughter turned to hysteria. I was gasping, crying, screaming – until a plump woman with dark eyes wrenched open the carriage door, jumped in, and slapped me hard across the face.

PART FIVE

Chapter Forty-Six

France — June 1913

For days I hardly knew whether I was alive or dead – until they brought my baby to me. Then, as her warm lips closed firmly on my breast and began to draw sustenance from my body, then I knew I was alive.

All day she lay in her cradle beside my bed, and as soon as she began to whimper Anne-Marie would put down her sewing and bustle over. 'Ah, la petite – elle vient de se réveiller.' She would lift the swaddled bundle of my baby and rock her against her chest, talking to her in French until she was soothed. But often the baby cried more urgently, making the warm milk gush into my breasts so that my nightdress was damp even before my daughter was placed in my waiting arms. And as she began to suckle so I would come alive again – for a little while.

The door of my room was always left ajar, and whenever she passed the Widow La Roche would put her white-coiffed head around it, smiling her warm smile. 'You are well, Madame Donne? Good, good.' And for a little while I would feel safe. When the helpless tears came Anne-Marie would come and bend over my bed, patting my shoulder, but if the Widow La Roche was by she'd go straight to the cradle and lift the baby out. 'Come, ma petite, wake up – your maman needs you.' And I would lie cuddling her against my breast, until the worst of the darkness had passed.

Twice a day the Widow would bring my dress and shawl and shoes. 'Time for your outing, Madame.' When I turned my face to the wall she would click her teeth and say, 'Madame – the doctor, he insists. It is the routine; you must walk outside or he will scold me.' She would walk slowly beside me, holding my arm as she took me out to circle the little grassy plot in front of the farmhouse or, after the first week, down the path to the field where the cows grazed. The doctor gave his orders and we obeyed them.

Sometimes it was as though I watched my body eating, dressing, walking, while I hovered above it like a ghost. I was frightened that one day the ghost I had become would wither away and my body would go on without me – empty. Only as long as the baby was close by me, then she kept me anchored to the earth with her warm, strong mouth.

But when evening came Anne-Marie carried the cradle away and the key turned in the lock, leaving me alone. At night they only brought her to me when she cried loud and long; it was the orders of the doctor, so I could sleep undisturbed, he said. In practice I hardly slept at all, for when I did I was back swaying on the windowsill, and in my dreams I stepped forward, falling into blackness, so that I no longer knew whether I were alive or dead. I would lie terrified with the imprisoning walls of my glass coffin shimmering all around me in the darkness, my body rigid with fear: fear that I was dead, fear that I would be buried deep in the earth until, at the last, just as those fears were about to totally destroy me, huge paws would grip my shoulders while a harsh voice roared in my ear – and broke the spell. The Beast – the Beast had saved me.

Yet when Lord Warminster came to see me each day it seemed as if it was that first night at the inn which had been the dream. I couldn't believe that this formal, black-coated gentleman carrying his top hat and cane had ever reached into the coffin and shaken me, or held me close against him while I fed my baby. The first time he came he asked me questions – how I was, whether the doctor had come, was the Widow La Roche kind to me, did I wish to stay? I answered only yes or no. There was a long pause during which I saw his glance veer to the small window, only feet above the ground, then his gaze returned to mine as he said, 'You must promise, you must promise me – not to – do anything foolish.' He pointed with his cane to the cradle by the hearth. 'The child – needs you.'

I whispered, 'I do promise, my lord.'

He moved closer to the cradle, bending over it, and I saw his face change, soften, as he spoke to her. Every time he came he spoke to her, and always without the slightest trace of hesitation. 'Good morning, my Flora – how are you today?' He would wait, as if listening to her answer, before replying, 'Good, good.' Then he

398

would smile. I'd never seen him smile before – but he always smiled at her. Reluctantly he would draw away from the cradle, and turn towards the door; then he would say to it each time before he went, 'If there is anything – I can do – to help you?'

And each time I would reply, 'There baint nothing, thank 'ee my lord.'

Mr Wallis came every day, too. He'd sit down in Anne-Marie's chair and chat about the weather and the peculiar ways of the French and the primitive facilities at the hotel. He didn't seem to mind whether I listened or not. Then he'd lean over the cradle and tickle her before straightening up again and coming to where I lay in bed. 'All right, Amy?' I'd nod in reply, then he'd reach out and squeeze my shoulder gently, giving me a smile and saying, 'Keep your pecker up, then, my girl,' and I'd try to smile back.

After I'd been in France a fortnight Mr Wallis came first one day and told me that Lord Warminster was going back to England. In a matter-of-fact tone of voice he said, 'His Lordship wants to see Lady Quin. She took it very hard, him marrying you – said she'd rather he didn't call any more after His Lordship had written to tell her what he'd done. Only now her Ma's sent a letter – seems like Lady Quin'd like to see her father-in-law again after all. Besides, her baby's due next month, so all-in-all he's keen to go and make it up with her and see how she's keeping.' Mr Wallis added, 'From the way His Lordship spoke she's none too well.'

I began to cry tears of weakness and Mr Wallis came over to the bed. 'Look, he said I was to get the truth out of you – are you happy here with the La Roches? If you aren't there's still the hospital in Paris.'

'No! I don't want to go back to hospital – not never.'

'Do you want to stay here, then?' I nodded. 'Are you sure?'

I said, 'They be very good to me – and I do like to hear the chickens clucking outside.'

'All right then.' He paused before telling me, 'His Lordship said he'd leave me here, if you wanted. Thomas could look after him for a few weeks.' I watched Mr Wallis' face as he continued, 'But the Widow La Roche seems a sensible body, and with the doctor coming regularly . . . If there were any problems he'd telegraph to Eston at once.'

I said, 'Everyone here be very kind, Mr Wallis. You don't have to stay if you'd rather not.'

His face cleared. 'Then I'll go back with His Lordship. It took him long enough getting used to me after his previous gentleman left. He hates anyone strange around him when he's dressing, especially youngsters – he thinks they're going to make fun of him behind his back. And I wouldn't put it past that Thomas, to tell you the truth – cocky little whippersnapper, he is. Right, I'll say cheerio for now then, Amy – Look after the young 'un.' He bent over the cradle. 'Pretty little thing, ain't you – just like your Ma.' He straightened up with a wink to me, then added, 'We'll be back in a week or so, lovey – he won't be able to keep away from his precious grand-daughter for long, I'll warrant.'

They came back quite soon, just as Mr Wallis had predicted. Lord Warminster brought an ivory rattle for the baby, and as he crouched over the cradle shaking it for her I could almost believe that he was the kindly Beast again, but when he turned to where I sat in the chair and said, 'The doctor – has sent me – satisfactory reports – of your progress,' then he was Lord Warminster once more, grave and formal. And guilt pierced me, because I had not died as he'd expected me to, wanted me to. He questioned me and I answered only, 'Yes, my lord,' and 'No, my lord,' until he turned to leave. But before he went he shook the rattle again over the cradle and smiled, before telling her, 'It will soon be time for your shortening, my Flora, so your Papa has brought you a box of new clothes.'

I said, 'Thank 'ee, my lord.'

He looked around in surprise, as if he'd forgotten that I was in the room too, then he told me, 'Wallis will bring the boxes round – this evening.'

Her new clothes were beautiful. There were Saxony flannel nightgowns trimmed with real lace, frilled muslin bibs and cream cashmere cloaks with matching bonnets and bootees. For warmer weather the nightgowns were of lawn with embroidered yokes, and there were silk pelisses edged with swansdown – together with lace veils to protect her from the dust of the road. Delving further I unpacked short frocks of washing silk and nainsook – every one trimmed and embroidered – and for wearing underneath all this finery there were knitted wool vests and pilches, binders and quilted flannel stays, petticoats and soft flannel drawers.

Mr Wallis laughed at my expression as an exclaiming Anne-Marie unpacked them all. 'He sent for a Harrods catalogue and chose every one himself – nothing but the best will do for our Lady Flora.'

The other box was for me. It held all my belongings from Lambeth, including my sewing machine – and Esau. I showed him to my baby and she reached up a hand, gurgling, but I soon put Esau away because she preferred the ivory rattle Lord Warminster had bought her. They only stayed two nights, then they went back to England. Mr Wallis told me Lord Warminster was still worried about Miss Annabel – she was very near her time now. After they'd gone I lay and wept, because Miss Annabel had a mother to look after her, and two men who loved her – but nobody cared for me.

It was three weeks before Mr Wallis came back again, and when he did he was alone. After greeting me quickly he went straight to the cradle. 'Well, she looks healthy enough, anyway – that'll relieve His Lordship's mind.' Then he told me that Miss Annabel's son had been born – and had died the same day. I couldn't believe it at first, then I bent over and snatched up my own baby, and wept hot tears on to her downy head.

Mr Wallis didn't stay long. He said Lord Warminster was living at Kew and going daily to enquire after Miss Annabel, who was very ill. She'd gone down with a fever after her baby died and there were three hospital nurses caring for her round the clock, and big London doctors coming every day.

After Mr Wallis had gone back I realised that although I still felt the guilt, the shame and the despair, none of them were important compared with the one overriding fact – that my baby was alive and healthy. Before, I had merely watched listlessly while Anne-Marie played with her – now I held her on my own lap, talking to her. I insisted on bathing her myself, soaping her firm silky flesh, and as she splashed her chubby legs I walked my fingers up her bare stomach – and smiled at her crow of pleasure. Then I would lift her out, wrap her slippery body in a towel and hug her close against my breast.

I began to carry her through into the farmhouse kitchen where she could watch the comings and goings of the Widow La Roche's big family. I watched too, and listened, and gradually I realised that although they spoke in a foreign language I could understand some of what they said. Madame La Roche began to speak to me in French and almost without noticing it I found I'd picked up a word here, a phrase there, until gradually I began to reply in French myself.

When he came, the doctor would nod his head approvingly and tell me he could send good tidings to His Lordship in his weekly letter, and now the key was no longer turned in the lock at bedtime. I asked Madame La Roche if my baby might sleep beside my bed at night and she agreed – once the doctor had given his permission – though she said that soon Anne-Marie would not be earning her wages! I knew Anne-Marie was saving up for her dowry – her *dot*; she had been planning to go to England to be a nursemaid, just as her mother had done before her. She was pleased to be able to stay in France and earn, because she could see her Pierre of a Sunday. He only lived in the next village, but they could not marry until she had earned her dowry. With a rueful smile she told me, 'You English girls are lucky – an Englishman will marry for love alone, but in France . . .' She shrugged. 'However pretty a girl is, even as pretty as you, Madame, still she will need a *dot*.' She leant forward. 'I have heard it said that some families of high birth but little wealth will send their girls to England to see if they can catch the eye of an English milord, because if he is rich and falls in love he will marry her without a sou. English gentlemen, they are so romantic!'

In the warm late days of August I would carry my baby down to the field, to show her the patient, doe-eyed calves, then I'd take her under the green canopy of the big elm tree to let her watch the flickering shadows of the leaves. But the guilt would always be with me: I had betrayed Miss Annabel, and now she'd lost her baby and was so ill – perhaps dying. I remembered with shame how for one terrible moment in Lambeth I'd hoped for her death; now that memory racked me.

In the middle of September word came that the English gentleman with the humped back had arrived at the hotel. I waited, heart pounding, and soon I heard the uneven footsteps on the path outside. Madame La Roche tapped on the door of my room then held it open; as he walked through, my eyes went at once to his right arm – there was no black band encircling it. She was still alive. I felt giddy with relief.

But he didn't even cast one single glance in my direction – he went straight to the cradle. Putting down the parcel he carried he drew a string of coral beads out of his pocket. He didn't greet her, as he'd always done before. Instead, he swung the beads over her face, backwards and forwards, without saying a word. She gave a gurgle of interest, then one hand shot up to seize hold of them – and as she did so his whole ungainly body seemed to sag with relief. Gently he prised the beads from her hand and put them down on the chest of drawers. 'Later, my Flora – you shall have them when your teeth begin to grow. Here, this is what Papa has brought for you now.' He unwrapped the parcel he'd been carrying to reveal a beautiful brown furry bear. I heard her crow of delight as he set it down on her coverlet.

Then he turned away from the cradle and began to pace up and down the room, until all of a sudden he came to a halt in front of me. His mouth opened and his jaw worked – but no sound came. Finally, with an exclamation of anger and frustration he took a pencil from his pocket, tore off a piece of the parcel wrapping and bending over the chest scribbled a message. When he'd finished he thrust it at me and stood waiting. He'd written a question: *'Did you ever have intimate relations with Lord Quinham after his marriage?'*

I stared at it. I couldn't comprehend at first what exactly it meant, and then when I did understand my face seemed scorched with the heat of my blood – and I couldn't reply. He crouched down, so his eyes stared directly into mine. 'Tell me – the truth!'

I stammered, 'No – never! 'Twould a' bin adultery. I did never commit adultery, I do swear it.' He snatched up the scrap of paper, crumpling it in his hand and thrusting it into his pocket, then he almost threw himself out of the room.

Mr Wallis came later. I jumped up. 'Be she still poorly – Her Ladyship?'

'She's not in good shape, Amy, but they reckon she's out of danger. His Lordship's been allowed in to see her, so she must be a bit better. As soon as he came back he told me to pack to come over here, but I doubt he'll stay long – he's still fretting over her.'

Lord Warminster came again that evening. I had my baby on my

403

lap, and when he saw her there he stopped, hesitant. I held her out to him. 'Mebbe you'd like to hold her, my lord.' He took her from me and lifted her up so she was resting against his shoulder where he could look into her eyes and smile at her. Seeing him standing there, holding her, gave me the courage to say what I'd been thinking about all day. I took a deep breath. 'My lord, what you did ask me this morning,' his body stiffened, but I rushed on, 'my lord, I did do a terrible wrong, but – Miss Annabel, she'd quarrelled with – with him. She'd sent his ring back, and when he asked me if he could – I did think – I know it were a sin, only I thought, I thought he did want to marry me.' My voice faltered, then I said loudly, 'It were only that one night, and the day after – when you did see me.' I gulped. 'I didn't know he'd already made it up with –' My voice trailed off into a despairing whisper as I confessed, 'But I did love him so.'

I couldn't bear to look up into his face; instead I stared at his hands, holding my baby – under the black mat of hair they'd gone as scarlet as my cheeks. I didn't speak and nor did he. I just watched those hands until suddenly they reached out, offering her back to me. I took her from them and he turned and left without a word.

He came again the next morning and asked me how I was and whether I would be happy to stay with the La Roches over the winter. I said I would be, then, with one last lingering look into the cradle, he left. Mr Wallis put his head round the door later to say, 'His Lordship sends his regards, and says to tell you he'll be over again before too long. Cheerio, Amy – must dash for the train now.'

Chapter Forty-Seven

Early in October Mr Wallis came again. He was carrying two packages, the smaller of which he put down by the cradle. 'That's for Lady Flora, though I dunno what she's going to use it for, seeing as she's still only sprouting a few wisps – but he would send for it.'

When I opened the leather case I found a small hairbrush – for a baby. I held it up so she could see the flash of light on the silver back and she reached for it, chortling with glee. When I turned round Mr Wallis handed me the larger parcel. 'And this one's for you, with His Lordship's compliments.' Inside the wrappings was a second leather case, and I pushed back the lid to see a pair of silver-mounted hairbrushes nestling against the blue velvet lining, with a matching silver-mounted tortoiseshell comb.

'Oh, baint they lovely!' Lifting one of the brushes gently out of its nest I looked more closely at the chased pattern on its back – and saw the roses. There were four of them, entwined around the shining silver oval panel at the centre, with their leaves and buds flowing on a curving stem up the handle of the brush. 'Oh Mr Wallis, they be so pretty! Do 'ee tell His Lordship thank you.'

He grinned. 'You can tell him yourself. He's at the hotel now and he told me to say he'll call in half an hour, if it's convenient.'

I jumped up. 'I'll change her, now.' I dressed Flora in one of her best silk frocks and matching bonnet, then hastily tidied my hair with my new silver brush and comb. We were only just ready when the rap came at the door. I called, 'Entrez,' before remembering and quickly amending it to, 'Come in.' He came in with his hat and cane in one hand and stood awkwardly just inside the door while he asked the wall above my head if I were well. Even as I answered him his gaze was veering over to the cradle by my side and I continued, 'And Flora be well too, my lord. I just changed her, so she be quite dry if you did want to pick her up.'

At once he dropped his hat and cane and lurched forward, his hands stretching out to lift her. He held her cradled against his broad chest, rocking her gently as he murmured his usual greeting, 'Good afternoon, my Flora – and how are you today? Good, good.'

I said, 'She do be main fond o' that bear you brought her, my lord. And, my lord, the hairbrushes you did send for me, they be beautiful, the most beautifullest brushes I ever did see, especially with thic roses on the back.'

His face reddened before he replied haltingly, 'I know – you are fond – of roses. So – the child – is flourishing?'

'Aye, my lord. She be trying to sit up already – she do like to watch what's going on, and she do smile and chatter all the time. Well, she baint exactly talking yet, 'tis more of a babble, but she do understand what's said to her, even if 'tis spoken in French. Madame do say as she's a clever little maid, and main forward for her age.'

'Good, good.'

'And she be beautiful, baint she?'

'Yes, she is.' Then he swung round until he was looking directly at me. 'The doctor tells me – that your health – is much improved.'

I nodded. 'Yes, my lord. I be brave and well now.'

'He also tells me that – you are conversing – in fluent French. Who taught you?'

'Nobody, my lord.' He looked surprised, so I told him, 'Except if I baint picked up a word I do point, then Anne-Marie, she tells I.' He still seemed puzzled so I explained, 'They do all speak French here, so 'tis easier for I to do the same.'

He looked almost as if he wanted to smile, and as his gaze returned to Flora he told her, 'It is not to be wondered at that you are a clever girl, my Flora. You obviously take after your Mama.' I flushed with pleasure.

He held Flora a little longer, then he left. Mr Wallis told me next morning that it was only to be a brief visit. 'He's like a fish out o' water when he's away from his precious garden. And then there's Lady Quin – she seems to rely on his visits while she's poorly. And o' course, he don't like France – I can tell that, soon as he steps off the gangplank.'

When Lord Warminster came later he told me, 'I have spoken to my lawyer – and he advises that you stay in France – until the child's first birthday – next May. Is that arrangement – satisfactory – to you?'

'Yes, my lord.'

'Good. I will be returning to England today – unless there is anything you wish me –?' He broke off, waiting for my reply.

'No, my lord.' He bent over the cradle and carefully lowered Flora down into it, tucking the covers around her. Then, with a parting caress, he left her.

After Lord Warminster had gone I felt relief: I could stay safely at the farm with my baby. Next May was a long time away – I wouldn't think about what was to happen then. I shut the future up in the little house in my head and leant over to tickle my baby's hands. At once she seized hold of my finger, and wouldn't let it go. I smiled down at her and she smiled up at me, her mother.

The autumn winds blew and the golden-brown leaves went swirling above my head, but I didn't leap up and catch them as I'd done as a child. I carried my baby in my arms now. Besides, there was no point in catching wishes: my lord was married to Miss Annabel and I to his father – but I would not think of that.

Each day when it was fine I would wrap my shawl around us both and take her out walking along the paths and country lanes. I loved the feel of her warm body close against my heart, and under my shawl I would leave my blouse undone, so she could suckle whenever she pleased. As long as my baby was safe at my breast I did not think beyond.

But one afternoon as I came back towards the farm Michel, the Widow La Roche's eldest son, called to me from the barn, 'Faites vite, Madame! Le milord vous attend dans votre chambre.'

Bracing Flora against me I quickened my steps, my heart beating faster. Why had they come back so soon? Had Miss Annabel –?

I stopped dead in the doorway, my heart drumming in my chest at the sight of the man sprawling in the armchair. He looked up, his face unsmiling as he said, 'I've come to see my child.' Slowly I walked towards him. His hands reached up. 'Let me have her.' My arms trembled as I held out her firm, warm body. He took her on to his lap – then thrust her quickly back. 'Ugh, she's wet!'

'I'll change her.'

He didn't speak until I'd fastened the safety pin and replaced her pilch, then he ordered, 'Give her to me – give me my daughter.' He held her awkwardly, but she didn't seem to mind.

She reached out a small, chubby hand, trying to catch hold of his nose. He caught her fingers in his and she crowed with delight at the game, smiling up at him. His face softened as his lips curved into an answering smile. Watching his sleek fair head bent so protectively over her drove the breath from my body; I felt as though I would suffocate – my lord, my love.

Then she began to wriggle. He lifted her up. 'She's as slippery as an eel – you'd better put her back in the cradle before I drop her.' She protested, but I jiggled Lord Warminster's rattle and she grabbed hold of it and began to play.

I straightened up to stand in front of him, and his face changed, hardened, as he asked, 'And how are you – *Lady* Warminster?' I couldn't answer. He continued, in a voice made harsh by anger, 'He wrote to Annabel, but she didn't tell me – the first *I* knew of it was in the marriage columns of the *Times*. I sat over breakfast and read that my mistress had become my step-mother.' I shrank back as his tongue lashed me. 'And a countess, to boot. You always were ambitious, weren't you, Amy? It didn't take you long to toss that young gardener aside when you saw the chance of something better.'

I exclaimed, 'Joe – he didn't want I!'

He raised his eyebrows in disbelief. 'No? I bet he'd have wanted you if you'd lured him with the right bait – after all, you landed an earl with it, didn't you? The old man swallowed it, hook, line and sinker? No wonder he kept on going up to Kew. Tell me Amy, how does it feel, that grotesque body covering yours while he thrusts his cock into you – is that twisted like a corkscrew, too?'

Frantically I shook my head. 'No – he baint never touched me, I swear it!'

He said flatly, 'I don't believe you. No man in his senses would turn down what you can offer.'

I drew a deep breath – I was almost sobbing. 'He did. I did offer, at Kew, before she was born. I thought I had to because he'd given me money, but he said he didn't want I. He said he were too old.'

He was watching my face intently. I saw his scowl beginning to lighten as he exclaimed, 'Good God, I really believe you're telling the truth! So the old man's impotent. What a jest by the gods – married to a woman with your face and figure and he can't make use of you.' He laughed, but there was an unpleasant edge to it, and soon I saw his face darken again. 'But it doesn't make sense. If he knew he was incapable, why on earth did he marry you? You've got nothing else to offer a man like him.'

I turned to the cradle. 'He wanted her. You'd told him you'd take Miss Annabel's baby away, so I offered to give him mine.' My voice broke. 'I did offer to give her to him, afore she were born – because he be her Granfer.'

He frowned in puzzlement. 'But –'

I went on desperately, 'The doctor told him I were dying, so His Lordship did marry me, so she'd be his, and to give her a name.'

He shook his head. 'No. To take her away from me – that's why he did it.' His face was like a thundercloud again. 'And of course, you – you couldn't resist the thought of being called "my lady", and of being able to buy all the jewels and fripperies you wanted – you greedy little fortune-hunter! So even though he was an impotent cripple, and twice your age, you jumped at the chance of marrying him.'

I exclaimed, 'No! No – I never did jump. I didn't *want* to marry him, it were all a mistake. I didn't even know it was him until it were too late. I thought I were marrying you.'

His blue eyes were hard. 'Pull the other one, Amy – it's got more bells on it.' Desperately I collected my wits together and began to explain: how ill I'd been, how when Lord Warminster came to the hospital the doctor had thought he was my baby's father and so he'd told me: 'Your precious "my lord" has agreed to marry you'; how he'd said that 'my lord's' wife was dead – and I'd thought it was Miss Annabel who'd been so poorly – so when the doctor asked if I were willing I'd said yes.

'But –'

His voice was blank with disbelief. I hurried on, 'I knew *you* wouldn't never want to marry a servant, but I thought he was making you, to give his grand-child a name.' I explained how I'd tried to ask the doctor, but he'd misunderstood. I was so ill and confused, I'd believed what I wanted to believe. And then I told him how I'd been wheeled up so close to the altar steps, and the words I'd overheard about the ring, so still I'd believed. Then I'd heard the footsteps, Mr Wallis' footsteps, Mr Wallis who trod so light and quick, like a much younger man – and never realised. I'd never realised until I heard that terrible, halting, 'I – will.' And then I knew, but it was too late.

'No Amy, it won't do,' his voice snapped out. 'If you were able to say your vows you were able to say "No"!'

I whispered, 'I did.'

Astonishment was replacing anger on his face; he shook his head. 'I don't understand – he wouldn't have been allowed to browbeat you at the altar.'

'My pains had already started. One came just then.' I faltered, shuddering, 'So they all thought that were why I was crying "No!" and they speeded up, trying to get it done in a hurry – for *her* sake.' I touched the cradle, and stumblingly tried to explain again how ill I'd felt, how confused I'd been. 'Like a dream it was, a nightmare – not real any more. They told me to say it so I did – I said "I will". I didn't know what I was doing, I said whatever they told me, as the pains got worse – and then just as soon as it was over I fitted. It were days afore I knew what I'd done, and then it were too late.'

I was weeping by the time I'd finished. He just sat staring at me, then he leant forward and touched my wedding ring – like a manacle around my finger it was. He said softly, 'He doesn't want you, and you don't want him. God, what a mess.'

I turned my head to look at her, in all her pink and gold perfection, and then I told him, 'But she do have a name now.'

His head snapped up. 'She'd have got that if you'd simply married that gardener fellow.'

I shook my head. 'Joe – he wouldn't give her a name.'

'No, not once your foolish little tongue told him someone else had already begotten her on you. Whyever didn't you do as I told you to?'

'It weren't honest.'

'But did you never think what your misguided honesty would cost *me*? And what of *her* distress? I thought you cared for her? If you *had* to tell that gardener you were already up the spout couldn't you at least have kept *my* name out of it? And the old man – he wouldn't have contemplated marrying you if he hadn't known whose child it was you were carrying. Now he's stolen her from me. He refused even to tell me where she was – I had to wait until he was up in Town and then sneak down to bribe a footman, Wallis being determined on playing the seagreen incorruptible. My own child, and I wasn't to be allowed to see her! But he wasn't clever

410

enough; France is *my* country, he couldn't hope to hide her from me here – and now I've found her.'

He jumped up and strode over to the cradle, looking down at Flora. She gazed back up at him, crowing and smiling. Folding his long limbs into a graceful crouch he brought his face close to hers – and slowly his lips curved into an answering smile, so that the child and the man were one: mirror images reflecting each other. 'God, she's beautiful.' He held out his hand and at once she reached up, seizing hold of his finger. He laughed aloud like a young boy. 'See, she knows me – she knows who I am.' He glanced up, including me in their smiles. Bending over her I reached down into the cradle – and at once her other hand seized mine, so that we were all three linked together. Then she dropped his finger to pick up her rattle; his freed hand left the edge of the cradle, moving towards me – and before I'd realised what he was about it was sliding inside my unbuttoned blouse. I sat motionless as his fingertips caressed my breast, before encircling my nipple with a firm, strong pressure. Even as I made myself pull back he withdrew his hand – and laughed at the white drops of milk beading his fingers. 'I can see she's being well fed, my daughter.'

Rocking back on his heels he licked his fingers clean. I fastened my blouse with hands that shook, then whispered, 'She be a fine, healthy baby.'

He said, 'Yes,' then his face changed, becoming still. 'Not like my son – he died within the day.'

'I be terrible sorry.'

'So am I.' Then he took hold of himself and shrugged. 'Well, these things happen. There'll be others, I'm sure.' He glanced down into the cradle again. 'In the meantime, at least I've seen her.' Springing to his feet he looked round for his hat and gloves; I ran to pick them up for him. As he took them he told me, 'I must be going now, Amy – I want to catch the evening boat.' He bent over Flora in farewell. 'Au revoir, ma petite.' His eyes came back to mine. 'Look after her for me, Amy – until we meet again. Goodbye.' For a fleeting moment his warm lips brushed mine, then he was gone. At once I lifted her out of the cradle and put her to my breast, desperate for the comfort only she could give me.

I took her to bed with me that night, cuddling her against my breast, and all next morning I held her on my lap; but in the

411

afternoon Anne-Marie took her from me and put her in her cradle to sleep. Desperate for occupation, distraction, I got out my sewing machine. My figure had changed since Flora's birth: although my waist had gone back to the same measurement my bust was fuller – it was time I altered my dresses. When I took the cover off the machine I found a little bag tucked underneath; it was made of wash-leather and weighed heavy in the hand. I undid the drawstring – and inside there were gold coins, sovereigns and half-sovereigns, each one wrapped in a piece of rag so that there would be no betraying chink. At the bottom was a folded note from Beat: *'Dear Amy, Here's your savings. I hope you won't need them, but every wife should have a bit of cash of her own put by. All the best, duck, love from Beat.'*

That evening after I'd put my sewing away I wrote a letter to Beat, thanking her for looking after my things and telling her where I was and what I was doing. Except that when I read it through again it seemed to be mostly about the doings of my precious baby daughter – but I knew Beat would want to know all about her. I added my best wishes to the boys and Uncle Alf, then gave it to Michel to post when he went into the village the next day.

I sewed a little every day after that, but only after lunch. In the morning I would carry the cradle through into the big farm kitchen and set it down by the hearth, then I would offer to knead the dough or pluck the fowls for the pot. It was good to be busy again, and gradually I learnt to cook the French way: omelettes instead of scrambled eggs, cassoulet instead of stew. Besides, his visit had unsettled me, and having my hands occupied helped me not to keep remembering it. Reading was a distraction too. Juliette, Michel's wife, liked to read stories of an evening; she read them aloud to us while we sat round the big table sewing, and often I would put down my work and peer over her arm, fitting the printed words to the spoken ones. She offered to lend me her old magazines, so I took them off and puzzled over them in my room until I could read French almost as well as English. I decided that next time Lord Warminster came I would tell him what I'd learnt to do, so he'd be pleased with me.

One day I went with Anne-Marie to the market in the town, and there I bought soft woollen cloth and lace. I set every tiny stitch by hand, making my daughter a dress fit for a princess. But I didn't sew as fast as before, because the minute I heard her stirring I would put my work down and go to her. As soon as she saw me she would hold her arms out to me, smiling her beaming smile – and my heart would turn over as I picked her up. She'd reach out to take hold of my hair, pulling me close, and I would kiss her soft cheeks and rub her button nose with mine until her whole body quivered with laughter. My baby, my own darling daughter.

It was the middle of November and her first pearly tooth had come through before Michel told me that the English milord with the twisted shoulder had come to the hotel. I changed Flora, dressing her in her new dress and cashmere pelisse, then I tidied myself and sat waiting. But Mr Wallis came alone. He gave me only the briefest of nods in greeting. 'His Lordship says will you send Lady Flora over for an hour, with the French girl.'

I stood up, reaching for my shawl. 'I'll take her myself – 'tisn't far.'

Mr Wallis shook his head. 'No, Amy, he doesn't want to see you. And he assumes the feeling's mutual after what you told Lord Quinham.'

I exclaimed in dismay, 'He didn't *tell* His Lordship, did he?'

'O' course he did.' Mr Wallis spoke almost roughly. 'What else did you expect? The way the pair of 'em don't get on, how could he resist throwing something like that in his father's face? Soon as Lord Quinham got back he went straight down to Kew – he could hardly wait to get through the front door before he started on his tale. My Lordship had just come out of the drawing room, so I heard the lot. His Lordship tried to say as you'd been asked, and you'd said you was willing – but Lord Quin laughed in his face. Then he told his father exactly what you'd told him, word for word. O' course, I could see how the confusion had arisen. I was there in the chapel myself, I'd heard you cry out "No!" just like His Lordship did – so he stopped arguing then. He just stood there looking stunned until Lord Quin had said his piece and left, slamming the door behind him before I could get to it.' Mr Wallis paused to look me straight in the eye. 'Amy, maybe you did marry him by mistake, but surely he deserved better than that of you? At least you could have had the decency to tell him the truth to his face.'

'I – I wasn't going to tell anyone, not never. Only Lord

Quinham, he –' I was almost sobbing as I whispered, 'I never thought he'd do that.'

'No, you never have thought, have you? Well, maybe it's time you did, because you're a wife and mother now, whether you like it or not. Now, where's that Anne-Marie girl? His Lordship's waiting, he won't be staying long.'

Lord Warminster returned the following month. He brought Christmas presents for Flora: a teething ring, new clothes and a tiny necklace of seed pearls. He stayed two days, and asked for her to be carried over to the hotel each morning and each afternoon. I did offer to take her myself once, but I was relieved when Mr Wallis said Lord Warminster didn't want to see me. I was frightened at the thought of his anger.

He came again in the middle of January; this time I didn't offer to take her, and while Anne-Marie was away Mr Wallis stayed a while talking to me. He seemed more his old friendly self. He said the crossing had been a bad one, and made Lord Warminster seasick – he always was in rough weather, but he'd insisted on coming. 'He couldn't wait to see his grand-daughter.' Mr Wallis laughed. 'He thinks the sun shines out of her bonny blue eyes. He can't put his mind to anything except babies, these days – he's even got a book in his bedroom called *Advice To Young Mothers*. When he saw me looking, he pushed it under a couple of his Rose Annuals!'

After Mr Wallis had gone I remembered Beat saying, 'I'd been so upset for you, thinking you'd have to go through what Aggie did – and there was the answer staring me in the face!' And for the first time I was glad of that answer, glad that I'd misunderstood the doctor and agreed to marry Lord Warminster – because I couldn't have borne it, having to give her away to him. I began to dream again: when Flora had had her first birthday then we could go back to live in England, to a cottage in a village that was not too far from Eston. It would have roses round the door and be just big enough for Flora and I. I would cook and bake and wash and iron, and keep it spotless – and once or twice a week Mr Wallis would come to fetch her in the gig and take her to Eston, to spend a couple of hours with her grandfather.

By February she'd learnt to shuffle along the floor on her bottom, and I'd chase after her, trying to stop her pulling over the wood piled by the hearth, or tipping up my work-basket. Often I'd catch her just as her inquisitive fingers closed on their prize, and as I detached them she would yell with indignation, until I shook the rattle or gave her her hairbrush to play with. Then she'd reach up to tug hard at my hair, pulling me down on to the floor beside her, so that we collapsed together into a tumbling, laughing heap.

Whenever the day was fine I took her out for an airing after dinner, her pink cheeks peeping out from the safety of my shawl, her blue eyes watching. 'Look, Flora – a cow, une vache . . . See the birdy, Flora – l'oiseau . . . Listen, Flora, un cheval – horsey, horsey's hooves.' Clippety-clop, the horse came cantering round the bend of the lane, and the fair-haired man riding her saw me and reined in.

'Hello, Amy – the old man hasn't arrived yet, has he?' I was so stunned at the sight of him I could only shake my head. 'Good, I thought I could overtake him if I played my cards right.' He swung his leg over the horse's back and sprang down beside me. Flora struggled to get her hand free, calling to him. His face softened as he looked down at her. 'She's grown, hasn't she? Good morning, little Lady Flora.'

I whispered, 'Say "Good morning" to your Papa, Flora.'

She gazed up at him with her big blue eyes, and he reached out one hand to gently chuck her under the chin with his forefinger. Crowing with pleasure she grabbed at his finger and caught it in her small, dimpled fist. Holding him fast her face broke into a beam of triumph – and he smiled back. 'Aren't you pretty, Flora my pet?'

Proudly I corrected him, 'She be more'n pretty, she be beautiful – my baby.'

He looked up at me, and the smile had gone. 'Yes, she is beautiful – but she isn't your baby any longer, Amy. The old man's coming to take her away.'

Chapter Forty-Eight

I just stood there in the lane, staring at him. 'But he said – His Lordship did say as I maun stay here until Flora's birthday!'

He shook his head. 'He isn't taking *you* back, Amy – only your baby. He told Annabel yesterday, he didn't want her to hear it from some gossip. He's engaged a nursemaid and she's on her way with them – I actually caught sight of her on the boat with Wallis and had to dodge behind the funnel. He's taking Flora back to England tomorrow while you stay here the full year – then he'll make alternative arrangements for you.'

'No! He can't do that.' Remembering Beat's words I exclaimed, 'He can't take her away from me now, because I be his *wife*.'

'Amy, that's why he *can*,' He looked at me with eyes that were the same vivid blue as my baby's and explained, 'If you'd never married him he wouldn't have had a shred of a claim to her, she'd have been yours for life. But by marrying you he made himself the legal father.'

'But – I be her *mother!*'

He spoke gently now. 'Amy, didn't you realise? In law a child born in wedlock has only one parent – and that one is the father. That's the price you paid for her name. You have no rights over her at all now, and if he chooses to take her from you,' he shrugged, 'that's it.'

His words were hammer blows upon my heart. 'But – won't I even *see* her again?'

'Not if he doesn't want you to. It's true that the courts may grant a woman the right to visit her child, even care for it while it's still so young, but –' and the fair skin of his face became tinged with red '– only if there is no stain on her moral character.'

And for a moment I was back in the housemaid's closet at Eston, staring at the cistern and the chain that dangled from it – then I pulled my frightened wits together and tightened my grip on my baby. 'I'll take her away, now. I'll fetch my sewing machine – I can work and earn enough to keep her. But I don't know where to go.' Frantically I cried, 'Thee maun help I!'

He stood looking down at us, and she wriggled her other arm free, holding it out to him, laughing. He took both her hands in his, and held them tight, before saying, 'That's why I came, Amy.' Relief flooded through me. Then he added, 'But I can't, not now I've seen her again.' His blue eyes were very serious as they looked into mine. 'I don't want him to have her – I hate the thought of him, of all men, stealing her from me. But if he takes her then she'll be brought up at Eston with everything she wants, and when she's grown-up she'll take her proper place in society – the place her rank and blood entitles her to. So I can't be selfish, Amy – I must put her interests first.'

I whispered one last time, 'Please – do 'ee help I.'

But he broke across my despairing plea. 'No, Amy – it wouldn't be fair to her. Don't worry, he'll make you a generous allowance, he told Annabel that, and he said he'd arrange to set you free by annulling the marriage – there are sufficient grounds. Then you can marry some young man who cares for you, and have other children.' Other children – what did they matter besides this one, my own precious daughter! But he was still speaking. 'Goodbye, Amy. I'm glad I saw you with her this one last time.' He bent down and his lips brushed my cheek, then gently kissed hers before disengaging her clinging fingers and turning away. He put his foot in the stirrup and swung himself into the saddle; turning the head of his horse he rode off, back the way he'd come. I stood looking after his straight, slim back – and the clip-clop of the hooves seemed to be chanting: 'Take-her-away, take-her-away.'

No! She was *my* baby, no one would take her away from me – no one! I spun round and began to run stumblingly back to the farmhouse. But suppose he'd already arrived? My lord had been on the same boat – perhaps I should go now? The road to the station beckoned – but I had no money with me. Besides, I might meet them coming down it. No, I must go back to the farm for her clean nappies, her clothes – and the money. The money Beat had hidden in my machine. And my machine, I must take that with us. I would pack her clothes up in a bundle, tie it around my back so I had one hand free to carry my machine. When they arrived they would go to the hotel first, and then I could escape, go to the station – take the first train that came, go anywhere – but escape.

No one saw me as I slipped into my room. Quickly I dropped her

417

down into the cradle. 'Be good, Flora – please be good.' I thrust her bear at her and she put its snout into her mouth and began to suck it, gazing up at me trustingly with her wide blue eyes, and my heart seemed to turn right over in my chest, leaving me shaking and panting. I must get her away, I must. I scrabbled in the chest for the bag of gold coins and rolled it up in her nappies before beginning to fold her clothes – then a voice spoke outside, Mr Wallis' voice. He'd not gone to the hotel first, he'd come straight here. But perhaps, if I begged him, Mr Wallis would help me . . . then I heard it, the heavy, irregular tread of Lord Warminster's boots.

But there was a delay: Madame La Roche was outside, they didn't come straight in – and that few minutes' grace gave me time to think, to plan. When at last the tap came at the door I called, 'Entrez,' and looked up from my sewing as I sat in the chair by the window. I stood up and bobbed to Lord Warminster – but I did not meet his eyes.

I listened to his halting voice as he spoke of how I'd promised my child to him before her birth; of how he would set me free as soon as he was able. I listened as he quoted his lawyers: 'A marriage can be rendered – null and void – if one party is proved to have been – in a state of mental derangement – at the time of the marriage – and so unable to understand the contract.' I had been in such a state, because of my illness; I would merely have to swear an oath that this had been the case, and then I would be set free – but I could keep his name and title if I so wished, and when I came back from France I could live where I chose. He would make me an allowance, as much as I wanted. It was all about my choice, and what he would give me – how he would give me whatever I wanted: money, title, freedom – but I didn't want any of those, I only wanted my baby. I would have lived penniless, and a slave – if only I could keep her. But as his halting words finally came to an end I made my voice reply, 'Yes, my lord, I understand. Thank you, my lord.' But I did not meet his eys.

There was silence. I thought he'd finished. Then he added, 'You – are – young. You – will – marry again.' There was a pause after every word as he said, 'And – have – other – children.' I could not answer. But then he added, 'I will send the nurse – to collect her.'

And now at last I raised my face to his and spoke very quickly.

'But, my lord, she baint weaned yet.' He looked nonplussed. I plunged on, 'If you could wait just a couple o' days, then I could wean her, afore she goes.'

He hesitated, uncertain – then, as if sensing my desperation, Flora began to cry: her hunger cry, her breast cry. I went to the cradle and lifted her out. At once she began to tug at my blouse with her small, strong hands, and his face was suffused with blood as he backed towards the door saying, 'Two – days,' then he'd gone. I opened my blouse, whispering, 'Thank 'ee, Flora, thank 'ee,' as her mouth took hold of my nipple.

I planned my escape very carefully. He sent for Anne-Marie to take Flora to the hotel, and while she was gone I carried my sewing machine the three miles to the station. Just before I got there I hid it deep in the hedge; then I asked the time of the first train to Paris.

Long before dawn next morning I crept out of the farmhouse door with Flora tied in my shawl across my breast, her firm body resting on one arm, my basket carried on the other. I had dressed in two of everything, just as Grammer had made me do long ago in Borrell, when she sent me to London, to Aunt Agnes. I could only carry Flora's things in my basket so Esau, the faithful companion of my childhood, had had to be left behind – there wasn't room for him as well as her bear. I left a full two hours before the train was due: I knew I could only walk slowly, burdened as I was, and I had to pick my way carefully because the moon was only a faint glimmer in the sky, hiding behind the racing clouds. As I passed the byre a cow lowed – she was calving, and I saw the flicker of a lantern inside. My foot stumbled on a stone – the lantern came to the doorway and swung up high – I crouched back against the wall as I recognised the stocky figure of Michel, but after a moment the cow lowed again, and he went back inside. My heart raced as I walked on and out into the lane.

I left my basket at the station and returned for my sewing machine; it was still there. My arm was aching with the weight of my baby – but soon we would be on the train, and safe. The minute the office opened I went to the grille and asked for a single ticket to Paris; he would never find me there. The porter picked up my sewing machine and escorted me across the line to the other platform. Thankfully I sat down to wait for the Paris train, cuddling my sleeping baby.

419

And then I heard it – the clippety-clop of hooves, coming through the village and up the road to the station – the hooves of a horse being ridden fast, too fast. Further away a whistle sounded: the train – the train was coming! The hoofbeats, they were nearer, but the train was faster. I jumped up and peered down the line. In the pale dawn light I could see the plume of smoke; turning I looked the other way, down the road – and saw the man on horseback dipping and swaying as he rode, unbalanced by his twisted shoulder. The train – the horse, skidding to a halt, the man almost falling from its back, but retrieving himself, setting off in a stumbling, ungainly run. The train was very close now, but he was running faster and faster, along the platform to the crossing. There were cries, shouts – but the man ignored them, plunging down to the rails. The train and the man, meeting – I heard the squeal of brakes, shouts of 'Monsieur! Monsieur!' And then above the noise of the shouts, I heard the footsteps, lurching on, towards me.

Dropping my basket, I clutched my baby and ran to the train as it steamed in – but even as I pulled open the door he dragged the handle from me. I turned to the next – but strong hands reached out, tore my arms apart – and seized my baby, taking her from me. I had lost her.

The porter came up with my basket and sewing machine. He swung open a door for me. 'Madame, voulez-vous prendre place maintenant?'

On the platform behind me stood Lord Warminster, his face dripping with sweat and his huge arms clamping Flora to his chest, trapping her. He swung round and lurched away down the platform –and then I heard her start to cry, crying for me. I turned and followed him. Outside was the same station fly we'd arrived in all those months ago. He climbed in with her in his arms and sat down on the dusty seat; I stepped up behind him and sat down opposite, my eyes fixed on her tear-stained red cheeks. The porter stowed my basket and sewing machine tidily away at my feet, before asking, 'Monsieur, que voulez-vous que je fasse avec le cheval?'

A coin was tossed and deftly caught. 'Attachez-le.'

'Bon, Monsieur.'

The carriage started with a jerk, and we jolted forward. At the movement Flora's wails subsided into plaintive whimpers, and at last he spoke to me. 'Where – were you – taking her?'

I whispered, 'To Paris.'

'To – Lord Quinham?'

'No! He did come, but he said I maun give her to you, but – I couldn't, I couldn't. So I thought if I took my sewing machine then I could set up as dressmaker, and earn enough to keep her.'

He shouted at me, 'You little fool – you'd have finished up on the streets!'

I cried back, 'I dussent care. I'd even a' done that – so long as I could keep her!' And as I said it I knew I spoke the truth – and so did he.

He said angrily, 'You offered her to me, you *gave* her to me – before she was born.'

I struggled against the tears as I told him, 'I didn't know her then.' I looked up at him, for the first time. 'She by *my* baby – she be all I got.'

And as I spoke she began to cry again. He jogged her up and down, speaking to her. 'Flora, don't cry. Don't cry, little Flora – your Papa will look after you.' But she didn't want him, she wanted me. She struggled to get to me, fighting against his restraining arms. 'Flora – please.' But she was screaming now, louder and louder, and somehow she managed to get her arms free and fling them out towards me, her eyes fixed piteously on my face.

Her screams pierced my heart. Holding out my arms I begged him, 'Please, let I hold her – just to calm her. I won't try and take her away, I do promise. Just let I hold her.' At first he wouldn't, but she was gasping and frantic with trying to get to me and at last, very slowly and reluctantly, he leant forward and let me lift her rigid body into my arms.

I felt her desperation, and now all my mind was concentrated on soothing her, calming her. 'My baby, my sweetheart, my liddle rose – sh – Mama hast thee safe – shush, shush.' I held her against my breast, my cheek pressed to her head, rocking her, loving her – and slowly her frantic sobs subsided into hiccups and snuffles. Her hand began to pull at my blouse, and at once I unfastened my buttons and gave her my breast – and was pierced with love and anguish as her mouth took hold and began to suck. For the last time. I felt the warm milk rush tingling into my breast; my final gift to her – my baby, my daughter. And as the milk flowed from my breast so the tears streamed down my cheeks, but I fought to stay calm for her sake – and to remember. Sharp as a scythe came the thought of Aunt Agnes. Just so must she have fed me for the last time at the station, while Granfer waited to take her away – as my baby's Granfer waited, now.

The cab jolted to a halt. I heard the driver climb down and come to the door. A harsh voice ordered: 'Attendez,' and my baby sucked on. I wanted her to suckle forever, but I felt the strong pulls lessen, and knew she was satisfied. When she'd finished I lifted her up, holding her body to my bare breast and her cheek against mine as I whispered my farewells in her small, perfect ear. 'Goodbye, my Flora, my sweeting, my dear one.' She buried her hands in my hair, tugging at it – and although she was too young for memory I knew I had to tell her: 'Thee maun remember, my maid, that thy mother, she never did want to give thee away – and she do love thee, always.' Then I gently disentangled her clinging fingers and took a deep, painful breath before telling her, 'Now thee maun go to thy Granfer.' With trembling arms I held her out to the man opposite. He did not move. I told him, 'Take her – she be quiet now.'

Still he was silent, until my arms were shaking uncontrollably, then, speaking as slowly as if every word were being dragged out of him he said, 'You – may – keep – her.'

I couldn't take in what he was saying. Bewildered, I asked, 'Don' 'ee want her?'

'I – I –' His mouth was working but he couldn't get the words out until finally he almost shouted, 'Keep her! She is – your child.'

'Do 'ee mean I can keep her forever?'

He tried to say yes, but could only give a grotesque sideways nod before wrenching open the carriage door and almost falling out. I followed as if in a dream.

Back inside the farmhouse I sat cradling my baby in my arms, my legs shaking with relief, while outside the window came the sound of boots, tramping up and down, up and down, up and down – in a ferocious, lopsided patrol.

Long after, he came in and told me I was to stay at the farm with Flora until her first birthday. Then he would send Mr Wallis to bring us both back to England. He would find me a small house and engage servants for me, and I could live there with my daughter.

In my relief I offered, 'If 'twere not too far from Eston – near a station mebbe – then you could come and visit her, regular.' He didn't answer; he just stood staring bleakly at the wall. Then he sent for a priest to bring a Bible, and made me swear on it that I wouldn't take Flora away from the farm without his consent. I put my hand on the big black book and swore, willingly. Afterwards he demanded that I hand over my money, and I gave it all back to him. It was his money, after all.

The next day he left. He hadn't asked for her to be sent to the hotel again.

Chapter Forty-Nine

For days I clung to my baby. I could not bear her to be even as far away as the cradle beside my bed. As soon as Madame La Roche and Anne-Marie had wished me 'Bonne nuit' I would lean over and lift her into my bed, and sleep all night with her warm young body nestling close to mine. Sometimes in my dreams I heard the clatter of hooves and the shriek of the engine's whistle, and would wake in a panic to hug her to me in a frenzy of relief.

But gradually my fears subsided and I could relax and enjoy her gleeful laugh and the strong tug of her fingers as they entwined themselves in my hair. Now when I changed her nappy she would wave her arms and legs, inviting me to tickle her fat little feet until her whole body came alive with joy. We played pat-a-cake, and round-and-round-the-garden: the simple babies' games I'd seen mothers playing with their children at Borrell and in the Buildings. And now it was always my face she turned towards, my voice she listened for, and my words she answered in her soft, murmuring babble – until that wonderful morning when she held her arms out to me and said, quite clearly. 'Mama.' I hugged and hugged her.

Two days after she'd spoken for the first time Mr Wallis came, alone. He only stayed an afternoon and evening, but as the weather was fine he came out with us on our afternoon walk, and carried Flora back for me. Just before saying goodbye, he said casually, 'Lady Quinham's gone to America. She's never been right since she lost the baby, so her mother's taken her to Boston, to see the doctors there. I'll go and pay Madame La Roche up until the little 'un's birthday, Amy, and tell her I'll be over to collect you both then.' He swung Flora up in his arms. 'Give us a smile, sweetheart. My, just look at those teeth!' Putting her down again he grinned at me. 'Cheerio for now, Amy – I'll see you in May.'

Although I still gave Flora my breast whenever she wanted it she was eating solid food now. She sat on my lap at the big kitchen table and Madame would mash and mince, talking to me of what babies liked to eat while I listened avidly to every word. I wanted

424

to learn all I could, because when we went to live in our little cottage together I would be looking after her by myself. Lord Warminster had talked of engaging servants, but I wouldn't need those, nor would I need a house, however small. A cottage would be quite big enough. I began to daydream in earnest of that cottage: it was thatched, and had pink roses growing all round the front door and a vegetable plot at the back. Indoors a fat, contented cat sat purring on the red-brick floor, and sitting on the rug by the hearth was my baby – always there was my baby – watching me, listening to me, loving me, needing me.

Sometimes I would imagine Lord Warminster coming to see his grand-daughter; I would have polished the furniture in the little parlour until it shone and he would sit in there with Flora while I was busy in the kitchen. Then I'd carry through his tea tray and set it on the small oval table, before bobbing politely and withdrawing; as soon as he'd drunk his tea he'd go home again. At other times, guiltily, I dreamt that her father had come to see her, and we were sitting either side of the shining parlour grate while I told him how clever his daughter was. As I imagined his laughing smile my heart seemed to turn a somersault in my breast.

I had all her clothes starched and pressed and ready for packing by the day of her birthday, and in the morning we gave her her presents. I'd sewed her a soft rag doll and dressed it, right down to its miniature pair of corsets. Madame La Roche gave her a teething ring, Anne-Marie a brightly coloured ball, while from Michel came a wooden bowl and spoon that he'd carved himself. She crowed and gurgled with delight, hitting the bowl hard with the spoon and beaming at the noise it made. Over and over again I kissed her satin cheeks and silken hair – she was so beautiful, my baby.

I didn't expect Mr Wallis until the afternoon, when the slow train to Paris stopped at the station – but he arrived suddenly in the middle of the morning. I looked up in surprise and he explained, 'I've come up from Rouen – I sailed Southampton–Le Havre so I could travel overnight. Look, Amy – do you think you could be ready to leave at midday? Then we can connect with the one thirty-two from Amiens. It's a fast train, goes straight through to Calais to catch the afternoon boat. That way we can be in London this evening and get straight down to Kew.'

London – by this evening? I could hardly take the idea in, then I pulled myself together and told him, 'I be all ready to pack, then I've only got to put Flora's outdoor things on. I won't be long.'

'Good girl. We'll make it, then.'

'But, His Lordship did say a small house, in the country. Be I going to Kew now, instead?'

Mr Wallis nodded. 'For a few weeks, yes – or it might be longer. We're all at sixes and sevens at Eston, what with His Lordship's accident.'

'Accident!'

'He came off his horse, nearly three weeks ago now, it was. That stupid oaf Butty Williams with his traction engine came round the corner too fast, steam everywhere, straight at His Lordship. The mare panicked and tried to bolt but she put her foot in a pothole and fell – then she rolled over, right on top of his leg. Clara's mother saw it happen, and she said you could hear His Lordship's bones snapping. And o' course, it would be his good leg, not the short one.'

'Be he hurt bad?'

'I don't suppose you'd be feeling too chipper if a horse had used your thigh as a mattress, Amy. Luckily the doctor was visiting at the post office and he came straight out, and got His Lordship carried back on a gate – but it was an awkward job, with him being so big, and twisted too. But then Dr Matthews said as he daren't set the leg himself, it was in such a mess, so he telegraphed to a doctor in Liverpool who's got a name as a bonesetter – Welshman, he is – and he sent back word as he'd come down and likely operate.' Mr Wallis dragged my box out into the middle of the floor. 'You'd best get started on this packing, or we'll miss that train.'

Mechanically my hands began to shake out and fold as I asked, 'And did he?'

'Oh, yes. He said there was no way he could set it without using the knife first.' I shuddered. 'A right to-do we had getting everything ready. His Lordship's bedroom had to be cleaned from top to bottom and all the curtains taken down, and the kitchen table carried upstairs and scrubbed with carbolic. Mrs J. was in a real four-star tizzy by then, as you can imagine. His Lordship came through the operation all right, but he'll be bedfast for months – Dr Matthews said his thigh-bone was all crushed. So the faster we can get away, Amy, the better I'll be pleased.' Flora's rattle landed with a clatter at Mr Wallis' feet. As he handed it back to her he added, 'To tell the truth, I didn't want to leave him to come here, but he insisted – seemed to think you might make off to Paris with the youngster if I didn't arrive on the dot.'

I flushed. 'I'll be as quick as I can, Mr Wallis.'

When I'd finished packing Mr Wallis said would I ask Anne-Marie if she'd come to England with me for a while as nursemaid to Flora. 'His Lordship was going to engage a nurse hisself, but then this happened.'

I shook my head quickly. 'She won't want to leave all of a sudden like that. Besides, I don't need no nursemaid – I can look after my baby myself.'

'I daresay you can, Amy, but . . .' then he shrugged. 'Well, there's no time to argue.'

I had to hurry to get Flora fed and changed, then there were all the goodbyes to be said, so I had no time to think again until we were at the station; after all the rushing we were early, and had to wait. I looked at the bench on the opposite platform – the bench on which I'd been sitting when I'd heard the hoofbeats and the whistle – and remembered how the train had come closer and closer as Lord Warminster ran along the platform, and right in front of the train. Despite his short leg and twisted body he'd managed to run; but now he lay in bed with his good leg shattered.

Turning to Mr Wallis I asked, 'His Lordship – he will be able to walk again, won't he?'

'Dr Matthews reckons he likely will, if he's lucky.' Mr Wallis looked me straight in the eye as he added, 'But then he don't have much luck, does he? Poor old so-and-so. After all, both his wives left him – and the first one took his son away from him, while now the second one's making off with his grand-daughter.'

Quickly I defended myself. 'I baint! I did tell him, last time he were here – I said I'd live in a cottage not far from Eston so he could visit her, regular.'

Mr Wallis shook his head. 'No, he won't do that. If she's not to be brought up under his roof then he don't want to see her again, ever.'

'But – he were main fond of her!'

'He *is* fond of her, Amy, very fond – but that's not the point. He don't want her turning against him, see, and that's what he thinks'll happen if she don't get used to him when she's young. I wouldn't have realised how he felt but for what he said that night after that accident of his. Some gentlemen, they talk to their valets, confide in 'em, even – but Lord Warminster doesn't. Never has done in all the years I've been with him. I don't think he confides in anyone, to tell you the truth. But he got near to it just that one night. I sat up with him; Dr Matthews'd told me to, but I'd have done it anyway, him being in that state. I could see he was in a lot of pain, and worried about what the next day would bring – and who wouldn't have been, in his position? Anyway, I thought he'd nodded off at last when suddenly he opened his eyes and said, "Bring me pen and ink, and a piece of paper." He managed to scrawl a few lines then he handed it to me to read: it was a note to his agent, saying that in the event of His Lordship's death I was to be paid six months' wages. And then he said to me, "She's provided for in my will, her and the child – but if things go wrong tomorrow I want you to find her somewhere to live and engage reliable servants, then stay with her until she's settled in. Make sure she doesn't try and go back to live in that slum – it's no place to bring up a child, but she's young and silly, she won't think." '

'He looked so grey and haggard I spoke out of turn. I said, "Look, my lord – you're being too gloomy by half. You'll live to see your grand-daughter grow up, don't you worry." But he just stared at the wall and said, "No." So I tried to cheer him up. "My lord," I said, "this Welshman's reckoned to be a dab hand with the knife – you'll pull through tomorrow, I'd put my shirt on it." Then he started to get irritated and snapped, "I daresay I'll survive – but you're wrong, I won't see *her* grow up. I won't see her any more." So I told him, "Amy – Lady Warminster, that is – she won't run off again. She'll let you visit the little 'un – or even bring her here to see you, if you can't get about so easily." '

'And at first I thought he wasn't going to answer, then he started to speak again, but with even longer gaps than usual, as if the words were only coming out because he couldn't keep 'em in, rather than because he meant to say them. "No," he said. "Only a child who'd grown up in my house, under my roof, could ever bear to tolerate my presence." And then he added, almost under his breath, "Because I am monstrous." At first I couldn't believe I'd heard him aright, then I answered, "With respect, my lord, you're exaggerating. Your appearance is – unusual, but –" And he just broke in, shouting: "You're wrong, Wallis, you're wrong! Besides, you're a man – females see things differently." He'd got himself so agitated that he jerked his leg right up and started groaning, so I had to concentrate on easing his position. When I'd settled him a bit he muttered, "Leave me, I want to sleep." But I'd never seen a man looking less like sleeping, only I reckon he regretted having spoken so freely to me. So I went and sat in his dressing room, with the door ajar.' Mr Wallis took out his watch. 'This train's late, even by French railway time – and where's that dratted porter got to?' Then we heard the whistle.

Flora was dazzled by the train; when I held her up and pointed out of the window she shrieked with excitement – and then kept trying to wriggle off my lap and crawl along the seat. The other women in the carriage were ladies – their own children were safe with their nurses in the second-class – and although they found Flora's antics amusing at first little frowns soon appeared. I put her to my breast to soothe her, and overheard their murmured conversation. They were saying that a wetnurse shouldn't be travelling first-class – it wasn't 'convenable'. I redoubled my efforts to amuse Flora, but by the time we reached Calais over-excitement had made her whining and fretful.

On the boat she finally tired, and dropped off to sleep in my arms. As I held her I thought of how we would soon be living in our little cottage, with its roses round the door: but as I day-dreamed the small building seemed to become frail, shadowy – and the roses were no longer glowing and pink; their petals had begun to fade and droop. I thought, Lord Warminster would know how to cure my roses, when he came to see Flora – but he wouldn't be coming to see her; Mr Wallis had explained that. And her real father, Lord Quinham, he wouldn't be coming either. It wasn't proper for him to come to tea with me because he was Miss Annabel's husband, not mine. And the thought came unbidden into my mind that it was Lord Warminster who was *my* husband. At once I thrust it from me and began recklessly to jiggle Flora up and down until she woke up and claimed all my attention.

It was just after seven when the boat-train drew into Victoria. Flora had fallen asleep again and didn't wake as I carried her through the barrier and out to the cab rank. We were soon at Kew, and as our cab pulled up outside the main entrance Mr Wallis took out his watch. 'I'd like to get over to Waterloo for the nine-fifty. It's a snail of a train, goes all round the houses and doesn't reach Eston until three in the morning, but I'd be happier getting back as soon as I possibly can. I'm worried about His Lordship. He don't much care for me giving him a bedpan, and I reckon he'll do hisself a mischief before he asks a woman for one! And you know what Mrs J.'s housekeeping's like – he could be starving for all the effort she'd make – so if you can manage . . .'

'Yes. Yes, o' course I can.'

'Soon as we arrive I'll put the kettle on and ring down for a bite.'

There was a cot beside the bed in the room I'd had before; I only took Flora's outer clothes off and then slid her between the sheets. She whimpered, but she didn't wake up properly; I'd fed her on the way to London and now she was tired out with the journey. When I went along to the kitchen Mr Wallis was sitting at the table in his shirtsleeves, a cup and saucer in front of him. I moved to pull up a chair but at once he jumped to his feet. 'I've laid the table,' he said, and before I realised what he was about I'd been ushered into the dining room – Lord Warminster's dining room. There was one place laid. Mr Wallis whisked out the chair for me and was back in seconds with a loaded tray. Scrambled eggs, bacon, mushrooms, toast – all were deftly served then he asked, 'Do you require anything more, my lady?'

The title hit me like a bolt of lightning, and I could barely stammer a reply, 'N-No, thank you, Mr Wallis.' I saw his almost imperceptible shake of the head at my use of the 'Mr' – but I couldn't bring myself to drop it. My hands were trembling as I picked up my knife and fork.

So I sat in Lord Warminster's place in Lord Warminster's dining room, then I allowed myself to be shepherded along the corridor to Lord Warminster's drawing room where I sat in Lord Warminster's chair with his coffee pot on the table beside me. I could shelter behind 'Madame Donne' no longer; we were back in England now.

Mr Wallis returned with his bowler hat in one hand and a salver in the other. 'I'll be leaving now, my lady. I expect His Lordship will be sending me up in a few days to make further arrangements.'

430

He put the salver down on the table; there was a large envelope on it. 'His Lordship instructed me to leave these with you. He said you would no doubt prefer to have them in your possession. Good night, my lady.' It was almost a relief when I heard the door click gently shut behind Mr Wallis – Mr Wallis who was not a friend any more, but a servant.

I opened the large envelope almost without thinking. I expected to find a banknote and there was one inside – but it was the other envelopes I saw first. Each one was neatly labelled – they were certificates. Before I could stop myself I slid my hand into the one labelled *'Birth Certificates'* – and the older paper came out first. I dropped it as though it were red-hot, and it was a long time before I could force myself to pick it up again and unfold it – and look. I never had looked at it, not even that day in Pennings Workhouse when Grammer had sent it down to me but now, at last, I did – and saw the blanks, those terrible blanks that proclaimed to the world that I was a bastard, born without a name.

I made myself read what pitifully little there was to read, and saw that it was even worse than I'd realised. Under the date of that birthday which I'd never been allowed to celebrate was named the place of my birth: the workhouse. I'd been born in Lambeth Union Infirmary: behind those high prison walls, inside that iron gate where the hopeless, ragged queue formed each evening, waiting for the spike. I threw the piece of paper down, the hot tears of shame burning my eyes.

Quickly I reached in for the other certificate, my daughter's birth certificate – and there were no blanks. Every column was completed, and the two that were empty on mine were full to overflowing on hers. Under *'Name and Surname of Father'* was written: *'Leonidas Arthur Hector Fitzwarren-Donne, 7th Earl of Warminster'* and in the sixth column, in a firm, clear hand: *'Peer of the Realm, of Eston in the County of Wiltshire.'* And when I read what was written in the space between, the column listing her mother, I saw that I had a name too, now: *'Amy Fitzwarren-Donne, Countess of Warminster, formerly Roberts.'* I picked up the first certificate from the floor and put the two side by side on the table: on the left with its ugly, betraying gaps, that of Amy Roberts, born in a workhouse, whose mother had not even been able to write *'formerly —— '*; and on the right the perfect

431

certificate of Flora Elizabeth Fitzwarren-Donne, my daughter –
my daughter who had a name, a gift from the man who was her
legal father. In my pain and anguish I had begged him to give her a
name, and he had done so.

I opened the second envelope, labelled *'Certificate of Marriage'*,
and there it was, dated that one vital day before my daughter's
birth. The certificate of marriage between Leonidas Arthur
Hector, 7th Earl of Warminster, and Amy Roberts. There were
gaps on that one too, of course; but set as they were beneath the
name and rank of his father they did not seem so blankly obvious
– but they were there. I would always be branded, even though I
was Lady Warminster now – but my daughter would not, because
of this certificate I held in my hand. Then I read in the fourth
column the single word *'Widower'*, and Mr Wallis' words came
back to me: 'But then he don't have much luck, does he? After all,
both his wives left him . . .' Lady Warminster, she'd left him long
ago and besides, she was dead now, but I, I was living – and his
wife.

I put those certificates down, not wanting to think about the
implications, and picked up the third envelope, which was
unlabelled. When I opened it I saw that it contained my Labour
Certificate. Looking at it I remembered how Granfer had brought
it home from the schoolhouse at Borrell and shown it to
Grammer. Just as eleven years earlier he'd brought me home to
her – a babe in arms to be tended and reared. I knew more of the
demands of a child now, and I understood what it had cost
Grammer, old and bent-up with rheumatics as she was, but she'd
tended me and reared me because it was her duty. Duty, 'Stern
daughter of the voice of God': Grammer had hearkened to the
voice of God and done her duty – just as now I must do mine. I had
a husband who was bedfast, perhaps for the rest of his life; a
husband in need of care and tending and, above all, needing his
grand-daughter, to whom he'd given his name, by marrying me,
his wife.

The roses that clustered around the door of the tiny cottage
withered and fell; their crumpled petals dropped to the ground
and one by one were blown away. As I watched, the walls of the
cottage crumbled to dust, and my dreams crumbled with them.

Tomorrow I would return to Eston.

Chapter Fifty

As I walked through the barrier and on to the platform at Waterloo I felt as though my feet were made of lead; but I forced them to climb up the step and into the train. I was frightened, terribly frightened. Not just of Lord Warminster, but of his servants. They knew what I was and they knew what I'd done. The whole of Eston – house, village, estate – would have heard of my sin. The certificate packed in my basket said I was Lady Warminster, but they all knew I had no right to that title – no right even to the status of a married woman. Mrs Johnstone, Mrs Procter, Clare, Bertha, Mary; Mr Tims, Thomas, Henry – their accusing faces swam before my frightened eyes as I gazed unseeingly out of the window. And Joe Dempster – Joe who'd cast me from him with that contemptuous blow – how would he look at me now? I was soiled goods, and I was returning to the one place above all others where everybody knew it.

Waiting for the connection at Salisbury I almost turned and ran down the steps over to the other platform, where passengers were boarding the train going back to London – but I didn't. The weight of Flora in my arms restrained me; she was his grand-daughter and he loved her. Besides, he was ill, bedfast. He needed nursing, caring for – he needed me. I clung to that thought all the rest of the journey.

Henry was on hall duty, and as he opened the door to me his jaw dropped in astonishment. Gathering all my courage together I said, 'My luggage, 'tis at the station. Do 'ee arrange for to collect it.' Then I rushed on through the hall and up the stairs – those front stairs which seemed wider and longer even than I'd remembered; and every step of the way a red-coated general glared at me angrily. But when I'd reached the top and turned into the corridor where the main bedrooms were my headlong rush faltered – I didn't know which one was his. Then I saw a golden head raise itself from the floor, and a golden tail waved – it was Nella, marking his door. I took a deep breath and walked towards it. I

433

was so wrought-up I didn't even knock – turning the handle I stepped straight inside. He lay on the bed facing away, with a great hump in the bedclothes over his leg. He didn't move. Then as Nella streaked past me Flora cried out, 'Doggie, doggie!' and the whole top part of his body suddenly heaved round to face the door. He gasped in pain, but his eyes remained fixed on her, his grand-daughter. I saw how drawn and haggard he looked and said loudly, 'I be come back – I brought her to live under thy roof.' By now Nella's front paws were up on the edge of the bed, her tail wagging furiously, and he reached out his hand to pat her golden head – but his eyes never left Flora.

Then an outraged voice exclaimed, 'Whoever let that dog in here? Get it out at once!' And there in the dressing-room doorway stood a woman in a white apron and a frilled starched cap. She advanced into the room with a loud rustling of petticoats and clapped her hands. 'Out, dog – out!' Nella dropped down to the floor and slunk away as the nurse turned on me. 'However could you have been so foolish as to bring a child into the sickroom? An infant must never be subjected to the slightest risk of infection – remove her at once.' I turned and fled. As the door shut firmly behind us Nella dropped patiently back into her vigil, but I stumbled away down the corridor with my precious burden, tears filling my eyes. I'd been wrong; he didn't need me.

Clara found me and took me up to the nursery. She said Lord Warminster had had a nurse ever since the morning after the accident. She'd come down from London and she wouldn't allow anyone else in his room except Mr Wallis, and that was only because His Lordship insisted. I remembered Mr Wallis saying, 'He don't much care for me giving him a bedpan; I reckon he'll do hisself a mischief before he asks a woman for one.' I should have realised then. All my brave plans about being a dutiful wife had been so stupid; he wasn't a husband in the Buildings at Lambeth, he was a lord – of course he'd have engaged a proper hospital nurse.

Clara didn't look at my face as she spoke; she was embarrassed, and so was I. But at least she spoke; no one else did. The other maids turned their heads away when they saw me coming, and Thomas and Henry sniggered openly. When I went up and down from the nursery I used the back stairs, because I'd always used the back stairs – but I had to stop. Mrs Johnstone came out and barred my way. 'The front stairs are down *there*,' and then, after a very long pause she added, 'my lady.' In those two words she conveyed a whole world of contempt.

I wouldn't have gone out at all if Flora hadn't needed the fresh air. But for that I would have hidden in the nursery all day and never moved, except to pick up the trays Henry left outside the door. The food on them was not only carelessly cooked – it was cold, deliberately left to cool. Then one day Clara came instead with hot dishes under a silver cover; she carried the tray right inside and as she unloaded it she told the table that she'd had a word with Mr Wallis and he'd told Mrs Johnstone how devoted His Lordship was to his grand-daughter, and how angry he'd be if he heard she wasn't being properly fed. I was grateful to Mr Wallis. Once I saw him on the stairs and he stopped to smile at Flora and tickle her under the chin, then he looked at me. 'I'll tell His Lordship I've seen her. He can't stop talking about her now, it's made a big difference to him, my lady, you bringing her back here.' And he smiled at me before he moved on. I was so grateful I could have fallen to the floor and kissed his feet.

Mr Tims opened the front door for me once. Thomas was lounging in his chair and didn't move as I came into the hall, but Mr Tims shuffled quickly in front of me on his gouty feet and swung the door right open. He didn't smile, but his face was anxious, not angry, and I was grateful for that, too. Outside I only dared go into the park, where I'd exercised Earl – I was terrified of meeting one of the gardeners anywhere else, especially of meeting Joe. Although the weather was fine I never stayed out long; I only felt safe up in the nursery with Flora.

Then, a week after I'd come back, the nursery door opened and a woman in a brown felt hat and severely tailored coat marched in. She unpinned her hat, took off her coat and hung them both up. She was dressed in starched white and she walked briskly over to where Flora was playing at my feet and scooped her up. 'Dear me, we can't have Baby playing on the floor, can we? *Most* un-hygienic.' Flora's mouth opened in an 'o' of surprise. Settling my baby on her arm with practised efficiency the woman turned to me. 'You may return to the drawing room now, Lady Warminster.'

'But – I do live up here – and I cassent leave my baby.'

She shook her head, smiling but firm. 'We can't have Mamas in the nursery, Lady Warminster. So bad for Baby – it'll *quite* upset her routine.'

I said desperately, 'I be feeding her myself.'

'I will see to her meals now – I'm trained in the *best* scientific principles of infant feeding, as I've just been telling Lord Warminster.'

'But – she be still at the breast . . .'

'At the breast – at *her* age! Lady Warminster, how *could* you! Don't you realise that Mother's milk is *terribly* harmful for a child once it's had its first birthday? It'll stunt her growth. My goodness, she must be weaned at once.' Marching to the door she opened it wide. 'Good *morning*, Lady Warminster.' I didn't move. When she spoke again her voice was spiked with ice. 'Lord Warminster intimated that he had *complete* confidence in my professional competence, but if *you* are not satisfied you are free to express your opinion to His Lordship.' I stumbled out.

And so I lost my child. I was allowed to spend five minutes saying good night to her at half-past six each evening and, more grudgingly, I was permitted to enter the nursery and enquire about her health each morning. Other than that I had just one hour a day with her, from five o'clock to six o'clock, when she was brought down to the drawing room each afternoon at tea-time – just as Miss Annabel's niece and nephew had been. At first she was angry with me, my baby, because I'd left her and denied her my breast. The first evening I gave it to her, of course – but the nurse knew. She spoke to me sharply at bed-time, and cringing, I promised never to do it again. She was so sure of herself, so certain that I would be harming my child if I continued to suckle her; she quoted doctors, and other experts, and I forgot the healthy toddlers at Borrell who'd run to their mothers to suck, and accepted her words as Gospel truth. All my confidence had gone. She spoke to me as though I were a naughty schoolgirl, and at the slightest hint of protest on my part she talked meaningfully of 'consulting His Lordship' – and at once fear silenced me. Suppose she complained to him, and he sent me away? Better, a thousand times better, to have that one meagre hour, than nothing. But sometimes, as she was being taken from me, I hated him for what

436

he'd done, and once I even found myself remembering him running in front of the railway engine in France – and wishing there'd been another outcome. I shuddered with horror on the edge of the pit to which my thoughts had led me.

In a couple of weeks or so it was obvious that Flora had settled down with Nurse: she was contented, accepting the rigid daily routine of the nursery. She would hold her hands out and crow with pleasure when Dora, the nursemaid, brought her down to me, but when Nurse herself came to fetch her at six o'clock then she went to her arms quite happily, while I was left in the alien drawing room weeping with jealousy and frustration – and loss.

I couldn't bear to remain alone in that stiff, formal room, and five minutes later would see me creeping up the stairs to skulk in my bedroom. My bedroom, which was no more mine than the drawing room was. It was the countess' bedroom; Mrs Johnstone had put me there, and I hadn't dared to argue with her. It had a huge four-poster bed which dwarfed me, high ceilings, great windows with long heavy curtains – and a bare room opening off it that was furnished only with a cold marble basin and an even colder iron bath. And then there was the door, the door that led to his dressing room. I never opened it, of course, and nor did anyone else; but if I were near it I could hear the nurse sometimes, talking to Mr Wallis – so I didn't feel safe even in my bedroom.

I took to going out early and spending all day out if it were fine. Clara would bring me a slice of bread and cheese if I asked her, and then as soon as I'd come down from my brief morning glimpse of Flora I'd creep out and wander over the park and into the woods. I felt safer in the woods, because there I was hidden. Sometimes I'd stand in the shadows of the trees and look across to the pink and white blur that was the outer fringe of the rose gardens; it was June, so the roses were all in bloom – but I didn't dare go any closer.

Over on the other side of the woods the open downland began; sheep roamed on the close-cropped turf. I saw a shepherd once and asked him if there was a village nearby – my boots needed mending – and he showed me the way to a cluster of houses nestling in the shadow of the down. The cobbler soled and heeled my boots as I sat waiting. He talked to me in a slow, familiar dialect, and I answered him in the same, feeling at home for the first time in years. I went back again to buy thread at the village shop, and then went a third time, just so I could talk to people somewhere I wasn't known. But this time I had to wait, and the women at the counter were gossiping – and I realised they were gossiping about me. They didn't know me, of course, but they knew of me, and they spoke in shocked tones of Lord Warminster's new wife, and how he'd married a servant girl who'd gone astray – with his own son. I left the shop without buying and never went back to that village again. There was no escape, anywhere.

Yet one day I did find a refuge. I didn't keep to my usual path through the woods – I'd turned aside to smell a clump of sweet-scented honeysuckle, and listlessly I followed their starry trail – I had nothing better to do. No one needed me now, not even Flora; and he – far from needing me he'd taken my child away. My thoughts became trapped in the same deep rut of resentful bitterness – and then I saw the hedge of roses. They were wild roses, like the dog roses in the hedgerows around Borrell, but they were deep inside the wood. But the sun was shining through to them, and as I came nearer I saw that they were on the edge of a wide clearing – and just over the top of the roses I glimpsed walls. No roof, just those uneven stone walls, with the tip of a window-arch visible here and there. I stood in front of the hedge and it was as though I were in a fairytale – did Sleeping Beauty lie waiting for her prince within those ruined walls?

I threaded my way through the undergrowth along the side of the hedge until I found a gap, and slipped through it; inside were the ruins of a house. And climbing, rambling, sprawling all over the walls – were roses. Their bobbing pink blooms peeped into the spaces where windows had once been: one bold rose tossed her heads high upon a crumbling chimney-stack; another drooped, heavy with the weight of her blossoms, down over the curved arch of an entrance door. It seemed as if they were all beckoning me on, and walking forward I stepped under the arch into a roofless hall, where the roses had climbed through the empty windows and swooped down inside – beautiful invaders who made the whole place glorious with their scent. Crossing the uneven flagged floor I came to the door opposite and passed through it into a central courtyard – and there I saw her. She was standing right in the

438

middle of the court, with her head bent protectively over the sleeping child in her arms.

Rose petals lay all around her feet in drifts of pink and white; delicately I stepped onto that fragrant carpet and walked lightly up to her. She was taller than I was, and I had to reach up to touch the rounded curve of her shoulder; my caressing hand slid down to stroke the pink marble of her arm, warm from the sun, before tenderly cupping the head of her sleeping child. I stood there a long time, looking at her, and her gentle presence comforted me. She loved her baby, I could see it in the expression on her face – and so she understood my loss.

And as I stood there gazing at her in the sunlight, my bitterness and anger gradually drained away. I had not completely lost my child: I saw her every day, I played with her every afternoon, and I knew that she slept under the same roof as I did, safe in her nursery. I understood now why he'd done what he had. He had not meant to take her from me – it was just that he was a gentleman, a lord, so he had different ways. I should have realised that, I who'd been a lady's maid. If Miss Annabel's son had survived and come to Eston he too would have lived in the nursery, with a nurse and a nursemaid to care for him – because that was the way the gentry lived. I had tried to escape with my dreams of a cottage, but now I'd come back to his house I had to live as Lady Warminster had done, however unfitted I was to take her place.

As I looked at the statue I recognised her, for her lovely face was that of the French countess who had bent over me, praising my sewing; and by telling me I should be a lady's maid when I grew up had unwittingly set me on that path which had led me to this sunlit courtyard today. I had loved her son and sinned, and borne his child – now I was paying the price. But there was no blame, no shadow of reproach in her sculptured face – only compassion and understanding; and I was comforted.

When the sun began to sink behind the trees that ringed the ruined house and garden then I set off back, and on the path beyond the rose hedge I found a feather: it was speckled brown with bold black bars – and tinged with shining gold at the tip. I fancied that the marble lady had put it there for me, because she knew that every day I searched for treasures to take back for Flora to play with, in our precious hour together.

439

I longed for that hour, I lived for that hour. First we would sit down on the floor together while I made Esau dance for her; up on the sofa we would play pat-a-cake or round-and-round-the-garden, then I would take her on my lap to show her the treasures I'd found that day – and all the time I would be hugging her, cuddling her, loving her. But all too soon the door would open and in would come the rustling skirts of Nurse, coming to take her away. She was carried down to Lord Warminster's bedroom each day to see him, now the hospital nurse had left – Clara told me that. Dora, the young nursemaid, came from Eston village and she passed on little titbits of information from the nursery to Clara, who relayed them to me. I listened avidly, and so I learnt that my child had taken her first unaided steps – and wept because I'd not been there to see her do it.

It was Clara who told me that England was at war. I couldn't understand it. She said the Germans had invaded Belgium and France, and now our soldiers had gone to help drive them out. I thought of Madame La Roche and Anne-Marie, threatened by the German Army; it didn't seem as if it could really be happening. I stood in the rose-petalled courtyard and told the French countess that her country had been attacked, but her expression never changed – because she was made of marble. I knew that really, only I had to talk to her, because there was no one else.

Several weeks later Clara said that Thomas and Henry had both left and gone to be soldiers, then, staring harder than ever at the table as she unloaded my tray she added, 'Joe, he's gone too, with Jim Arnold and my cousin George who worked in the gardens. They went up to Salisbury and enlisted there.' But it was as though I were listening to a story: it didn't seem real. Often I thought I wasn't real either, as I flitted along the corridors and down the staircases of Eston trying to be invisible. Sometimes I felt as though I'd succeeded – and turned myself into a ghost.

Chapter Fifty-One

It was November, and the last of the roses in the ruined house had long since shed their petals.

I shivered as I stood in the courtyard, and the marble skin of the French countess was cold and hard to my touch. When I got back to the house I went down to the big, draughty drawing room and sat crouched over the fire until Clara came in with the tea tray; as she set it down she told me that Lord Warminster was out of bed and on his feet again. 'He's using two sticks, my lady, and he's still unsteady – but Mr Wallis says as he can walk.'

Now I was even more nervous as I slunk along the corridors and crept up and down the staircase, but it was days before I saw him. I was coming down the stairs to the ground floor, and as I turned the corner of the flight I saw that he was coming up. I stopped at once and pressed myself against the wall while he climbed slowly up, holding fast to the banister rail. As he drew level with me he paused as if to draw breath, then staring ahead he said slowly, 'How – do – you – do?' and I realised that he was addressing me. I couldn't answer. The unfamiliar, formal greeting confused me and besides, it was so long since I'd spoken to anyone other than Flora and Clara that my tongue had become rusty. When I didn't reply he swung his twisted shoulder sideways and his eyes flickered momentarily over my frightened face; then his mouth stiffened, and turning so that his humped back was towards me he resumed his laborious climb. It was only then that I noticed his boots – they were a perfect match: the right one wasn't built up any more. After that I hid every time I heard footsteps, becoming more like a ghost than ever.

On the Sunday after I'd seen him Clara told me at tea-time that Nurse had been invited to spend the evening with Mrs Johnstone, then she added, in a tone that was deliberately casual. 'So Dora'll be on her own upstairs, she says – except for Lady Flora, o' course.' I seized the hint eagerly, and crept upstairs like a thief in the night to the nursery. I was a thief, stealing time with my own daughter. Slipping through the inner door I crossed noiselessly over to the cot; the night-light gave only the faintest of glimmers, but it was enough – I could see her, my sleeping child. The curl of her hair, the sweep of her lashes, the curve of her cheek – the sight of those was like water to a parched throat, manna to a starving woman. I stood there all evening listening to the sweet sound of her even breathing – oblivious to my cramped calves and aching back until Dora's soft voice summoned me away from Paradise.

But like Eve, I had to pay the price for those stolen hours. Mrs Johnstone saw to that – the work of her viper's tongue showed in the contemptuous face Nurse turned towards me next morning. Nurse had always been patronising, pursing her lips as I spoke in my Wiltshire accent, but as long as I obeyed her rules she had been scrupulous in keeping to her side of the bargain. But now all that changed. Mrs Johnstone had told her who I was and what I'd done, and when I made my morning and evening visits to the nursery Nurse looked at me as if I were unclean, ostentatiously drawing her skirts aside when I passed near her, and barely replying to my timid enquiries about my daughter's health. But worst of all, when she sent Flora down in the afternoon it was always a little late – I would sit with my eyes fixed on the clock, grieving for every lost minute.

And Flora, she was changing too, growing impatient with my lap and my cuddles; she wanted to be always up and doing – and she wanted playthings. But there was nothing for her to play with in the drawing room. Once she clambered up on the back of the sofa and grabbed at a slender vase on the bureau. I had to take it from her and she howled in protest; when I offered her Esau instead she thrust him away. He was old and shabby now, not golden and furry like the bear Lord Warminster had given her. Once I plucked up the courage to ask if she could bring her bear down to the drawing room with her, but Nurse shook her head vigorously. 'Certainly not. It's *most* unhygienic to take nursery toys downstairs!'

I said desperately, 'But she does play with her toys when she do go down to His Lordship in the library – Clara did tell I.'

Her voice was tight and sharp as she replied, 'Lord Warminster has *special* toys which he keeps in his library. He *never* requests for nursery toys to be sent downstairs.' I dared not ask again.

I'd even have braved the village on the downs in search of toys, if I'd had any money, but the banknote which I'd received at Kew had all gone now. My clothes were worn and shabby – even the rags I used when my monthlies came were patched and darned – but still I cut up one of my two dress blouses and sewed a floppy rag doll. It was too floppy because I only had a few pieces left over to stuff it with, but I embroidered a mouth and nose and eyes, and stitched each tiny finger. Flora took it when I offered it to her, but she soon lost interest, and dropping it carelessly on the floor she headed for the coal scuttle, her mouth set in a determined line. She shrieked when I tried to take the coal away from her, so to please her I let her play with the shining black lumps – but when Nurse came to fetch her at six o'clock and saw the dirty smudges on her hands and her dress she was very angry.

The next day Nurse brought her down herself. Flora was grizzling as she was carried through the door and when I held out my arms to her she pushed them away. Nurse said, 'Perhaps I'd better take her upstairs again, Lady Warminster. She really *isn't* in the mood for the drawing room tonight.'

'No – she maun stay.'

She frowned. '*If* you insist.' Setting Flora down on the sofa she marched off. Flora wailed, 'Nursey, Nursey!' after her retreating back – and her cries pierced my heart. It was almost time for her to go upstairs again before I was able to coax her on to my lap, and then I held her gingerly, in case she took fright – yet she was my child. I cried myself to sleep that night; my daughter, my own precious daughter didn't want me any more. The following afternoon Nurse didn't bring her down until ten past five; the next day it was quarter-past. My precious hour was being whittled away – and Flora was awkward, cranky – I couldn't pacify her. The day after that I sat in the gloomy drawing room and watched the hands of the clock creep round to twenty-past – then Dora arrived alone, her face flushed and her eyes not meeting mine as she delivered her message: 'Nurse says as it upsets Lady Flora so much having to come down to see,' she stopped, her face a deeper shade of red as she amended, 'Come down to the drawing room, so she's not sending her tonight.'

I didn't stop to think. Leaping to my feet I ran to the door and straight to the stairs. Up and up – I was panting by the time I reached the nursery corridor but I wouldn't stop – nothing would keep me from my child. I thrust the door open. 'Lady Warminster! Whatever –' I rushed past her, and there was Flora playing on the rug. Swooping down I seized hold of her. 'Come to Mama, Flora – come to Mama.' She began to struggle. 'Flora – Mama wants you.'

Her struggles became stronger and she cried, 'No! No!'

'Flora, it's your Mama –'

She lashed out with one hand and thrust herself away from me, her body becoming rigid as she shrieked: 'Mama bad, *bad* lady – go 'way, go 'way.' She began to scream.

My arms went stiff and awkward, so that I almost dropped her. Nurse spoke sharply, 'Give her to me. I *told* you going downstairs was upsetting her!' She took my daughter from my arms with a, 'There, there. Look at the nice giraffe – Flora play with the nice giraffe.' And Flora buried her head in the starched white collar, seeking comfort from that square white shoulder. I watched her clinging to that other woman – her body softening, relaxing as the woman soothed her frantic sobs into calmness. 'There, you see, Lady Warminster? It's *much* better if you leave her to me.'

I whimpered, 'Flora,' but she didn't even turn her head. I backed slowly away; even now I couldn't believe it. At the door I tried to call her again, but my throat seemed to have closed up – I couldn't even speak her name.

I turned and stumbled out, and then I was running down, down – faster and faster – I couldn't stop. Twisting, turning, blinded by tears, I was using the back stairs but I didn't care. Nothing mattered besides this – my baby, my baby – she didn't want me. 'Go 'way – bad lady!' There were scorchmarks where her hands had pushed at my chest, my baby who'd fed from my breast. 'My baby!' I was sobbing aloud as I flung myself down the last flight. I could hear my voice crying: 'My baby, my baby – she dussent want I, she dussent want I!' Sobbing and panting I ran along the stone flags to the back door, the servants' door – I was leaving Eston by the way I'd first entered it. I threw myself at the handle but it wouldn't move – it was bolted. I began to claw at the heavy bolts, tearing my fingernails, but the pain in my heart obliterated all others. The last bolt shuddered back and I seized the handle, desperate to escape but there were rapid footsteps behind me, voices: 'What on earth?' ''Tis her!' 'What's *she* doing down 'ere?'

444

'Silly little cow!' A hand touched my arm. 'My lady.' I screamed, 'Let I out, let I out!' Then a man's black arm was pushing past me, forcing its way between me and the door, barring my path. 'It's raining cats and dogs out there – you'll catch your death.' 'I dussent care – let I go!' But he was forcing me back. I flailed at his chest. 'Let I out!' A voice spoke sharp and spiteful. 'She's gone mad – bad blood will out. Let her go, and good riddance. We don't want the likes of her in this house.'

'No!' His body was between me and the door now, and his strong hands gripped my wrists, holding them fast as I struggled to escape.

'Careful, Mr Wallis – she'll scratch your eyes out.'

'Amy, what's the *matter*?'

I raised tear-drenched eyes to my captor. 'My baby – my baby don't want I.'

'That *bloody* nurse!'

And as suddenly as it had come the unnatural strength left my body and I sagged back against the wall, weak and shaking. They were all there – Mrs Johnstone, Mrs Procter, Bertha, Clara, Mary – all watching me, accusing me, jeering at me, as though I were a freak in a fairground. I turned to Mr Wallis, my voice shaking, 'It were because o' you, what you said. I didn't have to come back, but you said, "Both his wives left him, and taken, and taken – " ' My voice broke, I couldn't speak of her. 'So I came back, I came back to nurse him, to be a good wife, but he didn't want I – and now, *she* doesn't want I either. She hates I, my baby . . .' Looking up into his eyes I saw the kindness there and desperately I appealed to him, 'Help I – please help I.'

'I can't help you, Amy.' I slipped down, down towards the floor – but he reached out and caught me, lifting me up into his arms. Then he said, 'There's only one person who can help you now.' He turned to face my accusers. 'Get out of the way, you lot – and stop gawping. Clara, you come with me, to open the doors.'

I was still sobbing and crying as he carried me – 'My baby, my baby' – then Clara's voice broke in, 'But Mr Wallis! We daresn't –'

'Get that door open, my girl – before I kick it down!'

And suddenly there was bright light and leaping flames – and a dark shape hunched behind a desk; we were in the library. 'What – on – earth –?'

445

'I've brought you your wife.' Mr Wallis' voice rang out loud and clear, then dropped to a whisper as he said, 'Down you get now, Amy.' I slid from his arms like a bundle of old rags. 'Clara, hold her up.'

I stood swaying and sobbing, 'My baby, she don't want I!'

As Lord Warminster rose slowly from behind his desk Mr Wallis turned to confront him, his voice bold with anger. 'She's been back in your house six months, and in all that time have you spoke one kind word to her? You miserable old sod!'

'How – dare – you!'

Clara gasped, and I shrank back against her, but Mr Wallis didn't stop. 'Have you stopped your wretched pack of servants from harrying her?' Lord Warminster's mouth was working but Mr Wallis ignored it, shouting on, 'No! You've not raised a finger to help her. All you can do is sit brooding over your own miseries while a young girl like this is being driven out of her wits because that nurse – that so-well-qualified hospital nurse that *you* chose – has poisoned your grand-child's mind against its own mother!' He turned and pointed to where I stood. 'Look at the state she's in now! She was frantic, and trying to get out of this damn place just as she is – no hat or coat on, and in this weather. If I hadn't've got to her when I did God knows what mischief she'd have done to herself.' He paused, then said clearly, 'But maybe that's what you wanted?'

And all at once there was silence, with only the sound of my sobbing, suddenly loud in the room. Then the man behind the desk reared up, towering over it and shouted, 'Get out, Wallis – get out!'

'I'm going – but I've got one thing more to say before I do. Now she's finally in the same room with you, *talk* to her – ask her this question: ask her *why* she came back to Eston. Because she didn't have to, and she's not stupid – she knew that lot down there'd peck her to pieces as soon as she set foot over this bloody threshold – but she still came back. So ask her, just ask her why.' He reached for my clinging fingers and gently detached them. 'Let go, lovey. He's the one who promised to love and cherish you – it's time he got started.'

I turned to Clara, and her arm tightened round my waist. 'Mr Wallis, she's terrible upset . . .'

446

'That's for His Lordship to sort out. Come on Clara, we're going.'

At the sound of the door closing my legs gave way. I sank down onto the carpet and crouched there in a sobbing heap. Then a warm tongue licked my cheek and a soft muzzle pushed its way between my hands; putting my arms around Nella's neck I wept into her soft fur. The light went out, and there was only the glow from the fire. Hidden by the merciful darkness I sobbed myself into an exhausted silence. Then a shadow fell across Nella's pale back, and a voice above me said, 'I am – sorry.'

I heard a chair being pushed forward behind me. 'You would be – more comfortable – in this. Nella, up.' Nella carefully rose to her feet, pulling me up with her, and I sank back into the chair. I began to shiver, and going to the hearth he crouched down to manipulate the poker and tongs himself so that the fire blazed up more brightly. Then he moved into the corner of the room and I saw the glint of glass; coming back to set a small table beside me, he placed a goblet of amber liquid upon it. 'Drink – that.' My tongue and throat burned as I tried to swallow and I spluttered. 'Another – mouthful.' Obediently I drank again, and the fiery liquid warmed my chest. I put the glass down too quickly and it rattled on the table, suddenly loud in the quiet room. I tried to blow my nose on my sodden handkerchief, and his hand came down and dropped a large square of white linen on the table beside me. 'Use – this.' My eyes were swollen and painful – I was glad he'd switched off the glaring electric lights.

The clock whirred and struck the half-hour. I whispered to the shadow beside me, 'You'll be wanting to dress for dinner, my lord.'

'Dinner can wait. May I – sit down?'

I glanced up in surprise. 'O' course you can.'

He crossed to the other side of the hearth and drawing up a second chair lowered his gaunt frame into it. The flames warmed my right cheek but I was still cold; the shivering came back and I couldn't control it. He pulled himself upright again and I watched in disbelief as he shrugged off his jacket and held it out to me. 'Put this – around your shoulders.' I pulled it round me; it was large as a cape and warm from his body and gradually my shivering stopped. He went back to his chair and sat down; in his waistcoat and

447

shirtsleeves he was a little less frightening, and the rapid beat of my heart began to slow. It was then that he asked, 'And why did you – come back?'

So I told him, 'It were because o' the certificates.' A coal fell sending a flame spurting up, and in its light I saw his mismatched eyebrows pucker in query. I explained, 'At Kew, Mr Wallis did give I the certificates, and I looked at my birth certificate and saw the gaps.' My voice quavered. 'I'd never looked at it afore – I never did open it when Grammer sent it down to me in the House.' And the memories came flooding back, washing over me, drowning me. 'I – I cassent –'

'Tell me – you must tell me.'

I obeyed him. There, in that quiet room lit only by the dancing flames of the fire, I told him what I'd told no one else. I told him of how I'd come back from London to find Granfer dead and Grammer in the workhouse, and had gone to get her out – but she'd spurned my offer. I'd told him about the second time I'd gone, how I'd walked along the canal, footsore and unhappy, desperate for Grammer to speak to me, to tell me what to do – but she'd refused even to see me. And that was how my birth certificate had come into my hands – but I hadn't looked at it. I'd always known what I was, ever since that first day at school – Grammer had told me then – but I couldn't bear to look at it.

I told him how I'd sat in the garden at Pennings, his garden, with that certificate folded in my pocket, and realised that nobody in the whole wide world had ever wanted me, and nobody ever would. And so I had taken refuge in my dreams – my foolish, pathetic dreams. In my dreams I would serve Lady Warminster who had praised my stitches and said I must become a lady's maid; and Lord Warminster – my dream Lord Warminster, tall and distinguished – he would find my father for me; my father who was a gentleman and who would be so pleased to have discovered me that he would want me, love me – and so would Lady Warminster's unknown son. Even that dream I told him. Then when Grammer died and I'd used all my savings for her funeral Miss Annabel had come to my rescue; as her maid I'd gone to London with her. 'And there I did meet Mr Dunn.' At the memory of his daffodil-yellow hair and laughing blue eyes the tears threatened, and my voice faltered.

The man opposite prompted me, questioning, 'Mr *Dunn*?'

I whispered, 'I should a' known – I did read it in the big red book called *Debrett*. I read it to Miss Annabel – she said as 'twere vulgar for ladies to read from thic book so I maun read it to her, only it were spelt "Donne" so I read it wrong. Miss Annabel, she would have read it right if she'd seen it, but she did have cucumber on her eyes.'

My own eyes were filling again, but Lord Warminster sat opposite, waiting. 'Tell me – you must tell me.'

'He did meet I in the Park, when I were walking Earl, and he took me on the river, and to the zoo, so I did think – I thought – as he were courting me. So then I'd changed my dream, because Lord Quinham, who was her son, he were courting Miss Annabel and I, I did love Mr Dunn. I didn't know as they were one and the same.' My voice faded.

'When did you – find out – the truth?'

'Not till I come here, to Eston.' And I told him of my distress and bewilderment, but then, when he and Miss Annabel had quarrelled, it had seemed as if it were all coming true – that my first dream, about marrying Lady Warminster's son, had been the right one all along: it was meant to be. So when Miss Annabel had sent me to give him back her ring, and he'd been so unhappy, wanting me, needing me – then I'd sinned. And so the dream became a nightmare because I had done to my unborn child what Aunt Agnes had done to me.

I stopped talking and drew his jacket closer around my shoulders. The faint smell of his body lingering in the silk lining tugged at my memory, reminding me of that night in France when he'd held me close so that I could feed my baby – his grand-child. His halting voice from the other side of the hearth prompted me once more. 'And – then?' I'd become confused, I didn't know how to pick up my story again, until he repeated my words. 'Because – of the – certificates?'

'Then I did open the second certificate – Flora's birth certificate – and 'twere perfect. There weren't no gaps, because o' the third certificate. You'd given her your name by marrying me – so I was your wife.' My voice dropped, but I made myself carry on. 'Mr Wallis, he'd told me about your accident, and your good leg being crushed, so you were bedfast now and mebbe wouldn't ever walk

449

again. And I thought, I thought you'd be needing a wife, to nurse you. Besides, there was Flora. I'd given her to you afore she was born, in thic same room in Kew – and now, in law, she were your daughter.' A coal shifted with a hiss. I turned to stare down into the flickering flames: castles, roses, dreams of love – all were consumed in the fire and burnt to ashes. I lifted my eyes to look into his. 'So I did bring her back to Eston – and now she dussent want I any more, nobody do want I.'

His dark, twisted shape was still as the statue in the old rose garden. Then he spoke. 'Would you mind – if I made myself – drunk? You see, Wallis told me – to talk to you – and he's quite right – I must – but I can only talk properly when I'm drunk. And there's something else – I will have to do – and I don't think I could bring myself – to do it – if I were sober. May I have your – permission?'

He spoke to me so politely, as if I were a lady. I answered, 'Aye, my lord. You do whatever you please.'

'Thank you. I will need – your glass. I only ever keep one – since I don't normally entertain – visitors in my library. No – don't get up. I will fetch it myself.' I watched him move from table to cupboard then back to his chair; he set the decanter down beside him, filled his glass and tossed the liquid down his throat. When the glass was empty he said, 'I don't normally allow myself – more than an eggcupful of brandy – the temptation to be fluent is too great. But I feel it is necessary tonight.' And already the hesitation in his speech was less noticeable. He drank the second glass more slowly, then began on the third. I sat waiting for him to speak, and when he did so he sounded like a different person: his voice had lost its harshness and become lighter, younger, with his words flowing smoothly as a swift-running stream.

'Firstly, I must make a confession. I knew the answer to that question already – there could only be one answer. Besides, you told me yourself when you broke into my bedroom with Nella. Before that virago so summarily ejected you both, you said, "I be come back – I brought her to live under thy roof." Nothing could have been clearer than that, though I didn't realise then the full extent of your intended sacrifice. But knowing the truth I naturally tried to deny it to myself. I sought other reasons, convincing myself that you'd come back to Eston to queen it over the servants as Lady Warminster, in some kind of revenge, or again that you'd come in order to make clandestine assignations with Francis. I rather liked that one – I could justifiably be angry with you while I believed that. But none of those reasons made sense, and in the end I had to accept the truth: that you'd come back with Flora for my sake. And having accepted that, then I had to accept the corollary, that I must send you both away again. But I couldn't bring myself to do it; now I must. You can go tomorrow and take Flora with you.'

I exclaimed in disbelief, 'Don't you want her any more?'

'Oh yes, I want her. I want her more than anything in the world. If I bred the perfect rose and she bent over it and pricked her thumb and cried I would rip it out of the earth and destroy it for causing her a moment's pain. That's how much I want her. But she isn't mine, she's yours.'

'But – she don't want I.'

'She will, once she's out of the clutches of her present nurse – you'd have realised that tonight if you hadn't been so distraught. You're her mother, she'll want you again.'

I felt a faint flicker of hope. 'Do you think so?'

'I know so.' The tears of relief began to trickle down my cheeks and as I wiped them away with his handkerchief he said quietly, 'You poor child, into what hell on earth has my quixotic gesture plunged you?' His voice rose again as he added, 'I really will have to stop marrying women. I'm a veritable Bluebeard where wives are concerned.'

I stared at him in astonishment. 'But Bluebeard, he did murder his wives!'

'Well, it's not all that different when they try to tear doors down with their bare hands to get away from me.' He paused as he poured out more brandy then continued, 'Or attempt to throw themselves out of windows because they can't face the thought of being my wife.'

I shook my head. 'No, that weren't why I did it. It were because you wanted me dead.'

His head jerked up. 'I! *I* wanted you dead?'

'Beat, she did tell I – you only married me because Doctor said as I were going to die and you wanted Flora. Only I wasn't dead, so I thought when I were well enough to get out o' bed then I had to –'

451

He finished, 'Rectify the omission.'

'Aye.' I added bleakly, 'And it were true, weren't it? You did only marry me because I were dying.'

'No!' His voice was emphatic, and he said again, 'No. Now listen to me carefully. Being as I am I wouldn't have offered to marry you had I not believed you to be dying – but I did *not* marry you *because* you were dying. Do you understand the difference?'

It took me a few moments to work it out, then I nodded. 'I think so. But then, if it weren't because o' that – why did you marry me?'

'I think I need some more brandy.' He raised the glass and downed its contents in one gulp, then coughed before pouring himself another measure. 'What a damnable way to treat good Cognac. Now, why did I marry you? Because you asked me to.'

'But –'

'Not in so many words, but you asked me to give your child a name. And you were only a child yourself; so young and so desperate – and so ugly. You were all swollen up like a piglet with bloat – I felt a fellow feeling for you. Even then I'd never have thought of it for myself, but when your step-mother came up with the idea I thought – why not? My name is of no value to me – but if it matters so much to her, then she can have it. Or rather, I didn't think. If I had done I suppose I wouldn't have done it – but I have a streak of the gambler in me, so I gambled on your life. Heads she dies, and then I will have her baby, or tails, she lives – and I have them both.'

'Both?'

'Yes. Your baby – and you. Only when I went to see you after the birth you didn't want me. I can scarcely blame you – I wouldn't have wanted me myself. Then later Francis enlightened me as to the true enormity of the wrong I'd done you. I'd rather you'd told me first, Amy – it wasn't very kind, was it? Still, I suppose you didn't think. I didn't think either when I was young – I don't think now, that's been the cause of your suffering, poor little Amy. Just fancy being married to me, of all men – that's an appalling fate in itself, but to have been married to me against your will . . . But I didn't mean to do it, I told that doctor he *must* ask you – only when he said you'd agreed then I thought . . . I must stop thinking, obviously that's a mistake, too.' He stopped abruptly, and shook his head, and his twisted shoulder moved in unison because he had

452

no choice. For a few moments the headlong rush of words was halted as he swallowed another mouthful of brandy, then it began again, faster than ever.

'I feel almost light-hearted now the Sword of Damocles has finally fallen. You've been terribly on my conscience. I've felt so guilty, and guilt is an awful thing. I've enough guilt to carry already, over Jeanette. She was my first wife, you know – of course you do, you told me you met her, dreamed about her – I used to dream about her, too.' He broke off, then said, 'I think I drank more than I intended to – I can't stop talking now I've started. You see, I don't get the opportunity very often. I wanted to get drunk while Annabel was here so I could talk to her properly but it wouldn't have been good manners – but you're my wife so perhaps you won't mind, just this once. And Amy, there's something I wanted to say to you before you go: forget what your grandmother said, forget all that rubbish about being conceived in sin and born in sin. You didn't ask to be conceived, or born – I expect there've been occasions when you wished you never had been – I certainly do, I wish it all the time. She was a dreadful old woman, your grandmother. You were quite right to leave her in the workhouse.'

'But I didn't!'

He held up his hand to silence me. 'You must listen to what I'm telling you. Guilt is so awfully corrosive. It gnaws away at your vitals, it eats you up – so don't feel guilty, Amy, please.'

'But I did sin!'

His voice rose, questioning. 'Did you sin? Or did you simply love too well? If loving too well be a sin, then let sin prevail – so that those of us who are not loved at all may hold out our hands to the reflected warmth. You need feel no guilt.'

I looked at him in disbelief, before shaking my head. 'But – I be a sinner, a terrible sinner. I be soiled goods –'

'Amy, do stop drivelling on about your trifling transgressions – you merely indulged in a little fornication. I don't suppose you enjoyed it much – you certainly didn't look as if you had when I saw you that time – who would, in a housemaid's closet? Especially that one – it smells; it's the drains, I think. My housekeeper isn't very good, I should pension her off but I don't like new faces – looking at my face. I'm drunk, Amy – I've miscalculated the dose. Amy, you said no one wants you. That isn't true. Flora wants you,' he drained his glass with a final gulp before adding, 'And so do I.'

Suddenly there was silence. I just sat staring at him, then I said, questioning, '*You* do want I?'

He spoke quickly, 'Oh, don't be frightened. I won't touch you – I'll never touch you, I'm too damaged to touch any woman.' His lopsided mouth curved into the ghost of a smile as he said, 'You're soiled goods and I'm damaged goods, so we're very well suited, don't you think? No, of course you don't think so! I'm drunk, I drank too much, Amy. Amy, Aimée, Aimée Vibert. Do you remember – I gave you the rose?'

'I thought it were for Miss Annabel.'

'No, it was for you – because you were talking to my roses. I talk to my roses – I don't have to be drunk to talk to them. And Flora, I can talk to Flora – but not any longer, because you're going away.'

I said loudly, 'No, I'm not.'

His head jerked forward. 'You're not – why not?'

'Because you gave I the rose – so I be under thy spell.'

'My spell?' His eyes narrowed. 'You're living in fairy tales again. Who gave the rose? I know! Only it wasn't given to Beauty but to her father, after he'd stolen it.'

'I baint got no father, so you did give it to me.'

'So I am the Beast!' He threw back his head and laughed. 'The Beast in his enchanted castle –'

'– with thy rose garden.'

'And the servants. Let's not forget those apes who were Beauty's servants – they've played their role, but how can I play mine? What do you want from me, Amy? Shall I give you jewels – is that what you'd like?'

I shook my head. 'I don't need no jewellery – but the Beast, he did talk to Beauty, every evening.'

His whole body became very still, then he said softly, 'But I can only talk when I'm drunk. And now I'm too drunk, far too drunk – I don't know what I'm saying. The Beast, Beauty, – what is beauty? "Beauty is truth, truth beauty – that is all ye know on earth, and all ye need to know." Amy is beautiful – but is Amy true? Or is she just a waking dream who will vanish in the morning, leaving me alone in my castle? Don't leave me, Amy,

454

please don't leave me. I promise I'll dismiss the Red Queen tomorrow. Flora isn't a piglet,' he laughed. 'You were the piglet before she was born, a little fat pig with tiny beseeching eyes! I'm drunk, very drunk – but I must remember about the Red Queen – have you read *Alice*, Amy?' I shook my head. 'Strange – I thought – perhaps you had.' He blinked, and blinked again, then very slowly slid off his chair to land with a bump on the carpet.

He lay sprawled on the floor, his body so still that I thought for a moment he was dead. Uncurling my cramped legs I stood up and lifted one of the brass candlesticks from the mantelpiece. I lit it at the fire and then went to stand over him, holding it up so I could see his face. His eyes were open, looking up at me. 'The face of Aphrodite.' He paused. 'What are we going to do, Amy? I'm an awful person when I'm sober – and I almost always am.' Shifting his humped back to ease it he added, 'You see, I won't want you when I'm sober.'

I said, 'Uncle Alf, he did get drunk every Saturday night.'

His unequal mouth curved in a fleeting smile. 'How wise of Uncle Alf. But it won't do, Amy – it won't do. There's my guilt, you see – I have a responsibility to my guilt; it's the fox I carry under my cloak and it has to feed every day – I can't abandon it now. Tomorrow I shall hate myself – and worse, much worse, I shall hate you. And you can't stand being hated, can you, my poor little Amy? I learnt that tonight. It'll upset you terribly. I can stand it – I'm used to it, but you aren't. Your Grammer did her best, but it wasn't quite good enough – you still used all your savings to buy her a proper funeral, foolish Amy. You won't like me hating you, so I think you'd better leave, tomorrow morning.'

I stood looking down at him and he blinked. 'Would you mind moving your candle, Amy. I don't like eyes looking at me, not even Aphrodite's eyes, not even when I'm drunk.'

I put my hand around the flame, so that his face was in shadow, then asked, 'Will you hate Flora, too?'

'No, I'll never hate Flora. She's the only creature in the whole wide world that I love – apart from Nella, of course. Mustn't hurt Nella's feelings.' The bitch, hearing her name, came padding over to where he lay and flopped down beside him. He reached out his black furred hand and stroked her sleek golden head. 'Nella won't leave me.'

I said loudly, 'And nor will I.'

His hand stopped stroking and became still. Then he said, 'I think you're being extremely foolish, Amy – I think you're a very silly girl.'

'Aye, I daresay. But then I do be a silly maid – there wouldn't be no Flora if I weren't.'

'No, I suppose that's true.' He drew a deep noisy breath. 'Amy, there isn't much time – I'm going to pass out soon, I can feel it coming over me.' His voice was slower now, and slightly slurred. 'Amy, if you insist on staying, then you must behave as Lady Warminster, as my wife. Only in public, of course – I won't come near you in private – but you must *be* Lady Warminster, because of the servants. You must – dine with me – every evening.' There were gaps now between his words again. 'It won't be – very pleasant – for you – and I won't like it either, I can't stand people – seeing me – eating. But it must be done, because of the servants. Do you –understand?'

'Yes, I understand.'

In the dim light from the shaded candle I saw his attempt at a smile as he said, 'Pretend you are Beauty. It won't be difficult for you, for you are beautiful, Amy. And you must pretend that I,' he stopped, then his voice became harsher and deeper as he exclaimed, 'No! You won't have to pretend – because I *am* the Beast!' His eyes closed as he slumped sideways. Nella whined and licked his hand, but he didn't respond.

I stood looking down at him – at his clumsy body, his twisted neck, his lopsided face already darkened by stubble – and he was no longer the remote, formal Lord Warminster. He was so ugly, so sad and so vulnerable as he lay there that I wasn't frightened of him any more. Instead I seemed to hear his voice saying again: 'Amy, you said no one wants you. That isn't true. Flora wants you – and so do I.' Setting down the candlestick I slipped his jacket from my shoulders and spread it over his humped back and ungainly arms, tucking it carefully around him to keep out the draughts. Then I whispered softly in his ear, 'Don' 'ee fret – I baint be a-going to leave thee.' But he only stirred in his sleep and began to snore.

I pinched out the candle-flame between thumb and forefinger before dragging out the guard and setting it around the dying fire.

It was large and fine-meshed – not a gentleman's fireguard at all – he must have got it because of Flora. Then I quietly opened the door and peeped out. Mr Wallis was sitting on a chair in the hall. I went over to him and touched his shoulder; he woke with a start. 'Mr Wallis, His Lordship be asleep in the library.'

He followed me back into the room and stood staring down at the sprawled body on the floor. 'Gawd – whatever've you done to him?' Then he went over to the empty glass and picked it up, sniffing at it. 'Ah, he's done it to hisself. I'm sorry, Amy, he ain't been on a bender like this in years – and in the past he always made sure nobody 'ud see him at it. He used to lock hisself in here – even put the dog outside. I'd hear him talking sometimes, but he was always on his own.'

'Can you get him to bed?'

'No, I certainly can't, seeing as I'm not the Giant of Wilmington – and Tims is too old to help. His Lordship'll just have to stay here – the state he's in, he won't notice the difference. I'll fetch down a pillow and a couple of blankets.' Nella stood up and came over to us, whining softly. Mr Wallis grunted, 'And she's not been taken out for her walkies, either. He always does that last thing, regular as clockwork – never misses. Still, I suppose he had something else on his mind tonight.'

'I'll let her out for a run.'

He hesitated, looking hard at my face before nodding 'All right, you do that. Just stay on the step – she'll be back soon as she's done what she has to.'

I stood on the doorstep waiting for Nella with the autumn wind blowing cold on my face, just as his words had blown into my head – like fresh blasts of air in a musty room, challenging all I'd been taught to believe in. 'Forget all that rubbish about being conceived in sin and born in sin. Did you sin? Or did you love too well?' I exclaimed aloud, 'But, surely . . .' And his voice seemed to answer me in the wind: 'If that be sin, let sin prevail!' The wind blew stronger and stronger, buffeting me, but I didn't flinch. Then there was the sudden patter of footsteps on the gravel and Nella came bounding back up. As she reached the top step she shook herself hard so that a shower of silver raindrops spattered my skirt. I laughed, reaching out my hand to pat her damp head. Then I closed the front door and walked with a firm step over to the

457

library, where Nella was already waiting to be let in. The minute I opened the door she trotted across to where he lay and flopped down beside him. Her fur shone in the firelight as she crouched there, a small golden lion guarding her master. I whispered, 'Good girl, Nella,' and softly closed the door.

Chapter Fifty-Two

I went to bed but I didn't go to sleep. His words whirled round and round in my head like leaves in autumn, tossed hither and thither by gusts of wind. I tried to catch them before they fell, just as I'd tried as a child to catch the leaves of the ash tree behind the cottage. Then my body had jumped and twirled in dancing pursuit, but now it was my mind which leaped and twisted, reaching out, trying to catch hold of his words – and to understand them. 'My quixotic gesture' – what did kwicksotic mean? 'The Sword of Damocles' – who was Damoklees? Afrodity? And why should he carry a fox under his cloak, especially one that bit him? Why had he called Nurse 'The Red Queen'? And how could anyone read an Alice – Alices were girls!

The leaves whirled faster and faster as desperately I leaped for them. I wasn't dancing for fun now, it wasn't a game – I had to catch them, I must. But even as my fingertips brushed the whirling brown flakes, so they were tossed away by the wind to drop beyond my grasp, until at last all I was left with was Bluebeard – and the Beast.

The minute I woke up the next morning my thoughts flew to Flora, then the tap which had roused me sounded again. It was Clara, carrying a letter. 'His Lordship says to give you this.' I tore open the flap. Inside was a sheet of the notepaper headed *Eston, Wiltshire* and on it was written only the briefest of messages: *'Nurse dismissed, as agreed. Supply substitute, instanter.'* Then underneath, a scrawled, *'Warminster'*.

I hesitated before asking diffidently, 'Do you know what "instanter" means, Clara?'

'No, my lady.' I bit my lip, then handed her the terse message. As soon as she'd read it she said, 'I think it must mean "at once", because Nurse is upstairs packing, Dora says.' She paused, then added, 'Dora, she's a steady girl, but she's only just fourteen. His Lordship won't want her left in charge of the nursery, not even for a couple of hours.'

I said, 'There baint no need for a new nurse. I'll go up and live in the nursery, like I did afore.'

Clara glanced involuntarily at the door, the connecting door to his dressing room, then replied, flushing slightly and with her eyes on the carpet, 'His Lordship wouldn't like that. And besides, he's given orders as you're to lunch in the morning room every day.'

'Does His Lordship lunch in the morning room?'

She shook her head. 'Oh no, my lady – His Lordship don't eat lunch, never has done. He don't take no tea, neither – but he says as you'll be taking tea in the drawing room, afore Lady Flora comes down. And then, he says, I'm to help you dress for dinner, because you'll be dining in the dining room, with him. So you couldn't be up in the nursery all day, could you?'

'No. But I dussent know any nurses.'

Clara looked at my worried face then said, 'There's Ellen.'

'Ellen?'

'My cousin Ellen. She's nursemaid now, up in London, but since she turned twenty she's been thinking about finding a place of her own. She baint fixed on one yet, though – I do know that. She wants to come back to Wiltshire, see. I'd've spoken for her to His Lordship back in the summer, only that hospital nurse got to him first wi' all her talk about "scientific training". Ellen, she baint got no scientific training, but she be main good wi' kiddies.'

I gave a sigh of relief. 'I'll ask His Lordship.' Then my eye caught the *instanter*. 'But even if she can come, she'll have to give a month's notice – and he do say I maun find someone straight-away.'

'I could ask my Mam to come up in the meantime.'

I looked at her hopefully. 'But wouldn't it be inconvenient, having to leave her own home?'

Clara shook her head decisively. 'Nothing's inconvenient for my Mam where His Lordship's concerned – and remember, it baint the first time she's been in Eston nursery, so she knows her way around!' She grinned, then said, 'I'll run down to fetch her this minute. I'll tell Mrs Johnstone you sent me.'

'But –'

Clara added firmly, 'My lady,' and I subsided.

I dressed very quickly and went straight up to the nursery. I spent all morning there. Flora was fractious and disturbed – she didn't want Nurse to go and she hardly seemed to remember who I was. She was crying, and it was all I could do not to cry with her as I petted and talked to her and made her bear dance for her. Then Nurse came in in her brown coat and hat to say goodbye to Flora, who clung to her weeping, 'Flora wants Nurse, Flora wants Nurse!' She struggled against my restraining arms as the door closed, then her small fists thumped at my chest. 'Go 'way. Mama *bad* lady!' I thought my heart would break.

I scarcely noticed the door opening and a woman coming in with Clara, for still I wrestled with my daughter – cajoling, petting, pleading – then a voice said, 'Thee maun give her thy tittie, my lady.'

I looked up, my eyes desperate. 'But she were weaned months ago.'

'They do remember – 'tis the smell, I think.' Frantically I unfastened my blouse and tore open my camisole. I hugged her red cheek to my bare breast and still she struggled – but her struggles became feebler, and at last she fell asleep, there on my breast.

But I had to leave her at lunch-time, my lord had ordered it. I sat and ate sawdust and ashes in the cold morning room. When I got up to leave Mr Tims said, almost apologetically, 'Coffee is served in the drawing room, my lady.' So I had to go into the even colder drawing room to drink that bitter brew before I was allowed upstairs again. By tea-time she'd consented to play with her Noah's Ark while I held out each toy animal for her to take – but then I had to go down to the drawing room again for tea. After that I rebelled. I didn't want to disturb her so I spent my official hour upstairs, and bathed her myself in front of the fire. She splashed in the warm water, and when I finally lifted her out she favoured me with one wavering smile; I hugged her towel-wrapped body close to my breast. But then the dressing bell rang, and I had to leave her again.

I put on my one remaining dress blouse; the blue was faded now and it didn't fit properly because feeding a child had made my breasts fuller. I remembered my own lord caressing my rosy pink nipples – then thrust the memory from me and went down to dine with his father. As I entered the hall I saw Lord Warminster standing by the fireplace, resplendent in full evening dress: high

461

wing collar, stiff bow tie, starched shirt front, rigid waistcoat – all shining, gleaming white – while his tailcoat and tapered trousers were as black as the night. I felt very small and shabby. Slowly he turned round to face me, and as I saw the expression in his eyes I shivered; not the kindly Beast tonight – but Bluebeard.

He didn't offer me his arm, he didn't even wait to see if I were following, but stalking across the hall he headed straight for the dining room. I had to run to catch up with him, so I could precede him through the door. At the threshold he stopped dead, glaring at the table where two places had been laid, his at the head and mine to his right. He pointed to my place. 'Tims, Lady Warminster will sit in her proper seat.' Mr Tims glanced at me in apology, then I had to stand waiting while the knives, the forks, the spoons, the set of glasses and the folded damask napkin were all moved down to the other end of the long table and re-set there, as far away from him as they possibly could be.

I walked down to where I'd been banished with as much dignity as I could muster – which wasn't very much. Mr Wallis came and stood behind my chair, murmuring so that only I could hear, 'The miserable old sod. Keep your pecker up, Amy.'

Lord Warminster never addressed one single word to me as baked sole succeeded oxtail soup, and chicken cutlets succeeded sole. The remains of the saddle of mutton had been removed and the roast partridges were on the table before I could pluck up the courage to speak. 'My lord,' – his fork stopped in mid-flight –'about the nurse. Clara did suggest her cousin Ellen – would that suit you?'

He dropped his fork with an impatient clang. 'It is – your decision. I engaged the first one – you had her dismissed. You engage the next one – then it'll be my turn to dismiss her.' He picked up his fork again.

'But my lord, I cassent ask her to come if you're a-going to decide to turn her off again!' He continued eating, ignoring me.

Mr Wallis came through the door and up to my chair. 'My lady . . .'

Lord Warminster threw down his fork, his face furious. 'What do you want? I didn't ring!'

Mr Wallis turned to face him. 'Mrs Chandler's sent down from the nursery, my lord. Lady Flora's howling fit to bust, she says, and could Her Ladyship come upstairs, please.'

I sprang to my feet – then a loud voice from the other end of the table said, 'Lady Warminster is dining. She does not wish to be disturbed.' He reached for his fork again. There was silence, but in my head I could hear his voice as he'd told me, 'Tomorrow . . . I shall hate you.' Now it was tomorrow, and he hated me.

I began to sink back onto my seat – but before I reached it my body snapped straight and I stood upright again. Addressing the hunched shape at the far end of the table I said loudly, 'Yesterday, yesterday evening, you said, "If I bred the perfect rose, and it pricked her thumb –" '

His angry shout stopped my words. 'Then go! Get out, get out!'

Behind me Mr Wallis murmured, 'And up yours too, my lord,' then, raising his voice he told me, 'I'll ask Mrs Procter to put the rest of your dinner in the hot plate, my lady.'

I walked up the length of the table and left the room without a backward glance. As soon as I was outside I ran to the stairs and rushed up them. I could hear my baby's screams before I reached the top. As I took her from Mrs Chandler her small fists hit out at me. 'Go 'way, go 'way!' She sobbed herself to sleep on my breast eventually, and then I was able to gently lay her back in her cot.

I knew I should go back downstairs again, but I didn't want to leave her, so I sat down opposite Clara's mother, who was peacefully knitting by the fire. The door opened behind us, and Mrs Chandler was already sketching a bob as she rose to her feet and thrust her needles into her ball of wool – so I knew who it was who'd come in even before her quiet, 'Good evening, my lord.'

'Good evening, Mrs Chandler. It's kind of you to come and help us out.'

She smiled. 'My pleasure, my lord. She's a bright liddle maid is Lady Flora, even when she's upset. But my lady's settled her, and she's sleeping sound as a bell now.'

'Good. I hear Ellen Watson is looking for a new position?'

'Yes, my lord.'

'If you give me her address, I will write to her tomorrow.'

Mrs Chandler's face broke into a beaming smile. 'She'll be main pleased, my lord.' He crossed to the night nursery, gently turned the knob and eased himself inside, pulling the door to behind him. As Mrs Chandler sat down again and pulled out her needles she said to me, 'His Lordship allus did think highly of Ellen. He wrote

463

her character for her when she first went out as nurserymaid – lovely character it were, too, the lady told Ellen.' Her needles resumed their rhythmic clicking.

I leant forward. 'Mrs Chandler, Clara'll be downstairs in the hall just now – mebbe you'd like to run down and take a cup o' tea with her? I'll stay up here with Flora.'

'Why, thank 'ee my lady.' The needles were rammed into the ball again.

As soon as she'd gone I very quietly opened the door to the night nursery. He was standing beside the cot, crouched awkwardly sideways so that his tiptilted face could look directly in at her, and my whisper of protest died on my lips as I saw his expression. He was gazing down at my daughter as though she were the first baby that had ever been born. Then he realised that I was in the doorway – and at once his expression changed from adoration to antagonism. He turned and came towards me, sidling along on the balls of his feet like a huge crab so as not to disturb her. When he was outside, with the door closed I asked, 'Why didn't you tell I you did know Ellen Watson?'

'Why – should I?' Then he gestured towards the night nursery. 'Was she – ill?'

'No, my lord – she were only throwing a tantrum.' I paused before adding, 'Like some others as are old enough to know better.'

His eyes narrowed in anger. 'I warned you – I warned you!' Turning to go he loosed his parting arrow. 'You should have – left.'

Chapter Fifty-Three

And that became the pattern of my life. Upstairs in the nursery Flora threw tantrum after tantrum; when she wasn't screaming in anger she was sulking. I coaxed and petted and cajoled, but she would not forgive me for first deserting her in the summer and now sending Nurse away; and whenever I finally did get her settled then it was lunch-time, or tea-time, or the dressing bell had rung – so I had to go back downstairs. Then when I came back again she hated me for having left her. While he, her grand-father, hated me for staying.

Some evenings he was bent on tormenting me, like a cat playing with a mouse before it gobbles it up. He'd order, 'Talk, you must talk – or what will the servants think?' So I would speak, as he'd commanded, saying something about the weather or what Flora and I had seen on our daily walk, then he'd pounce. 'Baint! That's not correct English. And 'tis – what does 'tis mean? Use *me*, not *I* – me is the accusative case of the first person singular – I is the nominative. Surely you know that?' But of course I didn't – and he knew I didn't. Then he'd start to interrogate me, deliberately using words I'd never come across before and didn't know the meaning of. Yet when I tried to ask him, saying, 'My lord, I baint never heard o' . . .' then his great paw would come down again. 'You say that you "have *not never* heard"? But a double negative means a positive, so you *have* heard – then why do you need to ask for an explanation?' I shook my head. 'But thic words –' 'You and your everlasting "thic, thic"! What does it mean? Thick? Thick as wood, thick as a plank? How can *words* be thick?' Then he'd pause, glaring at me before insisting: 'You must speak as Lady Warminster – do you understand?' I understood, but I couldn't.

Another evening it was my clothes. 'You must dress as Lady Warminster. That blouse doesn't fit, and you've worn it every night for a week.'

Reddening I told him, 'I know, my lord, but I cassent let the seams out any further – and I did cut up the other.'

'There is a dressmaker in the village. Go to her – order a decent evening gown.'

'But, my lord!' I shrank from the thought of even walking down the village street, with everybody looking at me in contempt – and he knew it, he knew it.

His eyes watched me, taunting me as he added, 'She cuts well, her scissors are sharp – but her tongue is sharper still; she's a great gossip, Maud Winterslow.' He put down his fork before commanding, 'Go tomorrow. Tell her I've sent you.' His eyes dared me, as leaning forward he exclaimed, 'Lady Warminster must be frightened of no one – *no one*.' His voice dropped and became harsher as he asked, 'Are you frightened? Are you frightened of *me*?'

'No, my lord.' But I was lying and he knew it.

On other evenings he never spoke as course after course was served. He sat at the other end of the table glowering into his plate until finally, after Mr Tims and Mr Wallis had left, he would rise to let me precede him from the room and then, just as I drew level with him, he'd say, 'You should have *left*.' He said it every evening without fail, whether he'd been mocking me or glowering at me; always there came that final, hostile: 'You should have *left*.'

Then one day he changed this refrain. As soon as I'd spread my napkin on my lap he began to torment me. 'Why aren't you talking? You must talk, because of the servants. We must convince the servants of our conjugal felicity.'

His eyes glittered and my carefully-prepared report on the weather fled. Instead I exclaimed desperately, 'My lord, I dussent understand you. What do thic words mean – "conjugal felicity"?' And even as I asked him my tongue stumbled over them.

'What a little ignorama you are!' "Conjugal felicity" is the condition that we two enjoy. "Conjugal" means married – like you and I – and "felicity" is happiness, the state of being happy – like you and I.' He twisted his mouth into a grotesque parody of a smile. 'You are happy, aren't you?'

I cried out, 'Why don't you get drunk? I were happy then, because you did speak kindly to I!'

'Ah, but sometimes when I am drunk I become vicious – and you wouldn't like that, would you?'

466

Misery made me reckless. I replied loudly, 'I don't reckon as I'd notice the difference.' I heard his indrawn hiss of breath.

He didn't speak again over the meal, but as I drew level with him on my way out he opened his mouth to deliver his final taunt – but it had changed. This time it was a challenge, 'Why don't you *leave*?' And that became his parting jibe now, repeated every night. I remembered the tale of Beauty and her Beast, and shed tears because I was trapped in this bitter travesty of it.

I was like a grain of wheat being crushed between the millstones of his anger and Flora's daily tantrums – yet those two were happy in each other's company. I asked Dora if Flora screamed when she went to him in the library. 'Oh no, my lady. All smiles she be when she sees His Lordship a-waiting at the door. Holds her liddle arms out she do, cooing and calling: "Papa, Papa!" – and the yellow bitch there, a-wagging of her tail – 'tis a pleasure to see it.'

I decided Dora must be exaggerating, but then I saw them together myself. It was Christmas Day and I'd gone upstairs early; I'd snipped the bottom off my petticoat and sewn a soft ball of cloth. She condescended to play with it for a little while, then he arrived with his presents and she lost interest in mine. The oddman carried in a dolls' house: it had eight rooms, from cellar to attics, and a brick and stucco front that opened. It was completely furnished and there was a family of dolls living inside: mother, father, boy, girl, baby, and all their servants, from scullerymaid to butler – there was even a miniature golden retriever like Nella. Flora gurgled with delight, although she was too young for it really, and then he gave her a small parcel to unwrap. She ripped the tissue off and as soon as she saw it was a book she exclaimed: 'Read – Papa read story.'

He lowered himself down into the creaking wicker armchair and swung Flora up on to his lap. She settled herself into the crook of his arm, nestling against his waistcoat, and it was obvious from the way she tucked her head into the space below his tilted chin that she sat like this every day. He began to read, his voice low and fluent – no trace of hesitation with her, of course.

'There was a little woman, as I've heard tell,
Who went to market her eggs for to sell.'

467

His large finger pointed. 'See her basket, Flora? What's she got in her basket?'

'Eggs!'

'Good girl.

> *She went to market all on a market day,*
> *And she fell asleep on the king's highway.'*

'There, there!' A chubby finger stabbed at the page.

'*Clever* girl.

> *And then came a pedlar whose name was Stout,*
> *He cut her petticoats all round about,*
> *He cut her petticoats up to her knees,*
> *Which made the little woman to shiver and freeze.*

'You'd shiver and freeze, wouldn't you, Flora, if a pedlar cut off *your* petticoats?'

Her head nodded solemnly. '*Naughty* pedlar.'

'Don't worry, my Flora – Papa won't allow it.'

I shivered as my petticoats hung limp to my knees – and the cloth ball they'd been sacrificed to make lay unregarded on the nursery floor. There was no room for me in front of the fire so I went and knelt by the dolls' house, and began to rearrange the family of dolls. I took the nurse and sent her out walking with the two children. Picking up Mama from where she languished in the drawing room I shifted her to the nursery, then I lifted the baby doll from its crib and set it down on her unresisting lap – her painted face looked rather surprised. I picked up Papa – what should I do with Papa? After a moment I upended him, and laid him sprawling on the floor of the wine cellar, with two tiny bottles by his side and the sleek golden retriever at the foot of the steps.

The story had finished, and the floor creaked behind me. He stood there with Flora in his arms, studying my handiwork – then he suddenly dropped her on to my lap and turned to go.

She called, 'Papa!' but he only replied, 'You will come down later, Flora – to the library.' Then he left.

Half-an-hour after, Clara came up. 'His Lordship says could

468

you be downstairs at a quarter before eleven, my lady, ready to go to Church.'

'Church! But he don't never go to Church.'

'Christmas and Easter he does, my lady.'

He never spoke in the carriage until it drew up at the lychgate, then he said, 'You must be – seen to be Lady Warminster.' But I knew that in my old felt hat and too-tight jacket I looked exactly what I was – a disgraced lady's maid. My legs shook as I climbed down the step.

A hush fell on the congregation as we came through the door and sly glances darted in my direction. My cheeks were aflame; he strode ahead so I quickened my pace to keep up with him – but he lengthened his stride until I was almost running, and then thankfully a door opened into a high box pew, and the prying eyes were left outside. It was like a little room, even to the small fire burning in the grate, and as I collapsed on the wooden seat he arranged his ungainly form opposite. The service began.

Other than the weddings at Bath I'd never been to a service in church, and I didn't know how to behave. A man had given me a prayer book but I couldn't find my place and I leafed desperately backwards and forwards searching, then all of a sudden it was snatched out of my hands and an open one substituted. Lord Warminster had given me his. I strained to follow each word, even while I was kneeling, repeating fervently, 'We have erred, and strayed from Thy ways like lost sheep . . .' After the Absolution I managed to disentangle the alternatives, until I found myself reading, 'I believe in God the Father Almighty,' while everyone else was saying, 'Whosoever will be saved . . .' The hand opposite shot out, pages flicked rapidly and the book was handed back. To my horror I saw that the next line said, 'And the Catholick faith is this . . .' Whatever would Grammer have said? But I read grimly on until, 'world without end. Amen'.

The Litany began, and following it carefully in the book I managed to answer until, 'As we do put our trust in Thee,' but then it was a different prayer. I looked up anxiously and the book made its rapid to and fro, and then I saw the reason for the change: it was a special prayer to be read 'In the time of War and Tumults'. I remembered with a shock that Britain was actually at war. Men like Joe Dempster and Thomas and Henry were fighting in France against the Germans, and lots of soldiers were being killed, Clara said. The prayer ended, then the Rector's voice changed tone. 'And now let us remember in our prayers those men of this parish who are serving their King and country, facing death and danger at the hands of our enemies: James Arnold, Leonard Arnold, Cyril John Alfred Beeston, George Chandler, John Chandler, Horace Chandler, Herbert Dawson, Joseph Dempster, Wilfred Dyson, Francis Peter John Fitzwarren-Donne,' – and my gasp of horror was audible throughout the whole church. Even the Rector's level voice paused for a moment before continuing, '– Viscount Quinham, Thomas Albert Hastings, Henry Hunter . . .'

As I fought to keep back the tears I looked across the pew and saw that Lord Warminster's huge body was as still as that of a cat, watching the mouse it has caught.

I didn't hear a word of the sermon. My lord was in danger, fighting, being shot at by the Germans – he was going to be killed, I knew it! If only I could see him again, just one more time . . . As the sermon ended I fell on to my knees and prayed fervently, 'Please God, punish me but keep him safe, please . . .' A voice hissed in my ear, 'Get up! You're keeping the entire congregation waiting!'

I stumbled to my feet and out of the wooden pen. I wanted to pick up my skirts and run like a frightened rabbit but I couldn't, I had to be Lady Warminster. So I walked up the aisle with Lord Warminster and stood in the porch beside him while people shook him by the hand – faces, so many inquisitive faces – but I managed to mumble some sort of reply to everyone that spoke to me, until at last I could follow him out to the sanctuary of the carriage.

The springs jerked as he sat down opposite me. I looked up at him, crying, 'You knew, you knew he'd gone to the war! Why didn't you tell I?'

'You should have realised – he's young, he wants to be a hero. Besides, the Fitzwarren-Donnes have always been an Army family. Every earl has served his country – except for *me*.' His voice was so bitter I didn't dare say any more. I sat upright with the tears trickling down my cheeks until we reached Eston. As soon as the carriage stopped I leapt up, wrenched open the door and jumped down on to the wobbling step. I rushed through the front door as Mr Tims opened it.

Panting I stood in the nursery doorway; she was playing with her dolls' house. Her hair was silken pale as the outer petals of a daffodil in spring. Just like his. And her eyes, her forget-me-not blue eyes – they were his eyes. I saw him, his face waxen above his scarlet tunic, lying on the battlefield. My lord, my love. And I'd never even waved him goodbye.

Mr Wallis found me there. 'Dinner's at lunch-time on Christmas Day my lady, to set the staff free later. And by the way, he's not in France yet – Lord Quin – he's still training, in England.'

I closed my eyes for a moment, and my legs trembled with relief as I said, 'Thank 'ee Mr Wallis – thank 'ee.'

'Actually it was His Lordship as told me to tell you – but not to say it was from him, so don't split on me.'

Christmas dinner was a roast goose followed by plum pudding. I could hardly eat any of it. Lord Warminster never spoke a word except for the usual terse query at the end: 'Why don't you leave?' I walked past him as if I'd not heard.

On Boxing Day he began tormenting me again. 'This soup's lukewarm. Speak to the housekeeper – tell her to reprimand the cook.'

'But, my lord, she won't take any notice of –'

'Speak to her! You must *be* Lady Warminster.'

I tapped on Mrs Johnstone's door and gave her his message. She just looked at me, then said, 'Is that all?' There was a very long pause before she added, 'My lady?' The door slammed shut in my face before I had time to reply, but not before I'd seen Mrs Procter sitting by the fire with a glass in her hand and a smirk on her face.

Upstairs, Flora was more fractious than ever, and then Clara's mother began to cough and sneeze. She became very anxious and said she must speak to His Lordship; Clara came back soon after to fetch her things. 'He won't allow Mam to stay while she's poorly, in case the liddle maid catches it.'

'Could *you* stay with her, Clara?'

Clara shook her head. 'I couldn't handle her, mood she's in these days. But 'tis all right. Mam says. Granny Withers'll come – she'll sort out anybody, she will.'

Granny Withers was stooping, with wispy white hair tucked under a mob cap and only two stained stumps of teeth – one at the top and one at the bottom. She moved with a brisk shuffle. 'Good afternoon, my lady.' Flora jumped up and ran to stare at her. 'Well, well. I knows who *thee* dost favour – spitting image o' thy grandma, thee bist.' Flora braced her legs and stuck out her lower lip. 'But I can see 'tis only skin-deep, though. Thee bist a little madam, by the looks o' thee and she, she was soft as butter afore it sets.' She glanced at me from under her wrinkled eyelids. 'He ran her ragged he did, His Lordship – till she upped and left him.'

I called, 'Flora, do 'ee come to Mama while Mrs Withers be unpacking.'

Flora spun round on her heel. 'Shan't.'

'Now Flora, please!'

'Go 'way, go 'way!'

I managed to calm her at last. Granny Withers settled herself down in the wicker armchair, took out a clay pipe and began to fill it. 'He's running you ragged as well. I knows – Grace Chandler's been telling me.' She bent creakily over and struck a match on the sole of her boot. Flora watched in fascination. When her pipe was drawing to her satisfaction Granny nodded her head towards Flora. 'Thic liddle maid, you wants to tap her. Not to hurt her, just to show her who's boss, see. She's playing you up 'cos she thinks you're soft, and soft folk, they can't be trusted – she knows that, little 'un though she be. Next time she tries it on, you tap her one, she'll be the happier for it. Be easier on my ears, too.' She cackled.

By tea-time Flora was watching intently as Granny Withers' gnarled old hands manipulated a piece of string in intricate fashions, then the tea tray arrived. I called to her, 'Come along, Flora, 'tis time to drink thy milk.' Flora looked at me – and I saw it, I saw that fractional moment of calculation in her round blue eyes before she opened her mouth and screamed. So I leant forward and tapped her lightly across the back of her legs. Her scream cut off in mid-bellow, she gazed at me in incredulous silence – then I held out my arms to her. 'Flora, I do love thee, Flora.' She ran straight into them and began to sob. 'Flora, Flora!' She put her arms around my neck and I kissed her soft cheek, hugging her; her sobs were lessening already.

Granny Withers said, 'There – what did I tell 'ee? She needed that.'

The soup was lukewarm again, but he was sulking tonight, so he said nothing except the final, inevitable, 'Why don't you – leave?'

472

I was still in the nursery later when he came up to see her sleeping. As he came back out of the night nursery he said, 'Good evening, Mrs Withers.'

'Evening, me lord.' He headed for the door, but Granny's voice called after him, 'Baint you going to wish your lady good evening?'

He stopped with a jerk and swung round to bark, 'No!' Then he was gone.

Flushing with humiliation I stared down at the floor – then I heard the cackle of Granny Withers' laughter. As I looked up she winked at me. 'Temper, temper! He's allus been the same – spoilt he were, spoilt rotten. Nobody never tapped him, more's the pity.' She poked at her pipe. 'Not the first time I been in thic nursery it baint. Many's the Sundays I used to come and take tea wi' Missus Fenton, his nanny – her being me second cousin on my father's side. I told her, I told her, although she were a lot older'n me, o' course, her having been his mother's nurse – I told her, "Thee wants to tap him, Aunt Alice – show him who's boss." But she wouldn't. Kept on about him being a poor little boy, with his Mam being dead and his father never coming to see him, and him having to be sent away to school soon as he turned eight, way the gentry do. She were afeard t'other boys'd tease him, wi' him being twisted an' all.' Granny shook her head. 'Huh! So who hasn't got troubles in thic world? I told her! But she wouldn't never take me advice. She'd let him do whatever he wanted; spoilt, he was. I said to her: "But what about when you go, Aunt Alice? He'll have to learn then." But she says as she won't never leave him. Only whiles he's away at school the first time, she has a seizure and drops down dead as a doornail in thic floor 'ere. Not so long after, he arrives home for his holidays – but nobody's thought to tell him, so he comes running up here, looking for her – and she's already been buried a week. They tries to tell him then, but he wouldn't listen. Ran over the whole house he did, looking for her, like a hare with the hounds snapping at its tail, for all his short leg, so they tells me. And then, when it finally gets through to him as she really has gone and left him – my, then there *was* a tantrum! He's never spoke right since – done hisself a mischief wi' it, I shouldn't wonder. I told her, I told her!' Granny Withers bent over to tap her pipe on the heel of her boot, then emptied it out on to a square of newspaper which she screwed up and lobbed into the fire.

Creaking upright she set the guard in place saying, 'If you don't mind, me lady, I'll be a-getting to bed now. Early to bed, early to rise – that's allus been my motto.'

Next morning as I came into the nursery Flora looked up from Granny's lap and opened her mouth for her morning howl of rage – then she closed it again abruptly, slithered off Granny's knee and came to me. 'Mama, Flora want pipe.' Lifting her up into my arms I hugged her close. 'Good morning, Flora.'

Granny Withers cackled, 'See – I told you! You want to sort him out next.'

That evening he started as soon as the soup came in. He leant forward to touch the tureen. 'It's cold – stone cold. Didn't you speak to that housekeeper?'

Mr Wallis interrupted soothingly, 'My lord, it's bortsch – bortsch is cooled by the addition of soured cream.'

'Mind your own business, Wallis.' He glared at me. '*Did* you speak to her?'

'Yes, my lord.'

'Then she obviously didn't take the slightest notice of you!' I could see him working himself up into a rage – or a tantrum. He exploded, 'You – you're supposed to be Lady Warminster. Go and tell her, now!'

I sensed Mr Wallis stiffen behind me as I replied quietly, 'No, my lord.'

His face went red with fury, just like Flora's had so often done. Then, taking a deep breath he bellowed, 'Why don't you *leave*?' I was stunned. He'd never said it in front of Mr Tims and Mr Wallis before. Then he shouted again, 'Why – don't – you – leave?' And this time, I heard it. Behind the fury I heard the note of despair, the voice of the small boy who'd come back from school to find his beloved nurse had died, and left him.

I got up from my chair and walked the length of the table to where he sat at the head, then I stood looking down into his eyes – the eyes of an angry, unhappy child. But I couldn't tap him, he was too big. He shouted up at me, 'There you are – you're leaving – I knew you would!' And his voice was the voice of that small boy who'd run frantically over this house, searching for his dead nurse. I moved closer, and reached down on to the table in front of him. He watched as I lifted the heavy tureen. 'Yes – take it with you –

474

take it to her before you go, tell her –' His voice stopped abruptly and he stared in disbelief as I raised the tureen as high as I could and upended it over his head.

He only just got his eyes closed in time as soup soaked his grizzled hair, ran down his craggy nose, splashed his tilted chin and cascaded on to his immaculate black tailcoat. I watched as a great tide of crimson flowed over his collar and tie, down his starched white shirt-front and on to stain his gleaming white waistcoat; then I put the tureen back down again. He shook his head, and a shower of beetroot-red drops spattered the damask tablecloth, then he opened his eyes and stared straight up at me. I looked down into them and said, very clearly, 'I baint leaving, not –' I took a deep breath and continued – not *ever*.' Then I went back and sat down in my place.

Mr Tims' face was ashen, and it was Mr Wallis who stepped forward to ask smoothly, 'Are you ready for your fish now, my lord?'

Raising his napkin to wipe his dripping face Lord Warminster replied, 'Yes, Wallis.'

He didn't speak again. He sat and ate his way through boiled turbot, braised ham, roast beef and a large slice of apple pie exactly as if the whole incident had never occurred. The only time he showed any awareness that he was drenched in beetroot soup was when a ruby drop trickled off his bushy eyebrows and on to his nose – then he simply flicked it away with a jerk of his head.

I made myself eat, but under the table my knees were knocking. In his massive, crimson-soaked dignity he was my lord again now, and I was terrified of his anger. Suppose he sent me away, without Flora? He had the power to do it. The meal dragged on through the final savoury of anchovy fritters to end in a curl of orange peel; still he hadn't spoken. I sat, awaiting my doom.

He stood up. I stood up too, and moved down the table towards him, as I did each evening. And as I drew level with him he began to speak, as he did every night – but the question had changed. Tonight he asked, 'Do you think we have now – sufficiently convinced the servants – of our conjugal felicity?' Then he went to the door and held it open for me to pass through.

I was so wrought up I turned the wrong way, and without thinking pushed through the green baize door into the servants' passage – and there I saw Mr Wallis, collapsed over the serving table in a paroxysm of laughter. He tried to draw himself upright when he saw me, but he failed, and slumped back against the table. 'Oh, my Gawd. You were magnificent, Amy – my lady! Your timing was superb – you should go on the halls! And the old boy, I had to admire him, carrying on as if nothing had happened.' He wiped his streaming eyes. 'But it was high time somebody did that to him. Am I glad I was there to see it.' A bell sounded above us, and Mr Wallis glanced up at the indicator board. 'That's him ringing now, wanting a change of clothing, no doubt.' He grinned at me. 'Still, I'll bet that's the last time he complains about the soup not being hot.' With a parting wink he sprinted off towards the back stairs.

I went straight up to the nursery; I couldn't face drinking coffee alone in that huge, gloomy drawing room. I stood by her cot for ages, just looking down at her sleeping face. Then I heard him coming in and slipped out with downcast eyes to sit opposite Granny Withers, who was peacefully puffing on her pipe by the glowing fire.

He came quietly out of the night nursery, closing the door gently behind him. As he drew level with us he paused and said, 'Good evening, Mrs Withers.'

'Evening, me lord.'

Then turning to face me he added, very deliberately, 'Good – evening,' and walked out.

Chapter Fifty-Four

He sent for Flora as usual the next day, but I never saw him until I walked into the hall as the dinner bell rang. He was standing with his blind side to the stairs, staring into the fire, just as he always did, but as he heard my footsteps he swung slowly round, and spoke. 'Good evening.'

'Good evening, my lord.'

'Shall we – go in – to dinner?' He didn't offer me his arm, but then I knew he never would; it was enough that he'd spoken.

At the dinner table he took three mouthfuls of soup, then lowered his spoon. 'The soup – is hot – today.' Looking directly at me he added, 'But then, it was warmer yesterday than I had – initially supposed.' He watched for my flush of embarrassment before picking up his spoon to continue drinking. By the mutton cutlets I'd managed to tell him of some saying of Flora's, when we'd been out on our walk, and as the Cabinet pudding was served he remarked on the unseasonal warmth of the weather. Fervently I agreed. As soon as he'd finished his dessert orange he stood up as usual, and as I drew level with him I saw he was about to speak. My heart hammered, but he didn't tell me to leave. Instead he asked, 'May I – join you – in the drawing room?' Adding quickly, 'Only for – a moment.'

So great was my relief I almost stammered my eager, 'Aye, my lord – o' course.'

He didn't follow me in at once, so when Mr Tims set down the coffee tray I asked for a second cup. Mr Tims glanced up in surprise, then a look of pleasure crossed his face. 'Certainly, my lady.'

Lord Warminster came in soon after, carrying a large book. As he put it down on the table I saw from the distinctive gold lettering on the spine that it was the Harrods' catalogue. 'Order what clothing – and other items you need – from this.'

As he turned to leave I called quickly, 'Would you care for a cup o' coffee?' Halting abruptly he turned to look back at me; he was

477

like a large, uncertain animal. I picked up the silver pot. "Tis fresh made.' He came very slowly back and sat down on the extreme end of the sofa opposite – as far away from me as he could possibly get. 'Thank you.' He lifted the cup to his mouth as soon as I'd set it beside him, although it was scalding hot.

I asked, 'How much can I order?'

'Order whatever – you need.'

'But I dussent want to overspend.'

He put down his cup and stood up. 'Whatever you want – send for it.' He headed for the door, but as he reached it he added, 'Get yourself a decent coat – that jacket is far too thin – for winter use.' He shot through the doorway.

I opened the catalogue. Picture after picture, page after page of delights lay before me, from china and glassware to motor cases and luncheon baskets. Truly it was an Aladdin's cave. I began to compose a list in my head: a diamond tiara; a crocodile-skin dressing case crammed with shiny glass bottles; a gold chain purse with a bobble fringe all round the edge; a Moroccan leather writing case with fifteen different pockets; a white straw work-basket lined with pink silk – and a blue velvet pincushion set in the back of a miniature silver elephant. It was a wonderful list; when I'd completed it I said it all through in my head again. Then I went over to the writing table, picked up one of the white sheets of notepaper headed *Eston, Wiltshire* and wrote: *'Vests, 2, natural wool, high neck, short sleeve, medium weight (Small) @ 4s 11d = 9s 10d'*. Although they were the cheapest they still seemed awfully dear, but he had told me to use the Harrods' catalogue. I added two pairs of woollen combinations before flipping through the rest of the underclothing; I would sew my own. Then I reached *Ladies' Towels*. I hesitated. They did seem expensive, but I had to have them – my old rags had been so patched and darned they hardly kept me safe each month. So I wrote: *'1 doz. 20-inch Russian diaper, not taped.'* I'd order tape separately and sew it on myself, to save the money. My old corsets were worn out, too. I ordered maids' ones because they were cheaper; they were really only corded bodices, but my figure was still quite slight – it wouldn't show.

I gazed longingly at the pictures of black silk stockings before writing down: *'3 pairs, black cotton, 8½-inch foot to allow for shinkage @ 1s 6d per pair = 4s 9d'*, followed by two pairs of white. I turned back again and recklessly added two long-sleeved white merino spencers at 6s 6d each – it was so cold at Eston in winter. I didn't know what to do about gloves – they were all so dear. In the end I settled for a pair of washable black kid, with six-button black taffeta for evening wear. After listing a dozen plain cotton handkerchiefs I moved on to *Capes and Mantles* to order a tweed coat. After that I jibbed at the prices and turned to the dress fabrics. Besides, I wanted to sew for myself, I was longing to have my hands occupied again. I ordered longcloth for chemises and drawers, flannel for nightdresses and petticoats, navy serge for skirts, cotton shirting for blouses – that would see me through the day. But in the evenings I had to dine with Lord Warminster, so I took the plunge and ordered two lengths of velvet – dark grey and dark brown – and plain white and grey satin for the summer. I moved on to *Haberdashery* for lining material, thread, tapes and all the other familiar paraphernalia of dressmaking; then a pair of boots, two pairs of shoes and a couple of hats completed my selection.

I took the list and the catalogue to dinner with me the next evening. Lord Warminster noticed and as soon as Mr Tims and Mr Wallis had left after serving the fish he asked for them. I said anxiously, 'Mebbe 'tis too much –'

At once he reached into his pocket for his spectacles, put them on and glanced down at the total. 'It seems extremely modest to me. Are you sure you have ordered sufficient?' Ignoring his halibut pie he quickly scanned the rest of the list. 'Much of this is fabric – do you intend visiting Maud Winterslow after all?'

I shook my head. 'No – I be making it up myself.'

He stared at me. 'You'll be in rags before this is all finished.'

'It won't take me long. I did serve my time wi' a dressmaker, and I like to keep busy.'

He went back to his halibut pie and we ate in silence until the cheese soufflé had been cleared away and the bowls of fruit and nuts were on the table. Then he clicked open his spectacles and picked up my list again. 'At least you've ordered the coat.' Then he frowned. 'Diapers – why more diapers? Flora is almost dry now.'

Embarrassment washed over me as I muttered, 'They be for I, my lord.'

'For *you*?' Then he turned brick-red, and shifting so that he faced the wall, asked it, with very long gaps between the words, 'Did – you – suffer – some – permanent – injury – at – the birth?'

My cheeks were almost as red as his as I answered, 'No, my lord – but I be a woman.'

With a face the colour of beetroot soup he crumpled up the list and rang the bell loudly. He hadn't even touched his orange.

The next few evenings he scarcely opened his mouth except to make some trifling remark about the weather while Mr Tims and Mr Wallis were in the room. I'd reply, 'Yes, my lord, 'tis warm for the time o' year,' or 'No, my lord, I did get Flora back from her walk afore it come on to rain.' At the end of the meal when he stood up and waited for me to leave I would walk towards him with my shoulders braced as for a blow, but each time he said only, 'Good evening,' and I began to relax.

Then the order arrived from Harrods – except that it wasn't my order, I realised that as soon as I unpacked it. Instead of the length of plain grey velvet there was one of midnight-blue chiffon velour, and the dark brown was now golden Lyons at twice the price. The navy serge had turned into fawn lambswool and the plain striped shirting had become lengths of embroidered linen and cream spun silk. I couldn't understand how they'd made such mistakes – then I found they hadn't. The original list had been returned with the order, but it wasn't my list: he'd written it out again, altering it. The coat and the fabrics had increased in quality and brightened in colour, and the gloves – the single pair of washable black kid had become half a dozen of the softest French suede, while the two pairs of six-button taffeta had been transformed into four of ten-button cream silk and another four of sixteen-button white! Quickly I looked for the hosiery, but my three pairs of black cotton stockings remained unimproved, as did all the under-clothing materials – he'd left them severely alone. But he'd added an extra item – a pair of dress combs for me to wear in my hair. They were of golden-brown horn carved very delicately into a pattern of roses intertwined with leaves. I thought they were beautiful, but when I tried to thank him for them, and all the other

480

items, he became impatient. 'It is your right. Next time, don't wait for me to tell you.'

Clara's cousin Ellen was due to arrive the next day, so that evening I cut out a petticoat, sewed the seams on my machine in my bedroom and then took my hand-sewing up to the nursery next morning, as I was worried about Flora having to get to know yet another strange face. She clung to my skirts at first, and I was constantly putting down my needle to lift her on to my lap, then later she seemed to settle. However, I told Ellen to send for me at once if Flora became upset, and she did – while I was at dinner. Mr Tims delivered the message and I half-rose, then looked up the table. 'My lord –'

He glanced up from his baked herrings and grunted, 'I suppose I'd better let you go – I don't want fishbones stuck in my hair.' I was off.

But by the end of the week she'd got used to Ellen and was happy in her company. Her grandfather knew that as well as I did and he said at dinner, 'Ellen Watson is a reliable girl. You are Lady Warminster – Lady Warminster does not spend all day in the nursery.' I took my sewing down to the drawing room instead. Flora was quite satisfied as long as I went up to see her regularly but I, I missed her so much.

I saved the evening dresses until last. Wanting them to be in fashion I asked Clara if she'd fetch me a threepenny Weldon pattern book next time she went into Tilton on her afternoon off, but then I realised I hadn't got the money to pay for it; so over dessert I asked him, 'My lord, could I have threepence?' I explained, ''Tis for a pattern book – fashions they do change every year.' He came to the drawing room later and placed a threepenny bit on the table by the sofa then, opening his other hand, he dropped a shower of notes on top of the small silver coin. I said, 'My lord, I dussent need –' But he was already walking out of the door.

After carefully studying the latest styles I drafted my own pattern, cut out the golden velvet and began to sew. By the time I'd finished it my dress clung as closely as those sixteen-button cream silk gloves. I was especially proud of the fit of the low-cut bodice; I'd boned it so that my breasts were lifted up, and now they looked exactly as they had done before I'd fed Flora. As hems

481

were higher this year I made two golden roses from the leftover scraps of velvet; and as I fastened them on to the front of my evening slippers I hoped they'd distract his attention from my white cotton ankles.

That evening I didn't pull my hair back and knot it in its usual plain lady's maid bun; instead I brushed it out and pinned it up in elaborate coils so it framed my face, just as I'd learnt in hairdressing lessons. Then, very carefully, I inserted my two dress combs; their golden roses seemed to be growing there, amidst the curling tendrils of my hair. When I'd finished dressing I twirled round in front of the long mirror. I didn't look small and shabby tonight.

As usual when he heard my footsteps on the stairs he turned to face me – but this time he stopped still, staring at me. He stood looking for a long time, while my face flushed, then he said, 'You are – indeed – very skilful with your needle.' He added, as if he'd almost forgotten what time it was, 'Er – shall we go into dinner?' He didn't speak, but he sat at slightly more of an angle than usual, so that he could see me every time he lifted his eyes from his plate. I basked in his admiration. But as the meal progressed his glances changed. Admiration gave way to a kind of morose blankness, and then I saw the frown develop. By the time the savoury was served he was glowering at me, and I lowered my own eyes to my plate. And then, as I came level with him at the end, he finally spoke. 'It would – have been better – if you'd – left.' I walked out as though I'd not heard him, but my eyes were stinging with the hurt of it.

That night the toothache started. Some days I'd concentrate very hard on my sewing and tell myself it wasn't really there, then I'd drink a cup of tea and the pain would stab through my temple like a red-hot hat-pin. I'd go up and hug Flora and try and convince my tooth that it didn't really hurt at all, but it wouldn't be convinced. And all the time the fear grew. Remembering the shilling surgery and the pincers coming towards me I knew that however bad the ache was now, the pain of having the tooth pulled would be a thousand times worse. I scolded myself sharply for being a coward, but it didn't do any good. I *was* a coward – the very memory of the pain terrified me. I forced my fingers to sew on, but I wasn't enjoying it any more.

At dinner Lord Warminster crouched sullen and silent at the

other end of the table, never speaking from the time he said, 'Good evening,' in the hall to the time he repeated it as I left the dining room. Once or twice I ventured a timid remark about the weather, but he just grunted, so after that I stayed as mute as him. Perversely the soup came up steaming hot each day, and I sat miserably waiting for it to cool while he was obviously impatient for his fish. One evening I felt so low and ill I simply put the spoon down and left it undrunk. At that point he erupted into speech. 'Don't you like artichoke soup? You drank it before.'

Involuntarily I put my hand to my cheek before muttering, ''Tis a mite hot.'

'It's not *that* hot.' Then his eyes sharpened. 'You've got tooth-ache, haven't you?'

After a long pause I confessed miserably, 'Yes.'

'My dentist is in Salisbury. Go there tomorrow.'

I looked at him in panic, 'But I –'

He put down his spoon. 'You will have to put your head outside the park gates some time. Catch the nine-forty.'

He didn't speak again and nor did I, but as I left he said, 'I'll order the carriage for tomorrow morning and write a note for Williams, so he knows who you are.'

I didn't go. I told myself it was better, and so acute was my terror it almost felt as if it was. I sneaked down first thing and told Mr Tims to cancel the carriage. That evening as he unfolded his napkin Lord Warminster said, 'So Williams didn't take your tooth out?'

'No.' Then gathering all my courage I admitted, 'I didn't go – 'twere better.'

He looked at me suspiciously but didn't say anything else until I began to shift my spoon to and fro in my soup, then he suddenly barked, 'Drink it!'

'But – '

'*Drink* it!'

I did – and cried out with the pain, clutching the side of my face. It was worse, not better. He said, 'Tomorrow – the carriage will be – at the door – at twenty-past nine.' I didn't eat very much: I didn't feel like it. As I was leaving he said, 'Clara will go with you. Good evening.'

I was awake all night with the throbbing pain. It was like a beetle

483

boring into my skull, but when Clara came to the drawing room at twenty-past with her hat and coat on I told her it was better, and I wouldn't be going.

That evening he rounded on me as soon as I entered the hall. 'I've spoken to Clara – and *don't* try and tell me it's better, I can see by your face it's not.' I didn't reply. He went on angrily, 'I suppose I'll have to take you there myself. Be ready in here, at twenty-past nine.' He stalked off to the dining room.

Next morning I ate my breakfast in my room as usual and then went straight up to the nursery, but even the comfort of holding Flora's warm young body couldn't take away the pain – it was continual now. I did go down to put my hat and coat on, but I felt as though I were going to the scaffold – I just couldn't face it. I rang for Clara and asked her, 'Would you mind telling His Lordship I baint going?'

Clara didn't move. Then she said, 'Well, to tell you the truth, my lady, I would mind.' She smiled at me encouragingly. 'Sooner you go, sooner it's out.'

'No – I baint going! Mebbe you'd ask Mr Tims if he'd tell His Lordship?'

She came back quite quickly. 'Mr Tims, he said he'd much rather not, and Mr Wallis says as it baint no use asking him – His Lordship's bawled him out once already this morning.' I knew that, I'd heard him doing it through the connecting door. Clara said, 'He's pacing up and down in the hall like a lion as is all set to burst out on its cage – you'll have to go, my lady.' So, very slowly, I went.

He thrust his watch back into his waistcoat pocket as I came down the stairs and by the time I reached the bottom he was halfway down the front steps. He sat in furious silence all the way to the station and when we got there the train was already in, but the stationmaster must have seen the carriage coming because he was keeping it waiting. I climbed up into the compartment as though it were a tumbril; Lord Warminster followed and immediately opening his *Times*, disappeared behind it. I began to cry in earnest. The newspaper opposite rustled angrily as I fought a losing battle with my sobs.

At Salisbury I had to break into a run to catch him up at the ticket barrier, and as the cab door closed behind us he hissed,

'Stop snivelling! You're making me look even more of a laughing stock than usual.' The force of his fury bludgeoned me into silence.

In a nightmare of terror I found myself sitting in a cold leather chair while shining metal instruments winked viciously at me. A man's voice said, 'You'd better stay in here, my lord. Her Ladyship seems a little distressed.' I glimpsed Lord Warminster's face scowling at me from behind the dentist's shoulder then a black mask came down – I couldn't breathe – and suddenly the pain had gone. I tried to scramble from the chair but a hand restrained me. 'Don't get up just yet, Lady Warminster.'

I exclaimed desperately, 'No, you dussent need to take it out now – it's stopped hurting!'

'It *is* out.' He gestured to one side and there on a metal tray was my tooth.

I stared at him in bewilderment. 'But – I didn't feel you pulling –'

'Naturally not. That's what gas is for, to prevent the pain.'

'But – the doctor at the shilling surgery, he didn't give I no gas. He just pulled and pulled.' My voice quavered. ''Twere like my head being broke in two.'

The dentist smiled. 'Dear me, no wonder you were so apprehensive.' I saw a tide of red wash over Lord Warminster's face as the man continued, 'You really should have gone to a qualified practitioner, Lady Warminster.'

I shook my head. 'Uncle Alf, he only gave I sixpence – it were all he could spare. I baint never been to a proper dentist afore.'

He tut-tutted and pointed at the bloody stump. 'And this is the result. Now, you've got several other teeth which need attention if you want to avoid further abscesses. Come back in a few weeks and I'll fill them for you. You may get up now, if you're feeling quite recovered.'

I was so euphoric with relief that as we got back into the cab I began to chatter to Lord Warminster. 'I can't believe it – I didn't feel nothing, nothing at all! I didn't even hear the bones crack.' The full horror of the shilling surgery came back to me and I shuddered. 'That time afore – oh, it did hurt! Thank 'ee, my lord. Thank 'ee so much for taking me to a proper dentist.'

An odd expression came over his face, then he said, 'Are you –

heaping coals of fire on my head?' I stared at him blankly. 'No, of course you are not. I owe you an apology, a profound apology. I should have put your mind at rest, before this visit. I have been – very culpable in neglecting to do so.'

'But it weren't your fault. You didn't know about the shilling surgery.'

'No, but if I had been more sympathetic you would have told me, then I could have allayed your fears.'

I didn't know what to reply. He'd said 'more sympathetic', but I couldn't imagine him being sympathetic at all, not when he was sober, so I was lost for an answer. But something in his expression made me sense that he knew what I was thinking – his face was brick-red and he looked awkward and unhappy. So I tried to reassure him, repeating firmly, ''Tweren't your fault. You didn't know about shilling surgeries but no more did I know about gas. 'Tis just –' I groped for words '– 'tis just that there's lots o' things you know as I dussent, and some things I know as you dussent – and we neither of us knows what they be.' I paused. 'Do you see what I mean?'

'Yes. And you're quite right – but I don't know what on earth we are to do about it.' The cab rattled to a halt outside the station and he picked up his top hat and cane before adding quietly, 'It really would have been better – if you'd left.' And the way he said it, softly, almost sadly, was more upsetting than all the other angry times put together.

I stumbled on the steps getting out, and the cab driver had to steady me. As we came into the station Lord Warminster said, 'Can you – manage?'

Knowing he'd do anything rather than have me take his arm I muttered, 'Yes,' and concentrated on keeping my legs moving.

By the time we got back to Eston my jaw ached almost as badly as it had done before the tooth had been taken out. Mr Tims had to half-lift me from the carriage and as I stood swaying in the hall my lord shouted, 'Fetch Clara, quickly.' She helped me up to my room and I spent the rest of the day huddled on the sofa in front of the fire, trying to sew while my head throbbed and a foul rotting taste filled my mouth. Flora came down to see me but she wrinkled her nose when I kissed her. 'Mama smell!' and Ellen soon whisked her away again. I went to bed straight after tea, but darkness had fallen before I finally subsided into an uneasy sleep.

Chapter Fifty-five

I woke; moonlight streaming through a crack in the curtains told me that it was far into the night. I'd been awakened by the discomfort in my mouth: it was unpleasantly full of salty-tasting saliva. I tried to swallow but there was too much to go down. Gagging on it I coughed, spluttering, and a stream of liquid gushed out of my mouth on to my pillow. As I struggled up I saw in horror a dark stain spreading out over the pillowcase and reached, fumbling, for the light switch – and even as the light came on I coughed again and saw the scarlet tide spew out – it was blood. Blood – Dimpsey's dying blood, Aunt Agnes' life blood and now, my blood. I heard my own screams, high and piercing.

The door burst open. 'What on earth!'

I saw the dark, lopsided shape and throwing myself out of bed ran frantically towards it. 'I be dying – I be dying!' Seizing hold of his pyjama sleeve I clung to it desperately, sobbing with terror as I gasped over and over again, 'I be dying, I be dying!'

Suddenly a voice bellowed, 'You are *not* dying, *listen* to me!' My panting gasps slowed as two grey eyes glared into mine and pronounced, 'It's your *tooth*, just your *tooth*.' And finally his words penetrated.

My whole body sagged with relief as slowly I unclenched my fingers from his arm, croaking, 'I did think I were dying.'

He replied grimly, 'So did I when I heard those screams. Whatever possessed you, making a noise like that! Surely you realised –'

I whispered, 'Aunt Agnes – she coughed and the blood came out all red and frothy. She looked at me, she just looked at me – and then she died. Like Dimpsey did.'

And the anger left his eyes as he said firmly, 'You are not in any danger.'

I felt hollow and drained, and there was blood spotting his pyjama sleeve from when I'd been screaming – and now my mouth was filling up again. 'But – I do be still bleeding – it won't stop!' I raised my face to his. 'Canst thee not stop it?'

'No, but the doctor will. I'll ring for Wallis. Here, hold this to your mouth in the meantime.' He thrust a towel at me. 'And go back to bed.'

I began to shiver. 'There be blood all over the pillow, and the sheets . . .'

'Just a moment.' I watched him drag the sofa round until it was directly in front of the dying fire, then he hauled a blanket off my bed and spread it over the seat. 'There, sit on that and wrap yourself up in it.' Still clutching the towel I did as he told me. 'Have you no slippers?' Involuntarily I glanced down at his own bare feet and saw the dark mat of hair growing on the top of them –even his toes sprouted small dark tufts – then I shook my head. He took a step backwards as he said brusquely, 'You should have ordered some.' Then he'd gone back next door and I heard the faint buzz of the bell.

When he returned he was wearing his slippers and a dressing gown tightly corded round his waist; awkwardly he knelt in front of me and began to revive the dying fire. I heard Mr Wallis enter my lord's bedroom, hesitate a moment, then come and tap on the connecting door where it stood ajar. Lord Warminster heaved himself upright and went to him. 'Go and 'phone for the doctor – tell him Her Ladyship is haemorrhaging after a tooth extraction. Oh, and bring a pair of socks before you go.' Mr Wallis returned with a pair of brown socks and held them out to Lord Warminster. He waved them impatiently away. 'For her, for her.'

The socks were enormous; when I pulled them on they came right up over my knees, but they were blessedly warm. Pressing the towel against my face I closed my eyes so as not to see the ominous red stain spreading over its white surface. I was so frightened. Suppose the doctor couldn't stop it, suppose I bled to death, like Dimpsey? I began to shiver, and heard the poker being vigorously wielded. Mr Wallis' footsteps came briskly back into the room. 'He was in – he'll be up in ten minutes. Shall I change the bed? I've just got time, and it'll save waking Clara.' When he returned from the linen cupboard he said, 'You'd best sit down by the fire, my lord – no point in your catching a chill.' Then, 'Beg pardon, my lord, but I'll need this chair for putting the bedding on.

You sit on the sofa, it's the warmest place.' The sofa creaked as my lord sat gingerly down on the extreme end.

Opening my eyes I saw the reassuring bulk of him there as the terrifying blood oozed into my mouth, filling it. I mumbled, 'I do need to spit it out.'

Mr Wallis came quickly over with the big china washing bowl. 'You'd better hold it steady for her, my lord – the way she's shaking she'll tip it all over herself.' I spat, and the blood was bright and scarlet, like Dimpsey's in the pail. I began to heave and shudder, I couldn't stop – then there was a glass at my lips. 'Swallow, swallow.' My teeth chattered and it burnt my throat, but I managed to gulp down the fiery liquid, and gradually the shuddering stopped.

Mr Wallis said, 'Best not give her too much, my lord, she ain't used to it. I'll just run down and see if that doctor's arrived yet.'

As the door closed behind him Lord Warminster crouched forward, reaching for the tongs. I watched his hands carefully setting the new coals in place – black-furred hands, the hands of Esau, the hands of the Beast. He eased himself back again on to the sofa, saying, 'Matthews is a very capable man – he'll soon put you to rights. There's no need to be frightened, Amy.' He sounded so calm and confident that my tense body began to relax.

The doctor came soon after; he was grey-haired with a kind face and a piece of pyjama jacket sticking out from under his collar. 'Now, have a good spit and a rinse, so I can see what I'm doing.'

The china bowl reappeared, clean and shining – I flinched back. 'Close your eyes, Amy.' My lord's voice was firm and at once I obeyed him, so this time I didn't see the terrible scarlet drops.

A hand took hold of my chin. 'Open up now.' With eyes still firmly closed I opened my mouth. 'Mm, there it is – we'll soon stop that.' I heard the snap of a bag opening, there was the strong smell of cloves and firm pressure against my gum. 'Now close your mouth and keep it shut tight on the pad. Good girl. We'll give it ten minutes and then have another look. Lie back, now.'

As I lay there with my jaw clenched shut I heard the murmur of voices. They spoke of unfamiliar names: Yprès, La Bassée, Cuinchy – they were talking about the war. The doctor sighed. 'Worrying times we live in, Lord Warminster – worrying times. Now, let me look at my patient.' I opened my mouth and gentle fingers peeled away the pad. 'That's stopped it. You can open your eyes now.'

'Oh, thank 'ee, thank 'ee!'

His mouth curved under his bristly grey moustache. 'You'll feel better in a few days, once the abscess has drained.' He shook his head, smiling ruefully. 'It's a terrible thing, toothache.' Then his brow wrinkled. 'I've just thought – is there a youngster on the way, by any chance?'

I didn't realise what he meant until I heard Lord Warminster's, 'No!' He was almost shouting.

The doctor said, 'I just wondered – there's nothing like carrying a child to set off tooth problems in a young woman.' He bent down to pick up his bag. 'I'll be on my way, then.'

I exclaimed in panic, 'But suppose it do start again?'

'I'll leave the oil of cloves and some gauze. You can stop it yourself then, the same way that I did.'

'I weren't watching.'

He laughed. 'No, but your husband here was, he'll see to it for you. Good night, Lady Warminster. I'll drop by to see how you are in the morning. Good night, Lord Warminster.' With a cheerful wave he was gone.

Mr Wallis came back out of the dressing room, barely suppressing a yawn as he asked, 'Do you require anything else, my lord?'

'No, Wallis – get back to bed. And thank you.' As Mr Wallis left my lord turned to me, 'And you'd better get back to bed, too.'

I said quickly, 'No. Suppose it starts again? He did say you was to stop it, so you maun stay wi' I.'

'Ah.' He sank down on the sofa again. 'You want – me, to stay with – you?'

'Yes.' I added, 'Please.' Then I ventured, 'And mebbe you'd like to drink some o' thic brandy, too?' He swung right round and looked at me, hard. Lowering my lashes I whispered, 'Then you'd talk to me.'

'You're not completely sober yourself, are you Amy?' And as he said it I realised I wasn't, or I'd never have dared to speak to him like that. He went on, 'I think one of us half-cut is quite enough. Besides, after my performance last time –' he broke off and gave a small shrug, then said, 'I wouldn't be much good for stopping your haemorrhage again if I were snoring on the rug.'

I could see the force of that argument so I changed tack. 'When I were a liddle maid and I were ill in the loft, after Dimpsey,' my voice faltered, so I had to start again. 'When I was ill in the loft, and couldn't sleep for the ache in my neck, Granfer did tell I stories, to make the pain go away.' I paused then added, 'My jaw, it do ache now – and you be Flora's Granfer.'

There was a little silence, then he said, 'But I'm afraid I can't tell stories.'

'You do tell stories to Flora – I seed you do it.'

'I *read* stories to Flora.'

'Then, mebbe . . .'

And suddenly he smiled. 'You're as determined as your daughter. Right, I'll find a story to read to you.' He stood up.

I cried, 'Don't leave I!'

'I'm only going next door – I'll soon be back.' He returned at once with a small brown book in his hand. Sitting down on the sofa again he took his spectacles out of his dressing-gown pocket and put them on. 'Now, I wonder which you'd like best? Let me see . . . Ah, the Sirens. Would you like to hear the story of the Sirens, Amy?' I nodded and he began to read of women whose songs were so beautiful, they lured sailors to their deaths on the rocks; and of a man called Odysseus who cheated them by putting wax in the ears of the men who rowed his boat, and telling them to tie him to the mast – so he became the only man who'd heard the Sirens' song and lived.

His voice was low and fluent as he read, and the story sounded almost like a poem, except that there were no rhymes. When he'd finished he turned to look at me. 'You're half-asleep, Amy. I should send you to bed.'

I shook my head. 'No – read me another, please.'

'Flora's cry. You don't look much older than her, with your hair in plaits and those absurd socks on your feet.'

'They be lovely and warm.'

'Good.' He picked up the book again and read of how Odysseus and his friends stumbled upon the cave of a one-eyed giant who took them prisoner. My head drooped, he paused in his story and said again softly, 'You're half-asleep, Amy.'

I jerked my head up. 'No, I be listening.' I managed to force myself awake once more, but then I finally surrendered to the seductive sweetness of sleep.

When I woke up I was in bed, with my cheek resting on a towel;

I peered anxiously at it, but it was unmarked. Morning had come and my tooth hadn't bled again; I lay back with a sigh of relief. As I lay there I remembered the events of the previous night: how Lord Warminster had come to my rescue and read me stories. I felt a warm rush of gratitude – he must even have carried me to bed after I'd fallen asleep.

A tap came at the door. It was Clara with the can of hot water. As she set it down on the wash-stand she told me that Lord Warminster had said I was to stay in bed all day. I felt rather shaky as I was washing, and was glad to climb back between the sheets again for my breakfast. I lay there half-dozing, remembering the tales he'd told me, but I hadn't heard the end of the story of the one-eyed giant. I'd fallen asleep just as he'd started eating the Greeks – had Odysseus escaped? And then I caught sight of the little brown book, still on the mantelpiece. I would read it for myself.

But I couldn't, because it was in Greek. It took me a while to work it out, I was so taken aback when I opened it. He'd read so fluently, I couldn't believe he'd been reading from a completely different language – even the letters weren't the same. I puzzled over the little squiggles and identified a 'k' and a 'b' with a tail, and an 's' without one, but I couldn't make any sense of it at all. Yet he'd read the story from this very book, just as though it were written in the plainest of English. I stared at the pages, fascinated by the shapes of the letters and the almost-recognition – and remembered him telling Flora that night in France that he'd teach her to read Greek. But she was much too young, she couldn't even read English yet, so perhaps in the meantime he'd teach me? Clara's tap came at the door again; the doctor had arrived.

The doctor barely looked in my mouth. He told Clara to wait while he examined me, then he made me undo my nightie so he could look at my chest. He put his stethoscope to it and listened, then he tapped and listened again. He went through the same ritual several times in different parts of my chest and by then I'd guessed why – I could remember the doctor with Aunt Agnes. He sat back, folding his stethoscope. 'There don't seem to be any problems there. Did you nurse your mother before she died?'

'Aye, but the doctor said I could, because o' the lumps in my neck from the poisoned milk.'

'Ah!' He leant forward, feeling my neck. 'Yes, you're very

lucky – those tubercular glands have conferred immunity.' He smiled, explaining, 'You had a milder form of the disease, so you didn't catch the more serious type; it's like being vaccinated. I'll tell Lord Warminster, and set his mind at rest.'

'But did thic lumps mebbe give I toothache?'

He shook his head, laughing. 'No, tuberculosis doesn't cause tooth decay,' then he paused before asking, 'But are you *sure* there isn't a youngster on the way?'

Out of the corner of my eye I saw Clara stiffen – she was listening. I said quietly, 'Aye, I be sure.' The doctor didn't look convinced, so I added, 'I've only just finished my monthlies.'

'Oh, so that's why your husband was so certain.' He looked down at me, his eyes kind. 'No need to fret, my dear. These things sometimes take a little time.' He patted my hand before easing himself off the bed. 'I'm sure you'll have some good news for him before too long.' He picked up his bag. 'Stay in bed today. You can sit up tomorrow, but don't go downstairs until I say so – we don't want any chills.'

After he'd gone I kept thinking of what he'd said. 'These things sometimes take a little time' – but however much time passed I wouldn't ever be carrying a baby again. Lord Warminster had made that very clear that evening in the library: 'I'm too damaged to touch any woman.' He was my husband, but he couldn't give me a child. I felt a great sadness. I made myself dwell on how wretched and ill I'd felt when I was carrying Flora, and the terrible pain of the birth – much, much worse than any toothache, and yet . . . There was the patter of footsteps outside my door and a voice crying, 'Mama!' I called back, 'I be here, sweetheart,' and there was Flora trotting over the carpet towards me, her face one wide, beaming smile. I thrust the doctor's words from my mind and opened my arms to her – my darling daughter.

Chapter Fifty-Six

When the doctor came again he said I could get up for a couple of hours and go down to lunch. I said, 'But His Lordship, he don't eat lunch, so mebbe I could wait and take my two hours at dinner-time?' Smiling, he gave permission. I was still a bit shaky so I took longer to dress than usual that evening, and when I arrived downstairs the hall was empty. Nervously I pushed open the dining-room door – and saw he was already seated, with no place laid for me. I was starting to back out again when Mr Wallis said loudly, 'Her Ladyship's come down, my lord.'

Thrusting his chair back Lord Warminster jumped to his feet and turned round to look at me. He was wearing a dinner jacket, so he'd obviously planned to dine alone and I faltered, 'I could go upstairs again.'

'Tims – lay a place for Her Ladyship.' Mr Tims picked up the silver and went to the end of the long table. 'Not right down there! She doesn't want to have to shout.' Mr Wallis gave me the ghost of a wink as Mr Tims came back and set a place for me on my lord's right hand. Lord Warminster waited until I'd sat down before dropping back into his own seat and asking, 'Are you – fully recovered?'

'Aye, my lord – I be much better, thank 'ee.'

'Good – good.'

Celery soup, baked sole, veal cutlets, roast duckling – they all came and went in silence; several times he glanced at me as if he wanted to speak, but he didn't. Cheese fritters followed the brown bread pudding, and then disappeared in their turn, and now only the dessert was left. As he peeled his orange I took the bull by the horns. 'My lord, there were something as I been wanting to ask you.' He looked at me, warily. 'Thic fellow Odysseus – did he get away from the giant?'

His face lightened into a smile as he replied, 'Yes, he did.' I looked up at him expectantly, and he went on, 'He and his men made the giant drunk, then they heated a tree trunk in the fire and drove it into his eye.'

I exclaimed, 'And he did only have the one!'.

'Exactly. But blinded as he was the giant sat guarding the entrance of his cave every day, after he'd moved the huge boulder, so they couldn't get past.'

I prompted, 'But you did say as they escaped?'

'Under his sheep. His sheep went out each day to graze, and he felt their backs, but Odysseus told his men to cling to the wool of their bellies.'

'They must have been main big sheep!'

He smiled. 'They were – but remember, those sheep belonged to a giant.' He dropped his napkin and stood up. As I drew level with him he asked, formally, 'May I join you in the drawing room – just for a minute?'

I asked Mr Tims for an extra cup and sat waiting. When Lord Warminster came in he was carrying the Harrods catalogue. He put it down on the table saying, 'Order yourself some slippers, and any other items of night attire that you need.' He turned to go.

Very quickly I called after him, 'Would you like a cup o' coffee?' Slowly he returned to sit on the end of the sofa opposite. I told him how Flora had climbed up to my dressing table all by herself, and put one of my rose combs in her own hair. He listened without speaking, but at least he wasn't burning his throat on the coffee this time. Only he was drinking it quite quickly, and I knew he'd go as soon as he'd finished, so I summoned up my courage and said, 'My lord thic fellow Odysseus, he were a main artful card, and I'd like to read them tales about him – so mebbe you could learn I Greek?'

He put down his empty cup and said, 'Don't you think you should learn to speak English first?' Then he got up and walked out.

I was crying as I opened the catalogue, then a tear dropped on the page and made a damp splodge, so I swallowed and swallowed until I'd managed to stop. I wrote down the cheapest dressing gown I could find, made of plain white twill flannel piped with navy. I didn't like the style at all – it was dull and middle-aged and all bunchy at the back. I added the plainest pair of navy blue carpet slippers then closed the catalogue; I didn't feel like making an imaginary list today. Instead I went upstairs to fetch his copy of *The Odyssey*, and when Mr Tims came in to fetch the tray I gave it to him along with the catalogue and the list, saying, 'Would you take these to His Lordship, please?' Then I climbed up to the nursery for a last peep at Flora before going straight to bed.

Next day at dinner he made several remarks about the weather. I answered only 'Yes' or 'No', and by the time the roast was served he'd stopped speaking. It was the same the following evening, except that he'd lapsed into silence before the fish plates were collected, and the third day he didn't speak at all, except for his opening and closing 'Good evening.'

On Thursday I was in the drawing room with Flora when Mr Tims came in with three parcels; one was obviously the dressing gown and slippers, but the others were smaller and heavier. Flora's chubby fingers helped mine with the knots, and she crowed with delight when we unwrapped a large brown volume. Looking at the spine I saw it was a dictionary. When I opened it there was page after page of words: words that I didn't know the meaning of and he would – but it wasn't a Greek dictionary, it was an English one. I put it down heavily on the table. I wouldn't bother to open the other parcels. Flora patted them hopefully. 'No, Flora, Mama dussent want 'em.' She tugged unavailingly at the knot, and I repeated, 'No, Flora.'

She stretched her arms right round the parcel and looking up at me out of her bright blue eyes said, 'Gi' her to I, gi' her to I!' The Lady Flora Elizabeth Fitwarren-Donne, speaking in Wiltshire dialect – like Clara, like Ellen, like me. The nurse Lord Warminster had engaged, she'd spoken properly. I realised now that that was one of the reasons he had engaged her, but he'd dismissed that nurse, for my sake – and now his grand-daughter was speaking in a way that would brand her for the rest of her life, just as I was branded.

I couldn't go on sulking any longer. Side by side with Flora I attacked the second parcel: when I shook out the contents she squealed with delight. First came a deep pink cashmere dressing gown, with a fitted yoke and a satin appliqué embroidery of leaves and flowers in paler pink all round the neck and cuffs; then came slippers made of soft glacé kid and adorned with pink satin bows: they wouldn't have been out of place in a ballroom. 'Pretty!' Flora hugged one to her chest as I unwrapped the third parcel. It was another book but this one had a green cover with a design of pillars and trees on it, all embossed in gold. The title was in gold too: *Myths, Legends and Histories of the Greeks*. I opened it to discover story after story – all in English, of course, so I could read them. There were pictures of statues and paintings, too, some of them even in colour. It was a beautiful book.

I told him that when I thanked him in the hall that evening, but he just waved my thanks aside, as he had done before – only this time I was determined not to give up. As he neared the end of his carrot soup I told him that I'd already been reading the story of the Siege of Troy, 'So I dussent need to know Greek, but my lord, I did wonder if you could mebbe learn I to speak English properly, instead.'

I watched a dull red flush creep up under his tilted chin. Then he said, without looking at me, 'Most people – would think – that I lack – both the – necessary patience, and the –' the last word took a long time coming, ' – fluency, to teach anyone – to speak English.' He rang the bell.

I waited until Mr Tims and Mr Wallis had taken the tureen and soup plates away and we'd begun on our baked herrings then I said, 'I wouldn't mind if you did shout at I.' He looked at me in disbelief. I amended more honestly, 'Leastways, so long as you didn't shout too loud.'

There was a long pause before he asked, 'And what of – the other – problem?'

'Mebbe, if I did speak, you could just correct me?'

He put down his knife and fork. 'Speak, then – I am listening.' And of course, as soon as he said that I couldn't think of anything to say. I sat biting my lip and blushing at my own stupidity until he came to my rescue. 'Tell me – what did you read about today?'

' 'Twere a story about a soldier called Ach – Achills –'

'Achilles.' I said it carefully after him and he nodded before asking, 'And what did you think of him?'

'I thought as he did behave like a gurt babby, sulking in his tent like that, so his friend had to go and get killed instead, just because the King took thic slave girl off of him. And her, what about her?' I felt my indignation rising. 'Her, thic Briseis maid, nobody did ask her which o' the two she preferred – *if* she preferred either o' 'em, which I doubt, the King being near as childish as thic Achilles. I doubt she did moon about all sulky. Besides, she wouldn't have had the time.' I saw his eyebrows go up and added hastily, 'What wi' cooking the food and washing the pots and, er, such-like.'

'Ah, but surely Achilles may be forgiven for sulking, since he was a hero.'

I exclaimed, 'He weren't no hero!' My lord frowned but I didn't pause. 'He knew, didn't he, as how his mam had dipped him in thic there River Styx, so he couldn't be killed – all but for his heel, being as she had to hold somewhere to keep him from drowning. Now any man wi' an ounce o' sense, knowing that, would 'a made hisself the most biggest, strongest boot out o' the thickest oxhide he could come by and put his foot in and laced it up tight as tight and never taken it off, not even when he were in bed. But this Achilles, does he do that? Oh no, he goes off to fight wearing sandals – sandals! Serve him right getting killed say I, for being such a gurt fool.' I sat back and looked at my lord, waiting for his corrections. He gave an odd kind of snorting sound and I leant forward anxiously, thinking he was choking on a fishbone – and then I realised he was laughing, actually laughing.

I said doubtfully, 'I didn't realise it were meant to be a comic tale.'

'It wasn't, but you made it into one.' He was still chuckling to himself.

I flushed. 'I'm sorry I did make a fool o' myself.'

He stopped laughing and said quickly, 'You didn't. You just saw it from a different viewpoint. It was most – refreshing.' I could still feel the expression of doubt on my face; he leant towards me a little and said, 'I enjoyed your tale. Thank you – Amy.'

And it was the first time he'd ever spoken my name downstairs without being drunk; now my flush was one of pleasure. Then I suddenly remembered, and said anxiously, 'But I did tell it in Wiltshire – and I was supposed to be speaking English.'

He hesitated, as if searching for words, then he said carefully, 'In point of fact, the Wiltshire dialect is an older form of English. It was the correct form once upon a time, so as Homer is an ancient storyteller it was appropriate that you should use archaic language.'

I knew that really I'd been slipshod, but I was grateful to him for covering up for me – and he had called me Amy. So I said, 'Thank 'ee, my lord,' and smiled at him. He picked up his knife and fork then looked up again – and smiled back.

After that evening I was much more comfortable with him. There were still some days when the black dog was on his shoulder and he only said 'Yes' or 'No' or simply grunted when I spoke; but I'd got more used to him by now and just chattered on without expecting anything in reply except snapped corrections. Other days when he was in a good mood he would explain as he put right my mistakes, and soon I was hardly making any, until one evening he said, 'You are speaking quite correctly now. You don't need me to listen to you any longer.'

I felt my face fall. 'But, there's no point in my talking, if you don't want to listen.'

He put down his knife and fork. 'I said that you didn't *need* me to listen – that doesn't mean I don't want to listen to you.' He turned his attention back to his chicken cutlet.

I thought over what he'd said then ventured, 'But that doesn't mean you *do* want to listen, either.'

Eventually he replied, without looking up, 'I think – I would find your silence rather oppressive. I have – become accustomed to your chatter.' He rang for Mr Tims.

So I had to be satisfied with that. Later as I drank my coffee alone in the drawing room I thought of the tale of Beauty and the Beast. Lucky Beauty, she knew the Beast liked talking to her, because he asked her to marry him every night. But then my lord could hardly do that, because I was married to him already. With a sigh I put down my coffee cup and went upstairs for my last glimpse of Flora. Her eyes were tightly closed and her hair spread its silken strands over the pillow, daffodil yellow in the glow of the night-light, just like her father's. I remembered his face laughing up at me from the pillow. It was wrong, I knew it was wrong – but I couldn't help remembering. Flora was growing up; soon she'd be two and not a baby any longer. I sighed again as with one last, lingering look I left the nursery and went back to my big, lonely bedroom.

I didn't feel sleepy, so I read from my book instead. I'd learnt a lot from that book; I'd learnt why he called the fairy rose Persephone – after the maiden who had to spend six months of the year in the underworld, with her dread husband, Pluto, and then when she came back to the earth above she brought spring with her. I read about Circe, the enchantress, who turned Odysseus' men into swine and, above all, I read about the Spartans. I knew now why Miss Annabel had said my lord was named after three great heroes. King Arthur I'd heard of before; Hector, so I discovered now, was the heroic warrior son of Priam, King of Troy, and Leonidas was the brave Spartan King who, knowing he was hopelessly outnumbered, had fought to the death at Thermopylae. I thought how odd it was that Lord Warminster of all people had been called by a Spartan name, because they were a cruel race who reared all their sons to be soldiers – and so any Spartan baby that was not physically perfect was left out on the mountainside to die. My lord would never have been allowed to live, had he been a Spartan. But then, I was no Spartan either, because even Spartan women had to be strong and brave – and I was neither. Yet sometimes, for all their bravery, I thought they were rather stupid, as in the tale of the Spartan boy who stole a fox and hid it under his cloak. Even when it began to gnaw at his belly, still he kept it hidden, because that was the way Spartans were – daft.

The following evening he said over the dessert, 'It's time you went to the dentist again.'

'What! But I haven't got toothache, truly I haven't.'

'You soon will have, if you don't go now. He told you you needed some fillings. You'd better go next week.'

'Will he give me gas?'

'Not for fillings, no.'

I asked, but I already knew the answer from his expression. 'Will it hurt?'

'It may do. Fillings vary.'

I dropped my eyes. 'Maybe, in the summer . . .'

'I'll write to Williams tomorrow and tell him you'll be in on Monday.' I didn't answer. He said firmly, 'I insist that you go. You don't want to have lost all your teeth by the time you're my age, do you?'

I protested, 'But that won't be for years and years!'

He frowned angrily. 'No doubt, but you may not be completely decrepit, even at my advanced age. You may still wish to chew the occasional bowl of invalid pap.' He jammed his hand down hard on the bell and turned on Mr Wallis as he came through the door. 'Where have *you* been?'

Mr Wallis said smoothly, 'Outside the door, my lord, waiting for you to ring.' My lord's face went even darker. When I left he didn't say good evening, just, 'Monday, the nine-forty.' I opened my mouth to plead, but he gave me such a ferocious glare I shut it again without a word.

The next evening he was still glaring as the fish arrived, so I said, 'My lord, I'm sorry I said that last night about you being old.'

As Mr Wallis slid a grilled mullet on to my plate he breathed, 'Be quiet!' I bent my head and pretended to be engrossed in searching for the mullet's backbone.

He didn't speak a word to me all dinner, but he shouted at Mr Tims for the water not being cold enough, and then bawled out Mr Wallis for being slow serving the gooseberry tart. After I'd left the dining room Mr Wallis beckoned me round the corner into the service corridor and said, 'My lady, if you must tweak the tiger's tail, please don't do it at dinner, for the sake of me and poor Tims. He's got enough worries as it is, with losing his footmen to the war.' Then he grinned at me. 'Use a bit of tact, do. When a man's married to a woman young enough to be his daughter the last thing he wants is to be reminded of it, especially by her.'

He didn't speak Saturday evening either except to say as I was leaving, 'Remember, the nine-forty train.'

I said desperately, 'My lord, I be terrible afeard. I mean, I'm very frightened.'

'Are you telling me you're an arrant coward?' He was still glaring.

'I don't know what arr –'

His bark interrupted me. 'A, double R, A, N, T. Look it up!'

As soon as the soup had been served next day I told him, 'My lord, I did look that word up and the answer is yes, I *am* an arrant coward.' He stared at me, then all at once he gave a snort of laughter. Mr Wallis turned to grin at me before closing the door behind him. I gabbled, 'My lord, will you come with me?'

His smile vanished. He'd nearly finished his soup before he muttered, 'I'll see.'

He was waiting in the hall on Monday morning; he didn't look at all pleased but he was there, and my fears subsided a little. He sat behind his paper all the way to Salisbury, but he did finally speak as I dragged my way up the steps to the dreaded door. 'Take your gloves off and pinch your finger hard while he's using the drill, then you won't notice it so much.'

There were two red dents in my forefinger when I came out again, but at least it was over for the time being. The dentist said he'd found another cavity and I'd have to come back the next Monday – but that was a long way off. In the meantime I trembled with relief. On the way back in the train my lord put his newspaper up as soon as he sat down, but when the other passengers got out at Tilton and we'd started off again he lowered the paper to say, 'It wasn't *that* bad, was it?' And I realised what he was up to. He wasn't using his paper as a barrier against me but as a shield against the other passengers; he couldn't bear them looking at his face or his twisted shoulder. I remembered how he'd asked me to move the candle that night in the study: 'I don't like eyes looking at me . . .'

Suddenly he barked, 'What are you staring at me for?'

And even as I opened my mouth to tell him I recalled Mr Wallis' warning and said instead, 'I was thinking . . . wondering if you'd come with me again next week?'

The tension left him. 'I suppose so. It's simpler than writing to Williams to explain why you failed to turn up.'

He did come with me, and the drill hardly hurt. In no time I was outside the door again. Then, just as the cab drew up, a man's voice called, 'Warminster! How do you do?' My lord turned slowly round and a gentleman came striding up to us. Although he was obviously as old as Lord Warminster he was wearing uniform – and his arm was in a sling.

'How are you, George?'

'Improving every day, now they've got all that damn shrapnel out.'

'Leonidas!' A small plump lady suddenly appeared at the officer's elbow. 'How nice to see you, Leonidas.' The feathers in her hat bobbed up and down as she swung round to look at me. 'And is this your new wife?' A pair of bulging blue eyes surveyed me from head to toe. 'Well, well – no wonder – but what a fool Annabel was to have a girl like this about her. One likes one's own maid to look presentable, but . . .'

'Mother!' The khaki-clad man broke in sharply, then said to my lord, 'Leonidas, old chap, you must introduce us to your wife.'

My lord was terse. 'Amy – Colonel Sir George Burton, Lady Burton.'

Plump hands seized mine and I was engulfed in a cloud of violet scent. 'Amy! Such a nice short name – I do like short names – so much more convenient. How are you, my dear?' I found myself being edged along the pavement. 'We'll let the men have a little chat – George and Leonidas were at Eton together, both collegers you know, so they saw a lot of each other even though there's a year between them. They'll want to talk about the war, men always do. Now, my dear,' her voice dropped, confidentially. 'Tell me, how *is* Leonidas treating you?'

I said, 'He's been very kind.' She didn't look as if she believed me so I explained, 'I were afeard of the dentist, so he came with me.'

'Oh.' She sounded almost disappointed. Then, shaking her head she added, 'You don't have to put on a brave face with me, my dear – I know what a bear he can be at times.'

I said firmly, 'He's been very good to me. Why, when I bled and bled after I had my tooth out he held the basin to catch the blood.'

The feathers jumped as she exclaimed, 'Of course! Just the thing – why didn't I think of it before? Leonidas, Leonidas!' She was rushing back down the pavement. 'Leonidas, I need you – for my hospital! The Vicar's daughters are such dear girls, but one shouldn't expect them to shave men, and as for bedpans . . . Sister's getting quite worn out, and Collins is really *so* sulky about lending a hand in the wards, though I suppose with the footmen joining up . . .'

Her son broke in, explaining, 'Mother's running a Red Cross Hospital at Belling – I expect you've heard, Warminster, and she's right, she really could do with more reliable assistance.'

'Your little wife has just told me how splendid you were when she haemorrhaged.'

My lord swung his shoulder round so as to give me the full benefit of his glower. I took a step backwards as he said, 'Lady Burton, I really don't think –'

One plump gloved hand descended on his arm like the talons of a bird of prey. 'You can't bury yourself in your roses now, Leonidas – your country needs you. After all, George is older than you and he's already been wounded twice in the service of his King.'

There was a charged silence. My lord looked like an injured bear at bay – I didn't know what to do – then Colonel Burton spoke, pitching his voice as though he intended to sound casual. 'You might as well give it a go, Leonidas – it's the only way to shut Mother up! Besides, she does need some help – the elder clerical daughter's a fearsome sight with a razor; she nearly sliced through one poor corporal's jugular the other day. He told me later he'd felt safer back at Yprès!'

Lady Burton said firmly, 'I'll expect you at seven o'clock tomorrow, Leonidas, then you can help serve the breakfasts. Goodbye, and goodbye to you too, my dear. So nice to have met you at last.' The officer raised his cane and they were both gone.

My lord rounded on me. 'You talk too much!' He was absolutely livid with rage.

I said, 'Mebbe he could shave the corporal – that Colonel Burton.'

'Don't be stupid! He's an officer.'

'But you be a lord!'

'As far as the British Army is concerned I don't exist – I am worthless.'

As soon as we were on the train he pulled open the *Times* with such violence that it ripped. He sat behind the torn pieces all the way back to Eston, even though there was no one else in the compartment; not a shield this time but a barrier – against me.

He held an invisible *Times* in front of his face all through dinner, too. Afterwards I went to find Mr Wallis. 'Mr Wallis, couldn't *you* go and shave the men instead?'

'No, it ain't my job. And no, I'm not offering. That really would put the tin lid on it, implying he couldn't even manage to do his bit by juggling a few bedpans around.'

'Then mebbe I –'

'Oh yes, you'd be a big success, wouldn't you? If one o' them so much as cut his finger they'd have to scrape you up off the floor.' My eyes began to prickle. Mr Wallis said firmly, 'Look, my lady, let him go. It'll do him good to see some other poor so-and-sos worse off than himself. Might make him start counting his blessings.'

505

I watched him leave from behind my bedroom curtain. Clara had told me it was four miles to Belling and he was going to walk it; he was having his breakfast at five-thirty and leaving at six. As the stable clock began to strike a hump-backed, lopsided figure emerged from under the portico and set off trudging down the drive, with Nella close behind. He didn't look like someone who was counting his blessings.

Chapter Fifty-Seven

I worried about him all day. However would he cope? He did so hate meeting strangers, and anyway he was used to people waiting on him, not the other way round; I couldn't imagine him serving breakfasts. And then, he was so set in his ways. His daily routine was all mapped out, right up to that final walk around the rose garden with Nella just before he went to bed. Even then he followed exactly the same route every evening; I remembered Joe Dempster telling me once that when Lord Warminster was at Kew he'd taken Nella out instead and she'd set off padding along the paths without having to be told, even stopping and sitting down at certain places where in summer there was an especially fine view of the roses, or a particularly sweet scent.

By now I'd learnt his daily routine too, so that I could keep out of his way, but although I never usually saw him during the day the house seemed quite empty without him. Flora was puzzled too. 'Papa – Papa? Nella?' I took her out myself at the times she normally spent with him, but she was obviously looking for him. Every time she heard a man's footstep she'd spin round, only to droop in disappointment when she saw it wasn't her grand-father after all. Then, while she was in the drawing room with me after tea, Mr Tims appeared and said, 'His Lordship is back, my lady. He asked if you could send Lady Flora to him in the library at six o'clock, just for a few minutes before she goes upstairs.'

It was only half-past five but I held out my hand to my daughter. 'Papa's home, Flora.'

She tugged me towards the doorway and all the way across the hall to the library. As soon as I opened the door she dropped my hand and scampered forward shrieking, 'Papa! Papa!' His usual lumbering movements suddenly accelerated as he almost ran to meet her, then she was swinging up in his arms, squealing with joy. I felt a spasm of jealousy, but when he turned to me saying, 'It – is not – six, yet,' I replied, 'It doesn't matter. 'Tis your turn now,' and closed the door behind me.

After his usual 'Good evening,' in the hall he didn't speak again over dinner, and I didn't dare ask him how he'd got on – he looked so tired and drawn. It took me until the dessert to pluck up the courage to say, 'Flora, she did miss you today.'

'And I – missed her.'

I nerved myself for the sacrifice. 'If you wanted, you could go up to the nursery at six, for when she's having her bath and getting ready for bed – instead of me.' I crossed my fingers under the table that he wouldn't say yes, because I did so love bathing her and towelling her slippery little body dry and then rocking her on my lap while I sang a lullaby – but it was my fault he wasn't seeing her during the day.

At last he replied, 'Perhaps, if she had a longer nap in the afternoon, she might go to bed half an hour later. Then she could come to the library until half-past six – and you would still be able to put her to bed.'

'Oh, thank you my lord.' Then I said all of a rush, 'I'm terrible sorry about my careless tongue – I wouldn't ever've spoken if I'd known.'

He didn't answer for quite a long time, then he said slowly, 'I am of very little use to my country, but now she is at war it is right that I should make some contribution, however slight.' Then he rang for Mr Tims and told him dinner would be at seven-thirty from now on. Mr Tims looked rather upset, and I knew why. Mrs Johnstone would be furious – she liked her routine, too. She'd never stopped complaining about dinner being served at eight the time when Lord and Lady Quinham had been staying at Eston last year. If I thought of them as Lord and Lady Quinham like that they seemed more distant. I could pretend that I didn't long for him so much, or feel so terribly guilty about Miss Annabel.

But it didn't work the next morning when I saw the letter. It was from America and I recognised her handwriting at once. I'd seen his letters to her waiting for the postman but I'd not seen her replies before; he must have picked them up straight away before he started going to Lady Burton's. Now the sight of her handwriting made me feel sick and ill with guilt.

My lord scarcely spoke to me for the next fortnight; it was if he opened an invisible *Times* over the soup and never closed it until he'd finished his dessert, when he'd stand up and say, 'Good evening.'

Then on the Sunday Mr Tims came to the drawing room and said there'd been a 'phone call from Lady Burton. My lord had been delayed and wouldn't be back until later. 'Shall I tell Mrs Procter to wait dinner, my lady?' When I said yes, he added, 'Do you wish to dine at the normal time, my lady, or to dine later, with His Lordship?'

I looked up at Mr Tims and asked, 'Which do you think he'd prefer?'

Mr Tims' usual anxious look deepened. 'I really don't know, my lady. Perhaps you'd like a few minutes to think it over?'

I didn't know what to say, so in the end I went and waylaid Mr Wallis. 'What do you think I should do, Mr Wallis?'

'I can't speak for His Lordship,' he held up his hand to prevent my interrupting him, 'but if I had a wife I'd want her to wait dinner and eat with me.'

I chose my words with care. 'Even if you never spoke to her when you were eating?'

He pursed his lips, then said, 'Mebbe, if I'd been hard at work all day doing things as I'd never done before – especially if I was a man who usually kept out of the way o' strangers – then mebbe I might not feel like talking in the evenings. But that don't mean I might not like to hear someone else chattering, about my grand-daughter, or my roses, for instance.'

I made up my mind at once. 'Tell Mr Tims to wait dinner for me, too.'

I sat in the drawing room in my evening dress; it was almost nine before Mr Tims came for me. As I went out into the hall my lord came down the stairs in his dinner jacket. He stopped in surprise, asking, 'Haven't you dined yet?' I shook my head. He came down the last few steps and said, 'Then shall we – go in, now?'

Over the tomato soup I told him how when I'd taken Flora out we'd seen a squirrel, just sitting on a branch nibbling an acorn, as bold as bold could be. I'd whispered to Flora to keep quite still so as not to disturb his breakfast and she'd been as good as gold, never moving an inch until the squirrel had finished his acorn and disappeared with a flick of his bushy red tail. I saw that my lord was listening. Mr Wallis had been right.

The next day I saw Mr Wallis ahead of me in the corridor as I was going up to the nursery, so I speeded up to overtake him. 'Mr Wallis, you were quite right –' then I broke off. His face was deathly white and he was shaking. Putting my hand on his arm I asked, 'Mr Wallis – whatever's the matter?'

He turned to look at me, tears in his eyes. 'I've just had a telegram – those bloody Huns have torpedoed Fred's ship. He's posted Missing, but we all know what that means.' He had to swallow before he could bring himself to continue. 'It wasn't a battleship – Fred's a merchant seaman. They were only carrying cargo, so they'd be sitting ducks . . .' He couldn't go on.

I took him down to the drawing room and made him sit in front of the fire, then I rang for Mr Tims to fetch him a large brandy. He drank it down in one gulp and began to cry, sobbing like Flora did. I went over to the sofa and knelt on the seat beside him so I could put my arms right round his shaking body. His head dropped down on to my breast and I cradled it there, stroking his hair and murmuring to him – just as I did with Flora when she was upset.

At last he drew back, and blew his nose hard before saying, 'You're a good girl, Amy – I hope the old so-and-so learns to appreciate you. I'd best get back to my work now – and thanks, lovey.'

Two days later he came to tell me he'd given in his notice. 'I'm going to enlist. I know I'm not as young as I was, but Fred, he was ten years older than me, and those bloody Boches still killed him. So I want to have a crack at them myself, for his sake – he was all I had left in the world.'

'I'll miss you, Mr Wallis – and so will His Lordship. I know he do rely on you – he won't take kindly to a new valet.'

Mr Wallis shook his head. 'He says he won't have one, not now he's given up the flat at Kew. Didn't he tell you? He let it go while he was in bed all that time with his leg. And of course the house in Belgrave Square is back on his hands now, so he's decided he'll use that if he needs to be in Town. But I doubt he'll go far these days – he's too attached to the little 'un. Anyway, that was what he really needed a valet for – the travelling and waiting on him at Kew, so he reckons that when I go he'll shave and dress himself, and run his own bath, even, as long as Mr Tims'll lay out his things for him and keep his clothes in order.'

'But Mr Tims, he's got more'n enough to do already, and he's old. Brushing clothes, that's a lot o' work.'

'You and I know that, my lady, but I doubt his Lordship does. And of course Tims said yes – obviously any butler's done that kind o' thing in the past – but I do feel as though I've dropped him in it.'

And that was when I had my idea. It took me a while to persuade Mr Wallis, and even longer to talk Mr Tims round, but in the end they both gave in. I would look after my lord's clothes, and tidy his dressing room and arrange his things – while he was out, of course – we were all agreed on that. We all knew he wouldn't like it at all if he discovered what was going on, but as Mr Wallis said, there was no reason why he should find out.

Lord Warminster had let Mr Wallis cut his notice down to a fortnight, so for the next two weeks I became Mr Wallis' shadow, learning what I had to do. The very first morning I walked into the brushing room I felt a lift of the spirits: those plain whitewashed walls, the huge scrubbed table, the sink, the flat-topped stove with the irons placed ready; everything spoke of a workroom – and I couldn't wait to get back to work again. Mr Wallis handed me my lord's jacket and I laid it out and picked up the brush: up the nap to get the dust out, then down it to make the cloth smooth and neat. The strong sweeping strokes, the firm flick of the wrist – it all came back to me as if I'd never had a break from it. Mr Wallis gave me his spare set of brushes, and a lovely bone – from a deer, it was – so I could get a brilliant shine on my lord's boots. Even the gloomy boot hall was a treat to visit, now I'd got a job to do again.

I was nervous upstairs, though. I'd never been in Lord Warminster's dressing room before, let alone his bathroom, but Mr Wallis explained the bath would have to be cleaned by me or Mr Tims. 'He won't let the housemaids come in here at all – I reckon it's because he sheds so much of his hair. You have to make sure it's not blocking up the plughole – look at it now.' Mr Wallis' fingers dislodged a fine tuft of black hair. 'He's as bad as the dog when it comes to moulting. Still, I suppose with him growing hair all over hisself he's got near as much to shed as she has. Now, he likes his towels folded just so – and then we'll go through and see to his shaving gear.' I wrenched my mind back from the fascinating thought of Lord Warminster being completely covered with fine

511

dark hair and concentrated on Mr Wallis' demonstration of all the paraphernalia of a gentleman's shaving. There was a little spirit Etna to heat the water in his shaving mug, an opal-lined soap bowl, a small rubber-rimmed lather pot, the shaving brush hanging in its stand so it could drip dry – and, of course, the razors. There were seven of them, in a leather case of their own: each one had an ivory handle and a wickedly glinting blade engraved with the appropriate day of the week. I remembered how Uncle Alf had only shaved on a Saturday night, but Mr Wallis told me Lord Warminster shaved twice a day. 'And even then it'll start gaining on him if he don't watch it.'

'They do look sharp. Where's the strop?'

'Ah, now that *is* a job for Tims. I'm not having you slicing your fingers off.' I shuddered as we moved on to the wardrobes and chests of drawers. Mr Wallis explained which clothes had to be laid out and when. There wouldn't be a problem in the day-time, now he was at Lady Burton's, but in order to turn his bed down and get his clothes and shaving things ready for the next morning, I'd have to sneak in while he was taking his final walk round the rose garden, Mr Wallis said. 'Lucky he's not as untidy as a lot of gentlemen, but he has his moments. When he's in a bad mood everything's thrown on the floor. Still, that's the way the gentry are.' I nodded; I knew. Mr Wallis shrugged. 'At least His Lordship don't expect me to put his socks on for him and kneel down to lace his boots, like my last gentleman did. Now, do you think you can manage?'

'Oh yes, Mr Wallis. It'll be less trouble than looking after a lady.'

Mr Wallis smiled. 'He certainly don't need any elaborate coiffures! He won't even wear dressing on his hair when he's in the country – says he can't stand the smell of it. Right, then. Tomorrow you can do everything, and I'll just check it.'

Next day I bustled around in his dressing room, laying out shaving things, toothbrush, hairbrush and comb. I'd already guessed Lord Warminster didn't use dressing at Eston, because his hair always looked slightly rumpled, not sleek and smooth like . . . Resolutely I turned my thoughts back to the task I'd chosen to undertake. Collar studs and cufflinks to be laid out next, waistcoat and shirt buttons to be fastened in ready for him to wear, tailcoat

– I paused to admire the skilful tailoring, cut to fit just so over his hump – high wing collar – except that it wasn't high on one side, that had been specially made, too – dress trousers, black evening pumps, vest, underpants. When I'd finished I turned to look at Mr Wallis, waiting for his nod of approval. As soon as it came I moved out of the dressing room, across the big bedroom – rather quickly, because I felt an intruder there – and on into his bathroom opening out of the other side, just as mine did. After tidying the towels I picked up the cleaning cloth, then remembered the plughole. As I scraped the small collection of fine dark hairs out of it I recollected what Mr Wallis had told me – fancy Lord Warminster growing hair all over himself like that! I tried to picture it as I sprinkled salt on the cloth and began to rub at the smooth white surface.

I tried to picture it again at dinner that evening, as soon as Lord Warminster's attention was firmly fixed on his soup. It wasn't difficult to imagine with him actually sitting there, because obviously that luxuriant growth of black hair springing up on the back of his hands was far too vigorous to simply disappear when it met his cuffs. 'All over', Mr Wallis had said – what a pity it was covered up by his clothes. I thought how nice it would be if just for once he took off his jacket and shirt and came for coffee in the drawing room in his vest; then I thought how it'd be even nicer if he'd let me stroke him, he'd feel so silken soft and warm . . . All at once I realised how improper I was being, and my face flushed scarlet.

He looked up. 'Are you – too warm?'

I managed to mutter a reply, 'Just a little, my lord.'

Those two weeks of working with Mr Wallis seemed to fly past, and then the morning of his departure arrived. I had a lump in my throat as I said goodbye. 'I'll miss you, Mr Wallis. You've been so kind to me.'

'I'll miss you too, my lady.' Then he added, his voice serious, 'I admire the way you've buckled down and tried to be a good wife to him, Amy.'

I said doubtfully, 'I don't think as I've been good enough though, Mr Wallis. There's times I know I've been a burden to him.'

He smiled at me. 'You get on and fill that nursery for him, Amy

513

– he won't think you're a burden then. Goodbye and all the best.' He shook me warmly by the hand.

After he'd gone I went up to see Flora. The nursery was far too big for her alone, but I'd never be able to fill it. The tears welled up for the friend I'd lost and the babies I'd never have.

Yet it was better now, now I had something to do each day. What with Flora and caring for his clothes I'd probably have gone on placidly for months – if it hadn't been for Lady Burton. I was in the drawing room after tea; Ellen had brought Flora's Ark down with her and I was kneeling on the floor beside her as she set it out. ' 'Nother giraffe, Mama, 'nother giraffe.' I replied, 'Here it is, sweetheart,' just as the door opened and Mr Tims announced, 'Lady Burton, my lady.'

I scrambled to my feet as she swept in in a cloud of violet scent. 'My dear, I do hope I'm not intruding. Ah, how nice to see the little girl!'

Flora looked up and stared, then put the giraffe in her mouth. I said quickly, 'No, Flora – giraffes do taste nasty.'

Slowly she took it out and offered it to Lady Burton. 'No thank you, dear, I've already eaten. What a pretty child – the image of her father.' Flora, hearing the word, exclaimed, 'Papa!' Lady Burton beamed at her. 'I can see you're going to be a charmer, just like him.'

I said quickly, 'She do mean Lord Warminster, when she says Papa.'

'Oh. Still, he's been a tremendous help with the men – Sister is so pleased with him. Never shirks any duty, however unpleasant, she says – and we can't all be blessed with good looks, can we? Now, you must be wondering why I've come. I've a message from Leonidas. He asked me to 'phone – his speech is so much better these days, I suspect we've you to thank for that, but he still won't use the telephone. Only as I was on my way to see Stella I thought I'd drop off at Eston instead and see how you were.' Smiling, she settled herself down on the sofa. 'May I sit down, dear?'

'Yes – yes, o' course.'

'And if you sit down too we can have a nice little gossip, can't we?' As I subsided on to the sofa Flora came and pressed against my legs, but when I bent down to lift her on to my lap she wriggled away and dropped down on the rug to play with her Ark. Lady

514

Burton leant towards me. 'It must be a little lonely for her in that nursery all by herself.'

I said defensively, 'She's got Ellen, and the nursemaid – and I do take her out for walks.'

'Now that *isn't* what I meant, dear. Leonidas thinks the world of her, he often talks about her – but it's not the same, is it? As one of his own. But perhaps you're in an interesting condition already?' I froze. 'Now dear, I know I'm being a nosy old woman, but you aren't doing anything to *prevent* it, are you? You modern young wives are so much cleverer than we were. My Joan insisted she couldn't face the trouble of another baby for at *least* three years, but in your case . . .' She leant further forward, waiting. I didn't answer. 'Don't you *want* another baby, dear?'

I burst out, 'I want it more'n anything in the whole wide world!' And the total truth of what I'd said shocked me into a quivering silence.

'Ah.' A violet-scented glove patted my hand. 'I'm glad to hear you say that.' She talked on, but I hardly heard what she was saying. 'I'm very fond of Leonidas, for all his funny little ways. I knew his mother well, you know. She'd waited so long – twenty-seven years she'd been married before she conceived – and then to die before she'd held her baby in her arms . . . She never even saw him – but I always thought that was a blessing in disguise, his being born the way he was. But my dear, I'm sure *you* won't have to wait so long. After all, you've already made a start, haven't you, with little Flora? Poor dear Annabel! And of course, there's not been much time yet. When you came back from France Leonidas was completely tied up with his leg, he'd hardly have been able to . . . Another blessing in disguise, the accident, after a lifetime of dragging that hideous boot around with him. *Such* a clever man, that Mr Jones. George's agent is Welsh, you know – very brisk. George depends on him utterly. He needs a reliable agent with his having always been in the Grenadiers – a Burton tradition, you know, just like the Fitzwarren-Donnes, except for Leonidas, of course. Such an inappropriate name under the circumstances, but poor dear Elizabeth had chosen it before he was born, so old Lord Warminster let it stand. Such a shock for him, after waiting so long – he was nearly seventy, you know. He left marriage late, with being in the Army, but he carefully chose a very young bride, thinking that . . . only these things don't always happen as planned. It was very difficult for poor dear Elizabeth. Still, she never complained – she was always such a loyal wife. And then, when Lord Warminster finally got the son he'd wanted, the baby was . . . Still, as I said, Leonidas' manner has been much better recently – he hasn't been so almost-normal since he was up at Cambridge, just before he met Jeanette. Well dear, I've enjoyed our little chat, but I must be going now. Stella will be expecting me.' She stood up, and I jumped up too, trying to collect my scattered wits.

'Lady Burton – the message from my lord?'

'Ah, I quite forgot. Don't wait dinner for him, he'll eat with George. There are some patients due on the late train so he volunteered to stay and help Sister settle them in. It isn't worth his while to walk all the way home and back again. By the way, I've told him to get a little motor – he's never been a good horseman but it's too far to walk every day, and he was soaking when he arrived yesterday morning. He can drive himself, people do nowadays, with all the chauffeurs enlisting – they're so useful in the Royal Engineers, George tells me. Leonidas was always so good at Latin as a boy – I'm sure he'll soon get the hang of a motor. Thank goodness old Wilson agreed to learn to drive when Andrews volunteered.' I was enveloped in a violet haze as she clasped my hand. 'He isn't very good at it. We jump, you know, every time he starts – and the noise when he changes the gears . . .' she shuddered. 'But I do find his habit of always saying, "Whoa" before he puts the brakes on so delightfully reassuring! Goodbye dear, must fly!' She turned back for a moment. 'And about the other little matter . . . Don't worry, these things sometimes take a little time, but it will happen, I know. Goodbye.'

I stood swaying by the door. She was wrong, it wouldn't, not ever – not even in twenty-seven years. He'd never so much as touch me, let alone . . . I turned to look at Flora's fair head, bent over the red-painted roof of her Ark. She was growing up, she was a little girl now. I loved her, I loved her so much – but I wanted a baby, a baby to kick in my womb and tug at my breast. Before, Lady Burton had forced me to admit that I'd felt a sense of emptiness, of something missing. But now it wasn't just a feeling of loss, it was a longing: a longing for what I wanted more than

516

anything else in the whole wide world – and knew I could never have.

PART SIX

Chapter Fifty-eight

Spring came. The new leaves on the trees were alive in their greenness, and birds sang of their joy in the reborn sunlight. I took Flora to see the new lambs gambolling in the fields around the home farm, and as I looked at the fat, contented ewes suckling their young I envied them. My longing was growing in intensity with each lengthening day.

While I sat sewing in the drawing room one afternoon my mind kept going back again and again to that one desire. I didn't want to darn stockings, I wanted to embroider tiny bonnets and bibs. Putting down my needle I slipped off my thimble and picked up the book Lord Warminster had given me. I would read, instead – anything to distract my thoughts from that one, all-consuming passion. But it didn't work, the Greeks had babies too. Zeus, the King of the Gods, never seemed to stop begetting children: he turned himself into a bull to run off with Europa, and then she had two sons; and there was Danae, whose father shut her up in a tower so she couldn't be wed – but Zeus came to her in a shower of gold, and so she had a baby too. I thought that I'd like to conceive in a shower of gold – it wouldn't hurt like it did when a man kept thrusting his rod into your cunny – but then I shut the book and admitted that although I was a terrible coward I didn't care how much it would hurt, so long as I got my baby. I turned over the pages again. Aphrodite: although she was a goddess she was no better than she ought to be. She was married to the lame and ugly blacksmith god, Vulcan, but she was always running around with other men and she had a baby by one of them, little Eros. I searched for the story of Penelope – I should be safe reading that, as I knew she'd only had the one child, like me, before her husband Odysseus went off to the war, just like the father of my child had done.

It was no use. The very name Penelope reminded me of that first

521

day I'd met him in the Park and he'd christened the parasol girl – and I lost control of my fingers so that they quickly turned the pages to find his picture. The statue was labelled *Adonis* – but the minute I'd first seen it I'd known it was him. He was naked except for a cloak thrown carelessly over his shoulders and a pair of sandals on his feet – those long, slender feet leading up to his shapely calves and muscular thighs. He was wearing something else too: it looked like a leaf off a fig tree and it was just big enough to cover his rod and balls – to make him respectable for the photograph, I suppose – but it didn't succeed. He was bulging underneath it and as I stared at the photograph it was as if that leaf was made of gauze and I could see what was there, all of it – my body seemed to melt. I slammed the book shut and scrabbled for my needle; darning was safer.

As I darned I forced my mind to dwell on how fortunate I was. I had my daughter, she had a name, given her by her Granfer, who loved her. He'd been kind to me, too – and Lady Burton was right – since he'd been helping at the hospital he had changed. He'd become less prickly, more ready to listen, even, on occasion, to talk to me. Back in the winter I'd have been so grateful for that, but now I wouldn't care if he snapped and snarled at me every night if only . . . Hastily I packed my sewing away. It was really too early to prepare his dressing room, but I had to distract myself somehow.

Upstairs my hands moved mechanically. Collar studs, cufflinks, braces, sock suspenders – I reached for his jacket, with that peculiar, distorted shoulder – and remembered his voice in the library saying: 'I'm too damaged to touch any woman.' Firmly I scolded myself. He'd given me the choice, he'd offered to set me free, even tried to send me away – it was *my* choice to stay. But I hadn't thought, I hadn't realised – and my mind kept repeating that hopeless refrain: 'I'm damaged, I'm damaged.'

I didn't mean to be angry with him. I tried to talk normally at dinner, but my thoughts kept veering off at a tangent. He'd bought a motor as Lady Burton had suggested, from the Vicar of a village over the Down. Mr Selby had arranged it for him and showed him how to drive it and he'd been using it for several weeks, but this evening it had been raining and I'd asked him if he'd got very wet – I'd completely forgotten about the motor. He sounded put out, almost hurt as he said gruffly, 'The Rover has a full hood, that's why I procured it.'

I stammered, 'Aye – yes, o' course. I did forget . . .' My voice trailed away in confusion.

He spoke again. 'Have I – offended you – in some way?'

'No – no, o' course not.' I flushed.

Putting down his knife and fork he watched my face as he said, 'These past weeks you have looked – unhappy. Is there anything I can do – to help?' There was a long pause, then he added, 'Amy?'

He so rarely spoke my name that now he did I felt the tears come to my eyes; frantically I tried to blink them away. 'No, thank 'ee, there baint nothing. I mean,' I was fighting for control, 'there isn't anything you can do.'

There was silence. He picked up his knife and fork and began eating again. Then, as he swallowed, he said, 'If there is, please do ask me.' But it was no use asking him, he couldn't do it; he'd told me so himself.

Clara gave me snippets of news about the war. The Germans had sunk a huge liner called the *Lusitania*, and Cyril Beeston, the Rector's nephew had been wounded in a big battle near Yprès. I knew now that Clara was worrying about Jim Arnold, who'd driven me to Eston that first day so long ago. Jim had been sent to Egypt, along with some of the other young men who'd joined up from Eston village. 'He did ask I to write to him, and I do, regular, but –' Unconsciously her hand went up to touch the port-wine stain on her cheek. She sighed, 'I frets. He never could abide the hot weather, Jim couldn't.' I fretted too. Sometimes a gesture of Flora's reminded me of her father, and fear sliced through me like a knife. Was he still in England? I didn't know.

I began to dream about him: running beside me again with Earl in the Park, or lying back in the punt as I fed him bite-sized morsels of food. Then one terrible night I dreamt I was with him again in the housemaid's closet – only now I was leaning towards him, pressing my body against his, catching at his rod with frantic fingers before thrusting it inside me, holding him close against me I gloried in his vigorous thrusts until at last I felt the warm gush of his seed and cried out for joy. I awoke hot and slippery between my thighs and for a moment I thought it had been true, it had really happened – then I realised I'd been dreaming and my whole body burnt with shame.

As the weather improved Lord Warminster began to take Flora out to the rose garden in the early evening; he must have talked to her about the roses because she repeated scraps of information about them and snatches of poetry he'd recited to her. She tried to take me there on our walks during the day but I was too embarrassed; even though Joe Dempster had joined up, other gardeners would be working there and I couldn't face them. Then one evening in the middle of May Lord Warminster arrived home a little earlier than usual, and came to the drawing room himself to collect her. She ran to him, then looked back to where I sat, calling, 'Mama come too. See the roses.'

I glanced up at his face and he said, 'It is a fine evening. The fresh air would do you good.' So I rang for my hat and jacket and walked out beside him.

I couldn't think of what to say in this unaccustomed situation, but Flora chattered and he answered her, so I simply trailed along behind them, with my thoughts sinking down in to the same deep rut – dwelling on the baby I would never have. We went further than I'd ever been since I'd lived at Eston, and came down a flight of steps on to a lawn where there was a pool with a fountain – a fat bronze boy holding a dolphin. Flora ran back and began tugging me forward to admire the statue, so I made myself take notice –but it was the bush behind the pool which caught my attention. Amidst the fresh green leaves there were buds. I exclaimed, 'The roses – they be nearly out!' He turned, half-smiling, then beckoned to us. We followed him through an archway and left, towards a sheltered corner full in the sun; and there I saw them, white heads dancing amid the greenery – roses in bloom. I quickened my pace – and as I came closer I saw she was a moss rose, and recognised her. ' 'Tis the Countess!' I reached out to touch her scented petals, and stroke the mossy coat of her bud.

Behind me Lord Warminster said, 'She is a French countess. Her full name is the Comtesse de Murinais.'

I gazed at her silken white frills before replying wistfully, 'Lucky Countess Murinais – to have a rose named for her.'

'You claimed Aimée Vibert.'

I replied flatly, 'But I was wrong, wasn't I? I didn't know French then, so I made a mistake.'

'Not entirely.' His voice was gentle. 'Amy is the English of Aimée, and they are both derived from the same Latin root.'

'Aimée' – I knew what it meant now: 'the loved one'. Aunt Agnes couldn't have known or she'd never have called me that – me, the unwanted child. The petals blurred. I saw a black-furred hand reach out beneath them, taking hold of the stem; there was a sharp snap, then he carefully wrapped his handkerchief around the thorns before holding the rose out to me. I looked up at him. He was not the Beast any longer, the Beast who'd become a young and vigorous prince and given Beauty all the children she craved. No, he was merely a misshapen middle-aged man with greying hair who was my husband – but who could never be a husband to me.

I took the rose from him. 'Thank you, my lord.'

Flora tugged at my skirt. 'Me smell, Mama.' I bent down, but before I could stop her, her chubby hand grabbed at the stem above the white protecting cloth. She jumped back, her mouth a round 'o' of dismay as she gazed at the red bead of blood on her thumb. Quickly I put her hand to my mouth. 'There – all better now, Flora.'

He bent over anxiously, and I heard the concern in his voice as he said, 'You must remember, my Flora, that roses have thorns.'

I looked up at him. '*My* Granfer, he did tell I that, when I were only a liddle maid.' For a moment our eyes met over Flora's golden head. He was not just my husband, but my daughter's grand-father. She was our rose of joy, binding us together – and we must both pay the price.

My eyes veered away, to the Countess, and I told him, 'In Granfer's garden she did grow next to General Jack in his red coat.'

'General Jacqueminot grows in my garden, too. Shall I show you where?'

And so he led me on a treasure hunt of memories. General Jack, York and Lancaster, the Rosamund rose, William Lobb, the Garland, Maiden's Blush – every one of Granfer's roses grew in his garden too, and I greeted them like long-lost friends. They were not in bloom yet – it was still a little too early, but their buds were plump with promise. We came to the Cabbage rose last, which had always been my favourite, and I told him so – and how I had tried to count her petals, but could never reach a total, because I was afraid of hurting her. He was smiling as he replied, 'I too encountered that problem, so now we will never know.'

I turned from my Cabbage rose and asked him, 'Which is *your* favourite?'

'Here.' He led us down the path and across the lawn to where a cluster of rose pillars stood, connected together with looping chains all twined around by the free-growing foliage of a rambler rose. There were only buds as yet, and he stroked one gently as he told me, 'She was the first rose I ever grew – and the most beautiful.'

'What's her name?'

He half-smiled. 'Like your Cabbage rose she bears a most inadequate one. She's called Blairii Number 2.' I moved closer, studying the leaf pattern and the buds as he told me, 'She's thought to be related to the China roses – her flowers are double, a pure pink at the centre, shading out to white. You must come and see her blooms for yourself in a week or two.' But I knew I'd seen them already – though I didn't tell him so. Then we heard the chimes of the stable clock, clear in the still evening air and he said, 'It's nearly bed-time, Flora,' adding, in response to her wail of protest, 'Papa will carry you in.' At once she held her arms up and he gathered her to him. We walked back to the house, together.

After that evening we spoke little. He had never talked much and I was still lost in my hopeless longing, but I felt less uncomfortable with him as we sat together at the dining table eating our way through soup and fish, entrée and remove, sweet and savouries – until we arrived at the conclusion of dessert.

Then at the beginning of June, he told me, 'My Blairii Rose is in flower – have you seen her yet?' I shook my head, not admitting why I hadn't. But he answered what I'd left unsaid. 'The young gardeners have all enlisted now, so the older men are busy in the kitchen garden – and because the women have their household duties to attend to they don't arrive until the afternoon.'

'The *women*?'

He replied, 'Yes, it is women who tend my roses now – why not? Their fingers are skilful, and they grow their own flowers. So, if you go down into the rose garden of a morning you will be quite alone.'

Next morning I walked in his garden. It was beautiful – more beautiful even than the fairy-tale garden of the Beast. I went straight down to the Blairii roses. They were full and fragrant; from the pink petals at their heart to the white ones at their brim they were generous roses, generous both with their beauty and their scent. As I spoke to them they danced in reply – just as they'd danced around the marble statue in the courtyard of the ruined house. He'd set up that statue deep in the woods, a statue graven in the image of the wife he'd lost, but not through death. He'd lost her long before that. Those roses had been planted when she'd first left him, and taken his child away. 'I used to dream about her, too.' That was all he'd had left, her marble statue and his dreams, so he'd planted the roses, to keep her company. I looked at the Blairii·roses in front of me, tumbling down from the pillars and twining themselves along the chains – chains of roses, chaining me to him. '– and, forsaking all other, keep thee only unto him, so long as ye both shall live.' I put my hand over my empty womb and wept.

In the evening I told him of the beauty of his roses, and he flushed with pleasure. 'You must visit the glass-houses and the trial grounds tomorrow.' As I opened my mouth to protest he continued firmly, 'I will tell Hicks to expect you at nine-thirty.'

I was apprehensive, but Mr Hicks greeted me politely, doffing his hat and addressing me as 'my lady' – and slowly my nervousness changed to interest. He showed me the new rose Lord Warminster had bred from rugosa stock: she was just coming into bloom, her pale golden heart opening out to a lemony frill of outer petals. She was a dainty rose, but her sturdy stem was already well-protected by close-set thorns – you could see she wasn't a rose as would stand for any nonsense despite looking so delicate. And her scent too, it was sweet – but the sweetness was spiced with the tang of lemon sherbet. I did like her. 'What's she called, Mr Hicks?'

'His Lordship hasn't named her yet. He likes to be sure a rose'll breed true before he gives it a name. Now we'll go back to the houses, my lady, and I'll show you the fairy roses.'

The first one we saw was Persephone. I remembered, oh how I

remembered – in Lambeth when I'd carried my baby alive and kicking inside me. I felt dizzy with loss. He could breed beautiful roses, but he could never give me the child I craved. I made myself turn to Mr Hicks and ask, 'Mebbe you could tell me the names of the others, so I can learn them?'

That evening at dinner as Lord Warminster ate his last segment of orange he said, 'I hear you have been learning names. Hicks was most impressed by your diligence.'

'I do like to know the names o' things.'

'Yes – so I have noticed. I'd also deduced it from Flora's chatter. She likes names, too, but she is not so obsessive about them as you are.'

His voice rose a little as he spoke, almost as though he were asking a question, so I answered without thinking, ' 'Tis different for her – she has a name of her own. You gave it to her.'

He watched me. Then he said, 'I gave *you* a name, too. You are Lady Warminster now. You don't need to be afraid of gardeners any more.' He dropped his napkin and rose to his feet, waiting for me to leave.

As I drew level with him I said, 'Thank you, my lord,' and went quickly through the door.

I knew I must not blame him: he'd been good to me, very good. And his rose garden was beautiful. Every morning I walked amidst the scented flowers greeting old friends and making new ones. June had come and it was fine and warm, so that one morning after I'd taken Flora back upstairs I couldn't resist a final peep, and ran out again before lunch. At the Blairii roses I knew it was time to turn back, but I buried my face in their blooms for one last time, murmuring, 'Thee bist beautiful, so beautiful.'

And a voice behind me said, 'You're not so dusty yourself, Amy.' I froze – it couldn't be – but when I turned slowly round I saw that it was. 'Hicks told me you were probably down here. He seemed somewhat reluctant to part up with the information but I pointed out that as I was on leave it was only natural that I should want a few words with my step-mother.'

I couldn't speak, I just stood looking at him: Adonis, Apollo, Snow White's Prince all rolled into one. The sun seemed to turn his uniform into cloth of gold and the sheen of his hair shone like a halo around his head. Then slowly my vision cleared. It was Frank, Mr

Dunn, my own lord – so straight and slim in his close-fitting khaki tunic with the brass buttons shining and the gold braid edging his cuffs.

Chapter Fifty-Nine

Replacing his cap he shifted his gloves and stick to his left hand and held the other out to me. As his warm fingers clasped mine he asked formally, 'How do you do, Amy?' Adding with a laugh as I didn't reply, 'Has the cat got your tongue?'

Finally I managed to stammer, 'I – that is – good day, my lord.'

He grinned. 'I think "Frank" will do once more – in view of our close relationship.' I couldn't take my eyes off him, and his smile became broader as he said lightly, 'It looks as if I really have taken you by surprise! I was so sure you must have noticed my arrival and been playing that pretty pantomime with the roses for my benefit, but it was absolutely genuine. What a silly girl you are, Amy, talking to flowers!' I crimsoned. 'Still, it gave me the chance to have a good look at you, and that's always worth something.' His voice dropped, becoming low and caressing. 'And I think, I really do think, that I've seen what I'd hoped for.' I stood there as if in a dream – but his next words woke me. Sharply he asked, 'Why did you come back here – to Eston?'

I half-whispered, 'Because of Flora. He do love Flora so much.'

His blue eyes hardened. 'Was that the only reason?'

'He – he was bedfast, an invalid and,' I swallowed, 'he's my husband, so it was my duty.'

'Ah.' There was silence, then he glanced at me from under his golden eyelashes. 'Duty's a cold bedfellow, Amy. But he isn't, is he, your bedfellow?'

This time I did whisper, but he heard my answered, 'No,' and his square shoulders sagged for a moment before he told me, 'When I found out you'd come back, at first I was in a fury of jealousy. Then I used my brain – he hadn't taken you in France, like any normal man would have done – so I didn't think having you under his own roof would make any difference – and it hasn't, has it?'

'He's never so much as laid a finger on me.'

He laughed. 'Perhaps that accident finished him off completely

– and crushed the withered remnants of his balls to tissue paper! Poor old sod, I could almost feel sorry for him.' His white teeth flashed in a smile as he added, 'Almost, but not quite – there's a world of difference. But you haven't asked me why I've come here.'

'Eston – 'tis your home.' He laughed again, but there was a sour note in his laughter so I went on quickly, 'To see Flora?'

'I do want to see *my* daughter, yes – but that's not the main reason. I've come to ask you a favour, Amy. Will you grant it to me?'

'Yes – yes o' course.'

'That's what I like to hear in a woman – instant obedience. Perhaps the old man wasn't such a fool after all, marrying a servant. But that's not why you agreed to my request so rapidly, is it?' Reaching out he cupped my chin in his hand, forcing me to look directly up into his eyes. 'You'll do anything for me, Amy, won't you? Because you love me.' I twisted from his grasp, dropping my gaze, and heard his soft chuckle of satisfaction. 'I thought so – women like you don't change. But before you do me that favour, how about inviting me to lunch? After all, it's perfectly respectable – you *are* my step-mother.' He was laughing again as he spoke. 'Come along, I'm deuced hungry.' He turned to stride off across the lawn, and I followed behind.

I scarcely touched my lunch; instead I feasted my eyes on him. He looked so different in his uniform, but then he would look up and smile, and it was as if we were back together in the punt, that long-ago day on the river. He knew I couldn't take my eyes from his face and as soon as the pudding had been served and we were alone he grinned, 'Makes a change from sitting opposite the old man, eh, Amy?'

Colouring I said quickly, 'Lord Warminster, he doesn't eat lunch – and besides, he's out all day, being an orderly at Lady Burton's hospital.'

'So I've heard.' He didn't say who from. 'Must give the poor devils nightmares seeing that ugly mug bending over them when they come round.'

'When I had my tooth out, he was kind to me.'

'I'm glad to hear it, not that – oh, forget him – let's pretend he doesn't exist. Let's pretend there's only the two of us in the whole wide world!'

531

'And Flora.'

'Yes, and Flora. I'm looking forward to seeing her. Tell me about my daughter, Amy.' So I told him how pretty she was, and how forward for her age, and the clever things she said. He listened, smiling, and then when I paused said, 'Your speech has changed – most of your dialect has gone. You've still got that soft West-Country accent – I don't suppose you'll ever lose that, but you're speaking grammatically.'

'I asked my lord to teach me to speak properly, and he gave me lessons.'

Frank threw down his napkin and burst out laughing. 'What a comedy that must have been! Fancy him of all people trying to teach anyone how to speak!' I felt uncomfortable; Lord Warminster had taken the trouble to help me, even though it must have been a nuisance to him. Frank drew out his cigarette case. 'May I smoke, Amy?' He'd asked my permission – just as though I were a real lady! I felt a glow of pleasure as he cupped his hand around the lighted match. He tossed it aside and inhaled deeply. 'The chaps who've been out already say there's nothing like a gasper for steadying the nerves, so I'd better get into the habit.'

Fear gripped my heart. 'Are you going to France soon?'

'It could be any day now. I'd have gone already if I hadn't had a bit of a do with bronchitis back in February. Close your pretty little mouth, Amy. What's the point of being in the Army, if you don't go to war? I certainly don't intend to miss it. And after all, it's the country of my birth those bloody Huns have invaded – now I want to do my share in driving the swine out.' He ground out his cigarette stub. 'Oh, forget the war, too. Let's go up to the nursery.'

Flora ran forward as soon as the door opened, then skidded to a halt, her blue eyes wide with astonishment. He squatted down on his haunches in front of her. 'Hello Flora, and how are we today? We have met before, but I don't suppose you remember.' She gazed up at him then walked forward until she was between his knees. 'How about a kiss then? For your – brother.' I heard Ellen's small intake of breath – being a local girl she'd recognised him at once – but he took no notice. All his attention was for his daughter. 'Come along, Flora. Don't be shy – give me a kiss.'

Flora glanced up at me, uncertainly, but it was Ellen who

replied. 'My lord, she baint kissed a gentleman afore. His Lordship, see, he don't never kiss her.'

Frank laughed. 'Then I shall be the first! Come closer, my pet.' And very gently he kissed her round cheek. 'There – it didn't hurt, did it? Now give me one back.' She gurgled with pleasure and suddenly began to cover his face with butterfly kisses; laughing, he swung her up in his arms and she put her chubby hands around his neck and hugged him tight. My chest hurt as I watched them. Gently he detached her clinging arms and set her down, then dropping on to the hearthrug beside her he began to rearrange the dolls' house. She leant against his arm, hanging on his every word – totally entranced by him. He glanced up to where Ellen and Dora stood waiting. 'We won't need you for a few minutes.' Dismissed, they went quietly through into the night nursery. I knelt down on the rug beside him and together we played with her – our daughter.

He turned to smile at me. 'She's a beautiful child, Amy – just as you must have been – but then, they say love children always are.' A love child? No a bastard – that was the correct word, the word I'd been called by, time after time in my childhood; the word my daughter would never hear – because of Lord Warminster. And watching those two golden heads together I felt like a traitor. Her grandfather was toiling at messy, unpleasant work at the hospital instead of being here playing with Flora, as he'd a thousand times rather be doing – because he loved her.

I said abruptly, 'She loves her Granfer, and Lord Warminster, he do think the world of her.'

For a moment his shoulders became taut – then he shrugged. 'He wanted a child of his own and now he's got one – mine. He can't begrudge me these few minutes.' I didn't speak of it again.

At last he got to his feet, dusting down the knees of his breeches with his gloves. 'It's time for a walk, Amy.' Flora heard the word and jumped up like an eager puppy, trying to tug him towards the door. 'No, Flora – not you.' His voice was firm.

Her mouth crumpled. 'Me too – Flora come too!' But he was already turning away.

I caught her to me, cuddling her. 'She's a good little walker.'

He swung round and shook his head. 'No, Amy. A nursery walk is not what I've got in mind. Put her down and call the nursemaid.'

I lowered her to the floor. He bent over her. 'Goodbye Flora. Give me a last kiss.'

'Shan't!' Flora stamped loudly.

'Goodness, wherever did she get that temper from?' He sounded amused. 'Come along, Amy.' I glanced back to where Ellen was already starting to soothe my howling daughter. 'Come *along*, Amy.' I went.

On the stairs I said defensively, 'She's only two. 'Tis natural she gets upset when she's disappointed.'

'Don't apologise. I know what little barbarians children are – that's why they have to be kept in nurseries.'

'Lord Warminster has her brought down to the library and she plays there good as gold.'

'I daresay. Annabel told me he doted on young children.'

He'd spoken her name quite casually, but my legs trembled as I asked, 'Is she well?'

'Oh yes, she's blooming with health. If you don't mind, Amy, we'll talk about her later, out of this house. It has too many memories.'

As soon as we got outside he set off at such a pace I could barely keep up with him. I'd thought he'd want to walk in the rose garden but instead he skirted the stables and plunged into the oak wood, striding ahead in silence; we didn't stop until we reached the rose hedge around the ruined house. He seemed to know the way in: he headed straight for the gap, holding the briars back for me to pass through. As we came on to the rough turf of the sloping lawn in front of the crumbling walls I saw that they were bedecked with a thousand bobbing pink heads – the Blairii roses were in bloom. He led me over to an old stone seat, and we sat down, side by side. It was very peaceful there, with the scent of the roses and the sound of birdsong – but my body was tense as a coiled spring as he began to speak.

'You asked me about Annabel – she came back this week. That's why they let me have leave. My dear wife, just returned from America – how could the Colonel refuse? I went up to Liverpool to meet her. She's got courage, I'll give her that – it's not much fun crossing the Atlantic these days, only a month after the *Lusitania* went down, but she walked down that gangway looking as fresh and lovely as if she'd just stepped out of a bandbox.' He

534

broke off for a moment before exclaiming, 'God, how I'd missed her! We spent the night in an hotel there – I thought that room was the Garden of Eden, and she, she seemed to want me as much as I wanted her.' I shrank back on the seat, but he seemed almost to be speaking to himself, as if he'd forgotten I was there. 'There are lots of other beautiful women in the world but I thought, she's my wife, and I love her so this is special. And when I was holding her I thought about going to France, and possibly my number being up there, but now at least I'd be able to leave a son behind me, an heir. In the morning I lay in bed watching her brush her hair – like dark silk velvet that hair of hers, with her lovely white arms slowly drawing the silver brush over it. And as I watched I told her of my hopes, that perhaps she'd already conceived – and she swung round to face me, still brushing her hair with those long, sinuous strokes and said, "I'll never do that, Francis. You see, I had an operation in Boston to remove my womb. I couldn't have it done in England, the surgeons would have insisted on having your consent, and I knew you'd never give it, but in America . . ." She shrugged her beautiful white shoulders, "Mama has friends." I just lay there. I couldn't believe I'd heard properly, so I begged her to tell me it wasn't true. I cried out: "I want a son, I want an heir!" And she replied quite calmly, "I'm sorry, Francis but you'll have to do without. I can't conceive now, and I don't intend to set you free." She turned back to the mirror and began coiling her hair up, her long white fingers stabbing in each hairpin as though it were a dagger, as her words were a dagger in my heart. "I have no intention of giving you a divorce, and even if I did – go astray – it wouldn't be any use to you because before I left London I took the precaution of collecting evidence against you. You never were very discreet in your amours, were you, Francis? First my own maid and then that woman in Kensington, and no doubt there've been others. Still, you can't harm me any more now." I told her – I explained to her that they didn't mean anything to me, just a release. It wasn't that I hadn't loved her, but obviously while she'd been confined I'd needed – and she just cut me short. "I'm not interested in your physical problems, Francis, I'm merely telling you so that you understand that if you ever did have the colossal nerve to try and divorce me on some trumped-up charge I would counter-petition – and then there'd be deadlock. So we're bound together for life, you and I, 'Till death us do part'. But as there'll be no procreation of children for me then there'll be none for you, either – not legitimate ones, and that's all you care about, isn't it? Isn't it amusing, Francis? I'm the only woman in the world who can give you a legitimate heir – and I'm barren, totally barren – and you know why." And she laughed – she laughed! Then she picked up her silver pot of rouge and began, oh so delicately, applying it to her lips.

'I couldn't bear to stay in the same room as her. I got up, threw some clothes on and went out. I walked the streets of that filthy city all day, raging at her and raging at fate, and those last words of hers kept repeating themselves in my head, until at last I realised that she was wrong – she'd made a mistake when she'd said what she had. She *wasn't* the only woman in the world; there's one other woman who can give me a legitimate heir.' He swung suddenly round on the seat so he faced me directly. 'And that woman is you.' I stared back at him, unable to speak, and mistaking my silence he began to explain, the words tumbling out of him. 'Amy, you're my step-mother, my father's wife, so your son would be my brother – and my legal heir. Do you understand? Do you understand now the favour I've come to ask of you?'

I understood; my whole body understood and trembled with longing. His eyes were blue and pleading as my head fought my body and my conscience wrestled with my heart. When I finally spoke it was as though the words were wrenched out of my mouth. 'No. 'Twould be a sin.'

He shook his head. 'You've borne me a daughter already. How can a second time matter?'

I would not let my hands reach out to him; I gripped the edge of the stone seat so hard that it hurt. 'Fornication, that be a sin, but adultery be one o' the Commandments. And it'd be adultery twice over.'

His quick tongue argued, refuting. 'No. Marriage is for the procreation of children – what she has done has invalidated that. And you, your marriage is no marriage at all. You owe him nothing.'

'Except our daughter's name.'

'He wanted her for himself – that's the only reason he married you.'

Why did I marry you? Because you asked me to. I shook my head. 'He gave me a name, too.'

'Oh, don't be frightened – you won't lose your precious title. He won't repudiate you, or the child – he'll never admit publicly that he's been cuckolded, especially not by me, of all men. No, he'll acknowledge my son, just as he did my daughter.' His voice dropped, becoming low and urgent. 'Look, Amy, I'm going to France soon, and who knows what'll happen there? I want to leave a son before I go. And you, you want another child, I can see the longing in your face. I saw it in the nursery as you held our daughter. You're a natural woman, not like –' he broke off, then said loudly, 'Why should you go through life unfulfilled just because you're married to a man who's incapable?' He shrugged. 'After all, you'll be doing him a favour, since he dotes on children but can't beget his own.'

'Then couldn't we ask him?'

'Ask who?' He sounded puzzled.

'My lord, Lord Warminster – ask him if he'd let us, then if he says –'

He was almost shouting as he interrupted me. 'Have you gone completely crackers? What the hell do you think he'll say – "Oh yes, Francis my boy, you can screw my wife any time you feel like it." Don't be so bloody stupid, Amy!'

'But – you said he'd acknowledge the baby . . .'

'If it's already *happened* – it'll be too late to do anything else then. But that's not the same as . . . Good God, he'll be livid at first. Even a man who's incapable of fucking his own wife doesn't want another fellow doing it for him.'

And, forsaking all other, keep thee only unto him..

I gathered all my strength together and told him, 'No. It wouldn't be right.' I stood up. 'I – I maun be going back to the house now.'

He sprang to his feet. 'Sit down, Amy.' He towered over me; I sank back on to the hard stone seat. 'You want a child as much as I do.' He spoke softly, but each word was distinct. 'Your body gives you away, your very expression gives the lie to everything you've been saying. You say no with your lips but your eyes say yes – they're yearning, pleading with me.' I put my hands over my face. 'It's no use, Amy – I've read their message and I'm going to act on it.' I heard the sound of a buckle unfastening as he continued speaking. 'Your scruples are those of a child, I shan't let them stop me. Open your eyes, Amy – you can't keep your head in the sand for ever.'

As I took my hands away I saw his tunic and belt were on the ground and his breeches were open, so that I could see his rod; it was swollen and ready for me. My 'No!' was barely a whisper.

'That's right, you can say no as many times as you like, so long as your body says yes.' He came to me and lifted me up in his arms before lowering me to the ground. I didn't move. I lay still, gazing up at him, standing like a Greek god above me. As he knelt down beside me my body was submissive before his. Softly he spoke. 'It's better like this – you can tell the old man I forced you. Then your conscience will be clear.' He smiled, his heart-breaking, boyish smile. I loved him, oh how I loved him. But I knew that to look at him as he did this to me would be the final infidelity, so with a great effort I turned my head – and saw the roses.

The roses Lord Warminster had planted, tumbling laughing over that ruined house, but they weren't laughing now – they shook their heads in reproach. Strong fingers took hold of my ankles and separated my legs; still I lay like a stone. Skilled hands slid under my petticoats and tossed them back before beginning to unfasten the buttons of my drawers, but in my mind I seemed to see another hand grasping the stem of a rose and snapping it, before holding it out to me. And I had taken that rose, so generously offered by the black-furred hand – the same hand I'd clutched at in my pain and terror as I'd made my vows. *I Amy take thee Leonidas Arthur Hector – 'Don't leave me, Amy – please don't leave me!' – and thereto I give thee my troth.*

The man above me groaned with pleasure as his fingers drove into my cunny, and at last I began to struggle.

'So you want to play the game to the full, do you, Amy?' His knee thrust between mine. Too late, I'd left it too late – I felt the pain as he held down my arms. I couldn't move – I didn't want to move, he was too strong for me, it wasn't my fault. Deliberately I thrust the temptation from me and went back far into the past, seeking the memory I'd kept hidden there all those years. And now it was Uncle Alf's knee between mine, Uncle Alf's hands pinning me down – and I began to fight in bitter earnest. 'No, no!'

But it was too late, I'd left it too late – and then suddenly I was free. I lay huddled on the ground, sobbing.

'Look at me, Amy – look at me!' A hand, hard and angry, pulled my head round. 'Look!' And there in front of my eyes was his rod, hanging down, limp and useless. 'That's what you've done to me, you and your blasted conscience.' As he began to button up his breeches he exclaimed, 'I can't take a woman by force – I never have, and I can't now. Fine soldier I'll make. Stop blubbing and pull your skirts down. You're in no danger now.'

I whimpered, 'I be terrible sorry, but 'twould've been a sin.'

His face was bitter as he accused me, 'You're a hypocrite, a canting little Pharisee. You wanted it. You know that as well as I do, but your narrow Biblical morality stopped you taking it.' His voice rose in scorn. 'When you cry at nights for the child you'll never bear, when your breasts tingle to suckle the son you denied me, then I shall laugh, Amy. I shall laugh in your face, as she did to me. You silly little fool.' He fastened his belt, picked up his gloves and stick and strode off.

I lay weeping on the ground, as the roses laughed and tossed their heads – mocking me for my folly.

Chapter Sixty

I dragged myself back to the house; there were tasks to be performed. Upstairs in the barren bedroom of my husband I took out his razor, cleaned his comb, laid ready his collar studs, cufflinks, braces – my hands moving mechanically. There was nothing to look forward to, nothing. The sight of Flora's round face as she came into the drawing room warmed me a little, but she was fretful and whining – she'd been rejected by the glamorous stranger. I cuddled her as we mourned together.

That evening at dinner I opened my mouth to speak over the soup, then closed it again; I did the same with the fish. By the time the mutton had arrived I knew I had to tell him, but I still couldn't bring myself to do it. When the door had closed behind Mr Tims, Lord Warminster swivelled round, so he could look directly at me. 'Whatever it is you wish to tell me, Amy, please do so.' He was half-smiling, and he'd used my name, so I knew he was in a good mood.

Taking a deep breath I said, 'Lord Quinham, he did come today.' The half-smile vanished. Tightening his lips he bent over the plate and stabbed at the mutton chop. 'He – I – went for a walk, with him.' The chop was torn apart. 'And he – did go up to the nursery, to see Flora.'

The silver knife and fork were flung down with a clatter. He raised his head, his face angry. 'Flora is *my* daughter. He has no legal claim on her whatsoever.' Each word was deliberately, emphatically enunciated.

'He do know that.'

'He *does* know that. Speak English, can't you?' He almost spat the correction at me.

I didn't open my mouth again, and nor did he, except to receive his loaded fork. At the end of the meal when he stood up as usual to allow me to leave his whole body was one huge glower.

That night I woke up to find I was damp between the legs; my monthlies had come. I got up and tied a diaper round myself, and then I began to weep. I could still feel the pain in my arms where

540

his hands had pinned me down. Why oh why hadn't he forced me? My mind cried out in horror at my thoughts and I burnt with shame. 'Grammer, Grammer – I didn't sin. Do 'ee help I, please!' I tried to conjure her stern, righteous face out of the darkness, but there was nothing there, only the scent of the roses through the open window, mocking me.

By the middle of the week there was a livid bruise on each of my upper arms. As the weather had gone cooler I covered them up with a light wrap, but it slipped off as I drank my soup. Hastily I bent down to retrieve it and pull it around me again, but Lord Warminster's eyes were on me. 'What have you done to your arms? Have you – hurt yourself?'

Quickly I answered, ' 'Tis only a bruise.'

He corrected, '*Two* bruises,' and waited. I looked down at my soup and didn't reply. I saw his frown from under my lashes, but he questioned me no further.

Then, as the door closed behind Mr Tims and the tureen he spoke again. 'Is there anything – troubling – you? You have seemed – disturbed – these past few days.'

I looked up at him and there was a light sheen of sweat on his forehead; making an enquiry like that always cost him an effort. I spoke without thinking. 'My lord, if I, if I did something wicked – really wicked – would you send me away?'

The door opened as Mr Tims returned with the fish. Helping himself to whitebait Lord Warminster said, 'The Garland Rose is in bud. You might care to visit it tomorrow.'

'Thank you, my lord, I will.' He talked on about the roses, and I listened, nodding mechanically, like a Judy in a puppet show.

After the dessert he pushed back his chair and stood up, as always. As I came level with him he spoke. 'The answer to your question is no, I would not.' He paused and almost smiled before adding, 'After all, I gave you the rose.' Moving to the door he opened it for me and I slipped quickly through.

That night I dreamt I was lying on the grass in front of the ruined house with my own lord, Frank, towering over me, but this time when I struggled he was too strong for me, he overpowered me and drove his rod hard into my body – so hard that I cried aloud with the pain of it and bled. But in the pain and the blood he gave me that which I longed for, and I was satisfied. Then I woke up and wept – not in shame, but in regret. In the morning conscience returned and I was hollow with guilt. However could I be so wicked as to regret not sinning? Adultery – that was one of the Commandments.

Misery made me forgetful. That afternoon I forgot to put out his sock suspenders, and had to go back upstairs; then later I realised I'd forgotten to replace his towels. I didn't want to be bothered but if I didn't lay them out before Flora came down it would be too late – he always bathed as soon as he came in now. So with a sigh I dragged myself upstairs again, fetched the towels from the linen cupboard and went along to his bedroom. I wasn't looking, I could think of nothing but my own woes, else I might have noticed, would have noticed some slight sign of disarray; I wasn't listening, either, or I would have heard splashing. Instead I simply turned the handle and walked straight into the bathroom – and there he was: he'd come back early.

He was already half out of the bath, with one strong leg planted on the mat, but because he was facing the other way he didn't know I'd come in. I saw him standing there with the hair of his back sweeping in two great whorls over his shoulders then running down his backbone to fan out round the curve of his waist before coming to rest on his buttocks in skeins of shining dark silk. I didn't move. I just stood staring at him. He must have heard the door opening because he called out, 'Tims – where the devil are my towels?' then lifting his other leg out of the bath he began to turn round. But because of his twisted neck he couldn't see me as he turned – and so I saw them. And there was nothing wrong with them at all. His rod hung down below its dark mat of fur, while his two balls nestled full and round between the thick black hair of his powerful thighs. I gazed at them, transfixed. All of a sudden there was a great splash and a flannel whipped across his groin, hiding them from my view. Slowly I raised my eyes, up over his flat stomach with the dark hairs clinging sleekly to it, on to his chest so thickly matted with black fur that I could scarcely see the pink of his skin behind, and up to his face – his furious face. He was bellowing, 'Get out! Get out!' but I was quite calm and composed.

I stepped forward and he backed away, retreating along the side of the bath, still clutching that absurd fig leaf of a flannel. Putting

542

the towels down on the cork top of the stool I said, 'Here are your towels, my lord,' then I turned round and went out.

I heard him ringing the bell, and then shouting at Mr Tims – so loudly that his voice carried through the dressing-room door. When the shouting ceased I went out into the corridor; the butler was there, trembling. I put my hand on his arm and told him, 'Don't you worry, Mr Tims, it wasn't your fault. I'll sort it out with His Lordship.'

I went up to fetch Flora and played with her for an hour in the drawing room, until Clara came to take her to Lord Warminster. He hadn't come for her himself – I hadn't really expected him to. I went out and walked among the roses, his roses, and then went upstairs to bathe Flora before coming down to dress for dinner.

He was already in the hall as I walked down the stairs, and his face went beetroot red as soon as he caught sight of me. But I was still quite composed so I spoke first. 'My lord, it wasn't Mr Tims' fault.' His mouth opened but I continued, 'When Mr Wallis left I decided to valet you – all except for stropping your razors. Mr Tims, he's got too much to do already, with losing the footmen.'

'But –'

I interrupted him. 'My lord, you didn't want a new valet, even if you could 'a found one, which I doubt, there being a war on.'

'Tims should never –'

I stopped him again. 'He obeyed my orders, because I am Lady Warminster – so you mustn't shout at him any more.'

He looked at me, baffled, then exclaimed, 'I can't let *you* act as my valet!'

'I don't see why not – I was a personal servant, and I like to keep busy. Besides, I don't see as it's that strange. I remember hearing once as that Lord Wemyss, who died just afore the war, he was always looked after by a maid instead of a valet, and he was an earl, like you.' I paused, but he didn't try and interrupt this time so I added, 'Besides, I am your wife. Shall we go into dinner now?'

All through dinner I talked to him as if nothing untoward had taken place. After a while he began to answer me, and Mr Tims' hands stopped their shaking. At the end of the meal he stood up and held the door open for me as usual; I said 'Good evening, my lord,' and he managed to mutter, 'Good evening,' back – he didn't add 'Amy' because he was still annoyed with me, still having a bit of a sulk. But I wasn't bothered because I was annoyed with him, for having lied to me. He'd told me he was damaged, but he wasn't, not damaged at all. He had everything he needed to act as a husband to me, and as soon as I'd seen that in the bathroom I'd decided then and there that he would. I slept soundly that night, and didn't dream at all.

But I'd lost some of my calm confidence by the time I woke up the next morning. I was sure now that he could be a husband to me – but how was I to make him? At first I thought of simply asking him. I rehearsed the request in my mind: 'My lord, I'd take it kindly if you'd act as a proper husband to me,' or the more discreet: 'Mebbe you'd care to visit my bedroom tonight, my lord?' But that evening as we sat at dinner and I looked at him sitting at the head of his table in gleaming white linen and formal black dress-coat the formidable reality of him silenced my tongue. Besides, he was still scowling; he'd accepted my argument but he hadn't forgiven me – it was no time to ask favours. Except it wasn't a favour, it was my right; that thought strengthened my resolution.

But later it occurred to me that any other man would have taken his rights by now, so perhaps he hadn't lied to me. Perhaps he really was damaged – but inside, in some way that didn't show. My spirits plummeted. But then that remark of Ellen's came back to me: it was true, he never did kiss Flora, much as he loved her – yet he must be able to kiss, everyone could – only he didn't, because of his mouth, because it was misshapen, like his body. I remembered those journeys to Salisbury, with him holding the newspaper in front of his face, behaving as though he were damaged because he felt himself so, believed himself to be damaged. But he wasn't, not really. His eyes were odd but he could still see perfectly well with them, and although his mouth was lopsided he could eat and speak; only his speech was halting, but now always, he spoke normally to Flora and he could shout more than loud enough when he was angry. It was only when he had time to think that his voice betrayed him. And likely it would be the same with his rod, so I must take him by surprise – but how?

I thought about the story of Ruth in the Bible. She'd wanted Boaz as her husband so she'd gone to him in the night when he was sleeping and crept under his coverlet to lie at his feet. The next day Boaz had made Ruth his wife and given her a son – so perhaps I could creep into my lord's bedroom tonight and climb under the blankets at the foot of his bed? But suppose he simply raised one of his large furry feet and kicked me out again? And at the thought of that I began to laugh. I could laugh now, because I had hope; I didn't know the answer, but I knew there must be one.

I was still puzzling over the problem while I was eating breakfast next morning, when Clara came in with a message from Mrs Johnstone. 'She says, "What does Her Ladyship want done with the pictures, as they're gathering dust?" ' Clara grinned. 'She's in a bad mood today. Thic pictures never bothered her afore, nor dust!'

'Which pictures?'

'They're His Lordship's, from Kew. He told her to put the crates upstairs when they arrived, and he'd decide about hanging 'em later. Only Mrs Johnstone had a tiff with Mrs Procter last week, so to annoy her Mrs J. took Billy the oddman off scrubbing the kitchen floor and sent him up to unpack the pictures instead. Took 'im all afternoon it did, Billy not being the fastest o' workers at the best o' times – and Mrs Proctor, she was blazing! Only now Mrs J. don't know what to do about thic pictures.' Clara leant closer. 'She says as they baint fit for us maids to dust, wi' one of 'em being a nekked woman. I reckons if they'd been nekked men she'd a dusted 'em herself!' Clara giggled and so did I. 'Anyway, my lady, shall I tell her as the problem's none o' your making, and she can get into her own hot water with His Lordship?'

I was tempted, but then I remembered the pictures of babies – Flora would like to see them, and to be honest, so would I. Flora loved the paintings; gurgling with delight she jabbed her fat finger at the plump baby lying on the ground beside its mother. I left her chattering to the baby and went over to see my favourite again. Still naked, as Mrs Johnstone had said, she stood there, beautiful and unashamed, smiling at me. I smiled back. Then I felt a tug at my skirt and lifted my daughter up in my arms so she could see the picture properly. She gazed at it, fascinated, then reaching out her hand to the painted face she exclaimed, 'Mama, Mama!' and so at last I realised why that picture had always seemed so familiar to me, why I'd felt sure I knew her face. It was the face I saw in the mirror every day of my life.

Flora began to wriggle, and I set her down on the floor. There, low down, was the title of the picture: *The Judgement of Paris*. It had puzzled me at Kew, but I'd learnt much since then. Paris was not a city, but a man – the handsome son of Priam, King of Troy. And the golden apple lying at the lady's bare feet – I knew what that signified, that he had judged her the fairest of the three goddesses, so I knew who she was: Aphrodite, the Goddess of Love. And I remembered his voice in the library that evening: 'Would you mind moving your candle, Amy. I don't like eyes looking at me – not even Aphrodite's eyes.' My eyes. 'The face of Aphrodite.' My face. I looked up again into her smiling eyes – and she gave me the answer. I whispered, 'Thank you, my lady, my goddess,' and her rosy lips seemed to curve in reply. Flora tugged imperiously at my skirt. 'Want to see horsies, Mama. Want to go to stables.' She began to drag me to the door; she was getting spoilt, it was time she had a brother.

As soon as I'd taken her back upstairs before lunch I returned to the picture, studying it. I'd fetched a mirror from my bedroom and now I checked carefully: her eyebrows, eyes, nose, mouth – all were correct. Her hair – it was golden and curling like mine, only it wasn't clear how it was arranged at the back, but then I wasn't going to turn my back, so I simply studied the way the soft curls clustered around the oval face until I was sure I could reproduce the style. Then my eyes fell to her breasts – and my spirits sank. Hers were round and pointed with small pink nipples – the breasts of a woman who'd never borne a child. It must have been before she'd had Eros – my breasts would never look like that again. But at least my stomach was still flat and smooth like hers; then I paused, because she had no hair on her cunny. I'd thought all women had hair there, but perhaps goddesses were different? I bit my lip, worrying – then I remembered Lord Warminster's razors. I'd borrow one of those and use it to make myself hairless and smooth. I moved on to the rest of the picture. Aphrodite had her discarded dress hanging from her left hand – it looked like a very simple design, made of patterned silk – it wouldn't take me more than an hour or two to run that up, and it was Clara's afternoon off today when she always went into Tilton, so I'd ask her to buy me a length of material. As far as the background was concerned, it wouldn't be any trouble finding a lawn – there were plenty of those at Eston – but the tree was more of a problem. It was obviously an apple tree in blossom, and we were already well on through June.

In any case, all the apples at Eston came from the espaliered trees trained against the kitchen-garden walls next to Mr Hicks' cottage – and that wouldn't do at all. Then I heard the bell ring for lunch and put the problem away. It would have to be solved later.

And it was solved later, that very evening and by Lord Warminster himself. He said, 'I see the first flowers are out on the Garland.' The Garland rose, which grew twining up around the gnarled branches of an old apple tree.

I felt my face break into a smile. 'Thank you my lord, thank you.'

He looked puzzled. 'What are you thanking me for?'

'For telling me about the Garland. I'll go and look at it first thing tomorrow.'

'It's not fully in bloom yet.'

'It soon will be, though.' I smiled at him again. He shifted awkwardly in his seat, and rang for Mr Tims, though he hadn't quite finished his tapioca pudding.

Next morning I went straight out to the Garland. It seemed only fitting that he should have told me of the place himself. And it was perfect: the short flight of stone steps ran down to the soft, petal-strewn lawn, with the fountain splashing nearby. As yet only a few buds had opened on the Garland, but by Sunday the whole tree would be a mass of blossom; Sunday, the day of the full moon. I needed the moon to be full, because he had to be able to see my face – the face of Aphrodite. I laughed aloud in joy. Next day I made the silken robe, sewing my hopes into every tiny stitch, like a bride sewing her wedding gown.

When I'd finished I went back to my book: not to the picture of Adonis this time but to that of the great god Pan. I'd noticed the resemblance before: Pan was sitting on a tree trunk with his shoulders hunched over the reed pipes he was playing so that he looked almost to have a humped back. The hair on his head was rumpled and curling over his ears while the high forehead and beaky nose jutting out from under bristling brows completed the likeness to my lord. He was sitting in profile, so there was no way of telling whether Pan's face was smaller on the other side – but it didn't matter anyway, the resemblance was so strong. In the statue Pan had a beard and moustache, but then so would my lord have, if he didn't choose to shave every day, and on Pan's body, even

547

carved in stone as he was, you could see the abundant growth of hair on his back and arms and chest, right down to where it disappeared under the goatskin he wore wrapped around his waist. Pan had hooves instead of feet, but his legs were covered with fur, just as my lord's had been when I'd seen them in the bathroom. And deliberately I allowed my mind to dwell on all that I'd seen then: the fascinating, swirling patterns of dark hair on his back, the curve of his buttocks, the strength of his muscular legs as he'd turned towards me – and the power of what lay between. I lingered over that memory as my cunny softened, opening ready for his rod when it rose at Aphrodite's command.

At dinner I watched his hands, those strong hands with their vigorous growth of hair running right up to the knuckles of his broad fingers. Not the Beast now – the Beast had been kind, gentle even – no, not the Beast but the great god Pan. As I watched him he put down his fork and raised one finger to his starched wing collar, tugging at it slightly; there was a light film of sweat on his forehead, although the evening was cool. He stared at me, and I smiled back – then abruptly wrenching his eyes away he told his plate, 'I shall be late back tomorrow, very late. George is running down from Town, so I'm dining with him. Don't wait up for me.'

So the final piece of the jigsaw fell into place. 'I'll take Nella out for her bed-time walk, then, my lord – I do like to smell the roses at night.'

The following evening Nella showed me his path around the rose garden, until we came to the top of the stone steps leading down to the sloping lawn in front of the Garland rose. She paused a moment there, lifting her muzzle, and I heard the soft 'kur,kur,' of the nightingale, warning his mate of our arrival. Then she padded down the first flight of steps to the seat placed on the terrace halfway down, and sank to her haunches beside it. So I knew now that this was where he sat every evening, looking down at the Garland and the fountain and the roses all around. I bent and hugged her. 'Thank 'ee, Nella. Thank 'ee, my beauty.' She wagged her tail in response; she understood.

It was Sunday, the day of the full moon. I took Flora down to the garden and we admired the Garland rose together. Spring had come again to the old apple tree in clusters of pink buds and sprays of creamy white flowers, each with a yellow heart. Standing beneath that mass of blossom it seemed the whole world was perfumed with the sweet scent of honeyed oranges.

When I'd taken Flora back up to the nursery I went along to his dressing room and lit the shaving Etna before starting to tidy up. The dress suit he'd worn last night was hanging over the back of a chair, so I put it on a hanger ready to take down for brushing. His discarded linen was lying in a tumbled heap on the floor, and as I bent to pick them up I could smell the lingering scent of cigars – he and Sir George must have been smoking over their port – but stronger than that was the smell of his sweat, still clinging to his shirt and vest. I lifted them up – and the sharp tang of his maleness quickened my breathing and made my pulses race; bending my head I buried my face in it, and as I did so I felt my body soften, readying itself for him.

The Etna began to hiss, and reluctantly I dropped his clothing into the dirty-linen basket; I still had one more task to perform. Selecting the razor labelled 'Sunday' I carried it through to my bedroom, then fetched the rest of his shaving tackle. I took off my skirt and drawers, hitched up my petticoats and reached for the razor – but I couldn't do it, I was too much of a coward. The steel blade winked at me, jeering, as I carried it squeamishly back to his dressing room.

When I was dressed again I went to have another look at the picture: it was so smooth, so very smooth – in fact the artist had hardly painted her cunny at all! I looked up at Aphrodite's face, and for a moment I was sure she was winking at me. And then I realised why: she was sharing a joke with me about that artist who'd been too prudish to paint her as she really was. Of course she'd had hair on her cunny, all women did – even goddesses. Standing there in front of her familiar smiling face my confidence returned, for tonight I would become Aphrodite, and mate with the great god Pan.

I sat with him at dinner, smiling and talking. At the end of the meal he stood up, as always; drawing level with him I smelt his male scent, and my heartbeat quickened with excitement. 'Good evening, my lord.'

'Good evening – Amy.'

It was a fine, dry night, but with a cool breeze; yet although I was naked under my silk wrap I wasn't cold. I was warm and glowing, glowing as I walked barefoot over the grass and down into the rose garden. The roses bobbed their heads and rustled their leaves in welcome, and I brushed their soft petals in passing, for the sheer joy of feeling their velvet touch on my bare skin. I saw the liquid silver of the fountain, the boy and his dolphin sharply outlined in the moonlight, and heard the flowing of the silver stream running into that silver pool. The Garland rose was more beautiful than ever tonight; each cluster of flower-heads dancing in the breeze which stirred their petals and sent their fragrant message to meet me. Slipping under the canopy of blossom I leant back against the living bark and waited. And as I waited Amy Roberts blew away on the breeze and I became Aphrodite; the spirit of the Goddess of Love entered my body and made it her own.

High above, the face of the moon smiled down, wishing me well as she bathed me in her silvery light – and my body glowed with heat. Then the nightingale called a warning, and at the sound of his footsteps I moved forward and saw him, black and white against the sky as he came to the head of the steps and began to descend, Nella a silver shadow behind him. He reached the terrace – and then Nella lifted her head and whined – she'd seen me. He stopped, turning his head to look, and at that moment I slipped the wrap from my shoulders and let it slide down until it hung only from the fingertips of one hand. Then I began to walk towards him in the moonlight.

He stood still as a statue as I walked on, the silken robe whispering across the grass behind me. When I reached the foot of the steps I looked up and saw his face – and in the shadows cast by the moonlight it was the face of Pan, the Beast God; and I was Aphrodite, Goddess of Love. My lips curved into her confident, generous smile and I began to ascend the steps, my eyes never leaving the harsh planes of his face.

As I drew level with him I tossed my robe aside and raised both my arms to him. Very slowly, as though in a dream, he bent his great head so that I could clasp my hands around his neck and hold him close. And even as I pressed my warm body to his massive chest his arms encircled me, holding me fast against him, so that we became not two statues but one, entwined together in the moonlight.

All at once he moved – and I was swinging up in the air into his arms, to be held close against his fast-beating heart. Then he began to run – running with me down the steps, running across the lawn, running deep into the shadow of the Garland rose – and so I came to rest on the soft grass and lay there, waiting. I heard the sound of his rapid movements and watched the black and white of his clothing tumble to the ground, then I turned my head to look directly up at him. He stood dark and powerful against the moon, with his pale rod risen and swollen with promise; and even as he swooped down so my body rose to meet his, and he pierced me without pain. We rose and fell together, our entwined bodies moving as one, he entering deeper and deeper and I drawing him yet further in; receiving him, welcoming him, enfolding him – until at the last, even as the fountain behind us flowed into the pool, so did he flow into me.

His heavy body lay spent across mine, the silken softness of his hair caressing my breasts as the weight of his chest crushed them, while his gift lay safe inside my body. And because he had given me that gift which I had so longed for I murmured my thanks – but at my words he tore himself free, rearing up above me and blotting out the moon as his hoarse voice cried: 'No! No!' His hand came down hard on my belly, pressing, clutching at it – but it was too late, he could not take back the gift he had given.

I lay gazing up at the gently moving blossom of the Garland rose, the moon a full silver disc high above – and heard the snap of his braces as he struggled to dress, and the soft worried whine of Nella. Heavy footsteps ran across the grass and pounded up the stone steps, to crunch away along the gravel path, then I was left alone in the moonlight.

I lay with my back cool against the soft grass and my warm hands curled protectively over my full belly, cradling it. I whispered my thanks to the honey-scented flowers of the Garland rose, and to Aphrodite who had helped me win my prize. Then I rose slowly to my feet, and went to find my discarded wrap; pulling it round my bare shoulders I walked back to the house, the scents of the rose garden all around me. Before I slipped in through the side door I turned and dropped three curtseys to the moon – it wasn't the right

551

time of the month, but I wanted to thank her, too. Then I went upstairs and fell at once into a dreamless sleep.

Chapter Sixty-One

He didn't come home for three days. He sent a message over from Belling asking Mr Tims to pack a suitcase as he would be going straight up to London that evening, and staying for the summer Rose Show in Regent's Park the next day. He had mentioned the Rose Show over dinner once, but as he wasn't exhibiting this year I'd assumed he wasn't going. Now that he had gone I wasn't disturbed by his sudden change of plans. All my unhappy restlessness had evaporated, and I was as placid as a young heifer grazing in her field. As I walked in the rose garden with Flora I could hardly believe that that scene by the Garland rose had really taken place – except for a momentary flash of embarrassment when Flora's sharp eyes spotted one of his collar studs lying on the grass by the fountain pool.

It was Wednesday evening before I saw him again. He was standing by the hearth in the hall, with his humped back towards the stairs, and he didn't turn round, even though he must have heard me coming down them. As I walked towards him I asked, 'Did you enjoy the Show, my lord?' Very slowly he shifted his body so that he was half-looking at me. His face was brick-red. 'Were there any new roses?' His mouth opened but no words came out. I told him, 'Flora did miss you, but I kept her with me both evenings. Has she told you about Tabby-cat in the stables having her kittens in the manger?' He tried to nod. 'Tabby, she's a good mother, but she did let Flora handle them. Shall we go into dinner now?' I led the way to the dining room.

The gooseberry tart was on the table before he spoke, and then it was only to say yes, when I asked him if he'd been at Belling that day. He was permanently red in the face and he kept his eyes fixed on his plate. It was obvious he didn't know how to behave with me after Sunday night. Yet I wasn't flustered at all. It had been Pan who'd mated with me in the rose garden, whereas it was Lord Warminster who was dining with me, just as he did every night. It was as though the scene beside the Garland rose had been only a dream – except that my body no longer yearned; it was satisfied now and I slept soundly in my bed.

But that night the dream became a nightmare. I woke up; the silver moonbeams shining through the open window cast eerie shadows into the room – and out of those shadows came a monstrous shape. It lurched slowly but purposefully towards the bed – towards me. The hump on its back reared up as it bent over the bed, one huge black claw closing on the sheet and throwing it back. I heard its harsh breathing and looked up with frightened eyes to see the talons reach out again – and the frill on my nightdress hem showed white against their blackness as they wrenched it up and dragged it high above my waist. I trembled from fear and cold, but I was fully awake now and knew who he was and what I had to do, so slowly, reluctantly, my mind gave orders to my legs and they began to part.

When they were fully open I heard his groan of longing, then his weight drove the breath from my lungs as he threw himself down on to me. I felt his rod forcing its way inside me, and then he was thrusting again and again until my whole body was buffeted by the force of his demands. But I made myself lie still and acquiescent beneath him, accepting the mounting pressure of his desire, and his need to slake it in my body.

Urgency made him clumsy. As his body lifted from mine his rod began to pull out, so in my anxiety to meet his need I raised my cunny to enclose it again – and even as I did so I felt the first shudderings of his peak. At once he threw himself back – and the slimy seed came spurting over my thighs until with a sideways lurch he almost fell off the bed and on to the floor. Turning my head I saw him crouched there on the rug, and the moonlight shone on the seed still oozing from the tip of his rod. Frantically he tried to catch it in his hands, until the trickle slowed and finally stopped. He stayed there, crouching, his hands still cupped under his rod, with the dregs of his seed white in the palms of his hands – then he raised his head, and for a moment his mismatched eyes stared straight into mine. With a force that jolted the bed he flung himself to his feet and blundered away across the room. Desperately he fumbled with the handle until it finally gave and he almost fell through the door, slamming it shut behind him.

I began to sob with shock and distress. I was still crying as I forced my trembling legs out of the bed, stumbled to the wash-stand and sluiced my thighs with cold water. The rug beneath was sodden by the time I'd finished, but I was past caring. Back in my bed there were silvery stains on the sheets, and there, where he'd crouched on the rug the merciless moonbeams exposed a pale thread of slime, like the trail of a slug. I managed to clean it up with my face flannel, and then as I took that back to the wash-stand I saw the glinting on the dressing-room door handle – even that was smeared with his seed. My sobs began to choke me as my gorge rose and my stomach heaved. I only just got the lid off the slop bucket in time before I was violently sick.

Coming back from emptying the bucket in the water closet I had to pass the door of his bedroom; I shrank away from it, but not before I'd heard the steady thudding on the floorboards, almost regular, but not quite. It took me a moment to realise what it was: he was pacing up and down the floor of his bedroom. I could hear it faintly even in my own room, and when I eventually fell asleep it was to the vibration of that relentless pounding.

Clara woke me as usual with my morning cup of tea; the pounding had ceased. As she drew the curtains fully back she peered out saying, 'His Lordship didn't take the motor today. I do hope it don't rain, else he'll get wet through, walking all that way back.' She sounded concerned, but all I felt was relief that he'd gone.

I went up to the nursery to say good morning to Flora. As I cuddled her warm young body Ellen told me, 'We're a bit fretful today, my lady – His Lordship didn't come up to say goodbye like he usually do. I told Lady Flora it were with him having to leave so early. There maun be something amiss with his motor – thic things can't be trusted, not like horses can.'

I was reluctant to leave the nursery, but my breakfast would be waiting downstairs, though I had no appetite for it – I still felt queasy and ill. As I sat down at the table I saw there was a small package beside my place. It was tied with string and sealed with wax, but it hadn't come through the post since there was no address on it , nor name, either. 'His Lordship left that for you, my lady.' I dropped the packet as though it were red-hot. I couldn't bring myself to open it until I was alone in the drawing room later. I peered at the imprint of his seal set in the red wax – the swan arching its neck above the three mailed fists – and then reached for my sewing scissors and apprehensively cut the string. But inside there was only a key – a plain doorkey that might have fitted any of the locks at Eston. Eventually I went to find Clara. She was coming out of the housemaid's closet upstairs and when I held the key out to her she said, 'Good, you've found it, my lady. I seed it were missing this morning. It must've dropped out o' the door.'

'Which door?'

She looked at me in surprise. 'Why, His Lordship's dressing-room door, o' course, the one as leads to your bedroom.' I felt the blood rush to my face until it burnt like fire. Clara looked at me, puzzled, then I saw comprehension dawn. Mr Tims would have told the other servants about the unusual event of a parcel – a small key-sized parcel.

I whispered, 'Whatever shall I do with it?'

Clara reached out and patted my arm. 'My lady, he does have his funny ways – he baint like other men, His Lordship. Best put it back in the door and say no more about it. Likely he'll've got over what's fretting him in a day or two.'

I went back to my room and looked at the door handle he'd fumbled with last night. I didn't know which side of the door to put that key. Eventually I took it over to the bedside table, and sat down to think on the edge of the bed – the bed where he'd come to me last night – and remembering that night I shuddered. Under the Garland rose it had been so different. I'd been Aphrodite then, and fired with all her longing, but now I was Amy once more, and I was frightened. The girls taunting me at school in Borrell, the bedsprings creaking nightly in the Buildings, Uncle Alf, Peg . . . they'd all done their work well. But it was more than fear. I remembered that afternoon in the housemaid's closet – and the night that had gone before, and admitted that even with Frank, whom I loved, I had felt only pain and revulsion as he took me. And now I longed to seize hold of that key and lock the door against Lord Warminster for ever.

But there was another memory from last night. There was the memory of that moment when I'd looked into his eyes as he crouched beside my bed, and of the desperate shame and humiliation I'd seen in them. The same shame and humiliation which had driven him to send me this key today. But that shame, that despair – it was my fault. He was suffering because of my actions. Once he'd been a young man, with all a young man's urgent desires, and in the heat of his youth he'd fallen in love with the French countess and begotten a son on her – but then she'd left him. And so he'd retreated from life, and all its lusts, to take refuge in his roses, his books – and his pictures, letting the hot coals of his young desires die down into cold embers. *Child, it is so long since I associated with a woman.* But I had chosen to rekindle those embers, breathing on the dying coals and fanning them into unruly life, and now the flames from them were blazing so fierce and furious they could not be quenched – save only within my body.

I didn't put the key back in the door – he might think that Clara had simply changed it over – instead I took it down to dinner with me. But as I came nervously down the stairs I could see no sign of him waiting in the hall. I walked over to the dining room and peeped in; there was only one place set – mine. I hovered uncertainly outside until Mr Tims arrived and told me, 'My lady, His Lordship asked me to take a tray along to the morning room. He said he thought you'd prefer to dine alone tonight.' He opened the dining-room door wider so I could go in.

I hesitated in the doorway, then turned and said, 'Please tell His Lordship that Her Ladyship'd prefer for him to dine with her, as usual.' Mr Tims went off to deliver his message, and I stood waiting, wondering if he'd come.

He did come, but walking almost sideways, so his face was turned right away from me, and when we sat down his eyes stared straight over my head. As soon as Mr Tims had served the soup and left us I stood up. At once my lord leapt to his feet, his spoon falling with a noisy splash into his tomato soup. I walked the two paces to his side and set the key down next to his plate, then returned to my chair. He slumped down into his seat, his head turned at an awkward angle, so he could look at the key. I said firmly, 'My lord – I don't want it. 'Tis a husband's right to visit his wife's bedroom.'

He didn't pick it up, but all the time he was drinking his soup he kept darting glances at it. Mr Tims must have noticed it as he cleared the soup tureen and returned with the fish, but he gave no sign. I quailed at the thought of the gossip in the Room tonight, but still my lord did not pick up that key, although by now he couldn't take his eyes away from it. Then, just as the roast lamb came in, he reached out his hand – but before his fingers touched the brass he snatched them away again. He went through exactly the same performance after the strawberry tarts were served, and again as the anchovies arrived on their small squares of toast. By the dessert his face was a mask of agonised indecision, and I knew I'd have to speak again. When Mr Tims had left us for the last time I said, 'My lord, 'tis only natural for a husband to want to –' seeking frantically for a word I found one in the farmyard and finished – 'to want to serve his wife from time to time.' There was silence. Then the hand reached slowly out, to come to a halt on the tablecloth, an inch away from the key. It didn't move any further. I said loudly, 'My lord, in the Bible, St Paul he did say, 'tis better to marry than burn, so you'd best come to my room sometimes of a night.' His eyes met mine for a second, but I couldn't read his expression – then his hand moved so fast he almost snatched up the key, thrusting it into his pocket. At once he jumped to his feet, although his orange was still only half-eaten.

I stood up as well, and walked along to pass him, but as I did so he asked abruptly, 'When?'

I repeated stupidly, 'When?' Then I realised what he was asking and said quickly, 'Whenever you do need –' He still stood there, waiting, so I gathered my wits together and remembering this past week suggested, 'Mebbe Sunday – and Wednesday – would suit you.' His head dipped in acknowledgement, then he left the room without even saying good evening. Apart from that one barked 'When?' he hadn't spoken a word to me the entire evening.

On Friday he left a message to say he was going up to London as soon as he'd finished at Belling, and wouldn't be back at Eston until late on Saturday night, so I was not to wait dinner for him. By Sunday I'd not seen him since I'd given him back the key, and I wondered if perhaps he'd be home early, and maybe come into the drawing room at tea-time, or suggest that I join him and Flora on their early evening walk around the rose garden – but he didn't. And at dinner he sat unspeaking, but I realised he was watching me. Not openly, but whenever he thought my attention was on my meal then I would sense his eyes on me – but if I looked up to meet them they would swerve quickly away. Yet the minute I bent my head again I knew he was staring at me once more. By the dessert I could almost feel the heat coming from him: St Paul had said, better to marry than burn – but he was both married and burning. As I left the dining room I said, 'Good evening, my lord.' His lips moved but no reply came. Instead his gaze dropped to my breasts, and for a moment he lost control of his eyes and couldn't tear them away. As I walked out I knew he was staring at me.

Upstairs I heard him come back from his walk around the rose garden far too early. I ran to the bed and dived under the covers. He came in almost at once in his pyjamas and dressing gown, and without looking at me walked to the light switch and snapped it off. In the darkness I pushed back the covers as I heard the soft rustle of his dressing gown falling – then I only just got the skirt of my nightie pulled up before he was on top of me. The whole time he never touched me except to pull my cunny open so he could get his rod well in. After he'd reached his peak he held himself braced above me, and although part of his body was deep inside mine he never touched me. The minute he'd finished spending himself in me he pulled away, picked up his dressing gown, and left.

I dined alone on Monday and Tuesday. He came back to visit Flora in the nursery at his usual time, then returned to Belling, leaving a message that I wasn't to wait up for him. On Wednesday he dined at home, but apart from a muttered 'Good evening,' as I came into the hall he never spoke to me, ignoring my timid efforts at conversation as though he'd not even heard them. But he looked at me. Over and over again I would raise my head to see his eyes veer quickly away – but always I knew they returned.

As I left the dining room he said, 'It is – raining. I will not – be taking Nella for her usual – walk – tonight.' I understood and went straight up to my room. This time I turned the light off before he came in, but otherwise everything was the same as the previous Sunday.

The next morning my monthlies started. I stared at my bloodstained drawers disbelievingly, and then I began to cry. I'd been so sure, so very, very sure. Then I remembered that I'd bled at first while I was carrying Flora, so perhaps it would only be a brief show. But on Wednesday I was still bleeding, and I realised I'd have to tell him. As soon as Mr Tims had served the soup and left us I said, 'My lord . . .' He tore his eyes away from my breasts

559

and stared at the wall above my head, so I knew at least he was listening. My face crimson, I muttered to my spoon, 'Tonight – I be unwell.' I looked up, to see if he'd understood. He was staring into his spinach soup, his twisted shoulder sagging sideways. I whispered, 'I – I be sorry, my lord.'

He replied haltingly, 'It – isn't – your fault.'

I faltered, 'Likely – that is, I'll likely be over being unwell, say by Friday?'

'Sunday.' He didn't speak for the rest of the meal, and nor did I.

On Sunday the weather was cool so I put on my golden velvet evening dress; his eyes went at once to the curve of my breasts, and he barely lifted them all evening. Along with the dessert Mr Tims brought in a flat leather case which he put down by my plate. My lord gestured to it. 'I haven't forgotten that it's your birthday today.'

I looked at him in astonishment, because of course I had forgotten. Or rather, I'd simply not remembered – it'd always been such a shameful secret. 'How did you know?'

His lips curved a little as he replied, 'From the – certificates.'

And he'd taken the trouble to buy me a present! 'Thank 'ee, my lord, thank 'ee.'

'Aren't you going to open it?'

I put my fingernail under the brass clasp and opened it slowly, savouring the moment – it was only the second birthday present I'd ever received. The lid came up, and there, nestling against its blue velvet bed – was a pearl necklace. I stared at it.

'Aren't you – going to put it on?'

Picking it up as though it were a poisonous snake I fastened it around my neck. It had three rows of pearls, just like the one my own lord had given me, but it wasn't quite the same because it had a pendant studded with more pearls that hung down into the cleft between my breasts. I said, 'Thank you, my lord,' and reached for an apple. He began to quarter an orange – and nearly cut himself with the silver fruit knife as he did so because his eyes were riveted on that pendant.

Upstairs he came to me quickly, and left just as rapidly. I heard him call Nella, and then he went out for his postponed walk. I got up and went to the window, and looked out at the moon; she was waxing again. Leaning my head against the window frame I told myself it was as well that he was coming to me regularly – if I hadn't conceived under the Garland rose then at least now I soon would. But I felt so deathly tired I hardly seemed to care any more.

Much later I awoke to find him standing by my bed; he'd cleared his throat to attract my attention, but he didn't speak. He'd obviously come to claim Wednesday's dues; after all, he'd paid me well this week. Pushing down the covers I pulled up my nightie and opened my legs for him. Clambering on to the bed he straddled me, then began to push in his rod. It seemed to go on for ever, and all the time behind my closed lids I saw Peg with all those men in the alleyway, as they coupled casually against the wall. He was coupling with me on a bed, but otherwise it was no different; he was simply using me as a vessel for the satisfaction of his carnal lusts. There was no talking, no loving – only the repeated uncaring invasion of my body in search of release.

He achieved that release at last; but even as he was spending himself in me so the nausea was rising from the pit of my stomach – and the minute the door closed behind him I half-fell out of bed and stumbled to the slop bucket, trying to retch over it soundlessly.

The immediate sickness passed but I felt no relief, and back in my bed I huddled shivering under the covers. It was the height of summer, but I was so cold. It was a long time before I slept.

Chapter Sixty-Two

I felt myself to be no better than a harlot, for so he used me. At dinner he barely spoke to me but sat at the head of the table, a great brooding presence, seeming to resent my very existence. But every Wednesday and Sunday there were those snatched, hungry stares, and my whole body burnt with humiliation – while his pearls branded my flesh, reminding me that he'd paid for my services.

The Garland rose had shed her petals, and now there was just a gnarled apple tree beside the leaden fountain; it was as if that moonlit evening had been merely a dream, but the nightmare – the nightmare became real twice every week. I told myself I was behaving like a foolish girl. He was my husband, every stitch of clothing I wore, every mouthful of food I ate he had paid for, and so he had bought the right to my body, too. Besides, it was I who had chosen to awaken his dormant instincts, and by so doing made a rod for my own back. Then I thought – a rod for my own cunny, more like – and forced a smile at my silly joke. But when the evening came, the joke was a joke no longer, because that was all he cared for, all he wanted. That night, as always, he pulled away and left me without even a backward glance, and his rapid, scuttling gait made it humiliatingly obvious that he couldn't bear to be in my bedroom a moment longer than necessary. I remembered Uncle Alf, and the nightly creaking of the bedsprings – but he'd loved Aunt Agnes in his way, talking to her and never failing to greet her with a kiss when he came home from work each day. I told myself that Lord Warminster did not kiss – he never kissed Flora, even – but he took her on his lap and held her close against his chest, just as my Granfer had done with me. If only he'd just for a second reached out and touched my hair or stroked my hand before he left me – but he never did.

My monthlies came again at the usual time the second month and I shed tears of disappointment; though he used me every week he could not give me the child I longed for. But by September my breasts had grown heavy and full, and I almost began to hope.

Monday – Monday would tell me. If I didn't bleed on Monday. But first there was Sunday to be endured. I walked in the rose garden with Flora before taking her up to the nursery so she'd be there ready for when her grandfather returned from Belling. Back in the drawing room I picked up my mending and began to darn; my hands were busy with my needle but my thoughts were all for tomorrow. Maybe, maybe . . . Then the door opened and as I looked up Mr Tims announced, 'Lord Quinham, my lady.'

I stared at him as if he were a ghost. 'Good afternoon, Amy.' He walked in and threw himself down in a chair, his blue eyes never leaving my face as he dropped his gloves to the floor.

At last I found my voice. 'Would you like some tea?'

He shook his head. 'I haven't come here for tea.'

'Then, Flora? Shall I ring –'

He cut across my words. 'I haven't come for Flora, either.' His gaze didn't waver as he said, 'It's you I've come for.' I couldn't answer, but I managed to move my head in a gesture of refusal. He leant forward in his chair, his face fixed on mine. 'I need you, Amy – you know why. So I'm asking you again, and this time you must say yes. It may be my last chance – I'm going to France on Wednesday.'

'No!'

'Yes. I'm on draft leave – so I came here, for you.'

'No – I won't, I mustn't, I can't!'

He shook his head. 'It's no use your protesting, Amy – I'm not taking no for an answer again. I know my wretched cock let me down last time and I fumbled it – but I won't fumble it again. I've left my kit with Tims and told him I'm staying overnight, then I can come to your room under cover of darkness, in the respectable way. You can go through the motions of resisting me, just to appease your conscience, but you see, Amy, you gave yourself away last time. I know you want another child, so I'm going to give you one, tonight.' Sitting back in his chair he reached into his tunic pocket and took out his cigarette case.

As he snapped it open I blurted out, 'You can't – 'tis Sunday.'

He glanced up from his match. 'Yes, it generally is on the day after Saturday.'

'My lord –'

Striking the match he said, 'Oh, call me Frank, for goodness sake!'

'No. I mean, my lord –' I drew a breath and said loudly, 'Your father – he'll be coming to my room tonight.'

'What? But he can't be!'

'He's my husband, and he do be a proper husband to me now.'

As the colour drained from his face the match burnt down until the flame licked his fingers. With an oath he flung it into the hearth before exclaiming, 'It's not true. You're lying!'

'No – he's been coming to me regular, as a husband, since midsummer.'

'Since midsummer.' His eyes narrowed. 'And I came to you at the beginning of June, and you refused me – then the old man started coming to you . . .' He broke off, his face hardening. 'No, I've got it the wrong way round, haven't I, Amy? He never came to you – he wouldn't know how to after all this time. Besides, he swore to Annabel he'd never . . . No, you went to him, didn't you – asking for it, begging for it?' The hot blood rushing to my face told him the answer. 'Even he managed to get it up when it was offered to him on a plate. How could you, Amy? How could you?'

I tried to explain, excuse – but his angry voice rose louder and louder, drowning mine. 'Did you enjoy it, Amy? Did you enjoy having those great hairy paws mauling you? How does it feel now, you little slut, to have that huge crooked hump-back sprawled over your belly thrusting his twisted cock into you?' I put my hands over my ears but he was looming over me, shouting so that I heard every word. 'And how does it feel when that twisted cock finally manages to spew its vile gunk into you?' The tears were running down my cheeks. I tried to hide them but his hand caught my wrist and wrenched it back so that his glittering eyes stared into mine. 'Do you enjoy it *now*, Amy?' He read the answer in my face and suddenly his gloves came down in a stinging slap across my cheek. 'Serves you right, you little whore!'

He turned away and stood facing the hearth, his whole body shaking. When at last he was still I whispered hopelessly, 'I baint a whore – he be my husband.'

He threw back his head and laughed, jeering, bitter. 'Then tell your *husband* that I shall be dining with him tonight. Quite a family party it'll be, won't it? Father, son, step-mother – what a pity my daughter isn't old enough to join us.' He spun round abruptly and headed for the door. 'I'm going up to the nursery.'

'But, my – Lord Warminster, he do go up when he comes in.'

'Then I'll be able to say "How do you do" won't I? No doubt he'll be pleased to see me.'

I waited until the last possible moment before going down to dinner; slipping noiselessly down the stairs I stopped on the last step, unable to go on. They were standing either side of the empty hearth, each slightly turned so that they did not have to look at each other. But from the shadows I looked at them as they stood there – father and son. The son was straight and slim in his uniform, and his fair hair, catching the slanting rays of the sun through the high window, glowed like a golden halo. The father, with the upper part of his ungainly body twisted to one side, forcing the opposite shoulder up into that misshapen hump, stood away from the light, trying to merge his black bulk into the shadows – but I could still see the grey hair at his temples and the harsh lines on his face. My eyes travelled from one to the other: light and dark, young and old, straight and crooked, Adonis – and Vulcan.

I forced my unwilling foot to step down into the hall, and at once they both turned towards me. I looked at the two of them: the son with his handsome, regular features and the father, whose face seemed to have been squeezed by a giant's hand, until now nothing matched. For a moment both were still, then Frank glided lithely towards me, his arm extended. 'May I escort you into dinner, Amy?' Lord Warminster stayed still as a statue. I placed my hand on the khaki sleeve and allowed Frank to lead me across the hall and into the dining room; heavy footsteps followed.

Mr Tims stepped forward as usual, but Frank waved him back and drew out my chair himself; I almost fell down on to the seat – my trembling legs would support me no longer. Frank strode round the far end of the table to his own place opposite me, and with a scraping of chair-legs the two men sat down and unfolded their napkins. The soup was served, Mr Tims withdrew and both men lifted their full spoons. Frank swallowed his soup in a swift, graceful movement before smiling directly at me and saying, 'You look beautiful tonight, Amy – quite beautiful.' As the warm blush veiled my cheeks he laughed softly. 'You're absolutely delicious. Do you know, I feel great sympathy for that wolf in the tale of Little Red Riding Hood – I'm sure I could gobble you up for dinner in one big bite.' His smile broadened as he swung his supple body right round so as to face Lord Warminster directly. 'She does look tempting tonight, doesn't she . . .' there was a pause, infinitesimal yet still too long, before he added smoothly, ' . . . sir?' His bright blue eyes turned back to me, and Lord Warminster's grey ones slowly followed until both pairs were focused on my face for a moment; then, simultaneously, they dropped to the swelling curve of my breasts. But in that moment I'd read the same message in each – both of them wanted me. I was a hind caught between two rutting stags, and I could only wait fearfully for the clash of their antlers. It soon came.

The younger stag used his voice as his weapon. Lightly, fluently, he addressed his father directly, demanding answers – and always at the moment when Lord Warminster was about to put his spoon to his mouth, so he had to either drop it back again or miss his cue while he tipped his spoon at that awkward angle into his mouth under Frank's mocking gaze. Once he tried to reply and drink at the same time, as Frank was able to do, but the attempt failed in a spluttering cough while Frank laughed lightly for just a fraction too long before saying, 'Don't you fancy any more, sir? Then I'll ring for Tims.' And the plates were carried away, only one of them empty.

Battle recommenced with the fish. 'How's Nella, sir? Lovely dog – bitch, I should say. That Great Dane certainly knew her sex, that time in the stable-yard! Do you remember, Amy? Of course you do – in fact you must look back on it now as being an omen for the future, mustn't you? How I laughed when Tyson told me the story.' He turned to the head of the table. 'You certainly moved quickly that time, sir, didn't you? Just as well – what a terrible mismating that would have been.' Lord Warminster's mouth was working, searching for words as behind him I saw the first tremor of the door-handle, signalling Mr Tims' return; quickly, skilfully, Frank thrust in his rapier, bitter and sharp. 'Nearly as bad as your marriage. Still, you couldn't blame Amy that time, could you? *She* was too ill to know what she was doing.' Mr Tims entered the room and at once Frank's voice became light and casual as he added, 'You soon recovered though, Amy, didn't you? By the time I ran into you in France you were chatting away nineteen to the dozen.'

I cringed before Lord Warminster's furious glare. If only, if only

I'd not told Frank, but it was too late – he knew, and that knowledge sharpened his antlers for the next bout. But the old stag moved first. As the door closed behind Mr Tims his harsh voice spoke. 'I had a letter this week – from your wife. I respect the work she is doing.' For a second Frank looked disconcerted; I saw it, and so did Lord Warminster who looked at him directly as he added, 'You must be proud of her.'

'Yes, yes of course I am.'

He bent over his plate, but the heavier antlers would not be deflected. 'Tell me, Francis, I've temporarily forgotten – which VAD unit is she serving with?'

'I – can't remember myself, sir. You know I was never any good with figures.' The grizzled eyebrows lowered but Frank was recovering his poise. 'She looks a treat in that dinky white veil the nurses wear, though she's not keen on the apron – she says it makes her feel like a servant.' He smiled, confident now.

Lord Warminster spoke slowly and distinctly as he said, 'VAD clerks do not wear veils – or aprons.' The triumphant clash of the heavier antlers seemed to echo round the room as Frank's face flushed in humiliation.

But as course succeeded course it became clear which of the stags was gaining ground – the younger. He was swifter and more skilful; he launched his darts with impeccable timing so that again and again they found their mark just as Mr Tims' return thwarted the old stag in his efforts to retaliate. When the door closed again he would charge – but he was losing control of his temper, and relying on weight, not skill, so that as the antlers were about to lock, the younger stag with an adroit twist of his head would disengage himself, moving back out of danger by the clever use of his quick tongue and leaving the old stag baffled and frustrated.

And as they fought I knew that I was their prey. Locked in their verbal battle they didn't bother to speak to me – but they looked. At first only cautious, covert glances, but as the meal progressed they became more reckless and whenever Mr Tims' presence silenced them they would both turn to stare at me; blue eyes, grey eyes – both pairs wanted me. While I, I was acutely aware that I had been possessed by both of them. The son had taken me and I had borne him a child, a daughter; now his father took me, and would again tonight. And as I sat there through that terrible meal

567

the urgent need to pass water told me what I had not allowed myself to believe before – that I was carrying a second child; this time not the child of the son, but of the father.

By the dessert they were fighting their private war on the public battlefields of France. Frank made a comment about the guns and Lord Warminster disagreed savagely. 'You never could grasp maths – you don't know what you're talking about.'

'But *you're* hardly in a position to judge the strength of the German artillery are you – sir? Since your disabilities so fortunately preclude your participation.' Lord Warminster tried to reply but before he could find the words Frank said with a charming smile, 'However I must say I really admire the way you're doing your bit over at Lady Burton's.' Lord Warminster hesitated, thrown off-course by the unexpected compliment. Frank leant forward and selecting a hazel nut from the dish set it between the jaws of the silver nutcracker; he held it poised as he added, 'But then, I know you're not incapable – not totally *impotent*.' There was a loud crack as he brought the handles sharply together. I heard Lord Warminster's indrawn hiss of breath even above the sound of Frank's laughter. Still smiling he turned to me, 'Why so silent now, Amy? I couldn't stop you chattering this afternoon, could I?' I quailed before the fury in Lord Warminster's face: he was shaking with anger and his hand caught the glass by his plate so that it rocked and began to tilt. In a flash Frank had reached out and steadied it. 'Careful, sir, you mustn't *fumble*, must you – not tonight!' He laughed, and there was no mistaking the jeering note in it. Then his hand travelled to the bell and punched it hard. As soon as the door opened he ordered, 'Tims – Lady Warminster has invited us to take coffee with her in the drawing room – it'll be so much more cheerful in there. Shall we go?' I stood up, and the men rose after me, but as I walked to the door Frank exclaimed, 'Damn, I've left my cigarettes upstairs – must pop up and get them.'

I turned away from the direction of the drawing room and almost ran to the cloakroom; I couldn't face Lord Warminster alone, and besides I was desperate to use the WC. I huddled in the safety of the cubicle but I couldn't stay there for ever, so at last I pulled the chain and opened the door out into the cloakroom, and as I came out an arm seized hold of me from behind and clamped me against a hard male chest. A voice in my ear said, 'Don't be frightened, I'm not going to take you properly – but I don't see why the old man should have all the fun tonight.' Still holding me fast he backed up against the wall – and I saw the white blur of my face reflected in the small mirror over the wash-basin opposite. He saw it too and said mockingly, 'What a pity the mirrors aren't much cop at Eston. I enjoyed our little game before – until you ran away – but you're not going to escape this time.' As he shifted his grip I tried to wriggle free but at once his arm tightened again. 'No, Amy – don't struggle, I'm much stronger than you are. Best be a good girl and get it over with quietly. You won't be breaking any Commandments, that I can assure you.'

So I stood unresisting while his hand forced its way down inside my dress and under my camisole. He squeezed my bare breast so hard I wanted to cry aloud with the pain – but I didn't care. His other arm pressed across my stomach so that my buttocks were full against his crotch, and then he began to move. Rhythmically he rubbed himself up and down, up and down – his grip tightening all the time until my belly hurt with the force of it. At last, when I thought I could stand it no longer, he gave a final thrust forward, murmuring in my ear, 'Nice, Amy, nice – ah!' He held me fast against him as he throbbed and jerked against my buttocks. When he'd finished he pulled his hand out of my dress and released me with a casual push to one side. I sagged against the wall as he unbuttoned his breeches, took out a sodden handkerchief and tossed it casually into the waste-basket. 'Thanks, Amy – that should do the trick until I can get into Salisbury later,' he looked me directly in the face with hard blue eyes as he added deliberately, 'and find myself another whore. You cut along to the drawing room now while I nip up the back stairs and fetch my cigarette case.' He laughed. 'Funny – I really *had* left it upstairs, but when I saw you coming in here I couldn't resist the opportunity of relieving myself too.'

The minute he'd left I ran to the mirror, twisting and turning in front of it, but there was no damp patch on my skirt. Reaching for the taps I turned them full on. I wanted to climb into the basin and scrub myself all over – I felt soiled, dirty – but there was only time to wash my hands before going along to the drawing room. I was shaking as I went in, and when Lord Warminster looked across at

569

me I felt as though he could read my shame on my face. He stood there, watching me as I fought to control the tears, then Frank's footsteps sounded in the hall and I backed away from the door, trembling with fear.

Frank seemed completely unaware of my distress. 'Pour me a cup of coffee, Amy.' My hands shook so much the coffee spilled into the saucer as I handed it to him, but he took no notice. 'Thank you, Amy my pet.'

The carelessly used endearment was like a slap in the face and I flinched away from him – then Lord Warminster's harsh voice exclaimed, 'Don't call her – by that name!'

Frank's face was a mask of innocence. 'What name, sir – Amy? Has she changed it?'

Lord Warminster tried to say, 'Pet,' but he could barely get the word out and Frank laughed. 'Surely *I*, of all people, have the right to address her so familiarly?' There were no servants now to keep the duel within bounds and he turned deliberately round so he could cast his eyes over my body in one lingering, insolent glance.

As I shrank away, my cheeks burning with humiliation, Lord Warminster stammered, 'How – dare, how – dare – you,' he gulped, scarcely able to get the words out but he fought on, 'How dare you insult – my wife!'

Frank raised his coffee cup to his lips before replying, and even that simple move was performed with studied impertinence. He swallowed slowly, smoothly – then looking up at his father said, 'Oh, I dare, old man. I dare because before she was *your* wife she was *my* mistress.' I couldn't move.

'You – you –' Lord Warminster lunged towards his son, but Frank sidestepped, casually, gracefully, before saying, 'Don't get excited, old chap, I quite understand why you ignored her little slip-up – how else could you have got a girl with her looks? I don't begrudge you. After all, I'd already taken what mattered – remember, I was the man who had the pleasure of pricking her rose.' He threw back his head, laughing. 'How she did bleed, this girl. *You've* never seen anything like it! Oh yes, there was no doubting that I was the first man to enjoy her, but she's not so fussy these days, is she? She'll satisfy herself with whatever she can get – won't you, my pet?' He wasn't smiling now, and he spoke as if he hated me. He moved forward to look directly at me. 'Don't cry, Amy, it'll spoil your good looks – and what use is a whore without a pretty face?'

I stared back at him, mesmerised – and then suddenly Lord Warminster thrust his way between us so that his black-coated back hid me from those sneering blue eyes. 'Leave her – leave her alone.'

'Don't worry, old man, I'm not going to take her away from you – you're welcome to make use of my left-overs.' The black bulk lunged forward but slipping to one side Frank made for the door and with his hand on the knob called, 'If you *can!*'

Lord Warminster found his voice at last in a great bellow of rage. 'Get out! Get out of my house!' But it was too late, Frank had already gone.

His father, his face still working with anger, swung round to where I huddled sobbing on the sofa. I couldn't bear to look into his furious eyes – I hid my tears of shame in my hands. But when he finally spoke the anger had gone from his voice and he said quietly, 'Go up to your room now.'

Chapter Sixty-three

Somehow I got myself undressed and washed and into bed, my hands moving without thought because of the turmoil in my mind. I saw again the heavy, black-coated figure at the head of the table with the agile, khaki-clad body twisting and turning as it attacked its cumbrous prey – only I'd been wrong, they were not a pair of stags at all. I'd never seen stags fighting, but I'd seen a battle like this before – I couldn't remember where, but the flicker of memory was painful and sharp. The pain stabbed again harder at the thought of how Frank had used my body and then thrust me aside with those cruel words: 'And find myself another whore.' That's all I was, a whore to be fought over, a bitch pursued by panting dogs. I remembered their eyes at the dinner table, both pairs of eyes wanting me, lusting for me, fighting over me – and then my frantic thoughts slowed a little. No, not fighting over me – at least, not in the drawing room later, for by then Frank had taken what he could get, and having taken, despised me. No, in the drawing room Lord Warminster had been fighting his duel on my behalf, trying to defend me from the merciless attack of his son. 'How dare you insult my wife!' Because I was his wife and he'd always treated me so.

I'd been wrong these past weeks, quite wrong. He'd never treated me as a harlot: he'd burned for me, but only as a husband burns for his wife. The pearls, those hated pearls, had been a birthday gift, not payment. And with that realisation came a measure of calm. He knew my past, better than anyone – but he'd never thrown it in my face. Never once had he taunted me with my bastardy, with the folly of my dreams; and never, ever, had he condemned me for my sin, not even tonight, when Frank had used his knowledge of that sin as a weapon against me. Instead Lord Warminster had tried as best he could to defend me, fighting an unequal battle with his stammering tongue and clumsy body – until the inevitable defeat. Both of us – we'd both been defeated by that quick-moving tan body, and again the past tugged at my memory – but at that moment the dressing-room door began to open.

He came straight to my bed. I heard his dressing gown slither to the floor; he snatched the skirt of my nightdress up ready as he climbed on to the bed. His hand opened my cunny and then his rod began to push – but when it was halfway in it seemed to stop. He pushed harder – and even as he did so I felt it wilt and shrivel inside me. He brought his hips hard down on mine, thrusting frantically, desperately – but there was nothing there any more. For a moment he lay slumped across me, breathing heavily, then he raised himself a little and I felt his fingers fumbling with my cunny again, opening it once more before pressing his body so close against mine that I could feel his balls warm between my thighs – but his rod remained limp and useless. In my head I heard again Frank's jeering taunt: 'If you *can!*' – but he couldn't, for he was impotent now.

Slowly, hopelessly, he eased his body off mine and turned on his side with his back to me. Shifting to the edge of the bed he leant over it for a moment, then his arm came back up and I saw it moving in the dim light from the window; as the mattress began to vibrate in a steady rhythm I guessed what he was doing. He was handling himself in the same way his son had made me handle him in the housemaid's closet – and for the same purpose. I lay, waiting, but while the son had been young and confident, the father was middle-aged and uncertain, and before long the movements lost their rhythm and began to slow until finally, they stopped altogether, and he just lay there, slumped on the edge of the bed. And now the memory which had been teasing the fringe of my consciousness came flooding back: the bear and the dog. I was back in Lambeth again watching the dancing bear that was too old to dance any more, and the young tan dog that had been set on to it for sport. The snapping jaws of the lithe young animal, the clumsy movements of the old grizzled bear – too old and toothless to defend itself properly despite its superior size – I saw it as sharp and clear as though it had only happened today. But it *had* happened today, this evening; in the drawing room downstairs the very same battle had been fought and lost – but the old bear had not died in the gutter, he lay beside me on the bed – and even as I realised, I was turning towards him and putting both my arms

573

around his twisted neck. For a second he became stiff as a statue – then with a sudden convulsive movement he seized hold of me and pulled me close against him. He held me so tightly clasped in his arms that it was as if his heart beat in my body – then his desperate grip relaxed a little, and I felt the tenseness in him gradually slacken until we lay cuddled close and warm together, drawing comfort from each other's nearness. But as soon as I tried to ease my cramped arm from under the weight of his neck he at once released me, and before I could move he'd backed off my bed and left.

I slept at last, only to wake in the morning to the memory of Frank's cruelty – and that memory crushed me, because I knew that however much he hurt me I still loved him, and always would. But I forced myself to remember too that his father had tried to defend me – his father who was my legal husband. The two memories hung in the balance as duty fought with love, until Frank's own words helped me to win the battle: 'Duty's a cold bedfellow, Amy,' he'd said – but last night, just for a little while, duty had not been cold but warm, as Lord Warminster had held me close in his need. And he and I were husband and wife, before God and man; moreover as I felt the fullness of my breasts I knew that now I was bound to him by even closer ties, for I was carrying his child. So I knew what I must do.

Slowly and painfully, brick by brick, I built the little house in my head then, taking Frank by the hand for one last time, I led him inside and closed the door behind him. I wept tears for my loss but even as I did so I knew they were the tears of a foolish girl, for I had lost him long ago, to Miss Annabel. No, I was wrong – I hadn't lost him because he'd never been mine to lose. He'd never loved me, he'd only wanted from me what all men wanted – and in my sinful folly I had given it to him. I forced the door shut once more. I would not think of him, I must not think of him. All my loyalty now was owed to his father, my husband.

I was so unhappy that all day I kept trailing upstairs to the nursery. My only comfort was in my daughter, and as I held her firm young body I reminded myself again and again of that day when Lord Warminster had given her back to me. She broke away and went to fetch her new doll to show me; I'd never had a doll in my life, but she had half-a-dozen, and a bear, a dolls' house, a

Noah's Ark – I couldn't number the toys in the cupboard of that bright, airy nursery. And even those which had been gifts from me he had paid for; I had given her life, but he had given her everything else, including her name.

I didn't expect him back to dinner, but he came. We ate in silence, both constrained by the memories of the previous evening, while that fleeting moment when he'd held me close in the night seemed only a dream now. But by the time the apple pie arrived I realised that he wanted to speak but couldn't find the words, so with an effort I began to talk instead, telling him about Flora, and how when I'd taken her to the stables old Mr Tyson, the coachman, had lifted her up to pat the lawnmower pony. 'She loves the horses, does Flora.'

He replied, 'As soon as she is old enough to ride I will get her a pony of her own.' Another gift.

On Tuesday he managed a few halting words, but on Wednesday he simply told the wall, 'Not – tonight.' I was almost sorry, but although my monthlies hadn't come at all this week I was too embarrassed to tell him he could come if he wished – and besides, I wasn't sure whether he wanted to. But at the end of the meal, as I walked past him to leave the dining room I managed to whisper, 'Friday, mebbe?'

His reply was so low I barely heard it. 'Perhaps.'

By Friday I wanted him to come. He was my husband, it was right that he should – and his coming would help me keep that treacherous door in my head closed. As soon as I arrived in the hall before dinner I knew that he wanted to come, too – I could see it in the way he looked at me. But as course followed course I realised that he was nervous and uncertain, so in between our brief, formal conversational exchanges I would look down at my plate, or at the wall in front of me – allowing him to sneak those covert glances at my breasts; I understood now that he needed to do this. At the end of the meal I tried to think of some way of letting him know I was expecting him to come, but all I could manage was a murmured, ' 'Tis damp outside, my lord. You'd best not spend too long on your walk tonight.' By the reddening of his cheeks I knew he'd understood what I was trying to say, so with a formal, 'Good evening,' I left him – but I still wasn't sure that he'd come.

Upstairs I lay in bed for a long time, waiting – but the dressing-room door did finally open. At once I pulled back the covers and lifted the skirt of my nightie. He stood by the bed, hesitating, so I lifted the frilled hem even higher and then I heard the familiar sound of his dressing gown dropping to the floor. This time his rod did not betray him, though when his movements changed to the small quivering shudders that told me he was spending himself I felt profound relief. The minute he'd finished he withdrew his rod, slid off the bed and left the room at once – just as he always did. Once the dressing room door was closed I pulled my nightie down over my chilly backside and dragged the covers back up. The relief had faded by now and I felt only a cold emptiness – so cold that for a moment I was tempted and began to open that little door in my head. I only just managed to stop myself in time; I knew that once I let him out I'd never get him back in again. But no sooner had I forced it shut than the gentlest of clicks told me that another door had opened – a real door, this time, the door into my bedroom.

Peering into the darkness I could only see a pale blur, but I knew who it was who was moving so slowly across the floor towards me. Once he seemed to stop altogether, and half-turn round as if to retreat, but then he came on again. As he reached my bed I saw that he was only wearing pyjamas, and the absence of his usual, all-enveloping dressing gown confused me, so that I was slow in pulling back the covers and before I'd had time to draw up my nightie he diverted from his normal pattern by sitting down on the edge of the bed. As I watched his lopsided bulk against the paler oblong of the window I realised he wasn't approaching me – he was simply lowering himself down on to his back; and when he was lying as flat as he ever could lie then he simply stayed there, on the extreme edge of the mattress, still as a statue. And yet for all his stillness he seemed to be waiting for something.

I was so puzzled by his unexpected reappearance and this unusual behaviour that I couldn't think what he was waiting for – and then, at last, I understood. Yet, understanding, I could scarcely believe I was right, and my first moves were so tentative and slight they were scarcely moves at all as, very gradually, I began to inch my way across the bed towards him. He never moved as I came closer, but I heard his breathing quicken as my body met his. We lay side by side in the darkness, only our hips and shoulders touching; I had no clues as to what to do next. Even if the moon had given enough light I couldn't have seen his face – it was turned away from me, as it always must be when he lay to my left. But where my body touched his I sensed a tense expectancy, so slowly, gently – as though he were an untamed animal who might easily be frightened – I turned on my side towards him and slid my right hand around his chest. Then at last he moved. Just as slowly, just as cautiously as I had he slid his right hand under my body so that I lay in the curve of his arm. As he held me I pressed closer, until I could hear the drumming of his heart. The heat of his body warmed me – but my uncovered shoulders became cold in the chilly night air and I shivered. At once he set me free and went back to his room, leaving me regretting that unthinking shiver.

I was still regretting it the next day as I wondered whether he'd come back to dinner; he did come but he was very formal – almost speechless – though he watched my face intently as I told him of how Flora had seen two squirrels and a jay. And then it was Sunday. I almost welcomed his covert glances that evening because they told me he would come to my bedroom – but would he come twice?

At last my straining ears heard that gentle click and my body relaxed. Again he'd left his dressing gown behind for his second visit, almost as if he wanted to tell me it was for a different purpose. Once again he walked across the floor very slowly, and when he arrived at my bed he simply lay down and waited. But I was more confident tonight and moved straight over to him, pulling the sheet and blankets with me so that as my arm came round him the bedclothes came too until we were both enclosed in their warmth together. Then, with my hands holding him fast by the shoulders I wriggled around in search of a comfortable resting place – and found it in the hollow of his shoulder. Settling my cheek there with a small sigh of contentment I felt him pull me close – until he was holding me safe and warm in his arms. It was much later when he finally eased himself gently from me and left; I curled up in the space his body had warmed and fell instantly asleep.

Chapter Sixty-four

I no longer dreaded Wednesday and Sunday; instead I looked forward to them. The first time he came each night I would put my mind on other things – my sewing, which of his suits needed an extra brush – then as soon as he'd finished and left the room I'd move across to the side of the bed to warm the space for him, and wait. He always came back, and as soon as he'd climbed into my bed I'd reach out to him; his arms would come round me in return and then we'd hold each other close in a warm cuddle.

Once I was lying a little more across his body than usual and I felt his rod begin to swell again in arousal. I shifted uncertainly; immediately he realised and put me away from him, and then we simply lay side by side until he left. Coupling and cuddling were different, they mustn't be mixed. I understood – although he'd said nothing – because I felt just the same; and next time I was careful to keep my legs a little to one side of his, so I didn't touch him there. He said nothing, he never did say anything – he never spoke a word and nor did I, we simply lay close and warm together, drawing comfort from each other's nearness. Occasionally I gave a soft murmur of contentment, and then his grip would tighten for a second to show he'd heard and understood – but we never spoke.

At dinner we did speak, although we were not so much at ease with each other as we had been back in the spring; yet there was an understanding between us. Day-time and night-time were completely separate. He wanted them separate – and I was careful never to say anything which would link the two and spoil that delicate, unacknowledged equilibrium. But sometimes he would look up suddenly and catch my eye, and instead of looking away as he'd always done before, his mouth would curve into his awkward, difficult smile – and seeing it I would smile back.

I wasn't happy – how could I be happy when I struggled every morning to force Frank back into the little house? Perhaps if he'd really been safe in that house of his boyhood over at Pennings then

I could have settled; but he wasn't, he was in France, in danger – and the little news that filtered through only increased my anguish. There had been a big battle at a place called Loos, and Clara told me that a man from Tilton had been killed there. 'And there's many more of 'em gone, so they says.' Then we heard that all the men from Eston who'd been in Egypt were being sent back, and likely going to France, and all of a sudden the first of them came home on leave – Mr Tyson's grandson. He'd come straight up as soon as he arrived to see Mary, and the next thing Clara was telling me how annoyed Mrs Johnstone was because Mary was leaving at once to get married and so there'd have to be a new housemaid at Eston. 'There baint no cottage free so Mary's going back to live with her mam. Her being a widow they'll be company for each other, and then,' Clara's face clouded, 'if so be something did happen . . .' She didn't finish the sentence but I understood and my fears winged their way to France, to Frank: he might already be wounded, dead even – and I wouldn't know. But surely, a message would be sent to Lord Warminster, and there'd be some sign on his face. After all, they were still father and son, however badly they argued. If only Mr Wallis were still at Eston I could have asked him, but now there was no one, except Lord Warminster himself.

Eventually I couldn't stand the suspense any longer and at dinner I plucked up the courage to ask if he would please to tell me: 'If Lord Quinham – if he were – if anything happened . . .' My voice stumbled to a halt as I saw the expression in his eyes. Desperately I added, 'He do be Flora's father . . .' And knew as his face darkened that I'd said the unforgiveable. He didn't open his mouth again that evening, not even to respond to my timid, 'Good night, my lord.'

The following day Ellen told me he'd driven back in the afternoon to see Flora and was returning to Belling as soon as he'd brought her back to the nursery. There was only one place set at dinner; Mr Tims said His Lordship had insisted that I wasn't to wait for him. It was the same the day after, and then it was Wednesday – but he didn't return for dinner then, either. I went to bed and lay awake, waiting – hearing him moving about next door. But he never came, and I cried myself to sleep.

By the next day I was so desperate I asked Mr Tims to tell me as

579

soon as my lord had come back to see Flora in the afternoon – then I went straight up to the nursery. He was there, but he didn't want to stay when he saw me, only Flora wouldn't let him go. I sat over my sewing while she showed him how she built a house with her wooden bricks, and gradually I could see the tension drain out of him as she chattered away. When he stood up to go I rose too; Ellen was in the night nursery so we were alone, but for Flora. I said, 'I'm sorry, my lord. I won't ask again.'

Holding my daughter in his arms – his son's daughter – he haltingly told her fair head, 'If anything – were to happen – it would be known. Clara would tell you.'

As he turned to go I almost ran after him. 'Will you be back for dinner tonight?' He stopped at the door, then after a very long time he half-nodded his head.

That Sunday I dressed in my golden velvet. It was too tight now with the child coming but I managed to fasten it, and because it was tight my breasts swelled up from the bodice, rounded and full. Deliberately I used them to tempt him, turning towards him, leaning forward over the table so that he could not help but see the promise I offered. Then as I passed him at the end of the meal my ankle gave way and I stumbled. The accident was genuine but the way I swayed forward until my breasts brushed his arm – that was not. I glanced up into his face, and knew by the expression I saw on it that he would visit my room tonight.

He came the first time, but I'd almost given up hope of his return when the door clicked gently open a second time. At once I sat up in bed, holding my arms out to him – and he came straight to me. I pressed myself against him almost crying with relief, and he hugged me tight in response. But we never spoke.

One night soon after, I was lying close against his chest half-dozing, and fell into a fragment of a dream – a dream of him in the bathroom that time. Then he shifted his arm slightly, easing his position and as I came awake again I remembered how afterwards at the dinner table I'd longed to stroke that soft dark hair which grew on his body – and because now he held me in his arms, it seemed only natural to undo his top pyjama button and slip my hand inside. It was just as soft and silky to the touch as I'd imagined, only with the warmth as well from the living skin below. My fingertips stroked him gently, and his arms tightened round me in response; when I fell asleep my hand was still there, touching him.

On the following Wednesday as I put my arms around his neck I realised that his top button was already undone. At once I unfastened the second, and the third. He didn't stop me – I hadn't thought he would – after all, he'd given me the hint in the first place. By the Sunday I was bold enough to undo all his jacket buttons and push the cloth back so I was lying on his bare chest. But then my exploring hands reached his shoulder to discover a place where the hair stopped abruptly, giving way to a long ridge of skin; as I ran my fingers over it I realised it was a thick, raised scar. All at once he pushed me sideways so that my questing hand was jerked away, and hearing his low grunt of warning I understood; I must not touch him there. I lay still – and after a little while his hand on my back shifted in the lightest of caresses, and at this signal I resumed my steady stroking. When I became sleepy I settled my cheek down on the silky hair of his chest and gave my small sigh of contentment. All at once I was asleep.

The leaves swirled from the trees in dancing showers of gold as October gave way to November. I was becoming languid and slow-moving, and often of an afternoon I slept on the sofa in front of the drawing-room fire. Once I half-woke to see him standing in the doorway with Flora in his arms – she must have asked him to bring her down – but now he shushed her and closed the door firmly behind them both; I dozed again.

Every Sunday and Wednesday now I fell asleep in his arms, my cheek pressed against the firm softness of his chest. Sometimes I half-woke to feel his hand on my cheek, gently cupping it, or on my hair, stroking it with long, soothing strokes; but I learnt not to move. If I stirred and seemed to be waking, always his hand dropped back and he would leave me. So I lay half-dreaming against his heart as he held me close – just as I held his child. I was almost certain now. I hadn't bled the fourth month, either, though he'd assumed I was doing and waited until the Friday before coming to see me. Again early in November at the time when my monthlies should have come he said to the wall: 'Friday – this week.' I could have told him then, but it wasn't the right time or the right place. Besides, I wanted to be completely sure, and I could only be that when I'd quickened; and then I didn't want to tell him downstairs in the chilly dining room, I wanted to wait until he was holding me close in the warmth of my bed – and then for the first time I would break my silence. I day-dreamed of his pleasure, and how he would hold me closer than ever, cuddling me. I was both excited and fearful those early November days, looking forward to the spring when I would hold my baby in my arms – and yet afraid too, because sometimes the memories of Flora's birth came back, haunting me – and then I would long for the nights when he came to me, because in his arms I felt safe. Friday, Sunday, Wednesday – each night he came to me to satisfy himself while I thought of trimming cots and sewing tiny bonnets, then each night he returned to hold me close and cuddle me. On the Wednesday I fell asleep on his chest almost as soon as he took me in his arms, and dreamt of butterflies' wings brushing my face. Next morning I went at once to the mirror and saw it reflected there, sweeping up over my cheekbones – the faint brown shadow of a giant butterfly.

All day I hugged my secret to me, then early the following morning I felt that faint, unmistakeable fluttering, which grew stronger even as my hands stroked my belly. I had quickened. I lay in a mindless trance of delight as my hands caressed my baby for the first time. As I dressed later I decided I would tell him this coming Sunday.

On Sunday he came home a little earlier than usual. When I heard the motor I sent Clara to say he could have Flora now, but he came himself to the drawing room to fetch her. As soon as he arrived Flora tugged him over to look at her Ark, with the animals marching in two by two; she didn't want to move them, all arranged as they were, so I said, 'Why don't you stay in here with her today, my lord? The room's nicely warmed.' I curled up on the sofa watching as he talked to her, solemnly entering into her game of make-believe as he crouched on the hearthrug beside her – ungainly-looking but relaxed, because he was with her, and had forgotten I was there. I remembered how he'd held her, that first night in France, falling in love with his grand-daughter. In the spring I would offer him another child to fall in love with – but this child would be of his own begetting.

I must have nodded off, because his voice woke me, speaking my name. I sat up blinking and he realised I'd been asleep and said, 'Are you tired, Amy? You have been looking tired these last few weeks.' He sounded so concerned that I almost told him then – but Flora was there, so I said simply, 'A little, my lord, but I haven't forgotten 'tis Sunday.' His cheeks went ruddy red in the firelight.

I knew he hadn't forgotten either by the way he looked at me as I came down into the hall, but over the soup I began to feel queasy. The beef was too rare and pink to settle my stomach and the tapioca so slimy I could hardly force it down; then Mr Tims brought in the savoury. It was devils on horseback, and at the sight of the rolls of bacon I jumped up and ran from the room with my napkin pressed to my mouth. Out in the cloakroom I was violently sick, then Clara came running in and fetched me a towel and a glass of water – he must have rung for her. He was hovering at the door as I came out. 'How – is – she?' As Clara murmured an answer I started to shiver and he exclaimed, 'Put her to bed, now!'

Clara chivvied me up the stairs and helped me out of my evening dress in front of the fire. I began to unbutton my camisole and as she came back with my nightdress her eyes dropped to my breasts; then she looked up into my face with a broad smile of satisfaction. 'Granny Withers swore you were carrying when she came up to see Mrs Tyson the other day. You were in the stable-yard with the little maid and she's got sharp eyes, has Granny!'

I said quickly, 'I baint told His Lordship yet.'

She grinned. 'He'll be like a dog with two tails – but you'd best not leave it too long, or Granny'll beat you to it!'

'I'll tell him tonight, only – only you must say as I'm quite better now.'

She pursed her lips. 'You don't look better to me, my lady. You look shaky.'

I felt shaky, and still rather sick, but I said firmly, 'Say that I'm better.' I did so want him to come – I was longing to tell him.

The dressing-room door opened soon after, but before I could pull down the covers he went to the main door and switched on the light that I'd told Clara to turn off – and as he did so I saw that he was still wearing full evening dress. I waited as he came slowly towards the bed, and then I began to lift the covers, rather uncertainly. At once he shook his head, stopping me. 'No, not tonight – you're not well.' For the first time since he'd been coming to my bedroom he'd spoken.

I said, 'It'd be all right – if you wanted . . .'

'No.'

'Mebbe tomorrow, then?'

'Perhaps, if you have fully recovered.' He hesitated, then continued, 'I have noticed that you have not been your usual bustling self these last few weeks, and then, tonight . . .' He broke off, and I looked up into his grey eyes; they were anxious, concerned, and as I gazed up into them he slowly reached out to me, then stopped his hand halfway. I leant forward, moving towards him, and his hand resumed its journey to come to rest against the side of my head. I turned my face a little so that my cheek pressed into his warm palm, and his hand curved in response, cradling me; so I knew the time had come to tell him.

Gazing up at him so I could see the moment when his anxious expression turned to one of delight I said, 'I'm not ill, my lord – 'tis just that I'm carrying a child.'

And the hand cradling my face went rigid against my cheek as his expression of anxious concern changed – to one of horror. 'No! No!'

Confused I replied, 'Yes, my lord. I be near five months gone.'

'No – no, you can't be!'

I thought, it's because of the bleeding – he thinks there's something wrong, so I told him, reassuring, 'I did bleed the first couple o' months. I did the same afore, some women do – it don't cause no harm.' Still he tried to shake his head so I told him firmly, 'I be quite sure – I've already quickened.'

His fingers were like a vice on my jaw as he forced my head back full into the light; his eyes searched my face until he saw what he was looking for – then his whole body seemed to slump as he snatched his hand away. At once he turned his back on me and began lurching away like a giant lopsided crab. He was almost running by the time he reached the dressing-room door, and he slammed it shut behind him without a single backward glance.

Chapter Sixty-Five

I simply couldn't believe it. I must have made a mistake: he'd been taken by surprise, he hadn't understood properly and I'd misread his surprise as horror. Or perhaps it was shock – I should never have let him think my monthlies were still coming, no wonder he was disturbed. Besides, he'd always been a strange, difficult man – obviously he wouldn't react like any other husband. I was still telling myself this when I fell asleep.

I awoke in the morning convinced that I was right: he had his funny ways, but give him time and he'd be as pleased as any normal husband. After the doctor's visit I was even more convinced. Dr Matthews told me he'd been over the down at a confinement, and when he'd arrived back he'd found a message waiting for him from Lord Warminster, asking him to come up to the house straight after breakfast, to see me. As soon as the examination was over he told me there was no doubt that I was with child, but when I was dressed again and Clara had left the room he began to question me closely about Flora's birth – and then I understood. Lord Warminster had come to the hospital and seen me so ugly, so ill –and then, I'd fitted – I remembered Beat's description of what a terrible sight I'd been and how horrified my lord had looked; no wonder he was upset now – and so was I, as the memories came back. But Dr Matthews was reassuring. 'Don't worry, Lady Warminster, eclampsia's always more common with the first. Now you're on to number two it's far less likely. Besides, I'll be keeping a close eye on you, and even if you do become toxaemic there are steps we can take to prevent the poison from getting a grip.' He bundled his stethoscope into his bag saying, 'I'm due over at the hospital at Belling this afternoon. I'll see your husband then and tell him there's no cause for alarm – come April he'll be a proud father again.' He bade me goodbye with a smile.

I listened eagerly for the motor coming back after tea, and then went straight up to the nursery. As I came in he glanced at me quickly – then turned away. I went over to him asking, 'My lord – did the doctor see you?'

'Yes.' His face closed, and bending down to pick up Flora he called to Ellen, 'I'm taking Lady Flora down to the library.' He left without looking at me again. He was still angry.

I sat in the drawing room holding my cold hands out to the fire and decided that it must be because he thought he couldn't come to me as a husband, now I was expecting. He was angry just as Uncle Alf had been angry, that time in the Buildings. Probably the gentry didn't; or likely the doctor had told him not to because of my problems before, but he was always so careful never to put his full weight on me I was sure it wouldn't do any harm, no more than it had to the women in the Buildings. He'd already missed Sunday night, so the sooner he came again the sooner he'd stop being annoyed with me; I'd tell him at dinner.

But then Mr Tims arrived to say His Lordship was returning to Belling, and had said I wasn't to wait up for him. Jumping to my feet I hurried out to the stable-yard, and just managed to waylay him by the motor. He stood there, half-turned away from me, unwilling to listen but unable to pass. There was no one else about but my cheeks still flamed as I spoke. 'My lord, even though I be carrying it won't do no harm. You could still – that is . . .' I drew a deep breath and said quickly, 'I know men do have their needs and you've missed last night already, so if you did care to visit my room tonight you'd be very welcome.'

He turned round to face me, and I quailed before the expression in his eyes as he said, emphasizing every humiliating word, 'I will *never* enter your bedroom again.' As I shrank back from the force of his rejection he bent to the starting handle and swung it sharply; the engine clattered into life. There were tears running down my face as he climbed in and drove away – but he never looked back.

I ran straight up to my bedroom; between my sobs I kept asking my pillow why? *Why?* He'd looked at me, spoken to me, as if he hated me. Why, oh why did he hate me? Last week he'd held me close until I'd gone to sleep in his arms – he hadn't hated me then – and yet now, when I'd offered him a child, he hated me.

He didn't come back to dinner on Tuesday either, and by Wednesday I was desperate. I waited at the foot of the stairs until he came down from the nursery and then barred his way, asking him, begging him, 'Please, my lord – please will you come back to dinner tonight?' He stood there, his whole body taut with longing to escape, but I would not move. '*Please.*' At last he gave the briefest of nods.

It was Wednesday; a week ago today I'd been happy, though I'd not realised it at the time. I dressed very carefully and did my hair in an elaborate pattern of waves and curls. He didn't speak as I came into the hall but I knew I mustn't lose my nerve, so the minute the soup had been served I asked, 'My lord, would you please to get drunk tonight?'

He stiffened. 'Why should I do that?'

'Because I want to ask you a question.'

He was silent, and everything hung in the balance. Then suddenly his hand shot out and slammed down on the bell. When Mr Tims appeared he ordered, 'Bring wine – two bottles.'

When the butler returned he waved him away. 'I'll serve myself.' And as he tilted the bottle and filled his glass up to the brim I felt my whole body relapse into a fit of uncontrollable shivering. He glanced at me sharply, but said nothing, only drinking steadily as course succeeded course. When at last the cover was removed and the dessert bowls were set out he turned to me and spoke, his words flowing swift and fluent, without the slightest trace of hesitation. 'Upon which subject do you wish me to enlighten you?'

I forced my stiff lips to open. 'I wanted to ask you . . .' but the words wouldn't come out. I began a second time. 'I wanted to . . .' and again I lost my nerve.

'Continue.' There was impatience in his voice now.

Turning so that I could look directly into his face I cried desperately, 'Why do you hate me so?' His eyes flickered, trying to draw away, but I wouldn't let them go. 'Why? Why?'

At last he said, 'I do not hate you.' Despairingly my eyes dropped, and the sheen of the silver fruit-knife blurred before my gaze. He repeated, 'I don't hate you, Amy – any more than I hate one of my roses when it scratches me. It may cause me pain, but I do not hate it.' He pushed away his glass and put his hand to the edge of the table in the familiar gesture that indicated he was about to rise and leave me.

'Please – stay and talk to me. Thee didst get drunk to talk to I – don' 'ee waste it.'

The hand on the table edge tightened, then relaxed its grip. 'What shall I talk to you about?'

For a moment my mind was a blank, then the sight of those black-furred fingers prompted me and I said, 'Thy roses. Talk about thy roses.'

'I'm not sure I can tonight.' He was watching my face and I knew there were tears in my eyes. He offered more gently, 'Shall I tell you instead what others have said, of their roses?' I nodded, and he sat back in his chair until his face was in shadow before beginning to speak. 'Sappho, she was a poetess who lived in Greece, on an island, long ago.'

I whispered, 'How long ago?'

He paused to reckon before replying, 'Twenty-four hundred years ago.'

'Did they have roses then? In Greece?'

'Oh, yes. Why, your favourite storyteller Homer tells us that there were roses decorating the shield of Achilles – Achilles whom you thought did not deserve the title of hero.'

He half-smiled, remembering, and at once I pressed home my advantage. 'And what did she say, thic Sappho maid?'

He began to speak but I couldn't understand a word he said. My face must have mirrored my frustration because he checked himself. 'I forgot – forgive me. There are poetic translations, give me a moment to remember one.

> *Would Jove appoint some flower to reign*
> *In matchless beauty on the plain,*
> *The rose, mankind will all agree,*
> *The rose the Queen of Flowers should be.*

'Do you agree, Amy?'

'Aye, I did like Granfer's roses better'n all the other flowers he grew – and so did he.' My mouth quivered as I repeated, 'My Granfer, he did love his roses.'

My lord spoke quickly, 'Anacreon, who was a Greek too, composed an entire ode in praise of roses: *"Friends, join your voices with mine, in singing the season of flowers, and the Rose of spring!"* ' He stopped suddenly, and reaching for his glass drank deeply. 'Enough of the Greeks. Did you know that in Rome they made wine from roses? And scattered her petals over the couches they lay on as they feasted at their banquets? Theocritus called the rose the light of the earth, and Horace too sang her praises:

> *There be the rose with beauty fraught,*
> *So brilliant now, so soon to fade . . .*

"So soon to fade . . ." ' His eyes darkened and I shivered; at once he spoke in reassurance. 'You prefer the poetesses. Here, you will enjoy these verses:

> *For if I wait, said she,*
> *Till time of roses be –*
> *For the moss rose, the musk rose,*
> *Maiden-blush or royal dusk rose –*
>
> *What glory then for me*
> *In such a company?*
> *Roses plenty, roses plenty –*
> *And one nightingale for twenty?'*

Abruptly he stopped his chanting. 'The nightingale, it wasn't singing – but it did call. They call if there is danger, in warning – that nightingale tried to warn me . . .' He shook his head and said quickly, 'Keats – Keats wrote a poem about a nightingale. Do you know it?'

'No, but I'd like fine to hear it.'

'Then I'll try to remember; it's a long time since I learnt them but some of the words will come back to me if I cudgel my brain. It was night-time when Keats heard the bird singing.'

I tried to help. 'Nightingales do mostly sing at night, so you can't usually see 'em.'

'Ah – that's it!

> *I cannot see what flowers are at my feet,*
> *Nor what soft incense hangs upon the boughs,*
> *But, in embalmèd darkness, guess each sweet –'*

589

He broke off. 'But it wasn't dark that night – it was moonlit, a full silver moon hung in the sky, and I could see . . . Roses, you wanted me to talk of roses. He mentioned a rose in that same ode, let me recall it:

> *And mid-May's eldest child*
> *The coming musk rose, full of dewy wine –*

Only it wasn't May, it was June, late in June.' He shook himself as if trying to shake the memory away and lifted his glass high until it caught the light like a huge glowing ruby.

> ' " *Wine! Wine! Wine!*
> *Red Wine!" The nightingale cries to the rose*
> *That yellow cheek of hers to incarnadine.*'

He reached for the bottle again then stayed his hand. 'No, I must have a clear head with my loose tongue – how difficult it is to achieve the balance. You asked me – what did you ask me?'

But now I didn't want to know the answer and quickly I said, 'Thic Keats, did he write any more verses about roses?'

He was diverted. 'Yes, yes he did. There was another musk rose – he must have been especially fond of musk roses, that young doomed poet.

> *What is more tranquil than a musk rose blowing*
> *In a green island, far from all man's knowing?*'

He repeated to himself, ' "Far from all man's knowing," ' then jerked fully upright in his chair to proclaim:

> *Oh, lost green paradise,*
> *Were the roses redder there*
> *Than they blossom other where?*

A woman wrote that, she understood – and she can answer your question, your *first* question.' This time his hand took hold of the bottle and poured, but he didn't drink at once; instead he held the glass poised by its stem, twirling it round and round between dark-furred fingers,

> *'The rose saith in the dewy morn*
> *I am most fair:*
> *Yet all my loveliness is born –'*

He raised his glass, repeating, 'Is born – upon a thorn.' He drank. 'The thorns, the thorns – do you understand?' He looked directly into my eyes. 'A price must be paid for every pleasure, and sometimes the price is too high – like the price you demanded of me.'

I flinched away from the anger in his face. 'I – I don't understand.'

'You – don't – understand.' The spaces were deliberate now. 'Then let me tell you a tale – you like hearing tales. This tale is of a man long ago who entered the Garden of Mirth and saw there a rose bud, a beautiful rose bud close by the Fountain of Narcissus. And she is so beautiful, so lovely that he cannot resist her, though he knows he should.' He was still looking straight at me, and as I saw his face darken so I heard his voice become harsh and grating as he recited:

> *'But anguished and full of thought*
> *I felt more woe than wounds 'ere wrought.*
> *And yet I felt I had to go*
> *Towards the rose that pleased me so.'*

He drew a deep breath before continuing:

> *'Towards the rose tree fast I drew.*
> *But thorns much sharper then than now*
> *Were there – and thistles thick*
> *And brambles too to scratch and prick.'*

He began to speak very quickly. 'That man, he became the slave of Eros – Eros, son of Aphrodite. You see, the rose is the chosen flower of Aphrodite – did you know that? Of course you know that – maybe not by education, by learning – but you know

591

instinctively, just as every beautiful woman knows. Besides, *you* bear the face of Aphrodite – Aphrodite who brought Eros into this world, and whose son gave a rose to the God of Silence, so that the shameful deeds of his mother might be hidden – under the rose. It's Aphrodite who teaches women to enchant, to entice, to seduce men – to seduce them to surrender to their basest desires.' His breathing became fast and uneven and his words disjointed. 'Withchcraft – sorcery – Circe – she was a witch. Do you remember Circe?' His grey eyes hated me as he said loudly, deliberately, 'When Circe bewitched Odysseus' men and turned them all into swine then I think she too must have sidled out from beneath a rose – a *Garland* rose.' His angry eyes held mine as he asked, 'Have I answered your question now?'

I shrank back into my chair and the tears caught in my voice as I whispered, 'I be sorry, I didn't mean – I be terrible, terrible sorry.'

His voice changed as anger gave way to pain and his voice was low now as he said, 'You couldn't help it. You are as you are.' Reaching into his pocket he pulled out a square of white linen and pushed it across the table. 'Dry your eyes, child – there's no point weeping now.'

After I'd mopped my face and blown my nose I whispered again, 'I do be sorry – terrible sorry – but I still don't really understand.'

He didn't reply at first, then he said, 'Listen – listen to one more poem. Shakespeare will be my voice, and tell you what *I* cannot say. Listen carefully now.'

He began to recite slowly and clearly:

> *'No more be grieved at that which thou hast done:*
> *Roses have thorns, and silver fountains mud;*
> *Clouds and eclipses stain both moon and sun,*
> *And loathsome canker lives in sweetest bud.'*

I shivered, and he stopped a moment, his eyes anxious. 'No listen to me, listen:

All men make faults, and even I in this,
Authorizing thy trespass with compare,
Myself *corrupting,* salving *thy amiss,*
Excusing their sins more than thy sins are:'

He paused to draw breath, but my eyes never left his face.

'For to thy sensual fault I bring in sense,
Thy adverse party is thy advocate,
And gainst myself a lawful plea commence:
Such civil war is in my love and hate,
That I an accessory needs must be
To that sweet thief which sourly robs from me.'

There was silence. Then he said in a low, clear voice, 'So you see, I don't hate you – I can't hate you. I hate myself, but I don't hate you.' With a scraping of the chair he rose to his feet and left the room without waiting for me to precede him.

I still sat on at the table; my legs were trembling so much that I was afraid to stand, in case they wouldn't support me. I understood now. I'd heard what he'd said: '*thy* trespass, *thy* sins, *thy* sensual fault' – but he'd already told me, he'd told me as soon as he talked of Aphrodite, because I had been Aphrodite that night –and he'd recognised me. Aphrodite, the goddess who bore Eros as her son – but not to her husband, the lame, misshapen Vulcan. No, her son had not been her husband's child. No one knew who'd begotten Eros on her, but there was only one man whom my husband could believe to be the father of my unborn child – and that was his own son.

Frank had come to Eston in the summer, then, within the month, I had gone to Lord Warminster from under the Garland rose enticing, seducing – just as a woman would have done if she'd cuckolded her elderly, impotent husband and been desperate to conceal her sin. So he'd been angry, hating his adulterous wife – until tonight, when he'd forgiven me for that sin he believed I'd committed. 'No more be grieved at that which thou hast done.' But I *hadn't* done anything. He was wrong, quite wrong. I'd never committed adultery, and the child I carried was of *his* begetting. Somehow I must convince him of that.

I'd been sitting so long at the dining table my legs were cold and numb, but I made them take me to the drawing room to find what I needed, then I went straight across the hall to the library, where Nella lay on guard outside the door. Gathering all my courage together I knocked and went in. There was no light on, but the flames from the fire shone on the bottle at his elbow, and as my eyes adjusted to the dimness my nose caught the reek of brandy fumes. He didn't stand up, he only raised his great head to ask, 'What do *you* want?' There was no mistaking the hostility in his voice.

Shutting the door carefully behind me I moved a few paces towards him, gripping the book in my hand like a talisman; I dared not go any closer. 'My lord, I be sorry to intrude, but there be,' I corrected myself, 'there *is* something I must say to you.'

There was a long pause, then I saw his dark-furred hand reach out to the bottle and refill his glass. He lifted it to his lips and his Adam's apple jumped as he gave a long swallow before replying, 'Then say it.'

I began to speak in a rush. 'My lord, when Lord Quinham came,' I saw his body stiffen, and faltered before repeating, 'When Lord Quinham did come in the summer, he asked me to – to –' my voice stumbled. 'He did ask me to give him a baby, a son.' The hand holding the glass clenched tight around its stem. I rushed on, 'I told him no, 'twere adultery, but . . .'

I couldn't go on and there was the sound of the glass hitting the table as he set it sharply down. His voice was jerky. 'But he forced you. I saw the bruises on your arms – he forced you! But why didn't you tell me the truth before, instead of –'

'No! No!' I broke across his words. 'He did try to, but I saw the roses – *thy* roses – and I wouldn't let him. Then his rod fell, and he couldn't make me. Only I did want a baby so much – I was aching for a baby – so I came to you.' Walking forward on to the hearth-rug I raised the Bible so he could see the gleam of the gilt cross, and said, 'I swear by the Holy Book that I baint never committed adultery.' Lowering the Bible I begged, 'I be telling the truth – thee maun believe I.'

Out of the shadows a voice answered me, saying, 'Yes, I believe you.'

My whole body sagged with relief as I whispered, 'So thic baby I be carrying, 'tis yourn.'

And the voice replied, 'Yes. And I wish to God it were not.'

I couldn't believe I'd heard aright. 'But surely you do want –'

His bitter exclamation stopped me. 'If you had to play the part of Aphrodite, why ever did you cast *me* in the role of her mate?'

I shook my head, confused. 'But it were only right you should give me a child. You be my husband, just like Vulcan were hern.'

His voice was low and bitter as he told me, 'Then you don't know your mythology well enough – you don't know the nature of Vulcan's children.'

The room was quiet, with only the hiss and splutter of the fire breaking the silence. Then, suddenly, the huge dark shape of him reared up, towering over me. As I flinched away his hand reached for the poker and he stirred the coals until the flames blazed up; then he moved full into their light. 'So *I've* given you the child you wanted – *I!* Look at me, look at me!' I looked up at him – and the shadows leapt and shifted over the monstrous hump of his back, the crooked, twisted shoulder, and that grotesque travesty of a face. 'What manner of child do you carry in your womb?' And his unequal eyes held mine as he shouted his last dreadful question. 'What monster have I begotten on you?'

Both my hands closed in terror over my swelling belly as I stared in horror at the huge distorted shape – then I turned and fled.

Chapter Sixty-Six

Up in my room I flung myself down on the bed, my hands still clutching at my belly as his bitter cry echoed in my head: 'What monster have I begotten on you?' And yet even as I clutched I felt the familiar fluttering, so that my hands began to unclench, to cradle, to protect – protecting my baby.

I fell asleep with the tears still wet on my cheeks, and woke early to hear sounds of movement next door – clumsy, hurried movements as he blundered into the wash-stand and sent a shower of small objects clattering to the floor. I knew I wouldn't sleep again and it was too early to go up to the nursery, so as soon as I'd heard him leave I went through to tidy up. His dressing room looked as if it'd been struck by lightning: the marble top of the wash-stand was askew and its surface was a mess of spilled tooth-powder and slopped shaving water. His razor had been flung down still open, and the steel blade was smeared with blood. As I picked it up to wipe it clean on the discarded towel I saw that it was the one labelled Sunday – but this morning was Thursday; I'd never known him make such a mistake before. Last night's clothes were tossed in a tumbled heap on the floor, and as I picked up his tailcoat I smelt the reek of brandy, and saw the distorted shape of it. Once I'd admired that skilful tailoring which sought to minimize his deformities – now the very sight of it made my stomach heave, and I barely got to the slop bucket in time.

When I'd splashed my face with cold water and finished tidying up I went straight to the nursery; it was too early but I couldn't wait any longer. Flora was still in her nightgown, but at once she came running to me. I put my arms around her warm, sweet-smelling body and buried my face in her soft hair, hugging and hugging her. I didn't want to ever let her go, but she soon broke free, clamouring to show me some lost nursery treasure that Ellen had just found for her.

I sat watching as Ellen dressed her in front of the fire; she stood so sturdy and straight, just like her father. Her father – and suddenly my breath caught in my throat, because her father was straight-backed and unflawed; her father who was Lord Warminster's first-born son. And Flora, my beautiful Flora – she was Lord Warminster's grand-daughter. A great weight fell from my shoulders to be succeeded by a surge of pure anger. How dared he frighten me so, speaking as he had last night? But the anger passed almost as quickly as it had come. I'd seen the anguish on his face – he'd believed what he said. For so many years he'd brooded over his physical deformities that now, on this subject, his mind was as warped as his body.

I sat in the morning room that afternoon, so that I'd hear the motor, and as soon as it came spluttering past I went to the side door and waited in the small lobby there. When I stepped forward he shrank back against the wall, as if in fear of me, so I spoke firmly, as though to a disturbed child. 'My lord, what you said last night, it wasn't sensible. You'd taken too much drink and it'd addled your brain. Now you think about Lord Quinham – there's nothing amiss with him, nothing at all. And Flora, she's straight and beautiful – so it's downright silly to get all het up, the way you did.'

'Yes, yes.' He spoke much more quickly than he usually did when he was sober. 'You're right – everything you've said is true. I was a fool to speak as I did – I never would have done so had I not been drunk.' His voice dropped, as he added, 'Please, do forgive me.'

I gazed up at him; the dark scabs where he'd cut himself shaving stood out against the pallor of his face and he looked haggard and ill. No wonder with the brandy he'd drunk the previous night, on top of the wine, too. I said briskly, 'And another thing, my lord. Clara did tell me as you left afore breakfast this morning. Have you had anything to eat today?'

There was a long pause before he admitted, 'No.'

'Then I'll tell Mr Tims to take a tea tray to the library while Flora's with you. But toast and such-like isn't enough for a grown man, so you must come back for your dinner tonight in good time.' He stood staring at me, and I wondered if I'd gone too far, then his head moved in a gesture of acquiescence and I stepped aside to let him go indoors. He did come back, and I talked to him about Flora and the weather; he barely replied, but at least he ate.

As he rose after the dessert I said, 'I'll see you at dinner tomorrow, my Lord.'

'If you wish. Good evening.'

On Sunday I mustered my courage and told him as he quartered his orange, ''Tis Sunday, my Lord – so if you wanted to . . .'

'No! No!' I had a struggle to keep back my tears. Even though I knew he couldn't help himself the force of his rejection still hurt. Then on the following Wednesday he told me he was going to London, to stay.

I sat in silence as his halting words explained that he wasn't really required at Belling any more. It was only a convalescent home now that the military hospital at Sutton Veny had expanded. But a friend of Lady Burton's was running a Red Cross hospital for officers in London, and she needed a male orderly. He told me he'd been at school with her husband, who was now serving in France, so he'd felt he should offer his assistance. He'd already telegraphed to the caretaker at Belgrave Square asking him to open up a couple of rooms; but he would only be sleeping there, and when he didn't eat at the hospital he'd dine at his club. Then he stood up to leave. I said, 'Flora, she'll miss you.'

'And I shall miss Flora. I will run down for an hour or two when I can, to see her.' To see her, not me.

I packed for him and he left two days later. We ate in silence that last evening: he didn't speak and I couldn't think of anything to say. As I stood up to go he informed the wall above my head that he was catching the early train, so he would say goodbye this evening. I said my goodbyes to his gleaming white waistcoat then passed through the door he held open for me. But then he spoke behind me, and I turned quickly back. 'I am concerned about Nella. The Tysons always take her when I'm away, but they tell me she pines, so perhaps you would be so kind as to take her with you on your walks with Flora?'

'Aye my lord, I will.'

'Thank you.' He stood waiting until I'd crossed the hall and begun to climb the stairs, then I heard the library door opening and closing again behind him.

After he'd gone I felt hurt and rejected. I kept remembering Grammer spurning my offer to take her out of the workhouse and care for her – but then I told myself it wasn't the same at all. There was a war on; so many women had had to say goodbye to their husbands, and I knew by now how bitter he felt that he couldn't join the Army, like the red-coated generals had done. It was only natural he should want to do what he could. Besides, perhaps while he was away he'd come to his senses and realise how silly he was being about the baby.

Flora missed him, though – and poor Nella was completely lost without her constant companion, so I kept her with me all day long. The drawing room was much cosier with Nella curled up on the rug. When I took her back to the Tysons' cottage beyond the stable-yard one evening Mary was just leaving – and I noticed that her eyes were red with weeping. I looked at Mrs Tyson in alarm, but she shook her head. 'No, there baint nothing wrong, my lady. 'Tis just as she's missing her man, 'specially now when she's got the sort o' news for him as a wife'd rather whisper in her husband's ear than write in a nasty cold letter. And how be you keeping, my lady? Missing His Lordship too, I'll be bound.'

But I wasn't sure that I was. I'd only ever seen him at dinner, and after this last week or so it was almost a relief to be free of his brooding presence at the head of the table, and to be able to eat a simple supper in the morning room instead. But sometimes, at night, my bed seemed very large and cold, and all at once I'd be longing for the dressing room door to open and for him to come in and give me a cuddle.

But when he did come down after a fortnight he only stayed a couple of hours, and then he spent most of the time with Flora. He barely spoke to me except to say that although Dr Matthews had sent him good reports of my health he'd be arranging for a specialist to come down from London to examine me, as well. When he'd finished telling me this his eyes dropped to my waistline – and a flicker of pure horror crossed his face before he said a hasty goodbye and left. I was annoyed that he should look at me like that. After all, even if it had been me who made the first move that night under the Garland rose he'd then chosen to come to me regularly afterwards – so he must have known there'd be a child sooner or later. But my irritation soon subsided. He had one straightbacked son already, and when I presented him with another at the beginning of April then he'd realise how foolish he'd been. I relapsed again into placid contentment.

The next week he sent down for three books. Apologetically Mr Tims asked if I'd mind looking for them, since his eyesight wasn't so good these days – they were in His Lordship's bedroom. I went into the room feeling like an intruder and crossed quickly to the shelves. I found two of the titles and was looking for the third when I noticed a handkerchief box crammed in with the books – one of the maids must have put it there by mistake. I took it out and opened it to tidy the handkerchiefs – but there were no handkerchiefs inside, only rows of tiny little envelopes. Curious, I opened one – and was even more mystified. It contained a pink silk-elastic fingerstall. But whoever would want a box full of those? I looked at the envelope again. It was labelled in small letters: *Malthus Circular Sheath* – but I was still no wiser. Only when I found the piece of paper tucked in the side did I begin to understand. It was headed: *Instructions for the Use of the Appliance*, and I read them with growing amazement, right down to the final words which stated confidently, *When worn they are scarcely perceptible*. How right they were – I hadn't perceived them at all! But no wonder he'd always left me so quickly, and not come back until later for his cuddle. All that time he'd been deceiving me. If I hadn't taken him unawares under the Garland rose I'd never have conceived, not in a thousand years. That night of the nightmare he'd been intending to deny me his seed, but unwittingly I'd thwarted him – so the minute I'd given him back the key he'd gone straight off to London to procure these – these devices. Angrily I put the box back on the shelf. Even handling such things made me feel unclean.

Christmas was coming and I began to sew dolls' clothes for Flora and small gifts for Clara and Ellen. Then the week before, Lord Warminster telegraphed to say he'd be down the day after Boxing Day so I hastily asked Clara to buy me some fine linen and sat up hemming half a dozen handkerchiefs for him, then embroidered his initials in the corner of each. He arrived as planned, with a great box full of presents for Flora and a diamond brooch in the shape of a daisy for me. I gave him the handkerchiefs and we thanked each other politely, then he went straight up to the nursery and I hardly saw him again before it was time for him to go back to Town.

Soon after, the specialist doctor arrived from London. He was very imposing in a frockcoat and top hat and I was embarrassed when he rolled up his sleeves and examined me; but I felt grateful for his smile and confident reassurances that there was no sign of my previous trouble.

After he'd gone the outside world receded. In those long dark days of winter all that mattered was Flora – and my baby, kicking and growing stronger in my womb with every day that passed. He was a boy, I was sure of that, and when my Lord saw him he would forget all his foolish fretting and smile at me again with his rare, lopsided smile.

By the middle of January I could no longer fit into my skirts. I was planning to take off the waistband and let out the darts when I realised there was no need. Mr Selby, the agent, came to the drawing room with my pin money every week now on the orders of Lord Warminster – besides, he'd left me the Harrods catalogue. So I sent for two skirt lengths, cut them out and began to sew.

One afternoon I was hemming the navy skirt in the drawing room and dozed off, with my sewing still on my lap. It was twilight when I woke up with a jerk to hear the door opening and Mr Tims' voice announcing, 'Lord Quinham, my lady.'

I looked up in disbelief as he strode in and threw himself down in the chair on the opposite side of the fireplace. He dropped his hat and cane and gloves on the floor beside him then said, 'Hello Amy – sitting in the dark?'

He sounded so calm and casual that my racing heartbeats began to slow. 'I fell asleep over my sewing.' I clutched the folds of material around me like a shield, trying to hide my swollen waist in the shadowed depths of the big armchair.

But he scarcely glanced at me; he just sat staring into the glowing heart of the fire. By its light I watched the shadows chasing across his face: it was thinner and his nose and mouth were sharply etched above his drawn cheeks. I longed to reach out and gently stroke his shining hair – but I knew I must not. Finally he broke the silence. 'Queer how you see things in fires – fairy castles, my old nurse used to say. God, it's good to be back in civilisation again.'

I ventured a question. 'Are you on leave?'

'Mm – for a whole glorious fortnight. You certainly appreciate the comforts of England when you've been up to your eyeballs in

601

mud.' I shivered. 'Being out there – it makes you see all sorts of things differently.' He raised his head to look directly at me. 'I suppose I'm trying to tell you that I've come to apologise. Dammit, I *have* come to apologise, Amy – I behaved abominably last time I was here, I can see that now.'

I said quickly, 'It doesn't matter.'

He laughed softly. 'Generous Amy, what a forgiving little girl you are! But I'm not sure it's wise – you'll only encourage me to take advantage of you again, knowing you'll keep on forgiving me. No, Amy – this time, let me apologise. My behaviour was obnoxious.' He paused, then his voice rose again as he said, 'But you must blame him for it – the old man – he always brings out the worst in me. Maman made me promise on her deathbed that I'd play the dutiful son to him, but how can I, knowing what he did to her?' His eyes were deep and dark as he exclaimed, 'He killed her, Amy – he killed her!'

I heard my indrawn gasp of breath as his angry voice continued, 'If he'd strangled her with his bare hands he couldn't have done it more effectively. He knew just how to destroy her – and he did.' I didn't move, but the child, sensing my distress, began to stir uneasily as my ears strained to catch his every word. 'Maman was devout, totally devout, as only a Frenchwoman reared by the nuns could be. She asked him, when they were first married, and he made all sorts of offers – but then, when I was born,' he hesitated a moment, 'then he delayed. Perhaps I could have understood that, in the heat of the moment, but later he made the decision in cold blood. After she took me back to France he sent his decree through the lawyers – I was to be brought up a Protestant. She was devastated, but she obeyed. It was the nuns who'd taught her obedience, and they'd taught it too well.' His face was tormented as he told me, 'So my poor Maman spent the rest of her life believing I was damned. They wrote consumption on her death certificate – but she was murdered. *He* murdered her and I told him so.' His angry voice was harsh. 'She died while I was up at Oxford, and after her funeral I came back here, to Eston, and told him how she'd gone to her death in spiritual torment, still saying her despairing prayers for my soul. I told him what she'd made me promise, and that for her sake I'd keep that promise – but then I told him that I hated him for what he'd done to her, and always would. I saw it then, I saw the guilt on his twisted face – and I was glad. But it was too late, she was dead.'

He reached out and seized the poker, cracking it down hard on the largest coal so that it split apart with a crackling hiss – and his voice hissed in echo as he said, 'I know why he did it. Not because of any genuine belief – no, he wouldn't have cared if I'd been brought up as a Catholic or a Hindu. He did it because he wanted to hurt her – and he did.' His shoulders were shaking as he sat there crouched, staring into the fire. I dared not speak.

At last he threw himself back into the chair again, but his voice was still bitter with anger. 'I saw Flora outside. I stopped to speak to her and she told me her "Papa" was in London. Her Papa!' His eyes glittered.

I said quickly, 'He's gone to help in a hospital there.'

'I don't care where the devil he's gone – but I do care that *my* daughter calls him her Papa. He isn't her father Amy, and you shouldn't let her think he is.' His anger was turned on me now.

'In law, she is his daughter.'

He snapped back, 'But everyone at Eston knows she isn't. She's going to find out sooner or later – it's time you stopped this charade. Whatever the law says she's nothing to him, nothing!'

I said defensively, 'She's his grand-daughter.'

He broke in almost shouting, 'No, she's not!'

Trembling I exclaimed, 'I told thee true. She be *your* baby!'

'Of course she is. I've never doubted that for a minute – she's the image of me. I saw myself reflected in her eyes today, that's why it hurt so much to hear her – oh yes, I'm her father all right.' The tension left my body – until he added flatly, 'But the old man isn't mine.'

I stared at him in disbelief. 'But – he must be . . .'

'Why ever do you think a beautiful woman like Maman would have married a creature like him, unless she was desperate for a husband? She'd never have accepted him otherwise, however hard my great-aunts tried to persuade her.'

Now my mind was like Flora's jigsaws when she'd tumbled all the pieces together and they didn't fit any more; I tried desperately to make sense of what he was saying. 'Poor Maman, what she must have suffered those first few months here, having to submit to him – and all the time terrified in case he suspected her condition. The aunts did their best. They invited her over to France, claiming she was homesick – they planned to keep her there on some pretext until I arrived "unexpectedly", then they were going to explain me away as merely premature, with some talk of a fall, or such-like story. But they hadn't questioned Maman carefully enough. They'd thought she was only two months gone by the time of her marriage – instead, she was over four. In any case, he insisted on staying in France too, claiming he couldn't bear to be parted from her. So he was there when I made my appearance – a huge, bouncing boy born less than five months after his wedding day!' He laughed cruelly. 'I wish I'd been old enough to see the expression on his ugly face when they brought his first-born son to him – and he realised how thoroughly he'd been duped!' Then his voice softened. 'Poor Maman, it was terrible for her. He forced his way into her bedroom, ranting and raving like a madman. She told me she thought her last hour had come. Luckily her maid managed to get him out at last – she'd been Maman's own nurse, old Thérèse, and was totally loyal. Then he disappeared. The great-aunts were on pins, disgrace stared the family in the face. He'd not known of her condition when they'd married so obviously he had the right to repudiate her, annul the marriage – and stigmatise me as a bastard. Maman wept for a fortnight at the thought of that. Then one evening he turned up again, offering to forgive her and to acknowledge me as his heir – on condition that she gave him a child of his own. She agreed – what else could she do? Besides, he was still simmering with anger underneath; old Thérèse said it was like having a volcano in the room. Why, he even told Maman she should be feeding me herself, and tried to send away my wetnurse – the aunts had to hide her downstairs until he went back to England!

'Then, after a decent interval had elapsed, he came and fetched us. No one at Eston ever suspected. He'd acknowledged me as his son and I suppose if anyone did think I was rather large for my age they simply assumed the old man had anticipated. He told her the past was over and done with, and they must make a fresh start, but of course it was hopeless. His conjugal demands had been almost more than she could stand when they were first married – she'd only endured them for my sake – she'd really thought he'd never guess. The nuns had left her appallingly ignorant. Now she couldn't bring herself to even let him touch her – then she had a stroke of luck. He went up to Town to consult some medico about the chances of an operation to make himself straighter. The chap told him there was a possibility of that – but then threw in the information that his condition would probably be passed on to any offspring. So the old man came back and told her that from now on he'd be a husband in name only. But it was no use, she couldn't bear to stay in the same house with him, so the next time he went up to Town for the day she told old Thérèse and my nurse to pack and we all escaped back to France. But he got his revenge; he used the power he possessed as my legal father – the power *she'd* given him – to insist I be baptised and brought up as a Protestant. By marrying him she'd secured my legitimacy, but at the cost of my immortal soul. And that guilt never gave her a moment's peace. I wasn't bothered, of course – boys aren't – it was only when she'd died that I fully realised what he'd done to her, and then I told him. Now he's the one to suffer guilt and I'm glad – *glad*. But I vowed there and then that I'd never let myself feel guilty over anything I did. I decided that when I heard the whole story from her own lips, on her deathbed. Guilt corrodes and destroys – it destroyed Maman, and now I hope it destroys him.'

Abruptly he stood up. 'I'm going now, this house oppresses me. Anyway, I'm dining with Tommy Grayson, he's on sick leave.' He moved towards me and I shrank back into the shadows. 'Don't worry, Amy – I'm not going to wreak my wicked will on you today, I've already said I'm sorry. But I just want one last look.' Tilting the shade of the standard lamp he pressed the switch – and the light shone directly on my face. Blinking I looked up at him, but I couldn't see his expression; it was hidden by the shadows. He stayed quite still for a long time before murmuring, 'You're as beautiful as ever, Amy. I'd better go or I'll start repenting my restraint. Goodbye.' I could barely see his slim back moving to the door, but I heard it close shut behind him.

My sewing slithered to the floor; I didn't need its protection now. I never had, he'd only looked at my face, not down at my belly where my child was growing. My child! And the full significance of what he'd told me finally sunk in. My child was Lord Warminster's child, his *first* child, and that doctor had said . . . The memory of Frank's voice was blotted out as those terrible words of my lord's drummed again in my ears: *'What monster have I begotten on you?'*

Chapter Sixty-Seven

For days I was racked with guilt. Again and again I remembered how I'd walked out from under the Garland rose, believing myself to be Aphrodite, but I hadn't, I'd been Eve the woman tempting her husband and persuading him to sin. He'd even offered me the key, so I could lock the door against him and keep him from temptation, but in my arrogant folly I'd given it back to him. Only it had already been too late by then – the damage had been done. And the damaged child moved within me, intensifying my guilt.

One evening I ventured into his library, searching – and found there a directory of ancient gods and goddesses. With shaking hands I turned to the end to find the entry labelled 'Vulcan': *'Most of Vulcan's children were monsters . . .'* I slammed it shut and ran upstairs. The nightmares came, night after night, and in my dreams I saw all my husband's deformities, grossly exaggerated – and borne by a child, my child. Guilt consumed me. Some days Grammer seemed to loom over me, her words shrill and accusing in my ear: 'You be conceived in sin and born in sin – you be a sinner!' And now my child would bear the punishment for my sins. Guilt was destroying me, day by day.

Then one afternoon, as Clara picked up my untouched tea tray she said, 'You maun eat, my lady, for the sake o' the child.' For the sake of the child – that child who was alive and moving within me, needing me – and who would need me even more if it were born crippled and deformed. I called Clara back from the door, and made myself eat the soggy toast and crumbled cake. When I'd finished I felt a little better, and sitting there in the same room I seemed to hear Frank's voice again as he told me: 'Guilt corrodes and destroys – it destroyed Maman.' But I must not, I could not let it destroy me. My children needed me, both the born and the unborn. And he needed me, too, the man who was my husband, because guilt was destroying him as well. 'I'm a veritable Bluebeard where wives are concerned,' he'd told me that night in the library. I hadn't understood then, but I did now. Yet, weighed down as he had been by his own guilt, still he had tried to release me from mine: 'Forget what your grandmother said about being conceived in sin and born in sin – you didn't ask to be conceived, or born,' and as I remembered his words Grammer shrivelled and shrank, until for the first time I saw her clearly for what she was – a sour, embittered old woman. I wouldn't let guilt destroy me, or him either.

With that resolution came strength and calmness. But then I remembered the other cause of his guilt, guilt towards the French countess who'd deceived him – and I was adrift again as my dreams of my idol crumbled to dust. Dreams, so many dreams – all gone . . . I caught hold of myself. Forget the dreams, remember the reality: she'd deceived him, yet still he'd forgiven her – and then she'd left him. Just for a moment I saw his face as it must have been that day he'd come back from London and found her gone – and then it merged with the much younger face of the small boy who'd returned from school to find his beloved nurse gone, dead and buried. Just as I'd come back to find Granfer – and found only his grave. I began to sob and rock in my distress, but the baby within me made anxious, worried movements and I had to force myself to become calm again, for the child's sake.

But it wasn't only the child who needed me – it was his father, too. That night in the library he'd said: 'Don't leave me, Amy – please don't leave me.' And so I'd stayed even though afterwards he'd done everything he could to drive me away once he was sober again – until that evening when I'd finally convinced him by upending the soup tureen on his head. I'd promised then, 'I baint leaving you – not *ever*.' But now I'd broken that promise – or rather, I'd allowed him to break it. I knew now why he'd gone. Guilt had driven him away and I'd let him go. But it wasn't just guilt; he'd gone to protect me, to leave me believing that comforting untruth. He was a man whose tongue didn't easily lie, and next time I might have phrased my question differently and then he'd have been unable to reply, 'You're right. Everything you've said is true.' So instead he'd left, taking the guilt on his own shoulders. But I knew the truth now, he didn't have to hide it from me and besides, the child I carried was *our* child. Whatever it looked like I would love it and care for it – and once he held it in his arms he would do the same. My legs were trembling when I stood up; I felt as though I'd travelled a long, long journey – but I made them carry me upstairs, to pack.

I told Flora, 'We're going to London, to stay with Papa.' She crowed with delight, but Ellen looked at me in surprise. 'Mrs Johnstone didn't mention it when I popped down after lunch, my lady.' Mrs Johnstone . . . suddenly I realised that I couldn't just pack my basket, pick up Flora and go. However much I hated it I was Lady Warminster now and a countess – and when countesses moved they took the whole household with them: butler, cook, nursemaids, housemaids, kitchen staff – I quailed at the thought of the upheaval I would cause. But then my resolve stiffened; I wouldn't take Mrs Johnstone, at least – I'd leave her behind in charge of Eston.

I went straight down and knocked on the door of the Room. She didn't invite me inside and I stood awkwardly on the threshold telling her I was going to London, to live in the Belgrave Square house. She looked at me from her small mean eyes. 'The Germans've been dropping bombs on London, from them Zeppelins.'

I couldn't stop myself giving a shiver before managing to reply, 'Not – recently.'

'October it were, when the last one did its michief on London. Hit the theatres them nasty Huns did – more'n seventy killed, not to speak o' the hundreds left screaming in their agonies.' I swayed and she pressed on gloatingly. 'It were Birmingham's turn last week – more'n thirty killed there, the papers said. I always read about air raids, thinking of them folks all lying peaceful in their beds, knowing neither the day nor the hour.' She leant forward until I was forced back by the fumes of brandy. 'Don't you worry, they haven't forgotten about London – they'll be back killing people there. It stands to reason, wi' it being capital of the Empire.'

Desperately I interrupted. 'I'm not asking you to go, Mrs Johnstone. I thought if you stayed to look after Eston then Clara could come with us as head housemaid.'

'No, my lady.' Her voice was a flat refusal. 'Clara'll stay here as caretaker and I'll be coming to Belgrave Square.'

'I really don't think –'

Her little eyes were shrewd. 'If I gets direct orders from His

Lordship, that'd be different.' She paused, but there was nothing I could say and her voice was smugly triumphant as she continued, 'Otherwise I'll accompany you to Town – it'll make a nice change for me. 'Sides, I'd like to see some o' them buildings as was all smashed by the bombs.'

She held my gaze with her beady eyes until I looked down in surrender. 'If you wish, Mrs Johnstone.'

'I do wish.' There was the usual deliberate pause before she added, sneeringly, 'my lady.'

Over the next day my confidence ebbed away. I was frightened of Mrs Johnstone, frightened of the bombs, and frightened above all of the prospect of my lord's anger when we arrived – but I had to go. All the way on the train I felt sick and ill. Flora became overwrought and her shrieks of excitement pierced my throbbing head and annoyed the other passengers until Ellen took her from me and calmed her with a toy. I closed my eyes feeling a complete failure.

London had changed. It was drabber and harsher with so many men in khaki, and at Waterloo still forms on stretchers were being loaded into an ambulance with a red cross painted on its canvas side. Its driver was a woman, and she was in uniform too. So many people, so many voices – I'd been in the country too long and now I was bewildered and frightened. I looked at Mr Tims but he was shaking as well and even Mrs Johnstone and Mrs Procter had lost their arrogance. In the end it was Ellen who took charge, leading us to the cab rank and giving orders to the drivers. The streets were different, too. Again the uniforms were everywhere, and the women had altered as well. Hats were smaller and skirts shorter than I'd ever seen before, while their wearers strode purposefully along the pavement instead of strolling along under parasols as they had in that golden summer when I'd first come to Belgrave Square.

The house was the same, though – and I wished it wasn't. As soon as I saw it I became a servant again, but without the brisk confidence of the young lady's maid I'd been then. I scuttled guiltily up the front steps, which I'd never used except when I was escorting Miss Annabel, and at once all the servants disappeared back stairs while Flora was whisked up to the nursery by Ellen; they knew their places and had their jobs to do – it was I who was the intruder.

I stayed in my bedroom long after I'd finished unpacking, and it was only when the dustsheets had all been removed that a blank-faced Bertha summoned me down to the drawing room for tea. I was missing Clara already and I had to ask Mr Tims if he knew when my lord was likely to be coming home. He shuffled off, and then returned to report that the caretaker really couldn't say. His Lordship always went straight to his club and dined there if he wasn't on duty at the hospital for the evening; sometimes he didn't come back until very late, but as he had his own key and let himself in the caretaker never saw him until breakfast. Mr Tims looked anxious and suggested it might be better if I didn't wait up. He'd guessed by now that I'd moved us all up to London without a word to Lord Warminster, and he didn't want an angry confrontation any more than I did – but I couldn't bear to wait until the morning.

I was tired but I didn't dare lie down in case he came in early and besides, I was worried about how Flora would settle in this strange place so I went upstairs and helped Ellen bathe her, then sat telling her stories on my lap until she began unwillingly to doze off, still asking when her papa would be back.

The freshly-lit fire in the dining room did nothing to take the chill from the air, and I sat huddled over the piece of leftover pie that was all Mrs Johnstone had bothered to send up getting colder and colder as my courage ebbed away. Suppose he was so angry that he ordered me straight back to Eston again? But I had to stay here with him, at least until my baby was born and he'd learnt to love it. And thinking about the birth brought other fears, with the memory of the giant's hand crushing me and the terrible pain . . . I left the remains of the pie and went straight up for my sewing basket. In the gloomy drawing room I forced my needle to drive away the memories as I waited.

Eventually I heard voices in the hall downstairs and my lord's exclamation; Mr Tims had told him I was here. Heavy footsteps came dragging up the stairs and there was a long pause until at last the door opened. He stood outlined against the dim light of the stairwell, his hunched shoulder very obvious, then slowly he came in. I stood up and as he saw my swollen stomach his face twisted into a rictus of horror. At once I told him, 'My lord, I know. Lord Quinham did tell I. I know he baint properly your son.' His whole body seemed to sag as I added, 'And he told me about what the doctor did tell you, about mebbe being passed on to your baby. So you don't need to stay away from me now, because I know.' My legs gave way and I collapsed back into the chair. He still stood in front of me – unmoving, unspeaking. I whispered, 'I've been thinking. Doctors, they're clever people – so mebbe when the baby's older they could do something – to straighten him.'

At last he spoke, his voice harsh and grating. '*I* – consulted a surgeon, and he – operated on me. For the first time – I looked people straight in the eye. Then – I twisted again, and became – as I have always been.' I remembered the ridged scar on his neck that my questing fingers had touched when we'd lain in bed together, cuddling – and it didn't seem possible that he was the same man. He was so far away from me now.

But somehow I had to talk to him, so I tried again. 'My lord, won't you sit down? 'Tis warmer by the fire.' Like a huge, jerky puppet he slumped into the chair opposite and sat hunched there, his head twisted away from me as he stared into the shadows. I gathered all my courage together. 'My lord, your – peculiarities,' he stiffened and I rushed on, 'They baint so bad as all that. I seen plenty worse in Lambeth. Likely the baby, he'll just be a liddle lopsided. And it won't matter so much because he'll be our baby, we'll still love him.' Remembering Dummy Drew and his mother I finished, 'Parents do allus love their own children.'

Turning his head awkwardly towards me he said deliberately, 'My father did not.' His bleak words chilled the room. Before I could reply he continued, 'I am not just "a liddle lopsided" – I am a hump-back and my neck is twisted, I have one short arm, I had one short leg, and my face is so repulsive that people turn and stare at it in the street. Also, as I think you are aware, I am completely covered with body hair.'

Desperately I seized on his final point. 'That don't matter –'tis manly.'

His voice was flat as he replied, 'But suppose the child – is a girl?'

Pure horror washed over me – a girl, with a humped back and twisted neck – covered in thick black hair. Then I cried out, 'No – no! 'Tisn't a girl, he be a boy, I know it. The way he do kick, so strong – no girl'd kick like that. He's a boy.' And as I said it I knew

612

it was true. 'I told you Flora was a girl, and she was. I'm right this time, too.'

I could scarcely hear his low-voiced reply. 'I do sincerely hope so.' But there was no hope in his voice, only despair.

I leant forward. 'My lord, I know 'tis my fault. If I hadn't come to you like I did from under the Garland rose you wouldn't ever have become a husband to me, and after Lord Quinham told me about what the doctor had said to you I felt so guilty I thought mebbe I were losing my reason from it. But then,' my voice became firmer, 'I remembered what you told me in the library that evening, about guilt eating people up, and you asking me please not to feel guilty – I remembered you saying that. And Lord Quinham, he said guilt did destroy his mother . . .' I paused to take a deep breath. I knew by his stillness that he was listening as I explained, 'So I decided I wouldn't let it destroy me. I couldn't, because of Flora, and the baby – he'll need me when he's born. And my lord, he'll need *you*, too, so you mustn't sit and brood about it either. Besides, it don't do no good.'

I waited for his reply: it was a long time coming, but when it did his voice was very gentle. 'Wise Amy. You are right – you must do as you say.'

'And you – will you stop feeling guilty too?'

'No – I can't. You're young enough to fight it, but it's too late for me. The fox has been gnawing at my vitals for so long now – it grows hungrier every day and I must feed it.' He stood up. 'You'd better go to bed. You've had a tiring day and you'll have another tomorrow, when you go back to Eston.'

'No.' My reply came at once. 'No, I'm not going back. I told you – I told you twice – that I wouldn't ever leave you, and I'm not going to.' There was silence and I said firmly, 'Besides, there's Flora. She wanted to come and live with her Papa, she'd be main upset if you sent her home now.' He was still silent, then he moved his hand in a small gesture of resignation. At once I pressed home my advantage. 'Mrs Procter, she's come too, to cook dinner, so I'll expect you back regular.'

'I am often required at the hospital in the evening.'

'Then when you're not, you can come back here.'

'Tomorrow – I think I should be free tomorrow evening. But I must go to the Club first, to bathe and change, otherwise there is the risk of infection being conveyed to you and Flora.'

'As you wish, my lord.'

'Matthews has sent me good reports of your health.'

'I been keeping quite well – and I've been remembering to eat plenty o' fruit.'

'Good.' He crossed over to the door and held it open for me. 'Good night, Amy.'

'Good night, my lord.'

I hadn't fully faced up to it until I'd seen him again, but I had to now. So that night before I went to bed I deliberately pictured my baby, with his small shoulder raised and his tiny neck twisted sideways – I'd have to hold him differently so he could suck. His small, lopsided face was looking at me anxiously, one eye bigger than the other, and I imagined myself smiling at him; his unequal mouth smiled back, happy now because he knew I was his mother and I loved him. In my imagination I cuddled his warm downy body close against mine, and deep within my belly I felt him move, settling himself down to sleep. My hands caressed him; he was my son, I loved him, and I always would.

Chapter Sixty-Eight

I slept well and woke calm and rested. Lord Warminster had already left for the hospital, but I would see him again that night. We would have dinner quietly together and gradually he would get used to me again. He'd told me he couldn't lay aside his guilt and I knew he'd been speaking the truth, but we were already in February; at the beginning of April our son would be born and once he held him in his arms he would fall in love with him, just as he had with Flora that night in France. I'd thought he loved her because she was his grand-daughter, but she wasn't – instead she was the grand-child of the woman who'd deceived and deserted him – yet he still loved her. How much easier it would be for him to love his own son, whatever his appearance. I only had to wait.

And while I waited I would be a good wife to him, conversing with him at dinner, caring for his clothes and making sure he ate regular meals. I wouldn't let this house frighten me, either. I wasn't a servant any more, I was Lady Warminster and I must act as such. After all, I'd been a lady's maid, I knew how ladies behaved. I would walk in the park and spend a long time dressing and visit big shops to buy ribbons and gloves. Meanwhile, I would go up to see how Flora was faring in her new home.

She ran to me, her face wreathed in smiles. 'Papa – Papa came!'

I smiled over her head at Ellen who nodded. 'His Lordship sent to say he'd be up before he left, so we got dressed early, didn't we Lady Flora?'

'In my *pink* ribbons.' She crowed with pride.

'But my lady,' Ellen continued, 'I know London be always a dirty place, but thic nursery be in a terrible state.' She gestured around the dingy room where the soot lay in a greasy carpet along the windowsills and smuts stippled the skirting board.

I'd noticed the grime last night, but I'd been too worried to do anything about it; this morning I felt strong and energetic. 'Send Dora for a couple of pails of hot water and we'll give these nurseries a thorough springclean. Could you lend me one of your

615

aprons?' As Ellen stared at me in surprise Flora tugged at my skirt, clamouring to help. 'So you shall, my pet – but first you'll have to put on your oldest frock and pinafore.'

We beat rugs and scrubbed floors and wiped down grubby walls all morning, while Flora splashed and squealed with delight at this new game; it was a long time since I'd enjoyed anything so much as I enjoyed cleaning those two nurseries. I ate lunch with a good appetite, and after a little sleep while Flora had her afternoon nap I was ready for an outing in the Square gardens with Ellen and Flora. Flora ran about on the sooty grass while I sat in the winter sunshine watching her. Then another lady came in with her nurse and two little boys, and Flora stopped her play to stand gazing at them in open adoration; at once they began to hit the ground with their sticks and throw their ball higher and higher into the air, showing off in front of her. When it was time to go we passed the bench where the lady was sitting, and she smiled at me. I smiled back, then took Flora's hand firmly in mine, crossed the road and walked straight up the flight of stone steps and between the white stucco pillars; I would not let the house subdue me.

I would have liked to have had tea in the nursery with my daughter, but I knew a lady wouldn't do that, so I kissed her goodbye, promising to see her again soon, then went to take off my hat and tidy my hair before going down to sit in the drawing room. That was almost as grubby as the nursery had been, and I quailed at the thought of asking Mrs Johnstone to give it a good turn out – but I would be brave, for my lord's sake. Bending down for the tongs I built up the fire, then I sat back in my chair, waiting until the hands of the clock reached four and I could ring for tea.

But at five to four I heard footsteps outside and a voice. I froze. Surely not in this house – I must be imagining an echo from the past, it couldn't be . . . The door opened. 'Lady Quinham, my lady.' It was Miss Annabel.

She stalked into the room, tall and beautiful – her dress a sheath of scarlet and her glossy dark hair piled high under the swooping curve of her hat. Scrambling awkwardly to my feet I dropped her a clumsy bob.

For a moment her eyes looked straight into mine, then they fell to my swollen belly and I saw two crimson patches flare up on her cheeks as anger blazed in her eyes. Putting my hands protectively over my stomach I backed away from her fury and stumbled against the chair, almost falling. She laughed, a high-pitched jeering laugh. ' "My lady" indeed! My lord's whore – that's what *you* are.'

I cried out in protest. 'No – he be my legal husband!'

For a moment she looked surprised, then she said contemptuously, 'Not *that* lord – not Leonidas. No, you're my husband's whore and bearing his bastard – except in law it won't be, will it? You scheming little bitch!'

Desperately I denied her charge. 'No. My child, it be Lord Warminster's, my husband's.'

'Don't waste time telling lies – Francis told me. He boasted of exactly where he was going and what he intended to do – and I prayed as I'd never prayed before that this time you'd be barren! But no, he offered you his seed and your greedy little womb snapped it up.'

Her gloved fingers covered her eyes and again I declared, 'I be carrying Lord *Warminster*'s child.'

Her hand dropped, and I saw the glistening tears of anger as she shook her head. 'No, he promised me, Leonidas promised me, after . . . He swore to me that his marriage to you would be in name only – and *he* is a man of honour.'

'He didn't mean to break his promise, but I made him. I did take off all my clothes and go to him from under the Garland rose –'

The expression of disgust on her face stopped my words. 'What a loose little strumpet you are. So you deceived him just as you hoped to deceive me, and now he thinks it's *his* child – except that I'm sure he suspects you've betrayed him. I could see that from the expression on his face when he told me today you were in Town.'

'Ask him, ask him if I baint telling the truth.'

'I'll never do that. He's worth a thousand times more than Francis. I'll never be the one to tell him he's been cuckolded by his own son. That'll be our secret, mine and yours – and I'll remind you of it every second of the day.' She reached out and tugged sharply at the bell. Mr Tims came in at once. 'I'll be sending my baggage round later, Tims – see that it's taken upstairs. And tell Mrs Johnstone I'm having the blue bedroom, and my maid will go in the one above. You may bring in the tea now.'

As Mr Tims left she turned to smile at my appalled face. 'I'm sure you'll be pleased to entertain me as your guest, *Lady*

617

Warminster. Every time I've seen your husband lately I've been complaining about having to put up at my club; I know he'll be delighted to have me here, since you're now available to chaperone us.'

She didn't speak again until Mr Tims returned with the tea tray. 'Thank you, Tims. Put it down there.'

He hesitated a moment before obeying, then turned and spoke to me directly. 'Have you everything you require, my lady?'

I could barely manage to stammer my reply. 'Yes – thank you, Mr Tims.'

Her mocking laugh rang out as she mimicked my accent. ' "Thank you, *Mr* Tims". Haven't you even learnt how to address a butler yet, Amy? What an embarrassment you must be to poor Leonidas. Still, I don't suppose *you* care, as long as you're addressed as "my lady". What a long way you've come since I picked you up out of the gutter. How smug you must be feeling as you sit there with a title and a butler to wait on you!'

With fingers that shook so much I could hardly control them I poured her a cup of tea, added the milk and held it out to her. She raised her hand and swung it sharply out to knock the cup from the saucer – the hot tea splashed over my skirt as the cup shattered in the hearth. She sprang to her feet and strode to the door, but before she reached it she swung round with her parting taunt. 'Remember Amy, you may sit there preening yourself but *you'll* never be a lady – you'll never be anything but a bastard countess.' Her voice dropped and became low with menace. 'You're a thief. You stole my husband, you stole him twice – and now I'm going to make you pay.'

And she did make me pay – over and over again.

After she left me that first afternoon I was shaking so much that the child in my womb sensed my distress and began to twist and turn anxiously as I knelt by the hearth picking up the broken pieces of china. I made myself sit down and ring for Mr Tims and stay outwardly calm while Bertha came in and mopped up the spilt tea, then I forced myself to eat and drink. I fastened my thoughts on the fact that Lord Warminster was coming back to dinner and we could sit at the table together and perhaps talk a little; I knew Miss Annabel would go out. She'd never dine with me, her former maid.

I dressed in my best golden velvet, the colour Lord Warminster had chosen for me, and sat at the mirror ensuring that every hair was in place, trying not to look at the betraying brown wings which spread their shadow across my cheeks. Outside the drawing room I drew a deep breath and then pushed the door open; he was alone. 'Good evening, my lord.'

'Good evening – Amy.' He'd addressed the door above my head, but at least he'd used my name; my spirits lifted a little. Then he spoke again. 'Annabel will be joining us tonight. I am so glad she has chosen – to forgive and forget past, past –' His hand moved as he sought for a word, 'Events. Her presence in this house will be – extremely valuable to you socially. You must be very grateful to her.' Before I could answer I heard quick footsteps outside and the door opening behind me; at once his gaze dropped from the wall to go straight to the doorway, and his lopsided face lit up with pleasure. 'Annabel – good evening.'

It was the same all through dinner. He never looked at me, and only occasionally at the wallpaper above my head, but he couldn't take his eyes off her. She was as beautiful as ever. With her shining dark hair, her flashing eyes, the imperious tilt of her chin – she looked every inch the lady that she was. I had prided myself on my ability to chatter to him, and sometimes elicit the odd word or comment – but she, she conversed. She spoke of politics and philosophy, plays and paintings, of the war, of the work they were each doing; he hung on her every word, and responded. Cleverly, skilfully, she drew out his opinions and called on his wide knowledge, until under her influence his speech gained in fluency and he became animated and interested as he could never be with me. I remembered my old dreams, woven in this very house before she'd become Lady Quinham. I'd dreamt that she and Lord Warminster would fall in love and marry each other, leaving Frank for me. I'd been a fool to think Frank would ever marry a bastard servant girl, but not so foolish about Lord Warminster: he had fallen in love with Miss Annabel – and he still loved her.

His voice changed when he addressed me. Losing its liveliness, it became formal, forced. 'Have you settled in – satisfactorily, Amy?'

'Yes, my lord, thank you.'

619

'Is everything in the house as you wish? I fear the caretaker hardly had time to prepare for your arrival.'

'The nursery, it was terrible grubby, but Ellen and Dora and I did set to and give it a good going-over, and now both o' them rooms are clean as a new pin.'

A peal of silvery laughter cut across my pathetic little boast. 'Really, Amy – you mustn't clean your own nursery! That's a job for the servants.' She glanced across at him with a smile on her lips. 'Imagine it – Lady Warminster down on her knees wielding a scrubbing brush!' His mouth twitched at the corners: he was laughing at me, too. Her voice sounded almost kind as she told me, 'You must speak to the housekeeper, and see that she makes the servants do their work properly.'

Lord Warminster said, 'I'm afraid Mrs Johnstone is not the easiest of women . . .' He didn't say that I was incapable of controlling her, but it was implied in that discreetly unfinished sentence.

Miss Annabel smiled, her teeth white in the lamplight. 'Then *I* will speak to her, Leonidas.'

'Thank you, Annabel.' He smiled back at her gratefully.

Afterwards, when Mr Tims served coffee in the drawing room she moved automatically to the silver pot; I didn't attempt to forestall her. While I drank my coffee they talked casually together, as people do when they have so much in common. As soon as I'd finished Miss Annabel glanced in my direction. 'You'd better go upstairs now, Amy. You look tired – from your efforts with the scrubbing brush, no doubt.' Her tone was light with amusement, but I saw the flash of contempt in her eyes – and the hatred which fuelled it.

I got up and moved towards him, desperate to make some sort of contact; he rose politely to his feet and stood staring into the shadows above my head. My voice slightly shrill I said, 'My lord, I – ' and his head shifted so that he was looking at me for a moment –then his gaze fell to where my waist should have been and the flicker of revulsion in his eyes silenced my attempted appeal. He shifted abruptly so that he didn't have to look at me – and seeing it, she smiled.

With a false note of warmth in her voice she turned to me. 'You look a little shaky, Amy – I'll help you upstairs.' Taking a firm hold of my elbow she escorted me from the room; as we mounted the stairs the grip of her fingers tightened until her nails bit into my flesh. She spoke in an angry whisper. 'I saw it – I saw the expression on his face as he looked at you. What a burden you are to him, what an intolerable burden!' She forced me on, faster and faster until I was breathless and panting; at the top of the stairs she thrust me from her. 'You little whore – but I'll make you pay for what you've done, you slut!' She was right; I was a burden, a terrible burden. It was a long time before I fell asleep.

Next morning I was up in the nursery with Flora when we heard footsteps on the stairs. Flora looked up, her face alive with pleasure. 'Papa!' The door opened and she ran straight into his arms – then I saw her body stiffen with surprise as she looked over his shoulder; someone else was with him. Miss Annabel came in, the colour high in her cheeks and her eyes stormy as she stopped and stared at her husband's child. Flora struggled to get down, and ran to greet her. Silently I begged, 'Please, don't let her hate Flora.' The round blue eyes and the flashing dark ones gazed directly at each other.

I watched emotions chase each other across Miss Annabel's face before she said, her voice slightly tremulous, 'What a beautiful child!' She dropped down, so that the fair head and the dark one were level. 'Good morning, Flora, I'm your Aunt Annabel. Will you give me a kiss?'

Flora's face broke into a beam of delight. Launching herself forward she planted a moist kiss on the glowing cheek before seizing an unresisting hand. 'Aunt N'bel, come see Bavins.' Together they went over to the cradle where Bavins sat in state, lording it over his harem of dolls. Flora picked him up and thrust him into Miss Annabel's arms. 'Kiss Bavins!' The beautiful mouth gently touched the bear's fur and Flora crowed with pleasure; seizing my lord by the trouser leg she explained, 'Papa give Bavins a hug.' Solemnly the ritual was completed, then he bent his huge frame down beside Miss Annabel's slender one and the two of them listened to Flora's recital of the latest exploits of Bavins. I stood watching them, excluded from that charmed circle. My husband loved her, and now my daughter had fallen under her spell, too.

She came to me later as I sat in the big, gloomy drawing room,

621

and in her hands she held the huge red book called *Debrett*. I recognised it from the time before, except that now the gold-embossed date on the cover was 1914. Flinging it open she thrust it in front of my eyes. 'Look – look at your disgrace, proclaimed for all the world to see.' Her finger stabbed at the entry: WARMINSTER, EARL OF – the one I'd read aloud to her upstairs in this same house. Only it had been altered now: under my lord's names and details it read: 'm. 1st., 1889, Jeanette Joséphine Marie-Louise, who d. 1910, only dau. of the late Marquis de Montjean, of St Valéry, France; 2ndly, 1913, Amy Roberts' – and then there was just a full stop.

The curved polished nail flicked page after page and stabbed at entry after entry – and always after m. came the words 'dau. of' – daughter of, daughter of, daughter of. The stabbing finger slowed to rest on one entry: POULETT, EARL. It travelled down to 'm. 1908, Sylvia Lilian, dau. of Fred Storey.' 'She was a chorus girl, married straight off the boards of the "Gaiety" – but at least she isn't a *bastard* countess! Here, look!' I read again: HEADFORT, MARQUESS OF m. 1901, Rose, dau. of the late Charles Boote. 'Another chorus girl – yet even chorus girls have fathers! Everyone knows now what you are, and what your mother was.'

The contempt on her face spurred me to defiance. 'My father, he was a gentleman and he was going to marry my mother, only he lost track of her afore the wedding.'

She threw back her head in a peal of scornful laughter. 'You little fool, your mother lied to you.' Her voice was full of spite as she told me, 'Because you'd spun that tale to Leonidas he made enquiries when you were first taken into hospital, to discover if there was someone who would take responsibility for you. He asked a woman called Harris if she knew anything of your father, and she told him that the man who begat you was nothing but a two-timing servant.'

After she'd gone I sat huddled in the chair. It wasn't true, I knew it wasn't true because I could remember the exact words Beat had used: 'She saw him galloping towards her on horseback.' Because she hated me so Miss Annabel had lied to me – but I would go and see Beat now and she'd tell me the truth, the truth about the gentleman who'd loved Aunt Agnes, but lost her before he could marry her.

622

Beat's face was one broad smile as she opened the door to us. 'Come in Amy duck, do. And how are you, young Flora?' She bent to give my daughter a hug. As she straightened up again her gaze travelled complacently over my swelling figure. 'I knew he'd come round, Amy – a pretty girl like what you was. Sit down 'ere and have a cup 'o tea while I tell you the news.'

She showed me photos of Albie and Ned, both in uniform. 'Albie's a sergeant already, and Ned's a lance-corporal – they're doing well. George and Jim are both in steady jobs, the war's been good to us in that way. I still do four evenings at The Rose and Crown but the pay's better now. It's got to be, else I'd be off down the munitions factory making them shells.'

When I saw the third photo I exclaimed, 'But that's Uncle Alf!'

'Yes, Alf's joined up an' all, even though he turned fifty last spring. Still, as he says, you can't keep a good man down. He said, "If my boys are going, then so am I. There's life in the old dog yet." I'm proud of him, and that's the truth.' She held out her left hand. 'And we got hitched the day before he went, so's I'd get the seventeen and six a week and be able to make a home for the boys. Not that I'd ever a' let them down, for your ma's sake, but Alf insisted – he's a good father.'

At once I seized on that last word. 'Beat, I wanted to ask you about – about my father. You did tell me once about how Aunt Agnes fell in love with him the first time she ever did see him – and he was galloping towards her on a horse. Was that true?'

She nodded. 'Yes, Amy – o' course it were.'

I gave a sigh of relief. 'Then he *was* a gentleman.'

She shook her head, half-smiling. 'Whatever gave you that daft idea, duck? Aggie, she'd never 'a let herself be led astray by one o' the gentry – she had more sense. No, he was a groom, out exercising his master's horse.' My last frail castle in the air crumbled to dust. 'Poor Aggie, he didn't play fair with her. They was going to get married in a year or two, when they'd both got a bit put by, but in the meantimes he would keep pestering her, the way men do, saying as if she really loved him she'd let him have his way. Eventually she gave in. Just the one time it was, and afterwards she felt so guilty she told him never again, not till they was wed. But him having got the taste fer it he wanted more, see, and when she wouldn't give it to him he went elsewhere. This

623

other girl, she'd had her eye on him fer a long time. He was a good-looking man, real handsome – he glowed like the sun, that's what Aggie told me once. Anyway, the other girl give him what he wanted straight off – so he got the pair of 'em in the family way within the month. Your Ma kept hoping it hadn't really happened, the way a woman do, but the other girl, she moved fast. She told him he'd got her up the spout and he'd got to marry her quick. Your Ma was there in church, sitting at the back with the other maids and still thinking as he was courting her – and suddenly she heard his banns called. She went to him straightaway and told him how it was with her and he said it were too late. This other girl, her father was a gamekeeper, and he'd threatened to take the shotgun to him if he didn't do right by his daughter. He'd 'a done it, too – by all accounts he had a wicked temper. So he had to marry her instead. He told Aggie he were sorry, he liked her the better o' the two – but what could he do? He said anyway, it were all Aggie's fault really, because if she'd kept on letting him have what he wanted he wouldn't have needed to go to the other girl in the first place.'

I began to cry. Beat picked up the teapot. 'No use crying now, Amy. Poor Aggie's dead and in her grave. Still, I reckon she must be sleeping happier in it now her little Amy's a real lady.'

But I wasn't, and I never would be. Miss Annabel had made that abundantly clear this morning – not that I hadn't known already.

Chapter Sixty-Nine

She knew where I'd been. One of the servants must have told her after I'd asked Mr Tims to call a cab for me. As soon as I came into the drawing room she taunted me with my failure. 'You know the truth now, don't you? You know you were nothing but the by-blow of a philandering servant – and that's who you take after.' She came closer until I cringed away from her anger. 'You deceived me, and you betrayed me – twice you betrayed me, and now you've done the same to Leonidas!'

Under the bitter frost of her contempt my small seedling of courage withered and died. I'd believed I could fight guilt and overcome it, like St George with his dragon – but I'd been wrong, I wasn't strong enough. Grammer had sapped my foundations long ago. Besides, I was right to feel guilty: I had deceived Miss Annabel, I had betrayed her trust. I'd betrayed my husband, too. He'd taken me out of the gutter and given me the protection of his name, and how had I repaid him? By forcing him to beget on me a child in his own image – that image he hated so much. I had to stay in London for the child's sake, but how I wished I'd never come. He didn't want me, he didn't even need me to care for his clothes any more. He'd sent a message by Mr Tims to say that the caretaker would clean his boots, and one of the club servants was looking after his suits, while Mr Tims himself would perform any other duties required. So even that role was taken from me, and now all I could do for him was keep myself out of his sight, to save him the pain of being reminded of the coming child; and that at least I did do. By listening to his movements I learnt his daily routine, then used my knowledge to avoid him. It wasn't difficult. He never sought me out and Miss Annabel told me it was not fitting that I should come down to dinner in my present condition, so I ate off a tray in my room while they dined downstairs, happy in each other's company. I didn't fight; I let her take my husband from me, just as once I'd taken hers.

She'd said she'd make me pay for that theft and she did. She made me pay in slights and humiliations, taunts and jeers. I had no weapons with which to defend myself and besides, how could I? I had stolen Frank from her, for that one night at Eston. I had borne his child, who now proclaimed her begetter in all her golden-haired beauty. I hadn't stolen him twice – she had accused me falsely there – but the fact of that first unwitting theft held my tongue. Anyway, my tongue could not fight. I had preened myself on learning to speak properly, on no longer using 'baint' or 'I' for 'me' – but the minute I became flustered I lapsed back into dialect again; and even if I spoke carefully and corrected my grammar my accent still remained unchanged. Among the servants at Eston I had not realised how noticeable it was, but in London, before Miss Annabel's smart friends, I proclaimed my lowly origins every time I opened my mouth. I'd been a fool to tell myself I could learn to be a lady. Ladies weren't taught, they were born, and I'd been born the grand-daughter of a country labourer – and worse, much worse – a bastard.

When her friends came to tea she would introduce me mockingly. 'Do you remember Roberts, my maid, Muriel? Leonidas took pity on her and married her in the hospital chapel – just in the nick of time! It *was* naughty of him – it's so difficult to replace servants these days, and she was good with her needle, too. My present maid's not half so adept. Still, she is totally trustworthy, which is much more important in a woman of that class. Come along Amy, say how d'you do to Mrs Ellis. You must pretend you're a lady, now!' And they would both wait for my stammered greeting, so that they could laugh at its inappropriate pronunciation.

Her friends knew all about me, and they smiled at my discomfiture, enjoying my humiliation. I had broken all the rules and apparently escaped without punishment – so now they set out to punish me. At first I tried to stay upstairs when they came, but she wouldn't let me. I was the hostess, she said, so I must be present to pour tea in my own dining room. I dreaded that tea-time hour just as a mouse dreads the tormenting claw of a cat – but I obeyed her, just as I'd always done.

Some days young men in uniform who were home on leave would come to tea. They were kinder, and they'd smile at me as I handed them their cups and make casual conversation about the weather. But under Miss Annabel's scornful gaze I could only mutter confused replies in my broad Wiltshire accent until they drifted away, and then I would see her mouth curve into a smile of derision. As soon as they'd left she'd turn on me. 'Now you've lost your looks the men don't want to waste their time on you. How ugly you've become, Amy. It's lucky for you Francis isn't here, even a tom cat like him wouldn't want you now. No wonder Leonidas can't stand the sight of you!' The brown butterfly had become an ugly, disfiguring moth, my hair drooped dull and lifeless and my body was bulging and awkward – but I knew that wasn't why he turned away from me in horror. But it was no use trying to tell Miss Annabel, who would never believe me. She was convinced I was carrying her husband's child, the child she couldn't bear him. I wondered again and again why she'd ever had that terrible operation and so could never have a child of her own.

Now she tried to take away mine. She used all her charm and energy to entice Flora from me. She spoilt her, flattered her, bought her present after present. Lifting her on to her knee she would read her stories: she read stories much better than I did, putting on funny voices, acting The Three Bears with mock ferocious growls until Flora squealed in gleeful fear. Sometimes the stories were deliberately aimed at me – the tale of The Princess and the Pea, for instance. 'You see, Flora, a princess is always a princess, and a lady always a lady – like you, you're *Lady* Flora, you were *born* Lady Flora – but peasant girls, they're never anything else but peasant girls, however much they pretend!' Flora nodded her head in solemn agreement. She was totally fascinated by her. It was 'Aunt N'bel, Aunt N'bel,' all the time. She brought Flora down to tea, introducing her as, 'My little sister-in-law,' and her friends petted my daughter and let her do just as she liked until her behaviour became more and more uncontrolled, but when I tried to check her then I was mocked as a spoilsport, and Flora would break free of my restraining hand crying, 'Naughty Mama – bad Mama.' All around me the adult voices would echo, '*Bad* Mama, *naughty* Mama,' and I would flinch from their knowing laughter.

One day I understood fully Flora's wilfulness. Ellen told me that when I wasn't there, 'Lady Quinham, she tells her as how her Mama won't want her when she has the new baby. Her Ladyship do keep on about it until Lady Flora gets upset, then she says to her, "Never mind, Aunt Annabel wants you. You'll be Aunt Annabel's little girl then and eat cakes whenever you want." ' I thanked Ellen and did everything I could to reassure my daughter – but the damage had already been done. If only I'd been a normal mother, able to look after my child all day, every day, then she'd never have distrusted me, but now I remembered how I'd almost lost her before, when I'd first gone back to Eston – and I was afraid.

As my time came nearer I was never free from fear. The London doctor who'd visited Eston came regularly to examine me, brisk and impersonal in his formal frockcoat. He spoke bland, reassuring words, but I wasn't reassured: I was frightened, frightened for myself and frightened about how my baby would cope, once he was born. On one visit the doctor asked me who I'd engaged as my monthly nurse, and when I admitted I hadn't engaged anyone he frowned and insisted I must do so immediately. Good nurses were booked up months in advance, and in any case, there were fewer available now because of the war. Seeing my hesitation he said forcefully, 'You must speak to your husband about the matter – this evening.'

When I asked Mr Tims he said Lord Warminster was dining at home. I knew she'd be there too – she always made sure she was when he dined at home – but I had to see him. I could barely struggle into my evening frock; I had to let out the placket to accommodate my clumsy misshapen body, and in the mirror I saw how disfiguring the blotched stain across my face was, and how lank and greasy my hair had become. I was so ugly tonight – and she, she was beautiful. My heart was thudding as I went into the drawing room and saw the look of anger on her face. She would have ordered me away, but he greeted me politely and so she held her tongue.

I didn't speak during dinner: she took care to keep the conversation on topics and people of which I knew nothing. His replies were brief at first, my presence disconcerting him, but she chattered on so gaily that soon his reserve faded. We were back in the drawing room again before I plucked up the courage to speak. As she paused to raise her cup to her lips I said, 'My lord, the doctor did say –'

Quickly he turned to me, 'Yes?'

'He said I must ask you about engaging a monthly nurse.'

He looked dismayed. Obviously he was as much at sea as I was. Then Miss Annabel interrupted, 'I'll find someone, Leonidas, leave it to me. I'll make enquiries about hiring a trained nurse.'

Her words reminded me of that trained nurse at Eston who'd tried to separate me from Flora – and panic gave me inspiration. 'Mebbe Clara's mother – she do look after folk when they be lying in.'

At once Lord Warminster picked up the suggestion. 'I'll write to her this evening.'

'Really Leonidas – an ignorant countrywoman!'

'She is experienced and competent. Besides, I would prefer a familiar face in the house.'

I knew the real reason why he wanted Mrs Chandler, who'd been his own nursemaid. She wouldn't shrink from our son. I whispered. 'Thank you, my lord.'

His glance rested on my face. 'You look very tired – Amy.' Just for once there was no horror in his grey eyes, only concern. I shifted awkwardly in the chair, putting my hand to my back which ached so much I couldn't get comfortable. At once he got to his feet, took a cushion from his own armchair and came to me. 'Lean forward.' As I obeyed him his hands moved behind me, plumping up cushions and rearranging them. When he'd finished he stepped to one side and I sank back into the comfortable nest he'd made for me.

I looked up and saw the kindness in his eyes, and for a moment I forgot Miss Annabel as I whispered, 'Thank you, my lord – that be main comfortable.'

'Good.' He still stood there, looking down at me – then Miss Annabel's confident voice called to him, and the moment passed.

During that night I was dragging my heavy body back from the WC when I stopped outside his bedroom door. Knowing he was there, lying in bed so close to me I wanted to go to him – desperately I wanted to. I longed to rest my aching back in the crook of his elbow and lay my tired head on his broad chest; I wanted him to hold me, cuddle me, comfort me. I reached out to turn the handle of the door, but as I did so the child inside me kicked, hard – and I drew back. It was no use: as soon as he felt that kick he would recoil in horror and thrust me from him. Standing there I suffered in my imagination the pain of his rejection, and there were tears on my cheeks as I crept back to my cold and lonely bed.

A couple of days later Clara's mother arrived, clutching her basket and bundle, overawed by London, but determined to do His Lordship's bidding. Seeing her installed in the nursery and hearing her soft voice murmuring to Ellen comforted me a little, but as soon as I came fully inside the room the chatter ceased and there was a bob, the duck of a head and a polite, 'Good day, my lady.' I didn't belong in the drawing room – but I didn't belong in the nursery, either. I didn't belong anywhere now.

Each morning I woke with swollen fingers and painful wrists, and the pricking of pins and needles tormented me as I dressed. Each evening I dragged my weary body to bed, and heaved my burden from side to side seeking the temporary respite granted by sleep. But my fears pursued me even into my dreams: I was Red Riding Hood shrinking in terror from the wolf's sharp teeth; Snow White biting into the poisoned apple; Jack running frantically to escape the giant – the huge hand of the giant reached out to seize me . . . and I woke panting with fright and clammy with sweat, feeling the child's frantic movements and fearing for the two of us.

It was the morning of the last day of March; more than nine months had passed since I'd waited for him under the Garland rose, naked and unafraid. I could hardly believe it had ever happened, except that I carried the fruit of that night in my womb. I was uncomfortable, restless, frightened – and when I saw the bloody stains in my drawers I knew it would not be much longer now. I sought refuge in the nursery early, though I knew today he was spending part of the morning with Flora, so he would be bringing her back up there. But when I arrived she was already back, and Clara's mother told me he'd had to leave already. 'Never mind, my lady – likely he'll be home earlier this evening, instead.' But I wouldn't see him then, I never did. Besides, it might be too late. She pulled up a chair. 'Sit you down and have a rest.' Her voice was kind as she bustled around finding cushions and a footstool for my tired ankles, and for a while I felt safe, up there in the nursery with just my daughter and the two countrywomen for company.

But after lunch Miss Annabel pursued me there. I looked at her in fear. She was as tall and slender and darkly beautiful as the Queen in Snow White – and burning with the same jealous rage. She envied me both my children, the born and the unborn – yet it was by her own choice that she was barren. I felt a tiny flicker of anger – she had no right to hate me so – then the flame was quenched by guilt, leaving me weaponless as she took my daughter from my side with promises of fairy stories. I could only sit by, listening as she read her one after another of the familiar tales. Cinderella sat weeping amidst the ashes until her fairy godmother sent her to the ball – and next day the Prince arrived to rescue her. 'But really she was just an ignorant serving girl, Flora, with only her looks to commend her. I've no doubt the Prince soon became *very* tired of her.' The dart winged its way to its target. 'I daresay her looks soon faded, too. Women of that type go blowzy very early – and then her prince would have found himself another pretty girl, handsome princes always do.' Handsome? Then I realised she was referring not to my husband, but to hers.

Flora clamoured for another story and Red Riding Hood walked innocently into the trap set by the wolf – but when her screams of terror rent the air the faithful woodmen seized their axes and ran to rescue her and take her safely home to her mother. But my mother was dead long since. No one would come to my rescue when I screamed. Then I heard the familiar words: 'There was once a rich merchant who had six children . . .' I sat back in my chair, listening to the tale of the merchant's beautiful youngest daughter who comforted him when he lost his money and asked him to bring her back from his journey just a single rose. The Beast threatened the merchant with death and Flora gasped – but I wasn't frightened, for I knew that despite his angry tantrums the Beast was a kindly Beast who would care for Beauty and never harm her.

But all too soon that story was over, and then it was the tale of Snow White, and the wicked Queen intent on destroying her little step-daughter in her jealousy. Miss Annabel's voice rang out clear and thrilling:

631

'Tell me glass, tell me true!
Of all the ladies in the land,
Who is the fairest? Tell me who?'

The dread day came when the answer was Snow White – and the jealous Queen began her relentless pursuit: suffocating corset laces, tainted comb, poisoned apple – until at last poor Snow White lay trapped in her coffin of glass. And then it came, the first sharp twinge of pain. I gasped.

Miss Annabel broke off from her reading to look sharply in my direction. Clara's mother jumped up and came quickly to my side, but Miss Annabel forestalled her. 'I'll see to Lady Warminster. You go down and prepare her room.' Her voice was firm – the voice of authority. Clara's mother drew back and left.

I sat huddled in my chair as Miss Annabel stood over me, watching me as a cat watches a mouse – before it pounces. When Mrs Chandler returned she was ordered to stay upstairs. '*I'll* take Lady Warminster down to her bedroom now, and send for you when you're required.' But she wouldn't, I knew she wouldn't. I was trapped with her, with this woman who hated me – and my unborn child.

The WC offered me a brief moment of respite, but as I sat on the wooden seat the flux seemed to crush me in a nutcracker of pain; there was no escape anywhere. Back in my bedroom she sent me behind the screen to undress. Clara's mother had left hot water and I washed myself before putting on a clean nightdress, then plaited my hair ready – but I had to come out and face her. She seized hold of my elbow and hustled me over to the bed, ordering me to lie there flat on my back. I didn't want to. The pains were closer now and I needed to move about, walk even – but her glittering eyes held me down.

Then she began to speak. 'Does it hurt? Of course it hurts – how well I remember. I'll never feel that pain again, but I'll never forget it, never! Like a spear – piercing, ripping, tearing . . .' I gasped and she bent over me, her face afire with anger. 'You must pay, you must pay for your pleasure. He took his and then left you to bear the consequences.' Her laugh was high and shrill as she exclaimed, 'Men always do that, always!'

I whimpered in pain, 'My lord, my lord!'

Her jeering voice cut across mine. 'It's no use crying to *him* – he's in France. And he wouldn't come near you even if he were here – he's got no patience with sickness. Besides, he doesn't care tuppence for you, you were just the vessel for his seed – if you'd been the most hideous hag in the world he'd still have used you because of who you were. But the minute you'd served your purpose you were forgotten. He'll be using French whores now – he's no more need for the English one. Only *you've* got to pay the price, just as women always pay for the vices of men. I know because I'll pay for his carelessness for the rest of my life.' I stared up at her in bewilderment, then her voice regained its menace. 'But I'll make you pay, too. It's late, isn't it? His child, it should have come more than two weeks ago – I've been counting you see, I've been waiting too. Oh, it'll be a boy – he'll get what he wants, he always does – but you, you won't live to see it because it'll tear you apart. It's grown too big, far too big.'

'No! It baint late – 'twas the end o' June when I went to my lord –' the pain caught me, crushing me.

She shook her head. 'Don't lie to me! I know it was earlier than that. I'd just come back from America, and I'll never forget him telling me what he was going to do.'

As the pain receded I told her despairingly, ' 'Tis my *husband's* child, I swear it. I did go to him at the end o' June.'

'No doubt, but it's Francis' child that's tearing you in two – he had you first.'

'He didn't! He tried to – but I did fight him, and he let me go.'

'*You* fight *him*? How could you? How could you refuse him anything when you love him?' She bent over me and I cowered back from her as she cried, 'Tell me the truth, tell me! You do still love him, don't you?' Her voice rose shriller and shriller. 'You do, don't you?'

And fear drove the whimpering truth from me. 'Yes.'

'I knew it.' She drew away from me contemptuously. 'I knew it. So how could you refuse him anything he asked for? You little fool!'

I began to sob, 'Please my lady, please leave I be.'

'Why should I, when you're labouring with the child I can't bear?' She stood above me, pale with rage and envy – and the tears shone sharp as diamonds on her cheeks as I writhed gasping in my pain. 'It was like a huge claw ripping me apart with its talons – I'll never forget it, yet I'd endure it again a thousand times if only –' I was moaning and panting with my parched mouth and crusted tongue. Suddenly she swung away. I heard the flowing of liquid and a glass was thrust to my dry lips – her glittering eyes – the poisoned apple – I dashed it from me and the cold drops that fell on my skin burnt like frost. 'You're a coward – an arrant coward.' I heard the scorn in her voice as the giant's hand closed to crush me and the spear pierced my body – but I must not cry out, I must be brave, for my baby's sake, to protect my baby: if once I screamed then all was lost. I must be strong, I must control my screams, else I would be in her power, the spell would be complete – and she would destroy me, the wicked step-mother, the jealous Queen.

The next pain came and I wrestled with the giant's tearing talons, trying to withstand them – the roses, remember the roses – then, at last, the pain receded for a little while. Her bitter voice stabbed me in its stead. '*You* may love him – I don't. I hate him, I hate him for what he did to me. And I hate you – how can I not hate you? You've borne him one child, now you're giving him another. I hate you!' Her voice cut off, then returned to almost shriek, 'I hate you, you coward. You're a coward, a coward!'

The pain was coming again. I must fight it, wrestle with it, defeat it. I used all my strength – but it wasn't enough, I *was* a coward. I heard my voice raised in a high-pitched scream of terror – I'd lost control and now I was in her power. She laughed in triumph. 'You coward, you coward!' I was at her mercy now, I'd failed. I'd failed my baby. I began to sob. 'It's too late for tears of repentance.' She towered above me, a dark column of menace – then the tap came at the door.

As it opened I heard Mrs Chandler's voice. 'My lady, mebbe I'd best come in to her now?'

Panting I lifted my head, but Miss Annabel's reply came fast and sharp. 'No, there's no need. Go back up to the nursery.' My head sagged back on to the pillow.

Then another voice spoke. 'Annabel.' It was deeper, stronger, a man's voice – my lord's voice. And even as my panic-stricken brain recognised it so I was heaving myself up, flinging myself off the bed, and running stumblingly towards the door. She turned, startled, then tried to stop me – but I escaped past her and arrived gasping at the doorway to throw myself down on my knees before him. Reaching up, my frantic fingers locked themselves on the edge of his jacket as I cried out, 'I be afeard, I be afeard!' Then my voice dropped to a pleading whimper, 'Don't leave I – please don't leave I.' My ever-tightening knuckles were white against the black cloth of his jacket as I whispered, 'Thee maun stay wi' I, for thee didst give I the rose.'

A hand gripped my arm. Strong fingers began prising mine from his jacket. 'Really, Leonidas, she's completely hysterical.' Sharp nails sank into my shoulder, digging into my flesh as the giant's talons ripped open my belly.

The strength of the pain tore me free from her clutching hands, and at once I flung myself forward to throw both my arms around his leg. I clung desperately to its strength, strong as the trunk of a young tree – and clinging I fought the pain – panting, gasping, sobbing – but there was no scream. As it ended I crouched on the hard boards with my face pressed against his bootlaces and whispered, 'Please don't leave I.'

High above me I heard him promise, 'I won't – leave you,' and I sagged at his feet, limp with relief. Crouching down he held his arms out to me, and I went into them. He raised me gently from the floor until my sweating face was pressed against his chest.

'Leonidas, you can't possibly stay with her – this is no place for you!'

'It is my child which – is causing her – such pain.'

My child, our child, his child. I tipped back my head to look up at him, but I could only see the hollow of his neck – his twisted neck – as I begged, 'He be *thy* son, and thee maun love him, whatever he do look like – *please.*'

'I will – try.' He lifted me up into his arms.

I heard her voice behind us, more uncertain now. 'Leonidas . . .'

'Go up to Flora, Annabel – she must sense there is something amiss. She will need you.' Turning away from her he carried me back into the bedroom.

Clara's mother pulled back the sheets and he laid me gently down. 'She'd do better sitting up, my lord – it does help the pain.' Her deft hands built up the pillows behind me. 'Do 'ee kneel if thee dost want – 'tis often easier so. And I maun put thy pads on

635

for when thy waters break.' He turned his humped back while she made me comfortable then looked awkwardly round as she told him she'd finished – but the next pain was already coming and I reached out to him, catching at his hand, clutching at it; at once his fingers closed round mine. I was straining forward – panting, sobbing – but the warm strength of his hand helped me to withstand the attack, and just as I thought I must scream so the giant's talons relaxed their grip. 'There! She's main better kneeling, my lord – and you be calming her. 'Tis fear as makes pains worse.' She drew up a chair behind him. 'Sit you down beside her.' He sat down and reached for the glass of water; as soon as he gave it to me I drank thirstily.

Setting it back on the bedside table he turned to Mrs Chandler. 'Send for the doctor.'

'Aye, my lord, though it'll be a while yet.'

'How long?'

Pursing her lips she told him, 'I doubt she'll deliver afore midnight – but doctor'll tell you better.' I heard the door close behind her.

I whispered to my lord, 'Don't leave I. Please don't leave I.'

He shifted his clumsy body so that his grey eyes looked directly into mine. 'I won't leave you, Amy – I promised.' His expression softened as he added, 'Or must I pour beetroot soup over your head to convince you?' Reaching out he gently lifted the damp hair off my forehead, pushing it back out of my way – and as he did so I turned my sweating cheek into the palm of his hand. He let it rest there until he heard Mrs Chandler coming back, then he drew his hand away.

As long as I could I made do with just his hand, especially while the doctor was there, the doctor who tried to send him away with a, 'This is no place for a man' – but my lord had made a promise, and he kept it. But after the doctor had gone away, saying it would be some hours before his services would be required, I soon needed more than that one hand. He was uncertain, but Mrs Chandler became my ally. 'You'd best sit on the edge of the bed, my lord, and put your arm around her back, here – she do need a bit o' support. Aye, that's right.' The pain came and I turned to grip his shoulder. It was getting worse now, jagged, relentless. I fought back until it ended and I could sag exhausted against his

636

chest. 'She do need to let it out, my lord – 'tis no use a-fighting of it, it maun come.'

'Amy, scream if you wish.'

I confessed in a whisper, 'I be a coward – an arrant coward.'

'So am I, Amy. So am I.' His gentle finger touched my cheek.

Sometimes I screamed, other times I didn't. But always I clung to him when the pains came. At first his body was hard and solid as a rock, anchoring me, but gradually I felt him soften and become more pliable, moving as I moved, drawing the pain from my body into his and so helping me to endure it. It was as if a tree had come alive and enfolded me in its living strength. We didn't speak again with our voices, but our bodies spoke – mine telling of my fear and need, and his replying with comfort and understanding.

I lost all count of time: my whole world narrowed to pain, and the brief cessation of it. Then came the gush of water between my legs. I turned my face to Mrs Chandler and she came forward at once. 'My lord, if you'd just leave her a moment.' Gently he unloosed my clinging hands. As she unfastened the sodden pads and changed my soiled nightie I kept my eyes on those humped shoulders as they shrugged themselves out of jacket and waistcoat. He came back, just in time to help me through yet another pain.

It was hot, so hot that the white front of his shirt was sodden with sweat and the darkness of his hair showed through. Reaching up I pulled open his collar and tugged undone the small buttons until I found the damp, dark fur of his chest. The Beast – the kindly Beast. The pain came and I clutched at him, then slumped forward to rest my cheek against the soft mat of his hair. Listening to the steady thudding of his heart, I smelt the warm tang of his sweat with its promise of salt and turned my face to lick it from him. Still he held me.

'It'll not be so long now, my lord. We'd best get the doctor back.'

Pain – and the cessation of pain; but the pains were longer, the intervals shorter. I began to panic. 'Amy, Amy.' Holding me, rocking me, soothing me.

The doctor was in his shirtsleeves too, now. 'Not much longer, Lady Warminster.' The pain changed, became sharper, jagged. 'Push.' I screamed. 'Push!'

'Push, Amy – push.' It was too big – I was burning, splitting. I screamed and screamed again.

'Stop pushing now, Lady Warminster.' My body no longer belonged to me; I was a burning coal pierced by a red-hot poker – then with a slippery gush of release my son was born.

I lay back, panting with relief – and a voice loud and clear exclaimed, 'It's a girl!' Relief became hopelessness – and I saw my despair mirrored in his eyes. A baby cried: a twisted, misshapen daughter.

Clara's mother spoke, her voice warm and happy. 'Thee bist beautiful, my maid, beautiful. Baint she a lovely liddle maid, Doctor?'

His reply was briskly cheerful. 'Yes, Nurse. It's a treat to see such a perfectly formed infant.'

My eyes were fixed on my lord's face as it swivelled to stare incredulously at his daughter – and I saw from the expression that transformed it that they'd spoken the truth. 'Amy, she's perfect, perfect. It's a miracle!'

'Every birth is a miracle, Lord Warminster. Now just stand to one side so I can attend to your wife.' As his hands touched me I felt only a great emptiness: my little downy twisted son did not exist.

Far away I heard the splash of water, and Mrs Chandler's murmuring voice, then the pain came again, squeezing me hard. 'Just the afterbirth, Lady Warminster. It'll soon be all over, and then we can make you comfortable.' The doctor's hands busied themselves with my body until I felt the binder being firmly wrapped around my waist. 'Now nurse, let the mother have her child.'

Pillows were set behind my back, the doctor raised me up against them, and then Clara's mother held out to me a white bundle. 'Here she be – thy liddle maid.'

Instinctively I held out my arms – and even as I took her into them I was overwhelmed with love. It surged through me like a great wave of water pouring over a weir – more and more and more. She looked up from her large bright eyes, gazing at me as if she already knew me. Her rosebud mouth opened wide and at once I tore apart my nightdress and put her to my breast. She seized hold and the firm tug of her mouth and the warm curl of the tongue were a mingling of pain and ecstasy. As she suckled I whispered over and over again, 'Thee bist beautiful – I do love thee, I do love thee.' Murmuring of my love and my delight I cuddled her close, tears on my cheeks and laughter in my voice: we were enclosed in a shining, iridescent bubble, just the two of us – together.

When her mouth let go my hands began to undress her. The doctor spoke as if to stop me, but a voice commanded, 'Let her – be.' Her silken skin was like rose petals under my lips as I kissed her warm face, her plump body, her firm limbs. I kissed each separate, perfect eyelash, each damp, dark curl on her head – and then my hands began to move: touching, stroking, caressing – telling her of my love. At last I gently replaced her small white bonnet and pulled her vest over her head before laying her on my breast. I pulled up the shawl that had fallen from my own shoulders to wrap it around us both, and as I held her there I felt her curl up between my breasts, settling close against my heart. Lost to all sense of time and place I lay in a mindless trance of joy.

I was scarcely aware of the doctor taking my pulse for the final time before telling Mrs Chandler, 'I can leave now, Nurse. There shouldn't be any problems.'

Clara's mother roused me with a gentle touch on the shoulder. ''Tis time thee were properly settled down to sleep, my lady.'

I looked up; we were alone in the room. 'My lord?'

'He's gone now. Likely he's getting some sleep hisself – 'tis nearly dawn. Give me the little maid and I'll dress her properly. Even though 'tis like an oven in here, you can't be too careful.' Reluctantly I let her take my precious baby. When she'd finished she asked, 'Shall I put her in the cradle?'

I reached out my arms. 'No, give her back to me.' And Clara's mother, who'd held her own babies close in her small cottage, smiled as she handed me my precious daughter. She lay cradled in my arms as we both fell asleep, together.

Chapter Seventy

My baby stirred in my arms, nuzzling me into wakefulness. I offered her my breast and she took it at once; the tug of her strong mouth brought pain to my belly, but even pain couldn't hurt me today. Gazing down at the curve of her cheeks pressed warm against my full breast I gloried in my love.

Mrs Chandler came soft-footed to my side. 'His Lordship's been in twice, just for a peep. Soon as he saw you was asleep he tiptoed out again.' She reached for the bell. 'I'll change her while you have a bite to eat, my lady, then I'll set you to rights.' Bertha arrived quickly with a tray and I ate ravenously while Mrs Chandler murmured to my baby: 'Now my liddle maid, let's put thee a clean bonnet on. My, who's got pretty black curls then, just like her Papa?' She carried her over to the cradle and laid her down. There was a whimper of protest and I called softly to her as Mrs Chandler began to unfasten my binder. The minute the bedpan had been taken away and the fresh pad was in place I held out my arms for my daughter; with a snuffling murmur of contentment she settled herself down against my heart.

Mrs Chandler rang the bell again. 'As soon as you've seen to those slops, Bertha, tell Mr Tims to let His Lordship know as he can come and see Her Ladyship now.'

While I waited embarrassment warmed my cheeks; remembering how I'd clung to him in my pains and how he'd seen me at such a time I scarcely dared raise my eyes to the door as he came in – and when I did so I saw his embarrassment was as great as mine. The hesitation in his speech was very pronounced as he asked, 'How – are – you?'

'I'm very well, my lord.'

'Good – good.'

Drawing a deep breath I whispered, 'Thank 'ee for staying with me when I were afeard.' His face went a deeper shade of scarlet and he didn't reply; we had nothing more to say to each other. Finally I offered, 'Would you like to hold her?'

He came to the bed and held out his arms. When I put her into them he shifted her sideways, holding her tilted so he could see into her face. They both stared at each other. His face changed, softening, and his voice lightened as he greeted her. 'Good afternoon, little one. How are you today, this very first day?' He stood smiling at her, as if listening to her reply; then his face lifted and his tone deepened as he addressed me. 'I chose Flora's name – it is your turn now. What do you wish to call her?'

At once my voice answered, 'Rose.'

He looked at me, startled – and I felt my cheeks grow warm as his reddened too. Then he half-smiled. 'I suppose it is – apposite. And her second name?'

'I don't know – mebbe you'd better choose.'

'I chose Flora Elizabeth because Elizabeth was my mother's name. Perhaps Rose – Agnes?'

'Thank you, my lord.'

'I'll register her tomorrow. Now, I'll go and fetch Flora. She is anxious to see you.' Glancing at my face he added with a smile, 'Just as you are to see her.' He bent down over the crib.

'Give her to me, so I can show Flora her new sister.'

He continued lowering Rose into the cradle. 'No. It is her mother Flora wishes to see – not her sister.'

The minute she saw me Flora broke free of his hand and ran towards the bed; he swung her up on to the coverlet and she flung herself into my arms. I glanced up for a moment and our eyes met; he'd been right. It was only when my reunion with Flora was over that I guided her to the edge of the bed and pointed into the cradle. 'See, Flora, God's sent you a little sister!'

After one perfunctory glance she said firmly, 'Don't want a little sister.'

I coaxed, 'You can play with her when she's older. Look, isn't she pretty?'

Flora peered into the cradle again. 'No.'

'But Flora –'

She turned away, her face ominously red. 'Don't want her. Send her back.' I caught his eye in a shared flicker of amusement then Flora stuck out her lower lip and said, '*My* Mama,' before slithering from the bed and marching over to Lord Warminster.

She wrapped her arms right round his leg and said loudly, '*My* Papa.'

His face changed, softening, as he bent and lifted her up into his arms. 'Yes, Flora – I'm *your* Papa.' He hugged her close before bringing her to me for a farewell kiss and then carrying her back up to the nursery.

I slept with my child in my arms, half-waking every time her determined mouth nuzzled my breast. As soon as Mrs Chandler drew back the curtains in the morning I gazed at my baby's face, drinking in its pink perfection. 'Rose, my Rose, thee bist the most beautifullest baby in the whole world.' She blinked herself awake, her bright eyes smiling into mine.

The doctor came soon after breakfast. 'No problems, Lady Warminster, no problems.' He shook down the thermometer and peered at it. 'That's what I like to see. In a few days Lord Warminster should be able to get back to looking after his wounded officers. I know that being confined to clerical duties these last few weeks has been irksome for him, but with a birth imminent we couldn't take any chances.'

The doctor had barely left when another tap came at the door: Miss Annabel. She marched in, head held high, as she announced, 'I'll stay with Her Ladyship, Mrs Chandler. You may go downstairs.' I pressed back against the pillows, my arms curled protectively around my baby. Her mouth twisted into a grimace. 'You needn't look so terrified, Amy – I know the truth now.' Then all of a sudden she collapsed into a chair, put her hands to her face and began to sob.

I sat watching her as she fought for control, then she sat up straight and blew her nose vigorously before saying, 'Amy, I'm so sorry, so terribly terribly sorry. Leonidas told me everything.' Slowly my tense body relaxed. 'He couldn't stop talking. I've never seen him like that before – he was drunk with relief and it all poured out.' She blew her nose again, then tucked her handkerchief into her sleeve and tried to smile at me as she said, 'I think I've been slightly unhinged these last months. I was so envious, so eaten up with jealousy – that's why I was such a beast to you. But after Francis told me what he intended doing I was totally convinced that it was his child you were carrying. Besides,

642

Leonidas had promised me – I was so sure he'd never break his promise.'

I found my voice at last. 'He didn't mean to. I made him – because I did want a baby so much.'

'Yes, I know that now. And I of all women should have understood the power of that all-consuming longing.' Her face contorted with pain as she told me, 'I believe I would mate with the Devil himself if only he could give me back my womb – but he can't, nobody can.'

'Then why, whyever did you ask the doctors to take it away?'

She looked at me, her eyebrows drawn together in puzzlement; then her face tightened. 'Is that what *he* implied – that I had a choice?' She leant forward. 'Amy, the only choice I had was between the chance of some sort of normal life without my womb, or living as a permanent invalid with a womb that was useless, scarred beyond repair.' Her voice was bitter. 'I don't know what lies he told you, but I'm telling you the truth now – never in a thousand years could I have borne another child.' I saw the glint of tears in her eyes. 'After the birth of my little son I was so ill I thought I was dying, and afterwards, when I'd supposedly recovered, I couldn't walk three steps without collapsing. But I still kept hoping, because you see *he* didn't want to believe the doctors, so he wouldn't let them tell me the truth. It was Mama who wormed it out of them: that I'd be an invalid all my life unless they operated, but Francis wouldn't give his permission. He always believed what he wanted to believe – like a child.' She made a sound that was like a laugh – but it wasn't a laugh. 'That's why I fell in love with him, for his boyish high spirits. I didn't realise it meant he hadn't grown up – and never would. So Mama took me to America. She told the surgeons there I was a widow; I think they knew really but they were sympathetic and they did what was required. I began to recover as soon as they'd – they'd . . .' She put her head in her hands; her voice was muffled but I could hear every horrifying word. 'But I can't ever forget what I've lost – and I wanted to punish him. So when he met me at Liverpool I didn't tell him, I went with him to the hotel and allowed him to act as my husband –' She broke off for a moment. 'You see, I knew that sooner or later he'd start talking about an heir, for that was what he always wanted, and next morning, when he did – I told

643

him. It was the most exquisite moment of revenge! But then later he came back and said he was going to get his heir – his *legitimate* heir – from you. I was in torment from that day on. It never crossed my mind that you'd deny him. I thought you'd already betrayed me with him over and over again. I didn't realise until Leonidas told me yesterday morning that Francis had deceived you, too. Masquerading as "Mr Dunn" – how typically puerile – trading on your ignorance.' She glanced at me. 'And the irony was you'd actually seen his name, you'd read it aloud to me – but you didn't know how to pronounce it, did you? I realised at Eston that you'd made a mistake, only by then it was too late.'

I blurted out, 'But I did know! I knew it were him when I let him – but you'd given him back his ring and I thought, I thought,' my voice dropped, 'I thought he did love me.'

She spoke harshly. 'We both made a mistake about *that*.'

I whispered, 'He did love you.'

'It isn't love, to behave as Francis behaved. We were both his victims, I can see that now – you with your hopeless dreams of marrying a lord and I with my natural dreams of motherhood. He gave you a bastard child and I – I,' her words caught in a sob, 'He deprived me of children for ever.'

At the bitterness in her voice I exclaimed, 'But my lady, women do get ill after childbirth – it weren't *his* fault.'

'Oh yes it was, entirely his fault. My illness, and the consequences, were all due to his carelessness.' She was fierce with anger. 'On my wedding night I went to him pure and untouched. I gave him my virginity – and in return he gave me a dose of the clap.' She stared down at her hands. 'It was gonorrhoea, not syphilis – I suppose in that respect I was lucky, if you can call it luck. I've read all about them both, you see. The doctors don't always tell you the truth and I needed to know – it was my body, my future. I'm quite a mine of information on the "specific diseases" these days – that's what they call them in Harley Street – so much more discreet. He knew he'd got something wrong with him. It flared up on our honeymoon – perhaps it was already too late then. I'd conceived so quickly and pregnancy makes a woman especially vulnerable, but in any case he behaved like an ostrich and put his head in the sand. He went to some quack and got the symptoms covered up so I wouldn't suspect – not that I would have done, I knew nothing then, nothing! He should have realised he'd infected me, he knew I was under the weather – but he didn't want to admit the possibility, even to himself. He was like a child with a new toy. And I wanted to please him, I wanted so much to please him . . .' Her voice broke. 'I wasn't a total innocent; even then I knew men had "experience" before marriage. We used to talk together, we girls – we thought it was natural, the right and proper thing for a man to do. God, what naive fools we were. He admitted eventually what had happened. Apparently he'd had a regular arrangement: he and two of his friends set some woman up in an apartment in Kensington and the three of them had keys to her door – all very convenient and cosy – and safe. Only the last night before our wedding he wanted to celebrate – celebrate our wedding by doing *that* with another woman! But instead of going back to this female in Kensington he decided he wanted a change – so he took a whore straight off the streets.' I began to shiver as she exclaimed, 'How *could* he have been so careless – so thoughtless!'

In a whisper I confessed, 'He didn't mean . . . it were I – he'd asked me.'

'You!'

Somehow I stumbled through the tale of that evening. She watched me, the shadows under her eyes becoming darker and darker; when I'd finished there was complete silence. Then Rose stirred and automatically I put her to my breast. Miss Annabel turned her face away before she spoke. 'The irony of it. I've spent so long hating the thought of him with you – and now, if only, if only you'd stayed with him that night. *You* were clean. After all, that's why I chose you for my maid.'

She began to laugh hysterically and I could only whisper, 'I be sorry, terrible sorry.'

With an effort she pulled herself together. 'Don't get into a state, Amy, it'll only curdle your milk. After all, how could you have possibly known what Francis would do? Besides, "if onlies" are useless. If only my son hadn't died. They said it wasn't because of the infection, he was healthy – but the cord came round his neck . . .' She put her head in her hands.

Rose's small hands reached out and touched me; she whimpered, sensing my distress. I cuddled her, murmuring reassurance. Then I heard the chair being pushed back and Miss Annabel came to the bed and stood looking down, not at me but at my baby. 'Yes, I can see Leonidas in her. Another irony, that he should finally gain a child of his own through Francis' thoughtlessness.' She glanced up at me. 'A third irony – that Francis is a bastard, like you. Except that his mother was cleverer than yours – she got Leonidas' ring on her finger, by deceiving him. No wonder Francis is as he is. How I hate him!' She moved away. 'Yet I can't hate his daughter, curious, isn't it? I thought I would, but I couldn't.' With a catch in her voice she said, 'Flora looks so like Francis must have done when he was young and innocent – before he became corrupted.'

I whispered, 'He didn't mean no harm. He just didn't think.'

She swung back. 'How can you defend him? After the way he deceived you and then cast you aside?' She watched my face. 'I was right, wasn't I? You do still love him, even now.' My face told her the truth. 'Lord, what fools we women be.' She came closer. 'Amy, he isn't worth your love, he isn't worth the love of any woman. Don't you realise, if you'd allowed him to seduce you after my marriage, Flora could have been blinded?' I gasped, remembering Lord Warminster writing that message in France after he'd held the coral beads above Flora's cradle. Miss Annabel was still speaking. 'Though I suppose her sight would probably have been saved because she was born in a public hospital. Do you know that what happened to me is so common – so many men infect their wives – that hospital midwives put drops of silver nitrate into the eyes of new-born babies as a matter of routine? How hateful men are. And yet he's got off scot-free, he's cured now and he can beget as many healthy children as he wants – but not legitimate ones, never legitimate ones – I'll see to that.' I flinched from the anger in her eyes as she exclaimed, 'I'll never set him free – never!'

After she'd left me I began to cry. Mrs Chandler came back and fussed around me, but of course I couldn't tell her why I was upset. I wept on and off all day; my joy in my baby was overshadowed by guilt now. I had two beautiful children while she . . . I tried not to cry, suppose it stopped my milk coming in? But I couldn't stop repeating 'If only' – if only I'd spent that last night with him – because I'd loved him, I still did love him. She'd torn open the door of the little house in my head and now he'd escaped. I kept seeing him again in my memory, I kept seeing him again in Flora's blond head and blue eyes as she played on my bed. He hadn't meant to hurt Miss Annabel. It was my fault. I'd made him angry and so he'd been careless and gone to that woman – and now Miss Annabel would suffer for ever.

I dozed off in the afternoon and when I woke Mrs Chandler was sitting by the fire reading a letter. When she saw I was awake she said, 'I just heard from Clara by the afternoon post – she says our Emmie's expecting! I be so pleased. She's been wed over four year and never a sign – and then just when her Bill's gone away soldiering and only come home for five days' leave – then it's happened!'

I managed to smile and look pleased. 'Be it your first grand-child, Mrs Chandler?'

'No, my lady. My older boy, he's married with a couple o' childern – but a mother feels different when 'tis her daughter's child. You know what they say: "A son's a son till he takes a wife, but a daughter's a daughter for the whole of your life." Just think, our Emmie wi' a babe at last! I do be so pleased.' She stood up. 'I'll ring for your tea, my lady – you must keep drinking to help bring your milk in proper.'

'A daughter's a daughter for the whole of your life.' But I'd spent so little time with Aunt Agnes – and I'd never even known she was my mother until she was dead and buried. Cradling little Rose Agnes in my arms I began to cry again, crying for my mother – my mother who'd married another man and borne his children and yet had loved my father until the day she died; she would have understood.

Clara's mother must have fetched my lord, because he came upstairs as soon as he got home from the hospital. He stood just inside the door, looking at me anxiously. 'Mrs Chandler tells me you've been – upset. What is the matter – Amy?'

I couldn't talk to him about Miss Annabel, or Frank, so in the end I told him half the truth. 'I do want my mother.' And as I spoke it became the whole truth and the tears came flowing down my cheeks while he shifted his weight from one foot to the other and back again. Then he tugged and tugged at the bell until Mrs Chandler returned. As he left he said, 'I will send Flora down.' I had to pull myself together while Flora was with me, but after she'd gone upstairs again I couldn't hold back the tears.

The following afternoon Beat arrived in her best straw hat with two bunches of cherries bouncing on the brim. She said Lord Warminster had sent a cab to fetch her. 'Lucky I was in, Amy – I'd only just got back from the Cut. My, ain't she a beauty!' She took Rose into her practised hands and hefted her up against her broad bosom. 'Well, what a little corker – diddly diddly then, *who's* a pretty girl?' She glanced up at me. 'Funny, ain't it duck – she's a real looker already and yet you can see who her dad is, plain as the nose on me face. Oo's a little love?' Rose seized Beat's finger, her mouth opening wide. 'Who wants her Ma then? 'Ere she is, Amy.'

When Rose was settled at my breast again I said, 'Beat, I been thinking about Aunt Agnes.'

Beat gave a gusty sigh. 'Ah, it's only natural at a time like this. If only she could see you now, Amy – lying in the lap o' luxury with another lovely little daughter and a good husband to take care o' you. Poor Aggie – she weren't so fortunate.' She added hastily, 'Not that Alf weren't a good husband to her, because he was – always tipped up the housekeeping reg'lar and never got drunk save of a Saturday night.'

'But he made her send me away.'

'Well, that was only natural – a man don't want cuckoos in his nest. It's different with His Lordship, little Flora being his grand-daughter, but you was nothing to Alf, only a reminder o' something he wanted to forget. And he did give in in the end.' She smiled. 'You've never seen anyone as excited as Aggie when he said she could send for you. All the time she was waiting she was like a cat on hot bricks – she thought your grandma might not want to part with you – and then when you arrived – I'll never forget that evening when you first came. We stood there on the balcony at the Buildings, me and Aggie, watching you dance round the barrel organ – and when she turned to look at me her eyes, they was shining like stars. "This is the happiest day of my life, Beat," that's what she said to me that evening.' Beat took out her handkerchief and blew her nose. 'But then things started to go wrong. Her losing the baby, Alf losing his job and all of you having to leave the Buildings – and by the time he did get work again she knew she'd got the consumption and hadn't got long to go – then she went and

648

fell in the family way again. Seemed like fate was punishing her, it did. She'd got her daughter back, and then, arter all them boys the one she had to get rid of turned out to be a little girl an' all.'

My arms tightened around Rose in shock as I repeated, 'Had to get rid of?'

Beat looked at me, her eyes heavy. 'You must've realised since, Amy, even if you didn't then. She asked me to take her along to this woman in Fairley Street, what was near as clever as a doctor. She saw to it for Aggie.'

The baby, the tiny baby in the bowl, fluttering its arm. 'But why?'

Beat's expression changed to one of surprise. 'For your sake, Amy – that's why. Poor Aggie, she knew she couldn't last much longer. The boys, they was older, but with a baby, you'd have had to stay. You'd've been trapped there – and she knew you was longing to get home to your Granfer. She said to me, she said, "I hate meself, Beat, for what I done – but what else could I do? I let her down once, sending her away – I couldn'l let her down again." ' Beat dabbed at her eyes then thrust her hankie firmly away. 'Still, it's all over and done with now – no use crying over spilt milk. I had a letter from Ned this morning . . .' She rattled on and I pretended to listen.

After she'd gone I lay and cried and cried, weeping for Aunt Agnes – and for what she'd done for my sake. I was still red-eyed and unhappy when my lord came home. Mrs Chandler spoke to him softly at the door, then after pulling up a chair for him she left us alone. He sat watching me. Then he said, 'I thought Mrs Harris' visit would cheer you up.'

'She – she did talk to me about Aunt – about my mother.' He still sat there unmoving. I said, 'You baint had your dinner yet.'

'I am not – hungry.' He paused to shift in his chair before adding, 'If there is anything I can do to help?' I shook my head. What could he do? Aunt Agnes was dead.

He spoke again. 'Flora is expecting me, she saw me come in. I must go up to her. But perhaps, when she's in bed – if you wished me to return . . .'

'No, my lord, don't trouble yourself. You have your dinner.'

He went away without another word. After he'd gone I wished I had asked him to come back again – but I was too tired and unhappy to chatter to him and he never talked to me unless he was drunk. Then I thought, I could have asked him to read me a story – but it was too late. Besides, I'd got two daughters now, I was too old to have stories read to me.

That night my milk came in with a rush; my nightdress was sodden and the more Rose suckled the more milk came. Feeling it coming, knowing I could give her everything she needed lifted my spirits a little. My lord came to the door early and Mrs Chandler let him in – but as soon as he saw me with Rose eagerly suckling he backed hastily out again. I heard Mrs Chandler's cheerful voice. 'Enough for twins, my lord – and then some over! Just as well, thic liddle maid's as greedy as she's pretty – wants her mam all the time, she do.' I heard the low tones of his voice and her brisk reply, 'Don't you worry, my lord. Now her milk's in Her Ladyship'll soon be a lot perkier.'

Flora brought her entire Ark down and I let her play with it on my bed. When I fed Rose she sat watching, her lower lip jutting ominously, then she said, 'Flora too.' I uncovered my other breast and let her suck beside her sister; Mrs Chandler winked at me over their two heads. Flora was soon satisfied, and returned contentedly to her pair of hippopotamuses.

After lunch we all had a nap together, and when I woke up Mrs Chandler handed me a parcel which had been delivered. Inside was a jewel case, and when I eased up the lid diamonds sparkled against midnight blue velvet – they were set in a delicate pattern of flowers on a gold chain, to form a pretty diamond necklace. Flora reached out a hand, 'No, Flora – only look.' We admired it together and Mrs Chandler exclaimed in admiration, then I put it carefully back into its case. How kind of my lord to have taken the trouble to choose it for me. When I was up and about again I would wear it with my blue velvet dress to dine with him.

Flora went back up to the nursery and Bertha came in with my tray. As I was thirstily drinking my tea the door snapped open – it was Miss Annabel. 'Good afternoon, Amy. How are you today?' She walked restlessly across the room to the window, not listening to my reply. Then she swung round with her back to the panes and said, 'I've decided it's time I stopped playing at war work and did something useful. I've been to Devonshire House and asked for a transfer – it's all arranged, I'm going to drive ambulances.' She turned away so I couldn't see her face and told the cold glass, 'I've just heard today. Tom Verney's been killed – he was Francis' best man at our wedding and always so full of life. Oh, isn't everything just too vile!' She stared at the curtains, her shoulders quivering, then they suddenly stiffened and her voice was pitched high and light as she asked, 'What have you been doing with yourself all day? Oh, what a stupid question to ask a woman who's just been confined!'

I reached quickly for the jewel case. 'Look at the present my lord gave me.'

She scarcely glanced at it. 'Oh, it's arrived, has it? I thought you'd like that necklace – nice and glittery. Poor Leonidas hadn't a clue, in fact I think he's scared of jewellers' shops – I had to positively drag him inside Cartier's.'

I snapped the lid shut. 'He doesn't go into shops much, my lord – he chooses from a catalogue.'

She gave a short, scornful laugh and mimicked, ' "My lord!" For goodness sake, Amy – he's your *husband*. However must he feel when he hears you grovelling like that!' She glared at me. 'You wanted to be Lady Warminster, one way or another, and now you are – so start behaving like her.'

I whispered, 'I'm sorry, I'm sorry.'

There was silence. Then at last she spoke, 'All right, Amy – I know. I'm being beastly again – I can't seem to help it. But I will try. It's just that seeing you with that baby . . .' She broke off. 'Anyway, there's many a true word spoken in jibe – it *is* time you started calling Leonidas by his name. You're not his servant, you're his wife.' She spun round and left before I could reply. I knew she was right – but I couldn't imagine how I'd ever bring myself to do it.

It was late by the time he got back and my head was aching. He came in and hovered over by the door. I said, 'I did get – I mean, I got, the necklace. Thank you, my lord.' I couldn't call him Leonidas, I just couldn't.

'Do you – like it?'

'Yes, thank you. It's very nice.'

He shifted from one foot to the other, waiting for me to speak

651

again but I didn't, so at last he said, 'I will – leave you – to sleep.' He went.

After he'd gone I felt more wretched than ever. I should have been more enthusiastic about his present – only it had been Miss Annabel's idea really; all he'd done was pay for it. Rose stirred in my arms and gave the smallest of murmurs. At once I felt the tingling warmth of my milk and raised her head; her small mouth closed firmly on my breast and as she suckled the shadows retreated – my baby, my beautiful baby. I touched the curling down on her head, dark like his – and the diamond necklace paled into insignificance beside this gift that he'd given me.

As soon as he came in the following evening I said, 'My lord, I did want to thank you, for giving me Rose.'

He looked startled, then his face flushed brick-red before he replied, 'You must – make the most of her. There will be no others.'

I exclaimed, 'But – she's perfect!'

He spoke slowly. 'This once – the gods were looking the other way. They will not be so remiss – a second time. We will not live as man and wife again.'

It was then that I remembered the wooden box – and remembering, knew that if I didn't ask now I would never be able to. 'I did find it, the box in your bedroom.' As his face changed I added quickly, 'I weren't prying – you sent for those books and when I went to get them, I found it. So if you wanted to . . .'

'No, there is still a risk.' Then he looked directly at me. 'Besides, *you* don't want to, do you?'

I felt as if I were naked before him. I whispered, ''Tis a wife's duty.'

'Her duty, but not her pleasure.'

He sounded so bleak that I tried to reassure him. 'You never did hurt me.'

He just stood looking down at me, like a great unhappy bear, then he said, so quietly I could scarcely hear him, 'I suppose I must at least be thankful for that.' He turned to leave.

I called out, 'My lord!' He paused, waiting. In a loud, firm voice I told him, 'But I did enjoy the cuddling.'

At first I thought he wasn't going to reply. His hand was already on the door knob, turning it, when he suddenly swung round again

652

to look straight at me. I saw his face working then he said, in a voice so low I could hardly hear his words, 'So – did I.' Then he almost flung himself out of the room.

Chapter Seventy-one

After he'd gone I kept hearing that halting: 'So – did I.' I remembered how he'd held me while we cuddled and how, when I'd turned to him in my pain and fear, he'd comforted me. Although we could never live as man and wife again there was a bond between us, a bond that would last for the rest of our lives. I had not chosen to marry him, and I'd only gone back to Eston out of duty, but I owed him more than duty now – and he needed more.

Next day I asked the doctor if I could get up that evening to sit on the sofa, and he gave me permission. I waited until the last minute before putting my clothes on because of the milk leaking through my blouse, but I was determined to put him at his ease by being properly dressed – and in any case, I wanted to wear his necklace. I thought very carefully about the positioning of his chair; I wanted him to be sitting so that his face was towards the sofa, but still in the darker part of the room, because I knew that was what he preferred. Rose's cradle was by my side.

It was late when he came in, but I was ready. He looked surprised. 'You are – feeling better tonight?'

'Yes, thank you. The doctor said I could get up.'

'Good – good.'

'Would you like to sit down?' He lowered himself slowly into the chair as Mrs Chandler slipped from the room. As soon as the door closed behind her I took a deep breath and said, 'Miss Annabel told me as you'd likely prefer it if I didn't say "my lord" any more, so would you like me to call you Leonidas?'

His reply was abrupt and decisive. 'No.' There was silence, an awful silence; I didn't dare break it. At last he said, 'It is true that I do not like your addressing me as though you were a servant, but –' he hesitated before adding in a rush, 'I have an intense dislike of my given name – it is so totally inappropriate.'

He stopped, and it was obvious he wasn't going to help me out so I ventured. 'Mebbe Arthur then, or Hector?'

'No. They are equally unsuitable.'

So now I was worse off than before, because there was nothing I was allowed to call him. He just sat there, sulking like a child because he didn't like any of his names – I could have shaken him. I said firmly, 'Well, I've got to call you something!'

'Then perhaps you could make a suggestion?' Seeing him sitting there with his lower lip jutting and looking as if he were still in the nursery I said, 'When you were a little 'un, what did your nurse call you?'

'As my father was then still alive she called me – Master Quinham.' My face reddened, and he said, 'I hardly think –'

'No.' But after my hasty refusal he fell silent again. Desperately I thought about names: Albie, Ned, Beat, Uncle Alf. 'People with longer names do often use just the first part – so mebbe I could call you Leo?'

'Leo?' He sounded surprised, but not displeased, then his voice darkened. 'But Leo means lion. I don't think –'

And I could see exactly what was in his mind. He was going to start objecting because the lion was the king of beasts, and Richard Lionheart was a hero – so I jumped in quickly and said, 'Then that's right, because you're covered in fur.'

He exclaimed, 'Fur?'

'Yes – and I did like stroking it.'

I thought I'd gone too far this time – and then all of a sudden he started to laugh. Throwing his head sideways he laughed and laughed. When he finally stopped he said, 'Yes – call me Leo.'

I smiled back at him. 'I'm glad we've got that sorted out.'

He was still smiling as he said, 'You are using your beetroot soup voice, Amy.' Then just at that moment Rose chose to wake up – I suppose his laughter had disturbed her – and she let me know exactly what she wanted so without thinking I unbuttoned my blouse and reached down for her. Jumping out of his chair he moved quickly towards the door, muttering, 'I will leave you now,' and he did.

Rose wasn't really hungry – I'd fed her before he came in: she just felt like a suck. I scolded her, 'You should have waited. Now you've driven your Papa away.' She gazed up at me with her bright eyes; she didn't care – but I did.

He was home for dinner the following evening, so I sent Mrs

Chandler down to invite him to take his coffee upstairs with Rose and myself. As soon as he walked through the door I said firmly, 'Good evening, Leo,' and he replied 'Good evening, Amy.' Mrs Chandler poured his coffee then slipped quietly away. Rose began to cry almost at once – she wasn't used to being on her own, in the cradle. He started to get up but I was firm. 'You stay and drink your coffee while I feed her.' He subsided, drinking his coffee far too hot and staring at the wall. But after a while he put his cup down and shifted his head a little; slowly his eyes came round until he was looking at her properly. I said, 'She won't be long. She baint really hungry – it's just that she don't like to go more'n half an hour without having a suck.'

'Don't you find that – inconvenient?' I stared at him in astonishment. However could suckling a baby be inconvenient? He began to smile. 'I see that that was a foolish question to ask you.'

'I was a mite worried about when Flora was here, but I do let her have a suck too if she wants, just so she don't feel left out.'

'I know – she told me.'

Then I suddenly remembered. 'That hospital nurse who did make me wean Flora afore she was ready, she did say it was bad for childern as are more'n a year old – but I don't reckon she knew what she was talking about. How could mother's milk harm a child?' Looking him straight in the eye I said, 'I baint weaning Rose till she wants to stop.'

'My dear Amy, you must do just as you please. Though perhaps it might be a trifle inconvenient even for you once she's up in the schoolroom doing her lessons.'

'But that won't be till she's four or five year old –' Then I broke off and stroked Rose's plump cheek. 'Thy dada be teasing me, Rose.' By now he was smiling properly.

I felt much happier by the time I went back to bed that evening, but next morning the doctor said my temperature was slightly raised. He frowned a little. 'And Lord Warminster tells me there are more patients due at his hospital tomorrow, so he'll be required for orderly duties again. I've already warned him that I might have to forbid his visiting you then; I'll tell him this morning that once he's back on the wards he mustn't come near you until I give my permission. We simply can't risk the chance of his carrying infection to you.' He put the thermometer back into its glass. 'Now, Lady Warminster, there's no point in your looking downcast. There's many a woman giving birth in England today who won't be seeing her husband for months,' his voice dropped so I could scarcely hear his added, 'if ever again.'

And at his words my thoughts winged to Frank – then I caught hold of them and held them tight, and shut them away in the little house in my head. I must not think of him, I had no right to think of him – but I couldn't forget.

I didn't ask the doctor for permission to get out of bed later in case he said no, but when I woke up after my nap I suggested to Mrs Chandler that I might dress, then if His Lordship came in early he could come up and see Rose before he had his dinner. She shook her head. 'He peeped round the door earlier, and when he saw as you were asleep he said not to disturb you, but to tell you he'd be late back tonight because he was a-going down to Eston.'

'Oh.'

She smiled. 'But then he did say as 'twas to fetch a present for you as he were going, so he'd like to pop in this evening just as soon as he gets back from the station if you're still awake.'

I said firmly, 'I will be.' Then I added, 'Did the doctor tell him?'

'Aye. Still, as his lordship said, you can't be too careful at a time like this. Don' 'ee fret, my lady – at the end o' the month you'll be up and about again, and then you can see him every day.'

As I smiled back at her I thought, yes, and dine with him each evening, just as I'd always done at Eston – and all of a sudden, remembering the beetroot soup and how he'd sat there eating his dinner with the crimson drops trickling down his forehead and soaking into his bushy eyebrows, I began to laugh inwardly at the memory. I wouldn't have to do that again. He knew by now that I'd never leave him – and there was no need for him to run away from me, either, because Rose was born now and she was perfect. And almost as if she knew I was thinking of her she stirred and began to nuzzle my breast – so that soon I forgot everything in the pleasure of her warm, strong mouth.

It was after nine o'clock when Bertha came to tap at the door. 'His Lordship sent me to ask if Her Ladyship was still awake –'

With a smile in my direction Mrs Chandler replied, 'Yes, Bertha. Tell him she's up and dressed and waiting to see him.'

He was still wearing his tweeds, he'd obviously only just arrived home, and he was carrying a large parcel. He glanced at me as he came in, then went to put his parcel carefully down on the table beside my sofa before asking, 'How – are you, Amy?' His voice was concerned.

I replied briskly, 'That doctor, he does fuss too much. I'm quite well, thank you – Leo.' Seeing his cheeks redden a little as I used his Christian name I added quickly, 'How were all the folk at Eston?'

'Flourishing, and very interested to hear of our daughter.' He bent over to look at Rose, but she stayed obstinately asleep in my arms.

'She'll likely wake in a minute.'

As he straightened up, his eyes lifted to my face, and he said quietly, 'You do – look well, Amy.' His cheeks reddened further and abruptly he turned round to his parcel. 'I have something for you.' Untying the string he pulled back the brown paper to reveal an oblong wooden box. The lid was hinged, so that from where I was sitting I couldn't see into the box as he opened it – but I guessed what was in it from the expression on his face, and the gentleness with which he slid his hands inside.

The rose he lifted out was golden-yellow; it was his new rose, that he'd bred himself. I exclaimed, ''Tis so early for her – 'tis only April!'

'I had a bush brought into the glass-house last year. Hicks had instructions to telegraph to me as soon as she came into bloom.' He swung round to face me, holding out the rose in his black-furred hand, 'This is for you, Amy.'

Settling my Rose in the crook of one arm I reached out my hand and took his from him. 'Thank you, Leo – thank you.' Lifting her silken petals to touch my cheek I breathed in their lemony scent, then I lowered her a little away from me so that I could gaze into her perfect golden heart. 'Thee bist beautiful, my rose – the most beautifullest rose I ever did see.' Lifting my eyes to his lopsided face I told him, 'She's far too beautiful to be nameless.'

His grey eyes looked steadily back into mine. 'Yes, she is – so I'm christening her this evening.'

'Then – what be her name?'

His slow, difficult smile curved his lips and transformed his face as he told me, 'I am giving this rose your name. It is to be called "Amy, Countess of Warminster".'